Glittering par...
passio...

Regency

HIGH-SOCIETY AFFAIRS

They're the talk of the Ton!

The Disgraced Marchioness
by Anne O'Brien

&

The Reluctant Escort
by Mary Nichols

The *Regency*

High-Society Affairs

Regency

HIGH-SOCIETY

AFFAIRS

Anne O'Brien &
Mary Nichols

M&B™ and M&B™ with the Rose Device
are trademarks of the publisher.
Harlequin Mills & Boon Limited, Eton House,
18-24 Paradise Road, Richmond, Surrey TW9 1SR

First published in Great Britain in 2005 and 2000

REGENCY HIGH-SOCIETY AFFAIRS
© Harlequin Books S.A. 2009

The publisher acknowledges the copyright holders of the
individual works as follows:

The Disgraced Marchioness © Anne O'Brien 2005
The Reluctant Escort © Mary Nichols 2000

ISBN: 978 0 263 86864 7

052-1109

Printed and bound in Spain
by Litografia Rosés S.A., Barcelona

The Disgraced Marchioness

by

Anne O'Brien

Anne O'Brien was born and has lived for most of her life in Yorkshire. There she taught history, before deciding to fulfil a lifetime ambition to write romantic historical fiction. She won a number of short story competitions until published for the first time by Mills & Boon. As well as writing, she finds time to enjoy gardening, cooking and watercolour painting. She now lives with her husband in an eighteenth-century cottage in the depths of the Welsh Marches. You can find out about Anne's books and more at her website: www.anneobrien.co.uk

The Disgraced Marchioness is the first book in Anne O'Brien's exciting trilogy, THE FARINGDON SCANDALS – look for *The Outrageous Débutante* next month!

And don't miss Anne's latest Regency from
Mills & Boon® Historical romance.
Compromised Miss is available next month.

Chapter One

The gentleman was apparently not expected by the inhabitants of Burford Hall. In no way discouraged by the silence, the lack of activity and the shuttered windows, he leapt down from the curricle with unhurried grace to stand on the gravel carriageway, as his groom ascended the shallow sweep of steps and rang the bell. With his back to the house, the visitor allowed his gaze to take in the familiar vista, noting little change over past months. Expertly and fashionably designed gardens with paved pathways and shaded walks. A rose terrace where fragrant blooms were just being tempted to open in the warm sunshine. Rolling parkland made enticing by groupings of trees, which had been planted at least a century ago for impact and perspective. All prosperous and well tended with the glaze of extreme wealth. The stables off to his left had been recently re-roofed and he could see the grazing herd of cattle, placid and fat, in one of the distant pastures beyond home farm.

He did not need to turn to face the house to appreciate every inch of the elegant façade in intimate and well-loved detail. Every pillar, portico and decorated frieze, from balustraded terrace to dominant central pediment, all constructed in glowing local stone or faced with more fashionable brick. It was a beautiful house and home, gracious and welcoming, mellow with the happy memories of a shared childhood.

Two years previously he had chosen to turn his back on it, to leave the guarantee of wealth and privilege, and social acceptance by the *haut ton*. Two years ago he had wanted to create for himself a quite different lifestyle. And nothing had given him cause to regret his choice. But now, by a mischievous and malicious quirk of fate, his life had been turned upside down.

He supposed it was all his now: house, land, title and all they could bring in terms of comfort and consequence. His brother's untimely death had, overnight, created him Marquis of Burford.

The thought gave him no pleasure. *I don't want it. I would never have wanted it.* Indeed, the deliberate rejection of his birthright screamed through his mind as he climbed the steps with outward calm to his ancestral home.

The door was flung open at the insistent ringing to allow entry to the unexpected guest. The footman, a young man in neat black, casting an envious and knowing eye over the stylish equipage and well-bred bays drawn up on the gravel, bowed the gentleman in without a flicker of recognition, but accepting of his quality and his right to be desiring entrance unannounced to Burford Hall.

'If I could take your coat, sir, I will inform Lord Nicholas of your arrival.'

The guest looked at the young footman. A new acquisition to the staff since his last visit. He smiled in courteous recognition of the offered service. 'Of course.' He handed over his tall-crowned hat and shrugged out of an eye-catching caped greatcoat.

'What name shall I give, sir?'

Before he could give a reply, hesitant footsteps echoed on the marble tiles of the entrance hall and an elderly man emerged from the servants' quarters. He hesitated on an intake of breath, blinked as if he did not quite believe the evidence of his own eyes, and then immediately quickened his steps.

'My lord, my lord. Thank God you are here. We were not expecting you.' The old man shuffled forward, in spite of the infirmities of advanced age, to take the garment from the footman, and search the face of the gentleman with eyes suddenly moist with powerful emotion. 'We did not know if the letters had reached you—perhaps you might not yet even be aware of the tragic events here.'

'They did. About two months ago.' The gentleman stripped off his leather driving gloves with brisk efficiency. 'But there have been difficulties in travelling—chiefly the vagaries of the weather—so it took me longer than I expected.'

'We are so glad to see you again, my lord. So relieved. If I may say, you have not changed in all the time you have been away.'

'Only two years, Marcle. Not so very long.' The accompanying smile was understanding but designed not to encourage further comment.

'Long enough, my lord. You have been missed here.'

'But what about you, Marcle?' The gentleman began to walk in the direction of the library, sure of his direction. 'You look well. I see that you still hold the reins, in spite of your threats to leave to live in retirement with your sister.'

'Not so bad, sir. I would not wish to leave the Hall. And certainly not now… But what a terrible occasion this is. I cannot tell you… An accident that no one could have foreseen…'

'I know.' The guest, clearly a very close and knowledgeable one, intimate with the family circumstances, touched the old man's arm in a brief gesture of comfort, at the same time hoping against hope to dam the flood of painful detail and the threat of overt sympathy. 'So Mr Hoskins informed me. And my brother. Both letters eventually found me.'

'What a terrible homecoming, my lord…'

His attempts, it appeared, had been futile. *He really could not take any more.*

'I will deal with it, Marcle,' his tone now a little brusque but not unkind. 'I presume Lord Nicholas is here?'

'Yes, my lord.' The butler concentrated on the more practical direction given less than subtly to his thoughts. 'He has spent some time in London, particularly with the lawyers, being a trustee, as you will be aware—but he returned last week. He is in the gun room, I believe. I will send a message that you have arrived.' He motioned with a rheumatic hand to the young footman. 'Silas…'

'No. There is no need to trouble yourself, Marcle. I will go to the gun room.'

'Of course, my lord. I would just wish to say that…' But he was already bowing to an empty hall as the gentleman made good his escape.

Chapter Two

The door to the gunroom at Burford Hall, deep in the west wing, opened on to a familiar and industrious scene. A young man in shirt sleeves, corduroy breeches and high-topped boots, all well suited to country life, presented his back to the visitor. A black spaniel at his feet, Lord Nicholas Faringdon leaned with hip propped against a bench on which were all the accoutrements necessary for oiling and cleaning the impressive array of sporting firearms. Head bent, he was intent on freeing the firing mechanism on a particularly fine but unreliable duck gun. He whistled tunelessly between his teeth.

'So this is how you are spending your time. I might have known it. Planning a day's rough shooting when you should be overlooking the acres!'

The young man's head snapped up and turned at the sound of the soft voice. He stopped whistling. There was a moment of stunned silence. Then he abandoned the gun on top of the rest of the detritus on the bench and pushed himself to his feet, a grin warming his features.

'Hal! I had no idea.' He approached the gentleman, hand outstretched in formal greeting, and then thought better of it and seized his brother in a warm hug, all the time firing questions. 'How long it has been! When did you arrive? Have you been back in England long? How long will you stay?'

Returning the embrace with equal enthusiasm, Henry—Hal

to those who knew him best—pushed back and the brothers, Lord Henry and Lord Nicholas Faringdon, stood at arm's length to assess each other. The family resemblance was strong. Both were true Faringdons. Dark hair, almost black and dense with little reflected light. A straight nose, lean cheeks, a decided chin and well-marked brows, they were a handsome pair. But whereas Hal's eyes were more grey than blue, stern and frequently on the edge of cynical, Nicholas, some three years younger, viewed the world through a bright optimistic gaze of intense blue. Their smiles on this occasion were also very similar, but Nicholas's mouth lacked the lines of experience, of ambition and sardonic humour that were engraved on Hal's features.

'You look well, for all your travels.' Nicholas gave his brother a friendly smack on his shoulder. 'Have you made your fortune yet? Is that why you are here, to brag of your exploits?'

'Not quite.' Hal shook his head, well used to the ribbing.

'Ha! I wager you are too fine to have anything to do with a mere landowner now. Faringdon and Bridges, is it not? Should I ask who is in charge of the business? Are you controlling New York yet?'

'No—and, no, you should not ask! Nat Bridges and I have equal shares and investment in this company. I see you haven't changed, Nick.' Henry looked at his brother, noting the faint lines of strain beside his mouth, until his attention was demanded by a nudge against his boot. 'And who is this?' He bent to pull the ears of the spaniel who had come to sit at his feet in a friendly fashion.

'Bess. She's young, but she's hopeful. As soon as she stops chasing and scattering the birds rather than collecting them.'

The dog sneezed as if knowing she was under discussion. The two men laughed.

'Hal. I don't know what to say to you about all this…' Nicholas was suddenly sober, as a cloud covering the sun, the smile wiped from mouth and eyes by a depth of sorrow.

Hal shook his head and turned away to run his hand along the polished stocks and barrels of the guns in their racks. It was all so familiar. But now it was changed for ever and he could do nothing about it. 'Any problems with the estate?' He kept his back turned.

'No.' Nicholas was relieved to return to plain reporting of facts. Emotions at the Hall were still too stark to allow for casual airing. 'All neatly tied up. The entail stands. There are no inheritance problems and Hoskins had finished his affairs when I was last in London. Thomas always was thorough, of course. He left everything as it should be.'

At that, Hal spun on his heel, his voice and expression harsh with pain. 'How the hell did it happen, Nick? A riding accident? I have never seen anyone sit a horse better or more securely than Thomas. And he was not even out hunting, if the letters speak the truth.'

'No.' Nick frowned at the problem that had faced him for the past few months. 'He went out across the estate to meet the new agent, Whitcliffe. He never arrived. His horse returned here riderless. Thomas was found later that morning on the edge of the east wood, no obvious injuries, but his neck broken. The horse was unharmed too. It must have shied—a loose pheasant, perhaps—and thrown him. His mind must have been preoccupied and…well, you know the rest.'

'Yes. Such a tragic waste of a life.'

'I still can't believe that he will not walk through that door and ask me if I wish to go…' Nick's words dried in his throat as the memories became too intense.

Hal saw and understood. He grasped his brother's shoulder, with a little shake. 'I know. Come to the library and tell me about everything. And a brandy would not come amiss, I think.'

'Yes—of course. And I would wish to know what you have been about.' Once more in command, Nicholas shrugged into his jacket and followed his brother from the room. As he turned to lock the door to the gunroom, the spaniel fussing round his feet, a thought came to him

'By the by…have you spoken with Lady Faringdon yet?'

Hal came to a halt and turned, brows arched.

'Who?'

'Lady Faringdon. The Marchioness.'

'You mean Thomas married?' Hal asked in amazement. 'I did not know…I had no idea…'

'Why, yes. And he has a son. Tom—a splendid child. Just a little more than a year old.'

'Well, now!' Hal leaned his shoulders back against the panelled wall of the passageway and let his breath seep slowly from his lungs as he felt a ridiculous sense of relief begin to surge through his body. 'So the child will inherit. He will be Marquis of Burford.'

'Of course. What else?' Nicholas eyed his brother quizzically and then his face cleared, became touched with sardonic humour as he realised. 'You didn't know! The letters after Thomas's marriage never reached you. You thought it had all come to you, the title and the inheritance, didn't you?'

'Yes.' Hal closed his eyes at the enormous sense of release from an existence that had taken on the weight of a life sentence. 'Yes, I did.'

'And are mightily relieved that it does not.' Nicholas took Hal's arm in a sympathetic grasp to urge him in the direction of the library and the brandy.

'More than mightily. It is something I would never wish for. I will happily be a trustee for the infant, but Marquis of Burford? Not to my taste at all. In America I am now used to being Mr Faringdon. And I like it.'

'Still the Republican, I see.' Nick's tone was dry, with more than a hint of amusement. 'But you are safe from the inheritance. We sent to tell you of the marriage, of course, not so long after you left. The letters must have gone astray.'

'Easy enough to do. They never reached me. I had no idea.' Hal was still half-inclined not to believe this stroke of fortune. 'Why did Thomas not tell me of his intentions before I left? I thought we were close enough. If he took a bride so soon after I took ship, surely he had already met the lady!'

Nick grinned. 'I think not, from what I remember. It must have been love at first sight. Or at least a sufficiently strong attraction. Not that you would have noticed particularly—our brother was never one to wallow in sentiment, as you know—but Thomas would have a quick betrothal and carried it all off with high-handed determination.'

'It must have been a shattering experience for him, to have fallen in love so completely.' Hal frowned a little. The picture did not quite fit with his knowledge of Thomas, his brother's over-riding interest in sport and hunting to the exclusion of almost everything else.

'I know it does not sound like the Thomas we knew.' Nick shrugged in agreement, reading his brother's thoughts with unnerving accuracy. 'But come. We will postpone the brandy and I will introduce you to the Widow. I warn you, she is taking Thomas's death hard, but she is very resilient and will come about. I expect that she will be in the blue withdrawing-room with her mother and the baby at this time of day.'

'Then lead on.'

They walked through the house in close accord, Hal's lightness of spirit, in spite of the untimely death of his brother, a shining bright strand woven through the dark skein of grief. He would not have to inherit the estates and the title. Thank God! He could return to his dealings in America with a clear conscience, leaving the care of the property with his fellow trustee Nicholas, who had no objection to rural life. The direction of his life had suddenly come back into clear focus, an enormous weight lifted from his mind. He was all set to be appreciative of and everlastingly thankful to his new sister-in-law who had produced so timely an heir.

'What is she like?' he asked Nick as they climbed the main staircase. 'Is she pretty? Amenable?'

'Not so. She is a Beauty. A Diamond of the First Water! Thomas showed far more taste than I would ever have given him credit for. But you will soon see for yourself.'

Nicholas opened the door into the blue withdrawing-room, a light attractive space with azure silk hangings that matched and complimented the fashionable blue-and-silver-striped wallpaper. The room had, Hal noted, been newly refurbished, remembering the previous drab greens and ochres of his mother's occupancy.

A fire in the hearth beckoned. Sun glinted on the delicate crystal chandelier and the polished surface of a small piano. It was undoubtedly a lady's room, a lady of style and exquisite taste.

And the tableau within the room that met the critical gaze of the two men was equally attractive. A young woman was seated on the rug before the fire, her black silk skirts of deepest mourning spread around her. A baby in the experimental stage of crawling was in the act of reaching up to take a red ball from his mother's hands, then tried to stuff the soft felt into his mouth. A grey kitten curled at their side. The lady laughed at her son, face alight with pride and delight in his achievements; she reached forwards to pick him up and cuddle him against her breast, pressing her lips against his dark curls. The baby chucked and grasped her fashionable ringlets with small but ruthless fingers.

It was a scene to entrance even the hardest of heart.

Then the lady looked round at the opening of the door.

'Eleanor! I though we would find you here,' Nicholas began. 'Can I introduce you…'

The tension in the room was suddenly palpable. It tightened, brittle as wire, sharp as a duelling sword, in the space of a heartbeat. The kitten arched in miniature and silent fury at the appearance of the inquisitive spaniel. The newly widowed Marchioness of Burford, always pale of complexion, became paper white, expressive eyebrows arched, eyes widening with shock, as they fixed on the gentlemen at the door. Her smile of delight for her baby vanished, leaving her still and wary. Lord Henry Faringdon simply froze on the spot, every sense coated in ice, spine rigid. His breath backed up in his lungs.

Nicholas looked from Eleanor to Hal and back again. What in the Devil's name was wrong here? He had no idea.

For an endless moment Nicholas stood uncertain between the two, his introduction brought to an abrupt and uncomfortable halt. He looked towards Eleanor where she still knelt on the rug for some illumination, brows raised. Once pale, her face was now flushed with bright colour, but he could not read the expression that flitted momentarily across her expressive features. Embarrassment? Perhaps. A flash of anger? But that seemed unlikely in the circumstances. It did not seem to Nicholas that it was grief. There was no enlightenment to be had here.

Meanwhile Hal, he noted, had no expression at all! His face was shuttered, unreadable, his eyes hooded, an expression Nicholas recognised with a touch of trepidation from their childhood and adolescence. His brother was a past master at disguising his thoughts and feelings if he chose to do so and could quickly retreat into icy hauteur. His lips were now firmly compressed. If he had been about to say something on his entrance, he had clearly changed his mind. He continued to stand, rooted to the spot, the open door at his back.

Nicholas gave up and, for better or worse, completed the formal introduction.

'Eleanor. You must know that this is my brother, Henry. He received our sad news at last and is come to… Well, he is here, for which I am relieved.' The bland stare from the Marchioness gave him no encouragement to continue. Hal's enigmatic silence was no better. 'Hal…this is Eleanor, Thomas's wife.'

The silence stretched. The tension held.

Then good manners reasserted themselves as if an invisible curtain had been lifted. The lady placed the child back on the rug and rose to her feet with graceful composure, shaking out her ruffled skirts. Hal walked forward and bowed as the lady executed a neat curtsy and extended her hand in dignified welcome. He took it and raised it to his lips. All formal courtesy, appropriate to the occasion, all social graces smoothly applied. So why did Nicholas still feel that the banked emotion in the room could explode at any moment and shatter them to pieces?

'My lady. I am pleased to make your acquaintance, but I regret the occasion. May I express my condolences. Your loss must be very great, as is mine.'

'Thank you, my lord. Your good wishes are most acceptable. I miss your brother sorely. You must know that I have received all possible support and kindness from your family.'

All that was proper was expressed with cool, precise formality. *But it was all wrong.*

At their feet the child, tired of the red ball and lack of attention, began to fret and whimper. The lady immediately stooped and lifted him.

'This is Thomas's son.' The Marchioness turned the baby in her arms towards the visitors.

Against his will Henry was drawn to approach the child. The Faringdon line had bred true again. The infant had thick, dark curls, which would probably straighten with age. And one day when the chubbiness of babyhood had passed, he would have the fine straight nose and sharply defined cheekbones of his father. Already the dark brows were clear, arching with ridiculous elegance in the infant face. But the eyes. They were not true. They were hers, his mother's. As clear as the finest glass, as luminous as costly amethysts. The baby smiled and crowed at the attention, stretching out a hand to the newcomer. He had a dimple, Hal noticed inconsequentially as he allowed the baby to grasp his own fingers, smiling against all his intentions as they were promptly gnawed by tender gums.

'His name?' Henry had his voice well in hand.

'Thomas.' Eleanor did not. Her voice broke a little. 'He is named for his father.'

Henry stroked the baby's soft hair, his grief for his dead brother swelling in his chest.

Eleanor immediately stepped back with the child, putting a subtle distance between them. 'Forgive me—I am a little over-wrought and the baby will be tired and hungry. If you will ex-cuse me, I will take him to the nursery.'

She turned away abruptly, never once allowing her eyes to meet Lord Henry's, and began to walk towards the door.

'My lady.' Henry's words stopped her, but she did not turn to face them as if the open door was a much-desired means of es-cape. 'I would request a meeting with you. A matter of business, you understand, as a trustee of the estate.'

'Of course.'

'In an hour, perhaps, if that is to your convenience. In the library.'

'Of course,' she repeated. 'An hour.'

The Marchioness left the room, taking the child with her.

Lord Henry's eyes never left her until her slim figure turned the corner round the sweep of the main staircase.

* * *

It was one of the longest hours of the Marchioness of Burford's life.

After leaving her son with a doting nurserymaid, she paced the fine Aubusson carpet in the library, oblivious to the splendour and comfort around her. The richness of the tapestries that glowed against the panelled wood left her unmoved. The leather bindings of the books with their gold and red tooling might be sumptuous, but failed to catch her eye. The polished oak furniture, well loved by generations of the Faringdon family, went unnoticed. Nor could she sit, not even in a sunny window seat with its view of woods and distant hills and the parterre which she herself was in the process of planting. Nervous tension balled in her stomach. She felt cold, yet her hands were clammy with sweat, even as she wiped them surreptitiously down her black silken skirts.

She had dreaded this meeting, fully aware that it could happen—was almost inevitable to happen—at some time in the future. But she had hoped, prayed even, that it would never come about. Or be so far into the future distance that painful memories would have faded, emotions stilled. And she had deliberately closed her mind to the consequences. But when she had looked up to see him in the doorway, tall and dark and magnificent, it was as if all time had been obliterated. Her heart had leapt. Her pulse quickened and raced before she had sternly reminded herself of the events of the past.

And as she remembered again now, anger flared, all-consuming, raging through her veins so that she trembled with the force of it. He would receive no welcome here from her.

But what would she say to him? Or he to her? On a thought she realised that he was just as shocked as she, more so since he had apparently been unaware of her marriage. At least she had known of the possibility of this meeting and had been able to prepare. From the immediate tensing of his whole body on setting eyes on her, as if facing the barrels of a shotgun, *he* had been stunned.

She laughed with bitter eyes at her own predicament. *You are a fool. You were not prepared at all. It took your breath away to see him again!*

But now she had her own secrets to keep, whatever her personal inclination in the matter. She took a deep breath to steady her nerves. There was no room for guilt here. She would keep those secrets until the day she died. The only one who had shared them with her, who had understood their significance, was now dead, and she would keep faith with the vows made.

Eleanor set her mind to rule her heart.

When he came to her she was ready, standing before the long window, composed, confident, a glossy layer of sophistication. She would hold this interview on her own terms as Marchioness of Burford.

He closed the door softly, advanced and stood for a moment. They might have been strangers, distant acquaintances at the most, except that at least then he might have put himself out to be sociable. As it was he looked at her with apparent indifference in his cold grey eyes and the stern set of his mouth.

And surveyed her in a detailed assessment from head to foot with an arrogance that chilled her blood.

How right Nicholas had been, he thought. The Marchioness was not pretty. He had forgotten how very beautiful she was. Heart-stoppingly so. All that glossy brown hair with its autumnal tints, caught up in fashionable ringlets. Any red-blooded man would dream of unpinning it, of allowing it to curl in his hands or against his lips. He remembered exactly how it had felt. Her perfect oval face with straight nose and sculpted lips was lovely indeed. Calm and translucent as a Renaissance Ma-donna—until he looked at her eyes. Amethyst fire, fringed with dark lashes, and at this moment blazing with temper and wilful determination. Here was no simpering miss, he acknowledged. The pretty and naïve debutante of his memory had vanished for ever. She was tall. Taller than he had remembered, the crown of her head reaching well past his shoulder. And the black gown, extravagantly fashionable, complimented her elegant figure and the natural cream of her complexion. Assured and polished, she had grown into her new status since he had known her as Miss Eleanor Stamford. His brother had indeed shown excellent taste in his choice of bride.

Eleanor found herself flushing under the sustained regard. It had the whip of an insult and she raised her chin against it but she would not retaliate. She would not!

The silence between them had lasted too long for social correctness. But when the lady almost felt compelled to break it, it was he who did so.

'My Lady Burford. I believe that you deserve my congratulations as well as my condolences.' He bowed with cold grace. Another calculated insult. 'At least I now know the answer to one of the many unsolved mysteries of this world! I have clearly been lacking in my understanding of the driving ambition of some of the members of your sex. I realise that with any real understanding of human nature, I should have been able to work it out for myself.'

'My lord?'

'You look surprised, my dear Eleanor.' Lord Henry's smile was an essay in contempt. 'It is simply that I now find it perfectly plain why you chose not to respond to my offer of marriage, in spite of your previous…shall I say, *encouragement* of my suit. You had your sights set on a far bigger and more important fish in your small pond. And a far richer one.' The slick of disdain could not quite disguise the underlying pain, but the words had the bite of a lash. '*I* could obviously offer you nothing in comparison. I am sorry that my brother's death has caused all your planning to go awry, my lady! As widow of the Marquis of Burford, your social position will be far less glamorous than you had plotted and planned for—if my brother had had the consideration to live.'

Eleanor found herself unexpectedly speechless.

Whatever she had expected him to say, whatever tone she had expected him to use towards her, it was certainly not this.

'I do not understand. You will have to speak more plainly, my lord.' Eleanor managed with an effort of will to keep her response cool, with none of the confused bewilderment that resulted from his words.

'I admire your composure,' he continued in the same conversational tone, 'but of course you must have anticipated that we would meet again at some point, given the family connection. Unlike myself, who had no notion of what you had achieved in my absence. Did you perhaps expect me to have the supreme good manners not to mention our past dealings? To behave as if nothing untoward had occurred?'

Eleanor reconstructed her thoughts with a little shake of her head, trying to ignore the heavy sarcasm.

'An offer of marriage, you say? You *promised* marriage, certainly. And I believed you. But I never received such an offer. It appeared that you had changed your mind.' She held him in that clear gaze, willing him to deny her challenge. 'I could wish that you had been sensitive enough to inform me of it. Instead you left me, left the country. No word, no explanation. Nothing. I was forced to learn of your departure from elsewhere. I admit, my lord, I had expected better treatment at your hands.'

'You have a short memory, my lady.' He was implacable in his response.

'I have an excellent memory, my lord! I expected to hear from you. You promised that you would write when you had arranged your passage.' Eleanor could hear her voice rising as the past flooded back and she fought hard to keep it controlled. 'And then I was left to learn that you had sailed. To America. With no intention to return in the near future. You obviously had no thought for me at all.'

'I sent you a letter. Telling you when I would sail. Asking you to join me as we had discussed. I gave you time and place.' Lord Henry turned from her to stand before the fireplace, the distance between them a little greater. She was so lovely with the sun gilding her hair in an iconic halo. It would be so easy to believe her. And so disastrous if he allowed himself to do so. Besides, he knew that she lied. He clenched his jaw. 'Don't deny it. I know the message was delivered to your home. The groom I paid to do it confirmed the delivery.'

'I received no such letter.'

'It would certainly be more comfortable for you to hold to that fact, would it not, dear Eleanor?' Lord Henry struggled to keep his tone flat, conversational even. 'I would be the first to agree that such problems arise. It is quite possible for letters to go astray, as I discovered only a few hours ago. After all, I had absolutely no knowledge of Thomas's marriage to you until Nicholas broke the news in the gun room. And yet Thomas had certainly written to inform me of the happy event.' He picked up a fragile porcelain figure of a shepherdess and lamb from the mantelpiece, contemplated for the barest second smashing it on the hearth, replaced it gently with the utmost control in exactly the same spot. 'But I know without any shadow of doubt that *my* letter was delivered to *you,* allowing you all the time you would need to join me at the vessel. My messenger was most reliable, as you could imagine for so important a delivery.'

'Such a letter, if it ever existed, never reached my hands.' She could find nothing other to say in her own defence.

Lord Henry shrugged, a gesture of cynical disbelief. 'If you insist on holding to that, my lady… Tell me. Did you know my brother before I left, or did you wait until I had gone before you put yourself in his way?'

'I…' She could not believe that he had actually said that—that he could think so little of her!

'It would not be very difficult to lure Thomas into marriage,' he continued to taunt her. 'You have a beautiful face, as I know to my cost. And my brother found it easy to trust those he liked.'

'I never lured Thomas!' How could the man whom she had once loved more than life itself be so deliberately vindictive?

'No? But he offered you marriage.'

'Yes. He did.'

'I expect your lady mother was delighted. Your family might be respectable enough, but you had hardly been groomed for the role of Marchioness.' He lifted a hand to sweep the room in an expansive gesture. 'And here you are, mistress of Burford Hall, a town house in the most fashionable part of London and a hunting lodge in Leicestershire. Quite a killing, my lady.'

'Of course. It was more than I could ever have dreamed of.' A frown marred her forehead as she attempted to catch his meaning.

'You must have been astounded at your good fortune. A Marquis as rich as Solomon in all his glory. Instead of a younger son with uncomfortably Republican leanings and an inclination to make his own way in the colonies.'

So! He thought she had callously rejected him in the interest of wealth and social position. She caught her breath at the injustice of the veiled accusation and stepped towards him with an unconcealed passion.

'I would have risked everything to go with you if you had told me!' Her hands curled into fists, at odds with her feminine appearance. 'My home, my family. I would have followed you anywhere. How can you possibly doubt that?'

Lord Henry raised his brows in eloquent disbelief.

'Are you possibly making a play for me again, my lady—now that my brother is dead? Is the role of mother of the heir insufficient for you?' The bitter words were all that he could manage to hide the depth of hurt that still had the power to move him. He had truly thought that it had faded, that he had done with that episode of his life. Now, faced with the reality of her, knowing her rejection, it was as sharp and lethal as ever.

She could hardly comprehend his words. 'How dare you! How dare you suggest something so degrading—so despicable!'

'I dare! I dare do all manner of things!' The past swept back in a submerging wave, allowing anger, frustration, desire, all long subdued, to take hold. A desire to possess her once more filled him and, if he were honest, not a little to punish her for her treachery. She was so beautiful, and she was not his! 'Did you make a good bargain?' His demands evaded his control, even when he saw the hurt in her eyes. 'Could my brother give you pleasure to compare with that which you claimed to find in my arms? Or did you lie to me? And set your teeth when I kissed you or allowed my hands to touch your silken skin? Shall we rediscover what, if anything, was between us?'

He pounced with the lithe strength of a hunting cat on an unsuspecting mouse. His claws might be sheathed, but his dominance was lethal and dangerous none the less. His fine hands grasped her shoulders, holding her when she would have pulled away, but the initial contact startled them both, a tingle of reciprocating fire. He looked down at his hands where they grasped her shoulders. Surely he was over all that. This was not supposed to happen. Not now. Not when he had fought against it for so long, not when he believed her to be guilty of betrayal. He looked up to see her watching him with similar uncertainty, similar shock—but set his mind against it.

He would have taken her mouth with his, hot and demanding, more in punishment than passion, if his attention had not been caught by the jewel that she wore on her breast, a pendant on a fine gold chain. Small and delicate, of no great intrinsic value, yet it was beautiful and wrought by the hand of a craftsman. Its setting was gold filigree, leaves and flowers, the centre of each bloom set with a tiny diamond that glinted in the light with each erratic rise and fall of her breast. The central stone was an amethyst, clear and shining, of a depth of colour that reflected Eleanor's eyes when she was radiantly happy.

But not at this moment, when her furious glare was the stormy intensity of indigo.

'So you still wear it?' Lord Henry's tone was deceptively conversational.

'Yes.'

'It surprises me. Some would say that it was hypocritical not to consign it to the back of a drawer, since you turned your back with such ease on the one who gave it to you.'

'Perhaps, after today, I will.' She almost spat the words, shocked to the core by his accusations. 'I thought the giver had some affection for me, love even. How wrong I was! I should be grateful to you, my lord, for pointing out the error of my ways.' She angled her head, disdain writ large in her slanted glance. 'Perhaps I should return it to you. You may find some other naïve lady of your acquaintance in New York to gift it to.'

His tenuous hold on his temper duly snapped.

And he lowered his head, his eyes all the time on hers, until his mouth, hard and angry, crushed her lips. When she mur-

mured a protest, he immediately raised his head, eyes glittering.
'Had you forgotten, dearest Nell? I thought you had enjoyed it.
You did not refuse my kisses in the past.'

He slanted his head to take her mouth again, without kindness or thought for her own wishes, but forcing her lips to part
against her teeth. Eleanor stood unresponsive in his hold, until
on a breath, and a sob deep in her breast, her resistance melted
away, her anger as insubstantial as morning mist. Instead of
pushing against his chest to achieve her freedom, her fingers
curled into the material of his coat and she clung to him. In response his arms tightened round her until her curves were moulded to his hard length from breast to thigh. Her mouth softened,
lips parting of their own free will, to invite invasion. He groaned.
And took what she was prepared to give, and more. The fire
burned brightly, leaping through their veins with unexpected
brilliance and heat, and seared them both.

When he finally released her, the anger had not been assuaged
at all, but still surged through his blood, not even calmed when
she swayed and would have fallen had she not grasped his fore-
arms for support.

'Well, my lady?' For a brief moment he allowed her to see the
temper that burned in his gut. 'What do you think? A title and a
fortune balanced against the pleasures of my hands and mouth?
I wager that my brother was not lacking in skills of love. But did
he satisfy you?' But then the pain in her eyes, sharp and beyond
her control, forced him to retreat. 'Perhaps he was kinder than I,'
he murmured. 'Perhaps you were wise in your decision after all.'

Confusion swept Eleanor's features as she pushed herself to
stand alone. She could not think, could not accept what had just
happened between them, what she had allowed to happen. Humiliation brought its warm colour to her throat and cheeks. She veiled
her eyes from him with a downsweep of lashes. Perhaps there was
the merest sparkle of a tear, but he could not be sure. But it brought
him to his senses as assuredly as a deluge of cold water.

'Forgive me. I should not have forced myself on you in that
manner. It is unpardonable.' He stepped back from her as disgust
rose in his throat at his own temper. And that she should be able

to rouse such longings in him again, revealing a weakness that he thought well and truly dead. Disgust at the betrayal of his body, which was hard and demanding for her. He now kept his voice low, but with no warmth in it, simply cold acceptance of the situation. 'You would seem to have a talent for falling on your feet, my lady. I am not available to you. But I should warn you. Keep your clever velvet claws out of Nicholas.'

The lady flinched as if he had slapped her with the outrageous comment. 'I will not continue this conversation.' Eleanor choked on a sob. 'I can only be grateful that fate spared me marriage with you, my lord. I could never have guessed at your capacity for inflicting such pain.' She swept past him, but when she had reached the door his voice stopped her.

'Eleanor?'

'Well?'

'I would be interested to know if you managed to persuade my brother that you were a virgin on your wedding night.'

Her whole body stiffened under the vile cruelty of the attack. She dare not face him again for fear that he would see the tears that had begun to track down her cheeks.

'The matter is entirely none of your affair,' she managed in a voice little more than a whisper.

'Of course not, my dear. You are not my affair any longer. And I thank heaven for it. And by the by, there is no need for you to be concerned. I shall not divulge our sordid little secret to anyone. I believe it is not to the credit of either of us. We must preserve your spotless reputation at all cost, must we not?'

On which vicious parting shot, the composure of the Marchioness of Burford finally disintegrated. She wrenched open the library door to hurry from the room, slamming it forcefully in Lord Henry's face.

His lordship merely stood, head bowed, eventually returning to stare blindly into the empty fire-grate, until moved to kick viciously against a half-charred log with his booted foot.

Well done indeed!

His intention had been to pursue the interview with icy and disinterested detachment. So how the Devil had he allowed him-

self to make such unwarrantable comments? To inflict such blatant intimacies on her, uncaring of her wishes in the matter? A
despicable act, unworthy of his birth and upbringing. Conflict-
ing emotions and images warred within his brain. Of course she
deserved every accusation. Had she not rejected and humiliated
him, casting his love into the gutter as so much worthless trash?
Her promises of love, protestations of devotion and a willingness
to throw in her lot with him, had been shallow and empty. Instead, she had chosen worldly ambition. How fickle women
were! And yet…the horror in her face when he had accused her
of perfidy demanded his attention. The hesitation in her voice.
The tightening of the muscles along her jaw as she had striven,
unsuccessfully in the end, to prevent tears gathering in those glorious eyes, spilling down her cheeks. She had not been unmoved
by his words. Or by his demands on her body. He closed his eyes
as he remembered the scent of her hair, the taste of her lips as
they responded to his insistent possession. But then, women
were skilled actresses after all.

But what did it matter? Lord Henry straightened, stretching,
allowing the muscles in his shoulders to relax as his pulse slowed.
He had not realised that he had been so tense. He walked slowly
to follow the Marchioness from the library. It was all in the past.
She had what she wanted. The inheritance was secure with an heir,
albeit very young. Nicholas would more than willingly play the
interested uncle and trustee. He was now free to return to America and wash his hands of the whole situation in England unless
something unforeseen arose to demand his presence in the future.
He need trouble himself no further over Eleanor Faringdon.

And in the short time remaining to him here at Burford Hall,
he would treat her with all that damnable courtesy and good manners worthy of a gentleman. Whatever the cost!

Chapter Three

Lord Henry Faringdon settled back into life at Burford Hall in the following days with consummate ease. Casting an eye over the splendid horseflesh in the stables, he chose himself a handsome bay hunter and rode the familiar estate with Nicholas.

'This is all very impressive, little brother. The livestock looks well. And you have drained the lower pastures at last, I see. Your doing or Thomas's?'

Nicholas laughed, the shadows of bereavement lifting in response to the bright spring sunshine and physical exertion of a gallop across the open parkland. 'Do I need to say it? I may be the *little brother,* but I have an eye to the future of the family. Thomas, as you are well aware, only had an eye to the next run of the fox in winter, or the next winner at Newmarket in summer. Or a flirtation with the prettiest girl in the room.' His smile became tinged with sadness as the loss was driven home by the memories, and he changed the subject. 'The stone quarry has been developed since your day, Hal. We have improved the surface on some of the roads. And we are beginning to manage the old woodland for timber.'

Hal snorted. 'Very efficient! I will leave all such matters to you.'

Nicholas was silent for a moment as they reined in their horses to take in the fine view of the lower lake with its ornamental planting. Then he fixed his brother with a determined eye.

'Hal. I know that you can tell me it is none of my affair—but is anything wrong?'

'How do you mean?' Henry betrayed nothing by glance or voice. 'I am aware of nothing. Apart from having to share the breakfast table with Alicia Stamford and her interminable opinions on every topic under the sun. She is enough to make a saint swear—and I am no saint!'

Nick grimaced in sympathy, but refused to be put off.

'I don't know what it is, but between you and Eleanor I sense unease, some distance between you. More than that, in fact—a definite lack of…of *tolerance.*'

'How so?' Hal's expression became even more bland.

'I don't know.' Nicholas rubbed his chin with his gloved fist. 'It is nothing that you say or do. Just that—you don't seem to like each other very much. And you seem to have deliberately kept out of her way—and she out of yours.'

Henry kept his gaze fixed on the landscape, lifting his shoulders in the lightest of shrugs. 'I was not aware. Perhaps Lady Burford is just wary of men, after Thomas's death.'

'There, you see. You are all cold formality, using her title. And I had not thought that she was wary. Nell is usually approachable and friendly enough.'

Henry shook his head, teeth clenched. Nicholas had called her Nell! A spark of jealousy gripped him before he could curse himself for a fool. Such suspicions were totally unfounded as he knew very well. And what was it to him? The Marchioness was free to give her affections where she chose.

He deliberately turned the conversation back to the engaging topic of the merits of growing beet for the overwintering of cattle, leaving Nicholas with a clear conviction that his question had been adroitly evaded.

Henry's relationship with Mrs Alicia Stamford, Eleanor's ever-present mama, edged to the glacial. They were scrupulously polite to each other with no direct reference made to the circumstances of their previous encounters, when he had been regarded by her as a most unsatisfactory suitor to her beautiful daughter.

The rules were clearly laid down between them during their first meeting after Henry's arrival.

'Lord Henry. We are pleased to see you back in England.' Mrs Stamford forced her lips into the semblance of a smile and inclined her head with condescending grace, as she smoothed her satin skirts and arranged the costly and delicate shawl round her shoulders in more becoming folds. She had been a beautiful woman in her youth, shadows of it still there in the rich auburn of her hair and her elegant figure. But advanced hypochondria and a fierce ambition dedicated to ensuring the social advancement of her daughter had taken its toll. Her once-porcelain skin was now finely lined, her complexion sallow. Her husband, a country gentleman of comfortable means but no social pretensions, had been dead some dozen years. The lady was now intent on enjoying her freedom and elevated status as mother to the Marchioness of Burford, secure in the knowledge that she lived at one of the best addresses in town and had the means to trick herself out in the latest fashions.

'Thank you, ma'am.' Lord Henry raised her cold fingers to his lips with impeccable finesse. 'I see that you remember me.'

'Of course, my lord.' A flush stained her thin features. 'I remember making your acquaintance in London during my daughter's first Season.'

'But our acquaintance, as I recall, was of very short duration.' *Since you did everything in your power to keep Eleanor out of my path!*

'You were very keen to seek your fortune in America, my lord, as I recall. I trust that matters went well for you.'

'They did.'

'And how long do you plan to remain here at Burford Hall?' *A matter of days, I sincerely trust!*

'I have not yet decided.'

'I am sure the estate can manage well enough without your involvement, if business demands your presence elsewhere.' Her lips curled unpleasantly that he might be engaged in something so common as *business,* no matter how lucrative. 'Nicholas has proved himself an excellent trustee for my grandson. And Mr Hoskins, of course.'

'I am sure he has. But it my inclination to remain here for a little while.'

Which was about as much as they could find to say to each other. Henry smiled and bowed. Mrs Stamford inclined her head once more. They understood each other very well.

And Nicholas, with half an ear to the exchange, was left with the uneasy impression that there was something here which he had missed, of which he was unaware. Conversation with Nell's mama was always an adventure, bordering on the brittle. Opinionated, critical, frequently acerbic and intolerant, she took no prisoners. But here… Nick could not quite put his finger on it. The sneer on Mrs Stamford's face, the edge to her voice as the exchange drew to a close could have cut through flesh and bone. And as for Hal… There was no love lost here, despite the exquisite politeness of the little episode. But short of asking either combatant outright… One glance at the closed expressions, the barely veiled hostility, convinced Nick that no man of sense or with an eye to self-preservation would risk such a foolhardy move.

In spite of Nell's determination to keep her mind on more important issues, her thoughts betrayed her with cruel persistence. And her dreams. She relived again and again that magical Season when her mother and an aged uncle had launched her into society, the only season which was possible, given their financial circumstances. Her mother had been intent on a good match, as advantageous a marriage as could be achieved. Once she had met Lord Henry Faringdon, Eleanor had thoughts for no one else.

It was at a soirée, at the home of a distant cousin who mixed in the most fashionable of circles, an ideal opportunity for Eleanor to meet the privileged members of the *haut ton*. Her mother had managed to pull strings to achieve invitations. Eleanor could remember the occasion in perfect detail when she dared allow her mind free rein. Sitting in her bedroom with her son on her lap, she abandoned her attempts to discipline her memories and simply let them sweep back unhindered, layer upon layer. The decorations of hothouse flowers with the intense perfume of jasmine and heliotrope. The music and dancing. And the dress she wore for the occasion. White muslin as would become a débutante with a delicately embroidered hem and silver ribbons at waist and neckline. Her hair in high-pinned ringlets, falling to her shoulders, and a string of pearls, the only jewellery she possessed.

And she had seen *him* that night. He had entered the room with his brother, the Marquis, but Eleanor had eyes for no one but Lord Henry. The Marquis, for all his consequence and good looks, might not have existed. Lord Henry filled her vision and her senses. Tall, dark of hair, handsome of face, elegant of figure, impossibly attractive in the formal splendid of black satin evening clothes and white linen. They were introduced. They stood up for a country dance. And her heart was lost before she could take a breath, somewhere between the cotillion and a reel.

Her smile was wry, a little sad, as she recalled that heady moment. The merest touch of his hand had quickened her pulse and when his lips had brushed her fingers she knew that she was his for ever.

Disastrously, she was now forced to admit, Eleanor had believed that he was as captivated as she. What a fool she had been! Carried away by the romance of snatched meetings, the delicious duplicity of a few stolen moments of time when they could close out the world. She had listened to his dreams of a new life, fired by his ideas and ambitions. She had believed in him. Trusted. They would go together.

And then he had simply left her with not one word of explanation or farewell. Humiliated and heartbroken, she had hidden her grief, determined not to be an object of interest or pity. Her pride and her spirit had come to her aid when she might have been totally devastated, and she had survived. With the kindness and compassion of Thomas. Dear Thomas. But she had learned in those cold days after Lord Henry's departure that there was a high price to pay for love and she would not willingly pay it again. To show emotion, to offer love, was to put yourself into the power of those to whom it was given. And when it was not returned...

Eleanor shuddered as she remembered the exact occasion of her open avowal of love and commitment to Hal, when a soft moon illuminated the summer house, casting deep and intimate shadows within, painting the leaves of the overhanging willow that enclosed them with silver hue.

When Thomas had offered marriage, her gratitude knew no bounds. She could not love him—he both knew and accepted that. She had never tried to dissemble or pretend to an emotion that was now beyond her capabilities. Deep affection, yes, without doubt. And trust. But love…that was not possible. And he in his turn had offered her friendship, kindness, respect, a marriage based on compassion and understanding. No promises of blazing passion. But she could—indeed, wished to—live without that, and had done so comfortably for two whole years. Why was love considered necessary to achieve a satisfying marriage? When Thomas had taken her to his bed and made her truly his wife he had possessed her with such grace and sensitivity, with a depth of care and tenderness that she still felt she did not deserve. He had quite determinedly allowed no room for either discomfort or embarrassment on her part, enfolding her in warmth and a gentle humour. Her heart swelled, tears threatened as she recalled those painful early days when Thomas had set himself to comfort and reassure. And she, in recognition of her debt to him, had set herself to be a good wife and mother, equally determined that Thomas should never fault her or regret the decision that he had made that desperate day when she had visited him at Faringdon House in London to cast herself on his mercy.

Eleanor, allowing her gaze to rest for a long moment on the miniature of Thomas which stood on her nightstand, believed in all honesty that she had kept her bargain and would mourn her husband's death with genuine grief for the loss of the dearest of friends.

All passion in her life was dead.

If only Hal had not touched her beyond a formal gesture of greeting. If only he had not kissed her, held her in his arms. And she had responded, encouraged him. And wanted him. She felt the heat rise in her cheeks as her senses relived the moment.

Eleanor straightened her shoulders and lectured herself with stern words. Lord Henry must never be given the opportunity to reawaken the passion. It would—it *must*—remain dead and buried. He must never know what she had suffered for his rejection. For the future, she would tolerate her mother's well-meaning interference and devote her life to raising her beloved son. She would find enjoyment and fulfilment in that. She dashed the tears from her cheeks with an impatient hand. Of course she would. She buried her face in her son's dark curls.

On a parallel course, though both would have denied it, Henry, too, found his thoughts returning far too often for comfort to those days when he had met and loved Miss Eleanor Stamford. His courtship of her had been carried on under the most difficult of circumstances, not least the suspicious glare of her mother who desired a far better marriage for her beautiful daughter. Lord Henry, although his birth might be impeccable, was a loose cannon with a desire to make his own way in the world and an uncomfortable lack of consideration for social standing and protocol. Mrs Stamford had watched him like a mother hawk, intent on defending her chick. But he and Eleanor had found the means to meet and the memories were bittersweet.

By God, he had loved her! And believed beyond doubt that she had loved him. Enough to disobey her exacting parent and travel to the new world where they would marry and make a life not bound by rigid convention. He had sworn his undying love, sweeping her along with his dreams of the future. Made preparations. Sent to tell her of the time and place of their sailing. And waited in vain on the windswept dock as the Captain made ready to sail.

No message. No note. Nothing. The minutes had ticked by, his idealistic hopes fading with every beat of his heart, yet still trying to believe that she would arrive at the eleventh hour. And then he could pretend no more. They needed to catch the tide and he had sailed alone. He had risked one further letter when he had landed, but received nothing in return.

So Mr Henry Faringdon had set himself to building his future alone, finding the time to curse Eleanor and all women for their capricious and inconstant nature. Without doubt, she had enjoyed the romance and the excitement of his wooing, been flattered by his declaration of love, but had no intention of keeping her own promises.

Perhaps she had enjoyed the power of having him at her feet. Henry grimaced at his youthful naïvety, his black brows snapping into a firm line. Very well. He too had learnt a hard lesson and would not in his lifetime forget the painful wounds. And it would not be something that he would put himself in the way of repeating.

Thus in his dealings with women since, trust and loyalty were never an issue. Definitely not love! He kept a mistress in some comfort and enjoyed her many talents, but it was a casual arrangement, both sides enjoying the benefits but recognising the lack of commitment.

He now smiled at the thought of her accommodating bed and welcoming arms. Rosalind gave him the pleasures of light conversation, feminine company and the soft delights of her body, with no demands on his time or emotions other than those he was prepared to give. He gave her financial security—and presumably some passing pleasure. But on that windswept dock as the *England's Glory* prepared to sail from Liverpool to New York, he had vowed that he would never again give his heart and soul to any woman.

He might marry in future, of course. But he saw it as a business transaction only to achieve an heir. He would never allow memories of Eleanor Stamford to cloud his judgement or unsettle his peace of mind.

Now, back at Burford Hall, where he must see his nemesis every day, Henry closed his mind against the image of the girl who had stolen his heart, against remembering the soft seductiveness of her lips against his, her delectable curves as he drew her close to imprint her body with his own. And he found a need to discover any excuse against spending time where she might be found in the house. But he could not prevent Nell from haunting him in his dreams with her shy smile and delicious perfume, her hair unbound in glorious disorder in his hands.

He should never have allowed himself to kiss her, to reawaken the desires and needs that now snapped at him with sharp teeth.

He set his teeth against the vivid intrusion and snarled at his valet after another restless night.

On a bright morning Lord Henry, this time alone, made a private and intensely painful visit to the church of St Mary the Virgin, which served the spiritual needs of the estate and the small village of Burford. There in the graveyard, dark head bowed, he stood beside a new grave, the turned earth still raw, although now softened with a faint sheen of spring grass. A simple plinth had been erected, its clean lines topped by a classical urn. The words and dates that recorded the life of his brother were sharply incised, all very proper and tasteful, but telling nothing of the vibrant life of the young man who lay beneath the earth in untimely death. Sorrow clawed at Henry's heart, regrets flooded his mind. It felt, as the sun warmed his skin and the dappled shadows from the elm trees flirted playfully across the mown grass, that he had lost a part of himself, which it would never be possible to recover. With a gentle finger he traced the letters. The depths of the tearing grief that stopped his throat and stung his eyes shocked him as he damned the monstrous twist of fate that had robbed his brother of his life.

But at least Thomas had left a son, to carry on his blood line and the family name, so that there might always be a Faringdon living at Burford House. It was some comfort, Henry supposed, as he brushed the smooth curve of the urn. It must be.

As he would have turned away, his loss in no way assuaged, his attention was drawn to the fresh posy of primroses arranged at the foot of the plinth.

Eleanor's work? Henry hoped so. His lips curved with a cynical edge as he remounted his horse, turned his back on the calm tranquillity of the dead. Whatever motives had driven Eleanor to reject his own love, to send her headlong into marriage with Thomas, he hoped that in the end she had cared for his brother more than a little.

At the beginning of the second week, the family gathered in the dining room for a late luncheon. During the first course of a range of cold cuts of meat, Lord Henry took the unusual opportunity to address himself directly to Lady Burford across the table.

'You should know, ma'am, that I have arranged passage for
America. I shall leave next week.'

'So soon?' Eleanor's gaze moved from her plate to his eyes
and she lifted her napkin to lips gone suddenly dry.

'Why not?' His face held no warmth, but perhaps a little surprise in the consternation that he read in Eleanor's momentarily
unguarded expression. 'My business will not prosper in my absence, whereas you do not need my help here. Nick is more than
capable and far more interested in developing the land than I. And
Hoskins has his finger on all the legal niceties. The inheritance
and your jointure are secure, ma'am. There is nothing to keep
me here.'

'Very well. I…we shall be sorry to see you go, of course.' Her
tone was low with no inflection but, to his disappointment, her
gaze now quickly fell before his. She rarely allowed herself to
look directly at him so that he had presumed her uninterest. And
yet he realised, beyond any sort of logic, that he had been hoping that she would care. It seemed from her reply that she did
not. He allowed himself a sardonic smile at his foolishness. If
Eleanor had been prepared to reject his offer two years previously
in the face of better prospects, she would hardly show any concern for his presence—or his absence—now.

But, on hearing Hal's announcement, Nell's heart had fallen
to the region of her fine kid slippers, her nerves skittering like
mice in an underdrawing. She did not want him to go. She was
afraid of him, of her reactions to him, but she did not want him
to leave Burford Hall.

Mrs Stamford took up the conversation, breaking in to her
daughter's distraught train of thought. 'I am sure that life in
America has much to entice you to return, my lord. And I expect
there are friends who will be missing you.'

'It has indeed. And, yes, there are some who will have
missed me.'

Eleanor heard and came to her own conclusions. Of course.
She should have realised. Her heart sank even lower, if that were

possible. There was nothing to hold him in England. And there would be a lover waiting for him there, a woman who loved him and fretted for his return. A woman who was without doubt beautiful and who enjoyed the intimate attention of his mouth and hands. Her own hands clenched on her knife and fork. Of course he would wish to go back. How ridiculous to think that he would even consider her own needs. Not that she had any true idea of what they might be!

She put down the knife and fork, the slices of chicken untasted, her appetite suddenly gone. And began a detailed conversation with her mama with respect to a planned visit to a neighbouring family during the afternoon. Should they take the landaulet or the barouche? And what was the possibility of inclement weather?

And Hal bitterly accepted that, yes, there was nothing to keep him at Burford Hall.

The plates from the cold collation had hardly been cleared from the table and dishes of fresh fruit and cheese set out when Marcle entered to approach Lady Burford.

'My lady. There are a lady and gentleman come here.' He frowned his disapproval of such lax adherence to acceptable visiting hours.

Eleanor raised her brows a little in some surprise. 'Now is not a very convenient time, Marcle. Perhaps you could show them to the red parlour and supply them with refreshment. We shall be finished here in half an hour.'

Marcle persisted, if reluctantly. 'The gentleman apologises for the unwarranted interruption, but claims urgent business. Of a highly personal nature, which requires immediate attention from your ladyship.'

'I see. Who is he? Do we know him?'

'Sir Edward Baxendale, my lady.' Marcle presented a neat visiting card on a silver salver. 'And Miss Baxendale, his sister, I believe.'

Eleanor looked at the tasteful lettering on the card and then across the table to Nicholas, who was in deep and detailed conversation with Henry about the merits of a favourite hunter. 'Do we know a Sir Edward Baxendale, Nicholas? Does he live locally? I think I have not heard that name, but he might be one of the hunting fraternity. In which case you will be acquainted at least.'

Nick shook his head. 'There is no one of that name who lives in this part of the county, I am sure.' He looked to his brother for confirmation. Henry shook his head, uninterested.

Eleanor decided. 'Very well. Since it is an urgent matter…' She nodded to her butler. 'Show them in, if you please.'

Within minutes, Marcle ushered the visitors into the dining room.

'Sir Edward Baxendale and Miss Baxendale, my lady.'

The gentleman was a man in his early thirties, perhaps a little older than Hal, of medium height and stocky build. Eleanor gained a general impression of quiet elegance and understated fashion in his clothing and appearance. He was without doubt a gentleman of some means. The lady who accompanied him was younger, slight of build, clothed in black as if recently bereaved, but again with a distinct air of fashion. Behind them came a young woman, clearly a companion or governess from her plain and serviceable dress, carrying a young child who squirmed to be set on his feet.

The gentlemen bowed. The ladies curtsied. Marcle hovered with interest in the background.

'Well, Sir Edward. What is this personal business that cannot wait?' Eleanor smiled to put the visitors at their ease. 'Perhaps we can offer you a glass of wine. If you would care to sit—'

'Forgive me, your ladyship, my lords.' The gentleman bowed to the assembled company, face grave, politely deferential but firm. 'I would not normally arrive on your doorstep without due notice. But this is not a social visit. Time is, I believe, of the essence. And what I have to say will certainly, I fear, be distasteful to you.' He allowed his gaze to linger on the faces around the table, his own face and voice strained with compassion.

'Then in what way can we be of help?' Eleanor approached the little group, now with some concern, noting that the young woman was nervous and kept her eyes fixed on Sir Edward, as if for guidance or reassurance.

'I fear that we are come here in some way under false pretences. This is my sister, Octavia.' He took the hand of the young woman beside him to lead her forward. 'She *was* Miss Baxendale. She is now, I must inform you, Octavia Faringdon, wife of the lately deceased Thomas Faringdon, and has been so for the past three years. She is the lawful Marchioness of Burford. And this child—' he indicated with a glance behind him '—is their son, John. Heir to the title and Faringdon estates. I believe, madam, sirs, that we have much to discuss.' Sir Edward bowed again and waited to see the impact of his declaration.

The silence that hung in the room was painful in its intensity, as enveloping as the cloud of dust motes that drifted around them in the sun's rays.

Until Mrs Stamford grasped the edge of the table and pushed herself to her feet in outrage. 'A marriage? Thomas's wife? I have never heard such disgraceful nonsense in all my life!' She glanced fiercely at her daughter. 'If I were in your shoes, Lady Burford, I would have nothing to do with this scandalous claim. It is my belief that it is merely a charade on the part of these…these *people,* to get their hands on the Faringdon fortune.' She paused to cast a look of pure disdain towards the pair, her lips curled in what, in a less well-bred lady, would have been seen as a sneer. 'If I were you, I would have Marcle show these impostors the door, on the instant!'

The company, robbed of any desire for further social platitudes, or to sample the fine array of cheese and fruit set out on the dining table, repaired immediately to the blue withdrawing-room in stunned and uncomfortable silence.

'Perhaps you would be so good as to explain your astounding claims, Sir Edward,' Lord Henry requested with remarkable calm.

The gentleman was now seated on the silk-covered sofa, his sister beside him, palpably uncomfortable with hands clasped tightly in her lap. Their companion chose to take the child into the window embrasure, away from the heart of the crisis, to look out at the park and gardens and be entertained. Eleanor had low-

ered herself to an oval-backed chair as if she did not trust her legs
to support her. Nicholas stood behind her, Mrs Stamford took a
seat at her side. Lord Henry, either deliberately or through natural inclination, took a position of authority before the fireplace.
When thoughts and impressions ran riot, spiking the air with
nerve-jangling tension, he took command in a cool, unemotional
fashion and broached the shattering development.

'We would all be grateful if you would explain the circumstances of this supposed marriage. My family, as you must be
aware, is ignorant of its very existence.'

'Of course, my lord. I can understand why you might consider
it all a matter of pretence and artifice. This is not an easy situation and not one that I would naturally seek. Forgive me, my
lady.' Sir Edward bowed his head to Eleanor, clear blue eyes
guileless and full of compassion. She watched him with a mind
frozen in disbelief, the fragile skin stretched over her cheekbones, tight with fear. It was as if his voice came from a great
distance, but anguish gripped her heart at what he might say.

'My sister came out four years ago with a Season in London,'
he began to explain. 'She was very young, but my mother was
alive then and wished to see her daughter well established. Octavia met Burford during the Season. And then later in the summer months when we spent a few short weeks at Brighton. It is
very simple. They met and fell in love, as young people may do
on such occasions.' He smiled understandingly down at his sister, who continued to sit, head bent, fingers worrying at her reticule. 'And they were married, quietly, in Whitchurch, the village
where we have our small estate. Their child, John, was born
there the following year.'

The information, clearly and lucidly delivered, dropped into
the atmosphere as hollowly as pebbles into the depths of a well.
Mrs Stamford found herself lost for words.

'But why was it not made public at the time?' Lord Henry
frowned as he weighed the details. 'Why did we not know of this
marriage? Why did my brother not bring the lady home as his
bride? I can think of no reason why he should need to keep this
marriage a secret from his family and the world.'

'I know not, my lord, but Burford spoke of family disapproval. We were not to know the truth of it.' Sir Edward lifted
his hands in acceptance of a difficult situation and the lowered
them to cover those of his sister in warm comfort. 'My sister presumed that your family would not accept his marriage to a lady
of so little social consequence. Our family is respectable enough,
of course, but we have never aimed to the heights of the *haut ton*.
And to enter into marriage with the Marquis of Burford was beyond her dreams, even as a young girl who did not know the ways
of society.'

Henry turned his attention to the lady who sat silently, eyes
on her clasped fingers. 'Is this so? Did Thomas indeed marry you,
then hide you away in—where was it?—Whitchurch?'

'Yes, my lord.' She raised her eyes, not flinching as they met
such stern questioning. 'Thomas and I…we fell in love and he
wished to marry me, in spite of his family, he said. So we should
keep it secret, he said, and I agreed. I was very young, you see,
and knew no better.'

'Then why did you say nothing when my brother entered into
a second marriage with…with Miss Stamford?' Incredulity coloured Henry's question. 'Surely it is beyond belief that you
should simply accept such a development.' *And why in heaven's
name would Thomas have done such a thing?*

'That was a mistake on my part, I confess.' Sir Edward came
to his sister's rescue, taking her hand again and holding it in a
warm clasp. 'My sister was very foolish and, I do not hesitate to
say, is easily led. She was given to understand that his marriage
to Miss Stamford—' he inclined his head towards Eleanor with
grave respect '—was a matter of necessity, desired and encouraged by his family. Burford asked that Octavia keep the matter
of her own marriage quiet in return for a substantial annuity settled on herself and the child. I could not persuade her otherwise.
She insisted on doing what Burford wished. But now she has seen
that much is due to her and wishes to make everything plain.' He
smiled down at the young woman who coloured prettily and returned his clasp, nodding her agreement.

'But if he loved you and had married you, regardless of…of

the differences in your social rank,' Eleanor spoke at last to the fair lady, 'and since you had presented him with a son and heir— why would my Lord Burford consider the complications of a second marriage to me? It does not make any sense! Most particularly as—' She closed her lips into a thin line, unable to continue. *Particularly as my birth and the social status of my own family is no better!* It simply did not make any logical sense.

'My lady…' Sir Edward hesitated, all deference and concern. 'I cannot tell you… Perhaps you are the only one here who might know the reason for such an unfortunate decision.'

'But why wait to make any claim until now?' Mrs Stamford interrupted, impatient as she pinned the fair couple with an eagle stare, clearly not believing a word of Sir Edward's explanation. 'My lord has been dead for four months. Why did you not speak on hearing of his death? It has been no secret, after all.'

Sir Edward turned to face the lady with calm purpose. 'We knew of Burford's death, of course. A great shock to us all. We expected that Octavia would have been considered in the will. And that clear provision would have been made for the child— who, after all, is the heir. And so we waited in anticipation. But there was no word from the lawyers, there was no settlement for Octavia or for the child.' His voice hardened and looked down at his sister's face with concern. 'As the will stands, she has been left with no income, no security…no recognition of her position as Burford's wife. That is not right, as I am sure you will agree.' His gaze swept his audience. 'She deserves what is rightfully hers after three years of neglect, of being forced to live as if she had a guilty secret. I have persuaded her to come here today to lay the truth before you, knowing that you will not allow her to go unheard. She must receive what is due to her under the law.'

'Is this indeed so?' Eleanor appealed to the young woman who sat so blamelessly in her withdrawing-room and threatened to destroy her whole life.

'Yes, my lady.'

'Did you love him?' *And what a ridiculously inconsequential question that is!*

'Yes. I did. And he loved me. He told me so.'

'Did he...did he visit you often in Whitchurch?'

'When he could. It was not always easy.'

Eleanor's blood ran cold from her lips to the tips of her fingers. Was that why Thomas had been prepared to enter into a loveless marriage with her? Because it would have given her the protection she needed? And, more importantly, because he had already given his heart elsewhere so a union without love was of no consequence? It could be so. It could all be terribly true. The thought struck her with terrifying power. But why did he agree to marry her at all if he was already legally bound? The cool voice of common sense impressed itself on her mind, insisting that she listen to its reasoned tones. Surely Thomas, whom she had respected and married, could never have taken a decision so unworthy of a man of honour. Eleanor no longer knew what to think.

'Forgive me, Sir Edward, if I put this bluntly.' Henry broke into her thoughts. 'Is there any reason we should believe this remarkable claim?'

'Of course.' Sir Edward released Octavia's hand and stood, a deliberate confrontation now. 'I am not so foolish as to believe that you would accept my sister's claim without legal proof. I have it. I have with me the proof of the marriage of my sister and your brother. And the registration of the birth of the child. At the church of St Michael and All Angels in the parish of Whitchurch and both witnessed by the Reverend Julius Broughton who is resident there. It proves beyond doubt that the marriage predates any other agreement that Burford might have entered into and that the child was born in wedlock. Thus he is your brother's legitimate heir.'

From his pocket he produced two documents and handed them over. Henry read them, noting places, dates and signatures. And passed them to Eleanor, who did likewise, holding them with fingers that were not quite steady. Yes. There it was before her eyes. She swallowed against the tight constriction in her throat as the truth sank home. The documents predated her own marriage and the birth of her own child. She was not Thomas's wife. Her son was not Thomas's heir.

'It predates my marriage,' she stated in toneless acceptance, as if her world and that of her son did not lay shattered at her feet.

'It is as I said.' Sir Edward rescued the papers from her nerve-less fingers. 'Octavia is Burford's true wife. Your marriage, I am afraid, my lady, is invalid.'

At these gently spoken but brutal words, Lord Henry took a step forward, an automatic gesture, to put himself between Baxendale and Eleanor, discovering an overwhelming desire to shield her, to protect her from these destructive insinuations, as if his physical presence could rob the words of their veracity.

It was a futile attempt. Pride came to the rescue as, choking back a sob, Eleanor rose to her feet. She could sit no longer and so walked to the window where the child chattered unintelligibly and pointed excitedly at the circling rooks. She stretched out a hand to touch his hair. Pale gold like his mother, so different from her own dark son. A lively, attractive child who clutched at the coat of his nurse with fierce fists. Then, disturbed by Eleanor's scrutiny, tears welled in the blue eyes and a wail broke the silence. Eleanor stroked his hair and the nurse shushed him, crooning to him in a soft voice until he hid his face against her shoulder.

Oh, God! How has all this come about?

Eleanor turned to look back over her shoulder at the tableau before the fireplace, with Sir Edward and Miss Baxendale—or was it the Marchioness of Burford?—at its centre. Both fair, well bred and respectable, Octavia appropriately clothed in black silk, a black satin-straw bonnet framing her lovely face—it was indeed difficult to suspect them of any degree of duplicity or trickery. And they had the documents with all the force of the law behind them...

'This is a matter that needs our consideration, sir.' Her attention was drawn back to Lord Henry, who had taken a hand in the discussion again. What were his thoughts on this untoward turn in family events? For a moment, his eyes caught hers and she thought that for that one second of contact he was not indifferent to her plight. And then he turned away. 'What do you intend now, Sir Edward?'

'It is my intention that we go to London and lay this evidence before your family's legal man. A Mr Hoskins, I understand. I would presume, in the somewhat peculiar circumstances, that we can take up residence in Faringdon House? I believe that my sister should have that right as we do not possess our own establishment in London.'

'What?' Mrs Stamford could take no more. She surged to her feet, fury on behalf of her daughter writ large. 'I think you presume too much, sir. You have no right whatsoever to take up residence in Faringdon House!'

A quick, startled glance passed between Nicholas and Henry, Nicholas astonished at the man's effrontery in demanding the Faringdon London residence for his sister's comfort, but Henry's frown prevented any comment. His lordship placed a warning hand on Mrs Stamford's rigid arm.

'Do not distress yourself, ma'am.' Turning to Sir Edward, Henry bowed his head in acknowledgement of the claim. 'Very well, sir. I shall ensure that you are expected there and given every comfort. Although I would suggest that you do not spread word of this…this unfortunate and highly sensitive affair until the legality of your claim is proved.'

'It is not our intention to provide food for the gossips, my lord.' There was the merest hint of a reprimand in Baxendale's quiet voice. He took his sister's hand once more and drew her to her feet to stand beside him. 'It would be of no benefit to my sister to be discussed in the streets and clubs more than is necessary. There will be enough scandal as it is. I shall present these documents—' he replaced them in his inner pocket '—to Mr Hoskins. I think that they will hold up under due investigation by that gentleman—and then they will ensure the inheritance for my sister and her son. The entail on the estate should confirm it.'

'Very well, Sir Edward. I must bow to your decision in this instance.'

'I must thank you for your compliance, my lord. Now. If you will excuse us. We are intending to stay the night at the Crown in Tenbury Wells. I am sure that we will be in communication again very soon to straighten out this unfortunate matter.'

'We shall.' Lord Henry's face was grim, every muscle in his body under powerful restraint. 'We too shall be in London before the end of the week.'

* * *

Eleanor sank down onto the nearest chair as the visitors, accompanied by Nicholas and a furious Mrs Stamford, left the withdrawing-room to continue their journey. She was alone with Lord Henry but seemed oblivious to this. Her eyes were fixed on the window where afternoon sun cast patterns on the carpet and gilded the edge of the shutters. But she saw none of it.

'Eleanor…'

She turned her head. Slowly, as if it took all her effort of will to force her body to obey, to focus on the man who stood before her. She studied his face with an intensity as if what she found there was of the utmost importance to her. But apparently she could read nothing to give her hope.

'Eleanor. I presume that you had no suspicion of this terrible débâcle. Not the slightest hint that Thomas might have a liaison elsewhere.' Henry's voice held a harsh edge, almost as if, she thought, perhaps he considered that she herself was to some extent to blame.

'No. How should I? I cannot believe it…'

'Nor I. It does not sound like Thomas.' He watched her carefully, aware of the white shade around her mouth as she skimmed the brink of control. Every instinct urged him to take her in his arms and let her cry out her frozen misery against his chest. To carry her off from this place so that she would never again have to face anything as shattering as the revelations of the past hour. But he could not, dare not, too unsure of her reactions to him if he made any intimate gesture. Too unsure of his feelings towards her. There was no place for pity here. And yet the bitter anger at her cold-hearted betrayal of his own love for her no longer seemed to weigh in the balance. A very masculine urge to protect took precedence.

'That he should already have had a wife and child when he…when he…' Eleanor swallowed hard and pressed a hand to her lips to stop the words. Then, 'I don't know what to do.'

'You do not have to do anything.' Henry attempted to reassure her. 'Now is not the time for hasty action. We need to speak with Hoskins before we accept the statements of Sir Edward

Baxendale or the weight of his documents. We know nothing of him. We knew everything about Thomas.' *I pray that we did, for your sake!*

She hardly listened, took in none of his soft words.

'How can I do nothing! I have no right to the name I bear. I clearly have no right to live here or in any of the Faringdon properties, if what Miss Baxendale claims is true. And there is no evidence to suggest that it is false. Indeed, the proof for the marriage would appear to be unquestionable.'

She rose to her feet as if she would flee the room.

'I will do all I can to help you.' Henry moved to stand in her path. 'You have only to ask.'

She really looked at him now. Contempt was clearly visible, swirled with the total despair in her eyes, their usual bright amethyst now as dark as bluebells in shaded woods.

'Will you? Will you indeed, Hal?'

'Of course. Nell…' He stretched out his hand as if to touch her arm in compassion, moved by her dignity in spite of her grief.

'Don't touch me,' she hissed the words, taking him—and herself—by surprise at the sudden vehemence. 'I do not want your pity!'

'Nell, I understand that you—'

'No, you don't. You talked of humiliation when you believed that I had rejected you. You did not know the half of it. If Miss Baxendale's marriage is indeed legal, imagine what a feast the gossip-mongers will have over that. I shall never be able to hold my head up in society again. And as for my son… I care not for myself. But what can you possibly do to save my child—an innocent victim—from the condemnation of a critical and judgmental society?'

'You must not allow yourself to contemplate such a possibility. It may yet all come to nothing.' What other could he say? He fought against self-disgust as he heard his own empty words in the face of her impossible position.

'No? But if it does stand the test of law, Miss Baxendale's document will proclaim me a whore and my son a bastard. And you tell me not to worry? You must be thanking God, Hal, for his divine retribution!' She gave a little crow of hysterical laughter. 'If I did indeed reject you in order to manipulate Thomas into marriage, as you so clearly suspect, then I have been punished for my sins beyond all belief.' The laughter shattered and she covered her face with her hands to catch the tears that began to flow.

Ignoring her bitter accusation, answering his own need, he stepped forward, intending to take her in his arms. 'Never that! Let me help you, Nell.'

'Go away!'

Logic told him that he should do as she asked, should simply walk away. To hold her would be too dangerous, reawakening the feelings towards her that he did not want to experience ever again. But conscience, instinct perhaps—and something in the depth of his soul that he refused to acknowledge—insisted that he stay and comfort. Henry went with instinct and enclosed her in his arms.

Eleanor was immediately conscious of the warmth and power of his body, enfolding her, holding her against his strength. How strong he was. How easy it would be to simply rest her head on his shoulder and allow him to lift the burden from her, to solve the whole monstrous problem for her. How tempting to curl her fingers around his broad shoulders and simply hold on, until the nightmare dissipated as disturbing dreams must with the coming of daylight. And how foolish it would be to allow herself that luxury! What a terrible mistake to allow him to come too close, to know the thoughts and feelings that assailed her heart and mind, refusing to let her be.

She froze in his embrace as if she could not bear his touch, and almost immediately fought to be free, pushing with frantic hands against his chest, lifting her head proudly, defiantly, regardless of her tear-stained cheeks.

'No. I do not think I will accept your help, my lord. I need nothing from you.' Her voice was suddenly cold, derisive even. Although it hurt him immeasurably, he had never admired her courage as much as he did at that moment, but her words struck with deliberate venom, stinging him with their power to wound. 'Go back to America, Hal. You are well out of it!'

Chapter Four

On the following morning Henry and Nicholas were the only two occupants of the breakfast table, although neither was showing much appetite. Desultory conversation occupied the first ten minutes about the value of breeding their own horseflesh. But finally Nicholas pushed the tankard of ale away across the table, leaned back in his chair and pinned his brother with an unusually stern expression.

'Do you believe it, Hal?'

'No.' His brother's uncompromising reply did not surprise him.

'Neither do I. But there is all that proof, with the power of Church and State behind it. Legal documents and such…' He frowned at Bess, who had placed one confiding and optimistic paw on his boot. 'Tell me why *you* don't believe it. The Baxendales certainly did not appear to be—'

'Rogues? Tricksters? No, they did not.' Henry steepled his fingers thoughtfully, elbows resting on the table. 'Thomas was always ripe for a flirtation with a pretty girl. And Octavia Baxendale certainly qualifies for his interest. I admit, I was surprised to know that he had married Eleanor so soon after I had left. But two wives? One of them in secret when we were all still living here under this roof? Unlikely, anyone who knew him must accept.' He pushed back from the table, and rose to his feet to pace to the windows, emotion suddenly raw in his voice as he stood with his back to his brother. 'Why did you have to *die*, Thomas? And in such a uselessly tragic fashion!' He leaned his hands on the window ledge and looked out at glorious nature with unseeing eyes. Then, on a deep breath with senses governed once more, he walked slowly back. 'Apart from anything else, as you very well know, Thomas never could keep a secret to save his life! The number of times he fell foul of our heavy-handed parent because he could not keep a still tongue in his head—he probably totted up one beating a week for one sin or another, whether it was mine or his own was irrelevant.' His smile was a mere twisting of lips. 'You were probably too young to remember.'

'So what do we do?' Nicholas prompted. 'Accept the proof and have Sir Edward Baxendale and the lady resident at Burford Hall?'

Henry eyed him with silent, brooding intensity.

'Perhaps I should sail to America with you,' Nicholas continued, 'if he asks me to move out. Which he undoubtedly will. I wager he would not want a Faringdon living under the same roof.'

'And you would be welcome,' was the prompt reply. 'The hunting is excellent—you would enjoy it.'

'That might tempt me. Is it the land of opportunity that you had hoped for, Hal? You have said very little of your life there— but then we have been taken up with other matters, have we not!'

'Very true—Baxendale has driven business from my mind somewhat,' Hal admitted. 'But, yes—the peace between Britain and America two years ago has ended American isolation, so commerce is free to develop and fortunes to be made. It is still an infant society, but progress is very rapid. New York is growing at a furious rate. Banks and businesses opening every day it seems. So, yes, the opportunity is there for those who are willing to throw the dice and bet confidently on the outcome.'

'As Faringdon and Bridges will do?'

Hal smiled, a hint of pride evident in his face, his present problems for the moment overlaid by the bright promise of the future. 'Yes…Faringdon and Bridges. It sounds good, does it not? Even if all we possess is tied up in investment, leaving us on a very uncomfortable precipice of poverty.'

'I have every confidence and shall come to you for a loan

when you have made your first fortune.' Nicholas returned the
smile. 'And the women of New York?' He slanted a sly glance
at his brother. 'Are they pretty?'

'I believe they would compare with London. I have found so.'

'So tell me, Hal. Is she a prime article?'

'Of course.' Hal's answer was as smooth as watered silk.

'And the name of this fair Cyprian?'

'Rosalind—and the rest is none of your affair, little brother,
although she would box your ears for you if you dared impugn
her morality with such a title.'

Nicholas laughed and Henry broke into a reluctant grin at the
exchange but then became deadly serious again and returned to
the Baxendale claim. 'But, no,. I don't think it would be politic to
simply accept the story that we have been fed so far. I think—'

The door opened. The Marchioness of Burford swept into the
room, carrying her son, her mother in close pursuit.

'I do not think, my dear Eleanor, that—'

'Forgive me, Mama, but I have made up my mind.'

Eleanor came to a halt before Lord Henry, mood confronta-
tional. She had no difficulty at all in meeting his surprised scrutiny this morning, meeting it with a bright gaze that issued a
challenge to anyone who might be sufficiently ill advised as to
stand in her way. A sleepless night with much time for reflection
had achieved a very positive effect on the lady. Yesterday, she acknowledged, she had been weak. Spineless, even. She shivered
in humiliation at the memory of her tears and her outpouring of
grief and disillusion in Lord Henry's presence. She must have
been out of her mind to do so—to show such weakness. She had
no excuse. Today she would grasp the nettle with both hands,
crushing the stinging stems and leaves at whatever cost to herself. She would not meekly accept this hideous development. She
would fight for her position, and, more importantly, the inheritance of her son!

Letting his gaze rest on her, Lord Henry had to appreciate that
the lady had dressed for battle. The arrangement of her burnished ringlets *à la Sappho* could not be faulted, nor the quiet
elegance of her high-waisted, narrow gown, long sleeved with

only one row of discreet ruffles around the hem. The black silk creation, rich and costly, gleamed in the morning sunlight, undoubtedly created by the hand of an expert. Probably Eugenie in Bond Street, he thought, unless this most fashionable of *modistes* had changed in his absence.

Eleanor certainly had, he was forced to admit. Composed and sophisticated, her presence reinforced the impression that he had absorbed since his return. She had grown into her role as Marchioness of Burford and he could not fault her in it, although he felt a strange sense of loss that the young girl he had known had changed for ever.

'I have decided,' the Marchioness now announced to the room at large. 'It is my intention to go to London to confront this problem. I cannot sit here, buried in the country, waiting for decisions on my future to be made without my knowledge. I need to speak with Mr Hoskins. I *cannot* believe that Thomas had married Octavia Baxendale, visited her and had a son by her without my being aware! Certainly not for the whole span of our marriage! Such deceit is completely unacceptable.'

'But where will you stay?' Mrs Stamford broke in, continuing her earlier objections, but for once unsure of her ground. She could not but agree with her daughter's basic premise that the whole matter could not simply be ignored. 'Surely not at Faringdon House, with the Baxendales in residence. Think of the mortification of having to meet them every day, of sitting down to breakfast with them. Do think, Eleanor…'

'I have thought, Mama. I have done nothing else but think all night long! I shall not, of course, go to Faringdon House. It would not be at all suitable. I shall put up at an hotel until I can make more acceptable arrangements. But go to London I will!'

She glared at Henry as if she expected him to join her mother in condemnation of her scheme. Would he dare to thwart her? She did not care! Her mind was made up!

Henry watched her with none of the indifference he would have preferred. The anger that now drove her rendered her magnificent. She might be dressed in deepest unrelieved mourning, there might be light shadows beneath her eyes from her sleepless night, but her face was vivid and alive. Her skin glowed with delicate colour, her soft lips firm and uncompromising in her decision. The deep amethyst of her eyes was dark and turbulent, rich as glowing jewels. He was held by them, a slow enchantment which barred him from damning her hopes of success in her cause.

'Of course you must go.'

Eleanor blinked, momentarily lost for words as she marshalled an impassioned argument to use against him when he denied the validity of her plan. Lord Henry's lips curled a little at her obvious discomfort, but he had the wisdom to suppress too obvious a smile.

'But there is no need for you to consider an hotel. Nor, as you say, would it be proper for you to stay at Faringdon House in the present climate—it is not fitting. I shall myself go to London and I shall rent a house. I make you free of it. Rather than the Baxendales, you may sit down to breakfast with *me* instead!'

'You?' Her brows rose in sharp disbelief. 'But you are returning to America!'

'No. I think not. I cannot leave you with this situation unresolved. My departure for America can wait.'

'I do not need your help!' Temper flared again in the sundrenched room. She would not be beholden to this man who had kissed her into desire and then rejected her! She would not come to depend on him again!

'So you informed me yesterday. You appear to have a very low opinion of my abilities and my priorities, my lady!' Henry noted her guilty flush with some satisfaction and drove the point home. 'But this is not merely for you. My brother's good name is in the balance. And my nephew's legal recognition.' For some elusive reason, as he looked at Eleanor and the child before him, recognising her utter determination to discover the truth, he suddenly had no doubts about his own convictions. The Baxendales, for some devious reason known only to themselves, had concocted a series of lies and deceits. He lifted a hand to stroke one gentle finger down the baby's satin cheek.

The result both surprised and unsettled him. Tom ignored the gesture and continued to grasp the black satin ribbon on his mother's dress with fierce and destructive concentration. The Marchioness took the smallest of steps back, a subtle movement and yet very obvious to Lord Henry. As was the fleeting emotion that clouded her eyes. He thought it was fear—yet could not imagine why. He was no threat to her or to her son. Stifling a sigh, he accepted that it was simply another mystery in the complicated weave but must be put aside until the more immediate concern with Octavia Baxendale had been dealt with. Henry deliberately lowered his hand, but not his eyes from Eleanor's face, which was now flushed with rose.

'I need to know that the inheritance of this family is in the correct hands, you see, even if those hands are still very small and as yet incapable of handling the reins,' he stated quietly. 'And I think the matter deserves some investigation. I cannot leave.'

'But I cannot agree.' Mrs Stamford stood her ground. 'I have told my daughter that hers is a foolish idea. She could stay in residence *here*. To be turned out of her own home is insupportable. Besides, it is not seemly that she should put up in your rented property in London, my lord.'

'And why in God's name not?' Lord Henry's brows snapped into a dark bar of extreme exasperation, temper finally escaping his control. He had had enough of his family for one day and it was hardly mid-morning. 'I presume you will accompany her ladyship to London, ma'am? Does she need more of a chaperon than her own mother? And what the *devil* do you expect for her at my hands? That living under my protection will sully her reputation? The Marchioness is under no danger from me! Your comment, ma'am, is as uninformed as it is insulting, to me and to your daughter.'

The brutal statement was met with stunned silence. Nicholas turned away to hide a smile. Eleanor looked as startled as her mother. Lord Henry was not normally given to such a show of emotion.

'Well… I never intended to suggest… I did not think that… But how can you have agreed to the Baxendales taking possession of Faringdon House?' Mrs Stamford was flustered, but reluctant to admit defeat and pursued her quarry with more energy than sensitivity.

'What do you suggest?' The reply was immediate, biting. 'That we get to haggling over property at a time like this? As if we were in the market place? I think not!'

'Of course not. I never—'

'No. Perhaps you did not. But your thoughts were not complimentary to a lady who already has enough to contend with, without her mother casting doubts on the morals and motives of members of the Faringdon family!' Then, before anyone could recover from so direct an attack, Lord Henry addressed his next words to Eleanor in quite a different voice. 'I think it is an excellent idea. See to your luggage, ma'am. We leave early tomorrow morning. You, too, Nicholas,' which effectively wiped the smile from Nick's face.

'But I thought it might be better if…'

'No, it wouldn't.' His lordship's voice was now clipped. 'You are not going to escape a short visit to town, so save your breath. I have need of you in London, little brother. We have a campaign to wage!'

Eleanor looked from one to the other of the Faringdon brothers. Their determination, their confident air of authority, the implacable manner in which they undertook whatever they set their mind on, touched her heart after all. Yes. She would join her efforts to theirs. They gave her more hope than she could have dreamed of. And Hal was not going back to America. Not yet! She hugged the thought to herself as she hugged her precious son, even as she reprimanded herself for her foolishness. Henry had defended her before her mother. Perhaps he would not abandon her, whatever the outcome of the case. 'I will not go without Tom, you understand,' she informed Henry, looking again for disagreement, perversely unwilling to appear too compliant. 'He comes with me.'

Henry sighed and ran a hand through his hair at the prospect of arranging transport for a large party. The unnerving experience of being regarded by two identical pairs of deep lavender eyes, one openly critical, the other innocently curious, decided the matter for him. 'I suppose you must. Very well. I will arrange for the cleaning of the chaise. Be so good as to inform the stables, Nick. Be ready tomorrow morning, ladies.'

The Faringdon family was rapidly ensconced in a smart and stylish town house in Park Lane in the most fashionable part of London. By no means as spacious or as elegantly furnished as Faringdon House in Grosvenor Square, and lacking all personal touches, of course, yet it was proclaimed sufficient for their needs, even by Mrs Stamford, who was initially prepared to dislike it on sight. The proportions and furnishings of the main withdrawing-room, smaller parlours and reception rooms were declared adequate, the bedrooms comfortable, the furnishings suitably tasteful if a little bland. The address, of course, could not be bettered. The matter of staff was ably dealt with by Marcle, who had accompanied them, despite the state of his arthritic joints, and took charge of the lower regions with seamless competence. Eleanor did not bother to marvel at the speed or the smooth efficiency of the whole operation. If she did, she would have to allow considerable credit to Lord Henry who, she considered, carried it off with typical high-handed arrogance—and faultless style. But she was grateful. It was easier to take the comfort and concern for her well-being for granted and simply accept it when more momentous issues were to be faced.

The following morning, after persuading Mrs Stamford with a tact and a remarkable patience, which surprised everyone, that her presence was not essential to the success of the operation, Lord Henry escorted the Marchioness to the chambers of Hoskins and Bennett. Mr Edward Hoskins, a gentleman of advanced years and wide experience, had enjoyed the confidence and management of the legal affairs of the Faringdon family for many years, but his welcome on this chilly morning did not hold much pleasure for his noble employers. The low clouds, Eleanor surmised, accurately reflected the mood of everyone in the dusty, book-lined, wood-panelled room off Fleet Street.

'My lord. My lady.' The lawyer ushered them in with every

consideration and saw to their comfort, pouring a glass of canary for Lord Henry and ratafia for the Marchioness, even though no one had the heart for refreshment. 'What can I say? I could never have believed that such an occasion as this would arise in my lifetime. And certainly not with respect to your family, my lord, so correct and respectable as they have always been in my lengthy experience.'

He took Eleanor's black-gloved hand and pressed it in fatherly concern before taking his position behind his document-strewn desk. Such a lovely lady to be faced with the possibility of so much future heartache! And the Marquis of Burford had always struck him as a most conscientious young man. Mr Hoskins frowned down at the pages before him, hoping that Lord Henry could be relied upon to deal with the situation in a fitting manner. He knew little of the gentleman other than that he had left the country to seek his fortune—but this was sure to be a true test of his character. He glanced up under heavy brows at Lord Henry who stood behind the Marchioness's chair, a hint of the protective in his stance despite the lack of physical connection, noting the stern lines of his handsome face, the implacable will expressed in the cold grey eyes. Mr Hoskins suppressed a shudder. He would not care to make an enemy of this man. He trusted that the absent Sir Edward knew what he was undertaking.

'Sir Edward Baxendale and Miss Baxendale have been to see you, I surmise.' Lord Henry lost no time in broaching the delicate subject, meeting the crux of the matter head on.

'Indeed they have, my lord. Yesterday afternoon. A most personable pair, I might add, in spite of the reason for their appointment. I have heard their story and I have seen the documents. In fact, I have them here in my possession.' He laid his hand on them on his desk, as if with a degree of distaste for their content. 'Sir Edward left them so that I might check their authenticity.'

'And your opinion, sir? No dissimulation, I beg.' Lord Henry cast a quick glance at Eleanor's impassive features. 'I fear that they bear the mark of validity.'

Mr Hoskins noted again the strained but composed features of the Marchioness. She sat perfectly still to hear her fate, but her fingers, closed around the strings of the reticule on her lap, were bone white from the pressure.

'I believe that the documents are legal.' Mr Hoskins stated the matter without inflection. 'The marriage and the birth are recorded, as you are aware. It is simple enough to check the existence of the church and the priest concerned, and thus the signatures—which I am in process of doing. The marriage would appear to have existed.'

'And the witnesses?'

'Sir Edward himself, and Lady Mary Baxendale, their mother, were witnesses of the marriage. Lady Mary is now unfortunately deceased.'

Lord Henry nodded, keeping Eleanor under his close surveillance. 'So tell me, Mr Hoskins, in your legal opinion, where does her ladyship stand?'

Hoskins sighed. It would not be good news. 'There is nothing that I can tell you that you do not already know, my lord. The estate is entailed on the eldest son. A jointure is established for the widow to ensure her comfort for the rest of her life. The Marquis your husband, my lady, made no further will other than to give the trusteeship, if necessary on his death, into the hands of Lord Henry and Lord Nicholas and myself. He would not expect his untimely death at such an early age and so felt no compulsion to outline his wishes in more detail. If Miss Baxendale is proved to be the legal wife of the Marquis, then there is no legal recognition or provision for yourself, my lady, or your son.' He gave her the title, although now so clearly in doubt, through courtesy and compassion, his heart going out to the innocent woman who sat before him as if engraved in stone. 'The recipient of the widow's jointure will be Miss Baxendale,' he concluded, 'the Marchioness of Burford, I should say, not yourself. And the heir to the estate is the legitimate child of that marriage, John.'

'I see.' Eleanor felt as if the walls were closing in on her. She fought to stave off the blackness that threatened to encroach and rob her of all sense. Then, through the mists, she became aware of a warm hand on her shoulder, a firm pressure. The heat spread through the black silk of her spencer to reassure and comfort. As she turned her head to look up, there could be no doubting the depth of understanding in Lord Henry's face as he willed her to be strong. For one moment she covered his hand with her own and struggled to smile in reassurance.

It almost broke his heart.

His voice was harsh as he spoke again to the lawyer. 'Do you truly believe that my brother married Octavia Baxendale some three years ago, sir?'

'I do not like it, my lord. But on the face of it, yes. I am unable to argue against the evidence.'

So there it was. Eleanor covered her face with her hands.

'Forgive me, my lord, my lady. I would never willingly cause you such pain. If there is anything I can do…'

Lord Henry took Eleanor's arm in a firm hold, encouraging her to rise to her feet, then tucked her hand within his arm. She obeyed as if in a trance, all her hopes and dreams for the future destroyed. He fixed Hoskins with a flat stare. 'Will you be so kind as to do one thing for us, sir? Sir Edward claimed that an annual sum was paid to Miss Baxendale from the date of her marriage. A substantial amount, it would seem, to ensure her complicity in keeping the marriage secret. Is there any trace of such a sum being paid from the estate finances? I have asked the agent to look at the estate accounts at Burford Hall. It would be interesting to know if and when any large amounts of money were paid out and apparently unaccounted for.'

'I will certainly do that, my lord. But if there is no evidence of such, it may not prove that they were *not* made, of course.'

'I know. But it is a start and the best we can do.'

They returned home in pensive and uncomfortable silence, in a hackney that Lord Henry hailed outside the lawyer's rooms, to relay the depressing results of their morning's endeavours to Mrs Stamford and Nicholas who awaited their return.

'It is as we feared.' Lord Henry stripped off his greatcoat and strode into the front parlour to pour glasses of port. 'The documents would appear to be legally binding.'

Eleanor handed her spencer, gloves and bonnet to Marcle and

followed, determined to hold herself together. Henry cast one glance in her direction and stalked to her side to take her hand in a firm hold. 'It would be better if you sat before you fall to the floor.' His tone was harsh to cover the depth of his feelings for her. She looked so fragile, the impression enhanced by her black gown. Lost and vulnerable. He suppressed the fury that surged within him as he saw the result of their morning's work and felt the uncontrollable trembling in the hand that, for a brief moment, clung to his. 'Here.' He held out the glass of port. 'Drink this. Don't argue with me, just do it. You have had a most distressing morning, perhaps the worst hour of your life. It is not weakness to admit it and take a little stimulation!'

Eleanor looked up into his face, her eyes betraying her inner fears. She looked stricken—he realised that she must indeed be so, if she was willing to lay her emotions bare before him. All he wished to do was sit beside her and pull her into his arms to shield her from the cruelties of the world. Anything to smooth away the look of helpless desolation.

'Don't give up yet. This is only the first hurdle. We shall come about.'

Tears threatened at his gentle words but she would not, determined to keep her voice calm and composure intact. She sat at the pressure of his hand and obediently took the glass. 'But what hope is there? You heard what Mr Hoskins had to say. Thomas was in all probability wedded to Octavia Baxendale at least a year before I even knew him.'

'I am not convinced, in spite of the evidence to the contrary.' Lord Henry tossed back the port as if he needed it and poured another glass. 'Let us start from the opposite premise. That the claim is false. Consider this. If the whole venture is nothing but a deliberate trickery, a charade, why would they embark on such a risky enterprise in the full view of the *haut ton?* If they fail, and so are unmasked as frauds, the result will be a disaster for them. So what motives would they have to risk all on the turn of a card?'

'Money!' Nicholas stated without hesitation.

'Social consequence?' Eleanor suggested.

'The title!' Mrs Stamford added in flat tones.

'Money would seem to me to be the strongest motivation.' Henry cast himself into the chair opposite his brother. 'I wonder about the financial circumstances of the Baxendales.'

'An easy enough matter to discover, surely?' Nicholas lifted his brows.

'Do you believe,' Eleanor asked, considering a matter that had worried her since the first meeting at Burford Hall, 'that Miss Baxendale is strong enough to have stood against her brother if he wanted her to reveal her marriage to the world? Sir Edward said that she refused to do so when Thomas contracted to marry me, in spite of his persuasion to the contrary. Do you really believe it? She seems so biddable.'

'She might. If she loved my brother enough.' Henry acknowledged the point. 'But she is certainly not made of stern stuff. I think that we should get to know Miss Baxendale a little better. And perhaps without the presence of her more forceful brother. There is a role for you, Eleanor! You will not like it, I dare say, but I think you should further your acquaintance with Octavia.'

'But she is in black gloves.' Mrs Stamford pushed herself to the edge of her seat in horror. 'It is not yet six months since dear Thomas died. It is not fitting that Eleanor start going about in society. What will people say? I cannot condone a plan of action which would result in the Marchioness of Burford being considered *fast*. How can you suggest it?' Her eyes locked with Lord Henry's in accusation. 'I suppose that such casual ways are acceptable in New York…' she sniffed '…but they are not considered respectable in London!'

Henry turned his glittering gaze on Mrs Stamford without compunction. 'I both can and will suggest it. And I will suggest even more *outrageous* action. I think that you, Eleanor, should put off your full mourning and begin to go about a little. There is no hint of scandal yet, but there will be, and without doubt it will take the Polite World by storm. It is too salacious a story to keep quiet.' His lips thinned at the disagreeable prospect. 'We shall soon find that we are living our lives under full public scrutiny and, however unpleasant, I think we must not be seen to be

in hiding over this matter. We should go about as normal, make
no comment, presume that Eleanor is without question the Marchioness of Burford, and I think that you should try for an intimate relationship with the fair Octavia. If she wishes to confide
her troubles, you should be available with a sympathetic ear! I
am not asking your daughter to attend a full dress ball!' he informed Eleanor's outraged parent. 'Merely to show herself and
the child in public a little and pay some private visits.'

'That should be an interesting development!' For the first
time that day, Eleanor managed a faint smile, appreciative of the
plan. 'It is better to be active than afraid. I will do it.' Sipping the
port, which restored colour to her ashen cheeks, she signalled her
agreement. 'We should go about as if nothing were amiss. And
I will put off my mourning.' She frowned as her mama prepared
to interrupt. 'Better to be *fast* than a pawn at the whim of Sir Edward Baxendale.'

'Good.' Lord Henry had to admit to some relief. And a quiet
satisfaction at the success of his scheming, which had effectively
removed the stricken look from Eleanor's eyes. Action, as she
had observed, would take her mind from the anguish of her situation. Besides, Eleanor's involvement would be all-important
to the ultimate success of their campaign. 'And it will give the
interested something to consider when the gossips turn their attention to the Faringdon Scandal.'

'What do we say if we are asked why we are not putting up
at Faringdon House?' Mrs Stamford enquired, still unwilling to
capitulate. 'It will be sure to cause comment.'

'Say that it is no one's affair but our own!' Exasperation
cloaked his lordship, a heavy cloud. 'Say that redecoration is
being undertaken—if anyone has the temerity to question a Faringdon on so personal an issue. That the noise and dust is too
much for a young child. And since I am returned to London and
have hired a house for the Season, I have put it at your disposal.
Leave the Baxendales to make their own comments on the situation. If we remain calm and confident, the speculators will not
know what to believe.'

Which, Eleanor thought, appeared to be his answer to every

difficulty that arose. She could not help but be impressed, and terrified, as she found herself suddenly embroiled in little less than a form of war strategy. She felt a twinge of sympathy for Napoleon when faced with the determination of the Duke of Wellington at the Battle of Waterloo. Lord Henry appeared to have a very similar approach to such matters. Arrogance and a gift for detailed strategy.

'Meanwhile—' Henry had not finished but directed his keen gaze on his brother '—you, Nick, can visit the gentleman's clubs, starting with St James's Street. Find out where, if any, Sir Edward is a member. See if you can discover whether he gambles heavily. And, most particularly, if he is in debt.'

'Thank you, Hal! And how do you suggest that I discover such sensitive information?' Nicholas finished off the rest of the port in his glass and rose to his feet.

'Use your initiative, Nick. I am sure you can encourage the gossips.'

'Very well.' He walked to the door. 'I had better change into something suitable for such esteemed company as the Bow Window Set at White's. *Not* how I would have chosen to spend the day, but I will do my poor best. Perhaps I will look up Kingstone—he usually has his fingers on the pulse and is not beyond a heavy wager himself. And is never at a loss for the *on dit* of the moment.'

'I wish you well. Let us hope that our own situation does not reach his ears any time soon!' Henry grimaced at the prospect as Nicholas raised his hand in acknowledgement of the comment and made his exit with reluctant intent. 'Meanwhile you and I, Eleanor, and you too if you wish it, ma'am…' he glanced towards Mrs Stamford '…are going to pay an afternoon visit on Cousin Judith.'

'Lady Painscastle? What has she to do with this fiasco? The fewer people to know, the better, I would have thought!' Once again, Mrs Stamford frowned her objections.

'You must know Judith well enough to appreciate the advantage of having her as a member of this family,' his lordship replied again with commendable but hard-won patience. 'Her social life is hectic, I remember, and little passes her keen eye or ear, unless she has changed beyond recognition since I saw her last. It seems to me that Octavia must have come out in the spring of 1812. If my memory serves me well, so did Judith. I have no recollection of Octavia at any of the Season's main events, but Judith might. Thomas and I squired her to any number of incredibly tedious parties, balls and soirées when she was intent on fixing her interest with Simon Painscastle. Perhaps she will remember Miss Baxendale making her formal curtsy to society. And, more to the point, if there was any obvious close relationship developing between Thomas and the lady. Judith, I believe, is quite our best source of gossip.'

'An excellent idea.' Mrs Stamford's face brightened as she saw the value of the connection and so allowed a complete volte-face. 'Lady Painscastle is a lively and eminently sensible young woman. She might indeed have noticed something between the pair—which *you* did not.' Thus Mrs Stamford damning the inadequacy of the whole male race.

'Do you agree, my lady?' Henry took the empty glass from Eleanor's hand, noting the return of colour to her face. 'It might be a painful encounter.'

'It might.' She stood and raised her chin. He nodded at the air of determination and the bright sparkle in her eyes. She did not lack for courage, no matter the odds. 'I shall be ready immediately after luncheon.'

Judith Faringdon, now Countess of Painscastle and most eligibly married to her beloved Simon, was in residence in the family home in Grosvenor Square. She had made an excellent match, with love and affection on both sides, and was now enjoying life as a wealthy and fashionable young woman with all the freedom allowed to a married lady. She was a true redhead with green eyes, both characteristics inherited from her mother, and an abundance of energy all, on this occasion, attractively packaged in an afternoon gown of cream and white muslin. With a pretty face and a lively manner, coupled with an appreciation of the fashions that suited her and a wealthy, well-born husband who adored her and pandered to her every whim, she had entrée into the Polite World. Her love of the pleasures of London was immeasurable. As was her ear for gossip.

'Hal! I did not know of your return. You look wonderfully well. Life in the colonies suits you. I cannot imagine its attraction but…' She allowed him to kiss her hand and then opened her arms to clasp him in a warm embrace.

'And Nell. Mrs Stamford. A family party, no less. I did not expect…' She hesitated as she recalled the circumstances. 'I am so sorry, Nell. Forgive me. I did not mean to be so insensitive or unfeeling. Indeed I did not! I too miss Thomas dreadfully—but life must go on, you know.' She rambled on. All good humour and welcome, if a little shallow. All in all, it was difficult not to like Lady Painscastle.

'And who have we here?' She lifted Tom from his mother's arms and spun him round to his obvious delight, tickling his neck until he chuckled. 'What a charmer he will be. Another Faringdon, if I am not mistaken, to break our poor female hearts.' She kissed him enthusiastically. 'Just look at those dark curls and those eyebrows.' She frowned at Hal over the baby's head. 'And have you broken many hearts in America? I expect so.'

He flushed, the faintest of colours on his lean cheeks, but otherwise ignored her comment.

'He has your eyes, dear Nell,' Judith continued. 'How delightful. Perhaps it is time that I pleased my lord and presented him with a son and heir. You almost tempt me to do so!'

Out of which artless comment, it was clear that the Faringdon Scandal had not yet reached the Polite World!

The visitors seated themselves in a cream-and-gold withdrawing-room, stylishly and expensively furnished, tea was served with due ceremony and Tom returned to his mother's lap, where he proceeded to gnaw the carved ivory head of her parasol with serious intensity.

'You all look very grave.' Lady Painscastle disposed her embroidered and flounced skirts with casual grace as she surveyed her family.

'Yes. It is a delicate matter, Judith. And not one that we wish

to spread around.' Henry frowned discouragingly at his cousin.
'I believe that you can help us.'

'You can trust me, dear Henry!' She smiled winningly. 'Of
course I will help. And I am always discreet.'

'Judith! You are the most incorrigible gossip of my acquaintance.' Lord Henry could not help but smile at his cousin's naïvety.

'But not if it will hurt one of my family.' And however shallow she might be, they knew Judith was right. It made the forth-
coming conversation more bearable.

'Think back to your coming-out, Judith,' Henry prompted.
'Four years ago, I think, in the spring of 1812.'

'Yes.' Judith nodded, lifting up her bone china teacup with
an elegant hand. 'I have been married to dear Simon for three
years now.'

'Can you recall a young girl—about your own age. Octavia
Baxendale. Fair hair. Blue eyes. A little shorter than you, perhaps.
A neat figure. A quiet and unassuming girl, not one to take the
town by storm, but pretty enough. She would have been accompanied by her brother and perhaps her mother. I have no recollection of such a female, but you might.'

'Well, you wouldn't, Hal! Melissa Charlesworth came out in
that year. You were besotted, I remember. I doubt you noticed
anyone else!'

'Never!' His frown was definitely more pronounced.

'You even went to Almack's, drank tea and lemonade, danced
country dances and allowed yourself to be sneered at by the
Princess Esterhazy for making a comment about the war or some
such taboo subject! You were in love! Until Melissa threw you
over—a mere younger son as you were!—and married the Earl
of Saltmarshe. She always did have an eye to a fortune, no matter how ugly and old the husband.'

'Never mind that.' He rose to his feet to pace the room with
impatience and perhaps a little unease. Eleanor hid a smile in
spite of herself. 'What about Octavia Baxendale. Do you have
any recollection of her?'

'Well, now. Let me think. Perhaps I do recall… But it is so
long ago—and Thomas flirted with any number of ladies. I par-

ticularly remember one débutante—but she had curls as black and lustrous as a crow's wing. I believe I envied her, admired her colouring more than my own—foolishly, as Painscastle was quick to reassure me…'

Lord Henry sighed. 'Do try to concentrate Judith. Fair hair, blue eyes…' He looked to the ceiling in despair.

'Well!' She folded her hands and thought, the effort palpable. 'I think I might remember her at some of the occasions. With a brother, perhaps? The name *Octavia* seems familiar… But I am not at all certain. Why do you wish me to remember something so inconsequential?'

'Can you recall—did Thomas flirt with her? He escorted you to enough balls and soirées—he must have come across her if you did.' Henry ignored her demand for some clarification.

'I don't know… Well, yes, perhaps I do remember a fair girl, and perhaps he did. If it is the girl I am thinking of, she had a liking for *pink*. A colour I can never wear.' She bared her teeth as Hal's temper came close to boiling point. 'I know…I am trying, Hal. If it is the girl in question, I remember thinking that he could not be serious about her as a bride—a respectable family only. As Marquis of Burford he could look so much higher than a mere country miss…' She flushed with mortification as she heard her own words, the deep wash of rose clashing remarkably with her auburn colouring as she saw Eleanor blush with discomfort and Mrs Stamford's eyes flash a warning.

'Oh, Nell.' Immediately remorseful, the lady put down her teacup and stretched out a hand to touch Eleanor's cold fingers, 'My tongue runs away with me, as you know. I meant no criticism. Indeed I did not. Anyone could see that you and Thomas were so well suited to each other.'

Henry sighed and tried manfully both to preserve his patience and steer the conversation back into its previous channel. Neither was easy. 'Judith—did it ever occur to you that Thomas *was* more serious about the lady than a mild flirtation?'

'Perhaps. He once rode with a fair lady in the park, I know. And escorted her to supper…. He certainly stood up with a lady of such colouring at Almack's. And I think at my own coming-out ball in Faringdon House. But there could have been any number of fair débutantes. I suppose if it *was* the same lady Thomas must have been taken with her to single her out, mustn't he? Don't *you* remember, Hal?'

'No. Presumably I was still concentrating on Melissa Charlesworth! You are not a deal of help to us, Judith.' Henry set his teeth and continued to probe his cousin's erratic memory. 'Did Thomas go down to Brighton that year?'

'I have no idea.' Judith frowned at the close questioning. 'Why?'

'No matter. What happened to Miss Baxendale after the Season? Did she marry? Did she have another Season?'

Judith shook her head. 'If Octavia is indeed the girl I am thinking of, I believe that she might have left before the end of the Season, before my own engagement to Simon, I understand. Rumour said—I think!—that she had contracted a more than suitable marriage—with money. But more than that I know not. You should talk to my mother. She has an excellent memory. Too good, sometimes, when I wish she might forget some trifling indiscretion from my childhood.' Judith looked from Henry to Eleanor and back again in frustration, green eyes sharp as she scented gossip. 'But why all these questions about someone we do not know and events that happened so long ago? You must tell me! You are keeping me in suspense—which is unforgivable.'

She looked at the faces around her tea table. At the quick meeting of eyes between Lord Henry and Eleanor, Eleanor made the decision.

'It appears,' she informed Judith in a calm voice, 'that Thomas may have been the *suitable match* you spoke of, contracted by Octavia in the spring of 1812. Thomas, it seems, may have married her and kept her in seclusion in the country. And had a son by her.' She hesitated, touching her tongue to dry lips. 'It appears—it is possible that—I am not, and never have been, the Marchioness of Burford.'

Judith's eyes widened in horror.

'And we would be more than grateful if you did not spread that story around town, however tempting it might be to do so!'

Mrs Stamford added with a fierceness not usually encountered over an afternoon tea-drinking.

Judith, eyebrows arched in incredulous disbelief, was reduced, for once, to amazed silence.

Lord Henry trod the stairs late that night.

He was tired. A headache, which he could no longer ignore, however unusual it might be for him to suffer such a trivial affliction, lurked somewhere behind his eyes. A long day with nothing to show for their combined efforts but confirmation of their worst fears. The documents appeared to be legal. Sir Edward was not a member of any of the gentleman's clubs visited by Nicholas and, as far as they knew, did not gamble, whether lightly or heavily. There were the gaming hells next, of course… Henry sighed at the prospect. Nicholas would object, but he would do it with good grace. And Cousin Judith remembered a tender flirtation between Thomas and a pretty fair-haired girl who had retired from society at the end of her first Season with rumours of an advantageous marriage. A young girl whose name she *thought* was Octavia.

He groaned and silently cursed the cruel hand of fate.

It left Eleanor in an unspeakable position, any opportunities for optimism fast disappearing, as mist at the rising of the sun.

What the hell were you doing, Thomas?

Yet, curse as he might, Henry still found it difficult to see his brother in the role of treacherous, machiavellian husband to two wives at one and the same time, with a child by both. The subterfuge just did not fit. Far too complicated and devious for Thomas, far too insensitive to those involved.

Now for himself, Henry mused, well… A grim smile, a mere ghost, crossed his face. It would be more likely, at any event. But even he would draw the line at two wives!

The house settled into silence around him. Nick had gone out to join a party of friends to talk horseflesh and drink gin at Limmers in Conduit Street. Mrs Stamford—who knew? She had sufficient acquaintance in town to provide her with entertainment. Eleanor had retired early, probably worn out through trying to keep a brave face on the fact that she was fast becoming a bigamous wife and her child illegitimate, with no source of support, financial or otherwise. She had used harsher terms, he remembered, in a moment of anguish. *Whore and bastard.* He flinched at the deliberate brutality. It was certainly how the world would see it, and there was nothing he could say to make matters any better for her.

The lights on the first floor were low, one branch of candles left burning. And he was too tired to think any more. Tomorrow he would go to Whitchurch and find the Reverend Julius Broughton. He would verify that cleric's role in the proceedings. It might achieve nothing, but at least he would feel that he was doing *something.* And he would know if the marriage of Thomas with Octavia Baxendale had actually existed.

He yawned. And came to a halt on the landing. Further along on the right a door was ajar. The baby's room. A gentle light spilled out, very low. Probably the nursemaid come to check on her small charge.

Then a soft voice reached him, crooning a lullaby. A low voice, sweet and tender. He was immediately drawn to it and came to stand silently in the half-open doorway.

The child must have been restless. Rather than summon the nursemaid, Eleanor had come herself to comfort him. Of course she would, he acknowledged. The child was her only connection with Thomas, even more of an anchor in these stormy waters.

She sat in a low chair, a single candle on the little table casting its light from behind to rim her figure in gold. Apparently the infant now slept. Eleanor's song had become a gentle humming, her hand on the edge of the crib, rocking gently, her eyes fixed on the sleeping face.

Henry could not take his eyes from her, his thoughts and feelings suspended in that one moment. She had risen from her bed, her hair unpinned from its fashionable style but yet unbraided so that it fell in a glory of waves over her breast. A peignoir lay in soft overlapping layers of cream silk and lace from a high neck to cover her feet. Her face was calm. Her eyes hooded. Her lips curved in a tender smile. A Madonna, indeed.

His heart thudded against his ribs as the scene imprinted itself on his mind. She was so beautiful. And he had lost her to his brother. For the first time in his life Henry cursed the dead Thomas, even knowing that the blame could not in any way be heaped at his brother's feet. He had lost her. And yet for the past two years he had tried to persuade himself that his love for her was dead, destroyed when she had broken her promise to him. Wrong! Totally and utterly wrong! The voice in his mind and his heart would no longer allow him to pretend. His love for Eleanor was as strong as ever. And just as doomed. He must not allow it to be a burden on her—and so must bear it on his own shoulders, his emotions hidden.

A tingle of awareness touched Eleanor's spine and she knew that he was there.

She could pretend that she did not know, of course, conscious of a ripple of embarrassment to be discovered like this. If she kept her face turned towards the crib, he might walk away as silently as he had come. But she felt the compulsion of his eyes, felt her pulse pick up its beat in response. What did it matter that he saw her watching over her child in the dark of the night? After all, there was no one else to care.

She looked up, a slight turn of her head.

Her eyes, deeply violet-blue with love and compassion for her son, looked on his and could not look away, caught in his gaze.

Henry was drawn to her as a moth drawn to its ultimate destruction in the vibrant glow of a candle flame, against all his instincts to keep his distance from this lovely girl—woman, now—who had stolen his heart, and still held it in chains. Walking softly forward, so as not to disturb the child, his eyes never left hers. What compulsion drove him he did not know—and she made no move to stop him, equally trapped in the moment, to bring him to his senses. Placing a hand on the back of the low chair, he bent to allow his fingers to lift to her throat, to caress the graceful curve of her nape beneath her hair. She neither flinched nor resisted. If she had, he promised himself he would leave her. But she remained motionless, perhaps even leaned into his touch when he allowed his palm to brush and then cup her cheek, in the lightest of restraints. So he bent his head, slowly, deliberately, to take her lips with his. Whisper soft, mouth on mouth, encouraged by the small sound of pleasure in her throat. He savoured the sweetness of her breath, her mouth, her surrender to him.

It was a moment of impossible tenderness, recognised by them both, as the babe slept on by their side. Eleanor raised her hand to close her fingers round his wrist, a warm bracelet that held him, gentle yet burning him with its heat. Her breath caught as he deliberately allowed his tongue to trace the outline of her lips. She sighed against his mouth.

'Hal.'

Her perfume, the fine texture of hair and skin, her softness entrapped him, caught in that heart-stopping moment.

Then he eased back to look down into the beautiful face, a depth of emotion in his eyes. He could not have expressed his desires aloud for the world. But he captured her other hand from the side of the crib and lifted it to press his lips to the centre of her palm, marvelling at the softness of it.

'Nell…'

He murmured her name, the only word he had spoken since he had come into the room. A whisper of passion restrained. He ached with hard arousal, desire for her, a powerful need to touch and be touched, pulsing through every cell in his body.

When tears sparkled on her lashes he reached, without thought, to remove them with his lips.

Then he drew back and pushed himself to his full height. What could he say? It was a moment beyond words. So much promise, so much pain between them. So many broken dreams. He gave a little bow, strangely formal. Then turned and left the room as silently as he had come.

Henry's actions—and Eleanor's response—left emotions in turmoil. For both of them.

Chapter Five

On the following morning Lord Henry found himself alone in the sunny breakfast parlour. It was as he expected—and planned; it was still very early, but he intended to be under way to the village of Whitchurch before the rest of the household had risen. With good fortune he would return within the day. It crossed his mind with some force, and had done so more than once during a restless night of knife-edged introspection, that it might be to his advantage if he did not have to make conversation with Eleanor that day. What had driven him to such an unwise gesture towards her? He cursed himself once again for his blind stupidity. Within a few weeks this whole fiasco would be settled one way or another, and he would leave England. He would be out of her life for good—and he would be free to forget her and return to the attractions of Rosalind. But even though he swore at his uncontrolled actions, castigated himself for not keeping his distance, he was being driven to admit that he was not unmoved by Eleanor's plight. Unmoved? He swore again, brows drawn into a black bar. A magnificent understatement! He had loved her once and was bitterly aware that, however inappropriate and insupportable it might be, given their past history, he loved her still. Wanting nothing more than to take her to his bed, to undress her, to touch, to taste and to savour her for the rest of his life. To feel her stretch against him, beneath him, and hear his name on her lips when he roused her beyond thought and beyond sense. It would have taken a man of callous indifference not to respond to her plight of the previous night without tenderness and compassion. And where Eleanor was concerned, Henry was not that man.

So it would be better for everyone if he did not have to exchange polite conversation with her that morning! And doubtless Eleanor too would welcome his absence.

The door opened and there she stood.

They both became very still, Lord Henry with a teacup raised to his lips, Eleanor braced in the doorway. The previous night loomed between them, tension stark.

'Good morning, my lady. I trust you slept well.' Henry rose superbly to the occasion with the first bland comment that came to mind, wincing inwardly at his lack of polish. Then the emotional memories of the previous night were effectively wiped from his mind. With eyes narrowed he surveyed the lady from her head to her feet, momentarily taken aback.

She had taken his advice! And with stunning effect. He had not really expected it, but she had cast off her deep mourning and her black ribbons. The result took his breath, silenced any comment he might have been about to make. His memories of her had been as a débutante, certainly beautiful, but still ingenuously naïve in simple pastel muslins. And then in mourning, the stark black of her high-necked gowns highlighting her glorious hair and porcelain skin, grief adding a fine-drawn maturity to her face. But now he was struck anew by her beauty. Two years had added sophistication, elegance, confidence. An unfathomable grace. He had not realised the true worth of the woman he had lost that night when he had sailed without her. But he realised it now, with a blow to his gut, over the breakfast table with the sunshine pouring through the windows.

She had abandoned her black silk for a walking dress in dove grey spotted muslin, banded with a delicate interweaving of purple and amethyst flowers, the whole completed with a frilled hem. Its sleeves were long and tight with short puffed over-sleeves, the neckline high and pleated into a little frilled ruff. It fit to perfection, emphasising her slender figure, the embroidered decoration bringing out the intense colour of her eyes. She glowed in the morning sun, the fragile tints shimmering round her. It might still be mourning, demure and understated, but it complimented her colouring beautifully, her hair falling rich and burnished in a profusion of artless curls from a high knot to her shoulders.

His eyes came slowly back from their appreciation of her transformation, his mouth dry, words beyond him, to study her face. She did not look rested. Her pale skin still lacked colour, her eyes were strained and the shadows still left their delicate imprint. But she looked determined, a challenge in every line of her firm shoulders and the proud carriage of her head. She also looked apprehensive.

How fortunate, she realised, that he could not read her thought as she stood under his unnerving gaze. She had dreaded this meeting, needing all her pride and composure. But she had dressed for impact and raised her chin against any disapproval she might read in his face. She should never have allowed him to touch her. But she had, and had melted beneath the unmistakable tenderness of his touch. A mistake! Which she would not repeat, she promised herself—however great the temptation to do so. She would hide her trepidation behind a mask of fashionable unconcern. Yet she still found it well nigh impossible to lift her eyes to his or accept his critical survey with any degree of ease.

'My lady!' Henry rose to his feet at last, and bowed his head in acknowledgement of her gesture. But he did not approach her. Did not dare if he wished to mask the leap of heat in his blood as he studied her. He cursed again as the fire built and stirred in his loins. 'Allow me to say that you look lovely. And allow me to admit that I did not think that you would do it. What does your mother say?' His eyes narrowed again at the prospect of biting words from that quarter.

'Thank you, my lord. She does not know.' Eleanor still could not meet his eyes, unsure of what she would see in his face. If it was contempt or condemnation for her lack of respect for his brother, she could not bear it. Not after the unbelievable and exquisite cherishing of the previous night. 'I need to ask… I understand the reason for your advice, but I would not wish to show insufficient respect for Thomas. It is hardly more than four months... Do you perhaps consider it improper?' Now she lifted her troubled eyes to his. 'I hope that you would be honest with me. Indeed, I know that you will.'

Henry chose his words carefully to allay her anxieties. He could not take her in his arms as his heart might dictate, so he would use his mind to enfold her with comforting words, to soothe and calm. His face was stern, his voice firm with conviction, willing her to accept and believe. 'Your respect for Thomas can be questioned by no one, Eleanor. Your friends must know your qualities as wife and mother. As for your clothing, it is becoming and befits the situation. All you need is the confidence to carry it off. Yes, people will talk. Of course they will! Let them, until the next scandal raises its head to replace the sordid details of our family difficulties on their lips. We have nothing to hide and we will not allow society to dictate the behaviour of the Faringdons.'

'Even if I am not a Faringdon? It is a matter of some dispute, after all.'

There. She had said it aloud and waited, eyes closed, for his reply.

'There is no doubt in my mind, Eleanor. No matter the weight of evidence, I cannot accept that my brother would make such a terrible mistake with such painful and disastrous consequences for all concerned.'

She sighed and opened her eyes, blinking against the unexpected threat of tears at his firm declaration. 'That is what I needed to hear. I am in your debt, Hal.'

'No. You are not. You are in no one's debt! And besides, the dress is very becoming. You are a beautiful woman, Eleanor. Lift up your head and smile.'

She did just that. The smile might waver a little, but she would hold her own, of that he was certain.

Satisfied with his reply, Eleanor took a seat opposite to his place at the breakfast table and Henry resumed his seat. 'I hoped that I would find you here. I wished to know—what is your next strategy?'

He breathed out slowly. Now they were on even ground again,

without the threat of uncomfortable emotions to stalk and trap them. He could cloak his feelings in practicalities. 'It is my intention to go down to Whitchurch to speak with the Reverend Broughton. I know that Hoskins will be efficient in his investigation, but I would wish to see the village for myself, perhaps speak to some who know the family.' He frowned down at the scattering of crumbs on his empty plate. 'What I will discover I know not. Merely some knowledge of the Baxendale family, I suppose.'

Eleanor leaned forward, fingers linked on the table. 'Would you agree to wait until tomorrow and allow me to accompany you?'

'No.' His reply was unequivocal.

Eleanor was taken aback. 'Then I must go on my own.'

'To Whitchurch? Why should you? It is not a good idea.'

'If you will not drive me, then I will simply hire a carriage and go myself.'

Henry knew when he was being driven into a corner. She was quite capable of doing just that. Her lips were firm, her eyes ablaze with the certainty of her actions and there would be no gainsaying her. Lord Henry's mouth set with displeasure. He retreated but with little grace; the last thing he wanted was to spend the better part of a day in Eleanor's company.

'Very well, if that is what you wish. But, I warn you, I intend to take the curricle and travel fast. I would return within the day. And I will not tolerate your mother with us, so do not even suggest it!'

'You will not have to. There is insufficient room for her in a curricle!' Eleanor was maddeningly matter of fact in dealing with his objection and he suspected a spark of triumph in her eyes before she veiled them. 'Tomorrow it is.'

'Why not today?' he enquired brusquely.

Eleanor rose to pour herself a cup of tea, looking at him over her shoulder. 'This afternoon I intend to pay a visit on Miss Baxendale. I hope to take Judith with me for moral support. She may be able to discuss matters of which I know nothing. Perhaps Octavia will speak more openly if her brother is not present and I would know more of her supposed marriage.' She returned to her seat, her face pensive. 'The most difficult thing for me will be to face the servants at Faringdon House…but I must do it.'

Any ill feelings that Lord Henry might have been harbouring over his change of plan were instantly dispelled by the stark courage of Eleanor's proposed scheme.

'You have all my admiration, Nell.'

'Don't be kind to me or, even worse, show me *pity,* or I shall surely weep,' she snapped immediately. 'I cannot afford to be downtrodden over this. Even though there seems to be so little hope…' Her face was closed, shuttered against his careful scrutiny. She sipped her tea, holding her cup with hands which were not quite steady.

'I would ask a favour from you, Hal.'

Now she looked at him.

'Anything in my power.' He found himself stretching out his hand to her across the table, the lightest of touches on her fingers, a symbol of unity with her. Her reply astounded him, showing the lengths to which she was prepared to go to fight for her good name.

'Will you drive me around Hyde Park this morning? At a time when most of our acquaintance will be there? You said that we should be seen, and I wish to do so. The scandal has to break some time and I believe it will be soon rather than late.' She took a breath. 'I do not know how bad it will be, but I fear it. I cannot allow that fear to dominate my whole life. Will you drive me?' Her eyes pleaded with him, holding his until he would give her an answer. He could not but respond to such anguish, but she misread the brilliant glitter, the firming of the lines around his mouth as he was driven to acknowledge once again his love for her. She drew back a little and looked away. 'If you do not wish to, of course, Nicholas might.'

'You mistake me, my lady.' He kept his voice low. 'I am always at your service.' It was as much as he could say. Then a smile lightened his expression as he saw the possibilities of her plan. 'I will drive you round Hyde Park with great pleasure. And I think that we should go out of our way to make an impression. I will take Thomas's high-perch phaeton, which is sure to draw all eyes. Fine feathers indeed! It is in the stables at Faringdon House with some suitable bloodstock. Will that suit your intention?'

Eleanor shuddered, bringing the equipage to mind. 'If I must. An impression indeed! I...I will not let you or your family down, whatever the reception from the *haut ton.*'

'No matter. I will support you, Nell, whatever the outcome. You should know that.' Standing, he walked round the table, took her hand to urge her to her feet. 'You are not alone in this battle, you know.' He kissed her fingers with grave respect, holding her fingers still within his warm clasp.

'Of course.' Her words might be politely non-committal, but she returned the pressure of his hand, compelled by the instant warmth in the region of her heart.

Henry felt it and was satisfied. 'If *you* have the courage to visit Octavia, then I suppose that tonight *I* must join Nick in the gaming hells of Pall Mall!'

Two hours later, Eleanor presented herself promptly on the front doorstep of their house in Park Lane as Lord Henry manoeuvred the high-perch phaeton to a halt at the curb before her. Eleanor eyed it askance, but was forced to admit the excellence of Henry's scheme. In this carriage they would without doubt draw attention to themselves, as Henry had predicted. The woodwork gleamed glossily. As did the well-groomed coats of the pair of bays with their glittering harness. They pawed the ground with restive impatience, eager to be off. The huge hind wheels and the seat that overhung the front axle had been picked out with elegant simplicity in dark blue. Eleanor chose not to contemplate its height from the ground.

But it would suit their purpose. They wished to be seen and noticed. They could hardly help it.

And Henry himself had risen to the occasion, she was quick to appreciate, in the height of fashion with more care than was his wont. He was now sporting the palest of biscuit pantaloons, highly polished boots, a coat of dark blue superfine, which fit to perfection, and a discreetly striped waistcoat. His neckcloth might not be as extreme as some, but the folds were precise, tied by the hand of a master and secured by a sapphire pin. The whole ensemble was covered by a caped greatcoat, which hung negligently open with casual grace.

Eleanor found herself staring. With his striking good looks, he would draw any woman's eye. What hope was there for her poor heart when faced with his dark splendour? What chance to persuade herself that she did not care and that her heart did not beat faster merely at the sight of his dark hair and arresting features? She would have as much success in persuading herself not to breathe! And it was made even more impossible by knowing that his sometimes hard exterior hid a depth of kindness and understanding. Not to forget the burning kiss to remind her of what they might have meant to each other. She flushed and bit her lip as he reined in and leapt to the ground with fluid agility.

He looked her over critically.

'Excellent! A smile would help.'

And she did. It might be a trifle brittle, it might not quite reach her eyes, but it illuminated her face and would fool those who did not know her or did not choose to look closely enough.

Henry did both and felt his heart stir with compassion and longing.

She had completed her outfit with a close-fitting, highwaisted spencer in black silk. It added the perfect touch of sobriety to the silver grey of her gown. Her grey silk-covered bonnet tied beneath her chin with long ribbons, its brim framing her lovely face, the silk flowers in shades of violet and amethyst, detracting from the severity of the whole. A pair of flat slippers, grey kid gloves, a neat reticule and a silver grey parasol—and she was ready for the ordeal. She had exquisite taste, he acknowledged. Elegance and sobriety, layered in perfect harmony, not full mourning, but quiet and respectful. He could not fault her. And he was struck anew by her beauty as she turned her head to look at him.

He handed Eleanor up into the high carriage, mounted himself and waited as she arranged her skirts and unfurled her parasol.

'Ready?' He closed his hand momentarily over hers, knowing exactly what was going through her head, the pain of the anxieties that gripped her with fierce claws. 'Do we not look splendid?' His smile was wry. 'And highly respectable, of course! Not a whisper of scandal between us!' The groom swung up behind them as Henry took up the reins and the longhandled whip.

Before they could pull away, Nick appeared from the front door to stand beside them on the pavement, dressed to take a turn in Bond Street or stroll through Piccadilly, a quizzical expression on his face as he surveyed his brother.

'I am impressed, Hal.'

'So you should be. I hope the Polite World in Hyde Park will say the same.'

'Can you manage those bays? They can be lively. Perhaps I should offer to drive Eleanor round the park, for her own safety. You must be out of practice. Or do they have such sophistication in the colonies these days?' His lips curled in gentle mockery, hoping to drive away the strained shadows in Eleanor's face.

'I can manage. If you remember, I taught you to drive—to my cost! For your sins, you could find yourself a mount and come and ride with us.'

Henry's expression held a silent message. *A show of force in the face of the gossips would not come amiss. Eleanor would welcome it.*

'Very well. I will join you in the park—so don't crash the carriage before I arrive!'

A superior smile from Henry was the only answer.

'Thank you. You are very kind.' Eleanor's soft murmur told him that she was perfectly aware of his intent. He smiled reassuringly at her, before turning his attention to his horses.

In spite of Nicholas's barbed comments on his brother's expertise, Eleanor found herself in no danger at Henry's hands. He drove carefully through the crowded streets, skilfully avoiding a multitude of carriages and heavy wagons that thronged the centre of the city. He had the horses well in hand. She was left with the freedom to watch and admire his skill, the clever strength of his hands, with their broad palms and long fingers. They looped and wielded the reins and whip with casual and confident ease. She knew the gentleness of their touch for herself. And their power. She turned her face away in dismay.

* * *

Meanwhile, as Nicholas made his way to the stables at Faringdon House to acquire a suitable hack, his thoughts were taken
up, not with the complications and, probably, repercussions of
the Baxendale claim, but with the teasing matter of Eleanor and
his brother. There was some past history here. The more he
watched them together, the more he was certain of it. And it had
left a bitter residue. He tightened his lips as he remembered their
first meeting in the withdrawing-room at Burford Hall. The tension in the atmosphere. The crackle of shock, of controlled hostility, particularly from his brother. Nicholas had decided,
although he did not understand it, that it was simply a case of instant dislike, but now he was not so sure. Hal was so caring of
Eleanor. So concerned. He had altered all his plans, transported
them all to London and was intent on waging an all-out battle
campaign. Yes, to protect the family name and Thomas's integrity, of course. Hal could be expected to do just that. But there
was a far more personal involvement here. Nicholas saddled up
his hack, deciding that he would be prepared to wager five hundred guineas that Hal's feelings for Eleanor were not those of a
brother towards a sister. As for Eleanor, it was difficult to tell.
Who could ever read a woman's mind with any degree of accuracy! With a shrug, he pulled on his gloves, looped his grey's
reins and set himself to join the fray in Hyde Park.

Some ten minutes later Lord Henry Faringdon and the Marchioness of Burford turned into the formal gates of Hyde Park
near Apsley House, to be immediately swallowed up by a con-
stant promenade of those of the fashionable world who wished
to see and be seen. Carriages, riders, saunterers, turned out in
the height of fashion, ready to hail acquaintances, issue and accept invitations, chatter and gossip. Eleanor squared her shoulders and set to face the unknown beast in its den. Her smile was
securely pinned in place, her parasol positioned to a nicety as
she looked around her with commendable interest and confidence, not afraid to meet anyone's eye or raise her hand in
greeting.

It did not take long.

Veiled looks. Whispered comments behind gloved hands or hidden by the little feather muffs that had become so fashionable. Quick speculative glances from bright eyes.

'They know!'

'Yes. It had to happen.' Henry, too, was aware. 'But *we* are not concerned with trivial and empty gossip. We know the truth. You are the Marchioness of Burford.' He smiled at an acquaintance and nodded his head as he looped the reins to pass a curricle. 'Your son is the Marquis of Burford. Don't forget it.' He inclined his head with superbly arrogant condescension toward an elderly Dowager who raised her lorgnette in their direction.

The Marchioness promptly followed suit. She took a deep breath and set herself to follow instruction as Nick joined them on a lively grey hack.

'I see they're tattling.'

Which brutal words, Eleanor decided later, summed up the experience of the next hour.

It proved to be an education. Few people were secure enough in their knowledge to risk an outright snub to the well-born Faringdon brothers and their fair companion, no matter their doubts over the lady's present position.

The Princess Lieven, handsome wife of the Russian ambassador, did, of course. As her barouche drove past, she stared straight ahead, eyes cold, mouth unmoving, the epitome of cold disapproval of the English in general and the Faringdons in particular. The Faringdon phaeton might as well have been invisible. There was no recognition of a lady with whom the Princess had taken tea or exchanged cool pleasantries at Almack's. What would you expect from the most feared patroness of Almack's, so fixated with what was seemly and proper and good *ton,* Eleanor thought, her heart sinking.

'A disagreeable woman with an acid tongue!' Henry broke into her thoughts with a more forthright observation and lifted her spirits. 'All self-consequence and pride with nothing but contempt for those around her.'

'No more vouchers from Almack's from that quarter!' Nick, riding beside them, smiled wryly at the calculated snub.

'Thank God! A blessing in disguise!'

Eleanor laughed at Henry's irreverence and had to admit the truth of it. But it hurt.

Mostly the pleasure-seekers in Hyde Park were unsure. They were quite prepared to smile, wave or stop for a brief exchange of words. But eyes were uneasy. Glances interested, assessing the weight of evidence—or lack of it—that might suggest that the Marchioness of Burford was an impostor. And her infant son… Well! Knowing eyes slid away from too close a contact. Yet the Faringdons still received an invitation to a quiet evening party, from no less a personage than the Countess of Sefton. Just a small gathering. Perfectly proper for their present situation, with the loss of dear Thomas. Isabella Sefton's eyes were full of sympathy, her soft tones saying what her words could not. But the fact that she had gone to the lengths to instruct her coachman to rein in so that she could speak to them was balm to Eleanor's soul. Such kindness from one of the patronesses of Almack's threatened her composure.

They met Cousin Judith being escorted by the Earl of Painscastle in a smart barouche. The couple made a point of stopping to engage in animated conversation. Eleanor intercepted an eloquent glance between Henry and the lady, immediately alerting her suspicions. Henry had arranged the very public assignation, intent on leaving nothing to chance. A show of family unity and support could do nothing but good.

When the gentlemen fell to discussing horseflesh, Eleanor took the opportunity for a quiet word with Judith across the two carriages.

'It is my intention to pay an afternoon call on Octavia—I would be more than grateful if you could accompany me.'

'Octavia?' Judith's face lit up with sly enthusiasm. 'Of course I will come. I would not miss it for the world. What do we talk about?'

'Herself. Thomas.' Eleanor shrugged a little helplessly. 'Anything that might help me to understand.'

'Anything that might brand her as a liar?'

'Yes.' Eleanor sighed at the outspoken truth. 'That is what I could hope for.'

'I will definitely accompany you.' The Countess of Pains-castle opened her frivolous lace parasol with a definite snap. 'I will collect you in the barouche at three o'clock!'

They drove, waved, exchanged polite greetings under the intense scrutiny of the Polite World for more than an hour.

'Take me home, Hal. I have played out this role for long enough.' Eleanor furled her parasol with weary distaste.

'You were magnificent. You should feel nothing but pride.' Henry's quick glance at Eleanor confirmed his suspicion that the morning had begun to take its toll. If she would admit to it, a headache had begun to build behind her eyes from the strain of smiling and denying the effect of sharp, critical glances.

He would take her home. He would have liked nothing better than to take her away from London, from the whole sorry mess. To remove the hurt and the humiliation. But he could not. They must face it and defeat it if they were to restore Eleanor to her rightful place in society—and in her own eyes, a matter of even greater importance. Her spirit had been superb, carrying off the morning's exercise in full public gaze with considerable panache, but the threat of society's condemnation loomed on the horizon, as threatening as a thunder cloud.

They turned out of the gates, once more below the imposing façade of Apsley House.

'You did not stop to speak to Melissa Charlesworth,' Eleanor noted as a landaulet bearing the lady, now the Countess of Saltmarshe and once the object of Henry's gallantry, passed them with no change in speed.

'I did not see her.' His voice was surprisingly harsh.

Eleanor's brows arched. 'No?'

'No. She is not important.'

With which caustic comment Eleanor had to be content.

Eleanor and Judith arrived, as arranged, at Faringdon House to pay an afternoon call on Octavia Baxendale. The door was opened by Eaton, the Faringdon butler, momentarily lost for words when faced with the mistress of the house come as a visitor on a social call.

'My lady…' he stammered. 'It is not fitting that you should remain standing on your own doorstep…'

Before embarrassment could fall and smother both parties, Judith took the matter in hand, manipulating the situation in a high-handed and confident manner worthy of her mama, Lady Beatrice Faringdon, a lady of considerable presence and force of character, indicating that the Marchioness was staying with Lord Henry who had hired a town house in Park Lane, but only until he returned to America later in the month.

'It is more convenient, you understand!' But for whom and for what purpose the Countess of Painscastle made no attempt to explain.

And how was Eaton? As well as ever? And was Sir Edward Baxendale at home? No? How unfortunate… But perhaps Miss Baxendale was receiving visitors? She would no doubt welcome some company, knowing so few people in town! Perhaps Eaton could discover if…

Eleanor caught Judith's eye in deep gratitude—and then they were being shown into the familiar red-and-gold-striped withdrawing-room where Miss Baxendale sat alone beside the fireplace, a piece of needlework lying abandoned on the table beside her. The lady sprang to her feet as Eaton introduced the guests with a flourish. He did not know the full background to this development, and although common gossip was rife…he would dearly have loved to listen at the door, except that it was below his dignity. A pleasant enough young lady, Miss Baxendale, but not to compare with the Marchioness, of course. But the word in the town suggested deep doings. He shook his head as he departed for the kitchens to organise tea and inform the members of the servants' hall that *things were afoot* upstairs.

'Edward is not at home I am afraid.' Octavia looked rather nervously from one lady to the other. 'But if you would care to sit. And take some tea?'

The faint look of unease that hung about her black-gowned

figure suggested that she would rather they did not, but Eleanor came forward in friendly mode with hand outstretched and a smile on her face. There was nothing for Octavia to do but participate in the gentle social occasion with the lady whose social position, it appeared, she had every intention of appropriating for herself.

'We have come to see you, Miss Baxendale, to find how you are settling in,' Eleanor explained. 'I trust that we are not disturbing you. And my cousin Judith has come, with whom you might be acquainted.'

Octavia looked at the lively redhead as they made a polite curtsy. 'Perhaps… You were Miss Faringdon, were you not? And now the Countess of Painscastle? Pray take a seat.'

They did so.

'How uncomfortable this is…' Octavia picked up her embroidery and promptly put it down again, lost for words, unable to raise her eyes above her restless hands.

'But it will not stop us drinking tea together and having a cosy exchange of news.' Eleanor tried to put the lady at her ease, not for the first time wondering how Thomas could have possibly married this pretty but insipid creature.

'We came out in the same Season, Miss Baxendale.' Judith smiled encouragingly. 'I believe that we met at any number of balls and soirées.'

'Yes. I met so many people. But I think…I am sure that I remember you. I came to your coming-out ball in this very house. My aunt and uncle—and my brother, of course—chaperoned me. I remember thinking what a beautiful house it was. I never thought that I should be living here…' With which ingenuous comment she flushed and turned her head with relief when Eaton and an interested footman brought in the tea.

The ceremony was performed with nervous competence by Miss Baxendale, the tea was served, and the ladies chatted about a range of inconsequences of fashion and the events offered by London to ladies with a degree of leisure and affluence. Then Judith returned to her reminiscing over the glories of her Seasonal debut, Octavia agreeing and nodding but adding few of her own impressions.

'And how are you spending your time in London now?' Judith tried for another approach as the conversation dried.

'Sir Edward has been very busy,' Octavia explained. 'I have rarely been out.'

'And of course, you are still in mourning.' Eleanor sympathised with a sad smile, eyes keen and watchful.

'Why, yes…it would not be seemly for me to go about in public to any great degree. I see that you, my lady, have laid aside your black gloves.' She took in the glory of silver grey with some surprise.

'Indeed I have.' Eleanor did not elaborate. 'Have you perhaps driven in the park yet, Miss Baxendale? The days have been very pleasant. And I am sure Sir Edward would drive you to take the air. It would be quite acceptable for you in your situation.'

'No. I have not been beyond the garden.'

'Do you enjoy music or painting? To help to pass the time a little when your brother is from home?' Judith arched her brows.

'No. I do a little embroidery, as you see.'

'Perhaps you miss your garden in the country. Where is it that you lived?'

'In Whitchurch. And, yes, I miss it so much. The roses will just be coming into bloom. I shall not be there to tend them and wish I was…' It was the first animation that Octavia Baxendale had shown since her guests had arrived, her whole countenance blooming as did her roses, but only to be stemmed as if she feared an indiscretion. 'But, of course, it is necessary for me to be here.'

'You must miss it indeed. Now I have no interest at all in gardens, but I understand that it can be a great solace in times of grief.' Judith put down her teacup and leaned across the little table to pat Octavia's hand. 'Eleanor has been telling me about your little son. What a splendid boy he is. Could we perhaps see him? My lord and I are hoping for a child very soon…' She lowered her lashes in coy anticipation.

Eleanor hid a smile. Cousin Judith had a remarkable range of skills of which she had been unaware until now.

'Of course.' Octavia appeared a little surprised that her guests would wish to see her son, but rose to her feet to pull the bell hang beside the fireplace.

'Would you ask Sarah to bring the child down?' The footman bowed and departed.

Within minutes the door opened. In came the young woman whom Eleanor had last seen in Burford Hall. Fair and neat with a ladylike composure. Fair enough, perhaps, to be one of the family. A dependent of good birth, Eleanor decided, but most likely fallen on hard times, now holding the hand of the child, John. John Faringdon, if the documents were correct.

'This is Sarah,' Octavia said, confirming Eleanor's impression. 'She has been my companion and now acts as nurse to John.' The lady curtsied and released the little boy, who immediately ran to show his mama a wooden boat that he had clasped in his hand. Miss Baxendale patted his head. John thrust the precious possession into her hands, announcing 'Boat!' with a disarming smile.

'What a beautiful child.' Judith held out her hands. 'Come here, John. Let me see your boat.'

The child, aware of the possibility of a wider audience, walked shyly to Judith and then gurgled with shocked pleasure when she snatched him up and sat him on her knee. 'What a handsome boat. And so are you very handsome. All those golden curls and such blue eyes.' She pinched the end of his nose to make him laugh.

'He is a good child.' Octavia nodded and smiled as Judith stood him back on his feet when he struggled for freedom and restored his boat to his grasp. With a crow John launched himself back towards Sarah where she had remained beside the door, but, with uncoordinated enthusiasm, fell on the wide expanse of deep turkey carpet. For a second he crouched motionless. Then tears came to his eyes and a sob to his chest.

'There, now,' Octavia said. 'You are not very hurt.' Sarah swooped, picked up the child, kissing his cheek, smoothing away his tears with her hand, crooning to him in a soft voice.

'Is he well?' Octavia watched the little scene with a graceful turn of her head. So did Eleanor and Judith.

'John took no hurt, ma'am.'

'Perhaps you could take him back to the nursery, Sarah. He tends to get a little excited in company' she explained to the visitors. 'It is not good for a child.'

With a curtsy to the assembled company, Sarah walked to the door, holding the boy close, and left.

What else should they talk about? Judith tried fashions and the opening of a number of new modistes where the most ravishing hats and gowns could be purchased, but although Octavia was pleasant and smiling, she had little to say and shared little interest in what might or might not be considered *de rigueur.*

'I believe that it is time we left.' In desperation Eleanor was about to rise to her feet. 'My own son will be missing me by now, I expect.' Then the door opened to admit Sir Edward Baxendale. He greeted his guests with great charm and a warm smile, sat with them and accepted a hand-painted porcelain cup of tea from his sister. The talk encompassed the weather and Judith's new barouche, which awaited them at the door, but it was noticed that Octavia said no more.

'Well?' Eleanor and Judith were once again ensconced in the comfort of Judith's barouche after what could only be described as a frustrating and disappointing afternoon.

'That child is no Faringdon!' Judith pulled on her gloves with conviction.

'But he is very fair like his mother.'

'Faringdons breed true!' Judith insisted. 'Look at your own son. He might have your eyes, but his father's hair, his nose and mouth are very pronounced. There is no denying his parentage. I swear there is no trace of Thomas in that child!'

Eleanor flushed and hesitated at Judith's observations. 'But that is not proof. *You* inherited your mother's red hair and green eyes rather than your father's features.'

'Very true. But I have the Faringdon nose. And eyebrows. There is no mistaking them. The golden-haired child *we* have just seen bears no resemblance at all.'

'No. Perhaps not.' It had to be admitted. 'She is no doting mother, is she?' Eleanor commented. 'That surprised me a little.'

'Ha! Just because you are!' Judith smiled in understanding. 'We are not all born to lavish unbounded love and affection on our offspring. He is certainly a healthy child and well cared for.'

'I suppose.' Eleanor frowned at her recollection of the child's tears. *She* would not have been able to ignore them—to allow his nurse to lift and comfort him! 'I presume that Octavia's reminiscences of her coming-out were correct?'

'Yes…' Judith wrinkled her nose '…but she does not have much to say, does she?'

'No. And even less when Sir Edward arrived home.'

They were silent in thoughtful communion as the barouche made its steady way towards Park Lane.

'You know…' Judith ventured, brow furrowed in thought, 'Simon would make himself scarce if he knew a party of ladies were gossiping in his withdrawing-room. Wouldn't Thomas have done the same?'

'Why, yes…I hadn't thought. Thomas would have gone to the stables until they had all gone! Sir Edward joined us straight away. Why do you think that was?'

Green eyes met amethyst, their thoughts clear between them.

'But it does not add up to much, does it?' Eleanor queried. 'Merely that Sir Edward would prefer his sister not to be alone with visitors.'

'Or is it that he did not wish Octavia be alone with *you!*' responded Judith.

There was no answer to it.

The two ladies prepared to part company on Eleanor's doorstep. Judith leaned down from her carriage to where Eleanor stood on the pavement and clasped her hand in firm support.

'Have we proved anything?' Judith asked.

'No.'

'Except that Octavia was definitely not Thomas's usual flirt!' Judith tightened her hold to enforce her point. 'It is very difficult to believe, after spending such a tedious half-hour in her company, that he fell in love with her and married her. Whereas I can quite believe that he loved and married you, dear Nell!'

Eleanor took a breath. 'Sir Edward said that—'

'Tell me, Nell.'

'When they first came to Burford Hall—when they told us of the whole dreadful complication—Sir Edward said that Thomas forced Octavia to keep their marriage secret because of her lack of rank. That his family would disapprove.' A line deepened between her fine brows as her mind worried at the problem. 'But *my* birth, Judith, is no better than Octavia's, and I know that the Faringdons would never have chosen someone of so little consequence as myself for Thomas's bride, however supportive you and Aunt Beatrice might be now that we are faced with this scandal. Yet Thomas followed his own wishes in the face of family opposition and married me with as much public display as he could achieve.' She smiled a little sadly as she remembered the festivity and ceremonial of her marriage. 'All I am trying to say is that social standing does not seem to me to be a good enough reason for Thomas to hide Octavia away in the country—if he truly loved her and wished to marry her.'

Judith had flushed uncomfortably at her companion's devastatingly accurate reading of family opinion on her marriage to Thomas, but patted Eleanor's hand, for once all the careless flippancy quite gone from her face. 'Of course Thomas never married Octavia, dearest Nell. You must never allow yourself to think that. And as for your lack of rank—all I can say is that marrying you was one of the best decisions Thomas made in his whole life.'

'Thank you, Judith.' A faint smile touched Eleanor's pale lips. 'At least that is something for me to hold on to!'

In the entrance hall Eleanor's path crossed that of Henry and Nicholas as the two gentlemen prepared to leave the house and look in at Gentleman Jackson's Boxing Academy in New Bond Street before repairing to Brooks's for a hand or two of whist.

'Any fortune with your visit to the fair Octavia?'

'None. But tell me. If I were entertaining a group of ladies to tea and you arrived home, what would you do?'

'Head for the library and take a glass of port until they have gone.' Henry's response took no thought.

Neither did Nicholas's. 'Turn around and go back out to the stables.'

'Thank you. I would expect as much.' Eleanor nodded her head and proceeded to climb the stairs.

'Did we say the right thing?' Nicholas asked.

'I have no idea. Women can be very uncommunicative—and devious! But I am sure that Eleanor will let us know in her own good time. And since we have no library here in this house…' Henry turned on his heel towards the door of the morning room '…I think I need a glass of port before we depart!'

Later that evening Henry and Nicholas prepared to visit some of the discreet gaming establishments that opened their doors to those who had bottomless pockets and sought more excitement than the play offered at Brooks's and White's. There were any number of them with unmarked doors, opened by black-clad individuals who were careful whom they admitted. Some were more legitimate than others, some more honest, but the stakes were high and the play keen in them all. Some were the haunts of card-sharps, quick to lure young men newly arrived in London into the dubious delights of hazard and macao, where disgrace and ruin waited for the unwary flat. And if *point non Plus* was reached, it was always possible to patronise the fashionable establishment of Messieurs Howard and Gibbs, who were more than willing to lend at extortionate rates of interest. It might be that Sir Edward passed his evenings in such company. It might be that he had lost heavily and so was now in debt, sufficient that he would be prepared to risk an outrageous plan to get his hands on a vast fortune. It might provide them with a reason why he should put forward such a preposterous claim of marriage on behalf of his sister.

It proved to be a long evening.

By the end of it, after numerous hands of whist, reacquaintance with French hazard and roulette and too many glasses of inferior brandy, they had nothing to show for it other than lighter pockets and the lurking prospect of a hangover.

Sir Edward Baxendale did not spend his evenings or his money in any of the gaming hells they visited.

'So what does Sir Edward do with his time when he is in London?'

They strolled back to Park Lane in the early hours of the morning.

'Horses?' Nick suggested. 'But how we are to discover if he squanders his money on the Turf, I know not. I suppose we could look in at Tattersalls and see if he is known for betting on the horses. We do not know even if he is in debt.'

'No.' Henry fought off the looming sense of depression at the futility of the evening and the prospect of the long journey on the following day.

'Do you think he has a mistress?' Nicholas asked.

'To demand vast sums of money and diamond necklaces? A possibility.' Henry grinned at the prospect. 'Mistresses can be very expensive.'

'The voice of experience.' Nicholas returned the grin. 'And how would we discover that?'

'Have him followed, I expect!'

'That I will not do!'

'Go and talk to Hoskins tomorrow. Suggest to him that he make discreet enquiries with Howard and Gibbs—unless you care to? No, I thought not.' He laughed as he saw the expression on Nick's face They had arrived on the steps to their front door. 'But if Baxendale is short of the readies, and does not wish to advertise the matter, a moneylender would be his first port of call. Hoskins will know how to go about it, I expect.' He thought for a moment before opening the door, all humour drained in the dark shadows. 'But you might visit the other gaming houses. Meanwhile I will see what the Reverend Broughton has to say about our elusive gentleman.' He hesitated, but only for a moment. 'I don't suppose you would consider visiting Aunt Beatrice to discover her thoughts on the Baxendales four years ago. Judith reminded me that she has a formidable memory.'

'No.'

'Mmm. Then I will suggest that Mrs Stamford pay a morning call. They can enjoy a comfortable dissection of the manners and morals of the younger generation—and perhaps Aunt Beatrice will remember something of import.'

Chapter Six

Henry leaped down from the curricle, winced at the headache, cursed all gaming hells, and walked back into the entrance hall as Eleanor emerged from the breakfast parlour on the following morning. She had dressed in a smart travelling costume of deep blue, the fine wool double-breasted coat with its long tight sleeves and high waist already buttoned. She was in the act of arranging the wide collar so that it draped elegantly into a cape effect. If his lordship noticed that she wore a particular jewel on her breast, whether deliberately to provoke or through custom, he chose to make no comment.

'I am ready to leave.'

'Are you sure this is a good idea?' He frowned at her as she tied the bow of her neat straw bonnet beneath her chin to charming effect.

'Yes. There is no need to scowl at me, my lord. We have already had this conversation and come to an agreement.'

'I do not remember actually *agreeing* to anything—simply bowing to a stronger force when you threatened to go on your own.' The scowl did not lessen. 'I hope that you realise that we may learn nothing. I could see the Reverend Broughton myself and be back here within the day…'

She shook her head. 'You do not understand. I want to see the village…and hear what he has to say.'

'Do you not trust me to do the right thing?' The demand was brusque, Henry's mouth set in displeasure.

Did she? She looked at him consideringly, head a little on one side. All she knew for certain was that she must not rely on anyone, certainly not on Hal. She had trusted Thomas, had accepted his offer of marriage—which was more than she could ever have dreamed of and for which she would always be grateful to the depths of her soul—but look where that had got her. She must look to her own inner strength to weather this storm.

She turned her back on his lordship to pick up her tan leather gloves, thus evading the answer—which he was quick to notice with regret and a degree of hurt that jolted him. She did not trust him, not even to do all in his power to restore her good name.

'I simply need to go there,' was all that she would say.

The weather was set fair for travel. They made good time in the curricle on the main roads as they negotiated their way out of the growing sprawl of London. There was little conversation between them. Eleanor was too tense and could find nothing to say. Henry concentrated on his horses. When they took to the country lanes their progress was slower, but the pair of greys were excellent animals with strength and stamina and well up to the task. Henry drove them with patient skill to conserve their energies.

Eventually as the sun rose to the height of noon, they drove into the village of Whitchurch. They could see the cluster of stone houses nestling around a squat Norman church over to their left, calm and peaceful in the growing warmth, hardly the place where sordid schemes were in hand. Before reaching the village street, to their right, they drew level with a pretty stone manor house and Henry reined the greys to a walk. Jacobean in construction, behind its ornamental gates and stone wall with well-tended gardens on either side of the gravelled walk leaning up to the main entrance, it made an appealing picture. Behind the house were glimpses of a walled garden and an orchard with a rose-covered pergola leading to a sweep of open parkland.

Lord Henry halted the curricle before the wrought-iron gates.

'What do you think?' Eleanor sat and looked at the house where her husband might have spent time of which she knew nothing.

'It could be. An attractive little estate.' He studied the mellow stonework with a critical and knowledgeable eye. 'Well cared for. Prosperous enough.' A gardener was engaged in clipping a neat box hedge. 'There is someone who can furnish us with a little information.' Henry hailed him. 'Tell me. Does Sir Edward Bax-endale live here?'

The gardener, a man of advanced years, opened the gate to come and stand beside the curricle, pulling off his hat and squint-ing up at his lordship.

'Aye, y'r honour. But not at home—none of the family is. In London, so they says.'

'And his sister?'

'Gone with him, I expect. There's no one 'ere at any event—and not likely to be for the near future, so they says.'

'My thanks.' Henry tossed him a coin and watched him amble back to his box clipping. They sat for a moment and took stock.

'It does not suggest an immediate need for money, does it?'

Eleanor shook her head. 'Do you suppose…?' She hesitated, a deep groove forming between her brows. 'Do you think that Thomas came here to visit Octavia? Did he walk in this garden with her? Beneath those roses? Or sit with her in the arbour in the dusk of a summer's night? Octavia is very fond of gardens…'

'Enough, Eleanor. You must not torture yourself like this! Did I not warn you that it would have been better for you not to come here?' His voice was harsh and when she glanced up in some surprise, she saw no softness in his face. 'What is the point,' he continued, ignoring her distress, 'of *perhaps* and *what if?* It will only lower your spirits and drain your courage. It may be that Thomas did all of those things.' He looked away from the pain that filled her beautiful eyes and swore silently. 'But we still do not know the truth of it.'

She looked away from him and swallowed against the knot of fear and desolation in her throat, unable to find an adequate response. She had not expected such sharpness from him and yet had to admit that his words were justified. He had indeed warned her.

'So what do we do first?' Her voice was admirably controlled.

'We find the inn. It is after noon and you need food. And it might be to our advantage to talk with mine host before we tackle the servant of God.'

They left the curricle and horses in the charge of the ostler at the Red Lion Inn, which overlooked the village green. They were shown into a dark, dusty parlour where the innkeeper fussed over having the gentry call at his establishment. Not many people travelled through the village, the main post road passing to the east as it did. He could not remember the last time that a lady and gentleman of Quality made use of his inn, other than the people at the Great House, of course. But he hoped they would not find the Red Lion wanting. Certainly he could provide refreshment for his lordship and the lady. If they would care to be seated. He whisked ineffectually with a grubby cloth at the dust on table and chairs as his wife bustled in with bread, meat and cheese and a jug of local ale.

Lord Henry pulled out a chair for Eleanor to sit at the table and silently frowned at her so that she began to eat, or at least crumble a piece of bread on her plate.

'You are too pale. And I wager you did not break your fast before we left.' He took a seat opposite, cut a wedge of cheese and added it to the crumbs on her plate, ignoring her objections. 'I would prefer to deliver you back to your son in one piece and in good health.' She had lost weight, he thought. Of course she would in the circumstances, food would be her last consideration, but he had to try to do something to help her. When she had looked at the comfortable manor house and the pretty gardens, when she had envisioned Thomas living out a dream there with another woman, it had taken all his will-power not to drag her into his arms and blot out the cruel vision with his own kisses. He tightened his lips in a wave of disgust. So what had he done? Only snarled at her and increased the pain by his vicious words. He lifted his shoulders a little, discomfited by the thought that his command of his emotions when dealing with Eleanor was not as firm as he would like.

He took a mouthful of ale and then, tankard in hand, engaged the hovering landlord, who had returned to the room with a platter of fruit, in casual conversation.

'We had hoped to visit an acquaintance of ours in the village. Sir Edward Baxendale. We understand that he is from home.'

'Aye, my lord.'

'We do not know him very well. Have his family lived here long?'

'Generations of them, my lord. There's always been a Baxendale in Whitchurch, at the Great House.' Mine host, to Lord Henry's relief, was not reluctant to demonstrate his local knowledge and did not object to their interest in the local gentry.

'Do you see much of the family?'

'Quite a bit. With the hunting. And church. And the ladies walk in the village.'

'Are they well thought of locally?'

'Aye, my lord. Sir Edward's open-handed enough and a fair lord of the manor.'

'I am more acquainted with his sister,' Eleanor prompted, hoping for enlightenment on Octavia.

'Aye. Poor girl.' The innkeeper shook his head in ready sympathy. 'Not that we see much of her, o' course. But it can't be easy for her.'

'Oh?' Eleanor looked up enquiringly, hoping to encourage a more detailed comment.

Mine host nodded. 'What with a baby—growing up he is now—and a husband not long dead. Poor girl. And so pretty. But Sir Edward will ensure that she lacks for nothing—there'll always be a roof over her head. He's always been caring of his family.'

'Of course.' Eleanor smiled and nodded despite the tight band around her heart. 'Did you…did you ever meet the lady's husband before he died?'

'Don't know that I did.' The innkeeper scratched his head. 'Away from home a lot, as I remember, but the lady had made her home here with her brother.'

'Has she…has she gone to London with Sir Edward now?'

'Aye, ma'am. All of them. Saw them myself. And the baby as well. Not to mention the mountain of luggage. Seems like they intend to stay for the Season and the Great House all shut up. Pity you missed them.'

As the innkeeper prepared to return to the public room and leave his guests to eat their luncheon in peace, Lord Henry stopped him.

'One more matter, sir, if you would be so kind. The Reverend Julius Broughton—is he vicar here?'

'Aye, my lord. He is. If you wish to speak with him, the vicarage is the house next to the church, set back behind the stand of elms. But you'll likely find him in the church. They're burying old Sam Potter from down by the forge. So the Reverend Broughton will be doing the Lord's work today at least—you can't turn your back on a funeral if the body's coffined and waiting at the church door! He'll be there—at least for today.'

An interesting comment, Henry thought, not sure what to make of it. Or the slight undercurrent in mine host's voice. Was it dislike? Contempt?

'Do you know the Reverend well?'

'Some.' The innkeeper's smile was sly as he turned for the door. 'Some would say more than an innkeeper should! Likes his ale does the Reverend, and fine brandy. And he has a mind to other things many would say as he should not, being a man of the cloth. Some days he's in the Red Lion more than he's in the church! Not to mention his comforts at home!'

On which he left them.

With Eleanor's hand drawn through his arm, held firmly, Lord Henry stepped out of the Red Lion and strolled down the village street in the direction of the church. The village itself was small, not much more than a score of stone cottages at most, the village street merely hard-packed earth with grassy verges, but the church was impressive with solid walls and zigzag carving on the round-headed arches of door and window. When they came to the gabled lych-gate into the churchyard, they discovered that the innkeeper had been accurate in his information. A funeral was in progress with a small knot of mourners in the far corner of the churchyard where the coffin was being lowered into a grave. They could make out the black and white vestments of the Reverend Julius Broughton amongst them, his white surplice and ministerial bands fluttering in the light breeze.

'We must wait on Samuel Potter for the final time, it seems.' Henry led Eleanor to a sun-warmed seat beside the church door to wait. It was a tranquil spot, sunlit and restful, only the distant murmur of voices to disturb the silence and the nearer chirp of sparrows which were nesting in the roof above their heads. A tranquil place indeed. But one, Eleanor feared, where she might discover the indisputable evidence that she was not Thomas's wife, never had been. In this church Thomas could have been joined with Octavia Baxendale in the sight of God. His son named within those sun-warmed arches. She bit down on the panic that swelled beneath her breast bone. Her life would be shattered beyond redemption.

At last the mourners departed.

'Sam Potter returned to his Maker.' Henry took one of her hands in his, noting her calm outward composure. Perhaps too calm. 'Are you well enough to face the Reverend? I will speak to him alone if you prefer it.' On impulse he pressed his lips to her fingers. 'I do not doubt your courage. I never could. You have nothing to prove to me, Nell.'

'I know. And I know that you would take on this burden.' She smiled her thanks, but rose to her feet, smoothing the skirts of her coat with nervous hands as the clerical figure approached them along the path. 'We will see him together. He cannot tell us anything worse than the knowledge which we already have.'

Introductions were made, the cleric expressing polite interest. Henry, after a glance at Eleanor, opened the point at issue.

'We wish to speak with you, sir, concerning a marriage and a birth in this parish. It concerns a member of our own family.'

Julius Broughton raised his brows at the request, but smiled his compliance. 'Very well. Perhaps you would come to the vicarage where we can sit in comfort and I will see if I can help you.' No hint of unease here.

They followed him to the spacious vicarage, built in the previous century and tucked away behind the elms, to be shown into a library at the front of the house, overlooking the churchyard and the church itself. A pleasant room. Wood panelled, lined with books, a fire offering welcome from the hearth, the retreat of an educated and scholarly man. It was also spotlessly clean, the furniture polished with the books properly on their shelves and the papers on the desk in neat order. It gave the impression of care and order and efficiency, suitable to a conscientious man of the cloth.

The appearance of the man who faced Henry and Eleanor also confirmed this impression. Shorter than Henry, he had a spare figure, fair hair with a touch of bronze when the sun caught it, and pale blue eyes. His narrow face was also that of a scholar with fine, aesthetic features. He had an easy smile that made them welcome as he offered refreshments. Yet Eleanor felt uneasy in his company. She thought there was a slyness in his gaze, which did not sit and linger on anything for long. And his lips, which smiled so readily, were too thin.

The priest rang the bell beside the fireplace and the door was immediately opened by a young girl, as if she had been close at hand and awaiting the summons.

'Molly.' Julius Broughton addressed the girl. 'We have, as you see, visitors. Be so good as to bring brandy for his lordship and ratafia for the lady.'

She bobbed a curtsy, casting a sharp eye over the guests. A village girl, Henry presumed by her simply cut blouse and skirt, very pretty with dark curls under her white cap and attractive curves not in any way disguised by the white apron that enveloped her. Her smile revealed a dimple and she was not averse to a flirtatious glance from beneath long dark lashes. She had an air of smugness and her smile a hint of sly. Henry would wager that Mistress Molly was a most competent housekeeper, if surprisingly young for the position. He suppressed a sardonic gleam as he found himself remembering the innkeeper's enigmatic comments on their priest's interests. They were not difficult to understand,

The refreshments were dispensed, with graceful skill and

concern for their comfort, and then as Molly departed with a final swing of shapely hips the visitors were free to turn to business.

'We are looking for information, sir,' Henry repeated, wondering fleetingly if Mistress Molly was listening at the door.

'So I understand.' The Reverend indicated that they should make themselves comfortable in the charming room. 'I will try to help. Is it something that occurred within my holding of the living here?'

'Yes. The first event less than four years ago.' From his pocket, Henry took a number of gold coins, which he placed, without a word, on the desk beside him.

The Reverend's eyes fixed on them for more than a second, a flush mantling his cheeks. He pressed his lips together. It was, Henry knew, a gamble, based purely on first impressions. It crossed his mind that the priest could see it as an insult to his pride and standing in the community, and so refuse all co-operation with sharp words. Justifiably so if he were an honest man. But he did not. He answered, his eyes still on the money being offered so blatantly, 'Of course, my lord. As I said, I will do what I can.'

Lord Henry had read his man well.

'A marriage. At which you officiated. Between Octavia Baxendale and one Thomas Faringdon. Can you remember such a marriage?'

'Dear Octavia.' The clergyman took his seat behind his desk, resting his hands before him on the polished oak, fingers spread. His lips curled in a smile—or perhaps it was not. 'She is well known to me. A most beautiful girl. Indeed I officiated at her marriage. I remember it. A handsome couple.'

'Were you aware,' Henry asked carefully, 'that the groom was the Marquis of Burford?'

'No, I was not. Before God, a man's title has no relevance. And the law merely requires his name. You hinted, sir, that the matter concerned a member of your family.'

'I did. Thomas Faringdon was my brother.'

'Was he now?' A strange little smile again flirted with the cleric's lips. 'Now I begin to understand. Can I help you further in your search for truth, my lord?'

Henry frowned, but continued. 'I understand that Lady Mary Baxendale, who was a witness to the marriage, has since died.'

'She has. She is buried in the Baxendale tomb here in the crypt. I myself conducted the service.'

And Sir Edward Baxendale. He, too, was present at the marriage ceremony?'

'He was present.' Julius Broughton bowed his head in acknowledgement. Eleanor's brows arched a little. Was it her imagination, or were those clerical fingers suddenly clenched together?

But the Reverend was in no manner disturbed by the questions. His voice remained calm and assured. 'Why do you ask? There was nothing illegal or unseemly about the marriage of Octavia. I have known her, as I said, for many years.'

'And the birth of her son?'

Now there was the slightest hesitation, but the answer was forthright enough.

'You must mean John. I certainly baptised the child John in this church. He will be about two years old now, I surmise.'

'Yes.'

'And the image of his mother! I am sure she is very proud of him. He must be a great solace to her in her time of grief.'

Henry glanced again at Eleanor who shook her head. It was difficult to see where the conversation was leading.

'I presume that you know the Baxendale family well.'

'Indeed I do. You must know that the living here is in their gift. I have every reason to be grateful to Sir Edward for his Christian charity.' The lips that smiled at them were now drawn tight against his teeth. 'He has assured me of his continued benevolence, to the parish and to myself. I have always found him to be a man of his word.'

'If you will forgive me, sir, I hesitate to push the point but— this is a difficult question to ask—have you ever found reason not to trust Sir Edward? To question his honesty?'

'A strange question, if I may say so, my lord.' The Reverend continued to smile, but there was no humour in his pale eyes. 'Let me answer it like this. Octavia is as dear to me as any member of my own family. And I know nothing of Sir Edward that would make me question his integrity. Does that suffice, my lord?'

'Yes.' Henry stood and inclined his head. 'I must thank you for your time and patience, sir.'

They left the room, leaving the little pile of coins on the edge of the desk, glinting brightly and enticingly in the sun.

'I do not like him. I don't know why, but I would not trust him, clergyman or no.' Eleanor spoke her doubts as soon as they were out of sight and sound of the vicarage. 'He smiled like a snake.'

'I have never seen a snake smile, but I take your point. A wily character, I make no doubt. But equally without doubt, he confirms all we knew and feared.' Henry's expression was bleak as he replayed the conversation in his mind. 'Thomas married Octavia. And a son, John, was born.'

Eleanor could make no reply. After all, it was the truth.

The sun still shone. The sparrows still chirruped in the churchyard. And Eleanor's life, as she had feared, lay in pieces at her feet.

During their brief interview the heavy rain-clouds had begun to gather on the horizon and the evening drew close. Seeing the threat of poor travelling weather, Henry made a decision.

'We stay here tonight. I have no mind to be drenched before we arrive home. Let us see if the Red Lion can provide us with some suitable accommodation.'

The landlord at the Red Lion, by the name Jem Abbott, welcomed the return of the lord and lady to his inn with a greedy eye to their generosity. Yes, he could provide them with accommodation. Perhaps not what they would be used to, but comfortable enough. There was a private parlour they could make use of and an adjoining bedroom. Would that be sufficient for their needs? They would not be disturbed. He surveyed them with mild interest. There did not appear to be the stuff of scandal here, but you never knew with the Quality. A law unto themselves, they were! No matter how confident and assured his lordship might be in the settling of his affairs, no matter how elegant and composed the lady. Whether the lady was his lordship's wife was open to debate. But it was none of their concern, as Jem Abbott informed his critical wife, if his lordship had brought his mistress to their establishment. As long as their guests were prepared to pay with hard coin, who were they to judge!

So the landlord set himself to please. His wife could serve an adequate meal for them in the parlour—in an hour, if that would suit. They did not keep late hours in the country. If they would care to sit in the downstairs parlour until all was in readiness? And perhaps some refreshment for the lady, who looked a little tired after her long day? Lord Henry accepted. It was now far too late to return to London, having waited on the affairs of Sam Potter. And the burden of the Reverend Broughton's information pressed heavily on Eleanor.

They were soon ensconced in the promised private parlour, dusted more adequately than the public room, probably by the lady of the house. A fire warmed the room which was low beamed and whitewashed, provided with an array of old country-made furniture, which had seen better days but was not uncomfortable. Mrs Abbott was able to produce a raised game pie and a roasted chicken with various side dishes, more than sufficient for their needs, as promised, and a platter of fruits stored from the previous season.

'I hope it will be acceptable.' Mrs Abbot added logs to the fire, then, stopping to wipe her grimy hands on her apron, 'Not expecting your honour and the lady,' she apologised. And won Eleanor's heart by producing a dish of tea, albeit somewhat bitter, as well as the jug of ale. She smiled and thanked their hostess with real warmth. They would do very well.

Eleanor shed her coat and bonnet, determined to do justice to the simple meal provided for them and to banish the depressing outcome of their conversation with the priest until later. But there was no hope of her achieving either. In the event she picked at her food and Henry did not have the heart to remonstrate with her. Even so, by the time she had tried the pie and sampled the chicken, the food and the warmth from the fire had returned colour to her cheeks and her eyes were less bleak.

Henry disappeared through the door that led downstairs to the public rooms, returning with a dusty decanter of port. Without comment he poured two glasses and sat, beginning to pare one of the wizened pippins from the dish. He quartered it neatly and pushed the pieces to Eleanor. She thanked him with a smile and ate.

'Tell me about your life in America,' she asked suddenly, deliberately breaking the silence, pushing her chair back from the table. 'What is it like? What are you doing with your life there? Is it what you could have wished for?'

And so he told her. Watching her eat the sweet apple. Not so much to tell her about the momentous changes in his life since leaving England, but to distract her mind from the developments of the day.

'I live in New York. I rent rooms there, but it is in my mind to build a house for myself in the future. It is a thriving place and growing by the day. There is money there and it hums with energy. It is difficult to imagine unless you have experienced it for yourself.' He frowned down at the rings of apple peel as he let his mind return to his new life. 'One day New York will be as elegant as London. There are new people arriving every day. Different languages. Different customs. It has an excitement that stirs the blood.'

'Are you making your fortune—as you planned?'

'I am trying hard.' His face was lit by a sudden sardonic smile as a thought struck home. 'Your mother would sniff in disgust. I have become engaged in *trade!* She would certainly not approve! But there is money to be made, businesses to invest in, and I intend to make my mark. I would be a fool not to. Birth is less important than energy and initiative. I like it. It is novel to be addressed as Mr Faringdon.'

'So you will be a big name there?' She smiled a little at the subtle tension that gripped him, the shimmering ambition that she had not seen since he had left her two years ago.

'With good fortune.' His eyes now held hers, alive with subdued excitement. 'I am in partnership with Nathaniel Bridges—Faringdon and Bridges, no less. He is another young man of ambition and useful contacts—and a little capital, which he is willing to sink into the business, like myself. Now that the war with England is over our trade will expand. The treaty was made just before I landed, and it made expansion possible. This year we have a tariff to protect our own manufactures from foreign imports. We aim at self-sufficiency, which can be nothing but good for those prepared to invest in the future.'

She noted his casual identification with the new world, even if he did not. There was no doubt that he would return to New York when the inheritance was settled one way or the other. London, even Burford Hall, held nothing for him now except for memories of the past. She tensed against the pain around the edges of her heart when she acknowledged that he would leave again. Not that it should matter to her, of course. She turned her face away so that she could not see Henry's burning desire to be gone from England, away from her and the hideous complications left by his brother.

'Roads and canals are being developed,' he continued, unaware of her disquiet. 'And we are looking to develop trade routes further with Iberia and southern Europe. There is certainly a demand for wheat and we can produce it in huge quantities.'

'So you are making money, it seems.' She brought her thoughts back into line.

'It seems very possible—and we only pay a quarter of taxes compared to English tax payers. So it will leave us with more money to plough back into the business and into a comfortable lifestyle. But not yet! We are ploughing all our profits back until the company is more secure so there is little money to spare. Hence the rented rooms over a shop.'

'And when there is money to spend? What will you do then?'

'I intend to build a large house as befits my new status as successful entrepreneur and businessman!' Henry stretched back in his chair as he envisioned the future. 'There is plenty of timber and prime sites to be had. The Commissioners in New York have drawn up plans to rebuild the city on impressive lines. Nothing like London, all congestion with narrow streets and winding roads and dark alleys. It will be very splendid with wide avenues crossing each other into a grid. If fortune smiles on us—and a little business acumen—Faringdon and Bridges will be part of it.'

Eleanor watched him as he spoke, assessing the new Hal compared with the one she had known. All the old enthusiasm was still there, but now tempered with experience and knowledge and an edge to his maturity that had been missing when he was still enjoying a life of moneyed leisure in London. His eyes glowed, dark and vibrant, as he outlined the plans of Faringdon and Bridges, probably forgetting to whom he spoke. Her smile was a little sad as she realised that he might have been addressing Nicholas or the unknown Nathaniel Bridges. She had no doubt, no doubt at all, that he would be successful.

'We think we might invest in our own shipping.' His thoughts drifted through the endless possibilities for men with money and the willingness to take a calculated risk. 'And then there is the prospect of the opening up of the west. A lot of migration is under way and new states being added every year. And where people settle, they need goods and commodities. So much opportunity for those prepared to supply them… Forgive me.' His lips twisted in a grimace. 'I did not intend to bore you for so long. If you are unwise enough to ask, I am afraid that you pay the penalty.' The curl of his lips was apologetic.

'You did not. I would not have asked if I was not interested.' Eleanor looked at him consideringly. 'Will you marry?' Why she had felt the need to ask so personal a question, she did not know, but waited for his reply.

Henry regarded her with a quizzical look. 'Do you mean have I a lady in mind? No, I do not. But one day I shall marry.'

'Do you have a mistress?'

'Yes.' His brows arched at her question, perhaps a little amused at her directness.

'Is she pretty?'

'Rosalind. Yes. She has dark hair and green eyes.'

So now she knew. Eleanor reprimanded herself for initiating the subject. All she had achieved was a sore heart and a leap of jealousy that sank its claws into her flesh, even though she knew that she had no right or claim on him. But she envied the unknown but pretty Rosalind, with her dark hair and green eyes, with all her heart. He had smiled when he spoke her name. There would be no weight of guilt or betrayal from the past to hinder their love. Eleanor immediately knew that there was a harsh lesson here for her that she would do well to learn and act on without delay. Hal was not for her, and never could be.

She fell into silence, brooding a little, unaware of his watching her.

'What are you thinking?'

She blinked and withdrew her gaze from the flames, brought back to the present. Her eyes were suddenly clear and cold as she pushed herself upright in her chair, spine braced against its curved back. Her voice was equally cool and measured.

'Why, I was thinking about what I must do now. It is perfectly clear to me that my marriage did not exist. I can no longer deny it, even to myself. We have heard nothing today to undermine Sir Edward's written evidence and I must accept it.' She took a visible deep breath. 'I need to consider my future—I can put it off no longer.' Spreading her fingers, palm downwards, before her on the table, she contemplated them with a little frown. Then, without comment, she slid a gold ring set with a hoop of diamonds and sapphires from her finger and placed it carefully, deliberately, in front of her on the table between the empty plates and glasses. The sapphires gleamed balefully at their rejection, the diamonds glinted. She could not take her eyes from them, shocked at what she had just done, but she spoke firmly as if compelled by an unseen force. 'I need to make some decisions and act on them. And I may as well start now! It would seem that I have no right to wear that ring. Thomas gave it to me on the day that we were wed. I know that it is one of the Faringdon jewels and that your mother wore it as a bride.' She touched it with one finger, almost a caress, before drawing her hands away into her lap, fearing that in a moment of weakness she might snatch up the ring and replace it on her finger. 'I cannot wear it.' Her eyes, glassy with unshed tears, were no less bright than the stones that she had just discarded amongst the debris of the meal.

Her action stunned him. And painted for him, more clearly than words could have done, the quagmire that the future would hold for her. He opened his mouth to deny her words, to say anything that would restore a fragment of hope, but could not. He would allow her to speak her mind before offering any advice, before putting forward his own suggestions.

'So what will you do, Eleanor, if matters stand as Baxendale would have us believe?'

'I do not know.' A hint of panic nibbled at her determination to be strong-willed and positive, to take her future into her own hands. 'I do not as yet know where I will go.'

'Your family home, perhaps?' It was not a plan that would seem to hold much attraction, for any number of reasons.

'Yes. I can return to the village where I was born. My mother still has the house there, so there will always be a roof over our heads and we shall not starve.' She shivered a little as if a draught had suddenly crept into the room. 'I don't think I can do that.' Her courage wavered a little. 'Everyone in the village has known me since I was a child—they would know about my present…situation. What would I call myself? Miss Stamford? With a child, but with no claim on its father? And not even the right to call myself a widow?' She laughed, but there was a sharp edge to it, and her eyes were desolate. 'I cannot contemplate it. I will have to accept talk, of course, but not intimate knowledge from everyone I meet. It would be too humiliating, day after day.'

He remained silent, but filled her glass again and pushed it across the table. Her fingers toyed nervously with the stem as she allowed her thoughts free rein.

'Are you aware,' Henry enquired finally, when the silence stretched uncomfortably, her thoughts apparently bringing no joy, 'that Sir Edward has made the suggestion to Hoskins that the estate pay you a small pension?' How would she react to that? he wondered.

'No!' Her head snapped up, her eyes sparkling with quick temper. 'The thought of such charity appals me!'

'Are you in a position to refuse? For your son, if not for you?' He kept his voice deliberately gentle. 'You married Thomas in good faith. I suggest that the estate owes you enough and more to allow you and the child to live in comfort. Don't reject it out of hand, I beg of you.'

'No!' He watched her struggle for control, but then she sighed, and although she kept her head high in defiance against the agonies that the fates had flung in her path, her answer was bitter and plumbed the depths of despair. 'Your are right, of course. How could you not be? For my son's sake I must realise that I have no right to refuse. I must accept Edward's...*kindness!*'

'Can I tell you what I think?' Unable to remain seated, unable to bear her pain without sheltering her in his arms, Hal rose to his feet to stand beside the fireplace. 'I don't think you should shut yourself away in the depths of the country. It would be a terrible mistake. You are young. Very beautiful. There is no reason why you should not attract a husband and marry again. And find contentment, even happiness.'

She was silent, eyes wide as they connected with his.

'You look as if you had never contemplated the possibility!'

'No. How could you expect it? My situation would hardly attract a husband. No man would want his wife to be the subject of gossip and speculation. And without a dowry, not to mention an illegitimate child into the bargain.' She hesitated a moment. 'Apart from the fact that my experience of marriage would not encourage me to repeat it. I think not!'

Henry remained motionless, elbow resting against the heavy oak mantel, face set, no hint of the direction of his thoughts. Then, 'I would marry you, Eleanor.' He ignored her sharp intake of breath, as much surprised as she. 'I would protect your reputation from the world's censure with my name.' He stepped across to her, reached down to still her restless fingers with his own. 'Consider the advantages before you refuse.'

As he watched her reaction, one of utter amazement, he was forced to admit to his own astonishment at his words, which had come unplanned, unbidden, but at the same moment knowing in his heart that he wanted it more than anything—to protect and shield her from his brother's disastrous and ill-chosen course of action. But he was by no means certain of her response to his offer, and could have wished it unsaid as he saw the reaction sweep over her.

Eleanor flinched as if she had been struck, a sharp open-handed slap, her face becoming ashen as blood drained from beneath her fair skin. Her hands flexed under his. When she could find words to speak around the confusion of horror and intense longing in her mind, it was the horror and bone-deep humiliation that emerged to the surface, to colour her answer.

'Do you really think that I would leap at the prospect of marriage to you, Hal? After your deliberate and callous rejection of me?' Her voice was low, a bare whisper, but laced through with deadly venom.

'Why not?' Her refusal did not surprise him to any degree—but the tone of it hurt. 'I did not reject you…' What use going over this old ground? 'Surely we can deal well enough together, given the present circumstances. I can offer you security and respect, a comfortable life for you and your son.'

But not your love! 'Two years ago you did not want me.' She held up her hand, palm outward toward him, as he would have refuted this accusation once more. 'So why change your mind now? How dare you offer me pity!'

'I would never offer you pity, Nell.'

'No? It is the only reason I can think of, why you would offer me marriage now! Or do you think that our night here together might compromise my reputation? It may have escaped your notice, Hal, but I have no reputation.' The bitter irony lay heavily between them. 'You owe me nothing! I suppose I should thank you for making the grand gesture so selflessly, in spite of your attachment to Rosalind. You should feel proud of that. But you will doubtless be relieved to know I refuse your offer! There is no need to make the ultimate sacrifice for me.' Pushing back her chair, she stood, her eyes now level with his and full of contempt.

'Think what you wish, Nell. But don't be so quick to misjudge me.' There was a hint of temper in his voice, brows snapped together. 'I would give you and the child—Thomas's son—some security, some respectability—some recompense for the loss of all you had hoped for, if you wish. There could be worse scenarios, as you yourself admitted.'

'I don't doubt it! I could live in the gutter with the dispossessed of London!' He was taken aback by the sneer. The débutante he had known did not sneer. 'But to live in gratitude for *your* sacrifice for the rest of my life? For my son and myself to be dependent on *your* charity? I will not. Rather Edward's than yours!'

Tell her you love her, you fool. She is hurt and despairing and without hope. Of course she will refuse your offer! Take her in your arms and kiss that soft, sad mouth. Tell her that she holds your heart in her hands, and always will. And that Rosalind means nothing to you.

But in the face of such contempt he could not. He sighed, lips pressed together into a harsh line.

'Go to bed, Eleanor. Perhaps we have both said too much this night.' He turned away, so did not see her blink back the tears before she turned to the door.

Well done! You handled that magnificently!

Henry flung himself back into the chair with a curse, disgust riding him hard. He had been given a chance to make her life easier, with care and consideration, with compassion. Perhaps even at some time in the future to win her love. Instead she was under an indestructible impression that he had made his move through pity. The barrier that she had built between them in the last half-hour was formidable indeed. And to be honest, he could not blame her. He had, unwittingly, helped her to heap stone upon stone between them.

He swore again and reached for the decanter of port to refill his glass.

And, even worse, she would in all probability refuse out of hand *any* help offered by him now.

Subtlety? Finesse in his dealings with women? Ha! He did not know the meaning of the words! Instead he had ridden rough-shod over her feelings and sensibilities. To offer her marriage in such a situation had been crass in the extreme. But what man of honour could remain unmoved before so courageous and so lovely a woman in distress?

And he loved her.

He had tried to build her trust and, he thought, with some success. She had begun to relax a little in his company. He remembered her listening to his plans not an hour before, a smile on her face, a certain contentment in her eyes. Now all destroyed. He had hurt her pride—and she would feel that pride was all she had left. She was so sad and he had simply made it worse.

He drank the port, struck anew by the knowledge that, although she had now rejected his offer of marriage twice, he could still want her. And it had nothing whatsoever to do with pity!

What had she said to him? Hurtful things. Terrible things. She had meant none of them, but they could not be unsaid and now he would never forgive her. Eyes closed, she leaned with her back against the bedroom door, permitting the longing in her heart to sweep through her. What better future could she envisage than to allow him to take all her troubles on to his strong shoulders and let him stand protection against the world and its condemnation. And Tom. Her son would grow up with no slur on his name. As he should, as was his right.

And perhaps, one day, Hal might even return the love that burned so brightly and hopelessly through her veins.

The tears that she had battled against claimed victory at last. She removed her dress with fingers suddenly numb, her shoes, to stand in the centre of the room, in her chemise, hands by her sides, and weep helplessly, heartbrokenly for all that was lost.

Because she truly did not know what to do and Hal had offered her her dreams, to hold in the palms of her hand. And by the manner of her refusal, she had alienated him irrevocably. She knew that he did not want her, so she had refused his offer. Of course she had, as any woman of integrity must—but her pride was obliterated by bitter tears.

In the parlour, Henry rescued the sapphires and diamonds in their golden setting from the table. He held the family jewel in his hand as if it might give an answer to his problems, and then, with a shake of his head, slipped it into his pocket, to return it to her on a less emotional occasion. A thought struck him, chilling him to the marrow in his bones. He had offered Eleanor marriage carelessly and without consideration, acting without any thought other than his own desires, other than the simple expediency of rescuing her from her worst fears.

But it could not be.

The law recognised Eleanor's affinity to him only as his brother's wife and so in its wisdom frowned on any closer association between them. Certainly not marriage.

Eleanor had not realised it. Nor had he in the heat of the moment.

Marriage, with the possibility of further scandal attached to Eleanor's name, was no answer at all. The realisation stuck him with the force of cold steel.

The minutes ticked past in the Red Lion in the village of Whitchurch. Henry continued to sit by the fire, booted feet propped on an iron fire-dog, contemplating an uncomfortable and sleepless night, probably on the oak settle, when a faint sound from beyond the door to the bedroom brought him out of a morass of far from pleasant thoughts.

He sat up. And knew without any doubt.

Oh God, no! He rubbed his hands over his face, dragged his fingers through his hair and pushed himself to his feet.

The coward in him told him to ignore it. Eleanor would soon be exhausted and would fall asleep without any intervention from him. Any attempt to comfort her would solve nothing for either of them and might make the situation even worse with impossible legal complications that he did not feel up to explaining to her just at that moment. He bared his teeth in a grimace at the prospect of holding her in his arms and remaining unmoved by her softness and her beauty. *No! Don't even think about it!*

But he could not ignore it, of course he could not. Especially when he had in some sense been the cause of her emotional state of mind. His mouth curled sardonically. He had not expected that an offer of marriage would reduce any woman to a fit of hysterics! Rosalind, he thought, would leap at the chance.

With a sigh he walked to the door where he hesitated, listened, head bent. And then, without knocking, before he could change his mind, opened the door and went in.

She stood on the rag rug in the centre of the floor in her chemise, her feet bare. She was shivering with emotion and cold, but had been unable to make the decision to get into bed. And she wept, sobs that shook her whole body, tears streaming down her face. She made no effort to hide them or her tear-ravaged face from him, even if she were aware of his presence. He was not certain. She was beyond awareness, lost in a wilderness of insecurity and grief.

'Nell.' He felt his heart turn over in compassion, touched beyond measure by her wretchedness against which she had no defence. Courage she might have, but not the will to fight this deluge of pain. 'This is no good.' He stepped quietly to her. 'You will make yourself ill if you weep in this way.'

'Go away!' She choked out the words and now covered her face with her hands. 'I don't want you!'

'I will not.'

Without hesitation, he folded his arms around her, as any man must, and pulled her close, using one hand to press her head to his shoulder. She resisted, as he knew she would, standing rigidly against him, refusing to accept his comfort. But he persisted, until suddenly on a sob she melted and clung to him, turning her face against the base of his throat. Too sad to be embarrassed or to refuse the warmth offered by the one man who had possession of her heart and whose offer she had discarded with wounding and unforgivable words.

Henry stroked her hair, removing the pins that secured her curls as he did so, allowing it to tumble over his hands in a heavy fall of silk. He murmured and crooned, foolish words that promised the impossible, the unattainable, and yet soothed by their mere sound. He kissed her temples, the lightest of kisses, and let her cry, his cheek resting against her hair. She would have fallen at his feet if he had not held her.

'My love. My dear love. I will not leave you. I could not leave you to grieve alone. I will love and care for you, whatever the future brings.'

Momentarily horrified at hearing himself speak such sentiments aloud, he could not regret it, but fervently hoped that she would not remember when she awoke.

Gradually her breathing quietened, so that he was able to stoop and lift her high against his heart, carrying her to the bed where he placed her, sitting beside her to rock her in his arms until utter exhaustion claimed her and her lashes closed on her tear-stained cheeks. Only then did he turn back the covers, place her against the bank of pillows and tuck her in. He would not look at her. His instinct told him to leave, to go whilst he could still resist the lure of her fragile femininity and her need for comfort. But she held on to his hand, even in sleep, and it would be cruelty indeed to reject her now.

So be it.

He eased into a chair by the bed and let her be comforted by his presence, watching her now-sleeping face. Even when her fingers finally relaxed he still remained, unwilling to leave her for fear that she would wake alone in the dark and be unable to deal with the torment in her mind.

Eleanor…

Images flooded back into his mind from that night two years ago, that night that had haunted him every hour of every day since, no matter how hard he had tried to banish the painful and yet glorious memory. Images that swamped him with their clarity and intensity. He would like nothing better than to strip away the fine linen and lace chemise, to feast his eyes on the creamy white perfection of her exposed body. As he had in the summer house beneath the rose pergola, in the garden of Faringdon House. Escaping her chaperon, they had been intoxicated by the sense of freedom as he had pushed her gently back on the cushions. He had seduced her with tales of America and their new life there together. And with his kisses, the touch of his hands that awakened her innocent emotions, setting her blood on fire. She was virgin, of course, but as caught up in the silver enchantment of the moonlight, as he had been. He should have known better than to take advantage of her, he now admitted in that shadowy room in Whitchurch, but that night he had given in to youth and impulse and an overriding need to bury himself within her soft and tantalising heat. The scent of honeysuckle and jasmine invading the senses, robbing him of all integrity and responsi-

bility towards her. And yet she had willingly given him the greatest gift she could, clinging to him as he took her with less than
subtle skill. He smiled bitterly. He knew more about women
now. He might not be much older in years, but was vastly more
experienced in the arts of seduction. Now he knew how to
awaken passion, how to pleasure and delight. He must have hurt
her in that moon-kissed garden, but she had wrapped her arms
around him, vowing her everlasting love.

What had gone wrong? Why had she not joined him when he
had sailed for America? He could not believe that on that one
night, drunk on shared passion, she had not loved him to the exclusion of all else. And yet she had rejected him. Wilfully ignored, presumably destroyed, the letter that he had sent, which
he *knew* she had received, and thus turned her back on his offer
to share his life with her. And even if he had not been so very
certain of this letter, diligently delivered by his groom, there was
the one further note that he had hurriedly penned on his arrival
in New York. She had also failed to respond to that plea for an
explanation. She might deny their existence, but the evidence
weighed heavily against her. It would have been far better if she
had told him bluntly that she had simply changed her mind. It
would have sliced at his heart, but anything would have been kinder than the cruel edge of indifferent silence.

He breathed deep to still the beating of his heart, the pump-
ing of his blood to his loins. Because, in spite of everything in
their past, in spite of all her apparent duplicity, he could not get
her out of his mind, much less out of his blood where desire still
surged. He wanted her. Now. To show her again the splendour of
passion that could be awakened between a man and a woman.
To bury himself deep within her hot, velvet-soft body, so that she
could forget everything but the two of them. To drive her beyond
control so that she could forget uncertainty and grief. To claim
her as his own, bodies joined, slick with desire. To own her and
possess her, the one woman he desired. He wanted all of that now!

But he could not. And deliberately eased the unwitting tightening of his fingers around her hand. She was his brother's
widow. With a fatherless child, a reputation under attack and

complications on all sides. He must not allow himself to forget it, no matter the temptation to sweep it all aside and cover her body with his own, crushing her to the bed so that she cried out his name in the dark. She needed comfort and support. He would try to think as a gentleman, remember his duty towards her as a trustee of the Faringdon estate, and give her what she needed most. But, by God, he had given himself a hard task!

He looked at her, drawing on his memory and imagination. Tormenting himself but unable to fight the bittersweet longing. Long, slender legs that she had wrapped around him. High firm breasts, her nipples hardening under the onslaught of his lips. Shadowed secrets waiting to be discovered. He had not forgotten and wanted nothing more but to rediscover them again.

'I will care for you,' he murmured on a sigh of frustration, softly so as not to wake her. 'I will not let the world condemn you for some mischance that is no fault of yours. I will look after you, whether you wish it or no.'

Quite what he intended to do, he was unsure, but it was a solemn and binding vow, even though she slept on, unaware of it.

Eleanor awoke at some time in the night, disorientated and in discomfort from her long bout of tears. But even though her head ached, her first conscious thought was one of simple pleasure, that Hal had not left her. He was asleep in the chair beside her, head pillowed on one arm, resting on the edge of the bed. His other hand was still covering hers, even though lax in sleep. His face was turned away, hidden from her. She would have liked to touch his hair, the dark, vibrant strength of it where it curled onto his neck, but feared to wake him, nor did she wish to lose contact with his hand on hers. He had stayed with her, even though his stiff, cold muscles would be a matter for regret in the morning. But she would not reject his decision. Simply his presence comforted her. Thomas had been her friend, but Hal was the love of her life. She fell asleep again, holding the thought, as she held his hand, against the onslaught of disturbing dreams.

When Eleanor awoke again the next morning, with light creeping through the heavy swags, he had gone and the place where his head had rested was cold. She felt an instant chill of regret. He might comfort her, he might watch over her as she slept, but he had felt no desire to repeat the experience of two years before in the gardens of Faringdon House. An experience which she *would not* remember! Even after two years she flushed as the memories pushed their insidious tendrils into her thoughts, just as the wisteria invaded the balustraded terrace at Burford Hall. She could not imagine how she could have been so unmaidenly. A chaste kiss, perhaps, but she had allowed Hal far more intimacies. The flush deepened to flaming rose as she recalled the episode in the summer house with a ridiculous mix of horror and intense delight. He had handled her with such care, mindful of her innocence. Loved her, cherished her, left her in no doubt of his tender feelings towards her, except that they had apparently not been sufficiently strong to outlive the night! Perhaps he had been disgusted by her lack of skill, her lamentable lack of knowledge, the still unformed curves of a young girl. He had certainly discovered no desire to develop their relationship further! She had not seen him again until he had bowed before her in the withdrawing-room at Burford Hall. No matter the soft words and beguiling images he had painted of their future together, his promises had been empty indeed, proof that no man could be trusted!

Turning back the bed covers with a little huff of disgust at her wayward thoughts, she noticed, and remembered—and understood, with a sinking heart. Her ring. She had removed it in despair, leaving it on the table in the parlour, but now it was back on her finger. She twisted it so that the morning sun glinted on the edges and the tiny jewels. Hal must have restored it while she slept. She could not but admire his loyalty to his brother's name, even when she herself had despaired and denied the legality of her own marriage. But she also understood very clearly and knew that it would be wise of her not to forget. For the ring was a symbol of her union with Thomas, and Henry had replaced it where he considered it belonged. That simple action should tell her more plainly than any words that Henry saw her as his brother's widow, and nothing more in his life.

Chapter Seven

The gathering of the Faringdon family in the morning room of the house in Park Lane on the following afternoon, when Henry and Eleanor had arrived back in London, could not be described to be in a spirit of optimism or even qualified hope. They brooded over their lack of progress.

The visit to the village of Whitchurch had achieved nothing to their advantage, Henry reported. The Reverend Broughton might not be the most likeable of characters, with a shadow thrown over his morals and behaviour as a clergyman, but there was no reason to disbelieve him in the matter of the marriage of Thomas and Octavia. He had confirmed the events of marriage and birth. The documents appeared to be genuine. Sir Edward Baxendale was well known with a good reputation, and the existence of a sister with a recently deceased husband and a young baby was common knowledge. Eleanor said nothing, merely a silent witness to their failure to unearth any incriminating evidence.

The only outcome of the visit, in Mrs Stamford's unexpressed opinion, was a certain intangible tension in her daughter. As now, she thought, glancing across at her. Eleanor might have been alone in the room, with eyes unfocused as if her thoughts were far away, turning the ring on her finger round and round with terrible monotony. And there was a distinct unease between Eleanor and Lord Henry, for which Mrs Stamford was not sorry. Too much intimacy would certainly be unwise. But Mrs Stamford was wise enough to remain silent about the night they had been forced to spend in the Red Lion in Whitchurch. Given the circumstances, and her memory of the previous occasion of confrontation when she had quite clearly lost the battle of wills, she did not feel up to taking on Lord Henry on such a personal matter. Even if she was the Marchioness's mama.

London, likewise, had provided no scandal. Kingstone knew nothing of any interest about the parties. As far as Nicholas knew, Sir Edward was an exemplary character with no interest in gambling, horses or loose women.

Mrs Stamford frowned at his comment.

'For whatever reason, Baxendale does not appear to have arrived at *point non plus*. He has no interest in the turf. He does not own a racehorse. He is not known at Tattersall's. He does not frequent gambling dens. He does not keep a mistress. Nor does he visit opera dancers!' Nicholas deliberately expanded on the subject, his lips curled with mischief as Mrs Stamford stiffened and sniffed her disapproval. 'Sir Edward is a veritable pillar of society.'

'So I must accept the situation.' Eleanor had earlier returned from an emotional visit to her son in the nursery and, after holding him in her arms, watching his sturdy limbs as he pulled himself upright against his crib, she could not deny her duty to the child. 'I must take the offer of an annuity from Sir Edward—and thank him for his generosity!—and find somewhere for myself and Tom to live. Perhaps we should return to our house in Leavening, Mama.'

'No. It is too soon—' Henry immediately turned his head, intent on halting such a scheme, but Mrs Stamford interrupted, very much of the same mind.

'No, Eleanor. We should not. I went to see Lady Beatrice yesterday. Perhaps you had forgotten my errand in that direction. I swore her to secrecy, of course. I found her a most well-informed lady—not as flighty as her daughter. We had quite a detailed conversation and exchange of views.'

Henry avoided Nicholas's eye.

'I think you should not be in too much of a hurry to accept Sir Edward's offer, Eleanor. For once I am in total agreement with Lord Henry.' She smiled thinly at him. 'It is true that Lady Beatrice remembers a fair girl with whom Thomas was much taken. And she thought there was a brother with her on some of the social occasions. But she is not sure, and is not convinced that the name Baxendale rings true. She claimed to know no Baxendales. But she had to admit that she is better at faces than names—after all, it was four years ago.'

She looked round the circle of faces.

'I do not know if that helps us or not.' Nicholas rubbed his chin. 'I suppose that it is the only hint of doubt we have in an otherwise cast-iron case.' He looked to Henry. 'What do you suggest, Hal? Arrange a meeting between Sir Edward and Aunt Beatrice? Now that is an occasion which I would not want to miss.'

Henry frowned at him for a moment, considering the possibilities. Then: 'Very well. This is what we will do. We will entertain. A small party—we have sufficient rooms here. Very select—mostly family. Cards, music, refreshments—you know the sort of thing. Eleanor will be hostess.' He looked towards her, brows arched, not totally convinced that she would comply.

'Yes. Of course, if that is what you wish.'

'I do.' He smiled at her, an unusually tender smile, which was not lost on the audience. 'Don't despair, Nell. We still have all to win—but we will not wave the flag of surrender quite yet. And a family party will be quite the thing, in spite of Thomas's death. You need have no concern about that.'

She returned the smile, although a little sad, unable to resist such comfort. 'Thank you, Hal. I shall never forget your kindness, whatever the outcome.' As she looked down at the sapphires on her hand, they both knew that her thoughts were far from that room in Park Lane.

'And we will invite the Baxendales.' Nicholas picked up on Hal's suggestion to deflect attention from the pair, aware of Mrs Stamford beside him, rustling in displeasure at the unexpected intimacy. He would give a pony to know exactly what had happened between them in Whitchurch. He must make certain to ask Hal.

'We will stress that it is a family occasion. They will hardly be able to refuse since they are intending to fill their own niche in the Faringdon family tree. It will make for an interesting evening!'

'And I must be certain to invite Aunt Beatrice?' Eleanor asked, quickly appreciating the plan.

'Exactly!' Henry rose to his feet and strode towards the door. 'We will try every means we have to flush the bird from the covert. Even if it means spending an evening in Lady Beatrice's overbearing company!'

'Will you escort me to the theatre? Tonight, my lord?'

Eleanor confronted Lord Henry in the breakfast parlour two days later and made her request without preamble or explanation, even before she had closed the door behind her. She had positively erupted into the room in a flurry of muslin skirts.

'Well, I...' His lordship looked up from his perusal of the *Morning Post,* suitably taken aback.

'I realise that you might have other plans—and I would not normally ask that you put yourself out, particularly at such short notice—but I find that it is vitally important.' The words tripped off her tongue, indicative of strong emotion. She came to stand before him, determined to have his attention. Lord Henry promptly put down the paper to watch her warily, aware of the high colour slashed along her cheekbones. Now what was afoot?

Since their return from Whitchurch the strain between them had lessened a little, submerged under a cool sensible acceptance of the need to unite in their resistance to the Baxendales' claims. Although they were successful in keeping a distance, awareness of each other remained, a tangible thing. And so Henry was wary of Eleanor's request.

'Why?' He hoped the suspicion did not sound in his voice.

'We have not been invited—*I* have not been invited—to the Carstairs's Drum this evening, when we know that all the world and his wife will be present. I would not even have known of it, if it had not been for Beatrice asking if she would see us there.' Eleanor flung away from him to pace to the window, and back again. 'How long has Marianne Carstairs been closely acquainted with this family? For ever, I shouldn't wonder. She certainly counted your mama as one of her closest friends. And,' she interrupted, brows drawn together in an uncompromising line, as Henry opened his mouth to reply, 'don't tell me that they are being considerate for my state of mourning. I have been out and about so often recently that no one in town would be under any illusion about my present circumstances.' Eleanor sat herself in one of the straight-backed chairs with a flounce of indignation. 'It is a deliberate snub. I will not stand for it from a family I considered friends. So I wish to go to the theatre.'

'Perhaps the invitation has been mislaid?' Henry tried for a mild reply, to calm the seething lady before him.

Her stare of withering disbelief was answer enough.

'No. Of course, you are right.' Henry mentally postponed his evening, which had promised a leisurely hand of cards at Brooks's and a convivial drink with old friends. He managed not to sigh. 'So, what do you wish?'

'I wish to be seen at Drury Lane. I will not sit and hide at home when every other person of consequence in London is making merry!'

'Shakespeare?' His lordship mentally winced.

'By no means.' Eleanor was forced to smile at his reluctance. 'The Bard is distinctly out of fashion since you left these shores. Mr Elliston, who has taken on the management of Drury Lane, has decided that a more popular entertainment is more the thing—and will bring in more money to his pockets! So it is likely to be *The Beggar's Opera* rather than *King Lear*. Not as erudite, but more economically attractive, you understand.'

'Then I will escort you,' Henry agreed, amused at Eleanor's quick assessment.

'I can even promise you any number of opera dancers who will doubtless cast out lures to you. Your evening might not be wasted!'

He ignored her caustic comments, appreciative of her disordered spirits. 'And to escort so attractive a lady as yourself. It will be my greatest pleasure. How can I refuse?'

'How indeed.' Her brows rose.

'Ah—are we to be chaperoned to this seductive event?'

'Of course. It is not my intention to be seen alone with you at such a performance—to replace one scandal with another. My mother will accompany us. We shall all enjoy every minute of it!'

Thus a private box was procured at Drury Lane.

Eleanor made an appearance, spectacular in a new gown, guaranteed to catch every eye. The Italian silk and lace shimmered in the candlelight, its intense violet hue iridescent and sumptuous. A jewelled aigrette held a discreet spray of egret feathers in her hair. A rope of amethysts wound its shining path around her slender throat. She had even made judicious use of cosmetics to disguise the ravages of strain and sleeplessness. A little Olympian Dew to bring a sparkle to her eyes, the veriest hint of Liquid Bloom of Roses to enhance the soft colour in her cheeks. Her appearance at the theatre, Henry realised, was to be a deliberate challenge, a throwing down of the family gauntlet to all those who would dare to question the Marchioness's presence in London society. She looked magnificent, as had been her intention.

Henry dared make no comment, resorting instead to discretion, knowing that any compliment would have received a short reply. There was fire and temper in her eyes this night. So he merely bowed as he handed her and her watchful mama into the town carriage, quelling the desire with stern intent, desire that had run hot through his blood when faced with the glory of her appearance and her enforced proximity.

It was a tension-filled evening: more than one lorgnette levelled in their direction; more than one cold shoulder turned as Lord Henry ushered the two ladies with consummate ease through the crowded lobby; more than one half-heard whisper. But Mrs Stamford, well rehearsed by her daughter in her role for the evening, acted her part with undisturbed composure and dignity, set to ignore any unpleasantness as if it were beneath her notice. Eleanor was at her superb best. She bowed, smiled, conversed, sipped champagne—not everyone was at the Carstairs's

Drum!—gave her full attention to the performance as if nothing troubled her thoughts beyond the colour and style of the gown that she would wear on the following day. And she stared down those whose gaze she considered too insolent to be tolerated. She watched the remarkable Vestris in the role of Macheath, shapely legs scandalously clad in masculine breeches, with due admiration. She frowned at the courtesans who paraded in the lobby and sent flirtatious glances at her escort—how dared they!—and frowned equally at her escort, who was not averse to returning the smiles. And she engaged Henry in trivial and lively conversation to keep from dwelling on the critical stares of the Dowagers in their boxes.

Mrs Stamford found need to comment on young women—no lady here!—who *cavorted* on stage in male attire. She could not imagine why anyone of breeding and sensitivity would prefer such a performance to a production of *King Lear* with Edmund Kean—so talented as he was. The Darling of London indeed! Vestris was in Mrs Stamford's considered opinion no better than she should be! What was the world coming to! Eleanor turned a deaf ear.

Henry watched the performance with an amused smile and appreciative eye.

'I trust you are enjoying yourself, my lord?' Eleanor wielded her fan with considerable energy and expertise. Her mama was momentarily and safely occupied in conversation with a passing acquaintance.

'I am.' He slanted a glance at her lovely face.

'And you approve of Vestris?'

'Miss Lucy Bartolozzo? Definitely an asset to the production. It is everything you promised me. And the company of a beautiful woman, of course. You outshine everyone here, even the ladies of the lobby.' His smile was fast and devastating. Dangerous, Eleanor decided, lowering her lashes to hide her confusion at his compliment.

'Thank you, my lord.' Her lips curved in a genuine smile, despite her best intentions to remain censorious on the subject of the courtesans. 'Such a compliment lifts my spirits inordinately.'

'Is it possible that you are flirting with me, madam?'

'Certainly not!'

Henry laughed aloud, drawing more than one pair of eyes towards their box.

'Hush! I would not willingly give the town tabbies anything other to talk about! I was merely expressing my heartfelt gratitude.' Eleanor looked away, more than aware that her cheeks were burning.

'You must not, you know.' Henry covered her hand for a moment with his own, his voice very gentle. 'You are doing very well, Eleanor. It is not necessary to take the town by storm.'

'No? I think that perhaps it is. Smile, Hal.' Her own was brittle, but she held her head high. Once again, he could not but admire her spirit. 'The town is watching us. I will enjoy this evening if it is the death of me!'

At last the never-ending evening drew to a close. At last! Henry helped the ladies from their carriage and into the entrance hall in Park Lane.

'Satisfied?' he asked, with a quizzical glance.

'Yes.' Eleanor raised her chin, still vibrating with energy.

'Something you would wish to repeat?'

'No.' She could not lie. 'Not in the foreseeable future. If you wish to renew your acquaintance with Vestris, it will be without my company. But you have my gratitude, Hal. I felt a need to…to make a grand gesture and be noticed. I do not regret it.'

Mrs Stamford halted on the bottom step before retiring to bed, turning to look at his lordship over her shoulder. 'I have to thank you, Henry. For your unfailing support of my daughter. It should not go unsaid.' She spoke as if the words were wrung from her against her better judgement.

'My pleasure, ma'am.' Henry bowed, hiding his initial amazement.

'Not the easiest of evenings,' the lady continued, arranging her embroidered Kashmir stole more elegantly round her shoulders. 'And I am sure that you would have preferred to spend your time in other amusements.'

'Not when the comfort of her ladyship is a priority.'

'No. I realise that you have Eleanor's best interests at heart. I have not given you sufficient credit for that in the past, have I?' She gave him a considering look 'Perhaps I—' She broke off, redefining her thoughts. 'But no matter.'

She turned on her heel to precede them up the stairs.

Eleanor's eyes met Hal's in lively astonishment.

'Now that must be a first,' he murmured, when Mrs Stamford was out of hearing. 'Your mama's approval is a state that I had never hoped to achieve.'

'I advise you to treasure it,' was Eleanor's dry reply. 'In all probability it will never happen again.'

Before the Faringdon family could embark on their own social event, they were committed, the following evening, to the small soirée at the elegant London home of the Earl and Countess of Sefton.

'I would rather not go,' Eleanor stated, with every intention of following her statement with action, making a graceful withdrawal from the invitation. Taking the air in Hyde Park was one thing. So was an intimate family gathering. Even a private visit to the theatre. But appearing in public at so splendid an occasion, with the *haut ton* present, when she would draw the attention of, and need to converse with, any number of people without means of escape, was quite another matter.

'If you will take my advice…' Henry leaned heavily on the words, but with a bland expression '…you will present yourself with all the consequence you can muster as Marchioness of Burford and carry it off with the utmost assurance. I suggest you wear the diamond set, complete with tiara.'

'But I don't like the diamond set.' Eleanor was momentarily distracted. 'It is far too heavy, and the setting is very clumsy—it makes me feel like a Dowager of advanced years. And the stones need cleaning.'

'You *are* a Dowager—so wear it.' She silently dared him to mention her age, the glint of a challenge in her eyes. His lips twitched a little, but he desisted. 'If you are carrying a fortune of badly cut diamonds on your person, personally designed by my grandmother, no one will dare treat you with anything less than supreme respect!'

'But not the tiara!' She might be prepared to compromise, but only to a degree.

'Definitely the tiara!.'

'It is not my choice of an evening's entertainment either.' Nicholas also would gladly have cried off. 'Readings from somebody's recent masterpiece. One of Lady Sefton's protégés, I expect. A poet? Have mercy, Hal.'

But Henry took Nicholas aside when Eleanor had left the room with more than a suspicion of a revolt in her step. 'You should attend with the rest of us, Nick. It might not be the easiest of evenings for her—we cannot know—and Eleanor needs all our support if any of Lady Sefton's acquaintances takes it into her head to play the *grande dame* and turn the shoulder. Besides, it will be good to see the Faringdons out in force.' His lips curved a little as he anticipated his brother's reply. 'It is not necessary for you to stay for the whole evening. I give you permission to leave before the poet takes centre stage!'

'Very well.' Nicholas laughed. 'Whilst you, for your sins, can stay to the bitter end, to wallow in sentimentality and bad verse. Tell me, Hal. You seem to have come to some accord with Nell.'

'Do I?'

'Yes. Since your visit to Whitchurch.'

'Perhaps.'

'And you intend to tell me nothing.' Had Nick really expected his brother's confidence on this issue?

'Something like that.' There was nothing to be learned from the bland reply.

'Treat her gently, Hal.' Nicholas was suddenly serious. 'She has had an unenviable time since Thomas's death. And now all this…'

'I have every intention of doing so.' Nicholas flinched a little at Henry's fierce response. 'Do you consider me to be so insensitive?'

'Of course not.' Nick decided to take a step on forbidden ground. 'It's just that—you will be leaving soon—and…' He found it difficult to continue under his brother's intense stare, but then Henry shrugged and allowed himself a smile.

'I know. Don't worry, Nick. I will treat her gently.'

'Don't break her heart, Hal. She is very vulnerable.'

'I am aware.' An icy reply. There was no chance. No chance at all of that.

Nick changed the subject with ease when it became clear that his brother would say no more. 'I have discovered that you have a pronounced aptitude for management, Hal. I did not realise it— and must beware in future.'

'I can only hope it pays off.' But doubts crowded in. And not least that he was finding it increasingly difficult to disguise his emotions in his dealings with Nell. If Nick had his suspicions, he must be more circumspect. After all, who knew better than he just how very vulnerable she was? No, whatever was to come in the future, he must heed Nick's warning and ensure that her heart remain intact.

Eleanor chose to wear a stylish evening gown of amethyst silk. She knew it was beautiful and could not but enjoy the sensation of restrained good taste in the silk shell with its muslin overskirt, patterned with tiny flowers, falling in soft folds. The low scoop of the neckline served as a frame for the diamond necklace and she clipped matching bracelets over her long gloves. She even pinned the heavy ring brooch to the lace on the bodice. But wear the tiara she would not, the corners of her mouth lifting a little as she contemplated Henry's probable reaction. A lavender fan with silver sticks completed the ensemble. At the same time she cloaked herself in a veil of calm confidence, determined to smile and find enjoyment in the occasion since her family were so equally determined to support her. There would also be friends there, kind and supportive, as well as Lady Sefton's warm compassion. Nothing to fear, nothing to make her heart beat in her breast like a trapped bird.

They gathered in the front parlour, Henry and Nicholas splendid and austere in black satin evening coats and breeches, white linen and subdued waistcoats. The Countess of Sefton might promise a small soirée, but they knew her of old.

Eleanor thought that they looked stunning together. Tall, broad shouldered, lean and well muscled, their physical power and attraction enhanced rather than disguised by the formal clothing, she knew that they would take every eye in the room. They looked, she decided, dark and smooth and dangerous. How could she be nervous? They were quite magnificent.

Quietly elegant in deep blue brocade with a heavy lace overslip, Mrs Stamford ran a critical eye over her daughter. 'Very nice,' she admitted. 'Although, I have to agree, I have rarely seen so ugly a setting for fine stones. And so old-fashioned. What can your grandmama have been thinking of?' She frowned at Lord Henry as if he were in some indefinable way to blame for his grandmother's taste for the heavy and vulgarly ostentatious.

'Impressive!' was Henry's only comment as Eleanor innocently arranged an embroidered stole around her shoulders, refusing to meet his eye. His brows arched at the lack of the tiara and knew that she was waiting. So he said nothing. But privately thought that she would outshine every lady present that evening. Her eyes glowed, reflecting the tint of her gown and her nerves gave her cheeks a delicate colour, with or without the careful and subtle application of cosmetics. She was lovely. He raised her fingers to his lips and bowed his silent appreciation, since he was in a position to do no other.

Lady Sefton's town house in Berkeley Square, large, palatial and expensively furnished, and at the best of fashionable addresses, had been sumptuously decorated for the occasion with banks of flowers and silk swags. And as expected, the cream of society was present to hear the lady's fledgling poet.

The Earl and Countess welcomed the Faringdon party, the Countess with a warm handclasp and particularly understanding smile for Eleanor. 'Relax here tonight, my dear, and enjoy the company. I am well aware of what is being said. But you must not be embarrassed…' She tightened her hold in warm affection and leaned closer for a private word. 'I knew Thomas well. An estimable young man, of great integrity. As are all the Faringdons.' She cast an admiring glance to where the gentlemen were still in conversation with her husband. 'So attractive… My guests will respect your position, of course. I think you need fear no ill will here tonight.'

'You are very kind.' Eleanor felt her colour deepen as emotion welled. 'It has not been the easiest of weeks.'

'No. But you are here to enjoy the evening. A little conversation. Some music. A poetry reading, no less, by a remarkable young man. And here—' she beckoned a passing footman '—a glass of champagne. Permit me to tell you, dear Eleanor, your gown is quite beautiful. You must be sure to tell me who made it for you—later, when we have a little time.'

Eleanor felt a gentle warmth creep through her iced veins with the bubbles of the champagne, bringing her alive again. How valuable good friends were. She need not have been so concerned. Across the room she could see Lady Beatrice Faringdon, as well as the Earl and Countess of Painscastle. She wondered idly if Henry had once again exerted some influence on this show of support. He must certainly have bribed Nick to guarantee his reluctant presence.

'You must find your family most supportive.' Lady Sefton picked up Eleanor's thoughts before she moved away to greet more guests.

'I do indeed.'

'And I am interested to note a predatory look in Lord Henry's eye for anyone he suspects of showing you less than good manners.'

'Do you?' Eleanor looked across the room to Henry in some confusion.

'Of course. He is most attentive. And so very handsome. I am quite jealous.' She tapped Eleanor's wrist playfully with a pretty ivory-sticked fan and laughed. 'Perhaps you should try to persuade him to remain in London. There are so few *very* attractive men in comparison. And certainly none, I suggest, in the marriage market!' On a little laugh, seeing Eleanor's deepening colour, Lady Sefton made her departure.

Does she suspect me of flirting with Henry? With my husband dead little more than four months? Eleanor was horrified as she turned to look to where Henry was in conversation with his aunt,

Lady Beatrice Faringdon, a stout Dowager of considerable presence in sumptuous maroon satin and nodding ostrich feathers. Formidable indeed, as her mother had intimated. Then his lordship looked up as if he sensed her questioning gaze on him and, unsmiling, very grave, raised a hand in tacit recognition before bending an ear back to the Dowager, who was holding forth on some subject. *Yes. He is attractive. And he cares. No matter what was between us in the past, he cares. Whatever happens, I am not alone in this.*

And Nick watched the silent exchange. And understood. The flash of recognition, the almost intimate connection between them. Hal might as well have kissed her! The fierce heat, the intense possession in Hal's eyes were unmistakable. He had set himself up as Nell's protector, but there was far more involved here than family support in a potentially stressful situation. Just as there was no mistaking the delicate flush on Nell's cheeks as she turned away. They might deny it, as he was sure they would. They might succeed in hiding it from the fashionable world, as was doubtless their intent, but Nick could read the love between them as clearly as if they had shouted it from the rooftops. He swallowed against the dismay as he contemplated the terrible uncertainty of the future.

With a lighter heart, unaware of Nick's concern, Eleanor turned her thoughts back to the pleasures of the evening. Behind her a familiar voice took her attention and she soon found herself deep in conversation about the prevailing fashion for silk-edged bonnets with Cousin Judith and Miss Hestlerton, a pretty girl related to the Seftons and in her first Season. Perhaps the polite world was not so quick to judge after all.

But her renewed confidence was to be short lived. Lady Sefton requested in her gentle voice that her guests take a seat to listen to a poem, an 'Ode to Love and Romance', which was to be read by its author, a young man very much in the Byronic mode with ruffled dark locks and pale features.

There was some manoeuvring and much comment in the salon as guests took their places or attempted to withdraw to a little side salon, which had been set aside for those whose taste ran to a hand of whist.

'Eleanor.' Judith drew her notice with a hand on her arm. 'Can I introduce you to Lady Firth? I am not sure that you are acquainted. She has been out of town for some months with her husband who is a keen traveller.'

Before them stood a thin, fair lady of her mother's generation. Eleanor noticed that she had the coldest grey eyes. And for the first time there was no polite or welcoming smile, no exchange of light talk, nothing but contempt, barely concealed.

The thought flitted across Eleanor's mind. Lady Firth. No, she did not know the lady, but she knew of her. An associate of the Princess Lieven, which would explain much. The lady looked at Eleanor with a frown. She raised a pearl-handled lorgnette, with thin-lipped superiority. There was a world of distaste imprinted on her haughty features and in her gesture as she raked Eleanor from head to foot with condemnation in her eyes.

'No, my dear.' Lady Firth addressed herself to Judith. 'I do not think that I wish to be introduced to this person.' Her smile could have cut through glass, all edges sharp. 'I believe that she is here under false pretences and has no right to the title that she claims as hers through marriage. Lady Sefton really should have chosen with more discrimination for her guest list—but I suppose it is difficult to believe the depths to which some people will descend to be noticed.' The lady's voice had an unfortunate carrying quality that drifted across the elegant room, slicing through the conversations. Heads turned in their direction. Silence fell. All attention was drawn away from the budding poet.

Judith rose to the occasion without hesitation, eyes fierce, her red curls aflame with indignation. 'I am certain, Lady Firth, that it is no such thing. The Marchioness of Burford is my dear cousin and worthy of all respect.'

Eleanor drew herself together, all dignity and pride and glittering diamonds. She had expected to be overwhelmed with shame, but it was anger that surged through her veins in a veritable tidal wave. She would not bow her head before idle gossip and common innuendo. How dare this woman snub her in so public a manner! How dare she presume intimate knowledge on so delicate and private a matter! If Judith's eyes sparkled with indignation, Eleanor's flashed fury, entirely at odds with their beautiful, soft-violet hue. 'It is no matter, Judith. Do not allow yourself to be disturbed.' She bent her cold regard on the lady with a curl of derision to her soft mouth, spine held rigid. 'If Lady Firth is sufficiently ill mannered as to discuss my private affairs in Lady Sefton's salon, she does not deserve any word of explanation or apology from our lips. If she chooses not to recognise me, then—'

A cold voice, frigid and lethal as the wind from arctic snows, interrupted and finished the sentiment, '—then it is her loss.' A strong arm was placed beneath Eleanor's and a long-fingered hand closed around her wrist in a firm embrace. At the same time she was aware of Nicholas, unusually stern and forbidding, standing to her other side.

'Forgive me, Lady Firth.' Lord Henry bowed with impeccable grace and deliberate intent. 'Considering your ill-bred comment, it is not suitable that my sister remain in your presence. Come, Eleanor. You should not remain with one who listens to scurrilous gossip from the gutters and would give credence to it.' The silence in the room increased, positively crackling with tension as ears strained to grasp Henry Faringdon's words. He bowed again. 'Since the Countess of Sefton has made us welcome here tonight in her home, may I suggest that your own presence, Lady Firth, is suspect indeed if you would choose to be discourteous to one of her guests.' He turned his back on the astonished lady with deliberate and graceful arrogance and led Eleanor away towards a chair beside Lady Beatrice.

'An excellent response, my dear Eleanor,' he murmured through gritted teeth. 'There is no need for you to feel in any way discomfited by such ill manners. Just think of what is due to the fortune in stones around your pretty neck!'

'Of course.' And she smiled, a little startled at his barely repressed temper. 'Thank you for rescuing me, Hal.'

'I do not deserve your thanks! You should not have had to suffer such crude indignities. Permit me to say that you handled the whole affair magnificently. You have my total admiration, my lady.'

Eleanor made no reply, unless it might be the hot colour in

her cheeks, unwilling to exacerbate the rigid tension in the muscles and tendons of Henry's arm beneath her hand, masked by the softness of the satin. Conversation flowed on around them. Everyone keen to gloss over the slight to one of their number— for the moment at least. She took her seat beside Aunt Beatrice, who patted her hand whilst scowling at the distant figure and flushed face of Lady Firth. For the rest of the evening, Eleanor rose to the occasion superbly, with grace and assurance and humour, a residue of anger sending ripples of energy and exhilaration through her bloodstream. No one watching her would know the fear that lurked below the surface. But Lord Henry saw and understood.

'I know that you do not want my gratitude, but indeed, Hal, I—'

'I did nothing.' Henry interrupted, more than a little curt. 'You seemed to be perfectly capable of conducting your own affairs. Your demeanour and response to Lady Firth were both incomparable, sufficient to quell the most arrogant comment. A positive rout, I would wager, without any real need for intervention on my part.'

'Why will you not accept my thanks?' He saw hurt and confusion in her face, which strengthened his resolve further. He knew without doubt that this was the wrong time and certainly the wrong place for an intimate exchange of views between them. He had delivered Eleanor home to Park Lane and would now make himself scarce, for both their sakes. It would be too easy for emotions to run high.

'Any man of honour would have acted as I did.' His reply was thus even more brusque.

'Yet you have in the past accused me of treachery and betrayal. If true, if you truly believed me capable of such things, then you have no duty or demands of honour towards me. Yet you came to my defence with devastating effect and in full public gaze. I cannot let such kindness go unacknowledged.'

They stood facing each other, rigidly polite, uncomfortably distant, hostility sparkling between them as bright as Eleanor's hated diamonds, on the landing of the first floor of the Park Lane town house. Lord Henry had escorted Eleanor home from the Seftons' soirée with the intention of going on to relax over a hand of cards and a glass of brandy at Brooks's. The night, although it had been fraught with dangers both personal and public, was not too far advanced. The last thing Henry had wanted tonight was this confrontation with Eleanor where, against all his best intentions, all his determination to keep a circumspect distance between them, his self-control might be stretched to the limit—and beyond. But he must play out the present scene before he could leave her with formal courtesy and cool respect. Neither of which sentiments was responsible for the vicious and aching need that held him in an iron grasp. He wanted her, in his arms, in his bed.

'So I should leave one who bears my family name to be ripped at before the avid gaze of the polite world by the likes of Dorothea Firth?' Ice coated Eleanor's veins as she listened to Lord Henry's aloof assessment of the event. 'It was merely a matter of family honour, nothing more and nothing less. As I said, it does not require your gratitude. Nicholas would have done the same if he had been nearer to you.'

'Why are you so cold towards me?' Eleanor shook her head in a little movement of denial, unable to comprehend the chill that emanated from his lordship to settle around her. 'I find your attitude incomprehensible. You would condemn me, reject me in one breath and yet come to my rescue with the next. One moment you are caring and protective, the next your tone would freeze me to the marrow. You escorted me to Whitchurch and held me when it all became too much to bear and I wept in your arms. You have stood between me and society's condemnation here in London. But now…I do not understand. What have I done to earn your displeasure?'

She stood before him, tall and straight, yet intensely vulnerable. Challenging him. Demanding an answer. Yet it would be so easy to hurt her. Lord Henry groaned inwardly with frustration, a quick brush of temper. Why could she not simply retire to bed and allow the stresses of the night to calm before they must, by necessity, meet again over the breakfast table? He did not know what drove her. He only knew that desire and need had begun to simmer in his blood when he saw the proud light in her eyes, the indomitable spirit. Through narrowed eyes, he took in her flawless complexion, glowing in the soft light from the branch of candles at his right hand. Her soft lips, eminently kissable. The curve of her breast, enhanced by the low neckline of her gown and the glitter of precious stones. By God, he wanted her! He clenched his hands into fists and breathed carefully.

Eleanor stared at him, unable to interpret his stern expression, trying to clear her brain from the mist that engulfed it. Some unknown force seemed to be pushing her tonight. There was no need for this conversation, confrontation even. She should, if she were sensible, turn on her heel and leave him, ignore his ill temper, whatever the cause. She had played her role, held her head high through the whole nerve-wrenching proceedings, thanked him for his supreme moment of chivalry. And surely that was enough. But he stood there in the silent shadowed space where tension all but crackled around them. All dark power and male magnetism. And something kept her from sensible retreat. A need to provoke, she admitted to herself in that moment, honesty demanding that she see her motives for what they were. A need to strip away the polite exterior, the bland response. To discover what really lurked behind his cool, sophisticated, superbly governed outer defences. To see if this man before her bore any resemblance to the Hal she had known two years before, when she remembered his spirit and energy, his unquenchable thirst for a life of excitement and achievement that would cause his pulse to beat and his blood to run hot. When she remembered the heat in his eyes when he looked at her.

But did she know what she was doing? Unlikely, she decided, with a quick wash of panic that brushed the skin along her arms. It was like teasing a fireside cat, all fur and soft paws, only to discover a panther, sleekly elegant, but hiding lethal intent and deadly claws.

Emotion arced between them on that upper landing, unbidden, undesired and as yet unacknowledged. Created by their close proximity, the high, tension-filled emotions of the evening and their own past history. Alone, separate from time and space, they faced each other. Only themselves, so it seemed to be, in the silent, shadowed house. Caught, entangled in a fine web of silken strands, magical and unbreakable, which drew them together and bound them for ever whether they wished for it or not.

And they did. Albeit unacknowledged. The desire was there, unspoken, in their eyes, in the tingling awareness of their bodies, one for the other.

Henry was the first to speak, to break the spell.

'Eleanor…' He grasped at sense, control, honour, all of which seemed to be sliding inexorably beyond his reach. 'I must go.' He took a step back from her.

'Hal—' Stretching out her hand, that one word and the plea in her voice proved to be all that was needed to bring him to a halt. Was she really so wanton? The possibility astonished her, as did the answer in her mind. It did not seem to matter any more. Only this moment mattered. 'Ah, Hal—don't go. Don't leave me.'

'What do you ask of me, lady?' A hint of desperation crept into his voice.

'I don't know.' And indeed she did not. A suspicion of a tear escaped from the amethyst depths onto her lashes, as bright as any diamond, a rival to the brilliance of the fortune which clasped her throat.

It was his undoing. He answered the demand in his body rather than the sane advice of his mind, now completely overthrown. 'I know only one thing, Eleanor. I want you. I do not know if this is good or ill. Wise or unwise. But I can no longer deny it. I wanted you then—two long years ago. And I want you now—the feelings are no different.'

Before she could regret her ungoverned and blatant invitation, he took one stride towards her, grasped her wrist and stalked the length of the corridor, pulling her with him, deaf and blind to any resistance. Except that there was no resistance, which merely enhanced his desire for an ultimate fulfilment of this shattering revelation. Determined on privacy, he opened the door to his own room, pulled her through and closed it behind them. Locked it behind them. Then simply stood and looked down into her eyes, wide with anticipation, her lips parted, her breathing shallow.

'Tell me that you do not want this;' he demanded, 'and I will open the door and let you go free. But tell me now before it is too late.'

'You know that I cannot.' Her voice might be soft, but her reply was immediate. Her eyes never faltered.

'Have you then become a temptress, my lady?' She could not read the expression on his face, the edge in his words.

'No. Or perhaps yes.' She would not lie, caught in the force-field of his power. 'I am not the naïve innocent that I was, no longer a green girl with no knowledge or acceptance of the desires of my own heart. And I remember you, Hal. I remember what it was like to lie in your arms. I remember only too well. So, yes, I want you. I would be a fool to deny it.'

He could wait no longer but pulled her close, destroying the distance between them. Her body was held hard against his, that she would feel the strength and urgency of his desire for her. His mouth met hers, hot, feverish, her lips parting beneath his in willing submission as his tongue sought out the inner softness of her lips. Yet it was no submission. There was no force here. Her response was as heated as his, meeting fire with fire, as demanding and overwhelming as the need that surged through his own blood.

Now, although he released her to stand alone, he gave her no chance to retreat. They were beyond that. With clever fingers he dealt with the intricacies of her gown, removing it with all due care to her and the delicate fabric that she wore, all the while subjugating the force that drove him to tear and ravage, to permit the sensation of his hands against her skin. Her silk stockings were unrolled to reveal elegant calves and high-arched feet, as soft and smooth as their delicate covering. The diamonds were unpinned and unclasped to be discarded at her feet as so much dross. Until she stood before him in her chemise, her feet bare, her face naked and vulnerable before his searching gaze.

'I had forgotten how very beautiful you are.'

With neither reply nor response to the stunned amazement in

his voice, Eleanor bent her head and began to unfasten the ribbons to remove her own chemise. She would not allow him this final intimacy, but would accomplish it herself. The gesture stripped him to the bone. Took his breath—and even more, when the silk and lace folds slithered unhindered down her limbs to lie on the floor.

'I had indeed forgotten. I have longed to see you. How could I possibly forget such perfection?' He simply looked at her, could not take his eyes from her, transfixed for the moment by the magnitude of the gift she was offering him with such deliberate concentration. If she had been vulnerable before, now she was at his mercy, yet she met his gaze with her own, a challenge still in her raised head. He allowed himself the ultimate pleasure of his eyes lingering on every curve and dip of her body. Feminine with high breasts, the soft swell of hip and thigh from her slim waist, she had indeed matured into a beautiful woman from the shy débutante of the moon-shadowed summer house. Flickering light from the single candle on the nightstand illuminated and cast shadows as it would, to entrance and invite his touch. She simply stood, arms loosely by her side, and let him look his fill.

And he knew that it could not be enough. It pleased him that when he finally stretched out his hand she did not flinch from his touch or withdraw into shy embarrassment. Yet he did not touch her yet, still intent on savouring the moment to come, but removed the pins from her hair, one by one, until the lustrous glory of it cascaded into his hands and over her breasts in a shining fall. Until his own needs allowed him to hesitate no longer.

Then, stripping off his own clothes, leaving the single candle burning, he came to her. Without further thought of the sense of his actions, he lifted her high in his arms and tumbled her onto the bed. To join her there, flesh against flesh at last. 'Why can I not rid my dreams of you? You haunt me so.' A touch of anger here as he framed her face with his hands. 'I feel the touch of your hands on my skin, your lips on mine—both waking and sleeping. I can't get you out of my mind.' He crushed his mouth to hers, holding her as he wished, angling his head to take her lips more completely.

'I have dreamed of this moment through so many nights.' He rolled with her, pinning her body beneath him with his weight, braceleting her wrists with strong fingers to stretch her arms above her head. Even though his dominance might underline her vulnerability to him, Eleanor accepted it with a low purr of pleasure in her throat, secure in the knowledge that he would never be capable of hurting her. Only to drive her to the sharp edge of desire—and then over into dark delight.

Tracing a burning path with his mouth, Henry claimed her from her lips to slender throat, to satin shoulder, intoxicated by the heavy pulse that throbbed beneath her skin. He could not get enough of her, nor she of him. Here were no soft moments of tender reminiscence. No gentle interludes full of earlier memories. Only an onslaught of lips and hands to touch, to caress, to excite. Her wrists released, Eleanor was free to explore the man she remembered, as he explored her, hands stroking and moulding the taut muscles of his chest and arms, the flat planes of waist and hip and thigh. Ravaged bedcovers were pushed aside, as tangled and tumultuous as their emotions. Candlelight gleamed on sweat-streaked limbs that entwined, stretched, slid and clung luxuriously one against the other.

Relentlessly, refusing to let her rest, he brought her to the peak of arousal when her body shivered under his hands regardless of the heat. And raised his head as he felt the beginning of her response. Looked into her face.

'Look at me.' It was a demand from which she found no retreat, as she could find no escape from the glorious heat spreading from between her thighs, flushing her skin a delicate rose. 'Open your eyes, Eleanor. Know who owns you, who possesses you this night. You are mine. I took your innocence—now I claim you again. You will never forget me.'

'I cannot forget you.' Her admission was wrung from her on a sharp intake of break as his teeth closed around one taut nipple, driving her near to insanity.

'You torment me,' he murmured against the hollow between her breasts where he planted flesh-searing kisses. 'But I will not suffer alone. I will make you want me tonight.' Hands slid, held, fingers drifting over the gentle swell of her belly to search out the ultimate softness between her thighs. She arched her body on a cry at the intrusion, but in welcome. As urgent, as aroused as he. Hot and wet, she opened for him.

Oh God, he wanted her, must have her.

'Want me, Eleanor. Tell me that you want me.' Past and future held no meaning, only this one moment together in the flickering candle-flame. Perhaps the only moment they would ever have. A moment that should never have been theirs to claim. His conscience damned him for it, but he ruthlessly closed his mind against it, unable to see past the fierce call of his heart and body.

'I do. I want you.' Her reply, the rise and fall of her breasts on ragged breathing, destroyed any conscience which he might have held to. As did the immediate response of her body to his.

As she had given him her virginal innocence, now Eleanor gave him her maturity cloaked in fire and inner knowledge. Touched him, stroked him, set him ablaze with her fine but confident fingers, closed her hand around him, revelling in his groan of shock, of desire. Tomorrow was soon enough for regrets. Tonight she would relive all her hopes and dreams. She burned for him. Flames coursed through her as she enticed him, lured him, the very temptress he had called her. She had dreamed of a night such as this for so long, long nights when it had seemed such an impossibility and she had awoken with tears on her face. Now reality made it true and she would not hold back from him. Moulding herself against him, marvelling at his strength, his muscled power, his weight as he lowered his body to hers, the heat of his erection against her thigh, she laughed softly as she covered his face with kisses. Ah, yes. Henry wanted her as much as she wanted him. It was no time for maidenly blushes or shy hesitancy on her part.

On a breath, unable to delay further, Henry slid into her, lifting her hips to take her to the hilt. On a gasp of stunned amazement and delight she surrounded him in impossible softness, impossible tightness.

A sigh of completion united them. They remained suddenly frozen in time, all frantic demands stilled without words, lost in each other, held fast in each other's eyes, their bodies joined in this most intimate of joining. Taking his weight on his arms, he pressed her hands to the bed, linking his fingers with hers in perfect union, palm against palm.

'Yes, Eleanor.' He answered the question in her eyes, his voice harsh with emotion. 'You know you are mine.'

Only then did he began to move, slowly, deliberately, withdrawing and then reclaiming, watching her every expression as he filled her, stretched her, made her whole body shudder beneath his. It was his intention to keep the pace, to draw out the intense pleasure, but the fire was too great. Caught up in it, its urgency consumed him, the needs of his body overturning the planned campaign. More forceful, more demanding, hips flexed, thrust after thrust, he destroyed them both, carrying her with him to the end. He had no choice but to allow his body to rule.

Without control, Eleanor arched her hips for him, to take him deeper if that were possible. Heat built within her again, low and liquid and throbbing once more in her belly and she rejoiced in it.

'Say my name!' he groaned through gritted teeth as he still clung to the knife-edge of control. 'Say it.'

'Hal. Oh, Hal.' Her body convulsed in heat and light as a meteor shower erupted in golden spangles through her blood.

His control was at an end. Hal followed her into the darkness, losing himself in her, whispering her name as he buried his face in her hair.

Afterwards, when she would have curled into him, content to drift in a soft cloud of fulfilment, in his warmth and comforting presence, Henry exerted all his will-power to fight against the desperate temptation to allow it. Instead he left her warmth, shrugged into his gown to wrap her in a sheet and carry her back to her own room. It would be better so. To spend the night with her would be too painful. It was all too difficult. He should never have allowed such sweet but cruel-edged temptation to overcome him. Where was his much-vaunted control now? He steeled himself against the weight of her head on his shoulder as he carried her and the perfume of her hair that invaded his senses, aware

once more of the response in his loins. It would be so very easy
to give in and simply love her. To allow her to sleep in his arms,
to give himself the pleasure of kissing her awake and taking her
once more when dawn lightened the shadows of the bed.

'Forgive me if I have done wrong, Nell. You were far too enticing tonight.' He whispered the words as he relinquished his
burden and she slept in her own bed, hair tumbled in a ruffle of
curls onto her pillow. 'I could wish that you had repulsed me—
but the fault is undeniably mine. And how can I regret it?' He
gently touched a curl before withdrawing his hand as if it burned
his flesh to the bone. 'You are beautiful and desirable and I regret the events that separated us to the depths of my soul.'

Dousing the candle, he left her.

Only when he had returned to his own room, to spend a sleepless and restless night, did the thought come to him. Not one
word of love had been spoken between them during the whole
of their intimate coming together. Only of raw hunger and longing. It had been simply a moment of blazing need and desire for
each other, a passion that had carried them along in its torrent as
leaves in a fast-flowing stream, leaving them shaken and exhausted by the intensity of feelings at the end. But of love—not
one word.

Perhaps because there was no love between them. That was
the easiest conclusion to reach, the voice of cold sense and cau-
tion warned him. Perhaps the basic hunger of a virile man for a
beautiful woman had now been assuaged. Perhaps the burning
need to touch her, to possess her, had been cauterised by that one
moment of brilliant, diamond-bright madness.

Perhaps. But he could not believe it.

Yet it would be better if that were so. Too many shadows surrounded them. The past with its weight of guilt and denial.
Thomas, who had willingly taken her as his wife, a role that Eleanor had equally willingly accepted. And, not least, the pathway forward, which was too indistinct and uncertain to decipher.
He should pray that this shimmering need had indeed been
burned out in that final moment of glory.

But he had worshipped her with every movement of his body,

every caress. Shown her consideration even within the towering demands of his passion. Never pushed her beyond what she was prepared to give to him. And she had given him everything with a generosity beyond measure.

All he wanted was to take her into his arms and repeat it.

And what he could possibly say to her when they came face to face on the following day, he could not envisage.

Little wonder that sleep evaded him.

The house in Park Lane began to hum with unusual bustle at the prospect of a small evening party for members of the Faringdon family and a select number of close friends. Mrs Stamford, in her element at having been given *carte blanche* by Lord Henry, took it upon herself to organise a tasteful, even cosy, evening with the hint of expensive sophistication. Eleanor too found her thoughts given new direction, away from the looming catastrophe of her social status, but her activities did nothing to redirect her mind from thoughts of her outrageous behaviour on the night of the Sefton soirée. She could blame it all on Henry, of course, who had lured her into such a provocative response. Had she actually removed her own chemise? She closed her eyes against the vibrant recall, but her blood heated at the image of his fierce eyes on her exposed body. But honesty forced her to acknowledge her own very willing complicity. He would have left her if she had allowed it, had resisted him to any degree. And she had done neither. Rather, she had flung herself into his arms. She closed her eyes in delicious sensation, ignoring the lists of guests beneath her hand as she sat at the elegant little desk in the blue parlour. He had fired her blood and she had stepped into his embrace and into his bed without hesitation. And she very much feared that she could be lured again.

What must he think of her, of her wanton behaviour? She had no idea. And it had to be admitted, as she sat contemplating the sunbeams stealing across the paper before her, she did not seem to care. All that mattered was the image of his intense loving, the desire that had burned in his eyes and in the heat of his restless mouth. It had swept her beyond thought and conscience. He had wanted her and given in to the temptation. She hugged that thought close as she realised that she had discovered within herself the power to drive him beyond control. She held her breath at *that* thought, releasing it slowly as she also discovered an overwhelming desire to repeat the experience. It was, she acknowledged, a morning for unsettling revelation.

But he had uttered no word of love. Not once, in all the other words he had whispered in the dark expanse of his bed. But then, neither had she. Surely he must have some affection for her. The line between her brows deepened, as she once again demanded honesty from herself. But it was not affection she wanted from him. It was a blaze of love and passion to sweep all before it. Perhaps men were capable of such physical desire without the need for love and she must accept it. But she loved him—and knew it beyond doubt.

Her fair skin shivered at the thought and became suffused with colour. Yes, she loved him, but that did not mean that she wished every glorious detail to be imprinted on her memory every waking moment of every day! Or in her restless dreams. She huffed out her breath in frustration as she focused on the list on the desk, seeing Hal's name written again and again in the margin. With an unladylike hiss, she tore the page in two, consigned it to the flames, and began another. Then, she admonished herself, she must turn her mind to the far more important matter of staff to serve the food and wine to so many guests.

Although she would have preferred to take herself to the opposite ends of the house, even the attics, Eleanor found need to run Henry to ground in the small morning room which he had taken over as office, in lieu of a library in their rented home, and a masculine haven to escape the women of the household.

'I need to know about staff, my lord. Do we hire more footmen? Do I leave it to Marcle to decide what is necessary?' She kept her distance, remaining with her back against the closed door. She looked anywhere but at his face.

'Yes. You need not concern yourself. I have already spoken to him and, unless your mama decides to serve a seven-course banquet, God help us, we should cope more than adequately.'

'Very well.' She was well aware that Henry had hardly looked up from the table at which he was sitting. Which was perfectly acceptable as far as she was concerned! She would have left with a swirl of muslin skirts, but noticed a pile of letters spread before him, some distinctly travel-worn, through which he was steadily wading. They clearly took all his attention. It pricked her conscience and it enticed her to stay, to approach.

'Mr Bridges?' she enquired, remembering his enthusiasm when discussing his new partner and their fledgling company.

'Yes.' He smiled and answered abstractedly. 'I seem to have received a lot of correspondence, all in one batch. The post is still haphazard.' He discarded the top sheet and went on to break the seals on the next. 'A matter of new investments that we hope to take up. Nat has a mind to put some money into a new textile town in Massachusetts. He sees it becoming a second Manchester. And he could just be right. Power looms will make all the difference and there is plenty of water to drive them…' He gave his attention back to the letter under his hand.

She looked at his bent head. Tried not to think of the smooth texture as she had curled her fingers into his hair. Or allowed her lips to trace those elegant cheekbones. And she could not possibly look at his hands without reliving their demanding caresses on her own body. A little shiver feathered across her skin and she silently damned him for reawakening such heady desires.

And then she looked once more at the piles of correspondence, noting Henry's preoccupation with the advice of the absent Mr Bridges. It was all the proof she needed, as if she needed further confirmation, that he would go as soon as he could. The reinforcement of the knowledge destroyed all her remembered pleasure and her present composure in one fatal blow. Her heart ached in anticipation of the loss.

'I think you should return to New York,' she found herself saying brusquely, even though her soul shrieked its denial.

Henry now looked up, attention definitely captured by the harsh edge rarely heard in Eleanor's voice.

'Your business cannot wait for ever. Mr Bridges must feel the need of your presence.'

'Perhaps.' He had not expected this from her. The strain was showing this morning in her colourless skin and the shadows beneath her lids. Even her eyes had lost their sparkle. He realised that she was near breaking point and felt helpless to do anything constructive to alleviate it. Thus his answer was carefully worded. 'But Nat is quite capable of holding the fort for a little while longer. This is merely informing me of decisions he has made in my absence—and I would have done no different. My business is in good hands.'

'What use is there for you to remain here?' She was cold, so cold. 'There is no guarantee that our little event on Saturday night will produce anything of value. You cannot alter the demands of the law if Sir Edward's claims are genuine.'

'No.' Henry now rose to his feet, sensing her distress, intent on taking her hands to offer comfort. 'I trust the Baxendales have replied that they will honour us with their presence on Saturday?'

'Oh, yes. I doubt they could resist being introduced to the family, as you planned. But what will Aunt Beatrice remember? Perhaps nothing. It is a wild goose chase.' Eleanor took a step back.

He shrugged, allowing her to retreat against his better judgement, unwilling to damage the brittle shell which was holding her together. All she said was perfectly true.

'Go back, Hal.' Eleanor turned away and walked to the door.

'Nell.' His voice stopped her. 'I cannot go back. Not yet.'

She stood silently. He had heard the desolation in her voice—she had not been able to prevent it.

'Do you really wish me to do so?' he asked gently.

Now there was an impossible question. 'Yes. I think you should go.' How cold her voice sounded in her own ears. What would he think of her now?

'Nell…'

'No, of course I do not wish you to go! You must know that. But it might be better if you did.' The words, the stark truth, were wrung from her.

'Better for whom, Nell?'

But she closed the door behind her without reply.

Hal was left, hearing the echo of the sharp click as the barrier closed between them. The need to give comfort to her was so great it frightened him, as did the yawning abyss between them. Although he had to accept, with more than a little disgust, that comfort had not been uppermost in his mind when he had all but dragged her to his room. Possession. Need. The control that he had spent years in perfecting had snapped in that one moment when she had raised her eyes to his, had begged him to stay, begged him both with and without words, but none the less with transparent longing. And she had allowed herself to be drawn along, as a leaf in a whirlwind, answering his every demand.

His mind once more stumbled over the fact that he had not told her that he loved her. And perhaps it had been deliberate. And certainly sensible—probably the only commendable part of his behaviour towards her that night. To burden her with his love, against her wishes, would be cruel and insensitive. He hoped, in the inner recesses of his mind, that she would know that she held his heart in her keeping. Remembering her final words, he doubted it, and perhaps it was for the best. He would do all in his power to rescue her from the scandal created by Sir Edward Baxendale and then would indeed return to America for good.

By nine o'clock on Saturday evening, the rooms in Park Lane, perfectly arranged to Mrs Stamford's exacting standards, were soon flatteringly full. Not as elegant as Lady Sefton's soirée, of course. No music had been provided. No poet—thank God! But conversation, cards for those who wished it and an extensive supper, all hosted by Lord Henry at his most urbane and the Marchioness of Burford in softest dove grey, but without the Faringdon diamonds.

Sir Edward and Miss Octavia Baxendale had duly arrived, two of the earlier guests. Octavia was swathed from high neck to ankle in black, as severe and unflattering as ever to her slight figure and pale colouring, and seemingly reluctant to attend any social occasion, but she had smiled prettily and thanked Eleanor for the considerate invitation. She hoped that attention would not be drawn to them. They were simply friends of the family. Eleanor smiled reassuringly, but sardonically. Had Octavia given no thought as to why they should be putting up at Faringdon House when the Marchioness and the rest of the close family were living in Park Lane? Surely she could not be so naïve as to think that there would be no speculation or innuendo? Heaven only knew what people made of it! But Octavia appeared oblivious to the speculation and interested glances.

What did she and Octavia find to talk about as she led the lady to a seat and found some refreshment for her? Afterward Eleanor could not remember. Octavia was decidedly dull, with no opinion of interest to offer on even the most frivolous of topics, once the condition of her rose garden and neglected flower borders had been thoroughly discussed.

Eleanor delivered her with some relief into the safe keeping of Aunt Beatrice and found herself drawn into a few unsettling words with Sir Edward. It was an embarrassing, anger-provoking conversation, despite being quite private. Even though she was aware of Henry's hawk-like eyes on her in case he sensed her distress. She was angry, she thought, on any number of occasions recently, but put on her best sociable manner as hostess.

Sir Edward was as kind and compassionate, as sensitive to her situation as he had been throughout the painful developments. His fair countenance, with all the gravity of deep concern, should have comforted her. It did not. She took a step back when he would have touched her hand in sympathy. She found herself being complimented on her appearance and her fortitude under adverse conditions, which promptly set her teeth on edge. Henry might do so—but not Sir Edward. And her courage was remarkable in holding a social occasion—however informal—when the whole town was so obviously talking and smiling in derision behind its collective and judgmental hand. Eleanor held her breath until the urge to express her true sentiments in less than flattering terms had calmed.

Sir Edward bent his kind and understanding smile on her. 'I believe that Hoskins will have confirmed the legality of all documents by next week, my dear lady.' *How dare you address me with such familiarity! I am not your dear lady and never will be!* 'I have discussed the ultimate outcome with him, of course.'

How dare you!

'We must end this unsatisfactory situation soon. For your sake and for my dear sister's. To postpone the final settlement would be unwise.'

How dare you choose my social event for such a sensitive matter!

How dare you and your sister even exist!

'You are too considerate, sir.' Eleanor's clenched jaw ached.

'I have instructed Hoskins to offer an annuity for yourself and the unfortunate child. Will you take it?'

'I am considering it.' She marvelled at her even tones. At the smile which remained in place.

'There will be scandal, but it is unavoidable. My sister must take on her rightful title. She is very keen to be settled, as you might imagine.'

'Of course.' She continued to smile. She knew that Henry would bear down on them if she appeared in any way distressed—but her eyes were empty of emotion rather than unladylike, and rigidly contained, fury.

'And we must then discuss your moving to your own accommodation, of course. I believe that Octavia would wish to take up residence as soon as possible at Burford Hall. Life in town does not suit her. She enjoys country air.'

'I will inform Hoskins of my arrangements, Sir Edward. They are all in hand.' *But I will not discuss them with you!*

Still keeping a tight hold on the anger that seemed to be directed equally at Sir Edward, at Thomas and at fate in general, Eleanor moved through the rest of the evening like a child's puppet, automatically fulfilling her role. It seemed to be a success. She was complimented more times than she could count. She did not care.

After supper, at which she ate nothing but an asparagus tartlet without even tasting its succulent and delicate flavour, Eleanor made it her policy to find her aunt by marriage in a quiet corner where they would be undisturbed. Lady Beatrice had been able to watch and speak with Sir Edward and Miss Baxendale for a whole evening. She must have some recollection of any past meeting, if any such meeting had occurred. Eleanor had to know. Had Thomas cared for Octavia? Enough to have married her against family opinion and have a child by her? One more tiny nail in the coffin that was threatening to enclose her entire life. As cold as death itself, Eleanor faced the lady. Sensing her purpose from across the room, and not wishing her to be alone when his aunt delivered in typically forthright manner any bad news, Henry moved, silent as a ghost, to appear at her shoulder, to take up the initiative.

'Well, Aunt. You said you remembered Thomas flirting with a fair girl. You have had the opportunity to see the lady and her brother. Do you remember her?'

'Oh, yes.' The Dowager, remarkable in puce satin and lace with garnets, which did nothing to compliment her fading red hair, turned her critical gaze on the innocent object of their discussion. 'I remember her. She was a pretty little thing. Still is, of course but a trifle pale—understandable in the circumstances, whatever the truth of the matter. Thomas certainly had a *tendre* for her. Showed her a great deal of attention, in fact. Dancing with her on more than one occasion…more than I thought was appropriate. It does not do to raise pretensions and it was clear that the girl saw the glitter of a title within her reach. Judith was perfectly right. Thomas and the girl were infatuated—such a very unfortunate emotion, don't you think.'

'Oh.' Eleanor forced her mind to hold the dreaded words.

'I actually warned him off on one occasion—the child was far too provincial for my taste. Not suited to be Marchioness of Burford. Not like you, my dear.' She patted Eleanor's unresponsive hand with superior condescension. 'You have a touch of class, as I was quick to tell Thomas when some of the family expressed their disappointment at his choice of bride.' Realising what she had said, she coughed and spread her fan. 'Your paternal uncle is, after all, a baronet. Most acceptable, my dear. But that is all in the past.'

'So it is true…' Eleanor sighed '…Thomas did marry Octavia.' Henry took Eleanor's cold hand into his keeping and refused to let her pull away. At that moment he did not care who might see or pass judgement.

He simply needed to touch her.

'It may well be. He certainly did not take my advice, if rumours do indeed run true.'

Eleanor looked up at Henry, eyes over-bright. 'It is hopeless, then, as we thought.' But she tried to keep the smile. She would not weep. She would not shout her despair to the world. 'At least we know—it is better perhaps than all the uncertainty. False hope is almost impossible to live with.'

'There is one thing.' Aunt Beatrice reclaimed their attention with narrowed eyes. 'I do not quite recollect her name—Octavia, certainly—but I did not think that it was Baxendale.'

Henry sighed. What use to dredge up any more hope on such a flimsy point of order? He did not think Eleanor could take much more. 'It was a long time ago, ma'am. Even your prodigious memory might play tricks. I cannot think that it is strong enough to cast doubt on the whole question of the legality of their claim. We have to accept that Octavia is Thomas's legitimate widow.'

'Now don't be hasty, young man. Just like your father! Too impatient for your own good.' Lady Beatrice fixed him with a withering glance which he remembered uncomfortably from his youth, and she drew her stout figure up to its full height before delivering her final opinion. 'About the name. As I said, Baxendale I am not at all sure about. But there is one thing I can state for certain. And my memory is excellent when remembering faces! That man, Sir Edward Baxendale, is not Octavia's brother! He is without doubt *not* the young man who was introduced to me as her brother four years ago.'

'Are you sure?' Henry frowned. Whatever they had hoped for, this was most unexpected.

'Sure! Of course I am! I would wager my emeralds on it.'

'But she may have more than one brother.' Eleanor refused to believe that at the eleventh hour there might be the slightest chink of light, of hope, in the dark walls which hemmed her in. 'You may have met—'

'Don't be foolish, my girl. That is not the man who squired Octavia to parties in her London Season.'

'And I distinctly remember the occasion when Sir Edward said that he had been with Octavia when she had made her curtsy to the polite world!' Henry allowed the fact to filter slowly through his brain with all its possibilities. 'Why are you so sure, ma'am?'

'I remember the brother very well—because I took him in instant dislike. Octavia was charming enough, but no family would wish to acquire her brother around the dining table, take my word for it. He had the appearance of a gentleman and the manners were well-bred enough—but there was an unpleasantness about him. You would not trust him with a purseful of gold. Or with the reputation of any pretty young woman—he had quite an eye for them, I am afraid. Or so my husband informed me. I understand he frequented some of the more unsavoury gaming establishments in town. Also I was led to understand that he had an arrangement with a lower class of woman—if you take my meaning. Not that *you* would be acquainted with any such shady dealings of course, Henry.' She dared Henry to contradict her, but he recognised the glint of humour in her face.

'Definitely not, Aunt. Can you describe him—the gentleman introduced as Octavia's brother?'

'Rather like Octavia, I suppose. Taller than Sir Edward. Slighter. A thin face. Hair not quite as fair, perhaps. And cunning eyes, my boy. Not quite the thing at all.' Lady Beatrice furrowed her brow. 'I cannot remember his name—I wish I could. Thomas did not like him either,' she added inconsequentially.

'It is not much to go on, but perhaps enough.' Henry gripped his aunt's hand in gratitude. 'It may be that the whole family will owe you their thanks tonight for your part in overturning this cruel and malevolent plot.'

'Family is important, Henry, as you very well know! It delights me that you are giving your support to Eleanor in a time of trial. Why you should wish to take yourself off to some Godforsaken wasteland on the far side of the world, I shall never know. Much better to settle here, take my word for it!' Lady Beatrice, her mission completed, prepared to return to a cosy chat with one of her intimates. 'But there is one thing I think you should do.'

'And that is?'

'Come, my boy! Use your wits! Ask Octavia how many brothers she has, of course.'

They held a post-mortem in the early hours of the morning when the guests had gone, Aunt Beatrice's words heavy in their minds. Hope, so long dashed, began to run high, despite the essentially trivial nature of the information, and no one thought to claim exhaustion after so successful an evening.

'So who is Sir Edward, if not Octavia's brother?'

'I see you like to start with the easy questions, Nick!' Henry stretched out in a chair beside the settee on which Eleanor and her mama had taken up positions, his hands linked behind his head, ankles crossed. 'We do not know the answer to that one!'

'So what *do* we know?' Mrs Stamford demanded clarification. 'That her name was probably not Baxendale when Thomas met her. And Sir Edward is not her brother. Does it help us at all?' Doubts still drew a sharp line between the lady's delicate brows.

'Octavia only has one brother,' Eleanor put in quietly. 'I asked her about her family, a casual query you understand, over a glass of wine. She said that Edward was the only family she had remaining alive. Her parents are dead and she had no sisters. She offered the information that she and her brother are, and always have been, very close.'

'So we will work on the premise that Beatrice is correct.' Henry frowned down at his highly polished boots.

'But the innkeeper at the Red Lion—' Eleanor turned towards Henry, impatient with her memories of their visit to Whitchurch '—he said Sir Edward had a sister who had a young child. And that the sister's husband had recently died. A husband who rarely visited the Great House. Would he deliberately mislead us? I cannot see it.'

'No. I do not think he lied.' Henry found his mind working furiously with the scant evidence they had. 'He would have no reason to do so—he did not know the reason for our visit.'

'And they knew Sir Edward—both the landlord and the gardener,' Eleanor reminded him again. 'There was no dispute over his name or his living in the Great House.'

'There was in all probability no reason to do so. He most likely *is* Sir Edward Baxendale and I am certain that he does live in Whitchurch. So consider. If you are going to set up a fraudulent claim to a valuable inheritance, surely it must be safer to use as much truth as possible. The more truth, the less chance for the lies to be suspected and detected. It is *Octavia's* name which is in question after all, not Sir Edward's. And the identity of her brother—although how he fits into the puzzle I know not.'

'But Sir Edward has a sister with a baby,' Eleanor persisted.

'Yes. I don't dispute it. But not Octavia.'

'I still don't know where that leaves us.' Mrs Stamford lifted her hands and let them fall into her lap in frustration. She clearly spoke for them all.

'Tell me, Eleanor.' Henry now sat up and fixed the lady with a compelling stare. It appeared that he had come to some conclusions. 'When you first saw the child John, what was your first thought?'

'After I had recovered from the shock?' She laughed a little. For the first time in days it seemed that a weight had been lifted from her mind. They still knew so little, yet there was a distinct crumbling in the edifice built up by Sir Edward. He had lied. And how many lies he had been prepared to tell they had yet to discover. She must hold on to the fact that Thomas's marriage to Octavia was all a sham. And they would prove it! 'I shall never forget those first revelations!' she admitted. 'I suppose I thought that the boy looked nothing like Thomas. And later Judith said—'

'Judith said that Faringdons always breed true.' Mrs Stamford smiled, the slightest touch of triumph as she followed the line of thought. 'Look at dear baby Tom, the image of his father. And Judith is so like her father, apart from that unfortunate red hair which she inherited from Beatrice. But John looks like Octavia. Or even Sir Edward. Both very fair with blue eyes and fair complexions.'

'What are you thinking? Who is the child's father, if not Thomas?' Eleanor's face was suddenly flushed with a delicate colour.

'I don't know yet.' Henry lifted his shoulders and let them fall, but there was the fire of battle in his eyes. 'Who would know more about this?'

'But look, Hal.' Listening to the unfolding suppositions, sympathising with the need to destroy Sir Edward's case, Nick could still see one major sticking point. 'You have forgotten the documents. The marriage and baptism. All legal, signed and sealed, with witnesses. Guaranteed by Church and State. Can we argue round that? I don't see it. We can destroy Baxendale's credibility, but can we discount the documents in Hoskins' possession? He certainly believes them to be above question.'

'One witness of the marriage is dead.' Eleanor reminded him. 'Octavia's mother. It is very convenient, I suppose.'

'And do you remember the identity of the other?' asked Henry. 'It was Sir Edward. Even more convenient!'

'So was the priest also lying? Witnessing something that never happened? Forging documents? Is that what you are suggesting?' Mrs Stamford looked suitably shocked. 'A man of the cloth, too! What a terrible muddle this all is.'

'We need someone who can tell us more about the Baxendale family.' Nicholas returned to his brother's previous question. 'Someone who will know about relationships, scandals, whatever, and be prepared to talk to us.'

'That's easy!' Henry pushed himself to his feet to pour a glass of brandy, offering it to his brother. 'Servants. They always know more about the family than the family members themselves. If you ever wish to know anything about the Faringdons, for the past two generations at least, ask Marcle. Don't ever be under the misapprehension that you have any secrets, Nick!'

'There is only the nursemaid here with them in London. Sarah, I think.' Eleanor looked at her mama for corroboration.

'Perfect! Eleanor…would you care to pay a visit to Faringdon House again tomorrow?' Henry poured brandy for himself. 'On the pretext of enquiring after Octavia's health after her social introduction? And see if you can find an occasion to speak with Sarah.'

'But what on earth do I ask?' she demanded, startled at the

role suddenly thrust at her. 'Are your employers perhaps charlatans? Do they lie and cheat and——?'

'I will go with you.' Mrs Stamford rose to her feet. 'Come, my dear. It is late. We will think of something. And if words do not get the right results, gold might! In my experience, money will open a multitude of doors.'

'Well, Mama…' Eleanor failed to hide her surprise '…I shall certainly not refuse your offer. We will be able to enjoy another exciting conversation with Octavia about the state of her roses! If you will accompany me, it may give us the opportunity to distract her so that one of us can talk to the child and Sarah. I shall take Tom with me. What a cosy family party we shall make, to be sure!'

'Have faith, Eleanor. It seems that we have a mystery on our hands at last, rather than an open-and-shut case.' Henry walked with habitual grace to open the door for the departing ladies, bowing them out. 'And brother Thomas is beginning to look like an innocent pawn in an intricate and dangerous game of chance. More innocent by the hour.'

The ladies went to bed, deep in discussing tactics for the morrow. Hal and Nick sat on in the parlour, Hal deep in thought, a bottle of brandy between them.

'What is it?' Nicholas asked at last—his brother had spent the past ten minutes saying nothing, but staring into the fire.

'I have been thinking.'

'Never!'

Now he looked up, lips curving a little. 'The documents presented by Sir Edward. They must be false. And Aunt Beatrice's description of Octavia's brother…'

'So?'

'Little brother.' Henry smiled in gentle malice. 'Would you care for another tour of the gentleman's clubs and gaming establishments of London? And perhaps another informative conversation with Kingstone?'

'No. I would not!'

'I think this one may pay off. Just a hunch but… Say nothing to Eleanor. It would not do to raise her hopes until we have more concrete evidence than Beatrice's ramblings. Our aunt has more faith in her memory than I have. But I think…I just think that we may have been looking for the wrong person!'

Chapter Eight

At eleven o'clock on the following morning, Mrs Alicia Stamford, as promised, accompanied by the Marchioness of Burford and the infant Marquis, all suitably dressed for an informal morning visit, took the barouche to cover the short distance to Faringdon House in style.

'We must devise some means to encourage Octavia to bring the nursemaid and the child into the room. I doubt it will be too difficult.' Mrs Stamford settled herself in the carriage in a decided manner and unfurled her parasol. 'Since you have the baby with you, it would be natural to wish to praise and admire.' She removed the tassel of her embroidered reticule from Tom's inquisitive fingers with firm and well-practised skill. '*I* will engage Octavia in conversation. *You* may talk with Sarah about the family.'

'Thank you, Mama!' Eleanor's smile was wry. 'I am not sure who has drawn the short straw.' She distracted Tom from eating the fingers of her new kid gloves. 'I hope that she is of a confiding nature!'

As it happened, there was no need for devious plotting on the part of the two ladies. The morning was warm and sunny. There, in the private garden with its ornamental railing in the centre of Grosvenor Square, they spied Octavia Baxendale, her nursemaid and her son taking advantage of the mild temperature. Octavia sat comfortably beneath a tree, a little apart, a book open on her lap. On the grass some distance before her sat Sarah with the child John. High voices and excited shouts gave evidence that other families from the Square, both children and nursemaids, were enjoying the fine morning with childhood games.

'Fortune smiles on us so far.' Mrs Stamford gave her hand to their coachman and descended, all regal dignity, to take this crucial meeting with Octavia Baxendale under her control.

The ladies exchanged greetings. Enquired after their respective health. They had come, Mrs Stamford explained, to ask after the welfare of *Miss Baxendale* after the demands of the previous evening and her meeting the Faringdon family *en masse.* A most successful *at home,* was it not, as acknowledged by all. Lady Beatrice Faringdon had particularly commented on her enjoyment at renewing her acquaintance with Miss Baxendale. She clearly remembered their previous meetings very well, when Octavia had first made her curtsy, in spite of the passage of time. And had Sir Edward found it an amusing experience? Mrs Stamford had noticed that he played a skilful hand of whist.

Eleanor hid a smile and simply allowed her mother to continue unchecked. Octavia expressed no surprise, no recognition of, or response to, Mrs Stamford's subtle comments and answered in her usual calm manner. She smiled. Her eyes rested on her visitors with guileless acceptance. She was very well. No, she had not found it unduly stressful. Yes, she had enjoyed the evening, particularly her conversation with Lady Beatrice, who reminded her a little of her mother. So pleasant to have such a large family. Edward had said what an agreeable evening it had been. All so elegant and comfortable, as they had expected, of course.

Eleanor sighed inwardly and did not envy her mother her self-imposed task of bringing Octavia out of herself.

But Mrs Stamford sat beside Octavia, all determination, arranged her skirts and her parasol and set herself to entertain and elicit information. They discussed the care and design of gardens—of which Eleanor's masterful mama had limited knowledge, but yet approved as an interest worthy of a lady; and Byron's latest offerings of *Parisina* and *The Siege of Corinth,* both offered in the same volume—which she had never read but willingly condemned, as she did with equal fervency the infamous author for his scandalously wild life and lack of gentility, despite his elevated birth. There was no accounting for such aberrations in even the most well-born of families, she declaimed with a sharp glance at Octavia.

But Octavia had little to add beyond another smile and an inclination of her head. Nor did she claim acquaintance with the works of Lord Byron. Mrs Stamford quickly came to the conclusion that she had never spent so tedious a morning. Miss Baxendale might be a pretty girl with acceptable manners—no fault to be found in *her* upbringing, for sure—but she had absolutely nothing to say for herself. How Thomas could have married her, she would never understand! But then, she caught herself on the thought, she had to hold on to the conviction that he had never done so.

Meanwhile Eleanor, to the detriment of her figured muslin gown—but it was in a good cause, after all—sat on the grass with Sarah and the two children. Tom was intrigued, too young to enjoy the company of another infant, but content to crawl and to try to eat the daisy heads, which were opening in the sunshine. John ran about on sturdy legs, throwing a ball to Sarah when she encouraged him, but lured by the cries of the other children in the garden. Sarah allowed him to approach their game when the temptation grew too great to withstand, but kept a sharp eye on him. Octavia seemed unconcerned, deep in a discussion with Mrs Stamford of the value of auriculas for spring planting.

Here was Eleanor's chance.

Naturally enough, Eleanor tried to encourage Sarah to talk about children. Their ailments. Their diet. The needs of a tearful, teething baby and how to encourage an excitable child to sleep. It should have been easy, but Eleanor found it hard work. Sarah was, for the most part, monosyllabic. Not shy, Eleanor decided, so much as intensely reserved, although clearly knowledgeable about the range of subjects that they covered. She unobtrusively took stock of the young woman sitting on the grass. *Neat*, was the word that sprang to mind. Hair drawn severely back into a knot at the nape of her neck with no curls al-

lowed to flatter her face. Carefully dressed, without decoration
of any degree, but in good quality clothes. Fair skin, blue eyes.
As they talked she relaxed a little and was more willing to develop her answers to Eleanor's gentle enquiries. Her voice low
and well modulated, her speech evidence of a thorough education. And there was a certain confidence about her as she sat with
the sunshine dappling her hair and features, shining through the
leaves of the elms above them. Her eyes were reluctant to meet
Eleanor's at first, but gradually did so as she forgot her restraints
in conversation with the Marchioness of Burford. Her hands,
loosely folded in her lap, were long fingered and fine with none
of the roughness that might be expected in a domestic servant.

Eleanor was puzzled. And then realised that there was no
need. Here in all probability was a young woman from a good
family, fallen on hard times, and forced to take service as companion or governess with an established family. It was a frequent
occurrence, after all. She had Eleanor's sympathy.

Having wrung every possible detail from the topic of children,
Eleanor attempted to extend the conversation. To the matter of
the Baxendales. How loyal would the nursemaid be in the face
of pertinent questions? There was no way for Eleanor to know
until she tried.

Did she enjoy town life? Would she rather be back at home
in the village of Whitchurch? Did she find it very secluded there
or did the Baxendales have a vast acquaintance who might visit
the Great House with children for John to play with?

Sarah rapidly took refuge in monosyllables again, eyes downcast. Eleanor was getting nowhere, but persisted.

Did Sarah remember when Octavia came out? Was she in the
family employ? How long had she been with the family? Miss
Baxendale had said that Sarah was once her companion before
taking over the care of the child. She must have enjoyed being
in such a close relationship with her employer.

The Marchioness gritted her teeth. With no encouragement
from Sarah, it was fast giving the appearance of a cross-exami-
nation. So Eleanor gave up. If they were to learn anything about
the Baxendale family, it would not be from this girl who sat so

still and composed and *distant* beside her. And was intent on saying nothing but yes or no! But why did she get the impression that there was far more below the controlled surface, something that troubled the girl, her eyes strained, her lips pulled tight and thin in her otherwise serene face? It occurred to Eleanor that there was an indefinable sadness about the young woman, but there would be no confidences exchanged here, even without the social divide of Marchioness and servant.

They were suddenly interrupted by a squabble and sharp voices between the knot of children in the centre of the garden. Who should hold the lead of a lively brown terrier owned by one of the families? The result was much shouting and pushing. As the youngest and smallest, John came off worst. There was a howl, not of pain but frustration, when the children abandoned him to race off with the dog to their own nurse across the garden. John howled louder, tears of temper sparkling in his blue eyes when he could not keep up with their longer legs.

Eleanor watched the outcome, her interest caught.

Octavia did not divert for one moment from her discussion of herbs suitable for a kitchen garden, despite her son's loud expression of fury. Sarah immediately, without excuse or apology, leapt to her feet and abandoned the Marchioness. All her composure was gone in that moment of animation. She swooped on the child with expressions of concern, picked him up, wiped the tears away and promised a treat for little boys who were good and did not cry. The child's tears instantly receded, replaced by a bright smile of anticipation. Sarah nuzzled his neck, kissed his damp cheeks, John returning her embrace enthusiastically and beginning to giggle when she tickled him.

Eleanor's gaze became suddenly intent. Then she dropped her focus to her own child, who was attempting to crawl into her lap, taking in his dark hair and the promise of the striking Faringdon features. The differences were remarkable—there could be no denying it. So she stood, determined to seize the moment, smoothed down her skirts and approached the nursemaid who had set the child on his feet again, straightening his collar with loving fingers.

'Sarah. Tell me…who is the father of this child?' Eleanor bent to stretch out her hand, to touch the silky fair curls, to cup the soft curve of his cheek.

There was a flash of panic as the laughter in the nursemaid's eyes vanished. Sarah cast a glance towards Octavia, who remained unaware of any development. Then she gathered John up again into her arms, held close despite his sudden squawk of protest, as if she would shield him from some unseen physical attack.

'Sarah. I mean you no harm. Indeed…' Eleanor would have taken her hand, but Sarah stepped back out of reach.

'Excuse me, my lady. I must take him inside. He will be hungry…'

She fled, almost at a run, with a mumbled apology to Octavia in passing, and vanished through the doors of Faringdon House.

Eleanor picked up Tom, smoothing his hair reflectively. Sarah was afraid.

'I have spent so dull a morning! You cannot imagine.' The ladies were once more seated in the barouche, Mrs Stamford holding forth. 'She appears to know little and will say even less! Her head is stuffed with nothing but pergolas and French marigolds!'

'Sarah was even less communicative,' Eleanor admitted. 'I found out nothing other than an old wives' cure for an infant colic, which I would certainly never try on any child of mine! A poultice of common groundsel, applied to the stomach of the poor little mite—I shudder at the thought. But Sarah swears by it.'

'Which does not mean there is nothing to find out, of course.' Alicia Stamford turned her severe stare on her daughter, choosing to ignore the diversion into country remedies. 'Surely you could persuade her to drop some gossip about her employer?'

'No! I could not! What do you suggest? There is no point in scowling at me, Mama. Short of asking her if *Baxendale* is her mistress's real name, I could see no way of doing so.' She turned her face away, holding her son close for a long moment. 'But one thing is certain. There is some secret there that surrounds the child. And Sarah is not at ease.'

* * *

'Hal! You were right! I have found it!'

Nicholas erupted into Henry's bedchamber as the latter was putting finishing touches to his cravat.

'Come in, Nick!' His lordship continued to concentrate on his image in the mirror. He was no dandy, as he would be the first to admit, and was very ready to dispense with the services of a valet, but he knew that it was important to keep up some standards in London.

'A Waterfall, unless I am much mistaken.' Nicholas laughed and flung himself into a chair by the window to watch the operation. He was still in shirt sleeves and, although the morning was somewhat advanced, gave the appearance of not being long from his own bed.

'I like the coat—very Weston—and the sartorial elegance of the cravat is amazing for someone wedded to the undeveloped backwoods and social equalities of the New World. A pink of the *ton,* no less.' Nicholas smiled in friendly mockery. 'But that's not important! I would have come last night—this morning…it was only a few hours ago—but I presumed you would be asleep.'

'I was.' Their eyes met in the mirror. 'And don't sneer too loudly, little brother. New York may not yet be a centre of *sartorial elegance* as you put it, but neither it is the backwoods of anywhere. I can still cut a pretty figure.'

'So I see. And do the ladies of New York appreciate this jewel in their midst?'

'Rosalind has no complaints.'

'Ah. Rosalind. Is she a serious matter or in the form of entertainment?' There was more than a casual question in the voice that caused Henry to glance across from his task.

'None of your business, Nick.' Henry took a final glance at his reflection.

'Of course not.' He shrugged and grinned with easy acceptance of the rebuff from his brother. They knew each other very well. 'I only wondered if you had marriage in mind—to set up your own dynasty to inherit the vast fortune you are intent on making.'

'You will be the first to know when I do,' was the only dry comment he received in reply. 'Do I presume from your good humour that your efforts in the dens of iniquity paid off?'

'More than you could ever guess.' Nick settled himself more comfortably, one leg hooked over the arm of the chair, to regale his brother with the details. 'I managed to run him to ground. Our sly fox is a frequenter of White's, would you believe. And also the new establishment in Pall Mall—Whittaker's, I think. The place where the major-domo looks you up and down as if you might be up to no good and about to steal the silver.'

'So.' Henry anchored his cravat with a sapphire pin, smiling down at his brother's face, flushed with triumph. 'We have tracked him to earth.' His smile was not pleasant as he thought of the effect on Nell over the past weeks of fraudulent scheming. 'So what has our friend been doing recently?'

'He is not a frequent visitor to the clubs, but then puts in an appearance for a few nights in one week—as you would expect—when he escapes from his duties. He plays deep. *Vingt-et-un* is his poison. It does not need much skill—just a steady nerve, and our friend, it would seem, has neither. So he is in debt, I gather, to Spalding to the tune of 2,000 guineas. And perhaps to Robert Mallory—you remember him? You once bought a hunter from him—but I am not certain. But he owes something near to 5,000 guineas all told.'

'And where would he find money like that to pay off the debt?'

'Exactly. Shall I tell you more? I had a very busy night.'

'Please do.' Henry's eyes gleamed at the prospect of progress at last.

'It gets better. When I mentioned the name to Kingstone, he was an amazing source of information. It cost me a bottle of brandy, but it was well worth it. There was a scandal recently. We did not hear of it because I was at Burford and you were in New York. It involved a new young actress called Elizabeth Weldon. She was taken up by an admirer and had a child. Both actress and child were found dead in her lodging, their cause of death uncertain. Rumour connected our quarry's name with the girl, but there was no proof and his status would speak against it so the case was not pursued. But even so, Kingstone tells me that he is not liked. Hers was not the only name he has been linked with. It would seem that his appetite for pretty young girls is…shall we say, extreme.'

'Better and better.' Hal thought for a moment, toying with a silver-backed hairbrush. 'What you say does not surprise me. Aunt Beatrice hinted as much. He has a very attractive young housekeeper, I remember, with a pronounced invitation in her smile. Our esteemed aunt would definitely not approve.'

'Yes. Well, it would fit with the rest of the picture. And I only had to spend one night to get the information! Oh, and by the by, he drinks—to excess. Another reason for his being a poor gambler. Kingstone says that he has been asked to leave more than one club. His behaviour must have been vulgar indeed.'

'I am indebted to you, Nick.' Henry put down the brush and shrugged into the dark superfine coat which had attracted Nick's admiration. 'I think another visit to Whitchurch is called for. Tedious, but it will be worth it. Do you care to join me? This time Eleanor will be remaining in London, if I have to lock her in her room.'

'I will go to Whitchurch with you willingly. But restrain Eleanor? I will not volunteer to help—on your own head be it. Besides, she would forgive you quicker than she would forgive me.' Nick watched his brother closely, to see his response.

'I doubt it. The lady has not hidden the fact that she has a low opinion of both my involvement and my motives in staying to unravel this unholy mess!'

'Then you should not doubt it! The problem is, Hal, that you do not see what is under your nose where Nell is concerned. I thought you did not like each other at first. I admit I was wrong. Totally wrong. I am still not quite sure what drives both of you— or perhaps I am. In fact, I am convinced! But I know that you would not thank me for my opinions or advice.' With which set of blindingly enigmatic statements, Nicholas rose to his feet and made to depart.

Then Marcle knocked at the door and entered with a silver salver bearing a note.

'From Lady Beatrice, my lord.'

Henry sighed and frowned. 'Now what.'

He broke the seal, unfolded the single page and read the brief note of a few lines. And then re-read it.

'Well?'

He passed it on to his brother. 'I think that we have just dis-covered our pot of gold.'

My dear Henry,

I remember the name. It came to me at some inconvenient hour in the dead of night when I could not sleep, as is ever the case. Perhaps it came from seeing the girl and speaking with her at your evening on Saturday. Her name is—or cer-tainly was—Octavia Broughton.

I hope this information is to your advantage. I would hate to see the title fall into the wrong hands.

Your loving aunt,

Beatrice

'God Bless you, Beatrice!' Henry took back the note and stowed it carefully in his pocket.

'And the Devil take the Reverend Julius Broughton, Octavia's loving and expensive brother!' Nick added with some venom. 'When do we set out for Whitchurch?'

After Nicholas's departure, Lord Henry added a gold watch to his waistcoat and a signet ring to his hand, made to pick up gloves and hat, then simply stopped, standing to rub his hands over his face in frustration. Nicholas knew. It had become im-possible to disguise it. He had tried not to look at Nell. To touch her. To keep his distance when in the public eye. He had hoped, fought hard to hold his feelings in check. Not well enough, it seemed. Nick knew him too well. At least he could rely on his brother to be discreet. They both knew that they could not afford one whiff of scandal. If any word of an association between Lord Henry Faringdon and the newly widowed Marchioness of Burford got out to become the latest *on dit,* they would be all but destroyed. The censure of the *haut ton* would be damning indeed, for which he would never forgive himself. So he must guard his actions in future. There must be not the smallest hint of love or desire or need. He gritted his teeth. Nothing beyond brotherly affection and concern. But it was sometimes impossible when Eleanor looked so lost and weighed down by uncontrollable events. Or when she sparkled with courage and determination to fight back against the odds. Or when she smiled at him, her eyes glowing and her lips curving in just that way she had… Lord Henry groaned. In fact, it was simply impossible.

The morning visit to Octavia Baxendale at Faringdon House and her difficult but inconclusive conversation with Sarah gave Eleanor much food for thought. Sarah's protection of the child, her awareness of his needs, had been keen and instinctive. When he was in distress her response to him was immediate and loving. Quick to restore him to laughter. Whereas Octavia…she had continued her conversation after the briefest of glances towards the source of the youthful tantrum. Eleanor could not imagine being so uninterested in her son's concerns. But she lifted her shoulders in the slightest of shrugs. As Judith had been quick to point out, not everyone was blessed—or cursed—with strong maternal feelings. And, without doubt, the child was healthy and well cared for. There was no cause for concern for the well-being of Octavia's son.

The sunshine flooded the window embrasure of the little parlour at the front of the house where Eleanor stood, her own child in her arms, contemplating their uncertain future. She had been driven to rescue her son from his nursemaid in the nursery, to spend time with him, perhaps to reinforce her memories of Thomas and her marriage when the future had seemed so settled. So certain. She held the child close, enjoying the warmth of his small body, the grasp of his fingers at the neck of her gown. She rubbed her face against his, making him chuckle, so that those glorious eyes, not the dark blue with which he was born—indeed, they were now the most beautiful clear amethyst of her own— sparkled with innocent pleasure. Whatever the future would hold for him, she vowed that he would be safe. She could protect him and give him the best life that was in her power to give, what-

ever the outcome of Sir Edward Baxendale's assertions. And she
would love him with all the fierce maternal love that flowed
through her veins. The infant whimpered a little, his mouth
downturned as her possessive hold tightened inadvertently. Eleanor laughed a little as she loosened her grip and turned towards
the view from the window for instant distraction from tears.

'One day you will own a house as fine as this,' she told Tom.
'Finer, in fact. As fine as the King's own palace, if you wish it.'
Her cheek pressed against his hair as he leaned to stretch out his
hand to the world beyond the glass. 'One day you will own a
splendid bay stallion, just like that one.' She pointed as a rider
went past, the hollow sound of the hooves echoing on the hard
surface. 'You will ride as well as your father—all style and dash
and elegance. And you will look like him. I know it, even though
you are still so small. I see his dark hair and straight nose.' She
touched him with gentle fingers, savouring the curves of childhood that would disappear all too soon. 'Not his eyes—they are
mine—but those splendidly arched eyebrows. And the curve of
your jaw just there.' She ran her finger over the soft cheek. 'You
will be tall and handsome and when you smile the young ladies
will all want you to look in their direction. Just as I did when I
saw your father. You will break many hearts, I am sure—and you
do not care about one word I have said to you!' She laughed in
delight as she swung him round in a circle.

Then her thoughts drifted to Thomas, her husband, as the
baby dozed a little on her shoulder. The images rose before her
mind, crystal clear, finely etched, a painful and difficult mesh-
ing of contentment and grief. The morning she had gathered all
her courage to present herself at Faringdon House to enquire for
Hal. She had expected to be turned away, but Thomas had seen
her, invited her into the library to know the reason for her distress. Only to inform her that Henry had sailed two days before.
She had not believed him. She remembered as if it were yesterday the icy finger of despair that had traced its path down her
spine. She had felt almost faint with shock, disbelieving that he
could have left her, without word, without even a formal farewell. He had simply gone, in spite of all his protestations of love,

in spite of the promise implicit in his lips warm against her own. In spite of her giving him the proof of her own love. How empty his words must have been. How cold his heart—and she had never realised it until that moment when Thomas had said, 'But he is gone. Did you not know?'

Dear Thomas. Her lips curled sadly at the memory. His compassion and kindness had been overwhelming as he led her to a seat, helping her mop up her tears with his own handkerchief. She could not have expected such concern for her broken heart, but he had been open in his generosity.

And Thomas had married her. He knew that she loved Hal. Yet he had still married her.

Oh, Thomas. How unfair I was to you! She rocked the baby against her. *I gave you friendship and companionship, but I could not give you my heart. I never pretended otherwise, but I pray that you were satisfied. I think you deserved more. Perhaps you did love Octavia...but I can never accept that you would have treated me—or her—with such lack of respect. It was simply not in your nature to dissemble and hide the truth. We were always honest with each other.*

She brushed away the dampness from her eyes, determinedly refusing to let her thoughts return to her troubled relationship with Hal and his imminent departure. She cradled the sleeping babe more comfortably, humming softly, her cheek resting against his hair.

'You are so very young, still so unaware,' she murmured. 'And so you can never know your father—it will never be possible for you to grow up to experience for yourself his love and care. But I will tell you all about him when you are old enough to understand. I will never let you forget how splendid a man sired you, even though you will never be able to keep his image in your memory, and he will not know you as you grow to manhood.' Turning her face into the soft curls, she hid the anguish. 'And neither shall I forget. I shall remember him until the day I die.' Her voice was soft, even if the words were fierce. The baby snuffled and burrowed against her. 'You do not understand, but one day you will.'

* * *

Henry stood in the open doorway to the parlour. He had been standing there for some little time, having been dispatched by Mrs Stamford with an urgent request to her daughter. He could not help but listen and watch, uncomfortable at eavesdropping on so private a moment, but caught up in the situation. She was so loving, so tender with the child. The picture they made together, bathed in bright sunshine, gave them the glowing mysticism of a holy picture. Otherworldly. Beyond time. He would have liked to have walked in, enfolded them both in his arms in a symbol of love and possession, but could not, dare not, break the spell. He was shut out from this relationship by present circumstances and past history. His throat dried, his heart beat with a heavy pulse as he controlled the wave of regret and longing that compromised him with its intensity. Into his mind came the memory of the woman and the babe as he had once seen them, when Eleanor had leaned over the crib in candlelight and crooned a lullaby to a restless infant. The image was sharp, clear as the faceted crystals in the chandelier, and it rocked him to his very soul. Such love and tenderness between them. Henry was forced to turn his face away from the brightness before him, to close his eyes momentarily to shut out the promise of what might have been, and yet could never be. He would have retreated, leaving her undisturbed. After all, he did not know what to say to her and in that moment could not trust his composure.

Then, as he would have stepped back, she became aware and turned her head, a little startled. He had no choice but to continue with his errand.

'I did not mean to disturb you, my lady.' Eleanor apparently did not notice his hesitation. But his voice sounded strained, even to his own ears.

'You have not.' What was he thinking? His expression was bleak, the flat planes of his face stark with an emotion held in check. She hid her own discomfort behind a polite exterior, but could not look at him.

'Your mother seems to feel that there is urgent need for you below stairs. She accosted me in the hall. Some disagreement, I believe. She would not explain, but she is not happy.'

'Oh. My mother tends to see household catastrophes where they do not exist.' Eleanor managed a slight smile as she sighed.

'I dare not suggest such a thing. I think you had better go.' Henry's appraising glance took in her discomfort, her lack of ease in his presence. He wished that he knew why.

'It will be some trivial matter that Marcle will be able to solve without difficulty. My mama has a need to interfere!'

'I am aware. But dare not say that either!'

Now she laughed, the atmosphere lightened, as had been his intent. 'If you would ring the bell for Jennie to take Tom…'

'No matter. I can watch my nephew for a few moments without danger to him or myself, I expect.'

'Are you sure?' He did not know whether he saw amusement or uncertainty on her face as her eyes finally lifted to his, but either was better than her previous withdrawal.

'No. I can but try.'

She laughed again as she walked to the door, quickly turning her face away. How much had he heard of her foolish conversation with Tom? She was intensely aware of the hot colour that stained her cheeks, embarrassed by her vivid memories of a few moments before.

'Eleanor.' His voice stopped her. 'Will you return when you have dealt with the crisis? There is a matter that I need to discuss with you.'

'Of course.' She frowned. 'Should I be worried?'

'No. Not a matter of concern—rather one of hope. But there is something you should know that Nicholas has discovered.'

'Very well.' Eleanor tucked the child securely into the corner of a chair, supported by a cushion and, with the brief instruction to watch her son, left in the direction of her mother's raised voice.

'So.' Henry eyed the child with some disquiet. 'What do we do? I know nothing of babes. I suppose I can talk to you. Or perhaps I simply leave you to sit there until your mother returns. And pray that it will not be long!'

A whimper at the loss of his mother was the only response.

'Don't cry. Not that. I shall have failed and have to face your mama's wrath. Come here.' He bent and lifted the child with definite lack of expertise, but carefully enough, to carry him to the window as Eleanor had done. 'There—that is far more interesting.' He looked at the child, noting the features, his heart suddenly clenching in his chest. 'Oh, God! Thomas. I wish you had not died. You should see your son. So much like you.' He smiled as the baby blinked owlishly at him. 'Even to that innocent stare when there is mischief afoot. I predict he will be a handful as he grows—but with all the charm in the world.' The smile faded, his features taking on an austere cast. 'And his mother is exactly what you would have wished. I will care for your son—and Eleanor, if she will allow it. For both of them, as you would have done.'

Eleanor returned, the matter of responsibilities for ordering both household and kitchen candles quickly smoothed over, to see Henry in the window, holding the child. She came to an abrupt halt, much as Henry had done earlier. The breath caught in her throat at the unexpected scene. Both dark heads close together, some ridiculous conversation going on, which had caused the child to focus on Lord Faringdon with determined concentration and an instantly recognisable Faringdon frown. The object under discussion appeared to be Henry's half-hunter repeater watch, which he had opened to chime the hours and the quarters. Tom's frown suddenly replaced by a grin in which teeth were just beginning to emerge. He giggled at the bell-like tones.

She could weep for what might have been as Henry turned his head at her approaching footsteps.

'Eleanor.' The relief was palpable. 'As you see, I am entertaining your son. Not a tear in sight.'

'Thank you.' She was unintentionally abrupt, to hide the emotion that threatened her composure.

'You had better take him. I might drop him.'

'You look very competent.' She held out her arms, then turned her back, concentrating on the child, struggling to keep her voice light. Her heart ached. 'You said you had something to tell me.'

'Yes. It will interest you inordinately to know that Octavia's name is not Baxendale. It is Broughton. Aunt Beatrice remembered.'

'Broughton!' Eleanor became very still as enlightenment came to her, her eyes widening. The unexpected news overrode her wayward emotions and her discomfort in Henry's presence. She now turned to face him, features vivid with renewed hope, but still kept her gaze fixed on Tom's face. 'And so her brother? The Reverend Julius, I presume.'

'Yes.'

'Then…' she shook her head '…why did Sir Edward claim to be her brother? Why did the Reverend Broughton lie to us?'

'The details are not yet clear. But tomorrow Nick and I will go back to Whitchurch. The Reverend has an unsavoury reputation, it would appear. Nick has traced him to some of his London haunts. Debt is an issue. It might explain why he was willing to put his hand to documents so obviously fraudulent.'

'And you do not want me there.' She nodded once in quick understanding, but still disappointment.

Henry walked to the other side of the room, to put as much distance between them as was possible. He did not want to see the wild hope in her eyes. It was difficult enough to hear traces of it in her voice without surrendering to a need to hold and comfort her—in case their investigation came to nought.

'It would serve no purpose, Nell.' His words sounded cold, unfeeling.

'I understand. Whatever you wish, of course.'

'You amaze me, Eleanor.' Those well-marked Faringdon brows arched.

'Did you expect me to demand that I accompany you?'

'Yes. Nick and I thought we would have to lock you in your room.'

'I see. So you have already discussed the possibility!' And clearly not something that he wished for. Against her will, she was touched by amusement and decided to be charitable. 'No, I shall not be so difficult and uncooperative.'

'We could have the key to the whole secret by tomorrow night.' He tried to be encouraging.

'Yes. It will be a relief.' Her voice was colourless, disguising the thoughts that jostled in her mind, destroying the hope that should have been ignited by his words. *It will all be over. I should be overjoyed. My son's inheritance is safe.* She looked at the handsome man standing by the door. Noting the distance between them. Recognising his deliberate intent. *And then he can go back. Back to Rosalind. Don't think about it. Don't think about anything but the benefit for your son. Don't hope for the impossible. He did not want you before. He will not want you now. It is finished.*

Henry was shattered by the stricken look on her face, a fleeting expression of despair, seemingly incongruous with the news he had just brought her. Perhaps he misread it. Perhaps she was simply tired. But he doubted it.

He bowed and left. There was nothing he could do for her but unmask Edward Baxendale and Julius Broughton as the villains that they undoubtedly were.

He would do that, if he could do nothing else.

Lord Henry made the journey once more by curricle to the tranquil village where a malicious plot had been conceived and put into motion, accompanied as planned by his brother. It had to be admitted that he was not sorry; it was a more relaxed journey without the tensions and enticements of Eleanor's presence. But he had been more than a little surprised by her compliant willingness to remain in London, her uncharacteristically placid acceptance of his decision. Or perhaps it had not been placid but edgy, withdrawn, an unwillingness to be in his company, and he said as much to Nicholas as the miles sped past.

'She did not wish to come.'

'She seemed very calm about the whole affair at breakfast.' So Nicholas had sensed nothing untoward. 'You did not then have to lock her in her room.'

'No.'

Nicholas thought about it. 'You can't blame her. This will not be a pleasant interview and she would learn nothing that we cannot report back, after all.'

'No.'

But it worried him. Did she dislike him so much, a renewal of the hatred and contempt that had flashed in her eyes when he had first returned to Burford Hall? And if so, what had precipitated it? Had their night together, however unwise it might have been, not been what he had thought? She had quite deliberately refused to meet his eyes when he had told her of Nick's discovery, deliberately turning her back against him, when only the night after the Sefton soirée she had shivered in his arms. Arched her body against his and cried out his name with a fierce passion that had matched his own. And yet when she had returned to the parlour to take her son from his arms her response to him had been cold and aloof. He might as well have been a stranger to her. Women! How could a man ever be expected to follow their train of thought? He snapped his thoughts back to the present, tightening the reins, as one of the lively bays took it into its head to shy at a passing pheasant.

The minor skirmish and battle of wills over, his thoughts turned back to Eleanor whether he wished it or not. It was for the best. He could leave for New York with nothing to pull him back to England. No unfinished business, no untied ends, no tangled emotions. The bitterness might have dissipated from their relationship but, whatever Nick had intimated—and he was not perfectly sure that he understood his brother's comments—Eleanor was more than willing to turn her back on him as if there had never been any passion between them. So be it. It would be better so. There were no alternatives open to them under the law and it would be irresponsible of him to even contemplate anything other than a distance between them. Time and space would allow them to forget. To heal. Memories would fade. He would settle in New York, marry, produce an heir—and think of Eleanor merely as a pleasant if complicated interlude in his past, with no power to hurt or move him to unbearable need.

Not that time and space had worked any such miracle in the past two years! But it would. It must!

What could he possibly hope for in a future with Eleanor? The law and the church forbade any relationship between them, other than that of brother and sister. He set his teeth and concentrated on his horses.

They approached the pretty village of Whitchurch once more with its Norman church and cluster of tidy cottages. Past the Great House, still shuttered, where Sir Edward Baxendale lived with a sister and a baby—a sister who was not Octavia Baxendale. Or Octavia Broughton. And on to the Red Lion where Jem Abbott welcomed them, remembered his lordship and his open-handedness, stabled their horses and offered them tankards of ale. Henry refused and they walked the village street to where the vicarage was tucked behind the church in its leafy glade. No funeral occupied the churchyard this day to take up the Reverend Julius Broughton's time. It could be presumed that he would be at home to receive them.

The door to the vicarage was opened at their knock by the same village girl who had been present on Henry's previous visit. Young and comely, dark haired and dark eyed, with a flash of vivacious spirit and interest as she cast a less than servant-like glance over the two visitors. Her lips curled in welcome, her eyes sparkled with a sly flirtatious intent. She was very young, as Henry remembered, an unlikely choice for a housekeeper—but the house was undoubtedly well kept. Perhaps the Reverend had discovered a jewel. And yet, Henry admitted cynically, in the light of their knowledge from Kingstone, and Jem Abbot's knowing comments, perhaps housewifely duties had not been uppermost in the priest's motives when employing her.

'Come in, my lord.' The girl stepped back. 'The master is in the library.'

'Molly, is it not?'

'Yes, my lord. I remember you.' She gave him an appraising stare again at odds with her apparent role in the household. 'And could this be your brother? He has the look.' She dropped a pert curtsy and then with a swing of her hips she preceded them down the corridor and into the front parlour. 'I will see if the master is available to see you.' And left them, closing the door quietly behind her.

Nick raised his brows. 'I see what you mean.' He grinned.

'Not my first image of housekeeper in a vicarage. She is certainly nothing like Mrs Calke at Burford Hall.'

'Nothing at all! Don't let yourself be distracted, Nick!'

'No. I would not dare! But I wager that the Reverend Julius is, between writing sermons and burying the dead. She must be a great solace to him. Especially on a cold night.'

Henry snorted in appreciation and agreement, when Molly returned to usher them into the library with the sweetest and most innocent of smiles for the two gentlemen.

The room was as Henry recalled it. Bright with sunshine, polished with the faint aroma of beeswax and lavender lingering in the air, the books arranged with neat precision on their shelves. What had he thought when he had first entered it? The room of a scholar and academic? How wrong he had been. The gentleman in question sat behind his desk, light falling on his fair hair and finely chiselled features. Appearances were deceptive—they had been well deceived by the Reverend Broughton! Lord Henry controlled the surge of bitterness that threatened to choke him when he considered the results of this man's immoral meddling.

'My lord.' The priest rose from his chair, a faint but not unfriendly enquiry on his handsome face. 'How can I be of assistance?'

'Reverend.' Henry inclined his head in a cool acknowledgement. 'Can I present to you my brother, Lord Nicholas Faringdon? Nick, this is the Reverend Julius Broughton.'

They bowed, manners impeccable.

'I believed our business to be complete, my lord. I think I can give you no further information about the affairs of your late brother and Octavia Baxendale.' The priest's forehead creased in a slight frown, but the smile remained on his lips. He looked from one brother to the other for enlightenment, causing Henry to marvel at the man's ability to pursue the charade. How could anyone suspect a gentleman of such well-bred appearance and deportment—and a priest—of deceit and trickery?

'But I believe that you can.' Lord Henry's voice was cool and flat, revealing nothing.

'Very well. I will do what I can. Please sit. Perhaps I can offer you a glass of wine?' He stretched out his hand towards the bell-pull to summon Molly.

'No. This is by no mean a social call, sir.' But they took the offered chairs.

'So, my lords.' The Reverend Broughton lowered himself carefully to his own armed chair, his pale eyes moved between the two, but with no hint of discomfort or apprehension. No premonition of what was to come.

He is very sure of himself! Will he be willing to admit the truth, when we have no firm evidence? Only gossip and supposition that will prove nothing? Henry smothered the doubts, refusing to believe that they would fail in their mission. Too much hung on their success.

'It would appear that you have something of a reputation in town, sir.' Nicholas opened the conversation.

'I don't follow…' For the first time there were the faintest shadows of strain at the corners of the priest's mouth. His lips thinned marginally.

'I should tell you that after my brother's recent visit, I made it my business to ask questions in London.' Nicholas crossed one leg nonchalantly over the other. He might have been discussing the weather. 'Your name is well known, but perhaps not in the best of circles for the most altruistic of reasons.' He allowed his lips to curve in a faint but humourless smile. 'Some of my acquaintances were very ready to gossip about you, despite your position in the Establishment.'

'I fail to see… What do you imply, my lord?' Broughton picked up the pen from the desk, turning it in his fingers, as he kept his enquiry calm. 'My acquaintance in London is small. I cannot imagine that my infrequent visits make me an object of interest to anyone.'

'The word, sir, is that you are in debt. That you have a name for gambling, for hard drinking. And for unsavoury relations with certain women. Not what one would expect from a man of the church, I venture to suggest.'

'And you would give credence to such slanders? Accuse me without giving me a hearing?' The man to whom they had so casually tossed their accusations remained cold, austere, a man of principle, with just a touch of arrogance. He raised his chin to look down his aristocratic nose, his lips thinned with displeasure. 'There is no truth in it. And what possible bearing could this…this *gossip* have on your interest in the marriage at which I officiated?' The Reverend Broughton appeared to be genuinely stunned and outraged—until it was noted that his hands had clenched around the quill, to its detriment. 'It surprises me that you, my lord, would so willingly believe the gutter-sweepings of society gossip. Mere empty-headed nothings, without proof or conscience. And what business is it of yours? What right have you to interfere in my private affairs?' Broughton suddenly rose to his feet as if he could sit no longer, throwing down the pen as he did so, regardless of the spray of black ink that spread across the sheet of paper before him. There were high spots of colour on his cheekbones now. Of ill-concealed rage.

'I am not sure what bearing the gossip has yet,' Lord Henry chose to answer, his response as controlled as the priest's was not. 'But I think it will. You lied to me, sir.'

'Lied? I think not.'

'The marriage of Octavia to my brother.' He produced a copy of the document and laid it on the desk between them. 'It never happened, did it? This is a copy of your fraudulent document—bearing your signature—of an event that never happened.'

'You have no proof of that. On what grounds do you claim that the marriage never took place?' Cold anger burned in his eyes and he kept them fixed unwaveringly on the man who challenged his authority. 'You can have no proof!'

'No. I do not.' Henry admitted the fact with bland and unnerving assurance. 'But I do have proof that Sir Edward Baxendale is not Octavia's brother. That her true name is not Baxendale but Broughton, so that her name as written in the document is a fraud. And that therefore, I suppose by pure exercise of logic, *you* are Octavia's brother. If you are prepared to lie about that, then you would hardly balk at perjury over the matter of my brother's supposed marriage.'

Broughton had not expected this. His face paled, his breathing becoming shallow as he weighed the words spoken against him in such unemotional terms, but yet his voice calmed, his self-control remaining intact.

'A ridiculous notion.' He sat again and spread his hands. *They had no proof!* 'You can see the family resemblance between Octavia and Sir Edward. It is very clear.'

'No. I disagree. It is merely a matter of fair colouring. Indeed, it is the same as your own.'

'You have no proof.' Broughton fell back on denial.

'Oh, but I have.' Nick tried not to glance across at his brother at Henry's unexpected statement. It must be a bluff! He hoped it would work. 'Did I not tell you?' There was now an unmistakable undercurrent of menace in Henry's voice. His eyes were glacial and without mercy. 'Another lady travelled here with me today. An older lady. I have left her at the Red Lion, recovering from the journey. She claims acquaintance with you, Reverend Broughton.'

'Really?' His lips curled in a sneer of disbelief. 'And who might this ill-advised lady be?'

'My aunt. Lady Beatrice Faringdon. She remembers the Season when Octavia was presented into society very well since her own daughter made her curtsy to the polite world at the same time. She remembers my brother's flirtation with Octavia. And she remembers Octavia's brother who accompanied her to London. It was not Sir Edward. It was yourself, sir.'

'I deny it. How could she make such a false statement! It was four years ago!'

'Lady Beatrice has an excellent memory. She recalls that Octavia's name on that occasion was *Broughton*. If I escort her here, I am sure that she would instantly recognise you as Octavia's brother. She certainly had no recollection of Sir Edward Baxendale. Would you care to wager against it? As much as the 2,000 guineas which you owe Spalding? It would be a far safer bet for me than any wager which you might risk on the turn of the cards in *vingt-et-un.*'

Broughton said nothing, but sank back into his seat as if he needed the support, his hands clasping the edge of the desk in a vice-like grip. He contemplated the ruin of his life, spelled out in Lady Beatrice Faringdon's words of recognition.

'I suggest that this whole sorry affair is a sham, a cunning trick to take control of the Faringdon title and the inheritance.' Henry continued to hammer the nails into the priest's coffin. 'Thomas did not marry Octavia. You put your name to a false document.'

The statement was again met with silence. The Reverend Broughton took a deep and ragged breath as failure and social condemnation stared him in the face through the implacable eyes of Henry Faringdon.

'So, do we agree? This is not a genuine document. Or do I need to escort Lady Beatrice here to convince you?'

'No. There is no need.' The response was soft but quite clear. 'The document is not genuine.'

'Then the marriage never took place? You admit it?'

'The marriage never took place.' Broughton stared at his hands as if seeking an answer that would release him from the repercussions of his actions, but found none. His lips barely moved but he spoke the words. 'It never happened.'

'And are you willing to sign a declaration to that effect, sir?'

That brought the priest's head up, his eyes narrowed, a faint wash of panic.

'And if I do not?'

'If you do not, I would make it my business to spread the details of your dubious and scandalous affairs and your lack of integrity. I doubt that your position in the Church would remain secure in the light of such damning revelations.'

'Have I an alternative?'

'No.'

'Then I must.'

He pulled a clean sheet of paper towards him, picked up the pen, dipped it and began to write. For the next several minutes, the only sound in the room was the scratching of the quill on paper. When it was done, apart from the signature, Broughton looked up to find Faringdon's eyes on him. Questioning. Stark with contempt.

'Well?'

'Why did you do it?' Henry asked.

'Think about it.' Broughton laughed, a harsh sound in the sun-washed room. 'A fool could work it out—and you are no fool, Lord Henry. I am in debt to a sum far beyond my income. As your brother intimated, there is a shadow of scandal over my life. I am not proud of it, but neither will I grovel.' He shrugged his careless acceptance, without compunction. 'But it means that I am open to blackmail.'

'Sir Edward?'

'Of course. I am not the villain in this piece, much as you might wish to believe it. Sir Edward owns this living, which brings me a meagre income. Thus he holds me in the palm of his hand. To crush or to give freedom. If I agreed to support his claim to your family inheritance, he promised me security of tenure and money to pay off my debts and keep the style of life that I enjoy. If I did not…I would be destitute. He had the whip hand and I merely bowed to the stronger force. I would do the same again tomorrow given similar circumstances.'

'But now I hold the whip hand.' The curve of Henry's lips was not pleasant. 'So which is it to be? Sir Edward or myself?'

Broughton shrugged again. 'It seems to me that I am damned if I do, and damned if I don't. An interesting position for a priest to find himself in, I think! But I know that you will carry out your threat.' He read the determination in his lordship's face and gave a brief nod. 'I will sign to repudiate my actions.'

'Then do it.'

He did, with a final flamboyant sweep of the pen across the white surface, flinging the quill down at the end as if it burned his fingers.

'Thank you, sir.' Henry stood, bowed with heavy mockery and retrieved the copy of the marriage document and Broughton's written confession, folding them carefully and stowing them in his inner pocket. 'I doubt that we will need to meet again. I fervently hope that it will not be necessary. I will leave you to work out your own salvation with Sir Edward, and wish you well of each other.'

He walked to the door. Then hesitated and looked back.

'Why did you do it?' He frowned his incomprehension and his bitter disdain. 'How could you allow your sister to be used in this plot by Sir Edward? A young girl, easily manipulated by a stronger will. How could you allow it, even with the promise of money to pay your debts and a roof over your head? In effect, you sold your sister into Baxendale's hands to be used for his own purposes. It is despicable for a man to stoop so low.'

'I had little choice in it. How could you possibly understand?' Broughton was also standing, still the epitome of the cultured, educated cleric. He laughed bitterly. 'It is true that Octavia is my sister—but that is not all. She is also Sir Edward's wife!'

'His wife!'

'His wife. And has been for some little time.' The sneer on the priest's face was heavily marked. 'Which left me with no power whatsoever over his dealings with her.'

Henry looked at Nicholas, his gaze inscrutable, then back at the priest. 'So you told us the truth! You said that you officiated at a marriage at which Sir Edward was present. He was, of course. But not as witness.'

'Edward married her. Octavia's name truly is Baxendale. And, whatever your presumption, there was no force involved in her relationship with her husband. Octavia is a biddable girl and quite content with her lot. I do not believe that obeying her husband in this affair has been difficult for her.'

Henry weighed the words carefully. They had the ring of truth. It was easy for the priest to shift the blame.

'Then God forgive you, for I cannot.' He bit out the words. 'You have no remorse and deserve to be cast into the fires of hell. You do not know the pain you have caused to an innocent woman.' He turned his back and walked out of the Reverend Broughton's library.

Chapter Nine

'Hᴉs *wife?*'

Eleanor was incredulous, her voice rising, brows arched in amazement. Whatever she had expected from the visit to Whitchurch, it was not that.

'Octavia is Edward's wife,' Lord Henry confirmed. 'She was never married to Thomas. Your marriage is recognised in the eyes of the church and the law. You are, without any doubt, Marchioness of Burford.'

Eleanor and Henry faced each other across the morning room in Park Lane. The hour was nearing midnight, the ladies had already been retired for the night, the house quiet with only one branch of candles left by a conscientious Marcle to illuminate the hallway for the late arrivals. But on their return from Whitchurch, Henry knew that Eleanor would need to know the truth, no matter how late the hour. It would be cruelty indeed to withhold it. So, lingering only to strip off his greatcoat and gloves, whilst Nicholas returned the curricle and horses to their stabling at Faringdon House, Henry sought what promised to be an emotional audience with his brother's widow.

She now stood before him. It was clear that she had been awaiting their return, unable to rest, unable to sleep. He had not even needed to knock on her door. Now she waited, frozen into immobility, the heavy lace robe falling from throat to floor as she steeled her mind to hear and accept her fate. Her hair curled in a rich bronze mantle onto her breast, ends tipped with gold by the subdued candlelight, drawing his eyes to her soft curves. He could imagine that hair, as he had seen it, and saw in his dreams, pooling on his pillow, the sensuous silk of it curling onto his chest as she bent over him to lower her lips to his. He would have given the world at that moment to have the right to take her to his bed, to tell her the result of his journey as she lay in his arms, replete from the demands of his body, but pushed the thought away. Instead he stood at a little distance, watching her carefully as she took in the import of his words. Her eyes were huge, glazed with shock at first, but now the flicker of hope gave them an inner glow. She stood motionless, her mind focused somewhere far beyond him, weighing the repercussions.

'I thought you would wish to know tonight. You might rest easier for the knowledge. You can sleep again, knowing that your son cannot be disinherited.' He took a step back, away from the candlelight, so that she could not read his expression.

'Yes. Oh, yes. Thank God!' Without thought beyond the deluge of relief and gratitude that threatened to overturn her delicate control, she covered the stretch of Aubusson carpet between them and stretched out her hands to him. He simply had to take them in his own clasp. How could he possibly reject her? Drawing her closer so that their joined hands rested against his chest, even though his instinct warned him to keep his distance. But he could not.

'How can I ever thank you?' She tightened her grip, oblivious to their closeness, to his own struggle for mastery of his desires, and smiled up into his face. 'And my child? Is Tom truly safe?'

Henry took a deep breath in an attempt to restore some semblance of order to his thundering heart, without any noticeable effect. Surely she would feel the harsh rhythm that shook him to the core? But he kept his voice calm and unemotional in the eye of the whirlwind that prompted him to sweep her into his arms, to kiss her until all the sadness and heartbreak was finally obliterated. 'The child's inheritance is secure since you were Thomas's legitimate and only wife. The Reverend Broughton was persuaded to put his signature to his own confession, repudiating the documents presented to Hoskins by Sir Edward Baxendale.'

'Tell me why… How did it happen? How were you able to make Julius Broughton admit to such treachery?'

Henry drew her to the little couch, pushing her gently to sit and taking his own place beside her. He might resist taking her in his arms, but he would not willingly forgo his possession of her hands, which still clung to him as if he were indeed a lifeline in a storm. Her hands were trembling with the force of the relief, but she did not let go.

Henry explained, simply and lucidly, the content of the audience with Octavia's brother, the Reverend Julius Broughton, detailing all that he had revealed.

'So there we have it.' He smiled a little as relief and triumph chased each other across her lovely face.

'So. Sir Edward blackmailed him into forging the documents.' Eleanor frowned at the news, looking down at their joined hands. 'I did not like him. But I would never have thought him guilty of that. All the pain and turmoil he has caused. I know that he has admitted his fault—but I do not think I could ever forgive him. Or Sir Edward. Or those who turned their backs on me and wished me ill.' She glanced up, a bitter little smile twisting her lips, which touched his heart. 'You have no idea how vindictive I can feel when I think of the willingness of those *friends* to listen to poisonous unsubstantiated gossip. It shames me—but I cannot resist it.'

'It need not shame you, dear Eleanor.' He encircled her wrists with strong fingers, caressing the soft inner skin where the blood pulsed against his gentle clasp. 'A great wrong was committed against you. But it is over now. You must try to forget it and live out the rest of your life, secure in your social position, as if your status had never been questioned.'

'I think it will be difficult. I feel as if my good name and my position within the Faringdon family has been called into question and I have been left feeling—ashamed and unworthy.'

'I know it. But your family—those closest to you and those who knew my brother Thomas well—they never had any doubts.'

'No. *You* did not, I know.' She glanced up at him, a little shy, a little unsure.

'No. How could I?'

'Forgive me, Hal. I could weep.' She loosened one of her hands to brush a tear from her cheek. 'Even though the relief is great, I feel sad. Perhaps it is reaction. Perhaps I should be singing with joy!' Her laugh was a little tremulous.

'You need to sleep. You will feel better tomorrow. There is one thing, Eleanor.' His words were very gentle. 'It should not be a problem, but it would be as well if you were prepared.'

'What is that?'

'It may be that Octavia's son John is indeed the child of Thomas,' he warned, eyes sombre as he waited to see how she would react. 'We know that they were attracted and spent time together. But how far did their relationship progress? It could be that she carried Thomas's child before her marriage to Sir Edward, and it was that fact which gave Baxendale the idea to pursue the claim in the first place.'

'I see. I had not thought of that.'

'John could indeed be Thomas's illegitimate son.'

'Yes. Will it alter the inheritance?'

'No. The child will have no claim on the estate—indeed, there will be no actual proof of his sire apart from Octavia's own words. And how far should we trust her? I fear that she would follow Sir Edward's instructions to the letter without compunction. And Sir Edward could use the boy's existence to stir up scandal against the family if his darker scheme to disinherit you failed—as it now must.'

'Poor child. A pawn in everyone's game. Do you suppose anyone loves him for his own sake? He is very beautiful.' Eleanor remained silent for a long moment. 'If he is Thomas's son, I think the Faringdons should recognise him as such. And arrange an annuity perhaps.'

'You are very generous, Nell, and you humble me.' It took every inch of self-control not to lean forward and kiss away the furrow between her brows. 'Your spirit is as beautiful as your face. In spite of the agony they have put you through, you can still feel compassion.'

'He is only a baby after all.'

'Yes. Listen to me a moment. I think, if you are willing, we should try to speak with the nursemaid again. If we have some evidence to prove the relationship between Sir Edward and Octavia, she may be prepared to say more of what she knows about the child. She clearly cares for him and may be prepared to tell the truth. And perhaps if we met her away from the house, away from watchful eyes and the malign influence of Sir Edward. If I speak with Eaton, he will know if the girl takes the air at a particular time of day, and where. We should be able to waylay her without too much difficulty. Would you agree?'

'Of course. I truly believe that Sarah knows more than she is saying.'

'We may be able to persuade her, if she knows that it is for the good of the child.'

Henry raised her hands to his lips and kissed her cool fingers, first one hand and then the other. He could not resist. Even less when she smiled, her amethyst eyes glowing with an intensity of colour at the sudden restoration of hope. 'You are so very beautiful.' He turned her hands to press his lips to her palms, marvelling at their softness, the slender elegance of her fingers as they curled around his.

And Eleanor? The burning heat of his mouth against her skin made her breathing as ragged as his.

'Hal,' she murmured, closing her eyes against the feather-light brush of his lips, 'you are so very kind. To me. And even more to a child who may or may not be Thomas's son.'

'Perhaps.' She felt his lips curve against her wrist where he was pressing kisses against the pulse, which beat so hard that it took her breath away. 'But I do not think that I do it out of kindness. That is too mild an emotion.'

'Why do you care so much?' A whispered enquiry born out of the yearning in the depths of her heart.

'Because I…' he hesitated, aware of the words that he might have spoken but reluctant to break the spell of that intimate moment '…because I care about your happiness. And I suppose that I hold to a belief that every child has the right to know the identity of his father.'

She stilled, froze, the colour in her cheeks and the smile on her lips draining away. It was as if her blood had turned to ice. He watched the transformation with shock. And to be replaced by what? Fear? He could interpret the stark expression in her eyes in no other way.

Abruptly she pulled back, away from him, tugging her hands free.

What had he said? What had he done?

She rose to her feet, an edgy movement quite unlike her usual graceful elegance, backing away from him. 'I must go, my lord. It is late. You have all my thanks, of course.'

She almost ran from the room, leaving him totally at a loss.

Eleanor fled up the stairs, into her bedroom. She closed the door and leaned against it, her breathing uneven, not simply from her flight. She felt very cold, all the pleasure of the past hour destroyed by that one chance comment. She must think. Must decide. Dear Thomas—he had foreseen that some moment like this might arise in the unknowable future. And now it faced her.

What should she do? She could leave things as they were, the easiest option of course, Tom secure in his inheritance. Indeed, what had changed? Only her perception of the situation. And her knowledge of what was *right*.

Guilt pooled in her blood, her breath refusing to settle, cheeks ashen.

Every child has the right to know the identity of his father.

She pushed herself from the door to go to the dressing table. Sitting on the low stool, she pulled open the lowest drawer and lifted out a number of flat jewellery cases. The dreaded diamonds and other Faringdon family pieces. Below them was a small carved box, deeper than the others. As she opened it, it released the distinctive scent of sandalwood and she lifted out a silk-lined tray of smaller jewels. Worth a fortune, a king's ransom, but they did not interest her to any degree as she laid them aside without a passing glance.

Beneath them was a letter on thick cream vellum. Not very old, it was as clean and uncreased as the day it was written, the seals intact. Faringdon seals. The inscription, as she had known, was in Thomas's erratic scrawl. And the inscription was enigmatic.

Eleanor—

This is for Hal if you should ever consider that he needs to know.

She held it in her two hands, knowing exactly what it contained, torn apart by indecision.

What do I do, Thomas? Remain silent, safe in deceit, safe in the letter of the law? Or speak the truth and risk everything on the throw of this one dangerous dice? If the dice runs true, will the winning not be magnificent, worth every risk? But if it runs against me... What then?

She really did not know what Thomas would advise. Nor did she have any presentiment of Hal's reaction if she gave him the letter.

Somewhere in the depths of the house a clock struck the hour with quiet chimes. One o'clock. Eleanor sighed. Now was definitely not the time to be making so crucial a decision. With weary fingers she replaced the letter, then the jewels, back into the drawer

Whoever said that love brought happiness and contentment, she mused, as she took herself to bed, facing another restless night in spite of Hal's good news. It had brought her nothing but indecision and despair.

Now it threatened to tear her heart in two.

Discreet inquires of Eaton, butler at Faringdon House, elicited the information that it was customary for the young maid who cared for the child to take him for an airing in the park on fine mornings, before the fashionable crowd began to gather for their promenade. Armed with this knowledge, Henry and Eleanor took the barouche on the following morning to make contact with the girl. Whatever had disturbed Eleanor seemed to have released its hold on her, Henry noted, but she kept her distance from him, mentally if not in person. Approachable enough, but cool. And the shadows beneath her eyes were stark testimony to the fact that she still was not sleeping. Whatever relief his news had brought her, there was still something that troubled her. She would not confide in him, of course. So, waging a war against frustration, Henry decided to await the outcome of their morning's task and simply engaged her in trivial conversation and observations on their mutual acquaintance as they turned into the gates of Hyde Park.

They had not far to go before sighting the two figures whom they sought. Early as it was, it was very quiet with few interested parties to watch and comment on the scandalous developments within the Faringdon family.

'Stop the carriage,' Lord Henry requested his coachman.

They pulled to a halt near to where Sarah walked along the grass at the edge of the carriage drive, trim and composed as ever in a plain dark pelisse and an undecorated straw bonnet, holding the hand of the golden-haired child who attempted to pull her in the direction of the squirrels that hopped and chased around a distant stand of trees. She was laughing at his enthusiasm and inclined to follow his lead, but turned her head as the barouche drew up along side her and instinctively pulled the boy close to her side.

'Sarah.' Eleanor deliberately kept her voice low and undemanding as she leaned to smile down at the pair. 'A lovely morning for a walk. I think John would like to run rather than walk—at least he is still small enough that you can catch him.'

The young woman looked up, a fleeting shadow of concern crossing her features, but then as she recognised the Marchioness of Burford she smiled and nodded. 'Yes, my lady. He is always full of energy.'

Eleanor put aside her parasol and reticule and descended from the carriage without waiting for Henry to assist her. 'I would like to talk to you. It concerns the child.'

Sarah immediately stepped away, casting an anxious glance at Lord Henry who also joined them on the carriageway, and swept the protesting child up into her arms as if she sensed danger. Even, perhaps, an abduction.

'Don't be nervous.' Eleanor reached out to touch the young

woman's arm in reassurance. 'I intend no harm to either you or the child. This is a public place and you are in no danger from me. I wish you nothing but well. This is Lord Henry, brother to my late husband. You must remember him from your visit to Burford Hall.' Henry bowed, deliberately remaining beside the carriage. To approach might be seen in the light of intimidation. 'Perhaps you would consent to ride with us a little way. And then we will return you back to Faringdon House. I am sure John would enjoy to ride in the barouche. My own son likes nothing better.'

'It is very kind of your ladyship, but…' Sarah's anxieties were clear.

'Please, Sarah. It is most urgent.'

'Very well.' How could she refuse a request from the Marchioness herself? Reluctantly the young woman allowed herself to be handed up into the barouche with John ensconced on her lap, looking round with wide-eyed interest.

'We need to know, Sarah.' Eleanor took her seat and turned to face her as the barouche moved off at a sedate pace. 'You must know that it will not be to the disadvantage of yourself or the child. Will you help us?'

'If I can.' She was nervous. Her eyes moved from one to the other as she waited. 'But I do not understand what you could want from me. I am only the nursemaid, employed to care for the boy. How can I possibly help you?'

Henry's voice was gentle and full of understanding as he broached the issue. 'Let us be open and honest from the beginning, ma'am. You should know that I have spoken recently with Julius Broughton.'

There was now a distinct flash of panic in her eyes. Eleanor knew that if the barouche had stopped, Sarah and the child would have fled. But it was not possible so she simply sat, her hands white-knuckled as they clasped around the small body on her knee.

'I know that he and Octavia are brother and sister,' Henry continued.

'Oh.' It was little more than a sigh.

'I also know that there was never a marriage between my

brother and the lady. That, in fact, Octavia is the wife of Sir Edward Baxendale. The Reverend Broughton has admitted as much.'

Eleanor leaned forward to touch the girl's unresponsive hand where it clasped around the child. She was startlingly pale, but made no reply. There was no need. The truth was obvious in her face, in her teeth buried in her bottom lip.

'We need to know about the child, Sarah,' Henry continued. 'Is he Sir Edward's son?'

Sarah was silent for a long moment, studying the boy's upturned face as he laughed, enthralled by the speed with which they were travelling. Then she looked at his lordship, at his stern face but kind eyes. 'No.' She shook her head, compelled to reply. His eyes and voice might be compassionate, but she knew that he was determined to learn the truth. She made the decision to tell it. 'No. He is not Edward's son.'

'Then…is he…is John the son of Thomas, my husband?' Eleanor dared to ask the next question. 'Did Octavia bear Thomas a son out of wedlock?'

Sarah transferred her gaze to Eleanor's taut features, only able to guess at the emotion that surged within her at such a question, but could find no words to reply. She snatched away her hand from the comforting grasp, to hold the child close as she hid her face against the curve of his neck.

Watching them together, the light dawned for Eleanor. How could she not have made the connection? She had seen it before, and commented on it, without understanding its significance. It was as clear as faceted crystal in the morning sunshine.

'Of course,' Eleanor said softly. 'He is yours, isn't he? *You* are Edward's sister with the baby, who lived with him at the Great House.'

'I must not say.' Sarah's voice was muffled against her son's head.

'I should have guessed days ago,' Eleanor persisted. 'You are so loving, and caring of his needs. When Octavia was so uninterested—'

'Octavia cares nothing for him!' Eleanor's words brought an instant reaction. Sarah raised her head, lips thinned in anger, her words bitter. 'He is mine! Never hers! I should never have gone along with it. It was a terrible thing to do. I am so sorry…' Tears began to stream down her cheeks, as much in anger as in grief.

Eleanor produced a handkerchief and tried to calm the girl's anguish. Henry instructed the coachman to turn into one of the quieter drives where no one would be witness to her distress.

'Will you tell us, Miss Baxendale?' Lord Henry asked, giving her the respect of her true name.

'I dare not. Edward…'

'I will do everything in my power to protect you from Baxendale,' Henry tried to reassure her as the pieces of the puzzle began to fit together in his mind. Sarah's participation in Baxendale's intrigue, willing or otherwise, would prove to be the final key to the mystery.

'But I have nothing.' Her words were clipped and despairing. 'I need his protection. He warned me that—'

'We know so much already.' Eleanor tried to hide the urgency of her need. 'You must tell us the truth. It was a despicable thing for your brother to have done. I can see that you have been given cause for great suffering. If you will trust us, we can rescue you and make it right again.'

'Why not?' Sarah sighed, closed her eyes for a moment. 'What do I owe Edward now? I am so tired of all this deceit. It is true that I am Edward's sister and that John is my son.'

'Could you tell us how it was that you allowed your brother to make use of him?' Eleanor asked in her gentle manner so as not to distress the lady further. 'It must have been very difficult for you. Why did you agree to play the role of nursemaid?'

Sarah Baxendale looked at Eleanor for a long moment. Then nodded and began to explain the events which led to the deception.

'I was married to a naval officer, Captain John Russell,' Sarah explained. 'He was killed in action in the last months of the war against Napoleon. My son was born two months after his death—his father never knew him. The pension is very small and I had no resources of my own so Edward gave me a home and an allowance to bring up my child. I was companion to Octavia. He was very kind to me, you see.'

She bit her lip as the memories flooded back.

'And then he told me of his plan: for Octavia to pretend that she had been wedded to the Marquis of Burford, who had just died. And to claim that John was her child. Her brother Julius would provide the legal evidence, lured by the promise of a well-lined pocket. Even if he is Octavia's brother, he disgusts me…' Sarah frowned as she considered the sins of the Reverend Broughton. 'I refused, of course. How could I give my child into Octavia's careless hands? But Edward said that if I cared so much, I could take the role of nursemaid so that I could be with him. He threatened to…to turn me out if I did not comply. I would be homeless and without financial provision. I have no other relatives, you see. I did not know what to do. He knew that I had no choice and had no compunction in threatening me. But he told me it would not be for ever—perhaps only a few months at the most. So I gave in—for such a short time whilst we were in London. I know it is no excuse, but that is why I allowed myself to become involved in something that has filled me with guilt and a self-disgust beyond all bearing. I have shamed my own name and that of my dear husband.'

She dashed the tears from her cheeks with an impatient hand, determined to regain some of the dignity that had been stripped from her by her wilful brother.

'I don't think I realised that it would cause so much hurt. I did when we came to Burford Hall, of course. When I saw the effect of Edward's claims on you, my lady. But I closed my heart to it because I seemed to have no choice in the matter.'

She began to weep again.

'Mrs Russell,' Henry addressed her with due formality. 'Would you consent to tell this sorry tale to my lawyer, Hoskins? That is all that would be required of you.'

'I dare not face Edward,' she whispered in broken tones. 'He will punish me if he learns that I have spoken with you.'

'There is no need to face him, unless you wish it.' He looked to Eleanor for confirmation, an eyebrow lifted. She nodded, reading his thoughts. 'Nor will he harm you. I would suggest that you owe your brother nothing. He had no consideration for your feelings when he forced you to agree to so diabolical a plot against all your maternal instincts. We will acknowledge our great debt to you. You are free to live at Burford Hall with your son. Not as an employee, but as a guest. And the estate will provide you with an income. Until you decide what you wish to do and where you would wish to live. But you will never suffer for what you have done for us today.'

'No. I cannot…'

'Will you at least consider it? For the sake of John, if not for yourself?'

Sarah sat silently, looking at her son. She ran her fingers over his fair hair, so like her own, her lips curling into a reluctant smile when he looked up into her face and laughed with childish delight, lifting a hand to pat her cheek as if he would have given comfort. She would do anything for the safety and happiness of her child.

'Very well. I think that once again I have no choice.' She looked up, her eyes now clear and determined, and addressed Lord Henry. 'I fear that sounds churlish, which was not my intention. I know that I do not deserve your gratitude or your help, rather your condemnation. I have done you and your family a terrible wrong, helping to destroy the good name and integrity of your brother and his true wife.' She inclined her head towards Eleanor. 'But for the sake of my son, I will accept your offer, and thank you from the bottom of my heart. I will speak to Mr Hoskins.'

Henry took possession of one of Sarah's hands and lifted it in formal recognition of her intent to his lips. 'You must not blame yourself, ma'am. The wrong was Baxendale's—and you have now remedied it. My family's inheritance is no longer in doubt. The guilt is not yours.'

'And you have taken a terrible weight from my mind.' Eleanor touched the lady's hand in ready compassion. 'Your courage has ensured that the future of my son, as well as your own, is safe.'

If Mr Hoskins was surprised to see his noble Faringdon clients at an hour when they might normally be partaking of a light luncheon, he did not show it, but ushered them into his office.

He was unable to disguise his amazement, however, when he was introduced to the young woman who accompanied them. Why should the Baxendale nursemaid and the child at the centre of the controversy be on such terms with the Marchioness of Burford? She apparently was under no duress, but entered his rooms with quiet composure, holding the child tightly against her. He sensed a tension within the little group. But he did not express his speculative interest—instead he found seats for the ladies and fussed over a glass of ratafia for them and a brandy for his lordship. The child seemed content, in the short term, to sit on his nurse's knee and investigate the contents of the Marchioness's reticule.

Hoskins cast a sharp eye over the tall figure of Lord Henry as he took up a position beside the hearth with its smouldering fire. His reacquaintance with his lordship since his return from New York had given the lawyer considerable cause to re-evaluate the man who dominated the small room. If he had chosen to pay a visit at this time of the day, then there must be some pressing need. He remembered a young lad with vivid features, athletic build, and more energy and charm than was good for him. Always into mischief, but with the ability to extricate himself without too much difficulty. Always ready to challenge authority, to kick over the traces, but with a smile to win over those who might condemn him too harshly.

America had been good for him, Hoskins decided. Somewhere to channel his energies, without the rigid restrictions of birth and privilege to hamper his plans and dreams. Not for everyone, of course, but Lord Henry had done well. Confidence. Authority. Determination. They sat lightly on him, but made an immediate impression. He was still elegantly sophisticated in style and dress, still dramatically handsome, still capable of the effortless charm of his youth, but there was now an edge to him. Not a man to tangle with, as Hoskins had thought on their previous meeting in these very rooms, not a man to cross. From the look on his face at this moment, Hoskins would not have cared to be in Sir Edward's shoes. And as for the business with Faringdon and Bridges in New York, which his lordship had put temporarily into his hands during his stay in London—he would lay a wager that Mr Henry Faringdon of Faringdon and Bridges would do very well and make a fortune to rival that of his noble family in England.

'Well, my lord.' Hoskins finally took his own seat behind his desk. 'To what do I owe the pleasure of this visit?' He allowed his gaze to take in the ladies, but then returned his attention to Lord Henry. There was an air of anticipation here that he did not understand. He had no good news for them. There was no doubt in his mind now that Sir Edward Baxendale's claim was genuine. He frowned, contemplating the wound that he must inevitably inflict on the Marchioness, and wished that it was on an occasion of his own making. But she was here and he supposed that a final statement from him was necessary. It would not lessen the pain by drawing out the situation. 'I expect that you have come about the inheritance. A most unfortunate business, of course, as I have previously expressed. We have, I believe, to accept the truth of the Baxendale claim.'

'No.' Lord Henry spoke with quiet certainty, and moved to sit beside the Marchioness. 'No, we do not. The truth is this. We have undeniable proof, sir, that Baxendale's proposal that his sister was married to my brother and therefore that her child is heir to the title is nothing but a fraudulent sham.'

'Proof, you say?' Hoskins's frown deepened. 'I have to tell you, my lord, that in my opinion as your lawyer, the legal documents produced by Sir Edward are without question genuine.'

'No, they are not. They are fraudulent. I think that we should begin, sir, by allowing Mrs Russell to explain her presence here today.'

So Sarah Russell, née Baxendale, laid out before the astonished lawyer the nature of Sir Edward's scheme and her own part in it. Reluctant at first, with much hesitation, she grew in confidence as the enormity of her brother's behaviour towards her struck her anew. As she spoke, the persona of family employee and nursemaid dropped away, to be replaced by the quiet dignity and pride of both a lady of gentle birth and the widow of a naval officer.

Hoskins listened in silence until she had finished.

'I have kept silent when I should have spoken out,' she stated finally, impressing Hoskins with her admirable composure. The time for tears was past and she would follow her conscience. 'John is my child, the son of my late husband, Captain John Russell. Octavia is Edward's wife, not his sister, and she is childless. That is the truth of it, sir.'

'Well.' Hoskins leaned back in his chair, looking from one to the other. 'Well! I am speechless!'

He was rendered even more so when Lord Henry produced and laid before him on the desk the written statement from the Reverend Broughton, which explained further the source of the forged documents.

'So these documents…' his lordship finally indicated the ostensible proof of marriage and birth that had caused all the heartache in the first place '…are worthless.'

'Indeed. You have been busy, my lord. And very clever in your investigation.' There was more than a hint of admiration in Hoskins's shrewd eyes as he gathered up the documents.

'Not as clever as we should have been, I fear.' His lordship gave a rueful smile, 'We asked the wrong question. Or did not ask enough of them about Baxendale's family.'

'How so, my lord?'

'When we visited Whitchurch, the people who knew Sir Edward spoke of his sister and a baby, a sister who had lost her husband.' Eleanor took up the story. 'We did not ask if he had a wife as well. Since she was never mentioned, we presumed that he was unmarried and so came to the wrong conclusion. We thought the sister was Octavia.'

'I see. We have to thank Mrs Russell for her honesty in this matter. We are much in your debt, ma'am.' Hoskins inclined his head gravely towards the young woman.

'There would have been no need for the debt if I had been honest from the beginning,' she replied with shattering honesty, unwilling to accept a lessening of her burden of guilt. 'I simply hope that I have been able to make restitution, although the pain and grief will always leave its shadow.'

'Nevertheless, ma'am, without your courage, we would be unable to thwart Sir Edward's plans quite so effectively.' Lord Henry, who had risen to his feet, bowed in recognition of her admission. He smiled at her, a smile of great charm, hoping to allay her guilt. 'Do not be so ready to take the blame that your brother should bear.'

She looked up at him, cheeks now a little flushed, in gratitude for his understanding. 'Thank you, my lord. I hope and pray that you will indeed thwart my brother. I owe it to the memory and integrity of my husband's name. I have not done well by him, allowing his son to be used in so vile a scheme.'

'We shall unmask Sir Edward.' Hoskins stated with calm assurance, then glanced at Lord Henry from under his brows. 'So what is your plan of action now, my lord?'

'We need to see Baxendale. I suggest that you set up a meeting here. He will presume that it is to ratify his sister's position and the child's inheritance, and so will come without apprehension or fear of discovery. Then we will lay the evidence before him. I wish to be present. And her ladyship, of course. Mrs Russell if she wishes it.'

'Good.' Hoskins rubbed his hands together at the prospect of the completion of the unseemly business. 'Tomorrow?'

'Yes. Let us finish it as soon as possible.'

'It will be my pleasure, my lord.'

So tomorrow it would all be over.

Mrs Russell returned to Faringdon House with her son, to take refuge in the nursery, thus avoiding her brother and his wife, and to decide whether she would wish to be at that meeting. She did not know.

Eleanor acknowledged the relief that she could finally allow to sweep through her veins, as cold and clean and sparkling as a glass of the finest French champagne. She could hold her head up in public again, although she chided herself for allowing so foolish a situation to matter so much. The rest was far more important. Thomas's good name would be restored, no longer the subject of barbed gossip and sly innuendo in the clubs and fashionable withdrawing-rooms of the town. And her son... Tom would come into his inheritance in the fullness of time, as was his right.

Her cup should be full, her happiness complete. So why was there a shadow overlying her sense of achievement? Why was there a constriction, a tightness around her heart? She asked herself the question, her eyes unseeing of her surroundings as they drove home in the barouche, but she knew the answer. It was engraved on her very soul. Hal would leave. *Let us finish it as soon as possible,* he had said. She would lose him and her heart was sore. And, whatever excuses she could make to herself to explain away her behaviour, she was forced to acknowledge that she had not been honest with him

Henry watched the Marchioness in silence as she studied her gloved fingers so intently, wrapped in her own thoughts. It was almost done. He had fulfilled his duty as his brother's trustee and his success was on the verge of completion. The moment should have been sweet indeed. His family was secure and matters could easily be left in Nicholas's more than competent hands. That was it. His life in New York called to his blood and his imagination— and there was nothing to keep him here. No matter how much he longed to hold Eleanor and celebrate their triumph. The need to touch her as she sat with her face turned from him made his fingers burn. He accepted with the innate honesty so typical of him that the fact that she had rejected him for marriage with his brother no longer mattered, had not mattered for some time. Somewhere over the past days, his anger had drained away. He had loved her then. He loved her now. He would love her to the end of his days.

Chapter Ten

As agreed, they waited in Hoskins's office at eleven o'clock the next morning. Lord Henry, Hoskins and Eleanor. They did not know if Sarah Russell would attend. Perhaps not. It would be an unpleasant interview at best, possibly vicious in its outcome, and they had to accept that she might not feel strong enough to face down her brother, knowing that she was instrumental in his failure to achieve his nefarious goal.

Eleanor was nervous. But you cannot lose, she told herself. This is merely the final act in the tragedy, to expose the evidence before Sir Edward and thus accomplish his defeat. What possible evidence can he produce to refute the claims of his sister Sarah and Julius Broughton? She worked hard to keep an outward calm as she sat before the fire, resisting the temptation to fuss with her gloves, the strings of her reticule or the carved handle of her parasol. It could be seen, however, that she occasionally found the need to smooth her palms down the skirt of her deep blue muslin gown, and her cheeks and throat, above the delicately ruffed collar of her silk spencer, were more than usually, if becomingly, flushed.

Lord Henry stood beside her, immaculate and elegant in pale pantaloons, polished Hessians and dark superfine. Eleanor glanced towards him, intimately aware of his supportive presence, and privately considered him more devastatingly attractive than any man had the right to be. But that was not the first impression sensed by any casual onlooker. His face was cold, impassive, his eyes holding the glacial chill of mid-winter, his mouth grimly set. But when the door of the outer office was heard to open, and footsteps entered from the street, he leaned down to touch Eleanor's shoulder, fleetingly but with warm comfort. She looked up, unable to disguise her nerves as the muted sound of voices could be heard. His expression softened, his smile for her alone.

'We shall win, Nell. Never doubt it.' His gentle tones, his supreme confidence, warmed her cold blood like the finest brandy.

Sir Edward arrived to the minute of the hour, bowed into the room by one of Hoskins's clerks. As he walked in, it was clear from his demeanour that he had come intending to enjoy the final success of his risky enterprise. Immaculately dressed, well groomed, his blue eyes clear and smiling, he oozed confidence in the expectation of enjoying the Faringdon fortune through the enhanced status of his supposed sister. He bowed to Lord Henry and the lawyer with polished grace, his smile expressing magnanimous appreciation that he would win and they would lose and that he could afford to be gracious in victory. Then he turned to Eleanor, who had remained seated, took her hand to bow over it and kiss her fingers. Compassion was clear in every gesture, in the sorrowful expression in his intense gaze. Eleanor found the greatest difficulty in not snatching her hand away from his light grasp. Instead she gritted her teeth and kept her mouth curved in a semblance of a smile and hooded her eyes with downswept lashes. Henry did not even try for a pleasant expression, but regarded Sir Edward with a stony expression worthy of the Medusa. Although he gave the impression of arrogant assurance, he kept his hands clenched at his sides, eyes cold and flat, momentarily sorry that duelling was out of fashion. Or even if pistols at dawn were not an option, he would have liked to spread Sir Edward Baxendale out on the floor with a fist to the jaw.

Sir Edward, unaware of the latent hostility in the room, took a seat. Lord Henry did not.

'A delicate situation, my lord, my lady.' He sat with one leg crossed elegantly over the other, supremely at his ease. 'But I am

sure that we are all in agreement that it is time we settled the matter of the Faringdon inheritance. I presume that such is the reason for this meeting?' He arched a brow towards the lawyer.
'Then we can get on with our lives and allow the grief of the past
weeks to settle.' So accommodating. So reasonable. Eleanor felt
a sudden urge to scream her objections to her husband's name
being so vilified.

'Do you plan to remain in London, sir?' Hoskins enquired
with casual interest, as if nothing were amiss.

'My sister proposes to remain for a week or two at Faringdon
House. Then it is her intention to repair to Burford Hall.' He
turned his sympathetic gaze on Eleanor. 'Have you finally decided on your own destination, ma'am?'

'Not finally, Sir Edward.'

'And I presume that you, my lord, will return to America. So
much opportunity there for a man of enterprise such as yourself.
And Lord Nicholas?' His brows rose again in polite but pointed
enquiry. 'I think that Octavia will not wish him to stay on at Burford Hall. Or at least not in a permanent nature. Perhaps to visit
eventually… She considers that it would be somewhat…ah, uncomfortable in the circumstances. Until her position in the family has become more generally accepted, you understand. We
shall make our own arrangements for the administering of the
estate.'

And so all was to be very neatly arranged to Sir Edward's
liking!

'And I will discuss with Hoskins the matter of the annuity for
yourself and your son,' he continued with another sparkling smile
in Eleanor's direction.

'How thoughtful, Sir Edward. I am sure that I should be grateful for your consideration in the circumstances.'

Hoskins cleared his throat in a little cough to draw attention
back to himself. It was time, he decided, to end this cat-and-
mouse scene as he bent a fierce stare on Sir Edward. 'Before we
consider all these arrangements, sir, there is one small matter remaining for us to discuss.' Hoskins glanced up at Lord Henry
who had remained silent, allowing the lawyer to take the initia-

tive. His lordship could not guarantee the politeness of his words in the face of Sir Edward's overweening triumph.

Sir Edward caught the glance between them and his eyes narrowed in quick suspicion. 'Is there some problem here that I should be aware of? I cannot imagine what could now hinder the settlement.'

'There is indeed a problem, sir.' Hoskins lifted three documents from a pile in front of him and spread them on the desk. 'There is indeed.'

'Then perhaps you would explain—'

They were interrupted by a light knock on the door. One of the clerks from the outer office opened it to usher a lady into the room. 'The lady is here, sir. You said to show her in if she came.' He closed the door behind Mrs Sarah Russell.

Sir Edward turned his head in some surprise at the interruption, and then froze, the smile leaving his face. 'What is this?'

'The lady has some part in this discussion, it would seem, sir.' Hoskins rose to draw the lady into the room. 'She was kind enough to bring it to my attention yesterday.'

'I do not discuss my family's business before my servants.' Sir Edward's eyes were suddenly as icy as his insolent words, but there was a wariness in the clenching of his hands on the arms of his chair as he thrust himself to his feet.

'Then there is no problem, is there, Edward.' Sarah came to stand quietly beside her brother, to meet his supercilious stare with her own of sorrowful but calm acceptance. 'Since I am *not* your servant, the discussion can continue.'

'What is this?' he repeated, a tinge of colour now creeping into his face. 'You are my sister's companion and nursemaid for the boy. Why are you here?'

'You cannot continue with this masquerade, Edward. I have told Mr Hoskins the truth and my own shameful part in it.'

'No. It is not true.' He looked round, now uneasy, to assess the reaction of the other players in the game.

'Will you deny your relationship to me, Edward?' Sarah persisted, quietly but not to be intimidated. 'Do you deny that you are my brother and that I am no servant of yours?'

'No…no, of course not.' He looked across at Lord Henry and then at Hoskins, searching for a way out of the abyss that had suddenly opened up, dark and deadly and totally unexpected, before his feet. 'Yes, Sarah is my sister, fallen on hard times as a penniless widow. I have given her a home, as companion to my sister Octavia and nurse to the child.'

'And the child?' Sarah had no intention of allowing him to escape from the web of deceit that he had so carefully woven to catch the bright prize of the Faringdon inheritance. The web that had entrapped so many innocent people. 'Do you dare to deny that John is my son, not Octavia's?'

'You must understand.' Sir Edward grasped his sister's arm, fingers white, as if to silence her, and appealed to Hoskins. 'Sarah was overcome by grief at her husband's death. It overset her mind and she has never recovered. She came to believe that Octavia's son is her own, because she was never blessed with her own child. She needs sympathy…time to recover. The doctors tell me that there is no medical cure, only time and rest will ease her mind.' He tightened his grip so that Sarah was seen to wince. 'You should go home, Sarah. Octavia will care for you there. Let me arrange—'

'Let me go, Edward.' Sarah pulled ineffectually against the restraint, but Edward shook his head.

'Come now, Sarah. I will arrange for a cab to take you back to Faringdon House.' He would have pulled her towards the door.

'I suggest that you release the lady.' It was the first time that Lord Henry had spoken since Sir Edward entered the room. When Sir Edward hesitated, his lordship stepped forward with clear intent in his grim expression. Sir Edward allowed his hand to fall from his sister's arm.

'You do not appreciate, my lord—'

'We cannot accept this explanation, Sir Edward.' Eleanor's clear voice broke the tension between the two men as she stood to move between them. 'If Mrs Russell is indeed your sister, why should you imply that she is merely a nursemaid for the child, and treat her as such? When you first visited us at Burford Hall, you certainly gave the impression that she was a paid retainer, not a close member of the family. Besides, I have seen her with the boy. To me there is no doubt that he is her son. It could not escape my notice that Octavia appeared to have little interest in him.'

'You must not misread the situation, my lady—' Sir Edward tried to regain his composure, but his skin was waxy and sweat had begun to gleam on his brow.

'Enough!' Lord Henry intervened. 'The game is at an end, Baxendale.' He leaned forward, picked up two of the documents from the desk and tore them deliberately in half. 'These, sir, are your witnessed papers, proof of Octavia's marriage and John's birth.' Then he cast the pieces into the fire where they disintegrated in a shower of ash. 'This is what they deserve.'

'What have you done? They are legal documents.' Sir Edward looked on aghast, still unwilling to accept that all was indeed at an end.

'No, Baxendale.' His lordship held him, eyes resolute and pitiless. 'They are worth nothing. I know their true value because the Reverend Broughton admitted as much. In writing, so there would be no doubt, when he acknowledged that Octavia was his sister.' He lifted and held out the third document for Edward to read. 'I am certain that you will recognise the hand as that of your *wife's* brother. No more lies, Baxendale. I think we know the truth.'

Sir Edward's face was ashen as he stared at the incriminating admission in Broughton's recognisable hand. His lips twisted into a snarl as he witnessed the destruction of his plans and he turned on his sister. 'This is all your doing. How could you betray me? How could you show such ingratitude after I saved you from penury after your unfortunate marriage? I warned you of the consequences—'

'The lady no longer needs your support.' Lord Henry stepped forward to take Broughton's confession from Sir Edward's clenched hand. 'I believe that she would no longer choose to live under your roof. I shall make it possible for her to live with a degree of independence. Her duty to you is at an end as, I suggest, is yours to her.'

'Ha! You have come out of this very well, my dear sister. I should congratulate you.' Whipping round with a snarl, he lifted his hand and would have struck her if Henry had not intervened. With lightning reflexes he seized Baxendale's wrist and bore down, forcing him away from his sister, who had stood her ground, stricken at the unexpected attack.

'Don't give me an excuse to strike you down.' His lordship's words were low but none the less deadly. 'There is nothing I would like better, for the anguish that you have inflicted on my family as well as on your own sister.'

'Take your hand off me!' Sir Edward wrenched himself away, but made no further attempt to approach Sarah.

Shocked beyond words by the threat of violence, Sarah covered her face with trembling hands and began to sob. With a soft murmur of compassion, Eleanor moved to put comforting arms around her and to lead her to the door.

'I will take Mrs Russell to Faringdon House to collect John and then on to Park Lane. It would be better, I think. Will you…will you follow soon?' She looked anxiously from Henry to Sir Edward, caught up in the bitter mood between the two men, uncertain of the outcome.

Lord Henry nodded his agreement and smiled thinly. 'Soon. There is no need for your concern, my lady.' He strode to open the door for them, bowing with all courtesy as if he had not threatened physical violence a moment ago. 'All will be well.' So they left, accompanied by Hoskins, who would arrange a carriage for them, leaving Lord Henry and Sir Edward alone.

They faced each other across the room with its weight of law books and legal documents, the air still and heavy between them. As heavy as the unfinished business.

'Tell me one thing before we finish this.' Henry took up a stance behind Hoskins's desk. 'Why? Why Thomas? I presume your motive was money. But why choose to discredit him?'

'Of course it was money.' Baxendale had no hesitation in confession, a certain pride shining in his eyes as he expressed his illogical hatred for the family whose fortune he would have acquired without compunction. 'And Thomas Faringdon provided the perfect candidate. His unexpected death was most opportune. I knew about his liaison with Octavia when she was presented to Society. How he sought her out, and flattered her. He obviously thought her birth good enough for a light flirtation! He would have married her, Octavia believed, but he was warned off by interfering members of your arrogant family. So he rejected her because she was not good enough for him, her family not sufficiently well bred for a Marquis! He should have been whipped for his casual treatment of her! But, of course, that is not the way of the world.'

'But…' Lord Henry's brows drew together into a forbidding line. 'You would base this whole campaign, to discredit a reputation and destroy the security of my brother's wife and child, on something so tenuous as a flirtation that occurred four years ago? I find it difficult to believe any man of honour capable of such vindictive manipulation of a series of events that never even happened—that had not the slightest foundation of truth.'

'Why not? Your brother's death provided the perfect occasion for revenge. Octavia should have been Marchioness of Burford. Doubtless would have been if Lady Beatrice Faringdon had not stirred the mud in the bottom of the pool. So I would see to it that she achieved the recognition that was her due.'

'And benefit from her newly acquired status by association.'

'Of course.'

'And, had you been successful, Octavia would have had the whole Faringdon fortune fall sweetly into her lap.'

Sir Edward made no reply, eyes focused on some distant unpleasant vista, the muscles in his jaw tightening as he saw the destruction of all his hopes and intricate planning.

'With the financial reins in *your* capable hands, of course.' Lord Henry pursued the matter with the inexorable intensity of a knife edge.

'Yes!' It was a hiss of despair, of abject failure. 'Octavia should have had what she deserved.'

'So it was money. As simple as that. A desire to line your pockets with gold.'

'Oh, no.' The shrug, the sneer were unmistakable. Baxendale's eyes snapped back to his tormentor, filled with a cold hatred. 'There was nothing simple about it. Don't patronise me, my lord, with facile explanations. What do you know of genteel poverty, which grinds you under its unforgiving heel? When every coin has to be counted, but your status demands that you keep up a gracious lifestyle. Cushioned in wealth as you have been all your life, even though a younger son—what do you know of a father who drank and gambled away the family inheritance before dying in debt over a losing hand of cards and a glass of brandy in a gaming hell? A weak mother who frittered away what was left in meaningless luxuries. You have not the slightest idea!' His lips curled back from his teeth in a vicious parody of a smile. 'The house at Whitchurch will fall around our ears without an input of hard cash. The only way in which we could fund our stay in London now was through a small bequest from a distant cousin. And that is now spent to no purpose. There might be money in my mother's family, but there is no hope—' Becoming aware of the rising tone in his own voice, the uncontrolled outpouring of despair, Sir Edward snapped his teeth together to cut off the flow of bitter words.

'So you would cast the blame for your sins elsewhere. I should have expected it.'

'No. I will shoulder the blame, my lord. But necessity can drive a man to extremes.'

Henry turned his face from the harsh lines of naked greed and desperate failure. There could be no room for sympathy here. Edward Baxendale's glory would have cost Eleanor far too high a price.

'But the risk you were prepared to take was nothing short of fantastic. Did you think that no one would remember Octavia and her brother? Were you so sure that you could conduct yourselves so as to blind everyone to the truth?'

'Why not?' A gleam of sly cunning lit his face for a moment, displacing the bitter failure. 'After all, we nearly did it! If it were not for your interfering aunt, we would have carried the whole matter off in good style. People have short memories and mostly accept what they are told and what they see. No one other than your aunt thought to question my role as Octavia's brother. Scandal is the breath of life to many who would call themselves your friends. Like the vultures they are, they were more than willing to pick over the bones of the Faringdon family with gleeful enjoyment. If our luck had held, Octavia would have claimed the Faringdon inheritance and would be made welcome into society.'

And, although it sat awkwardly with him, Lord Henry had to admit to the truth of it. 'But after your confession, I can hardly believe that you were so idealistic as to do it all for your wife, can I?' He made no effort to hide the repugnance in his voice.

'Believe what you like. It no longer matters, does it? I think this conversation is at an end.' Sir Edward lifted his shoulders in an elegant shrug. 'It was worth the risk. And what do you intend to do? Drag the case through the courts? I doubt it! Think of the entertainment it would provide for the *ton!*'

'You disgust me. Get out of these rooms. And it would please me if you would remove yourself and your wife from Faringdon House at the earliest opportunity. No, I shall not take the matter further. You are not worthy of my consideration!' His lordship strode to open the door.

'Don't dare preach morality to me, my lord.' Baxendale did not move. The sneer on his face was heavily marked as he realised the depth of his failure. 'Your precious sister-in-law made sure that she ensnared your brother, did she not? She has been no better in her dealings with the Faringdons than the sins that you are prepared to heap at my door.'

'What?' Henry's hand closed on the door knob and was still.

'Don't tell me you did not know!'

'There is nothing to know.' But his eyes were watchful.

'So she has not told you? Well, I don't suppose she would. Females are always more devious than you would expect. And more mercenary, as exhibited by my dear sister Sarah, who has sold me for the price of her independence.'

'Tell me.' It took all Henry's control not to seize Sir Edward by the throat and shake him as a terrier would shake a rat, to wipe the contempt for Eleanor from his thin lips.

'Miss Eleanor Stamford was carrying your brother's child before their marriage,' Baxendale informed him, teeth glinting in vindictive pleasure. 'Of course he would have to marry her, as a man of honour, whether he wished it or not. Her birth is no more distinguished than Octavia's. A respectable gentry family, but with no claim to aristocratic supremacy. But Miss Stamford won the prize. You did not know?' He sneered again as he read correctly the tightening of muscles in Lord Henry's jaw. 'Ask her how long after the bridal nuptials the child was born, my lord. You were in New York and so would not see the clever scheme being unfolded. She and her ambitiously devious mother were determined to get the Marquis before the altar. Your dear brother was well and truly trapped by a beautiful face and the promise of a bastard if he did not act quickly. So he married her.' Sir Edward shrugged again. 'So don't talk to me about plotting and intrigue!'

'Your unsubstantiated opinions do you no credit.' There was barely a hesitation before Henry collected his scattered wits and replied, 'The Marchioness is a lady of unquestionable integrity and principle. If I discover that you have spread such gossip around town, I shall have no hesitation in making it a matter of law. Believe it, sir, before you choose to meddle further in the concerns of my family.'

He flung open the door and bowed, coldly and formally, the merest inclination of his head. But his thoughts were in a turmoil.

Hoskins returned, having delivered the ladies to a waiting cab. As he approached the open doorway, Sir Edward pushed his way past to storm out of the room.

'Get out of my way!'

They watched as he stalked to the door leading on to the street, flinging it back so that it hammered against the wall. Hoskins glanced at Lord Henry with raised brows.

'Let him go,' Lord Henry answered the silent question. 'He has no more demands on my family.' His voice was firm but a little weary as he eased his shoulders against the strain.

'What do you wish, my lord? To pursue the matter through the courts? To obtain recompense? I have to say that I don't advise it.'

'No. Let the matter die a natural death. I don't wish to provide the scandalmongers with any more salacious detail to discuss. I will make provision for Mrs Russell. The Baxendales will doubtless retire from town—I doubt that we shall see them again in the near future. They would not wish to draw further attention to themselves. And I believe that the Reverend Broughton's membership of White's will also lapse!' Lord Henry showed his teeth, more of a snarl than a smile. 'It will give me considerable pleasure to ensure that a man capable of such immoral dealings is no longer received at a gentleman's club.'

Hoskins was moved to smile at the prospect. 'It was well done, my lord.'

'Yes. And I have to thank you for your timely support.'

He left the lawyer's rooms with a lightening of the heart, but he could not dislodge a persistent worry that kept him on edge. He could not quite banish Edward Baxendale's final accusations from his mind. A sour note that spoilt his sense of completion. Baxendale had been mischief-making, of course. Eleanor would never stoop to such devious means. Surely she would never deliberately use the conception of a child to force his brother into a marriage—simply to ensure a glittering title and untold wealth. He would never believe it of her. And yet the malicious words, delivered in Baxendale's smooth, sly voice would not quite go away.

The Faringdon family chose to gather once more in the intimate family parlour in Park Lane. Sarah Russell, returning earlier with Eleanor, had retired to a guest bedchamber with her son and one of the maids who would look to their needs and act a nursemaid for the distraught but determined lady. Exhaustion had finally taken its toll. Although she had recovered from her bout of tears, she did not feel capable of sitting down with all the members of the family whom her brother had so ruthlessly pursued and exploited in his desire for wealth and revenge.

Exhaustion also laid its hand on the other individuals who came together to discuss and marvel at the recent development. There was a strange sense of emptiness, of anticlimax, Eleanor thought as she sank onto the sofa. She felt tired, but could not rest, could not quite accept that Sir Edward and Octavia no longer had any right to oust her from her home and rob her son of his birthright and herself of her widow's jointure. And there was a tension here, particularly in Henry, that she could not quite pinpoint. Perhaps she was simply tired, as were they all. Perhaps it was all imagination. The morning would bring calm and a sense of rightness and completion.

'What do you suppose Baxendale will do now?' Nicholas lounged in a chair to the detriment of his coat and yawned.

'Go back to the Great House in Whitchurch and live out his days in disillusioned reflection of what might have been, I presume.' Henry frowned as he leafed through a handful of letters that had been delivered that morning and were so far unopened. 'And his wife with him. And I expect he will find an excellent excuse to terminate the Reverend Julius's tenure of the living of St Michael and All Angels. I find that I cannot feel sorry.' His stern face was made no more approachable by the sardonic smile that touched his mouth. 'The wages of sin for our devious vicar could be homelessness and poverty.'

'And quite right, too. It is a disgrace that such a man should have a care of souls. I can find no Christian charity for him in my heart.' Mrs Stamford cast a sharp look at her companions, daring anyone to disagree with her.

No one did.

'I wonder what Octavia is thinking?' Eleanor picked up a forgotten piece of embroidery and instantly put it down again with nervous fingers. 'Nothing seemed to move or disturb her very much. Perhaps she does not care very deeply about the outcome. I doubt that she will miss John.'

'Her brother Julius suggested that she simply did whatever Edward told her to do, and was not unhappy with the situation,' Nicholas remembered with a twist of distaste to his mouth.

'I think they will not return to London any time in the near future,' Mrs Stamford gave her opinion. She was the only one of the little group with any energy about her. It burned in her face, in her eyes, a vindictive sense of triumph that flushed her narrow features with bright colour. 'Octavia will be able to return to her beloved rose arbours and trellises. I think that polite society would not make them welcome again if they knew the full story.'

'Perhaps. I think I do feel a little sorry for Octavia. Her life seemed to be so empty.'

'You should not, Eleanor.' Mrs Stamford's voice was sharp, her fixed gaze condemning. '*You* were the victim. The Baxendales deserve no sympathy, no compassion whatsoever. How can you even think it? What thought did they give for your comfort? None! They would have stripped you of your name, your title and your home.' She drew in a breath as she sought to control her damning words. 'But you are now vindicated, my love. And the dear child. What a terrible few weeks we have had, to be sure. I am quite worn to the bone.'

'I valued your support, Mama. It was not inconsiderable.'

'Of course. When would any mother not do all in her power to safeguard the future of her daughter?' Then, on a thought, 'Should we inform Lady Beatrice of the outcome? And the Countess of Painscastle? And perhaps some of our closest friends? Such as the Carstairses. We should not risk you being snubbed again, Eleanor, by those who are still motivated by ignorance or cruel inaccuracies.'

'No,' three voices answered in unison.

'I will not gossip about such private, family matters, Mama. It is not good *ton*.' Eleanor shuddered at the prospect, but her tone was decisive, all dignity. 'Let us simply leave it and forget it ever happened. I forbid you to be the source of any further scandal.'

Mrs Stamford flushed. 'Very well. If that is your wish. But I—' She caught her daughter's eye. 'Very well. But you should give thanks for your release from Sir Edward's clutches.'

Nicholas yawned again. 'We do—we do indeed.' He pushed himself to his feet. 'I feel as tired as if I have experienced a week of bad hunting, all hard runs, heavy going, a poor scent and nothing to show for it in the end.' He stretched his shoulders. 'But at least I need never darken the doors of a gaming hell again.'

'You have all my thanks, Nick.' Henry stood to grasp his brother's shoulder in gratitude.

'My pleasure.' He yawned once more and shook his head. 'I am going down to the stables—I need a ride, fresh air, easy conversation. Care to accompany me?'

'Later, perhaps.'

'I shall go and check on dear Tom.' Mrs Stamford, still a little put out, followed Nicholas to the door. 'At least he is too young to realise the dangers and be affected by them.'

Eleanor and Henry were left alone. She wanted more than anything to thank him, to express her gratitude for his strength and active support over the past days, but he seemed edgy and distant, fraught with an energy that made no sense to Eleanor. It was *not* her imagination. She did not know what to do or what to say.

'I would thank you—'

'I do not want your gratitude. We have had this conversation before.'

Eleanor flushed, remembering the occasion far too well, yet persisted. 'You have it anyway.'

Impatience lent his tongue an edge that startled her. 'Forget the whole episode, Eleanor. You have what you wanted. The title for your son. The estate is secure with the entail. The income from it will allow you to live in luxury. One day you may feel able to marry again. There is no more to be said—let that be an end to it.'

'Hal…'

She could think of no suitable reply, her mind a blank. This was not what she had expected or wanted. Why was he so brusque? What had she done? Silence lengthened between them as, with an intolerant shrug, Lord Henry put distance between them to stare unseeingly down into the remains of a fire. He tried to block out Edward's words. What the hell should he say to her? If Baxendale had intended to cause dissension between them, he was succeeding beyond his wildest dreams! Henry cursed himself silently. What a fool he was. Turning his head, he looked across at her, acutely aware of her troubled expression and confusion. And he grimaced at his own lack of finesse in handling her. He stood upright, his back to the marble fire surround and tried to put matters right between them.

'Forgive my ill temper. You are the last person who should be called on to suffer it. I have no excuse other than a surfeit of legal complications and Baxendale's sly smile!'

'Of course.' The taut muscles in Eleanor's neck and shoulders began to relax just a little. 'Don't apologise—there is no need' The weight on her heart began to lift just a little. 'Now you will go back.' A statement, not a query.

'Yes.'

'How long before you leave us?'

'I shall try for a passage next week from Liverpool.'

'Mr Bridges will be relieved to see you at last. He must have quite given you up, believing you lost to the dens of iniquity in London.' She tried to keep the tone light. A brief smile illuminated her face, forcing him to look away as he replied. Otherwise he might be driven against his better judgement to take her into his arms and kiss her until she sighed and melted against him. And then where would they be? He swore silently again, but his response was mild.

'Yes. I think he is beleaguered by business. He prefers action to figures.'

'Will Rosalind welcome you home?'

'She might.'

There was a moment of uncomfortable silence. Then,

'Tell me when you know of your departure. Otherwise I think I will take Tom back to Burford Hall. I have had my fill of London for the present, and I have no wish to live at Faringdon House yet. I will take Mrs Russell with me and see to her comfort—I expect she and the boy will enjoy life in the country.'

'Of course. Nick will see to any financial matters and your comfort.'

'He is very capable.'

'He enjoys it. If you will excuse me, my lady, I have some letters to write.'

Eleanor sighed inwardly. So coldly formal. Whatever the problem, it still troubled him. And the rift between them was as wide and as bottomless as it had ever been.

'To be sure.'

He looked at her, a searching glance that revealed nothing of his thoughts. Then, with a curt bow of the head, he turned and walked away from her, as she knew he would.

She had no right to call him back.

Edward Baxendale's bitter accusations against Eleanor refused to be banished from Henry's mind. Had she indeed trapped Thomas into an unwanted marriage with a child conceived out of wedlock? Without doubt, it would not be the first time that such a ploy had been used by an unscrupulous woman to gain a foothold into a noble family. But Eleanor? Never! And yet, how could he possibly discover the truth of it, if only to put his mind at ease. He could hardly ask Eleanor herself. Had she after all rejected him with the sole purpose of luring his brother into a far more advantageous union? Henry had decided that it no longer mattered, his love for her was absolute, no matter what had driven her to turn her back on him. But if she had used the child to spring the trap on his brother? He shook his head in disbelief. It simply did not fit with his image of her.

But sharp-edged doubts assailed him and refused to let up, and a far sharper edge that he should even contemplate questioning her honesty. He cursed himself for harbouring such doubts—but they remained. And there was no doubt, he knew in his heart, that Eleanor's doting mama would be prepared to take any step that would ensure the well-being of her daughter. He had heard such words from her own lips. How could he forget her almost unseemly delight over Edward Baxendale's fall from grace and Eleanor's social reinstatement?

He paced the morning room, self-disgust riding him with sharp spurs, his unfinished letter to Nathaniel Bridges lying forgotten on the desk as he wrestled on the one hand with his conscience, which insisted that Eleanor's honesty should not be questioned, and on the other the distrust created by Baxendale's vicious and well-aimed words. He loved Eleanor. By God, he did, beyond all thought and reason. But it might be that he had at last learned the truth behind her failure to join him on his voyage, committing her future irrevocably to his. Who could he possibly ask to gain further enlightenment? Whatever happened, he must do nothing to create more scandal, to spread any further shadow over Eleanor's name.

His head came up as he heard Nicholas's riding boots echo on the tiled floor of the entrance hall. Here was the only member of the family with whom he could share his thoughts. And even then, not totally. He opened the door and stepped out.

'Hal.' Nicholas swung round. 'Are you coming after all?'

'No.' He grimaced. 'Much as I would like to. Too much neglected business. Nat Bridges will write me off as dead!'

'Well, if you will sully your hands with buying and selling and the acquisition of something as common as money! By the by, I would not say it in front of the ladies, but…congratulations!'

Henry's brow arched in silent query.

'On burying the Baxendale plot so effectively…and without any fuss.'

'I would have dearly enjoyed burying Baxendale himself!' Henry smiled wryly at the prospect. 'You will never know how difficult it was to keep my hands from his throat when he tried to throw the blame in any direction but on himself, his own greed and ambition.'

'I expect it tapped the depths of self-control. Not something you used to be famous for!'

'It did. It was still hard. A sharp right to the jaw would have been much more in my line. Or even the use of a riding whip across his shoulders. He deserves far worse for what he did.'

Nicholas continued to head to the door, picking up whip and gloves from a side table.

'Nick…'

'Hmm?'

'Tell me…tell me about Eleanor and Thomas. Were they happy?'

'Now there's a strange question.' It stopped Nicholas in his tracks and he swung round to face his brother. 'Yes. To my knowledge. They seemed so.'

'Why did Thomas marry her?'

'An even stranger question!' He slanted a quizzical glance at Henry's face, but was unable to read the shuttered expression. 'I don't know. Speak with Eleanor if it matters. I don't advise it, though. Nell is a very…a very private person.'

'No. I wouldn't, of course.' He followed Nick to the door, unable to let the matter drop. 'It's just…'

'Something Baxendale said?'

'Yes. You are amazingly astute, little brother.'

'I am always astute, if you did but notice. But it's simply a matter of logic. Was it simply mischief-making?'

'I expect so.'

'Want to tell me about it?'

'No. I am not proud of my doubts! It will be best if I keep his poisonous words to myself, I think.'

'To share them could draw the poison. I can be a willing listener.' Nick angled his head, waiting for the reply. He had not often seen his brother so troubled.

'But not if it causes pain and even more hurt.' Henry frowned at the problem.

'True.' Nick shrugged slightly. 'Then you must perforce bear the burden alone. Do you want my advice?'

'I think I can guess.'

'Then forget it, Hal.' Nicholas for once was deadly serious. 'His intentions will have been malicious, for sure. How could you expect him to tell the truth about anything? You should not waste one moment's thought on any accusations he made. And certainly not anything concerning Thomas and Eleanor. Baxendale would be overjoyed if he knew that he had been successful in destroying your peace of mind. Don't let him!'

'Sage advice.' Henry turned as if to retrace his steps to the morning room, then with second thoughts, looked back. 'Was it a love match?' he asked bluntly.

'Well, if we are returning to Nell and Thomas…' Nick huffed out a breath and thought for a moment. 'Yes. They were attracted. The marriage was certainly arranged quickly. Perhaps not a grand passion, I would have thought. But they were happy enough together. They talked to each other, laughed together. You know…'

'And the child?'

'That's easy.' Nick smiled, a little sadly, as the memories crowded in, of happier times before his brother's death. 'Thomas doted on him. Very proud. As he should be. He was already planning when to teach him to ride and to shoot duck on the lake at Burford Levels, even though he was barely a year old. I never thought of Thomas in a paternal role, but it suited him. Why?'

'Nothing. I simply wanted to know.' Henry decide there was nothing more that he could ask.

'Problems?'

'No. Of course not.'

'Good.' On a decision, Nicholas stalked across the hall and took his brother by the arm. 'Come to the stables. Leave your letters for the afternoon—they will still be there tonight! Time you had some light relief.'

'Very well.' Henry smiled a little wearily, gave in and allowed himself to be led, grateful to have his mind taken from the suspicions that beset him. Perhaps Nicholas's remedy would push everything back into perspective for him and then he could be at ease again. At ease with Eleanor. 'Forgive me, Nick. I seem to have got into the habit of questioning everybody and everything—looking for shadows when they do not exist.'

'And very uncomfortable for us all it is, too. You need a drink and some convivial company.'

'True.'

'Easily done. Come with me.'

So much for business. Henry shut the door on the morning room and the affairs of Faringdon and Bridges and accompanied his brother to the door, more than a little reassured by what could only be described as a most inconclusive conversation.

Eleanor spent another sleepless night, thoughts in turmoil. Would she ever sleep well again? she wondered as she pushed her fingers through her hair, tangling the already disordered curls. Within a week Hal could have packed his belongings, terminated the rent on the London house and taken the mail coach to Liverpool. It was very possible that she would never see him again. Never hear his voice or feel the touch of his hands, in simple care or in passion. She stiffened her muscles to hold off the desperate sense of loss that swamped her mind and her heart and once again threatened to drown her in a deluge of helpless tears. She must not think of that. She breathed deeply and fought against the fear that stalked her through the dark hours. She must not allow it to colour her judgement. Her own loss was not the issue here.

For a little time she sat in her bed against the soft pillows with a book open on her lap, but to no avail. She could not read. The words on the page meant nothing to her when all she could see was Hal's stormy eyes, the groove between his brows when he was caught up in some matter, the utmost tenderness in his smile when he had kissed and held her against him, inflaming the needs in her body to match his own. Or the possessive fire when he had turned the key to imprison them together in his bedchamber. So she cast the book aside to pace her own room. Taking out Thomas's letter from her dressing-table drawer, she turned it over and over in nervous fingers—and then replaced it beneath the cases of jewellery. That, she decided, was not the way forward. He would either believe her on her own merits or he would not. It was a risk she would have to face. With that thought in her mind, she took herself to her son's room, to stand by the crib, silently watching him as he slept, fine lashes casting shadows onto his cheeks. How beautiful he was, what a splendid child she had been given. What a fine young man he would grow up to be.

The thought did not make her mind any easier. She had kept her secret for two long years, explaining it would be no easy matter.

By dawn, she had made her decision, for better or worse. Really, it was very simple. She did not know why it had caused her so much heartache, but her *toilette* took considerable time as she dressed with care, determined that she would look her best if she was to be on trial for her past sins. The exquisite silver-grey-and-cream-striped gown, demure and understated in its colouring, gave exactly the impression of sophistication and sobriety that she needed, the delicate ruffles at hem and neckline flattering but restrained. Her hair, charmingly arranged in ringlets, fell from a high knot to brush her white shoulders. She knew that she looked well enough, although nothing, other than the use of cosmetics that she determined to eschew on this occasion, could put colour into her cheeks or disguise the evidence of her sleepless night. No matter. It was important that she appear composed and assured, that her courage should not desert her in the face of Hal's amazed disbelief. Or his total rejection.

In spite of her clear intentions and her determination to be courageous at all costs, Eleanor could not face breakfast. She waited in her room until it was late enough in the morning for Henry to be engaged in business in the morning room.

Then she descended the stairs at last, breathing shallow, palms damp with latent panic. It was a dangerous game she was playing. She could win the glittering prize. Hold the moon and stars in her hands. Or her hopes and dreams could disintegrate, her heart broken. But she must do it. It was only *right*. Henry must not be allowed to leave England without the knowledge, without the opportunity to make a choice that could change the direction of his whole life. If she kept silent, the guilt would be too heavy and would hound her to the day of her death. She owed him the truth, even if he damned her for it and left her to face the future alone.

Henry ignored the timid knock on the door of the morning room. It would not be one of the family—they would not knock, so probably one of the servants who would go away if he made no response. He did not need an interruption. Marcle could find Nicholas if there was some urgent matter to be dealt with. The neglected business of Faringdon and Bridges still lay before him as he had left it on the previous afternoon. He must complete it. There was a sailing next week from Liverpool that he would take. With luck and a fair wind the letters could leave tomorrow and would make land before he did, informing Nat of his imminent arrival and the decisions he had made. Caught up in the planning, he did not notice when the door opened quietly and Eleanor entered.

She closed it silently and remained by the door, watching him for a little while as he sat, head bent, reading rapidly, before making a reply with firm characters on the page. There was a line between his brow as he concentrated, just as she had imagined in her thoughts the previous night. The bright sunshine kissed his raven-black hair so that it shone blue-black, but it was too dense to take any gilding. She knew its weight and its texture, its softness against her skin that made her shiver with remembered passion, and her fingers yearned to touch it again. Her mouth was dry, her pulse hectic.

'Hal.'

He looked up and immediately smiled. How could he not? How beautiful she was with the clear morning light teasing her hair with hints of gold and auburn, and bringing a jewel-like glow to her extraordinary violet eyes. He held out his hand to encourage her closer, his doubts assuaged by her presence and the fact that she had sought him out. He expected to see contentment in her face, an ease previously absent.

His gaze locked on hers. 'What is this?' He pushed back the chair and rose to his feet, approaching to take her hands in his, raising them to his lips, searching her face with instant concern. 'The Baxendale issue need no longer worry you. You must sleep and eat and regain your peace of mind. Nothing can harm you now.' He bent his head to press his lips to her forehead in a blessing, infinitely tender. 'You need not be unhappy Nell.'

Carefully, she disengaged her hands, which caused him to frown, and took a step in retreat. 'There is something I must tell you…'

Her low voice and the shadows in her eyes made his blood chill. There was something here… He set his mind and his will to remain calm.

'Come and sit,' he encouraged. 'Tell me what it is.'

She resisted still, remaining tall and straight in the centre of the room. He noted that her hands were clenched into fists at her sides, although half-hidden by the folds of her dress.

'No. I must stand… Listen, Hal. You must not go back to America without knowing…without realising…' Her words dried on her lips.

Hal's concern deepened, acquiring a sharp edge that sliced at his heart. 'Do I really need to know?' he asked gently. It was the coward's way, he knew, to prevent her opening her heart to him, but what good would it do? Was she indeed going to confess at last that she had rejected him to set her sights so much higher— and had achieved her goal through less than honourable means? He did not think that he wanted to know. He would rather live without the unpalatable knowledge of her betrayal and perfidy, rather carry the memory of her softness and sweetness as she turned to him in the night.

'I must say it,' she said simply, studying her fingers now linked before her, white with tension. 'It is on my conscience. And it could affect your future, your whole life. I must say it. By keeping silent I committed a great wrong.'

A pause. She moistened her lips with her tongue, then raised her eyes to his, a silent plea for understanding and compassion. For acceptance of a situation that had not been entirely of her own making, in which she had made the only choice possible.

'My son. Tom. He is not Thomas's child. He is yours…your son, Hal.'

The resulting silence echoed in the room, filling it from floor to ceiling with a tension that could be felt, tasted even. Lord Henry stared at her, blank shock imprinting his face, his brain repeating the words over and over again as if it might make for clearer understanding. Incomprehensibly, he could not grasp their significance.

'What?' The question was harsh, even though his voice was soft. He had suspected her of carrying Thomas's child and cursed himself for his lack of trust. But he had never suspected this.

'Tom is your child.' Eleanor never once took her gaze from his face, pinning him with her words, challenging him to deny it. 'That last night we spent together… I found that I was carrying him when you had gone…'

'My son.' The meaning took hold, searingly bright, as the implications began to leap into sharp and painful focus. As Henry recalled, suddenly with a terrible clarity, the words that he had overheard her speak to the child, his child, in the small sunlit parlour. Before he had held the infant in his own arms. *You can never know your father…you will never keep his image in your memory…* And he had not known, not understood. How could he have held his own son and not have realised? But then he had not understood her meaning. The powerful tangle of emotions threatened to choke him, but his eyes were stark, austere even, all emotion effectively buried when he turned his gaze on the woman who stood before him. 'Why did you not tell me? Why did I not know of this?'

'I did not know how to reach you. I wrote to you, but received no reply. And then it was too late—I was married to Thomas and it would have done more harm than good to tell you. And…' But there were no excuses, really. She gave up, eyes still searching his face to determine his reaction.

'Did Thomas know?' Henry rubbed his hands over his face, struggling to make sense of the incredible confession. 'When you married him, did he know that you carried my child?'

'Of course he did!' She grew pale with anger and not a little shame that she had put Thomas in such an invidious position. 'Would you accuse me of tricking him? Of course Thomas knew that Tom was your son.'

Baxendale's words returned to Henry like a blow to the gut. *Your precious sister-in-law made sure that she ensnared your brother, did she not?* This terrible scenario opening before him, revealed by the only woman whom he had ever loved, was even worse than the one painted by his enemy with such malicious intent. The shock wave rolled over him with remorseless power. It coated his next words with pitiless despair.

'Or did you allow my gullible brother to think that the child was his? Was that why he married you, to give his name to his own bastard child? Poor Thomas always did believe the best of everyone. Did you indeed trap him into marriage? Baxendale did not realise how far from the mark he was. Even he did not imagine that you would be capable of such a depth of deceit and trickery.'

Eleanor drew in her breath at the deliberate and ruthless assassination of her character. The pain in her heart was tangible.

How could he accuse her of such dishonesty? What could Edward Baxendale have possibly said to cause this volley of spiteful words?

'Why tell me now?' Lord Henry demanded, lips curled in a snarl. 'If you made so little effort to inform me two years ago, why now?'

She strove for calm in the midst of this storm of callous cruelty. There must be a way out of this maelstrom if only she could find it. 'Because with Thomas's death it has changed everything. The title is yours by rights. You should be Marquis of Burford. My son—your son—has no right to inherit before you.'

No! Oh God, no!

An icy hand closed inexorably round his heart with exquisite torture as he contemplated the one thing in life he did not want, had never wanted.

'I do not want it.' The denial was flat and instantaneous, disguising his fear. 'Neither the title nor the estate.'

'Perhaps not. But it would be wrong if you never knew, never had the knowledge to make the choice.' She swallowed against the lump in her throat. 'If you never had the choice to claim your son and recognise him as your own.'

'Do you really expect me to believe all this?' She would never have believed the flat denial in his eyes, in his voice.

'Why not? Why should you not believe me?' Anger began to replace shock in her veins and she lifted her head, drawing pride and dignity around her shoulders like a velvet cloak. 'I could have let you leave next week—without ever telling you that you had a child. Why should I make up a situation that would compromise my own honour? I have nothing to gain from this confession other than society's condemnation if it becomes known outside these four walls. It was my decision to allow you…intimacies without marriage. For that I certainly deserve censure. And how I paid the price!' She stifled a sob. She would not shed tears over this. Never again! 'I trusted you to marry me.'

Her accusation hit home, but he was too angry to give it credence, to contemplate it for more than a heartbeat. Even though a small part of his brain admitted that in all honesty she could not take all the blame for this. The child was the making of both of them in a moment of mutual love and desire. Hers had been the innocence on that occasion. How could he be so utterly selfish as to heap the blame on her? *If* the child was really his, of course, a nasty little voice insinuated in his mind. But he pushed away the uncomfortable thoughts and concentrated on the burning issue that raged, destructive and uncurbed, through his blood.

'You ask why I should accept your words. Perhaps you think your timely *confession* to be in your own interests. I suppose that it is just conceivable that, given the glad news of a son and heir, I would fall at your feet in guilt for my past actions and in gratitude marry you. That would restore all your status and wealth as Marchioness of Burford. An achievement indeed! Instead of the power being held in trust and your own income limited to that from the widow's jointure, however generous it might be.'

'Do you think so little of me, that I would deliberately lie to you?' Her cheeks were ashen, her eyes so dark as to be almost indigo as she regarded him with horror.

'Perhaps not, in all fairness.' The admission was forced from him. 'But I would not put it past your mother to lay out such a campaign! Her ambitions for you are outrageous. Whether you are compliant in her schemes or simply ignorant, I know not.'

Eleanor could find nothing to say. Her body seemed numb to all sensation. Nothing could be worse she thought, watching herself objectively, listening to Hal's harsh voice as if it were from a great distance, than this one moment in her life. She felt as if he had struck her, an open-handed slap, as indeed he had, with words if not with his hand. Her heart ached from the blow.

Lord Henry saw the effect of his attack. It had been devastating. It struck him instantly that he was in the wrong, but his disillusion was as bitter as gall, his wretchedness at being chained into a life that he detested was intemperate. Resisting the urge to enfold her close, to stroke and comfort, to fall on his knees to beg a forgiveness that he did not deserve, was almost beyond his power. Even though he raged against himself for his brutal insensitivity, Hal continued to lash out to cover his own hurt, his own vulnerability.

'Are you sure that you really know whose child it is?'

She had been wrong, Eleanor thought. This was worse. She shook her head as she struggled to find an answer to such an impossible question. 'I…I can't…'

Self-contempt now lodged in his chest to reproach him for so offensive an attack, disgust that he should make such an unwarranted accusation. Seeing the rigidity in her whole body, he reined in his temper and tried for a more moderate tone. 'Could you not have told me this any time before now, Eleanor?'

But Eleanor was beyond moderation. Fury leapt within her with all-consuming flames. She was past considering the effect of her words and struck out in her own defence. 'When do you suggest, my lord? The moment you arrived back at Burford Hall?' The sarcasm was biting, although she kept her voice low and admirably controlled. 'Welcome home, Henry. Let me introduce you to your son?' She laughed with a hint of hysteria. 'It would have put Sir Edward's news of an unknown wife, hidden away in the country, in the shade, I imagine. No, I could not. And I will tell you why. I was afraid.' She all but spat out the words. 'I was afraid to tell you. I knew that you did not want me. I could accept that—and have done so for two years. But I was afraid to discover that you would not want your son either. I thought that would break my heart.'

'Eleanor!' He had hurt her beyond measure.

'And I was right, wasn't I? You have no wish to know him or claim him and I cannot persuade you otherwise. It makes me regret that I ever tried, simply for the sake of my own conscience. It would have been far better if neither you nor my son knew. Thomas was more of a father to him than you could ever be.'

The hurt shimmered between them. Her eyes bright with unshed tears. His face ravaged with the deep lines of hard-held emotion. The abyss yawned wide and dangerous between them, impossible to bridge.

'Don't concern yourself, my lord.' Eleanor continued to pour out the anguish and the pain. 'Tom will never have to know that his father did not choose to acknowledge him, for I know not what reason other than that you doubt my honesty. From this moment,

Tom's father was Thomas, my husband. How could I have been so mistaken in my judgement? What a terrible mistake I made. And what a fool you must think me.' She laughed again, a sharp sound without humour that told him more than anything else of the depth of her despair. 'Go back to New York, Hal. Forget that Tom and I exist. I loved you to the depths of my soul and I gave you everything. I gave you a splendid child. But you are not worthy to be the father of my son. I wish Rosalind well of you.'

She turned her back on him.

Henry strode from the room, her final words, her merciless condemnation ringing in his ears. He thought that they would haunt him forever. He did not see the tears spangling her cheeks, despite all her good intentions. Or read the desolation in her face, not yet hidden behind a mask of hard serenity that would deny to the world that her heart had been ripped to pieces.

How could he have done it? How could he have been so deliberately cruel? So demon-driven, vicious as a wolf attacking its prey. Fear, he admitted. A title he did not want. A way of life that he had no desire for. But a son? The child whom he had held in his arms? He believed her, of course, every word that she had spoken. Her integrity was beyond question and she would not make up such a story. But he had hurt her so much. She would never forgive him, and rightly so. He was no better than Baxendale in his destruction of her life. Worse, in fact, since she had come to trust him and rely on him. And yet he had turned on her, cut her with taunts and vitriolic words. She had every reason to hate him. What the hell did he do now?

And he had a son.

'Hal…'

'Not now.' He strode past Nicholas with savage grace. 'Come and ride if you wish, but don't talk to me for a little while. Just don't ask. I am impossible company. I have just committed the worst sin of my life. I cannot undo the words I have said or the harm I have caused…'

Seeing the ungovernable torment and remorse in his face, Nick let him go, standing to watch as his usually impassive brother flung out of the house. At that moment, nothing would have persuaded him to restrain his brother, to question the reason for his distress. Nothing would have made him go into the room that Hal had just vacated, where Eleanor still remained. If he had needed any confirmation of his suspicions, his convictions even, it had just struck him with all the brutality of a slap to his face. Surely only two people helplessly in love could reduce each other to such devastating unhappiness as he had seen in his brother's face.

From the window of the morning room, Eleanor also watched with eyes as cold and empty as the hollow places in her heart. Could she blame him? Yes, she could! She had not deserved such condemnation, would never have believed that he would show such harshness towards her. But circumstances had conspired against her, she had kept her secret from Hal, and whatever Edward Baxendale had said to him in the aftermath of their disclosure of his deceit had borne fruit. She had played the game out to the full and must now bear the consequences of her shattered dreams and bruised heart.

But she had told Hal the truth at last. His reaction to it was within his own dominion—and, besides, he would be gone in a few days. Her damaged heart would heal, in a hundred years or so. And whatever she had told Hal in her wretchedness, in the desert of her wasted emotions, she *would* tell her son about his magnificent father. But never that Hal had rejected him, had rejected them both.

Chapter Eleven

'Nick. There is a ship sailing next week from Liverpool. I shall take passage on it.' Henry came to a halt at the bottom of the staircase as his brother was making his way down, dressed with fashionable, if unusual, flamboyance to go out.

'I supposed you would eventually.' Nicholas cast his hat and gloves onto the sidetable in the hall and followed Henry into the morning room. 'But I did not expect you to go so soon.' He took the offered glass of port. 'I shall miss you, Hal.'

'An important business deal has come to fruition—a lucrative contract that we wish to take up to ship raw cotton to the mills here in Lancashire and then return the finished textiles.' Hal made an obvious excuse. 'It is best if I am there. Besides, there is nothing to hold me here in London.' He bared his teeth in something that was not a smile and took a swallow of the port. 'Forgive me. I did not mean that as it sounded.'

'So I should hope.' Nicholas punched his shoulder in mock disgust, thinking that Hal looked as if he had spent a night of torment. No doubt the result of his conversation with Eleanor on the previous morning, the content of which still remained a mystery to him. Both parties had been at dinner, but so scrupulously polite to each other that it had been painfully unnerving to watch and listen. Like the silent shattering of fragile glass. The atmosphere had then glittered with shards of that broken glass, lurking to slice at the unwary—he had been more than glad to escape and join a party of friends at the theatre. What Henry had done he did not know and dare not ask. Eleanor had stalked from the room as soon as the meal had ended, leaving Mrs Stamford to stare with puzzlement from one to the other.

'So you are leaving me to manage the estate in your absence?'

'Yes. You will have to work for a living, for the first time in your life.' Henry put down his glass and took the seat behind his desk. 'Seriously, Nick. Would you dislike it too much? If so, it is unfair of me to leave you with it.'

'No. You know me better than that, Hal. There is nothing that I would like more. I have plans. When Tom inherits the estate in the fullness of time it will be a wonder to behold with sound investment. When he is older, I will see that he is up to scratch. He will not live off the estate, giving nothing back, if I have anything to say in the matter.'

Hal's answering smile was bleak. 'I know that he is in good hands.' *My son. My son.*

'And I know that you would not want to take it on. For you to have been born the eldest son would have been the worst possible destiny for you.' Nick grinned in some sympathy. 'Whereas I enjoy the life as a country squire. I shall not be sorry to leave town.'

Henry's smile vanished, leaving his face harsh and strained. 'Hoskins can be relied upon,' was all he said. He frowned unseeingly out of the window, arms folded before him on the desk. That was the key, of course, to his disastrous confrontation with Eleanor. Nick's comment that he would not ever want the title, the social hierarchy, the acceptance that the manner in which the world saw him should rest purely on an accident of birth. The idea that all men should have the same opportunities open to them, to construct a future for themselves dependent on their own efforts, suited him far better. And it was that which had pushed him over the edge. The title was legally his after the death of his brother, tying him into a social and class system that he was more than ready to escape. That, coupled with Edward Baxendale's vicious accusation and Mrs Stamford's determined and unseemly pleasure at the outcome, had driven him to heap the blame on

Eleanor. As if she were responsible for chaining him to a life that he detested as much as Nick enjoyed.

Not true. Of course it wasn't true. He knew it in every sinew of his body, heard it in every beat of his heart. And what had he done? He had made her cry! Humiliated her. Questioned her morality and her veracity. He deserved to be flogged. To be damned to the fires of hell.

It had not helped him when last night he had taken himself on an impulse to the baby's room. An astonished nursemaid had looked up from her seat beside the fireplace where she was sewing some small item of clothing. She leapt to her feet as if to leave the room.

'Don't go. I just need a moment.' *A lifetime.*

He looked down into the crib.

Hair, brows, nose—exact replicas of those that he saw every morning in his mirror. A sturdy frame that would become lithe and athletic. He would ride a horse with elegant grace. He would shoot with skill and accuracy. He would have dogs and horses as he grew from babyhood. He would look to Nicholas for his initiation into the rites and responsibilities of adolescence and adulthood. He would grow up not knowing his father.

The baby opened his eyes. Deep amethyst, fringed with dark lashes.

Henry held out his hand, drawn impossibly against his will to touch, to savour. The baby chuckled and clutched, delighted with the company, making contact in his small fist, drawing the offered fingers to his mouth to gnaw on them with half-formed teeth.

Henry's chest tightened, he found it difficult to swallow. His son. And Eleanor's. Whom he had rejected.

Oh, God!

What could he possibly say to Eleanor? She had borne this beautiful child alone, without him. He mentally thanked Thomas from the bottom of his heart for coming to her salvation. Knowing his brother as he did, he understood exactly what Thomas had done and why he had done it. Married Eleanor to give her the shelter of his name and consequence, so that no one need know that she had borne a child without the protection of marriage vows, and his brother's child would have all the benefits of being brought up as the Faringdon heir. Henry breathed hard against the flood of emotion that threatened to unman him, longing for that one impossible opportunity to tell Thomas of his gratitude.

And he had accused Eleanor of treachery and betrayal, of luring Thomas into a marriage to satisfy her greed and ambition. Nothing could be further from the truth.

But why had she not come to meet him, to join him on the voyage? If she had, their marriage would have legitimised the child and all the following complications would never have arisen. He would probably never know.

He stroked his hand gently over his son's hair, cupping his cheek, caressing the perfect fingers, the shell-like nails. Then turned and left the room, as quietly as he had come, with nothing resolved

'Does Eleanor know?' Nick broke into his uncomfortable musings, concerned for the stark misery in his brother's eyes.

'Yes.'

'What did she say?'

'Nothing of importance.' Henry shrugged and switched his focus back to Nick, replacing the inscrutable mask. 'Why?

Well! Nicholas hesitated, remembering. That was one statement palpably untrue if Hal's face, bleak with shock as he had exited the morning room after his conversation with Eleanor, was anything to go by. But should he interfere further? 'Nothing. Just that I had thought that you were not…not indifferent to each other.' Nicholas made his decision, for better or worse, and came to sit opposite the desk, to fix Hal with a stern expression. 'To put it bluntly, I had thought that you were more than half in love with her. That is, until whatever passed between the two of you yesterday afternoon in the morning room.' He waited the space of a heartbeat, seeing the shutters come down on any emotion in his brother's face. 'You are free to deny any or all of it if you wish, of course.'

'Ha! I wish I were free.' The words were wrung from Henry.

'What should I understand by that?'

'Nothing! Nothing at all!.' Hal sighed and drove his fingers through his hair. 'Yes, I love her. Of course I do. How can I deny it? I love her and I always will, even though I have hurt her beyond belief.'

'So why are you leaving her? Have you told her that you love her?'

'No.'

'I also thought Nell loved you. Is it because she is Thomas's widow that you have not spoken? I don't see that it has any bearing on your feelings for her or hers for you.' He frowned as he remembered their previous conversation. 'Is that why you asked me if theirs had been a love match?'

'Not really. There were other reasons at the time… But I have destroyed any hope of her love,' Hal answered quietly. 'She will never forgive me.'

'It can't be as bad as that.'

'It can—you have no idea!' *I questioned the birth of her child. I accused her of every sin possible. I humiliated her.*

'Are you going to tell me?'

'No. My feelings do not matter. Her life is here with the child. I have nothing to offer her. And—you cannot have thought…' Hal's face was bleak indeed '…there can never be any future between myself and Eleanor of that nature that has the blessing of the law. The church, little brother, in its infinite wisdom, denies the right of a man to marry his brother's widow.'

'I did not know…'

'Oh, we could find a minister easily enough, who would turn a blind eye and commit the deed. Particularly if we greased his hand with sufficient gold. Perhaps even the Reverend Julius Broughton could be persuaded on such terms!' His laugh was a harsh travesty. 'But anyone with ill intent or outraged morality could have such a union declared null and void. Imagine the scandal that would create! I will not do it, even if Eleanor would contemplate such a relationship between us. Which she would not, not after…' He shook his head and lapsed into silence.

'I see. I had not thought of that.' Nicholas decided to leap into the yawning chasm of Henry's reticence, to risk an outbreak of the banked temper in his brother's eyes. It would not be the first time that he had pushed and provoked until he had goaded his brother into disclosing what was on his mind. He might risk a firm and horribly accurate straight right to the jaw—a not infrequent retaliation in childhood when tempers had run high—but Nicholas was quite capable of holding his own, and it would be worth it if he could draw some of the pain from Hal's set expression.

'Look, Hal. I am not blind. To put it bluntly, the love between the two of you is as clear as a rising hawk at noonday. It shimmers between you when you are together in the same room.' He saw the glint of denial leap into his brother's eyes and stretched out a hand across the desk to grasp his wrist in strong fingers. 'Don't bother to deny it. She is as much in thrall as you. Why not simply take her with you? Marry her in New York where the family connection is not a matter of public knowledge. Surely it is better than committing yourselves to a lifetime of misery apart?' He hesitated, tensed his shoulders. He might as well say it. 'Do you have to be so damned noble?'

'Noble?' The icy flash in Henry's eyes heralded the expected eruption of passion. He snatched his wrist from Nick's light grasp, surged to his feet and strode to the window, his back turned against his brother's sharp gaze. 'Noble! Never that. This all started with an act of supreme selfishness on my part. Don't speak to me of nobility.'

Nick opened his mouth to ask his meaning, but did not. Too personal. Too painful. And perhaps, watching the unfolding events of the past days, he could guess at one of the problems which beset the two people he loved most. Hal could easily be Tom's father. But Hal would be protective of Nell and the child to the bitter end. It would be insensitive in the extreme for Nick to press him for an answer.

'I must not risk dragging Nell's name through the mire again. I won't do it, Nick. She will be safe here, with all due respect and honour. I know that you will care for her.'

'Of course.' His brother's anguish tightened cruel fingers in his gut. 'Are you indeed quite certain, Hal?'

'Yes.'

'You know your own affairs, I suppose.' Nicholas looked dubious but realised that he would get nothing more from his brother. Whatever had been said between Hal and Eleanor on the previous day was having a dire and lasting effect.

'Yes. I do. I shall leave for Liverpool in two days.' Henry strode to the door, opened it, thus bringing the conversation to an end.

And then I need never see her again!

As Lord Henry was engaged in deflecting his brother's interest and planning his future without Eleanor, the Marchioness of Burford was spending the day with a martial glint in her eye. Her mood alternated wildly between intense hurt and intense fury, the latter being in the ascendant. Sparkling anger ran through her veins, intoxicating in its effect, instilling her with magnificent energy. She railed silently at the pig-headedness and insensitivity of all men, and Lord Henry Faringdon in particular. So! She had lied to him, lied to Thomas, had she? How dare he accuse her of such perfidy—and without one scrap of evidence? How dare he believe that she had acquired wealth and a title through a devious and unscrupulous manipulation of Thomas? What had she done to deserve such an attack? Not that she cared! And what could possibly have driven Lord Henry Faringdon to use such cruel taunts towards her? Not that she cared about that either! She did not want an explanation from him. Or an apology. Or anything at all, ever!

Eleanor would not listen to the hurt of her broken heart. She would dearly like to break his lordship's head instead, with a particularly ugly Sèvres vase which stood on the mantelpiece in her bedchamber. Except that it would be a waste of the vase.

So she spent the day in a ferment of anger and bad temper. She contemplated throwing her breakfast cup of hot chocolate at the wall—except that Marcle would think that she had taken leave of her senses, as well as having to deal with the resulting sticky consequences. She thrust the pins to hold her curls in place with a savage turn of her wrist as if she were skewering Lord Henry's vital organs. She even snapped at her mother in unusual temper. No. She did not wish to go to Hookham's circulating library. If her mama wished to do so to exchange the latest offering from Walter Scott, then she must go alone. When Nicholas attempted to draw out the rigidly controlled lady by offering to escort her to eat ices at Gunter's in Berkeley Square, he was met with a coldly formal refusal and a flash of amethyst eyes, hardly the reaction he had anticipated for such a compassionate gesture and such an agreeable way to spend a morning. Eleanor noted the surprise, but she would not feel guilt—not even the slightest twinge. Presumably *all* Faringdon men were similarly obtuse and insensitive as Lord Henry Faringdon! She informed Lord Nicholas, in similar style to her conversation with her mama, that if he did indeed wish to stroll through Mayfair on so trivial an errand, he was free to do so, but without her. She was sure that he could pass the time far more profitably without her assistance. And then she turned her back on his amazed stare, leaving Nicholas to consider that perhaps ices had not been the best offering for so glacial a lady. And relieved that he did not have to spend any length of time in her company until her usual good humour had been restored to her. Whenever that would be. He bowed and retreated in poor order.

On meeting by chance Lord Henry himself, the chief culprit in the drama, Eleanor gratified him with an icy inclination of the head, the tiniest of movements, certainly one of her more effective set-downs, and then proceeded to walk past him into the parlour as if he were invisible, and closed the door in his face with considerable satisfaction.

Still restless and with time hanging heavily, she took herself off to spend a pleasurable interlude with baby Tom in the nursery. But the infant was tired and fractious with teething. When denied his own way over the delicate but potentially dangerous issue of cuddling the grey kitten who had accompanied them from Burford Hall, he wailed and fussed, his cheeks flushed with frustration and damp with tears. His mama kissed him and mopped up the tears, with fruitless efforts to deflect Tom's attention from his heart's desire, until she shut the kitten out of the room. The baby eventually fell into an exhausted sleep after another outburst of heartrending sobs, leaving Eleanor with the cynical observation that he was entirely like his father, bad tempered when thwarted to any degree. But his father need not think that *he* would receive any such sympathy from her, she vowed, as she crooned a soothing lullaby to her son and smoothed his ruffled hair.

By this time Eleanor felt the need to do something outrageous. She contemplated the possibilities with enjoyment. She could perhaps walk down St James's Street without her maid, under the ogling eyes and raised quizzing glasses of the bucks and beaux of the Bow Window Set. An action of complete impropriety that would surely damn her utterly in the eyes of the polite world and ensure that no one would be willing to receive her. What did it matter? Lord Henry Faringdon had believed the worst of her even when she was innocent!

The sooner Lord Henry Faringdon left these shores the better! Even if the rift in her heart throbbed with pain and widened a little further at the prospect!

Perhaps she should stroll along Bond Street, she mused, toying with the light luncheon served by a wary Marcle, who was more than a little aware of the remarkable unpredictability of his mistress's mood. She could fritter money extravagantly on any number of fashionable articles that she did not want and did not need. But perhaps not. In the end she took herself off to the Countess of Painscastle's *at home* where she regaled and entertained her hostess with a somewhat selective and censored account of the events of the previous day and her difference of opinion with Lord Henry. Judith's instant sympathy was balm to Eleanor's damaged soul, especially that lady's willingness to rise to her defence against all men, in particular her hapless cousin, Lord Henry Faringdon.

All in all, in spite of the satisfaction which she undoubtedly felt, it was one of the most exhausting days of Eleanor's life.

Later that same afternoon Henry returned from an equally exhausting visit in the company of Lady Beatrice Faringdon. She had insisted on hearing all the details of the Baxendale scandal, word for word, commenting at length and with much pride on her insight into that gentleman's perfidious character, and equally that of the disgraced Reverend Julius Broughton. Henry felt wrung out and decidedly irritable. And so groaned inwardly when Mrs Stamford accosted him in the hall, obviously lying in wait for his return. He had had enough of managing females to last a lifetime.

'I need to speak with you, my lord.' She saw his reaction, his inclination to retreat, and knew that he would make an excuse. She stretched out a hand to touch his sleeve in unexpected intimacy, but her words were all formality. 'Urgently, my lord. Or I would not trouble you.'

'Very well, ma'am.' They climbed the stairs, Henry wishing that he were anywhere but here, and he bowed the lady into the small parlour where a fire had been lit for his return.

She looked at him as he walked past her into the room, shocked by the weariness that he could not hide.

'I think I will ring for some tea. You look tired, my lord.'

'If you wish.' He would have much preferred a brandy, but it did not really matter. Nothing seemed to matter when he had so deliberately and callously broken Eleanor's heart and refused to recognise his own son. Nothing else mattered at all in comparison.

Mrs Stamford busied herself ringing the bell and informed Marcle of their needs. Then settled herself into a chair. Henry stood with his back to the fire, determined to hear her out and make his escape as quickly as possible.

'I have a confession to make, my lord.'

Not another! He stifled a sigh and raised his brows in polite enquiry.

As he cast a glance down at her, his attention was caught for the first time by her appearance. She was uncomfortable in his presence, not at ease. A deep line was engraved between her brows and she worried at her bottom lip with her teeth. She anticipated this conversation with even less pleasure than did he. A sharp suspicion crossed his mind.

'Did Eleanor send you?' he asked bluntly.

'Eleanor? No!' He imagined that she shuddered as a cold chill swept her skin. 'Eleanor knows nothing of this.'

'So. Tell me of this *urgent* matter, ma'am, which cannot possibly wait until tomorrow.'

They fell silent as a footman entered and positioned the tea tray on a small table to Mrs Stamford's right, placing the tea caddy at her left.

'Eleanor is very unhappy,' Mrs Stamford stated when they were once more alone, as if she had learned her words during the long wait through the afternoon. 'So are you, my lord, if I may presume to comment.' Lord Henry's gaze sharpened, but he forbore to reply. She had, it appeared, more sensitivity than he had previously given her credit for. 'I do not know the reason.' She held up her hand as she sensed his interruption. 'I know. It is not my concern. But I should tell you what I did. I think that I must. One moment, my lord.'

She opened the silken strings of her reticule and searched its contents, producing eventually four folded sheets. Clearly letters.

'I am not proud of this, but you have given such generous service to my daughter. And there is such unhappiness between you. You deserve to know the truth. And I think it would be wrong if this event from the past should cause further dissension between yourself and Eleanor. I think it casts a long shadow.' She wet her lips with the tip of her tongue. 'I think these speak for themselves, my lord.'

She held them out.

He took them without a word, turned them in his hands. He knew what they were, did not need to read the inscriptions. There were two letters in his bold hand, curled and much travel worn. Two were in Eleanor's writing, as clean and neatly folded as the day they had been written.

'You intercepted them.' It was a statement, not a question. Suddenly everything was very clear, inscribed with diamond brightness, the answer to all his questions and doubts.

'I did. I do not deny it.' Her eyes for the first time made contact with his, a challenge in their depths, daring him to condemn her, much as her daughter had done over the paternity of her child. 'I would probably do it again tomorrow in the same circumstances. Any mother would. I did not want Eleanor to commit herself to you—a younger son—and a risky life in the colonies. She was so young and I knew so little of you…so I intercepted the letters. Eleanor's never left the house. It was so simple—and Eleanor was so trustingly naïve. It was an easy matter to bribe her maid into handing them over. And equally simple to prevent yours from ever falling into Eleanor's hands. That was the reason she never joined you when you left the country. She believed that you had never written to her, had forgotten her, or deliberately rejected her.'

'As I believed that she had rejected me.' His voice held a weight of sadness.

'Yes, my lord.'

He turned the letters again in his hands, reading Eleanor's clear inscription of his name. Mrs Stamford awaited his response.

'Did you read them?' he asked finally.

'No.' Mrs Stamford flushed at the implied criticism. 'You might give me credit for some honour in my dealings with my daughter.'

'Why should I? You have no idea how much grief and pain you caused by your actions. Nor the present repercussions from your ill-judged decision.'

'Perhaps not.'

'Were you not aware of how much unhappiness you caused your daughter? How could you do it to her?'

'I knew. But I believed that she would forget.' Mrs Stamford raised her shoulders in elegant dismissal of her fault. 'Eleanor would soon meet someone else who would prove to be a respectable husband.'

'I blamed her, you know. And she blamed me. It has caused so much bitterness between us. How could you justify that to yourself, if you loved her?' Mrs Stamford had the grace to flinch from Lord Henry's accusation, but she stood her ground.

'A parent will do anything for her child.' Mrs Stamford rose to her feet to face him, as fierce as a vixen defending her young. 'I thought that she would be happier making a more stable marriage here. Settling in a comfortable house with husband and children. Not so far away—so that I could see her and enjoy her happiness and that of my grandchildren. She is all I have and I want only the best for her. But I do not expect you to understand, of course.'

But perhaps he did after the revelations of the past days, he thought. Acquiring a son gave a man a different angle on life. He would never have the right to enjoy his son's happiness other than from a distance and without recognition. Too many obstacles stood in the way. For the first time he understood in part Mrs Stamford's dedication to Eleanor's happiness.

'One thing.' He looked up from the letters, still folded in his hands, with a keen glance. 'When I had gone, did you throw Eleanor into Thomas's path?'

'No, I did not.' Mrs Stamford folded her lips in some indignation. 'I am no fool, my lord. I wanted her to marry well. She was a beautiful débutante, but not even I could look as high as a Marquis for her. It was a great surprise when he offered for her.'

'Had she known Thomas long?'

'No. A mere matter of weeks. What does that matter?'

It all fit together in his mind, with a sharp click of certainty, the final pieces in the puzzle. Thomas had indeed rescued Eleanor, a victim of his own thoughtlessness and her mother's meddling. His heart went out to Eleanor, who had been unaware of the forces that had worked so successfully against their union.

'It does not matter at all,' he now admitted. 'I am grateful for your telling me. And returning these.'

'I regret the pain I caused. She was devastated when she thought you had left her. And she is distraught now'

'Yes. I imagine.'

'I know not what will ease her pain. Will you tell her of the letters? Of my part in it?'

'I must.'

'She is at Lady Painscastle's now.' Mrs Stamford walked to the door, the tea forgotten, her errand complete. 'Judith is holding an *at home*. Eleanor will not be back until late. I doubt that she will choose to stay the night—not with the child here.'

'Then I must wait.'

'I am very sorry, my lord.' Mrs Stamford waited for a reply, but there was none, Lord Henry's concentration being fixed on the letters, the answer to all his uncertainties, held tightly in his hands.

Eleanor returned at a late hour from the Painscastles' town house. Word had begun to spread, discussing with intense enjoyment the Baxendale débâcle in every salacious detail. Eleanor had known as soon as she had been bowed into the room by Judith's butler, aware of the lightening of the atmosphere. Whispering, yes, but no hostile glances. Discreet asides behind fashionable fans, but no one thought to snub her. Judith had hugged her in delight, demanding a thorough gossip when time and opportunity allowed. Lady Beatrice had descended on her in full sail of mulberry silk and old lace, and had kissed her cheek. *So pleased, dearest Nell! And so brave of you to face all the past unpleasantness with such composure and assurance.* Eleanor had felt a sudden urge to shriek her fears and hurt to the room at large. How shocked they would be! But of course she did not, playing the role assigned to her of gracious lady of impeccable lineage and connections. She was back in the fold, after all. Accepted as Marchioness of Burford. Welcomed by the *ton* as one of their own as if her integrity had never been questioned, never been in doubt.

She knew that she should be rejoicing.

She returned to Park Lane, exhausted after her emotional day. By now her righteous fury had calmed to leave her aware only of the wretched emptiness that had assailed her since Hal had stalked from her presence, having accused her of disloyalty and trickery and malicious deceit. Nothing could fill the hollowness, just as nothing could prevent his words from circling over and over again in her brain. A headache lurked behind her eyes. She looked in on the baby, who slept in innocent ignorance of the impossible rift between his parents, then rang for her maid to help her disrobe. She was in process of stripping off a pair of elbow-length lavender kid evening gloves when a light knock was followed immediately by Lord Henry's entrance without further ceremony into her bedchamber.

Maid and mistress both looked up in amazement at the lack

of ceremony. Eleanor's anger found reason for instant and tumultuous rebirth. To be accosted in her own bedchamber! Whatever he had to say, she did not wish to hear it! She tightened her lips, but such sentiments were vividly expressed on her lovely face and in the dignified lift of her head—if her visitor had been in any way sensitive to appearance and atmosphere. Lord Henry simply ignored the accusing stares, wasted no words of greeting. He had been waiting far too long.

'I need a word with your mistress. Meg, is not it? If you would leave us.'

'I am tired, my lord. Can it not wait until tomorrow?' Eleanor was anything but accommodating.

'No.' Neither was he.

'Thank you, Meg. You may go to bed.' Eleanor bowed to a stronger force. 'I will undress myself.' Meg curtsied, a nervous glance at his lordship, and left.

'You should not be here.' Eleanor smoothed the gloves and placed them carefully in a drawer, relieved to have something to do with her hands.

'Do you wish me to leave?'

'Yes.' She would not look at him, but gave her attention to folding a spangled gauze stole with long fringes.

'This is the only place where I can be sure of your undivided attention—if you will put away that damned stole!' The frustration of the long wait surfaced, to be ruthlessly suppressed. Now was not the time for show of temper. This was going to be just as difficult as he had expected.

'I cannot think what you have to say to me, my lord. You have already destroyed my character and my morals. I think that is enough! I would be grateful if you would leave my room—now, my lord.'

Eleanor turned her back to sit down at her dressing table, raising her hands to remove her necklace.

Henry strode across the room to stand behind her, setting his teeth against her rigid formality. But, of course, he deserved no less. He deserved that she slam the door in his face!

Eleanor's hands froze in mid-air at his sudden proximity, at the stern set of his features, but she gave no quarter. There was not one spark of encouragement in her severe expression, brows simply raised in frigid enquiry.

'I will play lady's maid, if you will allow, my lady.' He was in control again, equally formal if that was her game, and bent with clever fingers to discover and release the gold catch on the string of sapphires. 'Not the diamonds, I see.'

'No.'

He laid the gems on the dressing table. Gently removed a pair of sapphire drops from her ear lobes to join them. Then, as she continued to sit, in frozen immobility, began to remove the clips from her hair until it tumbled in a profusion of curls and waves to her shoulders.

He resisted the urge to touch it, lowering his hands.

She wished that he had not resisted—but would not admit it, to him or herself.

'I do not need your help.'

His eyes connected with hers in the mirror. What she read there made her heart turn over in her breast, her throat tighten. Regret, certainly. A depth of self-disgust for his previous treatment of her, that too. But also lust. Desire. A fierce and burning passion that threatened to sweep away his careful command of words and actions.

But it did not.

'Turn around, Nell.' His voice was gentle. He took a step back from her, allowing her some space.

She watched him in the candle-lit reflection, considered refusing—but feared the result if she did. She would turn to face him as he asked, but did not have to listen or respond or cooperate. She did not have to listen to her senses that whispered intoxicating words of love for this man, that spilled jewels of heat and longing through her blood.

So she turned on the stool, hands folded on her lap, chin raised, her eyes pure ice, mouth set and unsmiling. No—she would not make this easy for him. The pain was still too sharp to be set aside. She doubted that it would ever be healed.

'What do you want, Hal? We have nothing more between us

that needs to be said. Your views of me were made perfectly clear yesterday. Nothing has changed that I am aware.'

'Nothing is clear between us, Nell.'

She would have risen to her feet, but he put out a hand, the lightest of touches on her arm, to stop her.

'Eleanor…'

'I don't want to know.'

'I know. And I can hardly blame you, can I? But will you at least hear me out? There is so little time left before I leave.'

There was no change in her expression. She was astounded at her ability to dissemble, to hide her thoughts. He was left uncertain and perhaps for the first time in his life a little afraid of a woman's response to him.

'If you must.' She shrugged a little, pleased with the result, as if it were of no consequence at all.

Taking one of the riskiest gambles of his life, Hal bent to lift Eleanor's hands from her lap, holding tight when she would have pulled away. And startled her when he sank to one knee before her.

'No!' she gasped.

'Yes! I must. What I said to you yesterday was unforgivable. I would give the whole world to retract those words, but I cannot.' For the first time in their relationship, she sensed his lack of confidence where she was concerned. 'This may seem overly dramatic, but it is the only way I can think of to gain your attention, other than throwing myself under the wheels of a passing cab.' There was no humour in his face, none of the arrogant assurance that the world might see. 'My words must always lie between us, to my intense regret. I know that I don't deserve your forgiveness, but must beg it none the less.'

'Please…' She tried again to pull her hands from his clasp. And failed.

'Will you at least listen? That's all I ask. Then I will leave you and embarrass you no longer.'

He waited, dark head bent, then looked up as she was silent. A little nod of the head was all the encouragement he got. He lifted her fingers to his lips. They were cold against her skin, she noticed, cold as ice.

'I accused you of so many things. I don't wish to repeat them. It shames me to think of what I allowed myself to say. I must have been out of my mind to even consider such things.' His hands tightened on hers, unaware of the strength of the pressure as he remembered his bitter accusations with undiluted horror. 'I know that Tom is mine. I know that Thomas married you in full knowledge, to save your reputation and cherish the child within the family. I know that you were innocent in all your dealings with him, that to trick or to manipulate is not within your nature. I also know, beyond doubt, that you did not reject me in favour of my brother's title and wealth. I was so wrong.' He sighed a little. Forgiveness seemed an impossibility.

'But why, Hal? Why did you do it? Why did you say all those dreadful things? I had surely given you no cause for such suspicions.' Eleanor frowned, mouth still set in an uncompromising line, but at least she was listening.

'So many reasons. None of them good. The worst is that…I allowed Baxendale to colour my view of…of events. He said that you had trapped Thomas by claiming to carry his child. And then when you told me…'

'I see.'

'No. I don't think you do. My reactions were appallingly, dishonourably self-interested. There is no excuse. I did not want the title. Or the weight of responsibility of the family estates. My initial response was to reject them. So I accused you of setting a trap to bind me to you and the inheritance. And by doing so harmed beyond repair the one love of my life.'

'So rather than be Marquis of Burford, you accused me of dishonour.' She would not let herself think of his last remarkable statement. But she kept it close, in her heart.

'Yes.'

'Oh, Hal! How could you? How did such divisions come between us?'

'Nell… Can you find it in your heart to forgive me?' As he felt a trembling in her fingers, he decided to put it to the test, to lighten the painful tension that held them so relentlessly apart.

'I would not wish to kneel at your feet all night, but will do so if it will give me half a chance.'

The resulting half laugh, half sob, gave him the merest touch of hope.

'Can you not give me the smallest crumb of comfort?'

'You do not deserve any!'

'I know it.' He was instantly sober again, but the painful weight in his chest, which had tortured him and compromised his self-control since their bitter quarrel, loosened a little. 'Anything that you say to me will not be any worse than the words I have used against myself. Yet I would ask that you have mercy. To know your hatred and contempt is unbearable.'

She made him wait a little longer. Not out of wilful cruelty, but because she needed to know her own feelings before she laid bare her soul. But she would do it. The time was past for hiding thoughts and feelings and she could bear no more secrets. There had been enough in past weeks to last a lifetime.

'Hal…I love you so much. Nothing will change that.' His eyes snapped to hers, not expecting such generosity, hardly able to believe it. He held his breath as she continued. 'How can I not forgive you? I swore that I would not. That if I had to suffer, so would you.' She laughed, a little sadly. 'But I love you and need to forgive you. I should have been more open with you… I accused you of rejecting me and your son…'

'No, Eleanor. You must not take any of the blame here for my irresponsibility towards you. My shoulders are broad enough to take the weight, as they should.'

She stood then, pulling him to stand with her. She did not let go of his hands, as if they were her only link with the reality of the moment.

'What now?' she asked, unable to see the future.

'You should look at these.' He released her hands, reluctantly, to take the slim bundle of letters from his inner pocket and handed them to her. With one accord, they moved to sit on the day bed in the window embrasure.

'What on earth…?' She turned the pages over, much as he had done earlier that afternoon. She needed no telling what they were.

'Can I guess where these came from?'

'I think you might.'

'My mother. I did wonder…but never really believed that she would do something so deceitful and wounding. Something that would hurt me so. She would, of course, if she believed it to be in my own best interests.'

'Yes. She did, with the willing conspiracy of your maid who thought you needed to be protected from my unprincipled schemes to snatch you from the country.'

'How did they come into your possession?'

'Your mother gave them to me. A fit of guilt. I think she felt that I had earned the truth after my efforts on your behalf. And because I had not seduced you and jeopardised your reputation when you were under my roof, under my protection.' He watched the immediate flush of colour in Eleanor's cheeks. 'She wanted to sever any connection between us, to see you comfortably established in England where she could take enjoyment from your success and your children. America was too far away for her to contemplate.'

'Oh, Hal. So much pain.' Eleanor pressed the letters between her palms.

The urge to draw her close in his arms was strong, but he could not. Not until the air between them was cleared. Not until he had fully understood the depth of her pain.

'Tell me about it, Nell. Tell me what happened when I left you.'

'You can guess, I am sure. You knew Thomas so well.' A sad smile tugged at the corners of her mouth. 'I came to Faringdon House. I had heard no word of you for days, weeks almost. And I knew by then that I carried your child. I was desperately unhappy…'

'I am so sorry, Nell. How supremely selfish I was, how arrogant, to take advantage of you as I did. I had the experience to know better when you did not.'

She shook her head but continued, the memories of those difficult days flooding back. He saw the lines of strain, the tightening of the muscles in her jaw, and knew that she would not tell him the full story of her sense of betrayal. 'I plucked up the courage to call at Faringdon House. What was I going to ask when I got there? I have no idea. But the butler would have been able to tell me where you were.' She brushed away a stray tear. 'I was not thinking very logically, you understand. When I arrived Thomas was there, in the entrance hall. He invited me in, sat me down in the library, and told me that you had sailed for America. Had been gone for some days. I cried. He dried my tears and…and before I realised, I found that I was telling him everything. I was so afraid. I didn't know where to turn. I did not dare tell Mama… And Thomas was so…approachable.'

'I know it. So Thomas offered you marriage.'

'Yes. He cared for me and did all he could to make me comfortable—for my sake and for yours. We had not heard from you—and he did not want scandal to touch either of us, or the child.'

'He would. Nell—I am so sorry that I accused you of wanting him before me—for his consequence only.'

'Oh, no. Thomas was so kind, so generous. He had no obligation to rescue me from my own stupidity.' Her innocent comment, unintentional in its power, made him flush, a twist of a knife in his heart. 'I told him everything. It was such a relief. I had no idea that he would… I refused his offer at first, but he persisted. And then I felt that I had no choice…I had the child to consider.'

'Can I ask one thing?'

'Of course.'

'Were you happy together?'

'Yes. He was the most caring of men. We were the best of friends.'

'I think you married the best of the Faringdons!'

'He loved Tom, you know. For himself as well as because he was yours.' In the resulting silence she stretched out her hand and touched Henry's cheek, sensing his heartache. 'He left something for you.'

She rose to her feet, moved to the drawer and extracted the letter, handing it to Hal. She stood before him as he read the inscription.

'Do you know its contents?'

'No. It is for you, if I deemed it necessary.'

He broke the seal and smoothed open the single sheet. It was very brief and typical of his brother.

Hal—
If Nell has given this to you, there must be a good reason for it. The child is yours. You have only to look at him to see it. He is a delight and I have looked to him as to my own. As I know you would do if our situation were reversed. Nell had been everything I could desire in a wife. It was your loss but I cannot regret it.
Ask her about the boy's name.
Thomas

Hal looked up to where Eleanor still waited, eyes sparkling with unshed tears and compassion, his own narrowed in anguish.

'Tell me about the child's name,' he asked quietly.

'Henry Thomas, of course.'

'Of course. I should have known that he would think of that.'

He laid the letter carefully on the seat and stood. He did not touch her now.

'You said that you loved me. Would you accept my own avowal of love in return? Despite all I have said and done, deliberately or otherwise. Despite the hurt I have caused you.'

'Yes.' Her eyes were wide and clear, allowing him to read every thought.

'You make it sound so easy.'

'I think it is—if we can put aside the past and trust each other.'

'Ah, Nell. I don't deserve such love. And the future for us is not a simple matter at all…'

'I didn't think you would ever love me again.'

'I have never stopped loving you.'

As one, they moved together, drawn by invisible bonds. Placing her hands, palms flat, against his chest, Eleanor marvelled at the strength of Hal's heartbeat, a heightened pulse that echoed her own. When she smiled at him, he accepted the final loving benediction from her and framed her face in his hands, pushing back the tendrils of hair that he had loosed, caressing her temples and fine cheek bones with gentle thumbs.

'You are so beautiful. Your face would torment me in dreams, the violet depths of your eyes would enclose me. I would wake, longing to wind my fingers into your hair, holding you so that I could not possibly lose you again. How could any man not love you?'

'It only matters that *you* do.'

'I do. I do.' For a long moment he rested his forehead against hers, to savour her closeness. Then, sure of his ground, he slid his hands down the graceful column of her throat to her shoulders, to clasp and pull her close, to allow his lips to touch hers. Gently, tenderly, as if she might resist such intimacy. but her lips were warm, soft and responsive under his. And he knew that they would open and welcome his invasion with little enticement from him.

He pulled back a little on hearing a soft murmur in her throat, but could not mistake the flush of pleasure in her cheeks, the glow in her eyes.

'Kiss me, Hal,' she whispered. 'Show me that you love me.'

'If you will kiss me, my lovely Nell. And show me that I am forgiven.'

She stepped into his arms, raising hers to lock behind his head, drawing him close. 'I love you.' She murmured the words against his lips. It was the flame to light the fire, the candle to singe the moth, and he needed no further invitation to show her with his body where words seemed so inadequate. He dragged her close, even closer, angling his head to fit his mouth more perfectly with hers and her lips opened to allow him to stroke and caress, claim her breath, swallow her shivers of delight. It was as if they had never been parted, never separated by the terrible rift of time and space and malicious intervention. Her body moulded to his, breast to breast, thigh to thigh, a fusing of flesh as their minds joined in demand and counter-demand. As he had dreamed, Hal wound one hand into her luxuriant curls and held her in his power—aware of nothing but her essential appeal to his senses, her total surrender. Eleanor felt his power and gloried in it, in his firm muscled flesh, in the hard length of his body.

When he finally released her, they stood, shaken by the emotion that thundered through their blood, their breathing laboured and uneven. Her eyes were blurred, swamped with love, lips soft and parted. He could not take his gaze from her.

'I love you, Eleanor.'

'And I, you.'

When Eleanor smiled up at him, her eyes shining with such joy and hope, Hal battled against his doubts and fears to draw her close again, unable to resist the overwhelming allure of the beautiful woman in his arms. He would kiss and hold her, convince her of his love for her, if only for a little time. She must not be left in any doubt, when he finally left her, that she meant more to him than life itself.

Eventually he put her from him, when the anguish in his heart grew too great to push aside.

'Nell. You are my beloved—my heart and soul.' His words were all that she had ever wished to hear, but the lines of his face were taut and stark. The intense grey depths of his eyes, cold and bleak, did not speak of love but fear.

'What is it, Hal?' She touched his face, the crisp outline of his lips, fingers trembling with the lingering aftermath of passion and with equal fear of the unknown.

'I said that nothing was simple between us.'

'I remember. But you love me. And you know that I love you.' She frowned a little as she tried to envisage the problem.

'Yes. And yes.'

'Tell me then. That I may understand.'

He held her again, resting his cheek against her soft hair. Arms enfolding strongly around her, his fingers spread wide to press her close. As if their proximity would take away the pain which he knew he must inflict.

'I cannot publicly acknowledge Tom as my son.' The statement was blunt, the tone flat, without inflection, not open to disagreement. 'I must not, whatever the temptation.'

'Why not? If—'

He withdrew a little from her, placed his fingers gently over her lips, desperately aware of the hurt in her eyes, but unable to prevent it, not if decency and principle had any meaning for him. Nor, God help him, the weight of the law.

'Think about it, Nell. Once, in despair, you told me that if Baxendale's claim was upheld before the law, they would brand you a whore and your child a bastard. I remember your choice of such brutal words and so should you.'

'Yes. Oh...' Enlightenment came to her, distressing in its clarity, a bright sword edge in her heart.

'If I acknowledge Tom as my son, will it not do the same as you feared? It will destroy your reputation as surely as any action on Baxendale's part, if I acknowledge that your son is mine, conceived out of wedlock. And it will make my brother a cuckold. It will proclaim to the world that you were my mistress and that my son was foisted on my brother, with or without his knowledge. Can you not imagine the consequences of such an admission from my lips? It is too terrible to be contemplated.'

'Hal!'

'I cannot do it, Nell—to Thomas or to you. I have too much honour to bring disgrace to you and to my family name.'

'You would put honour before love?' She might ask the question, but she already knew the answer, as strongly and assuredly as she knew Hal.

'You do not know what you ask.' Suddenly releasing her, he walked away so that she might not see the dilemma which tore him apart. 'I cannot risk your social and very public degradation. It is too much to ask.'

'Then let us come with you to New York.' Her mind sought furiously, feverishly, for some alternative to the living death that he proposed. 'No one will know. If you do not wish to marry me, I can accept that, but we could be together.'

'No. You must not say such a thing.' He regretted his harsh tones and gentled his voice, explaining the obvious but with little assurance that she would accept his reasoning. 'I have nothing to offer you, Nell. A new company that might fail as easily as succeed, with all my financial resources tied up in it. I have some responsibilities to my partner. I live in rented rooms. Law and order is still sketchy. And life is nothing if not dangerous and full of risks. Even the voyage has its dangers.' He walked back to her, to stand beside her again, sensing her resistance. 'It is not the life I would give you, darling Nell.'

'So we stay here—Tom and I—and you return to New York.' Her heart was cold. Her voice was cold.

'Yes. Your life is safe here. Tom will grow and learn, inherit the title and, when he reaches his majority, he will take on the Faringdon estates. Nick will be an excellent trustee, of course. You will live in style and comfort as befits your rank—and an untarnished reputation. That is what I would want for you.'

'You offered me marriage once—at the Red Lion in Whitchurch,' Eleanor reminded him, fighting against the wave of despair that threatened to engulf her. 'When I had nothing but a ruined name and an illegitimate child.'

'I know. I was wrong to do so—but allowed my heart to rule. You had nothing to lose then, Nell. Now you have everything to lose.'

'I would give up everything—'

'Nell.' He tilted her face up to his with gentle fingers. 'Listen to me, Nell. It is not simply a matter of my own wishes. We cannot marry, can never do so.' The words were forced from him. 'The church condemns it. You are my brother's widow. And unless there are grounds for an annulment of your marriage to Thomas, on the grounds of non-consummation…?'

She shook her head as she took his meaning. 'No. There are no grounds for annulment.' Bright colour flared in her cheeks. 'Thomas and I were truly man and wife. He…he came to my bed…'

'That is as it should be, my dearest one.' He stroked her cheek, the lightest of touches. 'Of course Thomas would want you. What man of flesh and blood could not?' Hal's smile was infinitely understanding. 'But it means that we cannot marry. My love. My life.'

'Would anyone have to know? If I came with you to New York—'

'Eleanor, listen to me.' His voice was gentle, but the words were cold and would brook no dissent. They lodged in Nell's chest with an unbearable weight. 'Yes, I could marry you. We could hide the true facts, find a minister who would carry out the ceremony. But what then would life be for us? For you? Flinching at every shadow, wary of every stranger who might know of our past and from either malice or outrage drag our affairs before the law. Our marriage could be declared illegal by anyone who discovered the truth and found a reason to stand in public and declare it void. Do you wish to live the rest of your life in fear that we shall be discovered? With all the resulting horrors of public speculation and condemnation? I will not tie you into a relationship that could bring you such shame and humiliation. Or even, quite simply, cause you to regret that you had ever chosen to walk that path with me.'

'I do not want to live the rest of my life without you.' She knew that she had lost the battle, but still could not let it go. 'I could never regret it.'

'I will not do it. I will not risk the possibility of more scandal attached to your name—or the children that we would have together.'

Henry took her hand, to link Eleanor's fingers with his own, as if it might force her to accept the weight of his argument. But she did not, would not. Not even in the face of such a final and irreversible judgement. The tender symbolism held no meaning for her.

'So my loss will be Rosalind's gain.' Eleanor could not disguise the bitterness. Indeed, she did not even try. Hal drew in a sharp breath at the lethal weapon that she had chosen to use against him in her distress. She had chosen well.

'Don't ever think that.' He lifted their joined hands to his lips. 'You should understand about Rosalind. We have an understanding. She gave me companionship, friendship, a human touch when I was alone and needed it. She is under no illusions. I never lied to her about my feelings for her, nor she to me. She knew that my heart was already given.'

'I see.'

'You have nothing to fear from Rosalind. But I cannot take you with me.'

'Hal…' How could she persuade him? She feared that his will would withstand any argument of hers. 'I would live with you in a gutter, with or without the blessing of the church, if I loved you enough.'

'And you do, of course.' He smiled, not doubting her for a moment.

'Yes.'

'But I will not ask it of you. It is too big a sacrifice for any man of principle to ask the woman he loves.' The smile vanished, leaving his face severe. 'It is enough to know that you love me. It has to be enough.'

She could not push him further. The set of his mouth and the sharpness of his cheekbones, where skin was tightly stretched, warned her that it would do no good. Her heart was banded with iron, unyielding and painful, her breathing difficult. Would it be like this for ever? Was there nothing she could salvage for them both from this morass of loss and despair? Perhaps…

'Will you do one thing?' She curled her fingers more tightly around his, willing him to look at her.

He did so and could refuse her nothing. 'If it is in my power.'

'If I have to live out the rest of my life without you, will you give me this one night together?'

'Nell…' For a moment he turned his face away from her in an intensity of emotion. 'How hard you make our parting.' Then turned to hold her eyes with his own, held fast by the passion of dew-drenched violets. 'Do you know what it is that you ask of me?'

'Yes,' she whispered. She would not back down from this one promise of shared glory. 'I can be thoroughly selfish—and will be if you would divide us asunder.'

Hal hesitated, acknowledging her strength of purpose. 'There could be consequences, as we know too well. Are you willing to accept that?'

Her amethyst gaze was implacable. There was no going back, not after offering herself to this man so blatantly, and without even the trace of a blush. 'There could.' She inclined her head in acceptance. 'I will face them if it should be so.'

'How can I resist such an offer. You know it. You are my only weakness.' His smile was a little wry, a little sad and he took a breath. To take her to his bed would make their parting so much more difficult. To know the satin glide of her skin beneath his, her softness moulding to the hard planes of his own body. To feel the intimate heat of her close around him in both possession and submission. It could destroy all his best intentions, unless he exerted his will to the utmost.

But he owed her that much, after all the grief in their past. And he would fulfil his obligation with every muscle and sinew in his body, with grace and finesse. 'Very well, lady. I will give you this one night with all the love and tenderness within me. I will leave you with no doubts about my need for you. I will promise that when we are apart you will remember this night with every waking and sleeping thought. You will know what worship and adoration, of a man for a woman, can be.' He bent to touch her lips with his own in recognition of his promise. 'I will give you this one night of love.'

And he would take it for himself.

So, because he was unable to give her any hope for a future together, Henry gave her the night she asked of him. Regardless of the bitter-sweet pain of separation, which a night of love-making would prolong almost beyond bearing, he could not refuse her. Nor, in all honesty, did he wish it. They would proclaim the glory of their passion and devotion one final time—and exalt in it.

Wrenching despair, soul-searing desolation, both were kept at bay, forbidden to encroach even though they knew that Hal's leaving would come to them as assuredly as the lightening sky of dawn. Such emotions would not be allowed to intrude into their room, into their bed, banished by the supreme quality of exquisite care that he lavished on her through the darkest hours. Love in every touch, in every caress, in every heated kiss. A tender wooing to construct an unbreachable barrier between the lovers and the approach of cruel reality.

Clothing was not permitted to be a hindrance, thus quickly shed. They had completed and overcome a long and hazardous journey through lies, deceit and deception, deliberately placed obstacles. Nothing should now come between the celebration of their mutual desire. Eleanor consented that Henry lift and carry her to the bed where the curtains were drawn back, the covers folded away and the pillows banked in soft invitation. Once there, she opened her arms to take him in, enclosing him to her breast, to imprint the essence of him on her mind and body for ever.

Slowly, thoroughly, Henry made love to her. There was no hurry, no demands on their time except to give and receive a precious gift. As if their lifetime stretched before them where they might sleep and wake together in joyous intimacy every night and morning for the rest of their lives. Eleanor had asked for a memory. Henry set himself to create one, as bright and as mystical as the beams of the moon that illuminated the room for them in its soft light. No candles were required to add to the glamour. Only silvered shadows, soft glimmering highlights on shoulder and thigh, hard-edged curls of hair and turns of hand, the deep velvet of secret, intimate places.

She was a man's dream, a fantasy of enchantment and fascination. Henry could not eat or drink his fill at the banquet offered in her arms. He touched and tasted, all those satin, seductive curves that tempted and beckoned, holding back when her immediate response, slim body arched against him in potent demand, would have driven him too precipitately to immoderate action. He framed her face with his beautiful hands to press gentle kisses on temple, eyes and finally her parted lips as her breathing quickened. Leisurely kisses possessed her, cleverly rousing her nipples to hard desire, tracing the soft hollows at her waist to make her shiver, anointing the tender skin between her thighs, which made her cry out. The taste of her skin, the perfume of her hair were branded into his memory for all time. Gentle but deliberate, he pursued the path that he had set himself, to awaken her senses to delight as he moved his body languorously against and over hers. Until his weight held her in thrall, aware of nothing but her allure as she smiled, a smile that stirred his body and blood as a sorcerer would create and use irresistible powers. Until he drove her to forgetfulness with skilful mouth and experienced fingers so that she shuddered in his arms, the heat becoming too great to withstand.

Eleanor felt the power ripple through her veins, turning her blood to red-hot gold as she stretched her body over his, hair falling on his chest so that he gasped, muscles tightening. She allowed her breasts to brush against the hard planes, delighting in the immediate response of his erection. As he had pleasured her, so she reciprocated with growing confidence and assurance. Her fragrant breath whispered against his skin. Soft lips, allowed to roam at will, dragged him to the very edge of reason. How amazing, she discovered, that she could reduce this powerful man to such weakness, that his body should quiver with such need as he strained hips and thighs against her in a gesture of dominant possession. How miraculous that she could compromise his proud self-control, as he could rouse her to mindless dependence. She stroked and smoothed, familiarising herself with the firm contours of muscle and sinew, lest in the endless years apart she should forget. As if she ever could forget.

She would not allow him to forget her.

No emotion, no passion was permitted to remain unawakened between them as the hours ticked inexorably past.

At last they came together in mutual demand. She opened to him and he slid gently into her, held deep in her tight velvet softness where he belonged. Slowly filling her and claiming her for all time. Eyes locking in pleasure beyond all words, drowning in the depths of love and a need to give and receive. He moved slowly to draw out the glory of it, until nerve-endings sang, blood raced, breath seared in lungs, pulses hammered with demand for release. But he would not. He kept the rhythm slow, hers matching perfectly, thighs clasping his hips, body arched to take him even deeper.

'Love me, Eleanor. Want me,' he murmured against her mouth, his lips a burning brand, breath ragged.

'I love you. I want you.' The stretching of her body beneath him echoed her words. Responding, he thrust deeper yet.

'No one will ever love you as I do.'

'Nor as I love you.'

Until passion grew too great. He waited until she reached the crest, hands tightening on his arms, nails digging crescents into his skin. Until she cried his name. Then thrust to hurl them both from the mountain peak, from where they fell together into hot darkness.

Afterwards she lay in his arms, head resting against his shoulder, but did not sleep. Time was too precious to be wasted without sensation, without awareness. Time enough for oblivion when she was alone. So she sensed his breathing, the steady rise and fall of his chest against her cheek. Absorbed his warmth and strength that wrapped her around to hold her safe. She would remember the splendour of loving and being loved with such intensity, with such unbearable tenderness, and rejoice through the pain of a future alone.

Eleanor wept a little, despite her intention to remain strong. For herself. For Hal. For their inevitable loss. For Thomas, whom she had not been able to love as he had deserved, but who had given her so much in full knowledge of her predicament. She had indeed been blessed. And Hal had given her a son.

Hal caught her tears with his mouth as they tracked down her cheeks into her hair, but said nothing, allowing her the luxury of weeping in his arms. Then, as desire built, he moved to take her again. And again.

Now he whispered words of love. Foolish words and avowals that reduced her to laughter and tears. All the words of love and care that had gone unuttered on the tempestuous and passion-rent night of the Sefton soirée were now given free rein. Whispered mouth against mouth, against silken skin, against scented hair. Every nuance expressed that neither might be left in doubt for all eternity. But no promises were made for the future. No words, no future. And she accepted it with a courage and fortitude beyond his imagining. His love for her was as boundless as the ocean that would soon divide them. As sure as the law that would stand in the way of their union.

Hers for him was as bright and durable as the stars that glittered in the night sky beyond their window.

In that one night of love they celebrated their eternal love—
but also set each other free for a future alone. To make separate
lives. To exist alone. Without the intimate knowledge of the
other's thoughts and desires. Without a familiar touch or caress.
The night was both a confirmation of love and a terrible sacrifice.

'I will love you until death, Eleanor.'

'Yes. Until death.'

With daybreak, they would never see each other again.

Chapter Twelve

Eleanor slept late. Exhaustion, mental and physical, had finally laid its irresistible hand on her. Henry had loved her, kissed her, held her, possessed her. Set her ablaze in a night of aching tenderness and overwhelming passion. Sleep had been far from their thoughts. Until they had fallen, deep under its calm surface, replete, at some little time before dawn.

But now she knew that he was gone.

Left London more than two days before he needed to catch the sailing. To lessen the agony and anguish of a drawn-out parting, for them both. He would think of that, of course.

The bed was cold. She ran her hand over the empty space beside her. No colder or emptier than the spaces in her heart. She buried her face in the pillow, breathing deep, to catch the lingering scent of him. How quickly it was gone. How impossibly short the night had been. And now her life stretched before her, impossibly long without him. Only one thought hammered in her mind, beating its message through her blood, through every vein. He loved her, but she must learn to live life without him again.

It drove her to rise from her bed. There, on the dressing table, were the letters where she had left them the previous night. Hers and his, hidden away by her mother all those months whilst she had craved news of him. She would read them one day. But not now. They were not important. She knew what was in Hal's mind and did not need words of two years ago to convince her of his love.

She simply stood in the middle of the room, remembering. A night of such splendour and magnificence. The glory of it still sent shivers over her skin, still tumbled through her veins with the cauterising heat of volcanic lava. She could taste his lips on her own, feel the brush of his hands against her skin, as if he were there with her. Whatever the future would hold, she would never regret this night. He had touched her soul and she knew, beyond doubt, that his heart was hers. It was enough.

It had to be enough.

And she had her son. Their son. To cherish and raise to manhood, as she and his father would wish.

On that thought Eleanor pulled on her robe and made her way to Tom's nursery. He was awake, gurgling with incomprehensible words when he saw her, pulling himself up by the sides of the crib to bounce on urgent feet. Soon he would walk. Soon he would run through the vast rooms at Burford Hall. And Hal would never see.

She lifted him, smoothing down his linen smock, crooning to him as he wriggled and pulled on her loosened hair.

'He has gone. But how he loved us,' she informed the infant in serious tones as if he would understand every word. Tom patted her face, fussing to be set down. 'He would not take us with him. He thought only of the dangers. I wish he had not been quite so honourable…'

She would have walked to the window to look down on the street where sparrows twittered in the cherry tree, but stopped when her attention was caught. The small night stand beside the crib. Beside the night candle.

She smiled then, although the glitter of tears was there if anyone looked closely. He had been here. He had been to say farewell. She closed her hand on the precious items and carried them and the child to the light of the sun streaming through the window.

Henry's gold half-hunter, which had entranced Tom as it repeated and chimed the hours and quarters, lay on her palm. And a seal, which she had never seen before, to be worn as a fob on a chain of gold. The body was amber, glowing in the light with yellow and deep ochre, tiny leaves trapped for all time in its depth. A beautiful object, of some history, beyond price to her. Its setting was chased gold, intricate, delicate, holding the resin securely with elegant claws. And carved into its flat surface was the Faringdon crest. Hal's own seal, left for his son.

'Look, Tom. This is for you.' She held out the seal to Tom, who immediately grasped the golden chain, transferring the links to his mouth.

'He left this for you. And the watch. But I don't expect he thought you would eat it!'

She laughed—and then on a sob, quickly swallowed, pressed her lips to the soft curve of his cheek.

Eleanor made the decision to return to Burford Hall. As she had told Hal, she had had enough of London and the shallowness of polite society to last her for some weeks, if not years. A lifetime even.

She must stop thinking about him! And dreaming. Waking to sense the brush of his fingertips against her cheek. The cool pressure of his lips, heating to an intensity of demand that caused her to shudder with longing. Expecting to see his tall figure every time she entered a room, his smile that illuminated all the dark places on her soul. Devastated when she realised anew that he would never be there. She was alone and must accept it.

The house in Park Lane was hers until she wished to leave. Nick would see to the rent and its eventual termination. She would not go back to Faringdon House yet, even though she believed that the Baxendales had departed for enforced seclusion in Whitchurch. It was all so empty without Hal. Her life was empty…

She must not think about him!

So they were packed, her clothes and all the many necessities for the baby, ready to depart on the following day. The ladies of the household gathered in Henry's morning room at three o'clock for tea and a final parting exchange of news and gossip as Cousin Judith joined them. Mrs Stamford planned to stay on in London for a few days with some distant relatives. Sarah Russell, more relaxed and at ease in her new surroundings, would go with Eleanor. Her guilt had begun to dissipate. She smiled more. Did not feel the need to apologise to Eleanor every day for her brother Edward's sins. Did not feel the need to watch John with an eagle eye every moment of every day. So she would go to Burford Hall and take up residence there. Eleanor had come to like the quiet, gentle girl. She thought she would be glad of her company in the empty hours and days ahead.

Eleanor had deliberately made no mention to her mother of the letters that now rested in a jewel case, replacing the one from Thomas that Hal had taken with him. What use? Nothing of the past could be changed and what could Eleanor possibly say that her mother did not know already? The confiscation of the letters had wrought a bitter rift between the lovers, as was intended, but Eleanor had made her peace with Hal, and he with her. No point in raking over cold ashes.

Mrs Stamford watched her daughter, wondering at her brittle composure, her dry-eyed determination to arrange her future to her own liking with no reference to her mother's opinion. Here was a young woman, chilly and aloof, with none of the softness of the past. Mrs Stamford eyed her askance when Eleanor kept her silence, but for once she did not dare broach the matter of the wayward letters. These days the Marchioness of Burford had a steel-edged maturity, a cold decisiveness, and had drawn a line of privacy over which her mama felt it unwise to cross.

Eleanor had read Hal's letters. And re-read her own naïve pleas for a word from him, a simple recognition that he had not forgotten her. An explanation for why he had sailed without her. She had wept a little. He had not forgotten her. She pressed his words to her heart. Regretted Hal's final decision to the bottom of her soul, and then put the letters away. She knew that he would not write again. Nor would she.

The chatter as the ladies drank tea was light, mostly inconsequential news of their mutual acquaintances. Judith promised to visit Burford Hall in the summer months. Mrs Stamford expressed the opinion that she might take herself to Brighton. Or perhaps to drink the waters in Bath. Sarah expressed her pleasure at the prospect of country life and fresh air. Open spaces for John to run and grow. Eleanor played her part. Yes, she anticipated the slow pace of life at Burford with calm approval. Unaware that her companions were concerned for her overbright eyes and pale cheeks. That she ate little and slept less. Unaware of their urgent conversations about her state of mind and the possible remedy. The only remedy. She would have been horrified if she'd known the depths of their concern, if she had realised that they could read her so well. She had been determined that she would not mope! She would rebuild her life and be perfectly content.

Of course she would.

Hal's departure had been accepted with little comment. He would be missed, of course, but it was no surprise that he had gone. It had always been his intention and his commitment to Faringdon and Bridges could not be overset. Perhaps he had not been expected to leave quite so precipitately, but then Hal was always a man of action and impulse. He had said his farewells to Nicholas and that was that. There was nothing more to discuss. And besides, such a conversation invariably brought a tightness to Eleanor's lips, an added pallor to her face.

As Nick had announced, 'It was always Hal's nightmare that he would ever be called upon to be Marquis of Burford. I wager he is plain Mr Faringdon in Faringdon and Bridges.'

And Eleanor knew that he was right.

'A visitor, my lady.' Marcle entered the room, disturbing the feminine chatter.

'Who is it, Marcle?'

He coughed, a warning. 'Lady Octavia Baxendale, my lady.' The butler's eyes and face remained amazingly bland, given the extent of knowledge below stairs. 'She is alone and requests a moment of your time.'

'Octavia!' Startled, Eleanor looked around the circle of faces. She was the last person who might be expected to pay a formal visit to Park Lane. 'I thought she had left London. They are no longer at Faringdon House, I know.'

'What on earth can that woman want?' Mrs Stamford was immediately hostile. 'I would have expected the lady and her despicable husband to have slunk back to the country. Will you indeed see her, dear Eleanor? I don't advise it. You should say that you are not receiving visitors—she will undoubtedly understand the snub.'

'Yes. I will see her.' Octavia's visit was intriguing and there was nothing to fear from it. 'Alone, I think. Would you perhaps give me a little time?'

The ladies withdrew to a parlour, reluctantly, wishing they could do something so lacking in gentility as to listen at the door.

Marcle, all cold arrogance and affronted dignity for the past treatment of his mistress, showed Lady Baxendale into the morning room, offering her the smallest of bows. Eleanor stood beside the fireplace, waiting with interest. How would the young woman react? What on earth was it that she wished to say? Eleanor had no idea.

'Lady Baxendale, my lady.' Marcle withdrew, as reluctant as the ladies in the parlour.

'Forgive me for encroaching on your time, my lady. You are very kind and…very kind to see me.'

Octavia was just as Eleanor remembered her at their last meeting in the garden of Grosvenor Square. Calm, placid, apparently unmoved by the unusual circumstances of this visit, showing neither embarrassment nor undue emotion of any description. She was carefully groomed, her fair hair in smooth, well-ordered ringlets, her dress fashionable—no longer black but in a youthful shade of eau-de-nil, her straw bonnet with feathered trim becoming, her gloved hands clasped lightly on the handle of her parasol. Her blue eyes gazed at her hostess with a strange guileless innocence, brow smooth, lips relaxed. She could pass for any young woman of respectable birth and independent means. Not one who had been integral to a dangerous game of fraud and deceit.

'I am at a loss to know why you should be here.' Eleanor broke the silence that had descended on Marcle's departure. She remained standing and did not immediately invite Octavia to sit.

'No. Of course you would wonder. I could hardly be welcome in your home.' Octavia's voice was light and pleasant, her expression accommodating. They might have been discussing the fashions of the day.

Eleanor mentally shrugged. There was no understanding this young woman who could stand before her with such apparent lack of awareness of the hurt she had wittingly caused. 'Please sit.' She gestured to the sofa.

Octavia did so, supremely composed, laying aside her parasol and removing her gloves with calm intent. She folded her hands comfortably in her lap and looked once more at her hostess.

'We will leave London tomorrow for Whitchurch. Edward does not know I am here. He would not be pleased.' A tiny frown creased her smooth brow. She looked, Eleanor thought, ridiculously young, little different, she imagined, from the débutante who had made her curtsy four years ago and caught Thomas's passing interest.

'I had to come,' she continued. 'I have tried to see Sarah, but she would not.'

'You cannot blame her.'

'No. I think that we did not deal well with her. Perhaps some time in the future…'

'I don't know. She will stay with me for the present, at Burford Hall.'

'Yes. I liked Burford Hall—I remember thinking how pleasant it would be to live there when I first visited you.' Such an ingenuous comment almost made Eleanor smile. 'I came here to say that I am sorry. I caused you much pain. And I remember Thomas with much fondness. It was wrong of me, perhaps, to pretend that he was less than honourable.' For the first time Eleanor caught a flash of discomfort on the delicate features.

'It was. Why did you do it? Why did you go along with such an outrageous charade? It could have worked, of course. But would you have been content, happy knowing that you had stolen what was not yours to take?'

'No. I don't think so.' Lady Baxendale appeared to give it some thought.

'So why?'

'It was Edward's decision. His plan.' The lady lifted her hands, then allowed them to drop back into her lap, as if her answer explained everything.

'But if you were uneasy with the lies and deceit, why did you not refuse?' Eleanor frowned her lack of understanding. 'I find it impossible to believe that you could be so…so accepting.'

'It is very simple, my lady. I love Edward. And I will do what he asks. It has always been so. I have known him all my life, you see.'

'And what will you do now?'

'Go back to Whitchurch, of course. It is my home. It will not be unpleasant to go back.' Octavia's reply was immediate and accepting of her changed circumstances, accompanied by the slightest of shrugs. 'It is Edward's decision. And I do not think that we will be made welcome in London when the truth is known. But Edward will take care of me, whatever the future might hold.'

With such an explanation, there was nothing more for Eleanor to say, nothing more for Octavia to add.

On that acknowledgement, Octavia stood. 'I have outstayed my welcome. I cannot expect forgiveness from you. Edward would say that I should not even offer my regrets. But I felt it right.'

'I admire your sense of justice. Your recognition that your actions were the cause of great harm and sorrow.' Eleanor's tone was a little dry as she too rose to follow her guest to the door.

'Oh, no.' Octavia admitted. 'I am sorry that I hurt you—but I would do the same again tomorrow if Edward asked it of me.'

She turned at the door, replacing her gloves, drawing them over her wrists with neat precision. 'I know that you will condemn me for my actions. But it seems to me that when your heart is engaged, then nothing else in life seems as important.' She gave another elegant little shrug, which sat quaintly on her young shoulders. 'Edward is everything to me. I would follow him to the ends of the earth if he asked it of me. It is not an excuse, my lady, just a fact. And I thought that you should know.' She dipped the slightest curtsy with impeccable grace. 'I doubt that we shall meet again. Good afternoon, my lady.'

Octavia Baxendale opened the door and left the room, closing it quietly behind her.

Eleanor found herself staring at the closed door, an arrested expression on her face.

'What did she say? What did she want? Was she indeed repentant for all the lies she told and all the misery she caused?'

Octavia had no sooner stepped out of the front door, escorted by a still disapproving Marcle, than the ladies quitted the parlour to return to the morning room, questions tumbling from their lips. To find Eleanor standing as Octavia had left her, eyes a little glazed, rigid tension in the set of her shoulders.

'What did she say?' Eleanor repeated, her thoughts clearly elsewhere. 'That she loved Edward more than anything in her life, had always done so. That she would follow him to the ends of the earth if he asked it of her.' She repeated the words as if they were engraved on her heart.

Mrs Stamford instantly bristled. 'Had she no shame? Could she not even offer the semblance of a heartfelt apology? Any true remorse? To you and to dear Sarah. When I think how she was prepared to use a child to achieve their fraudulent claims... A colder woman I have never had the misfortune to meet. She would appear to have no sense of right or wrong.'

'No.' Eleanor shook her head, turning away from the little group. 'I think she knows very well. She was sorry to cause hurt,' she said. 'But in her eyes her devotion to Edward excused everything. Even though she knew that what she did was wrong.'

'And I suppose you accepted her explanation, expressing your admiration of her fortitude.' Mrs Stamford stepped up to her daughter to take her arm in a firm hold, exasperation clear on her face. 'And probably sent her on her way with your blessing, if I know you! Eleanor, how could you!'

'No, Mama. Admire Octavia? How could I? But I do understand her—her love for Sir Edward...'

'And I suppose you told her that, too!'

'No. I…I did not… Octavia expressed her regret. Then just explained why she had done it…and left. I don't think she wanted my forgiveness. It did not seem to matter to her. Edward was the only one who…'

To the shock of everyone present, and to her own, Eleanor promptly burst into tears, covering her face with hands that shook. All the pent-up anguish flowed out, all her carefully constructed self-possession, held in place since Henry's departure, was obliterated in a storm of weeping. She sobbed uncontrollably, one thought only in her mind. She could not admire Octavia. But the lady's affirmation of unconditional love for Edward had touched her heart.

Judith tutted in sympathy, rushed to take her in her arms and to lead her to the sofa so recently vacated by the unrepentant Octavia.

'I am so sorry.' Eleanor sniffed as she tried to stem the sobs. 'What must you think of me?' She dabbed ineffectually at her tears with a small scrap of lace-edged linen.

Judith produced her own handkerchief and added it to the flow, making soothing noises and patting her shoulders. Until the sobs gradually abated.

'Nell. Look at me.' Eleanor raised her tear-ravaged face at the masterful demand from a usually easy-going lady. 'This cannot go on! Tell me what you most want in life. Be truthful!' Judith added as she sensed Eleanor begin to withdraw behind her habitual shield. 'What would you wish for, if any wish could be granted at this moment?'

'To be with Hal.' Tears threatened again.

'We thought as much.' Judith looked round to meet the eyes of the other interested ladies, a curl of satisfaction in her smile. 'Now don't cry again!'

'We knew that was the way of it.' Sarah nodded in agreement.

'But he has left me.' Desolation refused to loose its hold on Eleanor.

'Then follow him!' Judith gave her a small shake in frustration. 'Do it. Go to him!'

'I can't. He does not want me.'

'Nell—this is not like you. Where is your strength and

courage?' Judith's vivid Faringdon features, so like Henry's, were afire with determination on behalf of her friend. 'Of course you can. Being a man, he probably does not realise what he wants.'

'Oh, but he does. Indeed he does, Judith. But he must not marry me. The law forbids it…' Sobs threatened her returning composure again.

'There now. Such a little thing!' The Countess of Painscastle snapped her fingers in casual dismissal of the laws of man and God. 'You say that you love Hal. And yet you would live the rest of your life without him? Go to him, Nell. Anything is better than needless loss and regret.'

'What if he refuses to take me with him?'

'Are you going to give him the chance? I had thought better of you!'

Eleanor looked across to where her mother now sat. The lady's features were carefully schooled when she spoke. 'You love him, Eleanor. I should have known… I too did you a great wrong, as you know… And I suppose I would make recompense.' She winced a little at the sheer surprise that Eleanor could not disguise, but continued none the less. 'I don't like it. It breaks my heart to lose you and the child—but I can see in your face that you would be with him.' Mrs Stamford's eyes were bright, but no tear was allowed to escape, no expression of weakness. 'If you want him, Eleanor, then take Judith's advice. I will not put my weight of argument against it.' But she turned her face away.

'Octavia would do it.' Eleanor considered her previous conversation with that lady. *I would follow him to the ends of the earth if he asked it of me.* 'She would allow nothing to come between her and Edward.'

'There now. If she can, insipid creature that she is, so can you. It is settled.' Judith was now triumphant. 'And Sarah will go with you, won't you, Sarah?'

'Sarah?' Eleanor felt as if she were being swept along by a veritable hurricane, all her arguments ignored, all her reasoning disputed and thrown out. And even her mother… She felt momentarily helpless, but the feeling could not compete with the sudden surge of hope in her heart. *I can do it. I can go to him and insist that I go with him!*

'I would go with you.' Sarah's face lit at the prospect and she nodded towards Judith. 'We have talked of it and decided. I believe that Captain Russell might have liked the idea of his son to be brought up in America. I have a mind to see it for myself. Will you let me accompany you?'

'Oh, Sarah!' Eleanor dabbed once more at her eyes.

'Don't anyone say anything else to reduce her to tears again!' Judith instructed with a frown. 'Sarah—go and tell Nick that it is all decided. He will know what to do.'

Eleanor laughed softly. 'I have stopped weeping—I do promise you. What has Nick to do with it?'

'All your possessions are packed,' Judith explained. 'It seemed to us that you will have just enough time to take the coach to Liverpool and catch the sailing. Nick will arrange it, of course.'

'Have you been scheming behind my back?' Eleanor's fine brows rose at the extent of her family's duplicity.

'Yes. But only for your good.' Judith leaned to kiss her on both cheeks. 'It broke my heart to see you so unhappy. Go to Hal and make a new life for both of you, and for Tom.'

They left her alone with Nicholas.

'I see that Judith has been arranging everyone's life, as usual. And yours in particular.' He walked across the room to take her hands in his, lift them to his lips in formal salute, much as Henry was wont to do. The resemblance had never been so strong.

'Do you disapprove, dear Nick?'

'No. How could I?'

'Hal cannot marry me. Any union between us will not be legal.'

'I know it.' There was no condemnation here.

'Even if I take Tom with me? Out of the country?'

'Eleanor.' Nick's voice was gentle as he released her hands. 'He is Hal's son. Am I right?'

Bright colour suffused Eleanor's cheeks, but she would not deny it. 'Yes. Oh, yes. I did not realise…'

'No one gives me any credit for any percipience. You are as bad as Hal!' He huffed out a breath in mock annoyance. But smiled at her confusion and was quick to reassure her. 'I guessed long ago. Watching the two of you, it was not difficult to see the connection between you and Hal. The love that neither of you could deny, no matter how hard you might try. And Tom is as much like Hal as he resembled Thomas.'

'Oh.'

'And Thomas, being the honourable man he was, made you his wife and gave Tom a father because Hal did not know. Am I right?'

'Yes.' She sighed at his quick understanding and his calm acceptance of what many would have condemned out of hand.

'And Hal knows,' Nick continued, 'but fears taking you into hardship and danger.'

'Yes. That is it. You know us very well.'

'So it seems. You will join him in Liverpool and Sarah will accompany you. Or that was Judith's plan.'

'Yes. But what about the estate, Nick?'

'I will run it, with Hoskins dealing with all the legal business. When Tom comes of age, he can claim it. He can choose to live where he wishes.'

'But—'

'Before you ask, it will not be a burdensome task to me. I shall enjoy having a free hand.' Nicholas took her shoulders to shake her, much as Judith had done. 'Look, Nell. Do you love Hal?'

'More than life itself.' She found herself deliberately echoing Octavia's words, a tender smile touching her lips, leaving Nick in no doubt of the power of her love. He was quick to banish the sharp twinge of envy and turn his mind to the practical.

'Then go to him. You will catch the sailing. Everything is arranged.'

He took her hands once more and pressed a light kiss of farewell to her forehead, his smile a little sad at the anticipation of loss for himself.

'Thank you. Dearest Nick. I can never express my gratitude enough.'

'You do not have to…' But he spoke to an empty space. Eleanor had turned on her heel, to collect her son and begin her journey to Hal.

'Poor Hal.' A sudden grin lightened Nick's rather sombre expression as he envisaged the meeting in Liverpool. 'He does not know what fate has in store for him.' Then followed the Marchioness of Burford from the room to arrange the travel documents and the stowing of the luggage in the travelling coach.

Chapter Thirteen

In Liverpool, the days passed slowly for Lord Henry as the *Sea Emerald* made ready to sail. He put up at the Black Bull, a small but comfortable establishment close to the docks, and tried without success to exert some patience. Captain Armstrong and the ship's officers set about the supplying of the vessel with food and water, and the careful stowing away of trade goods, mostly cutlery and domestic hardware from Sheffield and the Black Country. Henry's impatience did not make it happen any quicker, but the ship's company was soon used to his interested presence on board. After all, the experience, invaluable in itself to a man newly engaged in trading contracts, took his mind off other issues. Or at least that was his plan.

He had done the right thing. Of course he had. He must not allow his impeccable reasoning to disintegrate into so much smoke and dust in the dark hours of early morning when sleep evaded him, to torment him over and over again with visions of impossible loss. He had made the only sensible decision. Taken the only honourable course. If he allowed himself to question his logic, he would begin to regret. And then it would be the easiest thing in the world to reject all honour and take the next coach back to London. Or Burford Hall. Or to wherever he could find Eleanor. No, he must not even consider such action. It was desperately important that she be kept safe in a life of cushioned luxury, her reputation untarnished, their child secure to inherit as was his right.

He cursed fluently as he watched the sun rise to herald a new painful dawn.

What had he done? His mind refused to listen to the sensible advice, his senses refused to be swayed by clear, cold argument, his blood refused to run quietly in his veins when he remembered their final night together. Her willing submission to his demands, her unquestioning response to his every caress, of hands and mouth and body.

He had been given his heart's desire. And wilfully turned his back on it. Not coldly, not with calm acceptance of the inevitable. By God, it had torn him apart. And continued to do so with the vicious claws of a predator, laying in wait with diabolical cunning for every moment that he allowed his defences to fall. But it had been madness to think that it was ever possible to take and to keep Eleanor at his side. And yet he could not get her out of his mind. Soft and naked and pliant in his bed. In his arms.

He groaned as he tossed and turned, sleepless once more, despite the renowned comfort of the Black Bull accommodation.

At least when the *Sea Emerald* sailed, there would be no going back. The decision would have been made, finally and irrevocably.

On the day before the proposed sailing, Lord Henry transferred his meagre luggage on board. It was a less than spacious cabin, but he had paid for the privacy it offered, and for that he would willingly tolerate the cramped surroundings as they sailed out of sight of land.

Later that night, before they would sail at dawn, he returned to the vessel after a final glass of wine with a group of associates at the Black Bull.

'Evening, sir.' Captain Armstrong touched his hand to his hat as he stood waiting on deck.

'Captain Armstrong. A clear night. Good weather for sailing.' The last thing Henry desired was a lengthy conversation, but resigned himself to it. He would spend many weeks in the Captain's company.

'Indeed, indeed. There's been a delivery for you, sir. I have sent the package to your cabin. A matter of urgency, I was given to understand.'

'Then I must go and investigate.' Henry bowed his departure and made for his cabin. He could not think what might have arrived with urgency. Letters forwarded from London? Had he mislaid something of importance that Nick had posted on with such speed? He shrugged, unable to guess. It really did not seem to matter. With such preoccupation, he did not notice the amusement in Captain Armstrong's face, or the knowing gleam in his eyes. Nor had he noticed the bustle on the dock. The smart coach and four, dusty from fast travel. Or the luggage being manhandled on board the *Sea Emerald.*

He went below, treading carefully in the ill-lit gangways below decks. It was well enough now, he thought idly, but what would it be like in a major storm after weeks at sea? His muscles tightened at the anticipation of such discomfort as he opened the door of his cabin. Stepped in and closed it behind him.

And halted, heart picking up its beat, breathing shallow. He was unprepared for this. The room—little more than a space—was small, dark and cramped, made worse by his recently disposed luggage. But someone had entered and had lit a half-shuttered lantern, which cast a circle of light onto the narrow cot against the bulkhead. The rest of the cabin was in deep shadow.

But on the cot, swathed in a soft shawl and blankets, and making every attempt to escape, sat a baby. A child with Faringdon features. A child who looked up at the opening of the door and blinked disconcertingly at him with amethyst eyes.

Henry halted, shocked into immobility by the totally unexpected. It was as if he had been robbed of all breath, of all power of thought and action. Then behind him, to his left, there was the smallest of movements.

He turned his head.

Eleanor.

She wore her fashionable travelling costume, high waisted, shawl-collared, eminently practical, a straw bonnet, feathered and be-flowered, and kid gloves, standing hands clasped before her, waiting for him. As if she had just stepped out of the house in Park Lane with nothing more important on her mind than to stroll through the gardens or to visit the expensive shops to spend a little money on fripperies in Bond Street. Her face was calm, her mouth relaxed and unsmiling, but her eyes were watchful. And fixed on him.

'Eleanor…' The words would not come.

'Lord Henry…' Now she could summon a slight smile at his obvious confusion, but her heart was beating fast, as fast, if she had but known it, as his.

'What have you done…?'

'I am coming with you.'

'I told you that it is not possible…'

'I do not accept your reasoning.'

She was so damnably calm, so assured and certain of the step that she had taken! He immediately sensed danger here. His gaze went to the baby, who appeared to be watching the scene with utmost fascination, and back again to Eleanor. Should he rage and curse? Or take her in his arms? Shake her or kiss her? Or simply ask her to leave, to take herself and the baby back to London. Perhaps that would be too cruel. But if she stayed… He knew well the limitations of his own control where she was concerned.

Eleanor could not read his face. It was severe. Harsh, even, with deeply engraved lines around his stern mouth as the consequences ran through his mind. Had she made the wrong choice when she had gambled everything on his needs being as great and all-consuming as hers? Icy fingers of dread began to tease their path down her spine, but she held them at bay. She would not make it easy for him to reject her again. She would trample on Hal's principles if she had to. But his honour was another matter…

'Nell…'

'If Octavia can follow Edward to the ends of the earth, then I can follow you.'

'Octavia? What has Octavia got to do with it?'

'Nothing, really.' With carefully controlled fingers, casually and without haste, she unfastened the ribbon bow of her bonnet, removed it and placed it on the cot with her gloves. Then unbuttoned her coat and disposed of it likewise. 'I have arranged everything and am here with the blessing of Nick and Judith.'

'Nick?'

'Yes. And you should know that Captain Armstrong has found a cabin for Sarah and John.'

'Sarah!'

'Even Mama waved me off,' she continued, smoothing down her fine woollen skirts, 'almost with good grace.'

'Your mother! Oh, God!' Henry ran his hands through his hair. 'It seems that within the last minute, lady, you have turned my world upside down and my wits have totally deserted me.'

'So I think. You sound like a demented parrot, my love.' She came to stand before him. But not too close. Not to touch. The ultimate decision here must be his.

'I will not take you with me.' The words were forced from him, but immediate.

'Hal. Look at me.' Still she did not smile. There was a challenge in her eyes. 'The only reason for me to leave this ship is if you tell me that you do not want me—that you do not love me enough to spend the rest of your life with me.'

He looked at her, a brooding quality in his eyes. How unfair that she should have done this, using his one weakness. But how magnificent. He was aware of nothing but her grace and beauty and the love that shone in her eyes. The love that he knew, without doubt, was for him alone. And he knew that she intended to fight for her happiness. He stifled a groan at the prospect.

'I cannot. You know that I cannot say that.' It was the only answer he could make in all honesty.

'Well, then.'

'It does not solve anything, Nell.' A hint of desperation crept in. 'It does not negate any of my reasons for leaving you in London. I have nothing to give you compared with what you have here.'

'My son needs his father far more than he needs a title and an estate.' Now there was the faintest snap of temper. 'And when he is old enough, he will tell you the same. You are not free to reject him, Hal. Nor me.' She played her final cards, flinging them defiantly at his feet. 'If you love me indeed, you must in all honour take me with you.'

'I should send you back.' Desperately, aware of his resistance crumbling before her deliberate and irresistible provocation, he held back.

'What? With my reputation even more besmirched, after joining you on board ship? What would the Princess Lieven say? I shall be banned from Almack's for ever! I cannot believe that you would do that to me, Hal.'

'Blackmail, Eleanor?' Now there was a spark of appreciation for her tactics in his sombre eyes, matching the glint in hers. Against his will, against all his intentions, he felt the tight knot of despair that had constricted his chest with tight bands begin to dissolve, replaced by an insidious warmth and hope.

'If it is necessary.' She raised her chin, accepting the blame, if blame there must be, but the flush that tinted her cheeks fluctuated deliciously. 'But I would rather you took me willingly, than under duress.'

'Your reputation is inestimable,' he stated, dropping his gaze because hers was too bright, too certain, with the faintest of sighs. 'It always will be. There is no duress for either of us.'

Suddenly, aware of possible disaster of a domestic nature, Henry turned from her with a rapid movement to scoop up Tom, determinedly attempting to crawl to investigate the space over the edge of the cot. With gentle hands and remarkable efficiency he smoothed the ruffled curls, then wedged the baby back into safety behind the barricade of a small travelling bag and the blankets, thoughtfully removing the enticing prospect of Eleanor's feathered bonnet out of reach.

She watched and smiled and waited. Perhaps the battle was almost won. When he turned back to her, she stretched her arm across the void still separating them, to touch his cheek in the lightest of caresses. Much as she might have stroked her son's cheek—but the result was intoxicating. Fire and heat sparked between them across the space.

'Do you love me, Hal?' Eleanor noticed with interest that she was suddenly breathless.

'Yes. As God is my witness. Yes.' All the doubt and uncertainty seemed to smooth from his face as he took a deep breath. 'I do not need to ask if you love me. If you have thrown in your lot with me, you must indeed be besotted, you foolish girl.'

'Will it be so bad?'

'Desperate.' Still he did not approach her. 'You will be Mrs Faringdon and live in a two-roomed garret above a business premises. You will have to learn to cook and clean and take care of money—no frivolous spending on gowns and kid gloves.' A faint sardonic smile tugged at his lips as he took in her stylish and expensive gown. 'We shall be forced to live on bread and soup—or something of that nature.'

'As bad as that?' It would be all right! Her pulse throbbed, her senses swam with relief. 'Should I change my mind, after all.'

'Oh, no.' He took one step closer. 'You had your chance and deliberately threw it away. You are in my power now, my lady.'

She veiled a satisfied gleam with long lashes, fighting to hold back tears. 'Thank God for that.'

Then he took another step. And she was in his arms. Held as he allowed his lips to claim his own. Hair, eyes, temples, lips, he kissed her with intense deliberation and growing urgency, halting only to murmur her name, to seek out the impossibly soft skin at the base of her throat where the pulse beat in tune with his. And Eleanor clung to him as the warmth in her blood was so effortlessly ignited into heat, to cleanse and burn, to obliterate all doubts for the future, all pain from the past.

'Hal—oh, Hal. I thought you might send me home,' she whispered as he tangled his hands in her hair, the better to seek and take possession of her mouth, slanting his head to capture and demand.

'You are home.' Drunk on heady passion, he tightened his hold, hands fierce, mouth scalding. 'You will stay with me! You no longer have a choice.'

His lips made their searing pathway along her elegant shoulder—then came to a halt as they brushed against a fine gold chain. He raised his head to look down at her, immediately lost in the shining depths of dew-sprinkled heart's-ease, but his desire was reined in and lightened with humour.

'I thought you would have brought the diamonds.'

She choked on a little laugh, putting up a hand to her breast.

'No. They are not mine to bring. But this is. It was given to me a little while ago. By an admirer. An admirer whom I choose to remember.'

'With fondness? With a little charity, perhaps?'

'With ecstasy!'

He lowered his lips to her breast, to press them against the fine amethyst jewel in its diamond setting, in recognition of the past before they put it from them for ever.

'I would give you more than this. I would give you my name, Nell.' His laugh was, for a moment only, heavy with irony, muffled against her hair. 'But you already have it.' His fingers encircled and tightened around Thomas's diamond and sapphire ring that she still wore, that he himself had replaced on her finger that night at the Red Lion with a silent promise to love and care for her. 'And you already have the Faringdon bridal ring.'

'You gave it back to me when I would have rejected it, Hal.' Eleanor bent her head to touch her lips to his hand, as it still enfolded hers, in recognition of that gesture.

'It is where it belongs. And where it will stay.' Hal's expression was stern as he spoke, his words a confirmation of his promise at the Red Lion, so that Eleanor might hear and know. 'I would give you the protection of my body. The worship of my soul. The adoration of my heart. Is that enough for you, my love, my heart?'

'I will accept all that.' She spread her palms against the solid beat of his heart, absorbing the comfort and the promise.

He put her from him, taking her hands and lifting them to his lips, first one and then the other, before looking down into her lovely face. 'Then this is all simply unfinished business, awaiting its completion for two long years. Your mother kept us apart. But Thomas kept you safe for me. Now you are mine. It is our destiny. And I would reclaim my own. In the eyes of God you, and Tom, are mine. With or without the sanction of the law, I claim you. I will love and cherish you to the end of my days. Will that be enough for you, my dearest and only love? It is all I have to give—and it is yours to take, if you will have it.'

Now Henry's hands folded around hers, encircling them in a gesture of strength, both comfort and protection. And the most tender expression of love.

'I accept, my lord.' Eleanor allowed her hands to rest in his as the heat spread urgent fingers to tint her skin with a blush of becoming rose. How splendid he was, how aware of her needs and anxieties, the weight of the past on her heart. How could he think that any woman would refuse such an offer? How could she possibly refuse?

'I will construct for you a house in New York. And build a life for you, worthy of you.' But he knew that she was now his, whatever the future would hold.

'I will live with you, Hal. With joy and contentment, assuredly. I will give you all the love that fills my heart and soul.' She hesitated, but only for the length of a heartbeat. 'And, Hal, I will give you back your son.'

His breath caught, moved unbearably by the generosity of her offer after all that had passed between them.

'A man could ask no more. Eleanor, my love.'

His lips once more took hers and sealed their future together.

* * * * *

Don't miss the second instalment of

THE FARINGDON SCANDALS,

The Outrageous Débutante
coming in December 2009

The Reluctant Escort

by

Mary Nichols

Born in Singapore, **Mary Nichols** came to England when she was three, and has spent most of her life in different parts of East Anglia. She has been a radiographer, school secretary, information officer and industrial editor, as well as a writer. She has three grown-up children and four grandchildren. Mary loves to hear from her readers and you can contact her via her website: www.marynichols.co.uk

Chapter One

1816

When Duncan first saw Molly, it was an early summer day, with the sun shining and the skylarks hovering above the heath. She was walking on the grass alongside the track with her shoes and stockings in her hand and the hem of her striped dimity skirt wet and muddy. Her cottager hat had fallen down her back on its ribbons and her soft blonde hair lay tangled on her shoulders. He took her for a child, a very pretty child.

She looked up when she heard the slow clop of the horse's hooves behind her and brushed her wayward hair from her eyes to watch him approach. Strangers were a rarity at Stacey Manor, it being on a promontory of land which was not *en route* to anywhere, and she concluded he was probably lost. His black stallion, seen with the eyes of someone who adored horses, was a beauty, strong and muscular and somehow out of keeping with the look of the man.

He was a rough sort of fellow, with a half-grown beard and clothes which were crumpled and dusty as if he had slept in them. But he held himself upright and his hands, holding the reins with a light touch, were brown and strong. There were lines about his dark eyes which could have been caused by frequent laughter or continually squinting in strong sunlight. A soldier home from the Peninsular War, she deduced, and immediately imbued him with the character of a hero.

In her mind's eye she imagined the heat and smoke of battle, heard the gunfire, saw the enemy hordes and the man, slashing this way and that with his sword and emerging triumphant. The only thing wrong with that vision was that the man's coat was not scarlet but a drab brown and he was not carrying a sword but a rifle in a holster on his saddle.

She waited, expecting him to stop to ask the way, but though his lips twitched into a smile as he passed he did not speak nor even acknowledge her, which piqued her. She hardly ever spoke to anyone but Lady Connaught or the servants and the chance of a little conversation with someone new, however brief, was something to be savoured.

She watched as he continued unhurriedly on his way and then sat on the side of the road to put on her stockings and shoes. Her feet were still wet from paddling in the brook and the footwear was tight and uncomfortable.

She had seen the green and blue flash of a kingfisher swooping along the bank and had waded into the shallow water to see it better. She ought to have known she would startle it and it would abandon its prey to sit in a tree overhanging the water until she had left its domain. And then she had spotted a trout under the bank and tried to catch it as she had seen Jeremy Bland, the poacher, do, but it, like the kingfisher, was gone in the blinking of an eye.

She had turned for home, knowing she would be in for another scolding from her godmother if she saw the state she was in. 'Molly Madcap', Lady Connaught called her. And though she grumbled and threatened, Molly knew her bark was far worse than her bite and she would escape punishment. Besides, what could her ladyship do, except lock her in her room? And that was easy to escape from. There was enough ivy clinging to the walls of the old house to make a secure ladder from her window to the ground.

There was no other punishment available, no social occasions she could ban her from attending, no friends she could be forbidden to see, no shops she could be barred from visiting, unless you went to Norwich or King's Lynn, which the old lady did twice a year. Molly hadn't been staying with her long enough to have enjoyed that experience yet, but she didn't hold out much hope that it would be the adventure she craved. She was bored. Even the stranger had ignored her. She might as well be invisible.

Once in sight of the big house, standing on its promontory, four-square to the North Sea, she hurried her pace, darting between the scattered shrubs which were euphemistically called a garden, and in at the kitchen door.

'Lord a'mercy, Miss Molly!' Cook exclaimed. 'What have you been up to now?'

'Trying to poach a trout for dinner.' Molly's smile lit her face; it was the kind of smile that made everyone around her feel more cheerful, however ill their humour had been beforehand. It started in rosy lips and even white teeth and ended in blue eyes, bright as cornflowers. Cook could not resist it, and even the Dowager Lady Connaught found it difficult to maintain her severity. 'But I'm not sad it escaped. It was too beautiful to be cooked and eaten.'

'Seventeen years old, you are,' Cook reminded her. 'Seventeen. Some young ladies are married at your age. Will you never grow up?' It was a rhetorical question. Cook knew perfectly well why Molly was still so childlike. It was her mother's fault. Harriet could never stand competition and Molly showed promise of being even more beautiful than her parent. So the poor girl had been kept a child for as long as possible, but when that would no longer serve she had been brought here to stay with the old lady while Harriet herself had set off for London to find husband number four.

'Has Aunt Margaret asked for me?' Lady Connaught was not really her aunt, but a cousin twice removed, but that was how Molly's mother addressed her and Molly, who had been named after her, had been told to do the same.

'No, but she will do so soon. We have a visitor…'

'A visitor?' Molly brightened, thinking of the stranger who had passed her on the road, and then wondered why her ladyship should entertain such a one. He had come to bring her some stupendous news: a long-lost love found. No, her godmother was too old for such fancies. Then news of some distant battle in which a relative had distinguished himself? But as far as Molly knew, her ladyship had no relatives except the Earl of Connaught who was her grandson, and he lived at Foxtrees on the borders of Hertfordshire and Essex.

Perhaps the stranger had been wounded and had come to be nursed back to health. Oh, that would be best, then he would stay a little, instead of disappearing as all visitors to Stacey Manor were wont to do. 'Who is it?'

'You'll see. I suggest you go and change and do your hair and be quick about it.'

Molly crept up the servants' stairs to her own room and stripped off her soiled clothes. She washed and dressed again in a pale blue sarcenet gown with a shawl collar of white lace, white stockings and blue kid shoes, then set about brushing out the tangles in her hair. When it was once again lying smooth and shining on her shoulders, she sat down and surveyed herself in the looking-glass, wishing she didn't look so young; Lady Connaught's guest would hardly converse with her unless she could make herself look interesting and intelligent. Perhaps it would help if she put her hair up.

She scooped it up in her hand and looked this way and that, then scrabbled in her drawer for combs and pins. Oh, if only she had a lady's maid to help her! But Mama had said it was not at all necessary at Stacey Manor where the simplest of clothes would be perfectly adequate. She had been right, of course. There was nothing to do, except walk and ride and read, and make occasional visits of a charitable nature to the local villagers.

Pinning up her thick hair was not easy but she achieved it in the end, though one strand refused to be confined and curled lovingly into her neck. She left it there and went down to the withdrawing room.

Lady Connaught, dressed as always in unrelieved black on account of being widowed thirty years before, sat in a high-backed chair by the hearth. Her visitor stood facing her, with his hand on the mantel. He turned when he heard Molly come into the room. She wasn't sure whether his smile was one of amusement or pleasure, but was gratified that he smiled at all.

He had changed out of the grubby clothes he had been wearing and was now in biscuit-coloured pantaloons and a blue superfine coat, beneath which was a canary-yellow waistcoat with brass buttons and a cravat of white muslin, cleverly tied. He had shaved and his hair had been washed and brushed until it shone. He was now Molly's idea of a man about town and the war-like fantasies she had been weaving about him faded to be replaced by others.

He was part of the Prince Regent's court and had been sent to rescue her, to take her to London to be courted by all the eligibles and marry the most handsome and attentive of them all. She might be presented to the Queen at one of her drawing rooms and everyone would say how well she looked.

She knew she should not indulge in these daydreams; it was foolish and childish, as her mother had told her often enough, but they lightened a dull afternoon when there was nothing else to do. Dreams were no substitute for reality and it was the reality she craved.

'Molly, come and meet…' Her ladyship paused and looked at him for a moment as if unsure of his identity, then went on, 'Captain Duncan Stacey. Duncan, this is Mrs Benbright's daughter, Margaret. You remember Harriet Benbright, do you not?'

Molly did not see the look which passed between them, nor did she hear his murmured comment as she dropped a very deep curtsey before moving forward, wondering if he recognised her as the girl he had seen on the road. She hoped he would not mention it, because it would spark off a jobation from Aunt Margaret and that would be too mortifying. Besides, she didn't want him to think of her as Miss Molly Madcap, but as a woman with whom he could enjoy social intercourse.

She looked up into his eyes and realised that he was trying to convey a message in them. It was a kind of reassurance and she gave him a conspiratorial smile which startled and then charmed him.

'Your servant, Miss…' In the middle of taking her hand and bowing over it, he paused. 'Forgive me, I do not know which one you belong to.'

He was referring to her mother's three husbands, she

realised. 'I should have thought it was obvious,' she said. 'The first one, Monsieur Martineau, of course. Mama was only seventeen when she married him and I was born less than a year later. It is why we are more like sisters than mother and daughter, so Mama says. If I had been the child of Mr Winters or Colonel Benbright, I would still be a child, would I not?'

'Of course,' he said, stifling an inclination to laugh. 'How stupid of me not to have worked that out for myself. Miss Martineau, I am pleased to make your acquaintance.'

'Sit down, both of you,' her ladyship said. 'Dinner will be served at three. We don't keep London hours here.'

'No, I did not think you would,' he said. He turned to Molly. 'Miss Martineau, are you enjoying your stay in Norfolk?'

'Yes, thank you,' she said.

'But it is somewhat dull, I think.'

'Sometimes.'

'How do you amuse yourself?'

She looked up at him sharply, wondering if his query was leading up to some comment about wandering about the countryside in bare feet. 'I walk and ride and read, and visit the cottages. The people are very poor, you know, and we must do what we can for them.'

'Indeed, I do know. It is commendable that you are concerned about them; isn't that so, my lady?'

'Yes,' her ladyship said. 'Though there is little we can do about the weather and it is the heavy rain that ruined last year's harvest.'

'And the end of the war,' Molly put in. 'All those soldiers coming home and needing work. No wonder they riot.'

'Do they?' he queried. 'Hereabouts?'

'Everywhere. You must have been out of the country not

to have known about it. But perhaps you are one of those soldiers yourself. I collect you are a captain.'

'I am, yes.'

'Were you in any big battles?'

'Indeed I was.'

'Which ones?. Tell me all about them. Have you ever seen Napoleon Bonaparte? Or spoken to the Duke of Wellington? How much do you think the different styles of leadership of Napoleon and the Duke contributed to the final outcome?'

'Styles of leadership?' he echoed, taken aback. It was not a subject he would have expected someone of her years to show an interest in.

'Why, yes. Napoleon likes to march to battle with a great deal of noise and show and banners flying, while the Duke hides his men away and does not reveal himself until the last minute. He also dresses in a very nondescript way and Napoleon struts like a turkey-cock. Is that not so? Do you think Wellington learned his tactics from Agincourt? Henry V hid his bowmen behind palisades until the enemy was almost upon them, didn't he?'

'Goodness, so many questions all at once,' he said. 'I hardly know where to begin.'

'I shouldn't answer any of them,' Lady Connaught put in drily. 'It will only lead to more. Molly's curiosity is insatiable.'

'But that is how we learn, is it not?' Molly said. Ever since she had been taught to read by her father, she had devoured everything she could lay her hands on, whether suitable or not. Simple moralising tales given to her by her nursemaid were soon replaced by novels, both good and bad, and the contents of her succeeding stepfathers' libraries.

Geography and horticulture and ancient history were

digested along with the rudiments of wine-making. And from Colonel Benbright's vast collection of military books she had read about war and military campaigns and those who directed them. 'I have read about such things,' she told the Captain. 'But it is not the same as talking to someone who was there.'

'Some things it is better not to know,' the Captain said. 'I shall certainly not enlighten you or I shall be blamed for giving you nightmares.'

'You think I am so lily-livered I have to be protected from anything disagreeable? I assure you, Captain, I am not so lacking in imagination that I do not realise that some things in life are very unpleasant. One must learn about the bad as well as the good.'

'But better not dwelt upon,' Lady Connaught said. 'Duncan, you may escort us in to dinner and I do not want to hear another word about the war. You may tell us what is going on in London instead.'

They moved into the dining room and over a frugal meal of turbot, game pie, vegetables and a fruit flummery Duncan regaled them with the latest gossip from the capital, including the Prince Regent's long dispute with his wife Caroline, and Princess Charlotte's love match with Prince Leopold, a story that delighted Molly, who had a very romantic streak in spite of her hoydenish ways. But he had been to no social gatherings and could tell them nothing of the latest fashions.

Duncan stayed behind to smoke a cigar and drink a glass of port after the meal but soon joined them in the withdrawing room where they played three-handed whist until it was time for Molly to retire.

'You will be staying?' she enquired, when she bade him

goodnight. 'I shall see you tomorrow? You can tell me all about your experiences then.'

'Alas, no, I must be gone by daybreak,' he said. 'But I shall look forward to meeting you again in the future.'

'Oh, must you go? We so seldom see anyone interesting at Stacey Manor. It is the most boring of places. Nothing ever happens here. Begging you pardon, Aunt Margaret, but there is so little to do and no one to converse with at all.'

Duncan's smile was a little crooked. 'I am afraid if it is social discourse you are looking for I am a poor one to provide it.' He stood up and bowed to her. 'Goodnight, Miss Martineau. May your dreams be pleasant ones.'

When she had gone, Duncan settled down again with his grandmother. 'The poor child must find it very boring here. Why in heaven's name did Harriet not take her with her to London?'

Lady Connaught smiled. 'And have everyone wondering how she can be old enough to have a daughter of seventeen? It would certainly be a stumbling block to her own prospects. Harriet has promised Molly a Season when she has landed a wealthy husband for herself. She is still a beautiful woman, not in the first flush of youth but not too old to want a husband.'

'She has had three already! I should think anyone contemplating marriage with her might well consider how long he might live after the ceremony.'

'Oh, that is unfair, Duncan. Her first husband, the French diplomat and Molly's father, was a widower and an old man when she married him. Unfortunately her expectations on his death were not realised; he left his fortune to his first family in France and only a small portion came Harriet's way.'

'And her second?'

'George Winters. He was a wine importer and plump in the pocket when they married, but the blockade of French ports ruined his business and he went to America to look for new sources of supply. He died out there of a fever in 1812 or 1813—I am not sure which it was. That marriage lasted eleven years, but it left Harriet no better off than before. Her third husband was Colonel Benbright…'

'He was killed at Waterloo. I met him once. An old stick-in-the-mud, who believed it was dishonourable to retreat whatever the circumstances. He had been ordered by Wellington to withdraw from his position, but he chose to ignore the order and took a great many good and brave men with him to their deaths.' He stopped, hearing again the sound of the unremitting guns and the cries and groans of the wounded men in that terrible conflict.

He had thought himself battle-hardened, but even he had been appalled and sickened by the carnage. And some of it was so unnecessary. Colonel Benbright's men, not knowing his orders, had obeyed his commands and died at his side. Duncan had been glad not to be one of them, even though, at the time, he had been feeling sick at heart and would have welcomed a good clean death.

'So now Harriet must find another husband.' His grandmother broke in on his reverie and brought him sharply back to more mundane matters. 'Her daughter is an encumbrance, if not a serious rival, so she sent her here to stay with me.'

'Fustian! She is no more than an attractive child; how can she possibly be in competition with her own mother?'

'She is not a child, Duncan. She is seventeen, nearly eighteen.'

'She looks more like fifteen. A mere schoolgirl.'

'That is Harriet's fault for trying to keep her young. Poor

Molly has not been allowed to grow up, but underneath that childish exterior there is the heart and mind of a young woman who could blossom into a real beauty.'

'I do not doubt it. It makes me feel like horse-whipping that selfish mother of hers.'

'That would not serve either. What Molly wants is someone to help her grow up. I can't do that; I am too old and set in my ways. And Stacey Manor is too isolated.'

'So?' he asked, wondering where this conversation was leading.

'You need to settle down, Duncan. It is about time you abandoned your scapegrace ways and made something of your life.'

'With Molly Martineau?' he asked in astonishment.

'Why not?'

'Grandmama, have you any idea what sort of life I lead?'

'Yes, and it is not to your credit. You did not have to abandon your inheritance and take to the road. It was done in a fit of pique...'

'No, Grandmama, it was not. When I came home and discovered I had been reported killed in action at Vittoria...'

'The report of that action was detailed enough for no one to doubt it,' his grandmother put in. 'You were seen to fall and a French officer dismounted and finished you off with his sword...'

'He meant to, but charitably changed his mind when he saw I was wounded and took me prisoner instead.'

'It is a pity you could not have managed to let anyone know you were alive...'

'I tried, but because I would not give my parole not to attempt to escape I was denied all privileges and no one would take a letter. When I did escape, I brought important intelligence and the Chief sent me back to discover more. I was not free to come home until after Boney surrendered. Too late. My father had died, my title had been usurped, the lady I was to have married had wed my brother and produced an heir.' He paused, remembering the consternation his return had caused.

If it had not been for that spell as a French prisoner of war and Old Hooknose sending him back behind the lines as an agent, he would have come home long before and claimed his birthright. He would have arrived before his father's death and there would have been no question of who was the heir. He would be head of the family, running his estates, married to Beth... Married to Beth.

He mused on that for several seconds. It was a prospect which had kept him going all the time he had been in the Peninsula. He had dreamed of it, sure that she was waiting for him. He had spent hours wondering what she might be doing, how she looked, whether she missed him and longed for his return as much as he missed her and looked forward to being reunited with her.

The reality had been very different. Coming home and finding her married to his brother had shaken him to the core. He had been angry and miserable and then anxious only to get away, to leave them to their happiness with each other. He had told them he did not care for the settled life, had not really wanted to be the Earl, that he was a soldier and would remain one. He would not bother them again; they might continue to believe him dead.

He had given a harsh laugh. 'You may even continue to mourn me,' he had said.

Hugh, though clearly discomfited, had not tried to dissuade him, but had offered him an income from the estate, saying it was the least he could do. He had refused it, being more concerned with salvaging his pride. He had wished them happy and reported to the War Office for further service. Napoleon's escape from Elba and the second phase of the war was fortuitous in that respect.

'What else was Hugh to do?' she demanded. 'He truly believed he had become the new heir and was entitled to inherit. We all did. And Beth had expected to marry the Stacey heir ever since she was a child; it was what both families wanted. You can hardly blame her for turning to your brother.'

Logic told him that Hugh and Beth were not at fault, but his heart was still sore. Beth had been so quick to change her allegiance that he began to wonder if, after all, it was Hugh she had wanted all the time and his reported demise had been a blessing. 'Oh, I can quite see how it happened. My return was an acute embarrassment to everyone. It were better I had stayed dead. I returned to my regiment to give Napoleon another chance to finish me off at Waterloo. 'Tis a pity he did not.'

'Don't be bitter about it, my boy,' she said softly. 'You chose to renounce your inheritance for the sake of Beth and their son, so now you must put it behind you and make a fresh start. Careering about the countryside getting into scrapes will not do. It just will not do.'

'How do you know I have been getting into scrapes?'

'Why else would you come here? And in the state you were in. I am not a fool, Duncan, even if you take me for one.'

'Oh, Grandmama, I know you are no fool, but it is better you do not know…'

'Running from the law, I shouldn't wonder, or your creditors. Using Stacey Manor as a bolt-hole…'

'Grandmama…'

'Enough. You are right—I do not want to know. But what about settling down? What about Molly?' She laughed lightly. 'Scapegrace and madcap, it might be the making of you both.'

'You are surely not in earnest?'

'Why not?'

'It's out of the question. You said yourself, I am a rake-shame, always on the move, getting into one scrape after another…'

'Precisely.'

'I cannot change into a fan-carrier overnight. We should both be miserable. And what do you suppose Miss Martineau would think of the matter?'

'She will be guided by her elders.'

'Her mother! I hardly think she would provide wise guidance with three husbands already dead and buried.'

'No, but as Harriet has left Molly in my care and Molly is an obedient girl she will listen to me…'

'Then she would be lacking in spirit and that would not commend her to me. Besides, it would mean taking Harriet Benbright as a mother-in-law and I do not think I could stomach that. Such pretensions I never did see in a woman of no consequence.'

'Harriet's father was a baronet and I hardly think you are in a position to talk of consequence now, my boy.'

'No, which is why Harriet would not entertain an offer from me for her daughter. I have nothing to commend me. And any children we had would have no prospects of inheriting the title. I could not go back on my word to Hugh. That alone would exclude me in Harriet's eyes.' He smiled disarmingly. 'Grandmama, I thank you for your concern, but I must continue to live my life in the way that suits me. I have a small pension from a grateful country and Hugh has been kind enough to make me an allowance from the income of the estate.' He did not want her to think ill of his brother, nor intervene on his behalf, and so he told the lie.

'So he should! It is yours, after all. Where are you off to tomorrow?'

He smiled, concluding she had not been serious or she would not have capitulated so easily. 'Wherever the fancy takes me.'

'But I collect it must be done under cover of darkness.'

'I am afraid so. I shall be gone long before you wake, so I will say my farewell now and retire.'

She sighed. 'Very well. But you know you are always welcome here, no matter what.'

'Yes, I know, but I would be grateful if no one knew of my presence here tonight. In fact, I should deem it a favour if you were to say, if asked, that you were unaware that I had survived the second war and returned to England.'

'That I will do, but I shall also pray that you come to your senses before you find yourself preaching at Tyburn Cross.'

'Oh, I do not think it will come to that,' he said lightly. 'Hanging is certainly not part of my plan for the future.'

'Then what is?'

'I do not know. Not yet. But undoubtedly something will occur to me. Now, if you will excuse me.' He bowed over her hand, putting it to his lips. 'Goodnight and God bless you, Grandmother. Tell Molly… No, tell her nothing, for there is nothing good you could say of me.'

He strode from the room and made his way upstairs to bed, though he did not intend to sleep for more than an hour or two. Long before dawn, he was up and creeping down to the back door, from where he crossed the cobbled yard to saddle his horse.

Molly's room overlooked the stables, and as she had

stayed up reading *Don Quixote* by the light of a candle she heard him leave the house. Going to the window, she watched him enter the stables. He was escaping, getting away on that beautiful black horse of his, and she was sure he would have many fine adventures and his life would not be at all boring, as hers was.

There was something a little mysterious about him; he had talked all through dinner without giving away a single thing about himself, not even why he had chosen to come to Stacey Manor in the first place, nor how he knew her mother. Until a few months ago, she had not heard of her mother's Stacey connections. And she was curious as to why it was necessary to creep away in the dead of night.

Without stopping to think of the consequences, she scrambled into her riding habit and hurried downstairs. She was in the kitchen, pulling on her boots, when she heard the quiet clop of a horse walking across the cobbles of the yard. By the time she had let herself out of the house, the sound of the horse was fading in the distance. She ran out to the stables to saddle her mare, Jenny. Lady Connaught had long since given up riding and there were only a couple of men's saddles belonging to the groom, who rode pillion when her ladyship went out in the carriage. Molly had used the smaller of these on many occasions and had become proficient at riding astride.

Two minutes later she was galloping after the enigmatic captain, without any idea of what she would say to him when she caught up with him. It was simply that she was wide awake and longing for something to give her life a little piquancy. She would follow him and solve the mystery of who he was and what he was about.

It was a quiet night and she could hear the hooves of his

horse ahead of her, cantering easily along the dry road. She would stay a little behind him until he stopped to rest his mount; she could catch up with him. Then he must either escort her back himself or share his adventure with her. Either way she would learn more about him.

She suddenly became aware that the hoofbeats had stopped and she pulled up to listen and look about her. She had left the familiar heath behind and was on a road with open fields on one side and a copse of trees on the other. There was a village not too far way, for she heard a dog bark. Close by an owl hooted, startling her for a moment, but there was no sound of man or horse.

Surely he could not have outrun her so completely? She began to walk her mare forward more slowly, straining to hear the slightest sound. Had he turned off? But she could see no other road or bridleway. Had he gone into one of the houses in the village? Could he have an assignation there? She ought to go back, but it would be so disappointing not to have her curiosity satisfied.

A mile or two further on, she became aware of the sound of a horse behind her. She stopped and pulled her mount into the edge of the wood, concealing herself behind a bush, refusing to admit she was more than a little afraid. The other rider approached at a walk, singing quietly under his breath. He stopped when he came level with her hiding place.

'Are we going to play hide-and-seek all night?' he asked mildly.

Recognising his voice, she gave a sigh of relief and emerged from her hiding place, ducking under the low branches of a tree. 'How did you get behind me?'

'I heard someone riding after me a long time ago, but when no one caught up with me I deduced I was being followed and that is something I do not like, so I hid in the trees to see who it might be. You are very lucky I didn't take a pot shot at you.'

He was annoyed; she could tell by the set of his jaw and the steely gleam of his eye in the darkness, and she supposed he had every right to be, but she was not one to back down from a confrontation. 'And when you realised it was me, why did you not show yourself?'

He chuckled, in spite of his annoyance. 'The follower became the followed. I wanted to see how determined you were. If you thought you had lost me, you might have turned back.'

'And now you know the answer to that, what are you going to do about it?'

'Send you home, of course. I cannot for the life of me think why you set out after me.' He paused as a new thought crossed his mind. 'Lady Connaught did not send you, did she?'

'Lady Connaught?' she queried in surprise. 'Why should she do that?'

He ignored her question. 'Then why?'

'I wanted to see where you were going. You are undoubtedly going to have an adventure and…'

He threw back his head and laughed. 'I am sorry to disappoint you, Miss Madcap, but I am simply going to join a friend…'

'In the middle of the night?'

'It will be dawn before I reach the rendezvous.'

'Is it a lady friend? You have a tryst?'

'Certainly not!'

'Why so adamant? Have you an aversion to ladies?'

'Not at all. I have known some very accommodating ones. Now, if you have finished interrogating me, it is time you turned back to Stacey Manor.'

'You are surely not sending me back alone? I might lose my way or be set upon and robbed. Or raped.'

He felt sure she did not know the real meaning of the word but, looking at her youthful figure and bright eyes, he conceded she might very well be right. But they had met no one on the road and in a quiet country district like this, so far from the evils of civilisation, she was safe enough. Besides, he had his reputation of being a hard man to consider and Frank waiting at the Red Lion in Aylsham for him. He did not have the time to go back. 'You came alone.'

'Ah, but I knew you were not far away and would have come if I had called for help.'

'You scheming little madam! Well, it will not serve. Back you go.'

He was angry again. His moods changed with lightning speed; one minute he was scowling, the next laughing, and it was difficult to know which it was likely to be, but that was half the fun of the adventure. She opened her mouth to answer him, but before she could do so he had reached down to take her reins. Turning her horse the way they had come, he slapped its rump. It set off at a canter.

She could easily have brought it under control, but decided to let it have its head and pretend it was bolting with her. She turned it off the road and they crashed through the trees, startling an owl which swooped down and skimmed so close to her head, she let out a genuine scream of terror. The horse panicked and reared and the next minute she hit the ground with a bump.

'Molly, where are you?' In a daze, she heard Duncan coming after her. She lay still, her eyes closed. She heard him pull up and dismount, felt his warm breath on her face as he bent over to see if she were breathing and then let out a shuddering sigh.

'Thank God! Molly, open your eyes, there's a good girl. Let me see you are not injured.'

She allowed her eyelids to flutter. 'Where am I?'

'Safe now. Are you hurt?'

'I don't know. My head aches.'

'Can you sit up?' He was surprisingly gentle as he helped her to sit. 'That's better.' He felt round the back of her head with gentle fingers. 'Nothing broken that I can see. Now stay there while I catch your mount.'

He disappeared through the trees, but he was only gone a minute because Jenny was cropping the undergrowth close by, calm as you please.

He walked both horses out to the road and tethered them, then came back to pick her up in his arms and carry her through the trees to sit her on the mare's back. She was still a little dizzy and not at all sure she could ride. Afraid he would set her off alone again, she moaned softly and fell forward on the horse's neck.

'Oh, damnation!' she heard him mutter. She was glad Jenny was being good because she had allowed her hands to fall from the reins.

He lifted her down again and put her on his own horse, then, leading Jenny by her reins, got up behind her in order to support her as they rode. She leaned back on his rough coat, wondering what he would do next.

'Can you hear me?' he asked. 'Molly, stay awake for God's sake.'

'Am awake,' she murmured. 'Bad head.'

'Very well, Aylsham is nearer than Stacey Manor and there'll be a doctor in the town, so we will go there, but as soon as you have sufficiently recovered I shall put you on the stagecoach to take you back.'

She did not argue. His arms were strong around her and the clop of the horse's hooves soporific; she was almost asleep.

'How did you come to be such a madcap?' he murmured, more to himself than to her. 'It was that silly woman, your mother, I have no doubt. You have to grow up some time, kitten, and I have a notion it will be very soon and very sudden. I wish I could protect you, but I cannot. I need protecting from myself, as Grandmama was quick to point out…'

'Grandmama?' she murmured.

'Oh, you are not as sleepy as you pretend, are you? Grandmama is Lady Connaught.'

She lifted her head from his shoulder and turned towards him. In the moonlight, his face seemed sombre beneath a large black hat. 'You are surely not the Earl of Connaught?'

He laughed under his breath, a harsh, rather bitter sound which troubled her a little. 'No, I am not the Earl of Connaught. I belong to a different branch of the family.'

'The poor side. Every great family has a poor side, does it not?'

'And its black sheep.' This time his laugh was one of genuine amusement.

'Oh, I see. But I should guess you are her ladyship's favourite, all the same.'

'Perhaps.'

'Oh, how romantic! I expect you have had hundreds of adventures.'

'So, your headache has magically vanished.'

'No, it is still there.' She hurried to assure him. 'It will be better tomorrow, perhaps.'

'It is already tomorrow. See, the sun is on the horizon and soon it will be daylight.'

'So it is.' She could see the road winding downhill to a group of buildings and a church. 'Is that Aylsham ahead of us?'

'Yes. The Red Lion is a respectable hostelry. We will stay there for a few hours until you are feeling better. Then I will see you safely on the coach to Cromer. If your horse is tied on behind, you will be able to ride from there to Stacey Manor.'

'Where are you going?'

'Wherever the fancy takes me.'

'That's sounds very indecisive to me and you do not seem to me to be an indecisive man. A secretive one, perhaps. Do you not want me to know where you are going?'

'There is no need for you to know. Your little adventure is at an end.'

She was silent for a moment. 'When you have seen your friend are you going on to London?'

'I might. On the other hand I might not. It depends.'

'On what?'

'On what transpires,' he said enigmatically.

'I should very much like to go there…'

'Perhaps one day you will. I collect my grandmother saying you had been promised a Season.'

'Oh, that will only happen if Mama finds herself a rich husband.' She sighed. 'I am afraid she is not very good at judging how wealthy a man is and may very well mistake the matter again. I hold out no great hope.'

'So young and so cynical!'

'Realistic, Captain. So, will you take me to London?'

He chuckled, unable to take her seriously. 'Minx! You have been play-acting the whole time. It will not serve, you know. What would my grandmother say if I were to carry you off?'

'We could ride back and tell her. She will be quite content to let me go with you.'

She squirmed to turn and look at him again when he roared with laughter. He laughed so long and so loud, the tears ran down his face.

'I amuse you?' she asked stiffly.

'Oh, I was not laughing at you but at myself. How anyone could be such a gowk, I do not know.'

'Gowk?'

'Fool, Molly. I am a fool. I have fallen for a ploy as old as time.'

'Then will you take me to London? To Mama?'

'I doubt your sudden arrival would please your mama.'

'Oh, she might ring a peal over me to start with but I shall turn her up sweet, then she will take me out and about with her.'

The idea amused him even more than knowing Molly had inadvertently played into Lady Connaught's hands. Harriet would be furious. It was almost worth considering just to discomfit her. But that would not be fair on Molly. And between the Red Lion and London were a great many miles and every one of them fraught with danger. Miss Molly Martineau must be returned to Stacey Manor.

He turned into the inn yard and dismounted before lifting her down and setting her on her feet. He ordered the ostler to look after the horses and escorted her inside. Not until he had bespoken a room and tipped a chambermaid to help her to bed did he feel free to go in search of Frank.

Frank Upjohn, once a sergeant in the Norfolk Regiment and now his servant, had taken two rooms along the corridor. Duncan tiptoed along and quietly let himself in, but Frank had been watching for him and was wide awake, sitting by the window.

'You're late, Captain,' he said. 'I had all but given you up for lost.'

'I was delayed.'

'Yes, I saw her. A pretty little filly, no doubt, but a distraction we could well do without.'

'You mistake the matter,' Duncan said. 'She is a distant cousin. I shall put her on the Cromer stage when she has rested.'

'No, Captain, you cannot do that, unless you want to upset all our plans. 'Tis the stage our target will be on.'

'How so?'

'He travels a day early. It were meant to confound anyone with an eye to waylaying him. He will be coming through here in two hours' time.'

Duncan swore roundly. Now what was he to do? He could not involve Molly in what he was about to do and he needed to get away quickly after the deed was done. 'She will have to stay where she is for another day and go on tomorrow,' he said, hoping Molly would be docile and do as she was told without further argument about sharing his adventures.

'We had no plans to come back here,' Frank reminded him.

'Then we shall have to change our plans.'

'I don't like it,' Frank muttered. 'Don't like it at all. Petticoats are the very devil…'

Duncan laughed. 'You never said a truer word, old friend, but what would we do without them, eh? But enough of that. Tell me all you have discovered and let's get down to business.'

Chapter Two

Molly woke with a start when a coach rattled into the yard outside her window. For a moment she lay staring at the ceiling, wondering where she was. And then it all came back to her—the ride in the night, the fall from her horse, the comfortable feeling of Captain Stacey's strong arms around her, and his determination to send her back to Lady Connaught. She sighed heavily. It had been a kind of adventure, she supposed, but only a little one and nothing of any importance had happened. She still did not know his secret.

She rose and went to open the window. The yard outside was busy with horses being changed on a coach and the passengers were coming into the inn for refreshment. She guessed it was late in the morning, for the smell of roasting beef wafted up to her and reminded her she was hungry. Without a nightgown, she had slept in her underwear and it did not take her long to wash, using cold water from the jug on the wash-stand, and put on her riding habit again. It was crumpled and dirty, but that could not be helped. Having secured her hair as best she could, she went downstairs in search of Captain Stacey.

'He and his friend left two hours since,' the landlord told her. 'He left a message that you were to wait here for him.'

She was puzzled. 'He did not say to take the stage to Cromer?'

'It left soon after the gentlemen, miss. If that was where you were bound, then you must needs wait until tomorrow.'

'Oh, I see.' She did not see at all. Unless the Captain had decided to take her to London, after all. But even she could see that was impractical; she had not thought of a long journey when she'd left Stacey Manor; it had been a spur-of-the-moment thing, coming to her as they rode together. She had no change of clothes, no baggage at all. No money either. In the unlikely event of him agreeing, they would have to return to Stacey Manor to make the proper arrangements for a journey.

Supposing the Captain had abandoned her? He was not at all a chivalrous man; he was the black sheep of the family; he had said so himself. He would have no conscience about leaving her to find her own way, especially if he had met up with a friend. 'Did he say where they were going?'

'No, miss.'

'But he did say he would be back?'

'Oh, yes, miss. Most particular he was as to that. And I was to see that you did not stir from the premises.'

'In that case, please bring me something to eat. I am starving. I am sure…' She paused. Was the Captain here under his real name? What was his real name? Would she upset some deep-laid plan by revealing the one she knew him by? 'My friend will pay.'

The landlord's smile did not reveal what he thought about young ladies arriving at his inn in the arms of gentlemen in the early hours; it was not his business, but if she had been a daughter of his he would have spanked her soundly. 'Do you wish to have it sent to your room?'

'No, I will eat in the dining room. And bring me paper and ink to write a letter, if you please.'

He conducted her to the dining room and offered her a table by the window where she could see everyone who came and went. Given the writing things she asked for, she sat down and scribbled a note to her godmother—telling her she was safe and well and under Captain Stacey's protection— which she gave to the innkeeper to put on the next mail-coach, before beginning her meal.

She had hardly begun to eat when a rider galloped into the yard and dismounted. He was obviously in a great hurry and very agitated. Molly watched as a crowd gathered round him. From their shocked expressions, she gathered he was bringing news of some importance. He left the crowd outside and came into the dining room, where he announced to all and sundry that the Cromer stage had been waylaid by highway-men on a quiet stretch of the road a dozen miles to the north.

'Was anyone hurt?' enquired the innkeeper while Molly reflected that if she had not overslept and if Captain Stacey had not decided to disappear she would have been on that coach. That really would have been an adventure and she was rather cross that she had missed it.

'No. But they made everyone get out and they searched the coach very thoroughly,' the man said. 'They took Sir John Partridge's gold and his watch and papers, but they let the ladies keep their jewellery.'

'Where was the guard? Did he not try to stop them?'

'The stage carried no guard. Sir John's man had a pistol but he was so slow fetching it out, he was useless. The high toby took it from him as easy as you please.'

'Then what happened?'

'They made everyone return to their seats and told the coachman to drive on. Sir John demanded to know their names, as if they would be foolish enough to give them to him. One of them laughed and said he was called the Dark Knight.'

'Where were you when all this was happening?' demanded mine host.

'I came upon the scene quite by chance, but there was nothing I could do. They had pistols and I was unarmed…'

'How many of them?'

'Two. Very big men, they were, and masked. I hid in the trees until it was safe to proceed.'

'Which direction did the robbers take?'

'To the coast, I think.'

The landlord sent a boy off to fetch a constable and there was talk of sending for the runners from London, but it was decided that by the time they arrived the highwaymen would be long gone. Doubtless Sir John would report the incident when the coach arrived in Cromer and constables sent from there to help search for the robbers.

In the middle of this discussion, Duncan strolled into the inn and sat down opposite Molly. He was dressed in soft buckskin breeches, a brown coat and a yellow and brown checked waistcoat. His boots and white neckcloth were pristine. She surmised that he could not have ridden very far, for the roads were dusty and there wasn't a speck of it on him.

'You have missed all the excitement,' she told him. 'The Cromer coach has been held up. They are even now sending for the watch.'

'Is that so?' He affected little interest. 'I'm devilish hungry.

Have you finished with that?' He pointed to a tureen of vegetables and a platter containing pork chops.

'Yes. Please help yourself. You will be paying for it, after all. I have no money.'

'Dear me! Not even for the coach fare?'

'No. I did not think I would need money. I was on horseback.'

'And what would you have done if I had not returned?' he asked, piling a plate with food. 'I could simply have ridden off and left you. The landlord would not have been pleased when he discovered you could not pay for what you had eaten.'

'He assured me you had said you would be back. I had no reason to doubt you.'

'No reason not to doubt me either. You are too trusting, my dear.'

'But you did come back, so I was right.'

'Tell me,' he said, tucking into the chops. 'What did you intend when you followed me last night? Not a journey to London, I'll wager, or you would have come better prepared.'

'No, I saw you leave and was curious as to why you travelled by night, that was all. I wanted to see where you were going. And riding in the dark is something I never tried before and I like doing new things. I did not think of Mama, until we started to talk about her. And then it seemed the very thing to join her in London.' She sighed. 'And you left me asleep, so I missed my adventure.'

'Adventure?'

'Yes, being held up by highwaymen. Do you suppose they stole a kiss from the ladies? But I collect the man said they took nothing from the ladies, only from Sir John Partridge.'

'What man?' Duncan tried not to let his real interest show.

'The man who saw it all. I think he must be a little nervous and not at all heroic, for he said he hid and only rode on when it was all over.'

'What else did he say?'

'There were two of them, heavily armed, and afterwards they rode towards the coast. Everyone seems to think they had a boat waiting for them and are long gone.'

'Very likely,' he said, allowing himself to relax. 'Now, what are we to do about you?'

'The landlord says the next Cromer coach is not until tomorrow. We shall have to ride back.'

'We, Miss Martineau? I cannot spare the time escorting a chit about the countryside; I should have been on my way long ago...'

Before he could go on, they were interrupted by the arrival of the local constable, who had come to take charge of the investigation into the robbery. He began by questioning the witness whose tale lost nothing in repetition. In fact, it gained a detail or two. The chief of the highwaymen was of a dark countenance, dressed all in black, and he rode a big black horse with a white flash on its nose. His accomplice was older and smaller by six inches and had a scar near his left eye, though it could not all be seen on account of the mask he wore.

Molly had pricked up her ears when she'd heard the description of the horse. She had ridden on the back of such a one not five hours since but, she told herself severely, there must be many black horses with white noses and many men with dark looks. She glanced across at the Captain who was placidly eating and told herself she was imagining things. To have arrived back in the inn so soon after the hold-up, he would, like the man who had witnessed it, have had to ride hard, but he was completely unruffled and showed every evidence of a leisurely toilette.

She noticed Duncan lift his head as another man came in. Did she imagine he nodded towards Duncan before passing through the room and out of the door towards the stairs? What was unmistakable was the scar on his face.

'Captain,' she whispered, reaching across and touching his hand to attract his attention. 'That man who just went out. He had a scar…'

'So have a great many men, I should think,' he said, without even bothering to look up from his meal.

'But one of the robbers…'

'Miss Martineau, you must learn to curb your imagination, you know, or you will land yourself in more trouble than a little.'

'You know him, don't you?'

'Miss Mar…' He stopped short when the bulk of the constable loomed over them.

'Sir, may I ask what you know of this matter?' he asked. 'I am told you have recently arrived and from a northerly direction.'

'If by recent you mean five hours or thereabouts,' Duncan said laconically, 'then I suppose you could say I have.'

'Hours, you say? I was told you entered the room but fifteen minutes ago.'

'So I did. From my bedroom. My man will vouch for me. He is even now packing for our departure.'

'It is quite true,' Molly said, turning her ingenuous smile upon the constable. 'I, too, can vouch for the Captain's whereabouts, though I own he did leave me for twenty minutes or so. He had to arrange transport for us.'

'Twenty minutes? No more?'

'Oh, no more, I do assure you.'

'And who are you, miss, if I might ask?'

'Why, I am Captain Stacey's wife,' she said, favouring the man with a dazzling smile and ignoring the sound of Duncan choking on his food. 'Who else would I be?'

The constable inclined his head towards Molly. 'I beg your pardon, ma'am, but I must leave no stone unturned.'

'And while you waste time turning over stones the thieves will have gone to ground.' Duncan, who had quickly regained his scattered wits, decided he could not embarrass her by contradicting her, but it put him in a devil of a coil. He could hardly put her on a coach to Cromer and ride off in the opposite direction if they were supposed to be husband and wife travelling together. 'Get out to the scene of the crime,' he said in his most commanding voice. 'Surely that is where you should begin?'

The man bowed again and left them and Duncan called the waiter to bring a pudding; he was still hungry, he said.

'Don't you think we should go?' Molly asked. 'If the constable sees your horse—or the man with the scar…'

'I see you have added two and two and made five,' he said, making inroads into the plum duff which had just been set before him. 'Have some of this; it is delicious.'

'No, thank you. I am no longer hungry. And I don't know how you can sit there and eat so calmly when you know…'

He smiled at her. Her blue eyes were looking troubled; surely she was not worried on his account? He felt an unaccountable frisson of pleasure at the thought. 'What do I know?'

'More than you are saying. If you were not on the road this morning, you know very well who was.'

'But you gave me an alibi. Surely you do not condone highway robbery?'

'I know nothing of it. If you were to tell me…'

'There is nothing to tell. And I wish you would not refine upon it. What I do is none of your business.'

'I think it is,' she said promptly. 'If you had not panicked my horse, I would not have been thrown and you would not have had to bring me here. That was your fault. And now, because there is no coach going to Cromer until tomorrow, we must stay here like sitting ducks. Besides, you have already said your man—and I doubt not he is the robber with the scar—is packing to leave and I have confirmed you have been out to arrange transport, so leave we must.'

'Of course we must; you made sure of that,' he said. 'We shall have to find another way of returning you to Stacey Manor.' He stood up unhurriedly and beckoned the landlord for the reckoning. 'Wait for me in the yard. I will be out directly.'

She went outside and, while waiting for him, wandered round to the stables. There was no sign of his horse, nor Jenny either; they had been spirited away. By the man with the scar? She turned as Duncan joined her. 'Where are the horses?'

'I did not like the stabling here; I have had them moved elsewhere where the fodder is better and the accommodation more to their liking.'

There was definitely something have-cavey going on and she was more intrigued than ever. 'Then how do we go on?'

'I have hired a curricle.' He stood looking down at her; she was completely unafraid, but that was because she had never in her life come across anything to be afraid of. He hoped she never would, but she was more astute than he had given her credit for and now he must protect her. He had commanded men in battle, been responsible for their lives, but never before had he had such an obligation as this and it was making him uncomfortable.

His experience with women was with women of the world, who asked nothing for their favours but money or costly presents. There were female relatives, of course, and Beth, whom he had expected to marry. But Beth would never put herself into the position that Molly had done; Beth was too aware of what Society expected from her and what it was and was not permissible for a lady to do. Chasing after a man in the middle of the night would not have occurred to her.

'Where are we going?' she asked, as he escorted her back to the front of the inn, where a spanking curricle and a small brown horse were ready and waiting for them.

'Norwich.'

'South! Why, that is halfway to London!'

'Not quite,' he said laconically, helping her onto the vehicle and climbing up beside her. 'But you have made it necessary for us to leave together and going north is not sensible, so Norwich it will have to be. Besides, the place is big enough for shopping and you need a change of clothes.' He turned to look at her as he spoke.

Her riding habit was of some dull silk material and the matching skirt was quite plain, not distinctive, except that it was unusual for a young lady to wear such a garment for riding in a carriage and the skirt was too long and cumbersome for her to walk comfortably in town. It would be noted and if, in her innocence, she let slip whatever it was she thought she knew, suspicions would be aroused. Once she was suitably attired, he could put her on the coach to Cromer, under the chaperonage of another lady passenger.

'We are going shopping! Oh, Captain, how very thoughtful you are! But I have no money.'

'So you have said before. My pocket is at your disposal.' He flicked the reins and they turned out of the yard at a smart trot.

'And is it a very deep pocket?'

'Not at all. We must be frugal.'

'But I heard Sir John had a great deal of gold…'

'You think I robbed that coach for gain?' The annoyance was plain on his face as he turned to answer her. 'Rakeshame I may be, but I do not stoop so low as to profit from another's loss, unless it be at the card table.'

He had not exactly denied his involvement, she noted, only that he had not gained by it; she was more curious than ever and determined not to be sent back to Stacey Manor until she discovered the truth. 'There are gentlemen highwaymen. I have heard of many instances where…'

'And I collect you are a great reader. Romantic fiction, I'll wager. The real world is not like that.'

'No, perhaps it is not. But fiction hurts no one, does it? And if it provides a little light relief and entertainment, where's the harm? I have my feet firmly on the ground.'

He laughed suddenly. 'And your head in the clouds.'

She was silent for a moment, but only a moment. 'What shall I be allowed to buy?'

'Whatever you need for a coach ride and an overnight stay. By the time we arrive, it will be too late to go on.' He knew perfectly well he was endangering her reputation, had in fact already compromised it, but it was her own fault; he had not asked her to provide him with an alibi. That was not to say he need not put his mind to finding ways and means of preserving her good name and he thought he might have the answer.

'Mama said she would buy me a wardrobe when I went to London,' she said rather wistfully. 'You know you need a great many clothes for a Season. You should have seen what Mama bought. Trunks full. She showed them to me. Gowns for mornings, afternoons and evenings, for riding in carriages and walking and habits for riding, and hats and bonnets and ballgowns. She said it was absolutely essential to be well kitted out.'

'Yes, ladies change their clothes a great many times a day, I believe,' he said, watching her upturned face and sparkling eyes.

'Mama's ballgowns are all very beautiful. Of course, she is taller than I am, so they would not fit me. And she said they were unsuitable. I am not…' She paused and treated him to her infectious laugh, which made the corners of his mouth twitch. 'I am not as well rounded as Mama.'

'No, indeed not,' he said, thinking of the voluptuous Harriet. 'But I think your figure is very pleasing as it is.'

'Do you? Oh, that is very civil of you. I think you are the most handsome of men, even if you are lacking in chivalry.'

'Am I so?'

'I have been reading *Don Quixote*. You know he was always rescuing damsels in distress. You are not at all like him. He would never have slapped Jenny's rump while I was unprepared for it.'

'He was also more than a little touched in the attic, I collect. He thought windmills were giants.'

'But it didn't stop him wanting to fight them, big as they were. He was very brave.'

'There are times, my dear, when bravery is foolhardy in the extreme. Have you never heard the saying "discretion is the better part of valour"?'

'Yes, but that is a very dull maxim.'

'Then I must be the dullest of men.'

'Oh, I do not believe that. Why, you said yourself you are a rakeshame and you cannot be that if you are too cautious. And I am sure you are not cautious at all. I believe you thrive on risk. Look how you came back to the Red Lion and sat and ate your dinner as calm as you please. And the way you answered the constable.'

He smiled. 'You didn't do so badly yourself, though I cannot think why you did it.'

'I was afraid they would go up to your room and find the man with the scar. Not to mention the gold.'

'Gold?' he repeated furiously. 'I have already told you I have no gold.'

'So you have,' she mused aloud. 'I wonder what you can have done with it?'

'Molly, you will make me very angry if you mention that again.'

'Very well, have your little secret, if you must, but how am I to help you, if I do not know the truth?'

He turned to her in astonishment. 'Help me?'

'Of course,' she said placidly. 'A man travelling to London with his wife is not the same as two masked men on horse-back, now is it?'

'London?' he repeated. 'Wife?'

'Oh, I do not mean you to marry me, but we could pretend. Just until we reached the capital.'

'I do not have to make an honest woman of you, then?' he teased. 'I thought in the best tradition of the lady novelists you would insist upon it.' Talking to her made a refreshing change from the horrors which often invaded his thoughts; she was like a breath of spring air, light and joyful, the fore-taste of the warmth of summer. And he had been too long in the cold.

'I am not such a ninny as to want to shackle myself to a man who has no great love for me. That would spell disaster. And besides, I mean to enjoy my Season if I am so fortunate as to have one, and how can I do that if I am already married?'

'How very sensible of you,' he murmured, smiling a little.

'You are laughing at me,' she said.

'No, I was thinking of your mama and what she might say when she found you on her doorstep.'

'She will be very pleased to see me.'

'Oh, I am sure she would.' And this time he did not hide his smile as he added, 'When she recovered from the shock. How are we to explain your arrival in my company? I am, after all, a rakeshame and you have no chaperon.'

She had no idea what she was talking about, he realised. The romantic reading which had been so large a part of her education might talk of ruined reputations, but he doubted if she had any conception of what it meant in practice. 'Have you any idea what would happen when we arrived in London and it became known you had openly admitted to spending a whole night in my company?' he asked.

'Two nights,' she corrected him.

'You would be vilified. Everyone would cut you dead. There would be no Season. Your mother would disown you. And every ne'er-do-well in the capital would take it into his head...' He paused. 'No, I will not go into that.'

'Then you must become a reformed character, concerned only for my welfare and good name. Lady Connaught charged you with bringing me safely to my mother and you discharged that duty faithfully.'

'She would never do that unless you were travelling with a female companion, a maid, who slept in your room.'

She laughed. 'Don't be a goosecap, Captain; even I know maids do not sleep in the same room as a married couple.'

'Not married,' he said. 'Being escorted, very properly escorted.'

'Oh, I see. But I have no maid. Mama said it was not in the least necessary for me to have one. Her maid always helped me when I was at home, but since she sold the house…'

'Sold the house?' he queried in surprise.

'Yes. The Colonel did not leave a great deal and all Mama had was a small pension. She was in debt and being dunned by everyone. She needed to realise all her assets to pay for her Season in London. It was an investment. She explained it all to me. She has rented a house in Holles Street and bought a carriage and horses. But when she has found her next husband we shall have a new home and everything we need.'

'I can hardly credit it,' he said, his fury with Harriet almost boiling over. He had always known Harriet was selfish and a gambler, but he had never thought she would treat her own daughter in such a ramshackle manner. 'Do you mean to say you are homeless?'

'I have—had—a home with Lady Connaught until Mama came about. And I suppose I could say I have a home in Holles Street. And if you are going to London…'

'Who said I was?'

'No one, but you are, aren't you?'

'No,' Duncan said firmly. 'The idea is out of the question.'

'Oh, please, Captain. I will not be a trouble to you, I promise. I will be as quiet as a mouse and do as you bid…'

'Impossible,' he said. 'I am ready to wager you could not keep quiet however hard you tried; I never heard such a chatterbox. And as for doing as you are told, give me leave to doubt that too.'

'Then I shall not promise it, only that I will try my best.' She turned a smile on him that made his heart turn over and almost took his breath away. 'I cannot say fairer than that, can I?'

'No,' he admitted.

'Then you will take me?'

'I cannot.' The further they went from Stacey Manor, the more difficult it would be for him to return Molly to his grandmother, but the young chit had been right when she said a husband and wife would attract less attention. They were still too near the scene of the action. But it was impossible. Out of the question. He had not yet stooped so low as to ruin a young lady's reputation.

She was silent for a moment, but only a moment. 'Have you been in London during the Season, Captain?'

'Many years ago, before I became a soldier.'

'And did you not find the lady of your dreams there?'

'I thought so at the time, but nothing came of it.'

'Oh, you were crossed in love. How sad for you. Is that why you have become a gentleman of the road?'

He laughed again but this time she detected a little bitterness in it. 'I have admitted to being no such thing. Now do you think we might change the subject?'

'Certainly, if you find it painful. Tell me, what do young ladies do during the Season? I have read some of Miss Austen's books and others on etiquette and it seems to me there are a great many pitfalls. How do they know who is eligible and who is not? So much of it seems to rely on hearsay. Surely one needs more than that? After all, everyone must have a different idea about what makes a perfect partner. And how can mere acquaintanceship turn to love if you are never allowed to be alone with a man even for a minute? After all, he might seem very charming and unexceptional when in company, but turn out to be the very opposite when it is too late.'

'That happens.'

'And once she is committed she must make the best of it, I believe.'

'That is another of your mama's truisms, is it?'

'Is it wrong?'

'No. But courtship works two ways. The lady might not turn out to be all the young man had hoped for. A pretty face and a fetching figure are not the only attributes for a good wife.'

'So, tell me what you think they are.'

He turned to smile at her. 'What do you think?'

'Love and compassion,' she said promptly. 'Gentleness, but not so much as to make her dull.'

'Oh, you are so right,' he said, only half teasing. 'I should abhor dullness in a wife.'

'I should not like a dull husband either. Not top-lofty or arrogant. I would expect him to be sensitive and kind.' She paused to look at him, a smile playing about her lips. 'And chivalrous.'

'Oh, dear,' he said mournfully. 'I should fail on all counts.'

'Oh, I wasn't thinking of you, Captain. You are far too old.'

'And that has put me firmly in my place,' he said, smiling a little ruefully as he flicked the reins to make the horse go a little faster. 'There is an inn ahead of us which I should like to reach as soon as maybe. And for your information I have seen but thirty summers.'

'Old,' she affirmed. 'But perhaps that is no bad thing. One would expect a man of thirty summers to have sowed all his wild oats and be ready to settle down.'

'The problem with that theory is that some men never want to settle down. Sowing wild oats is a deal more fun.'

'As ye sow, so shall ye reap,' she said.

'And what is that supposed to mean?'

'You will have a poor harvest.'

'Quite the philosopher, aren't you?'

'No, but I am interested in people and why they do the things they do. You, for instance…'

'I am a dull subject for your studies.'

'Not at all. You may be from the poor side of the Connaught family, but I believe you have been educated as a gentleman, you have served as an officer and you have a grandmother who is very fond of you, so you cannot be all bad. With a little instruction and application, you could become a real gentleman and find some more fitting occupation.'

'Heaven preserve me from reforming women! I am as I am and that is an end of it.'

'Very well,' she said meekly. 'I am, after all, in your hands to do with as you please. I have no wish to fall out with you.'

He smiled to himself as they bowled along. She was an amazing mixture of innocence and wisdom, child and woman, and one day, when she had learned the ways of the world, she would be a charmer, even a heartbreaker. And he did not want his heart broken again.

Unaware of his introspection, or perhaps deliberately ignoring it, she continued to chat happily to him until they turned into the yard of the Crosskeys at St Faith's just short of Norwich, and drew to a stop.

'Well,' she said, turning towards him. 'Are we to test my theory?'

'Theory?' he queried. 'It seems to me you have a great many theories. Which one are we to test?'

'Why, that it is Captain Stacey and his wife who will stay here overnight.'

'Good God, child, have you any idea what that means?'

'I believe it means we must share a bedchamber.'

'And what happens in that bedchamber?'

'How am I to know that?' she asked. 'I never did it before. But it doesn't signify, does it, because we are not really married but only pretending?'

'And if there is only one bed?'

'Oh, Captain, I am quite sure you can contrive something.'

Before he could find a suitable reply an ostler came out from the stables to see to the equipage. Duncan jumped down and reached up to help her alight. 'Come inside and we will decide what's to be done with you,' he said.

The inn was small and very old. Duncan had to duck his head to enter the doorway. He stood looking round the company, which consisted of a farmer and his wife who were quarrelling loudly, and four men, intent on playing cards. They were evidently playing very deep for there was a pile of coins on the table between them and their conversation consisted of grunts, unintelligible except to each other. The only other customer was the man with the scar. Duncan led Molly over to join him.

"Bout time too,' the man said. 'Did you stop to admire the wayside flowers?'

'No, but I had to answer questions from a bumbling town constable and I could not appear too eager to depart.'

'And you still have the trailing petticoats, I see.'

Duncan turned to Molly and took her hand to draw her forward. 'Miss Martineau, may I present my good friend, Sergeant Frank Upjohn? Frank, this is Miss Molly Martineau. We have spoken of her.'

'Miss Martineau, your obedient.' He did not seem particularly pleased to see her, she noted as he rose to acknowledge her.

The innkeeper came forward, wiping his hands on his apron, to ask their requirements.

'Food,' Duncan said. 'And plenty of it.'

The man went away to give the order to his wife and Duncan and Molly joined Frank at the table.

'You do not approve of me, Mr Upjohn,' she said, arranging her long skirt about her as she sat down; it was now more crumpled than ever. 'No doubt you think I am an encumbrance, but I assure you, I intend to help you both.'

'Whether we will it or not,' Duncan murmured, leaning back in his chair, a faint smile playing about his mouth.

'You said I did not do so badly,' she protested. 'And if you were escorting me from Stacey Manor to London you would not have had time to hold up a coach, would you?'

'Hold up a coach?' Frank repeated, looking sharply at Duncan. 'Who said anything about holding up a coach?'

'I certainly did not,' Duncan answered. 'Madam, here, has added two and two and made five, as I pointed out to her.'

'There is nothing wrong with my arithmetic,' she said. 'Two men, one bigger than the other, one riding a fine black horse with a white nose-flash, and the other with a scar beneath his eye. I cannot think of a better description of you both. You were absent from the inn at the relevant time and the horses were removed from the stable on a pretext I find unbelievable, not to mention the fact that you did not deny it when I said you had been with me all night.'

'I could hardly contradict a lady,' Duncan said, smiling at the look of astonishment on Frank's face at this statement. 'And if you were so sure, why did you not denounce me, instead of dreaming up another cock-and-bull story?'

'I was curious as to why you did it, if not for gain.'

'I thought you were going to send her back where she came from,' Frank muttered as the innkeeper's wife brought plates and tureens to the table.

'How?' Duncan demanded. 'There was no public coach, her mare had been hidden and I had no time…'

'It was necessary to put the constable off the scent,' Molly added. 'Besides, I want to go to London and I thought of a great ruse…'

He turned to Frank. 'She wanted us to pretend to be married; she even told the constable at the Red Lion that we were. I have persuaded her it will not do. We can't look after her. Quite apart from the practical difficulties, just think what it would do to her reputation.'

'And yours,' Frank said with a wry smile. 'The hard man who has no time for females, making a cake of himself over a chit. And we have work to do, or had you forgot?'

'No, I hadn't forgotten,' Duncan said, watching Molly pile her plate with roast chicken and vegetables. He disliked women who picked at their food in the pretence of daintiness. The longer they were together, the deeper became the coil he was in, and the inn, though perfectly adequate for him and Frank, was certainly not suitable for a lady. He wished he had thought of that before suggesting the rendezvous. It just showed how long he had been out of genteel society and how unmannerly he had become. 'But I must admit it would be easier to take her with us than try and return her to Stacey Manor.'

He could not tell Frank the other reason why he was even considering taking her with them because it had nothing to do with his own plight. He wanted to make her happy and if taking her to her mother made her happy, then why should he not do it? But not as his wife. Never that. 'We must make ourselves into a proper escort and that means another female and a coach and horses.'

'Oh, yes, please,' Molly said, brightening. 'That would be the very thing. I could enter London in style and no one would think any the worse of me.' She stopped and gave him a meaningful look. 'Nor you either. Everyone would admire you for it and your reputation would be quite restored.'

'What do you say, Frank?' Duncan asked him. 'Would Martha act the maid?'

'Martha?'

'Yes, why not?'

'Who is Martha?' Molly demanded.

'She is my wife,' Frank said. 'But she has never been a lady's maid. She would have no idea how to go on.'

'Oh, I could soon tell her,' Molly said. 'There is really nothing to it and I should so like a female companion. Do say you agree.'

'What is the alternative?' Duncan demanded of his friend. 'Turn and ride back to Stacey Manor and take our chances with the local constabulary, who will by now have been re-inforced by those from Cromer and Norwich, or leave the young lady here to manage by herself?'

'No, I am not so lacking in conduct as to do that. I'll fetch Martha.'

'Good. Where are our horses?'

'Fed and watered and grazing in a field nearby.'

'Then Molly and I will ride into Norwich in the morning with your mount. You take the curricle and bring Martha to us at The Bell.'

Molly, who did not fancy an evening spent in the company of the card players and the nagging farmer's wife, said she wanted to retire as soon as they had finished supper. Duncan cast a glance at the men, who seemed intent on their cards, but he knew they would hear any orders he gave; he could not let it be known she was a single lady and was left with no alternative but to ask for a room to be prepared for his wife.

Once this was done, she bade him goodnight with a great show of wifely affection. She was in a cheerful mood because he had fallen in with her scheme to pretend to be husband and wife, if only for one night. This was a grand adventure and so long as he remained with her she had nothing to fear.

As soon as Molly had been conducted from the room, Frank turned on him. 'Captain, you must be mad. Do you know how much this escapade is likely to cost? And we have nothing left, unless you have been holding out on me. Every farthing of what we took has been passed on as you instructed.'

'Good. I knew I could rely on you.' He was beginning to realise how poor people felt when their whole lives must be lived in search of money to buy food and shelter. There was never any time for anything else. No wonder some of the soldiers returning from the war with no way of earning a living and a family to care for turned to crime.

'But now we have pockets to let again,' Frank went on, speaking more bluntly than would have been considered fitting between master and servant in any other circumstances. 'It is always the same with you, Captain. It seems money is an embarrassment to you.'

'It is when so many of my fellows have nothing. They fought as hard as I did, and under more difficult conditions; they deserve all I can do for them. Especially for their widows.'

'So, how will you convey the lady to London?'

'With good luck, by post chaise, with a little less by stagecoach.'

Frank sighed heavily. 'I suppose it is useless for me to point out that petticoats are a bad omen…'

'Not this one. I have a feeling she will bring me the best luck in the world. Nor can you say Martha has brought you anything else.'

Frank owned himself defeated. 'Do you want me to leave now?'

'Yes, otherwise Molly will be unchaperoned yet another night.'

Still grumbling, Frank got up and left the inn. Duncan watched him go, then put the rest of the evening to good use by joining the card players when one of their number lost everything and was forced to stop. By dawn, he was richer by several guineas. It was enough to pay for their lodging and for Molly's shopping expedition, though he would have to warn her against extravagance.

Pretending to be too drunk to go to bed, he dozed for an hour or two on a settle. He could not join Molly and asking for a separate room would have looked decidedly odd. Besides, he risked over-sleeping and he wanted to be on hand if Molly took it into her head to do something foolish or talk to strangers; she could not know how risky that might be.

Chapter Three

As soon as Molly woke, she rose, washed in cold water from the jug on the wash-stand and, once more attired in the now bedraggled riding habit, went downstairs. In the corridor, she met the innkeeper's wife busy sweeping the floor. Molly bade her good morning and asked if the Captain was up and about.

'Yes, ma'am. Did you sleep so sound you didn't know he hadn't come to bed?'

She was momentarily disconcerted, but, remembering her role, smiled. 'I must have.'

'He's pacing the floor, chafing at the bit, waiting for you.'

Molly hurried to join him, but, far from pacing the floor, he was sitting at the breakfast table, apparently at ease. There was no one else in the room. He rose as she came towards him and pulled out a chair for her.

'Good morning, my dear. Did you sleep well?'

'Yes, thank you. But you did not, I believe. The innkeeper's wife told me you did not go to bed. Where were you?'

'In the next room, enjoying the company of friends.'

'Friends? I did not know you were acquainted with anyone here.'

'I used the term loosely.'

'Is that the usual behaviour of a man towards his wife when travelling?'

'It is certainly not so out of the ordinary as to excite comment and it was better than invading your privacy, my dear. Besides, I put the time to good use.' He jingled a pocketful of coins.

'Gaming.'

'Yes.'

'And did you win?'

'Naturally, I did.'

'Is that how you make a living?'

'It is one of the ways. Now, please have some breakfast. We must be on our way as soon as you are ready.' He indicated the platters of ham and eggs as he poured her a cup of coffee from the pot at his elbow.

She sat down and helped herself. 'And another way is holding up coaches. I cannot believe that someone as educated as you are should stoop to crime. I do believe there is more to it than meets the eye.'

'Is that so?' he asked laconically, wondering if she could possibly have stumbled on the truth. But no; clever she might be, but not that clever. 'And are you going to tell me your theory?'

'I don't have one, not yet. Of course, you could tell me and then I would not worry about you.'

'You worry about me?' he queried. 'Why?'

'Naturally I worry about you. You are family, even if it is I don't know how many times removed. And I am very fond of Aunt Margaret…'

'So, it is not for my own sake?' he asked, and wondered why he asked. Did it really matter what a chit of a girl thought of him?

'That, too, of course.' She smiled at him and popped a forkful of food into her mouth. 'Tell me, Captain, just what are you about?'

He smiled suddenly. 'I believe I am escorting a young lady to London to be with her mama.'

'Oh, so you do think I am a lady?' she said.

'I do not know what else you might be. Hoyden or school-miss might be to the point, but I give you the benefit of the doubt. Now, if you have finished, we must be on our way.'

'I should write another letter to Aunt Margaret before we go,' she said. 'I sent her one yesterday, but as I did not know our destination I could not be very precise. I shall tell her you are going to take me to Mama and that will set her mind to rest.'

He wondered whether it would, considering the jobation his grandmother had given him about his way of life, and decided to add his postscript to the letter assuring her he would take good care of the young lady. He could imagine the old lady's smile when she read it; he was playing right into her hands and if Molly had not assured him otherwise he would have had no trouble believing she had concocted the whole escapade to bring him to heel.

The letter was soon written and given to the landlord to put on the mail and they went outside where three horses stood patiently waiting for their riders. He helped her to mount Jenny, then picked up the reins of Frank's horse, which she learned was called Good Boy, and sprang nimbly into his own saddle.

They turned and rode towards Norwich, sometimes cantering and, now and again, when it was safe to do so, putting the horses to a gallop. She rode well, he noticed. He noted other things too: her softly rounded breasts and trim waist, her bright eyes, always so full of life, her pink lips and the way a strand of her hair curled so lovingly into her neck. And he asked himself what in heaven's name he was doing with her. Frank was right—he had run mad.

When they crossed the river and entered the city, she was so diverted by the size of it, the busy streets, full of carts and carriages, the pedestrians and hawkers crying their wares and the shops and taverns, she could do nothing but gape.

'I did not know it would be such a big place,' she said. 'Is it as large as London?'

'Not quite. But it is an important centre of commerce. You will find all you need here.'

He smiled indulgently as the road took them past the castle. She pulled up her horse to stare up at its looming grey wall. 'Is it occupied?'

'Oh, yes, by several hundred criminals.'

'It's a prison?' She shuddered, imagining the Captain being confined there, and it occurred to her that the life he led was dangerous in the extreme. If he were arrested and taken from her, what would she do? Might she be arrested too for aiding him? Adventure for adventure's sake was suddenly not so appealing. 'Then the sooner we leave it behind the better,' she said.

'We must wait for Frank and Martha. In the meantime we shall go shopping.'

'Good,' she said, looking down at her habit, which was so dusty and crumpled it looked as though she had slept in it. 'I tried to get the creases out but it proved impossible.'

'We need to refresh ourselves first and the horses need stabling,' he said, deciding that taking her as she was into a genteel establishment to buy the things a lady needed to travel to London would invite strange looks and he could not afford to arouse curiosity.

He took her to The Bell where the rooms were superior to any they had had so far: a well-furnished bedroom and a sitting room with a table and chairs and an upholstered sofa.

While she shut herself in the bedroom to strip off her clothes and wash, he changed into pantaloons and a clean shirt, tied a fresh cravat about his neck, donned waistcoat and frockcoat and left the building.

He returned just as Molly came out of the bedchamber into the sitting room. She had asked the chambermaid to press her habit and it was a little more respectable than it had been but still bore evidence of a long ride. She had cleaned her face and now it was pink and glowing and her blue eyes sparkled. She had evidently borrowed a brush and spent some time on her hair, because it gleamed with health and she had put it up into a Grecian style, which suited her piquant face.

His grandmother had been right, he decided; Molly Martineau would one day turn heads with her beauty. She was inexperienced and that was part of her charm, but he felt his loins stirring at the sight of her and realised he was not so impervious as he'd thought he was.

'Here,' he said, almost embarrassed, handing her the parcel he carried. 'Put this on. It is, I think, more suitable for a shopping expedition than a riding habit.'

She opened the package eagerly to reveal a simple round gown in turquoise muslin, with little puff sleeves and a round neck filled with lace. There was a little matching cape, white stockings, blue kid shoes and a reticule. 'Oh!' she exclaimed. 'It is very pretty. I could not have chosen anything I liked more. But will it fit?'

'There is only one way to find out,' he said, smiling at her enthusiasm. 'Put it on and we will go out and buy more.'

She needed no second bidding and disappeared into the bedchamber. Twenty minutes later she emerged once again, looking very fetching and smiling happily. 'You guessed my size exactly, Captain. How very clever of you. Except the shoes are a little tight.'

'I am sorry about that. Perhaps you could wear your riding boots…'

'Oh, no, that will spoil the effect. I shall manage.'

'Madam.' He smiled at her, offering her his arm. 'Shall we go?'

Laughing, she laid her hand upon his sleeve and together they went out into the street and strolled towards the centre of the city to the emporium where he had bought the gown and where he knew there were other establishments offering ladies' apparel, as well as things like fans and reticules, parasols and footwear, underwear and toiletries.

'Kit her out with everything she needs for a stay in London,' he told one proprietress, whose name, according to the legend above the door of her establishment, was Mrs Hannah Solomon.

'I am to have a Season,' Molly told her. 'Is that not exciting?'

'Yes, indeed,' the woman agreed. 'So very sensible of your uncle to buy your requirements in Norwich. The prices in London are much higher.'

Molly looked at Duncan when she mentioned her uncle and stifled a little giggle. He simply smiled and said nothing to put right the mistake.

The morning flew by as he sat and watched her parade before him in day gowns, carriage gowns, riding habits, gloves, shoes, half-boots, hats, bonnets, capes, spencers and pelisses. His resolve to limit her spending was abandoned in the face of her pleasure.

'Which shall it be?' she asked, looking from a carriage dress and matching pelisse in soft green velvet to an afternoon gown of blue sarcenet. 'I cannot make up my mind, so you choose.'

'Then have them both.'

'Oh, you are the most generous of men!' she exclaimed as Mrs Solomon began folding the gowns to pack into boxes before he should change his mind. 'I am beginning to revise my opinion that you are not chivalrous.'

He bowed towards her. 'And I am gratified to hear you say so.'

'Madam will need underthings?' Mrs Solomon queried, determined not to let this customer go until she had wrung every last drop out of the transaction.

'Naturally she will,' he said.

'And she must have at least one ballgown,' she went on. 'I have just the thing.' She disappeared through a curtain at the back of the premises and came back carrying a large dress box. 'This was made for a young lady who changed her mind about buying it. You are of a size, I think.' She opened the box and held the gown up against Molly.

The overskirt was made of the palest blue-green crepe with an open front which floated round her like shimmering water. It had puffed sleeves and a deep round neckline filled with rouched lace and the bodice was caught under the bosom with a cluster of silk flowers in pale colours of pink, blue and lilac; more of the flowers trimmed the hem. The underskirt was of white satin. Molly ran her hands lovingly over it. 'Oh, it is beautiful, but I do not know…'

'Try it on,' Duncan said.

He watched as she disappeared into an adjoining room to put it on, a procedure which had been going on all morning. He had thought he would be bored by it, but he was captivated. She was so easy to please and he guessed she had had few such pleasures in her young life. He was prepared to wager that Harriet had all the gowns she needed, while her daughter had nothing but what would suit a schoolgirl.

He looked up as Molly came back to stand before him. The gown fitted perfectly and her simple beauty took his breath away so that, for a moment, he could not speak.

'What do you think?' she demanded. 'Is it not beautiful?'

He swallowed hard. 'Indeed, yes.'

'It could have been made for the young lady,' Mrs Solomon said.

'But it was not,' Duncan put in. 'It has been left on your hands…'

Molly held her breath; she wanted to have the gown so very much and if the Captain haggled the woman might not let him have it.

'I am sure we can come to an arrangement,' she said with a simpering smile. 'For such a good customer.'

'Wrap everything up, put it into a trunk and send it to The Bell Hotel,' he instructed, pulling a purse out of his frockcoat. 'And I want a discount for cash.'

'Certainly, sir.' The sight of Duncan's hoard of hard-won coins was too much to resist.

Molly could hardly contain her excitement. Somehow or other, she was going to make an opportunity to wear that gown when they arrived in London. Already, she could imagine the occasion—the ballroom, the lights and music and the elegant young men clamouring to dance with her. Her mama would be very proud of her and not ashamed of her as she always seemed to be.

She chose to ignore the fact that they still had a long way to go before reaching the capital and she was almost sure the Captain was a wanted man. A more crucial problem was that she did not know how to dance. 'Captain,' she said, as they left the shop and turned back towards their lodgings, 'can you dance?'

'Tolerably well,' he said. 'But if you think I am going to take you to a ball…'

'No, not that; I was hoping you might teach me the steps. Mama always said there was plenty of time for that and so I never learned. And I should like to waltz.'

'I am not sure young unmarried ladies are allowed to waltz.'

'Why not?'

'I believe it is considered improper.'

'Why?'

'Because of the way the man holds his partner. It is a little…' He paused and smiled. 'A little too intimate for unmarried ladies.'

'Oh. There is a very great deal I do not know, isn't there?'

'Yes, I am afraid there is.'

'Then you must teach me.'

'Oh, no,' he said, laughing. 'I have undertaken to take you to your mother, nothing more. It is her place to instruct you.'

'Yes, but she is always so busy and it would be so much better if I could learn it all before we arrive in London. Then if an important invitation should come my way I would be ready.'

'No.'

'Why not?'

'I have more pressing things to do.'

'Like holding up coaches and gaming. I wish you would not do such dangerous things. I cannot bear the thought of you being shut up in that castle.'

He turned to look at her, trotting along beside him, trusting him completely, and a twinge of conscience smote him. What he was doing was highly improper and what was worse he was allowing himself to use her to allay the suspicions of the custodians of law and order. The fact that he had spent almost his last sovereign paying for her clothing in no way relieved his feelings of guilt.

'I have no intention of allowing myself to be shut up inside it,' he said brusquely.

'Why are you so blue-devilled? Is it because you have laid out more money on me than you intended? Mama will reimburse you, I am sure.'

'I have not laid out more than I intended,' he said, knowing perfectly well he would never accept repayment from Harriet, even if it were offered, which he doubted. 'What use are sovereigns except for spending?'

'Especially when they are not your own,' she retorted.

'I did not notice you refusing to take advantage of them,' he snapped.

'You said your pockets were at my disposal. I think it is very unkind of you to fly into the boughs just because I said I should not like you to be shut up in the castle.'

'Then there is no more to be said on the subject.'

'What are we going to do now?'

'Go back to The Bell and eat a good dinner.'

'Do you think Mr Upjohn will have arrived?'

'I certainly hope so.'

He shut his mouth so firmly after speaking, she knew it would be unwise to pester him. She walked on beside him, hobbling a little because the tight shoes were pinching her feet, and she wished she had asked if she might wear a pair of the new ones he had bought for her. But it was not the tight shoes which had spoiled the pleasure of the outing but his tetchiness. His mood was not improved when they returned to the hotel and found no sign of Frank and Martha.

'Perhaps Mrs Upjohn was not agreeable,' she suggested.

'Like all good wives, she will do as her husband bids her.'

'I should not like her to come against her wishes, Captain, and I should hope Mr Upjohn would not insist.'

'Then you would have to go back to Stacey Manor. I am determined we shall not continue alone.'

'I know what it is,' she said, speaking in a whisper, so that others in the crowded room would not hear her. 'You are afraid you will be forced into making an honest woman of me. That is not at all flattering.'

'And you are not at all consistent,' he said, also keeping his voice low. 'Yesterday you told me I am too old and you would not consider such a match. Now you seem to be saying the opposite…'

'No, I am not. I simply said you were afraid you might have to. Let me set your mind at rest, Captain. I have no wish to marry you, but, having come this far, it would be foolish to turn back, especially as we are like to run into more trouble going back than going forward.'

'How so?' he queried, wondering what she understood by the term marriage. She could have no conception of physical desire, the love and passion that, in his view, should exist between husband and wife. The novels she read and her mama's conversation had filled her head with nonsense. The man who married her would have a pleasurable time educating her.

'Why, Mr Upjohn may very well have been taken up; had you thought of that?'

'Yes, I had,' he said irritably. He was beginning to wish he had not drawn Frank into this escapade, though it had seemed like a good idea at the time.

They had shared so much during the Peninsular campaign, both the comradeship and the danger, but Frank had had enough of war by the time Napoleon surrendered in 1814, and decided to return home to his wife. He had not taken part in the Battle of Waterloo. Duncan had come back to England in late 1815, after recovering in a Brussels hospital from a wound in his side received at Waterloo, but he could not bear the thought of going home and so he had reported to the War Office, hoping to be given active service. Instead he had been sent to track down a traitor. His enquiries had taken him to Norfolk and it was in Norwich he had met Frank again.

He smiled, remembering the night of revelry they had enjoyed as they'd reminisced and talked about old battles and the people they had known. But it had been obvious Frank was in a bad way. He was thin as a rake and his clothes were in tatters. He had admitted he could not find work and had turned to crime. Duncan had been appalled and infuriated. There was something wrong when a good and valiant man like Frank should be so little thought of by the country for which he had given years of his life, while men like Sir John Partridge prospered. He had asked him to join him.

'There won't be regular pay,' he had warned. 'But there will be something at the end of it, if we are successful.'

And so they had joined forces. Becoming a highwayman and living the life of a ne'er-do-well had been one way of dealing with a personal situation he found difficult to come to terms with and he justified it with the argument that he was obeying orders. Taking risks was a way of finding release. Until he met Molly.

She had made him see life with a different perspective, had forced him to examine his motives. And in spite of her conviction that he was a criminal, which was only half true, she trusted him. Did he deserve that trust? Did he deserve anyone's trust? Martha's? Or Frank's?

'Do not look so cross.' Molly's voice broke into his self-analysis. 'It is not my fault you were seen holding up that coach. Indeed I have done my best to help you.'

He was about to tell her that she was more hindrance than help and that if she had not told the constable they were married he could have sent her back to Stacey Manor and forgotten all about her, but changed his mind. Not only would it hurt her feelings, it was palpably untrue. He could no more have sent her on alone than fly. Besides, he and Frank had brought their troubles upon themselves.

She smiled suddenly. 'Mr Upjohn might be here soon and I am hungry, so do you think we could have something to eat while we wait? I am starving.'

In the face of her imperturbability, he could do no more than take her into the dining room and order a meal, in the hope that Frank would arrive before they had finished it.

Molly hated long silences, and though she tried very hard not to speak she could not resist trying to bring him out of his ill humour. But he would have none of it and she turned her attention to the conversation going on at the next table, which was occupied by four men—tradesmen or perhaps farmers, judging by their plain trousers and gaiters, frieze coats and shallow hats.

'He says he gives them homes and educates them which is more than they had where they came from.'

'Don't make no odds,' another said. 'It's trading in human beings and I don't hold with that.'

'But they ain't exac'ly human, are they?' queried a third. 'They're savages. Black savages.'

'That's on account of they don't know no better.'

'Well, ain't that just what I've been saying?' the first man put in. 'He educates 'em in the scriptures and teaches 'em to work in the house.'

'Only so's he can get more money for 'em. Why, I heard he makes ten thousand a year.'

'You seem to know a lot about it.'

'My brother-in-law was on one of his vessels. In the navy in the war, he was, but had to come out at the end of it. Surplus to requirements, he was, even though he was in ten years and didn't know nothin' else. Grunston offered him a berth and he took it, but when he comes back the tales he told fair made me shiver, I can tell you. He didn't go only the once, said he'd rather starve than serve on a slaver again.'

By the time they had finished their meal, she had discovered that Mr Grunston owned two ships going out from Lynn to buy his human cargo, some of whom he sent on to the Indies, and the ships returned with cargoes of sugar from the plantations there—a double profit. Others he brought home and, having cleaned them up and taught them how to behave, he sold to Society ladies for whom having a black page or footman was the height of fashion. Two days hence he was off to London to purchase another decommissioned ship from the Admiralty to enlarge his fleet.

Molly leaned forward in order to whisper, 'Captain, did you hear that?'

'Hear what?'

'Those men at the next table. They are talking about a slave trader earning ten thousand a year. Don't you think that is disgraceful?'

'It is not unlawful…yet.'

'Well, I think it is reprehensible. I am persuaded the Dark Knight would have something to say on the matter.'

'The Dark Knight?' His only concession to being even slightly disconcerted was to raise one dark eyebrow quizzically. 'Is he another of your fictional heroes?'

'Oh, no, he is a real person, as you very well know.'

'Do I?'

'Oh, yes. I believe he models himself on Robin of Locksley.'

'Who is Robin of Locksley?'

'He is a mythical figure I read about. He lived a long time ago, in the time of Richard the Lionheart, and he was always holding travellers up and giving their gold to the poor.'

Duncan was diverted. 'And what would this Dark Knight do, if he were here now?'

'Hold the man up. Take his ill-gotten gains from him and set his slaves free.'

'That would be a crime,' he said drily.

'But justified, don't you think? You could distribute his wealth to deserving people and prevent another cargo of poor black men, women and children being sold into slavery.'

'Me?' he queried in astonishment.

'Why not?'

'Miss Martineau, I abhor the trade as much as anyone and I support those who advocate its abolition, but that is not the way to bring it about.'

'Oh, I did not think you were so pudding-hearted.'

'Molly, I wish you would put the Dark Knight from your mind. The Dark Knight is not Robin of Locksley, nor yet Don Quixote.'

'Indeed he is not, if he will not tilt at a few windmills.'

He laughed in spite of himself. 'Oh, you will be the death of me.'

'Oh, no, but you must admit you would like to do it.'

'Indeed I should,' he said. 'But that is not to say I will.'

'No, perhaps it would not be wise without Mr Upjohn to help you.' She liked to tease as much as he did and was gratified when he rose to the bait. 'I think we should have waited at the Crosskeys and not come here without him.'

'Do you? I recollect you wanted to go shopping.'

'That was your idea. I did not ask to go.'

'You could not go to London dressed in nothing but a filthy riding habit.'

'No, but I was not in such haste that I would want you to abandon your friend.'

'I have not abandoned him. He is well able to look after himself, which is more than can be said for you, who are young and vulnerable and whose head is filled with fantasy.'

'My head is not filled with fantasy. You do not know me very well or you would know I am a very practical kind of person.'

'Is that so?' He smiled for the first time for over an hour. 'I have seen no evidence of it so far.'

'Then I will prove it. I shall come back with you. We may well meet them on the way.'

'Not so long ago you were of the opinion we would run into greater trouble going back than going forward.'

'I am sure you are clever enough to avoid anyone searching for you if you go carefully, and I am not afraid of a little adventure.'

'No, that I had noted. And not above inciting a man to crime either.'

'Oh, that,' she said airily. 'I was bamming. But you must allow that you are troubled about Mr Upjohn.'

He sighed heavily, admitting she was right. He *was* worried and his conscience *was* troubling him. Frank must be in trouble or else Martha was proving difficult. But if that were the case Frank would have come on without her.

If it were not for Molly he would not have hesitated, but if it were not for her he would not have been in this predicament in the first place. He was not at all sure he liked being so accountable for another human being, and one who was so artless. 'Very well,' he said. 'We will go back, but only as far as the Crosskeys. He may be there.'

He rose from the table, leaving Molly to scramble under it in search of her shoes which she had kicked off.

'Now what?' he asked in exasperation.

'Nothing. I am simply looking for my shoes. They were tight and… Oh, there they are.' She bent to retrieve them and squeezed her white-stockinged feet back into them, to his unfeigned amusement. 'It will be a relief to go back to my riding boots.'

She went up to their rooms to change while he gave orders for Molly's new trunk to be kept for them when it arrived, and then they set off on horseback, retracing the route they had covered that morning, meeting a little traffic—a coach or two, several loaded haycarts, people on horseback and on foot—but not the curricle.

'Where are we going now?' she asked him when he'd returned from questioning the innkeeper at the Crosskeys and been told his friend had not returned there.

'To his home. We'll find out if he reached it.'

'How far is that?'

'An hour's ride. Are you tired? Do you want to rest?'

'No. I can keep up, never fear.'

They had been riding for perhaps an hour and were passing through a wooded area, when they came upon the curricle. It was tipped on its side in the ditch beside the road and there was evidence of a struggle, but of Frank or Martha there was no sign. Nor could they find the horse, though they stopped and searched the area.

'What do you suppose happened?' she asked him. 'Did the watch catch up with him? Or was it robbers?'

'Robbers?' he queried. 'What could robbers want with him?'

'Why, Sir John Partridge's gold, of course. They could have overheard the man who witnessed the hold-up of the coach and recognised Mr Upjohn from his description.'

'Don't be ridiculous!' he snapped, his concern for his friend making him speak sharply to her. 'There is no gold.'

'I am not being ridiculous. You are the most uncivil man I have ever come across. I am beginning to wish I had never consented to ride with you.'

He gave a bellow of a laugh at this statement. 'Consent to ride with me! Tell me, when did I ask you to?'

'Oh, well, if you are going to split hairs, then I might as well remain silent.'

'Do that. There is nothing I would like more than your silence. How a man can be expected to think with you chattering like a magpie all the time, I do not know.'

He went back to the curricle and examined it again but it revealed no more than it had before. From the direction in which it was pointing, he deduced that Frank had been on his way to join them and not on his way home. In that case, had Martha been with him?

Molly, following behind him and peering over his shoulder as he bent to move aside the splintered wood, spied a piece of torn jaconet attached to the broken door. 'Captain, would the watch have arrested Mrs Upjohn too?'

He sighed; his companion was determined to make her presence felt and it took all his self-control to keep his temper. If it hadn't been for her riding after him, none of this would have happened. He was angry with her but more angry with himself for allowing a slip of a schoolgirl to dictate to him.

'I do not think so; why do you ask?'

She pulled the tiny scrap of material from the wreckage. 'This. It is from a lady's gown.'

He took it from her. 'Come on, mount up. There is no time to lose.'

Not a word of gratitude, she noticed, not even an admission that she had seen something he had missed, just a curt order to get on her horse. She could almost hate him for it. Except, of course, that she knew he was very worried about his friend, even though he pretended not to be, and worry often made people crotchety. She must make allowances.

He almost flung her into her saddle and mounted himself with a curt, 'For goodness' sake, keep up.' And then he was off at a swift canter with Good Boy beside him. When he realised she was right behind him and grimly determined, he increased their pace to a gallop. She was too busy hanging on to call out to him to slow down or ask him where they were going.

They eased the horses into a walk as they entered a small hamlet and he picked his way over the village green and stopped outside the gate of a cottage. 'Wait there,' he commanded as he dismounted and went up the short path to knock on the door.

Molly watched as a young woman in a plain brown dress with a white apron and cap answered the summons. She stood for a moment, staring at him, then, recognising him, gave a little cry of relief. 'Oh, Captain Stacey, it is you. I have been praying you would come. The most dreadful thing has happened and I do not know what to do. Come in, please.'

She looked up and saw Molly. Her eyes darkened and she looked annoyed, but in the face of Molly's friendly smile she softened. 'The young lady too.'

Molly slipped off Jenny and joined them as Duncan ducked his head to enter the cottage. Mrs Upjohn stood to one side to allow her to precede her. Molly dipped her knee and lowered her head. 'Mrs Upjohn.'

Martha inclined her head in acknowledgement. 'Miss Martineau, I believe?'

'Yes. I suppose Mr Upjohn told you of me?'

'He did.'

'I am truly sorry if I have been the unwitting cause of trouble for you.' She stood and looked round the tiny cottage. There were two rooms downstairs, a small sitting room in which they stood and a scullery behind it. A ladder led up to a hole in the ceiling, presumably to a bedroom under the roof. It was very plainly furnished but was clean as a new pin.

'Never mind sorry,' Duncan put in as Mrs Upjohn indicated a sofa and bade them be seated. 'Martha, tell me what happened.'

'We were on our way to join you and the young lady,' she explained, standing by the hearth. She was very pale and trembling a little, Molly noted. 'It was a bright sunny day and we were not hurrying. Frank said we had all the time in the world. And then three men galloped up behind us. Frank drew to one side to allow them to pass, but they didn't want to pass. They surrounded us and forced us to stop.

'One said he was a constable from Cromer and he was arresting Frank for holding up Sir John Partridge's coach and stealing gold and other valuables. Of course that was nonsense and so I told them, but they took no notice of me. Another said he had been a witness and he would swear Frank was one of the robbers. I never heard anything so outlandish. Why, Frank would never do such a thing.'

'Then what happened?' Duncan asked, while Molly looked on, shocked into silence. Mr Upjohn had obviously been deceiving his wife about his activities with Captain Duncan Stacey. No doubt he had been lured into a life of crime by the Captain and that was very wicked of him.

'He struggled, but they overpowered him. They took the horse from the curricle and tied him onto it. They said they were taking him to Cromer to face charges. They said he would come up before the justices and one of them was Sir John Partridge. It afforded them a great deal of glee.'

'I'll wager it did,' Duncan said laconically. 'When did it happen?'

'This morning. About eight of the clock. Please, Captain, do something. Go after them, tell them it is all a mistake. Tell them he was with you the whole time. They will listen to you.'

'Of course we will go,' Molly said.

Duncan turned to her in astonishment. 'What are you saying, miss? There is no question of you going. If I go, I go alone.'

'But they will not believe you without me to vouchsafe your alibi; you know that.'

'I need no alibi. And if you continue to make public statements like the one you made at Aylsham it will ruin your reputation.'

Molly sighed. 'Why? I shall tell everyone we have done nothing improper and they will believe me. It is not as if we are running away to Gretna Green...'

'I should hope not!'

'You need not be so emphatic about that, Captain, it is not at all flattering.'

'Oh, Molly, Molly, what am I to do with you?'

'Take me to my mama, as you promised.' She paused and smiled at Martha. 'After we have rescued Mr Upjohn, naturally. We cannot let him languish in prison.'

Duncan had no intention of allowing Frank to languish in prison, nor of confronting magistrates, but that did not mean he would not do all in his power to free his friend and before he reached Cromer. Sir John Partridge would do anything rather than have Frank reveal their true interest in his baggage, which was certainly not the gold; he would make sure Frank never came to trial. His friend would meet with an unlucky 'accident'. Nor would Sir John rest until the damning papers Duncan carried in his saddlebag were once again in his possession.

The last thing he needed was Molly Madcap at his heels the whole time. It was time something was done about her. 'You are going back to Stacey Manor on the first available coach, which is what I should have insisted upon from the first,' he said. 'You are nothing but a liability.'

'Oh, that is not fair!' she cried. 'It was not my fault you are suspected of being a highwayman. That would have happened whether I was with you or no. You have just made a mull of everything and now you are blaming me. I begin to think I do not like you at all.'

In spite of the seriousness of the situation, he grinned. 'Only begin not to like me? Why, you have been ringing a peal over me these last two days.'

'I was bamming before, but now I am in earnest. You are not a hero, nor even a gentleman.'

'Then, miss, I wonder at your wanting to be in my company.'

'I did not know you were a rakeshame when I met you, did I?'

'Please, Miss Martineau, this is no time to be quarrelling.' Martha interrupted her. 'Let the Captain go. You can stay here with me until he returns.'

'Thank you, ma'am,' Duncan said.

Molly, who did not want to return to Stacey Manor and her dull life there, realised that it would be the best solution. 'Very well,' she said. 'I know we cannot go to London until you have rescued Mr Upjohn, so it seems to me the sooner you set off the better.'

He did not stop to argue about going to London but turned on his heel and left the cottage. They went to the door and watched him galloping away. Molly, who had done nothing but quarrel with him, even when he had been so kind to her and bought her a whole trunkful of fine clothes, felt suddenly bereft and miserable. Whatever he was and whatever he did, he had been her saviour and protector and if she never saw him again she would be sorry, very sorry indeed.

'Take care!' she called after him, but by that time he was out of earshot and did not hear her.

Chapter Four

'Now, Miss Martineau,' Martha said, taking hold of Good Boy's reins. 'Bring your horse round to the back of the house, if you please, then we will go inside and I will have your version of the story. You can tell it to me while I prepare something to eat. It will while away the time until the Captain returns and, please God, with Frank.'

They put the horses side by side in the makeshift stable, rubbed them down without speaking, after which Martha drew a bucket of water from the trough in the yard and gave them a drink. 'There's hay over there,' she said, nodding towards a small stack. 'I can see these poor beasts have been long on the road and deserve some petting.'

Molly, doing as she was told, reflected that she had been long on the road herself and was in need of pampering, but it was evident she would not get it, not from Mrs Upjohn, nor the Captain, who had ridden off without a backward glance. And now she had to explain herself to this woman and she had no idea how much she ought to tell. She wished the Captain had rehearsed her in it, but no, off he had gone, assuming she would know what to say.

Once the horses were settled she followed Martha into the kitchen of the tiny cottage where Martha bade her be seated. 'I've little enough in the house to eat,' she said. 'But you are welcome to share what there is. What Frank wants to be doing, racketing round the countryside with the Captain just as if he was still in uniform, I do not know. And how come you to be with them?'

'It was only meant to be a little adventure,' Molly began, sitting on one of four chairs set round the table, and watching Martha moving about with saucepans and vegetables and a large fish which she set about boning and skinning. 'I was so bored at Stacey Manor; there was nothing to do but go for walks and ride and read. I have read everything my god-mother—that's Lady Connaught, you know—had in the house several times over…'

'Yes, yes, but how did you meet Captain Stacey and my husband? Frank never said anything about Stacey Manor, nor no Lady Connaught.'

'I do not think Mr Upjohn was ever at Stacey Manor. Captain Stacey came to visit Lady Connaught alone. When he left, I followed him.'

'Why?'

'Why?' Molly considered the question with her head on one side, smiling a little. 'I was curious about him. And he was so set on riding off long before it was daylight and that seemed very mysterious to me. And though he bears the family name of Stacey he did not appear to be one of the *haut monde*.'

'Is that all? Just curiosity?'

'Yes. I followed him and he heard me and he said I had to go back to Stacey Manor, which I was not at all wishful to do. He slapped my horse and made it bolt into the trees and

I fell off and bumped my head so he was obliged to put me on his horse and we rode to the inn and went to bed.'

'To bed?' Martha asked, shocked to the core.

'Not together; of course not. It was at breakfast time there was a commotion about a robbery. Captain Stacey came in while everyone was discussing what to do about it. The constable questioned him, but I vouchsafed he had been with me all night.'

'But everyone must have thought…'

'I said I was his wife.'

'He allowed that?' Martha, in spite of wishing her guest would come to the point and tell her about Frank, was intrigued.

'He could hardly deny it once I had said it.'

'And where was Frank while this was going on?'

'I saw Mr Upjohn when he passed through the dining room but he was not questioned and he did not speak to us. I did not meet him until much later in the day after Captain Stacey had hired the curricle. He was waiting for us at an inn near Norwich, a long way from the scene of the robbery. It was then we discussed how I could be got to London without a scandal…'

'London?'

'Yes. I wished to join my mama, and Captain Stacey thought of you and the plan was contrived that we should all travel to London together…'

The fish had been put in the pot and Martha began peeling potatoes. 'But that does not explain why Frank was suspected of being a highway robber. Are you sure you have left nothing out?'

Molly hesitated and decided not to voice her conviction that the two men had had a hand in the hold-up; it would only upset her hostess and if Captain Stacey brought Frank safely back nothing need be said at all, but what he wanted to tell her himself. 'No, except the description the witness gave of one of the robbers said he had a scar beneath his eye—but Captain Stacey said many men have scars. After all, there has been a war and men were wounded.'

'That is true. Frank took a sabre thrust saving the life of the Captain at the battle of Ciudad Rodrigo. But that was some time before they were both taken prisoner.'

'They were taken prisoner? Oh, do tell me about that. I know so little and I am sure it must have been very exciting. Sometimes I wish I were a man and could go to war and ride about the countryside having adventures.'

Martha, who had labelled Molly as a hoyden at best and a strumpet at worst, began to revise her opinion. The girl was a simpleton. No, not even that; she was a grown-up child, which, she supposed, was the most dangerous of all. The Captain had obviously been captivated and she didn't think Frank had been so unaffected as he had pretended when he had inveigled her into going with him in the curricle. And what a farrago that had been!

'War is not an adventure,' she said. 'It brings out the worst in men as well as the best. It is bestiality and dirt and hunger and forced marches and danger of being blown to bits or cut to ribbons. And for what? Simply so that a man may say he has done his duty and not let his companions down. And I know, for I have been there…'

'To war?' Molly queried in surprise.

'Yes. I went with them. Two years I spent in Portugal and Spain, following in their wake, cooking and cleaning and looking after my man until he was taken prisoner along with the Captain.'

'Oh, I am sorry. It must have been hard for you.'

'It was better than being left behind in England with no means of support.'

'But when he was captured? What did you do? You did not go to prison with him, did you?'

'No, I waited. There was nothing else I could do. There was no way I could come home to England. As far as the army was concerned, I did not exist. It was hard. I had to find work to put food into my mouth…'

'How?'

'Cooking and cleaning for the single men. There were other ways but I did not stoop to those.'

'What other ways?'

'If you do not know, it is not my place to enlighten you, miss. I wish you would not ask me.'

Molly, who was used to being fobbed off when she asked questions, did not insist on being told. 'But you managed and the men escaped? Oh, do tell me they escaped.'

'Yes. Frank went back to his regiment but the Captain was put on special duties. I did not see him again until today.'

'You did not know the Captain and Mr Upjohn had met again?'

'Oh, yes, Frank told me they had met by chance in Norwich. He had gone there looking for work, but he had been unlucky and was just making up his mind to return home when he chanced to run into Captain Stacey. The Captain offered him a job but it was not the kind of work where he could take me because they would be moving about the countryside a great deal. And yesterday he came back and told me the Captain had a job for me too and we could be together again. I should have known it was all too good to be true.'

'But it is true. They are going to escort me to London to my mama, only the Captain said it was not at all proper for me to travel without a lady companion and he thought of you. When they come back, we shall still go. We shall be safe once we are out of Norfolk.'

'Safe?' Martha looked up in alarm. 'What do you mean?'

'Safe from all these robberies,' Molly said hastily. 'There have been so many, no traveller can be anything but anxious.'

Martha appeared satisfied with that explanation, much to Molly's relief, and they sat down to dine together. Molly regaled her new friend with the story of their shopping expedition and all the things the Captain had bought for her, which had sadly been left behind at The Bell, and Martha told her more about life as a camp follower in Spain and Portugal which had Molly's blue eyes round as saucers.

'And I thought riding in the dark was an adventure,' she said with a sigh. 'Why, that is nothing at all compared to what you have done.'

'You should be thankful that you have never had to endure it,' Martha said testily. 'You have never been hungry, never heard big guns and been afraid for your life, never eaten dog…'

'Dog?' Molly repeated, thinking of her mother's pet pug. 'Oh, no, I refuse to believe that.' She looked with distaste at her plate of food, though she had seen Martha put the fish in the pot.

'It is true. When I came home, I swore I would never let my husband go to war again. We would live in quiet seclusion until the end of our days. But Frank could not settle and when Captain Stacey offered him a chance to travel…' She shrugged. 'How could I hold him? He is a man, after all, and a soldier.'

'I think it was wrong of the Captain to tempt him. I shall speak to him about it.'

Martha smiled wearily; the girl spoke so confidently, as if she had some influence over the Captain, but she was sure that was not so. She could not imagine Captain Stacey under the cat's paw. 'I wish you would not. Knowing both men, I know it would do no good and might very well have the opposite effect. Frank will come to it in his own time.'

'How long do you think it will be before they are back?'

'I don't know, but I am sure it won't be tonight. I will make a bed up for you in the parlour. I think you will be comfortable there. Let us pray they come back safe and sound tomorrow.'

Molly could do nothing but echo her plea as she helped Martha clear away their supper and wash the pots, then she was given a blanket and a pillow to make herself comfortable on the sofa and Martha bade her goodnight and climbed the ladder to the upper room.

It seemed a long night to Molly, although she was tolerably comfortable and very tired. Never before had she been kept awake by worry and fear. Her childhood, though hardly privileged, had been serene, with nothing but the prospect of a scolding to trouble her. Now she was beset by thoughts of what might be taking place in Cromer.

If anything happened to the Captain, what would she do? Already her life had become so entangled with his she could not imagine living without him, bad temper, mocking smile, gambling and all. Was that love? She was not such a ninny as to believe that, but it was a feeling she had never experienced before, this concern for another human being, and she supposed it meant she was growing up.

She fell asleep at last and dreamed of the Captain brandishing his sword at windmills which turned into constables. The horse he was riding became a green dragon breathing fire. And the fire, orange and yellow and pink, licked about his feet and set his clothing alight. She saw him smiling as the flames consumed him and in her dreams she screamed.

She sat up suddenly, her mouth open, her eyes clouded by the memory of a dream so vivid she thought it must be real. The flimsy curtains to the room flapped in the breeze, revealing a huge red and pink sunrise. The shadows on the curtains made it look like tongues of flame. She breathed a sigh of relief.

She looked up to see Martha hurrying down from above. 'What is wrong? Why did you call out?'

'I had a bad dream. I thought the Captain was on fire.' She laughed shakily. 'I expect it was the sun through the curtains. I'm sorry if I woke you.'

'You didn't wake me; I could not sleep.'

'You are worried?'

'Naturally I am worried. And so should you be.'

'I am, but the Captain is a resourceful man and he will do his best for your husband.'

'But I cannot help feeling it might be too late. What will they do to Frank? Will he be sent to prison? Or hanged? Highway robbery is a hanging offence, is it not?'

'I do not know. But Captain Stacey will avow his innocence, an' if he is not believed I will repeat what I told the constable in Aylsham. The Captain was with me all night and Mr Upjohn slept in the next room.'

'Is that true?'

'It is not so very far from the truth, for we did not arrive at the inn until nearly dawn and though the Captain procured a bed for me I slept no more than an hour or two.'

'Not long enough for them to hold up a stagecoach?' Martha wanted desperately to be reassured.

'No, of course not. Put it from your mind. They will be back by the time we have breakfasted and you will have been worrying for nothing.'

But the men did not return. Martha and Molly sat about alternately talking and watching the road from the gate all day long and at dusk they had a silent meal before making ready for a second night of wakefulness.

Neither would voice the fear that was growing in their breasts that something bad had befallen them, that both men had been taken and would never return, though privately Molly vowed that if they had not arrived by noon the following day she would set off on Jenny to find out what had happened. Her longed-for journey to London was entirely forgotten.

Duncan pulled his galloping horse up in the shelter of some trees to wait for Frank to catch up with him. Caesar was a strong stallion and had carried him well all day but he was tiring and they must soon stop to allow both horses to rest, especially as the mare Frank was riding was more used to pulling a curricle than having a man on her back.

The night before Duncan had come upon the prisoner and his escort just short of Cromer. It had been late at night and, concluding that there would be no one awake to receive them, the constables had decided to light a camp fire and cook a meal before going into the town at first light. There was a skinned rabbit on a stick being turned over the flames by one of their number and the appetising smell had reminded Duncan he had not eaten since the midday meal he had shared with Molly at The Bell.

They had been very lax in setting guards, for all three were grouped around the fire, while Frank was tied to a tree nearby. The horses were tethered on a line a little way off and were quietly cropping the grass. He had left his horse and crept forward to assess the strength of the opposition and, if possible, to alert Frank to his presence without being seen.

'We'd have got into town before dark if he had been more of a horseman,' one said, jerking his head in Frank's direction. 'How anyone could keep slipping off a gentle creature like that is beyond me.'

'Well, I suppose he had the right of it when he said it was a draught horse and not used to a rider,' another said, staring into the flames. 'And he had no saddle.'

'We should have let him fall. Being dragged along the ground at a gallop might have taught him to keep his seat.'

Duncan, crouching in the darkness not a dozen yards away, smiled to himself. Frank had evidently been employing delaying tactics, hoping for rescue, because he was almost as good a horseman as Duncan himself.

'I wonder he has never been caught before if his seat is so bad,' the second man commented.

'It cannot be that bad,' the third man said. 'He was working in Sir John's stables for three weeks afore he piked off. I recognised him when he held up the coach, for all he was masked, and I saw him ride off.'

'I told you,' Frank put in from behind them. 'You've got the wrong man. I couldn't ha' done it for I can't ride, never could. When I was young we were too poor to own a horse and we lived in the city; how could I learn?'

'In the army. You were a soldier, weren't you?'

'In the infantry. The infantry march, they don't ride.'

'I saw him,' the valet persisted. 'And so I shall vouchsafe in court.'

'If he ever gets to court,' another mumbled, confirming Duncan's fears.

They turned back to their fire as one of their number drew the rabbit from it and began to cut it up and hand the pieces to the others on the end of the knife. 'What about him?' one asked.

'Oh, let him go hungry. It might help him to remember where he was when Sir John had his gold snaffled.'

They were obviously relaxed and confident and Duncan, keeping a close eye on what they were doing, risked crawling up to the tree where Frank was tied.

'Don't speak,' he hissed. 'It's me.'

'Yes, I saw you.' The answer was a whisper spoken through closed teeth. 'Get a move on, will you?' Then, remembering his place, he added, 'Sir.'

Duncan busied himself with the knots. 'Are they armed?'

'One has a pistol and another a musket.' He nodded towards the horses where there was a musket propped against one of the saddles. 'The third one is Sir John's valet. He recognised me.'

Duncan undid the last of the knots. 'Go for the horse and get going,' Duncan whispered, pulling his cravat over his mouth and nose. 'I'll hold them off.'

Frank was stiff from his cramped position, but he managed to hobble to the mare, untie her and set the others loose before throwing himself on her back. Although he moved swiftly and silently, it was enough to alert his captors. They did not see Duncan and assumed their prisoner had managed to free himself. One tried to catch the horses, while another ran for his musket, only to be beaten to it by Duncan who blocked his path, threatening him with his own weapon.

'Lie on the floor!' he commanded.

The man did not hesitate; he sprawled face down. The third man tried to come at Duncan from behind but he whirled round and hit him with the butt of the musket, sending him reeling. The valet did not see heroics as any part of his duty and simply sat staring at the scene with his mouth open and a piece of meat on the end of a knife halfway to it.

Duncan whistled up Caesar who came obediently and the next minute he was galloping after Frank, with the shouts and curses of the men ringing in the darkness behind him as they tried to recapture their mounts.

Frank was waiting half a mile up the road. 'You took your time,' he said. 'I was beginning to think we'd be in Cromer before you. It would have been devilish awkward to defend myself if I couldn't tell the truth about that traitor.'

'I was delayed. Now, let's be off before they come after us.'

'Where to?'

Duncan had been asking himself that question and there was only one safe place that came to mind. 'Stacey Manor.'

They took a roundabout route in order to put followers off the scent, but were there in less than half an hour.

It was half an hour in which Duncan began thinking about what he would tell his grandmother. She would want to know where Molly was and why he had returned without her and he had no idea what he could say. He had promised to protect Molly and take her to her mother; instead he was riding about the countryside at dead of night pursued by constables.

And supposing everyone had retired and there was no one to admit them? They could hide in the stables, but he did not think that would serve. The area might be searched. What they needed was a cast-iron alibi provided by someone no one would dare to disbelieve and that was his grandmother. And would she give them that, considering her poor opinion of him?

Not wishing to alert the servants, they rode up to the house as quietly as possible and dismounted outside the stables. Silently they led the horses into the stall and unsaddled them, then found hay and water for them. That done, they went back to the house.

There was a side door which was sometimes left unlocked to allow Brunning, her ladyship's butler, to return after a night out in the village. Duncan had discovered the man's secret quite by accident when he was no more than an adventurous stripling and had promised to keep it from his grandmother, demanding in return the right to use the door himself whenever he liked. The arrangement had always worked very well, but he wondered if Brunning still went out at night or if the practice had been discontinued.

He beckoned Frank to follow and found, to his delight, that the door gave when he tried the handle. They crept inside and along a corridor. Duncan, who knew the way, found no difficulty in the dark, though Frank stumbled now and again. In the large reception hall, they found that two lamps had been left burning and, picking up one of these, Duncan led the way upstairs to the room he always occupied when he was staying there.

'Now, we'll settle down for the night,' he told his friend. 'Tomorrow, we will convince everyone we arrived this afternoon.'

'I would rather we had ridden straight home,' Frank said, looking round at the huge well-furnished room. 'Martha will be beside herself with worry.'

'She knows we cannot return tonight. She has Molly with her. They will be company for each other.'

'I wondered what you had done with her. But I hope the chit will say nothing to Martha.'

'Molly knows nothing.'

'Give me leave to doubt that. She's a downy bird and not easy to gull. And I'll wager Lady Connaught ain't either.'

'You are probably right,' Duncan said morosely, stripping off his coat, waistcoat and cravat and sitting on the edge of the bed to pull off his hessians. 'But we shall see tomorrow. There's a truckle in my dressing room next door. Make yourself comfortable. I am for my bed.'

'I don't know how you can sleep,' Frank grumbled as he went to obey. 'We are in the devil of a coil.'

They were both awakened before dawn by a loud banging on the outside door. Frank was all for escaping down the ivy outside the window, but Duncan refused to allow it. It was as well he did, because a peep from the window revealed constables covering any escape from the rear of the house.

'What'll we do?' Frank asked. 'Will they insist on searching the house?'

'I doubt it. Grandmama can be very formidable, but I must put in an appearance.' He pulled on a pair of breeches and reached for a dressing robe, tying it about his middle before striding to the door. 'You are my valet,' he said over his shoulder. 'Make yourself useful laying out my clothes in case they insist on coming up here.'

'Which clothes?'

'It doesn't matter. I believe there are plenty in the wardrobe.' And he was gone.

Brunning, still half asleep, had answered the door to find the leader of the band of constables standing on the step. The constable was regaling him with horror stories of desperate criminals who were on the loose in the neighbourhood and would murder them all in their beds given half a chance.

He stopped suddenly when he saw Duncan descending the stairs. Brunning turned to see who was behind him. It was as well the constable could not see the butler's face because his expression of surprise was comical.

'I'll deal with this, Brunning,' Duncan said.

The servant recovered his wits with admirable swiftness. 'Very well, my lord,' he said. 'Shall I acquaint her ladyship?'

'No, there is no need to alarm her.' He turned to the constable. 'I have seen no strangers but if I do I will send for you at once. Tell me, what do they look like?'

The constable was at a stand. It was his opinion that the man who faced him bore a remarkable resemblance to the man who had turned his own musket upon him, but as it had been dark and the man had covered the lower part of his face he could not swear to it. 'Who are you?' he asked.

Duncan glanced at Brunning who was hovering nearby. He had addressed him as 'my lord', a title Brunning knew he had relinquished, but just for today he would resume it. 'I am the Earl of Connaught, which, if you had your wits about you, you would know. Now, tell me about these desperadoes.'

The man stayed only long enough to give a colourful account of the robbers' looks and the dreadful deeds they had perpetrated and took his leave, calling his men from around the house and riding off somewhat chagrined.

Duncan turned away, smiling. Desperado, was he, vicious, a man who would shoot you as soon as look at you? And as for his companion, he was so ugly no one could fail to be terrified by him. They would never be apprehended on that description.

'Duncan!' The voice was imperious and came from the gallery above. 'Come to my boudoir in twenty minutes.' Lady Connaught, disturbed by the commotion, had come out to peer over the banisters. 'I shall need an explanation. And, Brunning, tell Rose to bring my hot chocolate and washing water.' And with that she disappeared into her room again.

Brunning gave Duncan a rueful smile and shrugged his

shoulders before going to obey. Duncan went back to his own room to dress and make himself presentable.

The selection of clothes Frank had put out for him was extraordinary. There was a pair of cossacks, a cream shirt, a blue velvet waistcoat and a red satin coat with a huge cutaway collar and tight sleeves. 'Would you have me look like a play actor?' he laughed, picking up the coat and holding it up in distaste. 'I do believe this once belonged to my grandfather.'

He threw it into a corner and fetched out a brown riding coat of Bath cloth and a pair of nankeen breeches, cream stockings, a white shirt and a striped neckcloth, which he had left behind on his last visit for just such an eventuality. He needed no help to dress and Frank sat on the end of the bed in shirt and cord breeches, and watched him. 'They've gone, then?'

'Yes, but there is a greater peril. My grandmother wishes to see me in her boudoir. It will be like bearding the lion in his den.'

'She would not betray you?'

'Oh, no, but she will no doubt think of a worse fate for me. There is the question of Molly Madcap...'

Frank laughed. 'Who gave her that name?'

'Grandmama, but that does not mean she will not ring a peal over me about the chit.'

'What are you going to tell her?'

Duncan shrugged. 'I'll think of something.'

But when he had presented himself to an irate dowager and been commanded to sit down facing her he was apparently not required to speak.

'I knew you were a scapegrace,' she said, without waiting for an explanation. 'But I never imagined I should have a troop of constables banging on my door wanting to arrest you. I warned you. I told you you were heading for the gallows and now I am proved right. A Stacey hanged for highway robbery! We shall become notorious.'

'Grandmama, I must protest. I did no more than rescue my servant who had been unjustly detained. The constables were exceeding their duty.'

'Could you not let the magistrates decide that?'

'No, for that would have meant revealing my true purpose and I could not do that.'

'And why not?'

'Sir John Partridge is one of the magistrates.'

'What has Sir John to do with it?'

'Everything, ma'am.'

'Then you had better explain.'

He did so and she listened in silence, at the end of which she gave a bark of laughter which told him she appreciated his predicament. 'Does Molly know about this?'

'No, of course not. I left her with Sergeant Upjohn's wife.'

'While you fly about the countryside pretending to be a highwayman.'

Duncan smiled crookedly. 'Yes, but I have done nothing more reprehensible than taking from those who have betrayed their country and become rich by it and giving the proceeds to those who deserve to be looked after and who have been shamefully neglected.'

'So you say, but it is still unlawful. Will the War Department stand by you if you are apprehended?'

He shrugged. 'It was left to me to choose how I went about my assignment.'

'Then find some other way. I want to hear no more of this Dark Knight.'

'He is already superfluous. I have the information I need.'

'I am glad to hear it. Now what are we going to do about Molly? You have filled her head with nonsense, and no doubt she thinks you are her knight in shining armour.'

He smiled crookedly. 'No, I do not think so. She is forever ringing a peal over me and saying I am not chivalrous. She even tries to teach me manners.'

The old lady laughed aloud at that. 'I'll warrant she does. But I know Molly's character very well and she will see it as a perfect opportunity to indulge in what she calls adventure. And you did not help by keeping her by you when you could have brought her back at once…'

'She would not come. She had her mind fixed on joining her mama and she is very difficult to say no to.'

Lady Connaught smiled. She knew Duncan's difficulty very well but she was not going to let him off the hook so easily. 'You must prove to her that adventure is not what she needs. Take her to London as you planned, make yourself agreeable to her mama and marry the chit at the first available opportunity.'

'But, Grandmama, she is bound to refuse me. She told me I was too old. And, to be honest, I am inclined to agree.'

Even her ladyship's lips twitched at this, but she forced herself to remain severe. 'Fustian! She will do as her mother tells her. Try again.'

'And if I do not?'

'I cannot think why you are being so disobliging,' she said. 'Molly is a lovely child.'

'Yes, she is and that is half the trouble. She is a child and deserves better than me. I said so before.'

'I am biased perhaps, but I am persuaded she could find no one better. You are a man of good education and, until now, of good reputation. You are strong as an ox and could do anything if you put your mind to it. Why, you fought for your country. Wellington himself mentioned you in despatches.'

'It was that report forced me into this coil.'

'Forced, Duncan?'

'I could hardly refuse. I had nothing else I wanted to do and I needed the blunt.'

'You could have come to me. I would always stand buff for you.'

'Thank you, Grandmama, but I'd as lief be independent.'

'So what are you planning to do?'

'I must go to the War Department and make my report and then I have a fancy to buy a small property and breed horses.'

'Good. Go to London as you planned. Take Molly to Harriet and we will see what transpires. Perhaps, after all, you would not suit. I shall not insist.'

'Thank you.' He rose and bowed to her, anxious to make his escape before she added to her diatribe.

'You are a fool, boy,' she murmured to his departing back. 'You are just like your grandfather, as stubborn as a mule, but you will come to see I have the right of it.'

But he did not hear her; he was striding along the corridor to his own room to tell Frank to be ready to leave as soon as they had eaten breakfast.

Now, riding ahead of Frank, he found himself thinking of Molly. Why was his grandmother so intent on marrying him off to her? Molly, when she arrived on the London scene, would have the pick of the eligibles, young men of her own age, with titles and fortunes, who could give her everything he could not. He was too old, too disreputable, too set in his eccentric ways to make a good husband.

Besides, he had no wish to marry. He had tried to go down that road once, believing Beth loved him enough to wait for him. He had been wrong and the hurt he had received when he'd found her married to his brother and the mother of a son was still too raw for him to want to think about anyone else.

'Why the haste?' Frank demanded, coming up alongside him. 'You have been galloping as if the fiends of hell were after you. There is no one behind us and this poor beast will drop if you do not ease up.'

'Very well, we will walk a little.'

They dismounted and walked side by side along the leafy lane in silence until Frank said, 'I own I shall be glad to go home to Martha, but I am hungry. Do you think we can risk stopping at a hostelry for something to eat?'

'I was thinking the same thing, but unfortunately I have pockets to let…'

'That has never bothered you before. We have always contrived.'

'Yes, but after the jobation my grandmother gave me I have undertaken to mend my ways.'

'Did you not explain your difficulty?'

'Yes, and she offered to stand buff, but I told her I have a generous pension from a grateful country and an allowance from my family and I did not need money.'

'Do you? Have an allowance from your brother, I mean.'

'He offered it…'

'Oh, I see. You were too proud to accept it.'

'Something like that.'

'And I am afraid I cannot help. Those constables took every penny I had on me, said it was part of the proceeds of the robbery and must be produced in evidence, but I doubt any of it will go further than their own pockets.'

'Then we must go hungry. It is not the first time we have had empty bellies, is it, my friend?'

'No, but that was in the Peninsula and it was easy to take what we wanted and we were not branded criminals for doing it. Nor did we have two women dependent on us.'

'Then the sooner we rejoin them the better.'

They remounted and continued in silence for some time, each immersed in his own thoughts. Duncan was thinking about Molly, something he found himself doing more and more frequently, and cursing himself for being such a fool as to saddle himself with her. On the other hand, her company was delightful and he felt very sorry for her, having Harriet for a mother and being denied all the things that young ladies of her age should be enjoying.

She had been so happy and grateful when he'd bought her those clothes; many young ladies would have taken everything for granted, would have pouted and cajoled for more, but not Molly. She had been overjoyed when he'd told her she could have that simple ballgown. He could not imagine Beth behaving like that. The difference, he told himself with little conviction, was that Beth was a woman and Molly was little more than a child.

'Do you think the constables will have visited Martha?' Frank asked as they neared his home village. 'Is it safe to go home?'

'Do they know where you live?'

'I do not think so.'

'Then there is no need to worry. And tomorrow we will all four set off for London. We can lose ourselves in the metropolis.'

'You do not mean to return Miss Martineau to Lady Connaught?'

'No, her ladyship has washed her hands of us. We go on as planned.' He said nothing of the difficulty of finding a coach and horses or money enough for their bed and board on the way, though Frank must have been aware of it.

It was evening by the time they arrived and approached the cottage cautiously. Almost immediately the door flew open and Martha ran down the path to greet her husband, crying with relief.

Molly watched them embrace, standing a little shyly in the doorway, wanting to throw herself into Duncan's arms, but knowing it would never do. She smiled as he dismounted and walked towards her. 'You found him, then?' she queried.

'Yes.' She was looking especially lovely, though her eyes were dark-rimmed as if she had not slept, and he wondered whether he had been the cause of her concern and a feeling of remorse tinged with elation filled him, which he quickly stifled. 'All is well.'

'Then put the horses in the outhouse round the back; it will never do for them to be seen. And then you can tell us all about how you rescued Mr Upjohn while we have supper. Martha has been busy all day, cooking for you.'

Both men were ravenous and did justice to the meal they were given and afterwards they sat down to plan their next move, debating whether it was better to go by public coach or to have their own conveyance, concealing from the two women that they had no money to pay for either.

'Frank and I will go into Norwich tomorrow morning and see what is to be had,' Duncan said, rising from the table. 'If you would be so good as to allow Miss Martineau to stay with you again tonight, I will find lodgings.'

'At this time of night?' Molly exclaimed, suddenly realising that the little cottage could not respectably accommodate them all. 'Where will you go?'

'I can knock up the nearest innkeeper.'

'Sir,' Frank said, casting him a warning look which was not lost on Molly who guessed the reason for it. Duncan ought not to draw attention to himself. 'I think you should stay here. If Miss Martineau is agreeable, she can share with Martha while you and I will make ourselves comfortable down here.'

'The sofa is very comfortable,' Molly put in.

'And the hearthrug will do for me,' Frank said.

'Oh, please do stay,' Martha said. 'It is the least we can do since you spoke up for Frank and persuaded the constables to let him go.'

No one disabused her of the idea that Duncan had used reason and influence rather than force to free her husband and so they settled down for the night.

The sofa might have been comfortable for a diminutive figure like Molly, but Duncan, with his broad frame and long legs, found it decidedly otherwise. But it was not discomfort that kept him awake; he had slept in worse places. For the first time, he began to wish he could lead a straightforward sort of life which did not mean lying and subterfuge and living on his wits.

He should have thrown himself upon the mercy of his grandmother but that would have meant falling in with her wishes and his pride would not let him do that. His pride would be his downfall. After all, being married to Molly would not be such a hardship. In fact, it would be no hardship at all, especially if he could cure her of her madcap ways. But her madcap ways were part of her charm.

Charm was not love, he told himself sternly, and it was not

fair to Molly, who deserved to be loved and cherished and looked after, and he was not in a position to do that. If he had still had his titles and estates, that might have been different, but he had denounced them in favour of a life on the road.

He grinned ruefully in the darkness; he was a gentleman of the road which meant he was no gentleman at all but, in the eyes of the world, a ne'er-do-well, a rakeshame, a criminal. And the worst of it was that Molly trusted him and he did not deserve that trust.

Chapter Five

Duncan was not the only sleepless one. Molly, too, had been lying awake thinking. She was sure that Duncan and Frank, innocent or guilty, were wanted by the law and the constables would not give up while there was any chance the men were still in the area. It would not take long for them to discover where Frank lived, considering they had seen Martha and the curricle and would know she did not live very far away. If they came while the men were gone… The horror of that possibility convinced her she did not want to be left behind when the men went into Norwich.

It was while they ate a breakfast of bread and butter that she broached her idea. 'Captain, I have been thinking…'

'Thinking, my dear? I should not if I were you. Thinking will sap your strength.'

'Do not tease me; I am serious. Could the curricle be repaired? It seems to me that if it were repaired we could all leave here together. The sooner we are on our way the better, don't you think?' She paused, waiting for him to comment. He did not speak immediately but sat looking at her with a smile playing about her lips.

'Well?' she asked. 'If you and Frank ride and lead Jenny, I am sure Martha and I can drive the curricle. We would leave nothing behind for anyone to find.'

He had been thinking the same thing, but he could not resist teasing her. 'All the way to London?'

'If necessary.'

'I think, my dear, you would tire of that in half a day and London is two days away, even with a coach and regular changes of horses.'

'You said we might go by coach. You could obtain one in Norwich, I am sure. And we could pick up my trunk…'

'I do believe that trunk is your first consideration.'

'No, it is not, but as you were so generous as to buy it and as the clothes are meant for my Season it would be foolish to abandon it, would it not?'

'Very true,' he said slowly. He turned to Frank. 'What do you think?'

'I think Miss Martineau might be right. If we leave the curricle where it is, it will not be long before someone comes sniffing round it and asking questions in the neighbourhood. It would be wise to remove it and if it turns out to be re-pairable we might as well put it to use.'

'Why should anyone be interested in you or the curricle, if you have been cleared of any wrongdoing?' Martha demanded.

Duncan and Frank looked at each other, but before either could speak Molly answered her. 'The highwayman's description was so like Mr Upjohn's, others might make the same mistake,' she said quickly, casting a quick glance at Duncan. 'We would be delayed by having to answer questions all over again.'

Martha was not altogether convinced she had the whole story but she allowed herself to be persuaded and while she packed a few of her belongings the men went to inspect the curricle, taking the mare with them to bring it back. They returned in an hour, having discovered that, though the seating and door had been badly damaged, the wheels would still turn. They spent the next hour outside the back of the cottage, banging away with hammer and nails, and by the middle of the day pronounced it could be driven with care.

After eating the remains of the previous evening's supper they set off for Norwich in cheerful spirits. The day was fine, which was just as well, because the open carriage provided no shelter from inclement weather. Nor was it easy to drive after its makeshift repair and Molly soon relinquished the ribbons to Frank and rode Jenny.

She loved being in the saddle and riding beside Duncan along the leafy lanes of Norfolk was a joy. 'It will soon be time for haymaking,' she said, looking around her at the lush meadows where cattle grazed.

'Yes.' His mind was on other things, such as how to find the means to continue their journey, and was in no mood for trivial conversation.

'You are very quiet.'

'I am thinking.'

'What about? Are you afraid those constables will come back?'

'Why should they? Sergeant Upjohn is an innocent man.'

She laughed suddenly. 'And so, I have no doubt, you told them and I am equally sure they believed you. Mrs Upjohn might be easy to gull, but I am not. I wish you would be honest with me.'

'You know as much as you need to know. And I do not need a jobation from you. It is enough that Grandmama…'

'Lady Connaught?' she queried in surprise. 'You have seen her?'

'Yes.'

'Does she know the truth? Oh, my goodness, no wonder you are so blue-devilled. I'll wager she rang a thousand peals over you and made you promise to reform…'

'You know nothing of it, miss, except what your imagination has painted, and you will oblige me by keeping silent on the subject.'

'Oh, so my imagination painted the robbery, did it? There never was a hold-up, there never was a witness to it who described you and that horse you are riding so exactly, or a Sir John Partridge. You were never questioned by a constable. I never had to stand buff for you…'

'Stand buff? My dear girl…'

'I am not your dear girl and I wish you would not say it in that condescending way. My goodness, it is no wonder you were disappointed in love. No one likes a lover who is a cross-patch.'

'Molly, I do believe I shall strangle you if you do not keep quiet.'

'Then you will add murder to your other offences,' she said blithely. 'Did you promise her ladyship that you would turn over a new leaf?'

'Yes. Does that satisfy you?'

'Oh, then it is no wonder you are in the suds if you cannot have any more adventures.'

'This is adventure enough for me,' he said laconically, wondering why she was so unconcerned. Other young ladies would be in a quake or having a megrim at the mere mention of highway robbery. 'And I would have thought more than enough for a well-nurtured young lady.'

She sighed. 'Perhaps it is, for I should hate to see you

confined in prison. That would be even worse than being hanged, I think.'

He laughed at that. She was irrepressible and though he'd said he craved her silence he would be even more depressed if that bright spirit were to be quelled.

Thus they rode into Norwich and headed once again for The Bell, though Duncan, who had been given no opportunity by Molly to think as they rode, had no idea how they would pay for their overnight stay, nor how they would proceed the following day. The curricle was impractical for a long journey and he did not know how long the hasty repairs would last.

Something had to be done, and while Molly and Martha were upstairs in their room attending to their toilette before supper he left Frank to wait in the parlour for them and went into the town where he sold his gold fob and a ruby ring his mother had given him. He regretted parting with the ring but it was the only way out of their predicament. He smiled a little as he walked back. He was a highwayman who stopped short of stealing; Molly might be amused to know that.

He had no sooner returned than Molly entered the dining room and he was struck again by how lovely she was. She was wearing the green jaconet he had bought her and her hair had been brushed until it gleamed like pale gold. She carried herself with all the aplomb of a titled lady—something she had learned from her mother, he supposed. But her glowing cheeks and bright eyes were not those of a Society miss, who might often affect *ennui*, but of a lively, unassuming girl.

She was followed by Martha, dressed in a plain brown round gown trimmed with cream lace, which he assumed was her best dress, used only for high days and holidays. He supposed that if she was to act as Molly's maid she would have to be kitted out too, with at least one more gown and aprons and caps. Was there no end to the expense incurred in bringing a young girl out?

The two men rose to greet the ladies and escort them to their seats at the table.

'Oh, this is so pleasing,' Molly said as a delicious meal of turbot, chicken and ham, not to mention creamy sweets and fruit, was set before them. 'It is not often I have the opportunity to enjoy good conversation and good food in surroundings like these. Mother would never use a common inn, but always stay with friends.'

'Is that so?' He smiled, knowing that it was not the status of the inn which concerned Harriet so much as the expense. Friends did not need paying.

'Are the inns as good as this in London, Captain?'

'Oh, indeed,' he said. 'Perhaps better, but you are unlikely to see the inside of one, once you are safely with your mama in Holles Street.'

'Then tell us about Society. Tell us about the sorts of things we shall be doing. Whom shall we meet? Shall we see the Prince Regent? And the Queen? And will we ride in the park and flirt a little…?'

'Flirt?' he queried, unaccountably appalled at the thought. 'What do you know of flirting?'

'Why, nothing at all. I am hoping you will teach me.' And she looked in astonishment at Frank when he almost choked on his food.

Duncan grinned. 'I'm not much of a hand at that, Miss Martineau.'

'No, in with both feet, that's you,' spluttered Frank, which earned him a rebuke from his wife and a fierce look from Duncan. 'Well, you were a soldier and unmarried to boot,' he added to justify his remark.

'But I collect you once thought of marriage,' Molly said. 'Did you not flirt then?'

'Did no one teach you it is not polite to ask personal questions?' he retorted. 'Let us talk of something else.'

'Very well. I forgot you found speaking of her painful. What shall we talk of? The battles you have fought?'

'I never met anyone so blood-thirsty. We will not talk of the war. Tell us about yourself.'

'But I am so very uninteresting. Why, I have had more adventures in the last few days than I have had in the whole of my life. Tell me, how shall we go on tomorrow?'

Before Duncan could open his mouth to answer, there was a flurry at the door and an irate man in a cloth coat and nankeen breeches pushed his way past the waiter. He was followed by a constable. 'That's the man,' he said, pointing a pudgy finger at Duncan. 'I insist you arrest him.'

Martha gasped and Molly turned to Duncan, a question on her lips. He shook his head and she sank back into her chair, her heart pounding.

'What am I accused of?' he drawled, addressing the man who was now standing over him in a belligerent manner. 'Is my cravat not tied to your taste?'

'That's my curricle outside—the one with the yellow wheels—and it is my mare in the stables.'

'No one is denying it,' Duncan said calmly. 'You hired both out to me the other day.'

'One day's hire, that's all you paid for.'

'My business took longer than I expected, but I have done with it now.' Duncan reached in his pocket and drew out his purse. 'Another's day's hire should see us right, don't you think? There is no need for constables and threats.'

'What about the damage? It looks as though it was run off the road.'

'That is because it was. You are lucky I am not asking you for damages to life and limb for supplying a deficient vehicle.'

'Oh, please do not argue about it,' Molly said, worrying about the presence of the constable and glad he was not the one who had questioned them in Aylsham. 'Do give him enough to cover his losses, Captain; it is only fair. It was not his fault the coach driver ran us down.'

Once again she had jumped in to back his story, and with admirable swiftness. 'Very well.' He took out several guineas and handed them to the man. 'That should suffice.'

With no more than a grunt by way of a receipt, the man took them and turned on his heel, followed by the constable.

Everyone breathed a sigh of relief but Duncan was only too well aware that his funds had been seriously depleted. Now how were they to reach London? He did not have enough for the stagecoach fare, let alone the purchase of a coach and horses.

Molly, who had turned to look out of the window as the owner of the curricle departed with it, suddenly exclaimed in delight. 'Oh, just look at that! Did you ever see the like?'

The others turned to see a magnificent carriage pulling into the yard. It was a dark blue colour, its lines picked out in gold. It had a monogrammed door and brocade curtains at the windows and its metalwork gleamed with polish. It was drawn by four matched bays whose coats gleamed almost as much as their harness.

It drew up with a clatter and a flourish and down from its box jumped someone who could only be described as a tulip of the first water. He wore a long coat reaching almost to his heels. It sported three capes and two rows of pockets and enormous brass buttons. The coat flew open as he jumped down and revealed primrose-coloured breeches tucked into highly polished top boots and a black and yellow striped waistcoat. He wore a tall crowned beaver hat with a curly brim and a posy of flowers tucked into its huge buckle.

Another young man emerged from the coach, less flamboyantly attired, and followed the first into the inn. A third man, in livery, trailed behind them carrying a leather portmanteau.

'Andrew Bellamy,' murmured Duncan with a smile.

'You know him?' Molly queried.

'Only by sight and reputation,' he said. 'He is Lord Brancaster's heir and even more of a scapegrace than I am.'

'Will he recognise you?'

'I doubt it. We have not met in years.'

'Perhaps it is just as well,' she said. 'You would rather remain incognito; is that not so?'

Once more she had demonstrated her perspicacity but before he could agree the new arrivals entered the room and the landlord hurried to be of service. He conducted them to a table while everyone in the room stopped eating to watch their progress, passing close to where the four were sitting. Molly was delighted and smiled unashamedly at the young fop.

He bowed before her with a great flourish. 'Ma'am, your servant.'

Duncan was seething. Molly should not have smiled at him like that; it was almost an open invitation and one which Bellamy had not been slow in noticing. 'You do not need to be taught the art of flirtation,' he whispered fiercely at her. 'You are doing very well without instruction.'

She turned from gazing after the two newcomers and faced him. 'Whatever do you mean? He was perfectly civil.'

'He should not have spoken to you at all. But it is your fault for smiling at him.'

'May a lady not smile at a gentleman? And may a gentleman not acknowledge it?'

'Not in that way, not unless they know each other very well.'

'As you and I know each other, you mean? I may smile at you?'

'As often as you like. I shall not read more into it than you intend.'

'I intended nothing.'

'I know that, but he does not. He would infer that you wanted to further your acquaintance and without a proper introduction…'

'Oh, I see. You are cross with me again.'

'No, of course I am not cross, but it is not a good idea to draw attention to ourselves now if we are to arrive in London in the manner we planned…'

'And how are we to do that? Are you going to hire another coach or shall you buy one?'

'I have not made up my mind,' he said, wondering how either could be achieved. 'Now, I suggest you and Mrs Upjohn retire. We have a long day ahead of us tomorrow.'

The ladies rose dutifully, said goodnight and left the room, leaving Duncan and Frank facing each other.

'It would seem that providence is on our side, after all,' Duncan murmured, with a smile. 'I know Bellamy for a gambler and his father does not stint him. His pockets are deep. We can play our way out of our predicament.'

'We can't do that without a stake,' Frank said.

'I have a little left. Enough for a start.' He smiled suddenly. 'Don't look so Friday-faced; I can beat him easily, but you do not have to stay with me. I absolve you from any obligation.'

'You think I would turn my back on you just because you have lost your head to a petticoat...'

Duncan found himself grinning. 'It is not the petticoat, Sergeant, but what's inside it.'

'Then my advice is to watch out, for I am ready to wager she will turn the tables on you.'

'It is not a wager I shall take on, Sergeant, for I was only bamming. She is little more than a child and my grandmother's goddaughter. I could no more take advantage of her than I could a new-born babe.'

'Then I think you would do well to open your eyes, Captain. I saw no child.'

Duncan was watching Andrew Bellamy and his friend and did not answer. The two young men had finished their meal and were moving into a back room which Duncan knew was set aside for gambling should the clientele require it. He stood up and chinked his purse in his coat pocket. 'Come along, Sergeant, into the fray.'

The owner of the petticoat was sitting in it in front of a mirror, surveying herself with a critical eye, while Martha brushed her hair.

'I wish I looked older,' she murmured. 'No one takes me seriously.'

'I am quite sure Captain Stacey does.'

'Oh, he does not. He is continually roasting me.'

'Only because you provoke him. I wonder he has not sent you home long before now.'

'So do I, but then I can help him and he knows it.'

'How can you help him? You are not still thinking of that

robbery they took Frank for, are you? Surely that is all behind us?'

'Of course it is. At least, I hope it is. But people are continually mistaking Captain Stacey for the Dark Knight…'

'Dark Knight?'

'He is a highwayman, a very romantical figure, I have heard, who robs the rich to give to the poor.'

'And you think Captain Stacey is like him?'

'I think he must bear some resemblance to him,' Molly said, realising she was treading on dangerous ground.

'And does this man have a companion who resembles my husband?'

'I think he must have.'

'And is this Dark Knight a wealthy man?'

'No, I do not think he can be, or he would not need to take from the rich to give to the poor, would he? He could use his own money if he had any.'

'And the poor? What manner of people are they? Could they be soldiers and widows of soldiers?'

Molly swivelled round in her seat to face Martha, her expression one of dismay. Martha had tricked her into revealing more than she ought to have done about the two men and now poor Mr Upjohn would be in trouble with his wife. 'I do not know. I am only repeating hearsay, you understand. I am such a romantic I listen to every whimsical tale that is going around. Take no notice of me.'

'And do you think Captain Stacey is an honourable man?'

'Oh, I am sure he is, in spite of being the black sheep of the family. I think he exaggerates about that. Why, he is looking after me, when perhaps he would rather not, and he rescued Mr Upjohn…'

'But Frank has done nothing wrong.'

'Of course not.' She stood up and untied the strings of her petticoat and kicked it off when it fell to her feet. 'Now, I think we should go to bed. It is late and no doubt the Captain will want to leave early in the morning.'

'How? We have no conveyance. The curricle…'

'Oh, he will contrive, you may be sure.' She was not very good at dissembling and she did not want to be quizzed any more. Besides, she was very sleepy. 'Goodnight, Mrs Upjohn.'

Martha sighed, bade her goodnight and left to go to her own bed in the next room.

Molly found a new nightgown in her trunk, put it on and settled down in her bed, but sleep was slow in coming. The more she talked of Duncan, the more she became convinced that he was the Dark Knight. It was both exciting and terrifying. What would happen next? she wondered. How would their journey continue? Was he even now planning another hold-up?

But underlying that was a frisson of fear. She did not want anything dreadful to happen to the Captain as a result and there were many such possibilities. He could be wounded or killed if anyone was so brave as to take a pot shot at him; he could be captured, tried and hanged in spite of her willingness to perjure herself for him. It was enough to give her nightmares.

Holding up coaches was the last thing on Duncan's mind at that moment. He was playing a cat and mouse game with Andrew Bellamy and though his heart was beating very fast and his hands felt clammy he gave no outward sign of it. Not by the tiniest flicker of his eyelids, not by the lightest twitch of his lips, nor the minutest raising of an eyebrow did he betray the fact that he had a winning hand.

It was not the first he had had. Lady Luck had been with him and there was a pile of gold coins at his elbow and several scraps of paper on which Andrew had scribbled his signature against substantial sums. But the pile of coins was not enough to pay for four people to travel to London and the vowels could not be used as currency.

'I'm dished up,' Andrew said, in disgust. 'How anyone can have such luck as you have had, Stacey, I do not know.'

'It can't last,' Frank growled, pretending not to look at Duncan but receiving the secret message contained in the way he moved his hands when sorting his cards.

'No, for I am sure it is about to turn in my favour.'

'Then make your bid,' Duncan said.

Bellamy sighed. 'It will have to be another vowel.'

'No, no more of those.'

'But I have the winning hand.'

'If you are so sure, then back it with something worthwhile. What have you got?'

'You have everything. My ring, my fob, my purse. What more is there, but my watch and the clothes on my back?'

'Oh, I do not think they would fit me,' Duncan said drily. 'And I already have a good watch. But you do have a coach and horses.'

'You can't have those! They are my father's.'

'But you have said you have the winning hand. If you are so sure, you will not hesitate to put them up.' He smiled for the first time since they sat down to play. 'But perhaps you are bluffing.'

'No.'

'Then the coach and horses against all these.' And he picked up the slips of paper and slapped them down again. 'There's two thousand there.'

'As much as that?' Andrew went very white and his hands were shaking. 'Very well. The coach and horses against my vowels.'

Ten minutes later Duncan was the owner of one of the best equipages in the country and the now impoverished Andrew Bellamy was wondering how he was to pay for his night's stay and return to Newmarket from where he had driven that morning. He was inclined to bluster but his companion counselled him to accept defeat gracefully and the loan of five guineas which would see them safely back.

'I should not like to be in that one's shoes when he faces his father,' Duncan said as they watched the now deflated tulip toil wearily upstairs to his room, followed by his sycophant.

'But he will stand buff for him?'

'Naturally he will.' He laughed. 'He might bluster and threaten but Andrew is his only son and his lordship was a deep player in his young days. He once lost a thousand pounds betting on the colour of the Queen's gown at a soirée. He said it would be rose and it was green. I know because it was my father who won it from him.'

'What are we going to tell the ladies about the coach? I do not think Martha would approve.'

'We shall say Mr Bellamy was kind enough to lend it to us.' He paused. 'And, speaking of the ladies, I think we should be up betimes and on our way by dawn, so give orders for the coach to be made ready and brought round to the front of the house at first light.'

'Very well.'

Frank went to carry out his orders and Duncan went up to the room he had taken opposite Molly's. Ten minutes later, he was deeply asleep.

* * *

Martha, roused by her husband, went to wake Molly long before it was light. The young lady was disinclined to stir and simply pulled the covers over her head and grumbled that it was not fair to disturb her in the middle of the night.

Martha shook her. 'The Captain says we must leave in half an hour, unless you want to be left behind.'

Molly was up like a shot and scrambling for her clothes. 'How are we to travel? What shall I wear? Did he say?'

'Frank told me they have procured the loan of a coach and four. We are to go on in style.'

'Oh, wonderful! Then I shall wear my new carriage dress and the bonnet with the green feather and the kid half boots. Pour my washing water while I find them, please. Oh, I am so excited. How soon shall we be in London?'

She prattled on the whole time she was dressing and while Martha brushed her hair. 'Is the Captain waiting to go or are we to have breakfast first? I must have something to eat and drink for I cannot go the whole day without food. He is surely not in such great haste? Unless, of course—oh, dear, I do hope not.'

'What?'

'That those Cromer constables have not tracked us down.'

'Why should they? I really cannot imagine why you are so afraid of them.'

'I am not afraid of them. I was simply saying that it would be a great inconvenience to be detained by them again.'

'Frank said nothing of them, only that the Captain was in some haste to be in London.'

'Only so he may be rid of me,' Molly said morosely. 'I know he is looking forward to handing me over to Mama, so he may be free. I am an encumbrance.'

'Fustian! I am sure he thinks nothing of the sort. Why, I should not be surprised if he were to offer for you when he sees your mama.'

'Captain Stacey? Offer for me?' Her laughter pealed out as she stood before the mirror and set the straw bonnet on her curls and tied the ribbons beneath her chin. 'Oh, Mrs Upjohn, how can you say that? He is older than me; he did not deny it when I said it. He said he was thirty and, besides, he thinks of me as a schoolgirl; he has said that too.'

'Then more fool he.'

'Oh, you must not call him a fool, Mrs Upjohn, really you must not. He is knowledgeable and clever and brave...'

'That is no guarantee that he is not capable of foolishness, for I believe the contrary is often the case. Now, are you ready? I am sure I heard horses and coachwheels outside.'

They hurried downstairs where they were allowed by an impatient Duncan to drink a cup of hot chocolate and eat some bread and butter before he escorted them outside. Molly stopped when she saw the resplendent vehicle. Jenny and Good Boy were already tied on behind it.

'But this is the coach that came in while we were having supper last night,' she said. 'Surely it belongs to the young gentleman in the big coat and the yellow striped waistcoat? Did you not say his name was Bellamy?'

'Yes,' Duncan said, putting his hand under her elbow and guiding her firmly forward. 'He has been kind enough to lend it to us.'

'Oh, you mean we are to go on together. How agreeable...'

'No, he is going in another direction entirely. We are to have it to ourselves. Now please get in.'

'But I must find him and thank him.'

'There is no need for that. He is still abed.' He opened the door, let down the step and handed her in, allowing her no time to argue. Once she was safely in her seat, Martha joined her, Frank climbed onto the box, Duncan mounted Caesar and thus the little cavalcade left Norwich.

The coach was the height of luxury. It was beautifully sprung and had seats for four upholstered in red velvet, and there was plenty of headroom so that the feather in Molly's bonnet barely touched the roof. And with Martha the only other occupant they could both stretch out their legs in comfort.

They bowled along, drawn by the bays at a spanking pace, hardly aware of the uneven road. But one thing they could not do and that was change the horses. The bays were no ordinary post chaise horses and they had to be kept with the coach. Good Boy and Jenny were not draught horses and, besides, the stallion was very much bigger than the little mare and they would have looked odd between the shafts, so after a few miles Duncan slowed their pace to little more than a walk.

At midday they stopped at an inn at Scole for two whole hours, in which both humans and animals were fed, watered and rested. Molly whiled away the time watching the people coming and going, for Scole was a very important cross-roads and the roads in all four directions were very busy with traffic.

As well as public coaches loaded with passengers, who required meals or rooms or both, or to have their baggage moved from one coach to another, there were carts and riders and private carriages pulling in to change horses and the people were as varied as the vehicles.

Molly had something to say about each and her comments were pithy without being malicious, and Duncan, more relaxed than he had been since setting out on the journey, listened to her musical voice and watched her animated face and realised that he could happily do so for the rest of his life. The thought, as it flitted across his mind, shocked him to the core.

From shock he moved to irritation with himself for being such a numbskull. It was unthinkable. Falling in love had not been on his mind when he'd gone to Stacey Manor, only a few days previously. It had certainly been no part of his plan when his grandmother had talked to him about settling down. And even when he had agreed to take Molly to her mother it had simply been a mischievous notion to shock Harriet into being a proper parent to her daughter.

Molly was a handicap, preventing him from doing what he wanted to do. Her trust in him was an embarrassment. Her talk of adventure was simply a wish to escape her humdrum life; she did not understand the life he led and would be horrified if asked to share it. And he could not change. It was not in his power to do so. He had no money, no home, no roots; they had all been swept away by an unkind fate.

'Why are you so silent?' she asked him. Martha had persuaded Frank to go for a walk into the village and they were alone, if one could be alone in a roomful of people. 'You have been sitting there moodily staring out of the window for half an hour. What is out there that has thrown you into the dismals? I can see only another coach and the ostlers leading out fresh horses for it. And they are nothing like so fine as ours.'

He shook himself. 'I am not in the dismals, my dear. How could I be anything but happy in such enchanting company?'

'Now I think you are bamming me again.'

'Not at all. You must learn to accept compliments graciously, Molly. It is part of genteel society.'

'Oh, then I thank you and return the compliment. I am

happy to have such an agreeable escort.' She laughed lightly and added, 'Even if he is a little reluctant.'

'Reluctant? I would not say that.'

'Oh, I know you find me a burden. I am quite sure you would rather be the Dark Knight than Captain Duncan Stacey.'

'Really, Molly, you must not say such things. People will begin to believe you and you will have me arrested.'

'I am not such a goosecap as to tell anyone. I have not said a word except when Mrs Upjohn questioned me about how Mr Upjohn came to be arrested, then I told her you must look very much like the Dark Knight for everyone to keep mistaking you for him.'

'And what did she say to that?'

'Nothing except that the Dark Knight must have a companion who looks very like her husband. I do think it was wrong of you to encourage him to deceive her.'

'You don't know what you are talking about, miss, and I wish you would not refine upon it. Mrs Upjohn cannot possibly understand your vivid imagination and your longing for adventure.'

'Oh, she does, and she told me about being at war and how terrible it was. She does not wish for any more adventures, so perhaps it is just as well you promised Lady Connaught you would turn over a new leaf.'

'Did I?' he murmured, but he had ceased to listen to her for he had overheard a new arrival give his name to the landlord. It was Mr Grunston.

The man was fat, loud and overbearing and demanding that his horses be changed at once and food set on the table so that he could be on his way. 'I have important business with the Admiralty,' he said, loud enough for all to hear. 'I must insist on being given precedence.'

'What an unpleasant man,' Molly whispered to Duncan. 'I think we have heard his name before.'

'Have we?'

'Yes, do you not recollect those four men talking about him? Where was it? At Aylsham or Norwich—I forget which. They were saying he was a slaver and I said…'

'I perfectly recollect what you said. Fribble, all of it.' He looked up as Frank and Martha came into the room. 'Ah, here they are. I think we have rested the horses long enough. Come, Miss Martineau, back to the coach.'

It was while they were proceeding at a gentle canter towards Bury St Edmunds that Mr Grunston's coach came up behind them. The coachman was evidently in a hurry for he gave a blast on his horn to warn Duncan to give way before coming up alongside.

'Shall we give him a run for his money?' Frank asked as Duncan rode up on his nearside.

'No, my friend. Your wife would skin me alive, and as for Miss Martineau, she would likely be so excited she would be all over the place. Better let him go.'

Reluctantly Frank pulled the carriage up in a gateway and the slaver's barouche rushed past in a whirl of dust.

It was after it had passed that Duncan told Frank what he had heard about the man. 'It makes my blood boil,' he said. 'When our soldiers and sailors are without work and forced to beg, that fat pig lives in luxury. And, what is worse, it is condoned by the Admiralty. They provide him with ships.'

'He needs to be taught a lesson.'

Duncan smiled. 'Yes, but not by us.'

They stopped at The Angel in Bury St Edmunds for the night, only to find Mr Grunston there before them. He had eaten well and imbibed freely of claret and brandy, and was, in Frank's words, top-heavy, so much so that he was loudly calling for his coach to be brought round so that he might drive through the night.

'I do not like that man,' Molly said, after Duncan had procured rooms for them all and they were sitting down to supper. 'That is the third time he has crossed our path.'

'Possibly because, like us, he is going to London,' Duncan said.

'I hope we do not meet him again or I shall be constrained to tell him what I think of men who buy and sell human beings. Do you think that black man he had dancing attendance on him was a slave?'

'Undoubtedly.'

'I wish we could free him. Could we not buy him and set him free?'

'I doubt his master would part with him, and freeing one man would not solve the problem, would it?' Duncan said. 'What would the man do with his freedom? How would he live in a strange country where there are already thousands of men without work?'

'Your sensitivity does you credit, Miss Martineau,' Martha said as tureens of food were brought to their table. 'But the Captain has the right of it. Freeing one man is not the answer.'

'It is a job for the Dark Knight,' she said, then added meaningfully, 'Whoever he is.'

'Whoever he is,' Duncan repeated with a smile. 'Come, let us enjoy this meal and retire early. I am exhausted.'

They finished their meal without mentioning Mr Grunston again and afterwards the ladies went up to their rooms.

As soon as they had disappeared, Frank turned to Duncan. 'What do you say to one more jaunt? It seems to me that providence has taken a hand in this or why else would we have run into the man again and him so anxious to gallop through the night?'

'No, Frank. What we did, we did for a reason. That does not mean we are above the law, nor that I will allow you to fall back into your old ways.'

'But he is a sitting duck. There was only an old coachman and a black footman with him and I doubt he would lift a finger to defend his master. The ladies need never know, though I doubt Miss Martineau would turn a hair if we invited her to come with us.'

'Heaven forfend!' Duncan laughed.

'One more time, then you may go to London and act the gallant with the best of them.'

'No, my friend. We are already being pursued by the constabulary, and the last thing I want is for us to be apprehended for a whim of yours.' He stood up, yawning. 'I am off to my bed. I will see you at breakfast.'

'Yes. Goodnight, Captain.'

Duncan retired to his room, leaving Frank to follow more slowly. He was busy thinking about ways to replenish his funds and forgot all about Mr Grunston.

Chapter Six

At breakfast the next morning, both men appeared in very good spirits. Frank was smiling secretly to himself and Duncan seemed to have found a new lease of life; his tiredness had left him and he was bright-eyed and cheerful.

'You are in high gig this morning, Captain,' Molly said. 'You must have slept well.'

'Tolerably, my dear, tolerably.'

'That is more than Frank did,' Martha put in. 'He did not come to bed until cockcrow.'

'I told you,' Frank said, refusing to look at Duncan. 'Good Boy had the colic. I sat up with him.'

'Oh, does that mean we cannot go on?' Molly asked.

'No, he has recovered.'

The waiter came and refilled their coffee pot. He was obviously bursting with news. 'The Dark Knight has been at work again,' he said. 'The Newmarket mail has just come in and the passengers are full of it.'

'Oh, do tell us what happened,' Molly said, leaning forward eagerly.

'A private coach was held up between here and Newmarket last night.'

'Oh, dear. Was Mr Gr—?' She gave a little cough to cover her slip. 'Was anyone hurt?'

'No, though I fancy the gentleman's pride was injured. By all accounts, he was stripped of his fine clothes and arrived in Newmarket wearing his footman's livery. You may remember the gentleman, ma'am, he had a black man for a servant.'

'Oh, you must mean Mr Grunston. But surely the servant was much smaller than his master?'

'So he was. I believe Mr Grunston's arrival in Newmarket was a comical sight; his breeches hardly covered his knees and would not meet about his waist and his coat was so tight, he could not move his arms. The passengers on the mail were still laughing when they arrived here.'

'Oh, it is unkind to laugh at another's misfortunes,' Molly said, though she was laughing herself. 'And what was the black man wearing?'

'He has disappeared in his master's togs. Mr Grunston has offered a reward for the apprehension of the high toby and the return of his servant. But they will need better luck than they have had so far. The Dark Knight is as elusive as a ghost, here one minute, somewhere else the next.'

'Every Tom and Dick of a highpad scamp is labelled the Dark Knight,' Duncan said dismissively. 'It is nothing but rumour. 'Tis my belief there is no such person.'

In the face of Duncan's scepticism, the waiter left them to attend to new customers and Molly sat back in her seat and surveyed Duncan with eyes shining with laughter.

Martha looked from one to the other. 'I beg you share the jest with me.'

'Oh, it is only the thought of Mr Grunston bursting out of his slave's clothes,' Molly said.

'But being robbed is not a laughing matter, Miss Martineau. I am beginning to regret my decision to make this journey for ten to one we shall be the next victims, what with travelling in Lord Brancaster's coach and having so many fine horses with us. We shall be mistaken for Quality.'

'Oh, I do not think there is any fear of that,' Molly said. If Martha refused to go on, then the Captain would not take her to London and her whole adventure would come to an end. 'Why, we have the Captain and Mr Upjohn to defend us. No highwayman would dare to stop us.'

Duncan, watching Molly's performance with a mixture of admiration and fury, was startled when he found himself the recipient of a conspiratorial wink. It was the outside of enough!

Discomfited and irritable, he paid the innkeeper and hustled them all out to the coach which he had ordered up to the door. Frank was busy checking the equipage and refused to meet his eye. He strode over to him. 'Why, Frank, why?'

'I wanted to see the devil squirm,' the sergeant said, knowing perfectly well what he meant. 'I didn't take his valuables, only made him change clothes with the black man. It was Miss Martineau talking about the Dark Knight…'

'You were surely not influenced by Molly's madcap ideas?'

'Well, she had the right of it. It *was* a job for the Dark Knight.'

'Damn the Dark Knight!' he said fervently. He had laughingly invented the name when Sir John Partridge had demanded his identity; the night was dark and he had said the first thing that came into his mind. He had never expected the pseudonym to become so popular. Nor that Molly would find it so appealing. Somehow or other he must stop her mentioning it again. He left Frank and went over to where she was about to step into the coach.

'Ride Jenny, Miss Martineau,' he commanded. 'I wish to talk to you.'

The tone of his voice was ominous but she refused to be cowed and obediently allowed him to help her into the saddle. Hoping she might be given the opportunity to ride some of the way, she had dressed in her riding habit. Martha, disliking travelling inside alone, climbed on the box beside her husband and they set off again with Good Boy tied on behind.

'I am surprised we are taking this road,' Molly said as they turned towards Newmarket, slightly ahead of the coach. 'Surely it was down here that Mr Grunston was held up? Are you not afraid the same thing might happen to us?' Her laughing eyes were full of mischief.

His responsibility for her was weighing heavily on his mind. She deserved his total commitment, or as much of it as he could give her, considering neither Mr Grunston nor Sir John Partridge would take their losses with equanimity. If the latter ever discovered his identity he would send someone after them to retrieve his belongings and that might put everyone in peril.

The worst of it was he could not tell Molly the truth and she, as usual, was jumping to conclusions. To her it was all a great frolic and not dangerous at all. He could not disillusion her without frightening her. She was looking at him now, her lovely head on one side, waiting for a reply.

'Frank and I are a match for any high tobies.'

'I am sure you are,' she said, giving him an ingenuous smile. 'But I would have expected you to take a more direct route.'

'I never undertook to go the shortest way.'

'No, I concede you did not,' she said. 'But the sooner we arrive in London, the sooner you may be rid of me, and that is what you want, is it not?' There was a tiny note of wistfulness in her voice.

'Did I say I wanted to be rid of you?'

'No, but your whole demeanour proclaims it. I do believe you find me a hindrance to your calling, which is very disappointing, for I should love to be a highwayman. A female high toby would take the country by storm, would she not?'

'Certainly she would,' he admitted drily.

'What is the feminine equivalent, by the way?'

'I have no idea; I should not think there is one.'

'Highwaywoman is much too long, don't you think? Why, she would be a dozen miles away before the victims were able to utter the word.'

'I should think they would die of shock before that.'

She laughed, thoroughly enjoying teasing him. 'I would not want to be the cause of anyone's death. There is nothing for it but I would have to dress as a boy. Do you think I would make a good boy, Captain?'

'No, I do not,' he snapped.

'You are in a very disagreeable mood,' she said. 'And I had thought you would be in the best of spirits after last night. Indeed, when we met for breakfast, you were positively smiling, which is something you do not do very often.'

'If I am in a disagreeable mood, it is because you will persist in talking nonsense. It is enough to give me an earache.'

'Then I will be silent.' She spoke huffily and he was immediately sorry. He reached across and put his hand on hers.

'I beg your pardon, Molly. I am a crosspatch, I admit it,

but the truth is I am not used to being responsible for someone like you.'

'It is a heavy burden, I know.' She was aware of the pressure of his hand on hers but chose to ignore the sudden fluttering of her heart and the tingling feeling in the pit of her stomach; she was not experienced enough to connect one with the other. 'It is no wonder Mama was disinclined to take me to London and Aunt Margaret used to despair of me.'

'I am sure she did not. She spoke of you very affectionately.'

'Did she?' Molly brightened. 'But she often said the sooner I found a husband to knock some sense into me the better.'

'He would have a very hard time of it, I am persuaded.'

'Oh, no, for I am willing to learn. But I should not like him to beat me.'

She spoke so seriously, he burst into laughter. 'Oh, Molly, my sweet, he would be an unutterable cur to raise a finger to you.'

'Not even if he were provoked?'

'Not even then.' He turned to look at her and his heartbeat quickened. He would almost be sorry when they reached London and he had to part with her. A life on the road was beginning to be a far less attractive prospect than it had been two or three days before. 'But that does not mean I will allow myself to be provoked and do nothing. There is more than one way to skin a cat.'

'What a dreadful maxim. I beg you find a less distasteful image. I am very fond of cats.'

By this time he had completely forgotten what it was he wanted to scold her about, or, if he remembered, set it to one side. It was much more agreeable to listen to her chatter, even though he pretended he did not like it. He was almost sorry when they drew up at the Greyhound in Newmarket in the late afternoon.

Once they had procured rooms for the night, they were able to take a stroll round the town. Duncan had been there before and he was able to point out the important buildings and tell them about the stables and racehorses, some of whom they saw cantering on the heath in training for races the following day.

'Oh, do you think we might go to the races?' Molly asked as they walked together a little ahead of Frank and Martha. 'I should so like to see the horses running. Do they have lady riders?'

'Good heavens, no!' Duncan exclaimed.

'I do not see why not,' she said. 'Ladies are lighter than men and if they ride well that would surely give them an advantage.'

He grinned at her. 'Now I suppose you are daydreaming about being a lady jockey?'

She laughed. 'I'll wager I could ride as well as any of them.'

'And that is one wager I will certainly not accept.'

'What a pity,' she said, without rancour. 'But you will take me to watch?'

'Perhaps. If you promise to behave.'

'Oh, I will. I will be the epitome of decorum, the very stiffest, most upright lady you can imagine.'

'I shall look forward to seeing that,' he said with a smile which told her he did not expect it to happen. 'Now I think it is time to return to the inn for supper.'

Molly was delighted with the races. She loved the colourful crowds, the magnificent horses, the diminutive riders and all the tipsters and racegoers making bets, sometimes for thousands of pounds. Duncan gave her a few coins from those he had won at cards the previous evening. There was always a great deal of gambling in Newmarket and not all of it on the race course; it had been easy to find a game, which was his intention when deciding to come.

'I'm going to put it on that one,' she said, pointing to a chestnut filly.

'You will lose,' he said. 'She might as well have three legs for all the winning she will do.'

'Fustian! She is a lovely animal; she has such beautiful eyes.'

He laughed, thinking of Molly's expressive eyes. 'A horse does not run with its eyes. Look at its legs, its haunches, the depth of its chest.'

'Oh, that goes without saying,' she said. 'But the eyes show the spirit. She wants to win; you can see it there.'

'And like all females she gets what she wants—is that what you mean?'

'Yes. Please put a guinea on her for me.'

He smiled and took the coin from her outstretched hand and strolled over to lay the bet, adding several guineas of his own. He had no idea why he went against his own advice; the filly had no form and he should not gamble foolishly when his funds were so low, but if Molly fancied her, who was he to argue? Besides, she was called Brancaster's Bright Belle and that seemed a good omen.

They crowded as closely as they could to the edge of the course as the horses thundered past. Molly forgot her promise to act with decorum and jumped up and down in excitement, shouting the filly's name as it took the lead. To everyone's surprise, Bright Belle won her first heat and then her second. Everything depended on the last run. Molly hardly dared breathe as the horses lined up and took off.

This was a much harder race, for the runners had all won previous heats, and though Bright Belle kept with them for half the distance she began to flag. At the end of the second furlong, she was lying third and falling behind; it looked as though she had given her all. 'Come on, Belle,' Molly shouted. 'Show them what you're made of. You can do it.'

It seemed as though the filly heard her, or perhaps her jockey did and he wanted to please the vivacious young lady he had seen out of the corner of his eye. Whatever it was, Bright Belle put in an extra effort and passed the horse in front to run neck and neck with the leader. Molly was becoming hoarse with shouting and even Martha was caught up in the excitement and clasped her hands in front of her, muttering, 'Come on, Bright Belle,' as they approached the finishing line.

The crowds were going wild, urging one or the other horse on, and as they passed the finish with Bright Belle winning by no more than a nose there was a concerted sigh and then Molly grabbed Duncan by both hands and danced him round and round until both were dizzy. 'We won! We won!'

He tried to slow her by releasing his hands and putting them on her shoulders. Giddy, she stumbled and fell against him. He held her fast, feeling her heart beating rapidly against his chest, and smelling the fresh scent of her hair just below his chin. He wanted to go on holding her, to tip her head up and kiss her lips, to go on kissing her, to make love to her.

But it was only a momentary weakness. He allowed his lips to brush her hair before pulling himself together and holding her at arm's length. 'Steady, my dear; it is not a fortune you have won, you know.'

'Oh, but I do not care about that. It is the pleasure of seeing her win, when you said she had no hope…'

Reluctantly he released her. 'Oh, so it is your victory over me you are crowing about.'

'Yes. No, I did not mean that. It is the victory of the underdog which pleases me. You should understand that.'

'Should I?' he queried.

'Yes. I am persuaded you like nothing better than to fight for those who cannot fight for themselves.'

'Gammon! What evidence have you of that?'

'None but my eyes and ears…'

'Captain, I think you should collect your winnings.' Frank interrupted them. 'I fancy the fellow is about to depart.'

This was indeed true. The man who had taken a large number of bets besides Duncan's, and had obviously lost a great deal of money, was not going to pay up if he could avoid it. He was scurrying away through the crowds. Duncan and Frank went after him.

They were soon lost in the crowds who were milling about waiting for the next race to start. Molly, left with nothing to do, watched the people around her, some excited at winning, some disconsolate. She looked on in fascination as one finely dressed gentleman's pockets were picked and the thief made off with a watch, a fob and a purse. The man did not even notice his loss.

She walked over and tapped him on the shoulder. 'Sir, I believe you have just been relieved of the contents of your pockets.'

He swivelled round to face her. She gasped when she realised it was Mr Bellamy, but he did not notice as he patted his pockets and realised they were empty.

'I saw the man do it. He went that way.' She pointed. 'You will know him; he has a ginger beard and a long black cloak. Very thin fingers, which is why, I suppose…'

He did not wait for her to finish but dashed off in the direction she had pointed. 'Oh, dear,' she said. 'I wanted to thank him for lending us his coach.'

'He did not remember you,' Martha said. 'You should not have spoken to him.'

'Not told him I had seen his pockets rifled? Oh, that would have been very uncivil of me.'

They became aware of a scuffle breaking out a little way off and saw him tackling the thief, who was putting up a spirited resistance. It seemed that Mr Bellamy was having the worst of it, when Duncan and Frank, returning with their winnings, intervened. They held the struggling thief while Andrew went through his extraordinarily large pockets and retrieved several watches and purses.

'These are mine.' Andrew held up his belongings, while other victims hurried forward to reclaim their stolen property. 'I am in your debt, Stacey.' He smiled at Molly who was making her way towards them. 'And to the young lady.'

'Molly?' Duncan queried, looking at her. She was smiling back at Bellamy as if they were the best of friends and he felt a sudden stab of jealousy. Bellamy had everything in his favour: youth, looks, and the prospect of inheriting Brancaster's title and wealth. There was no cloud of rejection and dishonour hanging over him. He was what Society called one of the eligibles.

'I saw it happen,' she said, coming up to them and allowing Andrew to take her hand and put it to his lips. 'The thief was very deft, for he had the things out of Mr Bellamy's pockets in a trice.'

'You have the advantage of me, ma'am,' he said. 'You know my name but I am in ignorance of yours. Indeed, I do not think we can have met, for I would surely have rememberèd so delightful an encounter.' He bowed towards her, smiling in a way that infuriated Duncan.

'That is because you have not met,' he said coldly. 'Miss Martineau does not go out in the society you frequent.'

'But she has done so today and for that I give thanks.' He paused. 'Miss Martineau, you say?'

Duncan had no alterative but to present him. 'Miss Martineau,' he said, turning to her, determined to be formal, 'may I present Mr Andrew Bellamy?' To Andrew he said, 'Miss Margaret Martineau.'

He bowed with a flourish. 'Your servant, Miss Martineau, and a very grateful one, for I should have been penniless again if you had not seen the knuckle at his business.'

'Penniless again?' she echoed.

'Why, yes. Did my friend, Stacey, not tell you?'

'No. I am indeed sorry to hear it has happened before.'

'The circumstances were different,' Duncan put in quickly. 'It is getting late, Miss Martineau; I think we should be going. The racing is over for the day and I am sure you must be hungry.'

'Then please join me for supper,' Andrew said. 'It is the least I can do to show my gratitude.'

'I do not think so,' Duncan said coldly. 'Miss Martineau is fatigued.'

'Indeed I am not,' she contradicted him. 'Is there any reason why we should not accept Mr Bellamy's invitation? Besides, I wish to thank him for being so kind as to lend us his coach and horses.'

'Lend them?' Andrew queried, turning towards Duncan with a slightly puzzled frown. And then he gave a laugh that was mischievous if not downright malicious. 'Oh, yes, of course,' he said, speaking to Molly. 'It was my pleasure, ma'am. I hope you found it comfortable.'

'Indeed, yes. But it must have inconvenienced you a great deal to part with it.'

'I have other means of conveyance, ma'am. Think nothing of it.'

'It will be returned to his lordship,' Duncan said, stiff-lipped.

'Is that so? I wonder why you see the need?' He seemed suddenly more cheerful. 'But I had rather it were returned to me.'

'I am sure that can be arranged,' Molly said, while Frank and Martha looked on, Frank with secret amusement and Martha in bewilderment.

Duncan was feeling a little like a cornered animal, which was a state of affairs he was certainly not used to. And it was all because of Molly. Never before had he had to prevaricate to please a woman; they either took him as he was or they did not take him at all. Molly was different. He wanted Molly's good opinion even though he knew he did not deserve it, and he did not want her to know he had won the equipage in a game of cards.

'How about it, Stacey?' Andrew asked. 'You owe it to me to give me the chance to…' He paused and smiled. 'To express my gratitude to Miss Martineau for saving my purse.'

'But that is cancelled out by our debt to you for lending us your coach,' she said.

'Then that is the end of the matter,' Duncan said, snatching at this with relief. 'Come, Miss Martineau.' He took her arm and almost propelled her away, followed by Frank and Martha and the sound of Bellamy's laughter.

'That was most uncivil of you,' she scolded him when they were sufficiently far away for him to slacken his speed. 'Mr Bellamy was being polite.'

'Was he?'

'I begin to think he did not lend us his coach at all. I begin to think you held him up and took it from him at pistol-point.'

He grimaced; this was even worse than being accused of winning it at cards. 'He would not have stood there bowing and smiling if I had, would he? He would have shouted for help and had me arrested.'

'True,' she admitted. 'But perhaps he forbore to do that because I told him his pockets had been rifled and you helped him to overcome the knuckle.'

He smiled at her use of the slang word, which he was sure she had only just learned from Andrew's lips. 'The value of a purse is far inferior to the value of a coach and four matched horses. Frank will return them to Lord Brancaster after we have arrived safely in London. Now we will say no more of it.'

She opened her mouth to speak again, but desisted when she saw that he had set his mouth tight shut and was looking decidedly grim. If he was going to be a crosspatch, then she would not walk beside him. She slowed her pace to walk beside Martha. Frank took the opportunity to accompany Duncan.

'It was bad luck running into Mr Bellamy again,' Frank said to him.

'It is of little consequence. He would not renege on a debt of honour and force us to return the coach.'

'But he wants the chance to win it back. And he doesn't seem the kind of man to take no for an answer. If he makes a noise about it, he will have everyone on his side, baying for you to accommodate him.'

'If he comes looking for us, then naturally I shall comply, but I did not want to take him up on it in front of the ladies.'

'Forgive me for saying so, sir, but it seems to me you are paying altogether too much attention to Miss Martineau. It will end in tears. Hers, if not yours.'

'And I'll thank you to keep your thoughts to yourself.'

It was an answer which convinced Frank that his employer had lost his head, if not his heart, and he had better tread warily. He said no more and they arrived back at the Greyhound in time to change for supper.

Molly dressed in one of the gowns Duncan had bought her in Norwich, a froth of pink lace over a darker pink satin slip, and then sat down for Martha, who had already changed into her one good dress, to arrange her hair. 'Put it up,' she told her. 'Make me look a little older, if you please. The Captain is constantly calling me a child and I do not like it.'

'Perhaps it is not your looks but your behaviour which prompts that,' Martha suggested. 'You are as bright and eager as a child and speak before you think. You would do well to watch that.'

'Oh, do you think so?' She was thoughtful for a moment. 'I think you must be right, for Mama has said the same thing. She is always telling me I should hold myself aloof, that ladies never betray their feelings.'

'I know nothing of Society ladies,' Martha said. 'But it is wise to hold a little of yourself back. You must keep the gentlemen guessing; it is the only way to engage their interest.'

'Really?' She was astonished. 'You mean I must pretend indifference, even when I am far from indifferent?'

'Especially then.'

'How strange.' She looked at herself in the glass, turning her head this way and that and putting on a haughty expression which did nothing but make Martha smile. 'You see,' she said. 'No one takes me seriously.'

'Oh, I am sure the Captain does. Now, are you ready?'

Molly picked up her fan and they went down to the dining room, where the men were waiting for them. Duncan, who had very little in the way of baggage with him, had changed his coat and put on a fresh cravat, and Frank, apart from washing and brushing his dark hair, was wearing the same breeches and coat he had been wearing all day.

They had hardly begun their meal when Andrew Bellamy strolled into the dining room. He was attired in a green silk coat, white breeches and white cravat, exquisitely starched and tied so that its froth of lace filled the neck of his pointed shirt collar. His coat was open to reveal a pink and red striped satin waistcoat. His companion looked positively drab in a black tailsuit.

Molly caught sight of them first. 'Why, here is Mr Bellamy,' she said, with a delighted smile.

He saw her almost at the same moment and hurried over to make his bow. 'Miss Martineau, your obedient.' He turned to Martha. 'Ma'am.' And to Duncan and Frank. 'Good evening, gentlemen. I did not know you were staying here.'

'Yes, what a coincidence,' Molly said. 'Captain, do ask Mr Bellamy and his friend to join us.'

Duncan, forced into a corner, could do nothing but comply. Andrew accepted with alacrity.

'Let me present my cousin, Mr George Lampson, Miss Martineau.'

'Mr Lampson.' She bowed towards the black-suited man as he took his place at the table. 'This is Mrs Upjohn and her husband, Mr Frank Upjohn—my friends and travelling companions.'

'Mr Upjohn I have already met,' Andrew said, seating himself next to Molly, to Duncan's annoyance. 'Mrs Upjohn, it is my pleasure.'

Martha did no more than incline her head and Molly gained the distinct impression that she did not like the newcomers. Nor, she realised, did Duncan, which was very strange when Mr Bellamy had been so generous to them. Forgetting all Martha's advice to be more restrained, she set about redressing what she perceived as a slight.

For the rest of the meal, Molly's happy chatter and Bellamy's amused responses drove Duncan into silence. Occasionally he made a low comment when appealed to but most of the time he watched and seethed. He would not admit that the little green god was sitting on his shoulder.

'We are going to London for the Season,' Molly told Andrew. 'I am so looking forward to it.'

'The Season?' Andrew queried in surprise. 'But it is half over.' He looked at Duncan. 'I am surprised, Stacey, that you did not set out earlier.'

'Oh, it was a spur-of-the-moment decision,' Molly explained before Duncan could reply. 'But I shall soon catch up.'

Andrew smiled broadly. 'Oh, I do not doubt you will. Just when everyone is becoming fatigued and bored by it all, you will arrive and stir them into life again.' He paused, looking from her to Duncan. 'But I am puzzled. Stacey is no more than a soldier; he has no entry into the *haut monde*, so who will sponsor you?'

Duncan knew very well what the man was thinking. Molly was not a real lady and must belong on the fringes of Society; no self-respecting unmarried young lady would be travelling in such a fashion with a couple of ex-soldiers and a woman of no importance long after most of them were already in town. She was probably what was euphemistically called a 'little bit of muslin' and therefore fair game.

'Look here, Bellamy,' he began angrily. 'If you think…'

'Doesn't matter what I think,' Andrew put in. 'It's what the world thinks.'

'The world can go hang.'

'Dear me, so defensive! I assure you it is not in the least necessary. I understand.'

'It is more than I do,' Molly said.

'He is using you,' Andrew said, answering her and nodding towards Duncan. 'He is using you to gain entry into London's drawing rooms. But he will find it will take more than a pretty little nobody to accomplish that.'

'Oh, that is unfair!' Molly cried. 'He did not want to take me. I insisted. And besides, he is only my escort. I am going to stay with my mama. I do not need a sponsor.'

He bowed. 'Then I beg your pardon.' But he did not look in the least repentant. 'But if you are on your way to London, why delay your journey to go to the races?'

'Because I wanted to see the horses,' she said. 'And Captain Stacey was kind enough to agree. I was vastly amused. Do you know, I won several guineas?'

'Beginner's luck,' Duncan put in. 'A freak result.'

'Is that so? Or is the little lady a better judge of horseflesh than you are?'

'It was Brancaster's Bright Belle,' she told him.

He smiled knowingly. 'What made you choose that one?'

'She liked the filly's eyes,' Duncan said laconically. 'And who was I to argue with a lady?'

'You said she might as well have only three legs,' Molly reminded him. 'It is not my fault if I won and you lost.'

'Oh, I did not lose.'

'You backed her to win?'

'Yes.'

Her laughter pealed out, making one or two of the other guests look round to see the source of the amusement. They saw a lively young lady in the company of four very different young men, chaperoned by a drab woman who looked decidedly uncomfortable. If she had been their daughter she would have been locked in her room for her own safety, not let out to frequent coaching inns.

'How ironic!' she said. 'You expected to lose and you still backed her. Why?'

He shrugged. He did not know why. 'Sometimes you have to back your hunches. It felt like a lucky day. Mr Bellamy understands that.' He appealed to the young man. 'Is that not so?'

'Yes, indeed. And I backed her too, but it wasn't a lucky hunch; the filly belongs to my father and I have seen what she can do, if stretched.'

Molly clapped her hands. 'Then this is a celebration. Everyone is happy.'

Andrew grinned and Frank smiled and even Martha's lips twitched at her pleasure. Only Duncan seemed downcast. She could not understand it, but she did not mean to let it spoil her evening.

'Do you live hereabouts, Mr Bellamy?' she asked.

'No. My father's country home is in Huntingdonshire,' he said. 'I have lately been visiting there.'

'On a repairing lease, no doubt,' Duncan murmured.

Andrew threw him a look of pure venom. 'Unlike some, I have no need to flee the capital. I am never out of funds.' He smiled at Molly. 'I think you have not chosen your company wisely, Miss Martineau. Allow me to take over and escort you to the capital.'

Molly heard Duncan's quick intake of breath but he did not speak. She smiled at Mr Bellamy. 'I thank you, sir, but I am quite content with the escort I have. My godmother has entrusted Captain Stacey to take care of me and deliver me safely to my mama.' She paused and added, 'Besides, the Captain has your coach.'

Duncan, who had a glass of wine to his lips and was about to sip from it, spluttered into it, choking.

She looked from him to Andrew Bellamy who had lost his urbane smile and was glaring at Duncan, and decided it would be better to change the subject quickly. If the Captain had obtained the coach by deception… 'I do thank you, sir,' she said, pretending she had not noticed. 'Perhaps when I am settled in Holles Street we shall meet again. My mama no doubt will be taking me to all the right places.' She stood up and the men scrambled to their feet. 'Now, if you do not mind, I shall retire.'

She accepted their bows and murmured goodnights with what she hoped was cool aplomb and left the room, followed by Martha.

'Enchanting,' Andrew murmured to her departing back. 'Quite, quite enchanting.'

'And out of reach,' Duncan growled. 'Keep your grubby hands off her.'

'Grubby?' he queried, displaying perfectly manicured hands for inspection. 'Is it not a question of the pot calling the kettle black? What is your interest in her? Mama one of the *ton*, is she? No, that is not possible; no mother worthy of the name would have sent her off to London with a dis-charged soldier for an escort and without a conveyance, and little in the way of baggage.' He surveyed Duncan's thunderous face and smiled knowingly. 'You know, I do believe you are bamming her into believing you are taking her to her mama. You are not, are you?' He paused. 'Unless that air of innocence is all a sham and she knows exactly what she is doing.'

Duncan's fist caught him full on the jaw and he toppled sideways, taking the tablecloth and the contents of the table with him.

There was a moment of stunned silence from everyone in the room and then pandemonium as everyone crowded round. Andrew scrambled to his feet, wiping blood from his cut lip, and faced a furious Duncan, who stood with his feet apart and his hands clenched at his sides, ready to raise them should Bellamy attempt to retaliate.

'You have given yourself away, Stacey,' Bellamy said. 'No true gentlemen would resort to fisticuffs.' His emphasis on the word 'gentleman' conveyed his contempt.

'The Captain is a gentleman,' Frank put in, while everyone else in the room stood agog with curiosity. 'He is a Stacey.'

'So he is, though not one the family acknowledges. I am persuaded the connection is so remote as to be disregarded.'

Frank opened his mouth to speak again, but Duncan put a hand on his arm. 'Leave it, Frank. If our friend chooses to use my lack of breeding as an excuse not to challenge me, then let him. I have no wish to hurt him.'

That was too much for Bellamy to swallow. 'You will hear from my representatives, Stacey.'

'After we reach London and I have seen Miss Martineau safely reunited with her mother, I shall be delighted to oblige,' Duncan said, still angry, but fully aware that he could not take the risk of duelling with Bellamy while he was responsible for Molly. 'Come on, Frank; the company here is not to my liking.' And with that he walked from the room, followed by the sergeant. The spectators murmured among themselves and then, realising nothing more exciting was going to happen, dispersed.

Molly lay in her bed looking up at the ceiling, her head too full of images to sleep. It was less than a week since she had first set off after the Captain and inveigled him into being her escort and so much had happened it seemed like a lifetime.

It was an adventure of the first magnitude: coaches being held up by highwaymen; shopping and sightseeing; betting on the horseraces; pickpockets and Mr Bellamy joining them for supper. He was a real gentleman, handsome, well-dressed, polite, so why didn't the Captain like him? He had been as prickly as a hedgehog all evening. He was a strange man, was the Captain. One minute he was laughing and being the best companion in the world, the next he was growling and getting on his high horse over some little thing of no significance.

She was afraid it was her behaviour that brought on these strange moods, but as she didn't know how else to behave she could not do anything about it. She was still pondering on this when she heard a crash coming from downstairs and then a babble of voices. Curious, she crept from her bed and opened her door a crack to listen. There was silence. And then she saw Duncan and Frank come out of the dining room and begin to climb the stairs. Neither looked very pleased with life. 'What happened?' she asked. 'I heard a crash.'

'Nothing to worry about,' he said. 'I fell against a table. Very clumsy of me.'

Why did she think he was lying? 'Are you hurt?'

'No, of course not.' They had reached the landing and Frank gave her a nod and continued on to his own room. Duncan stopped and looked down at her. She was looking especially lovely with her hair flowing about her shoulders and the wrap she had put on over her nightgown falling open. He could see the outline of her firm young breasts and felt his loins stir uncontrollably. 'It is very late and we have a long day tomorrow. Go back to bed.' With an effort he resisted the temptation to kiss her. 'Goodnight, my dear.'

She bade him goodnight and watched from the doorway as he went along the corridor to his own room. He walked with a heavy tread, his head bowed, as if he was exhausted, and she supposed he was. He had all the responsibility of their journey on his shoulders and she had not made it easy for him. They were nearing their destination and he would be free of her; she was very sure he would not remain in London once his escort duty had been fulfilled; he would be off on the open road again, footloose and free of all encumbrances. And she would miss him.

No one could be so gallant one minute, so uncivil the next, so handsome and valiant and yet so infuriatingly condescending. Sometimes she longed to beat her fists upon his broad chest, to wipe the smile from his face with angry protests that he should see her for what she was, a young lady with sensibilities, not a child to be scolded or indulged as the fancy took him.

It just proved how far apart they were, not only in age, but in temperament. And though she had seen flashes of humour and light-heartedness he was, for the most part, a serious-minded man who did not suffer fools gladly. And she had been a fool. She had made it impossible for him to refuse her request for an escort without giving a thought about how inconvenient it might be for him. Was it possible to be more empty-headed? It was time she grew up. She fell asleep, promising herself she would try to be more understanding.

Chapter Seven

Molly was woken by Martha long before dawn. 'Dress quickly. The Captain is leaving as soon as it is light enough,' she said.

She dressed in her green carriage dress and set a feather-trimmed bonnet on her fair curls then hurried downstairs to find the others already there. Duncan looked grim and she realised that he was in no mood for her banter. She ate her breakfast quickly and then they went out to the coach, which was in the yard ready and waiting for them.

This time Caesar was roped on behind with the other horses and Duncan sat in the coach with Molly, while Martha climbed up beside her husband. It wasn't long before Molly realised that they were going at a cracking pace, much faster than on any previous days when Duncan had been careful not to overtire the horses.

After several minutes of being thrown about quite violently as the vehicle swayed from side to side, she turned to look at him, but he was staring straight out of the other window as if he could not bear to look at her. She was puzzled. Even when he was angry with her, he had never ignored her like this. What had she done?

'I am not at all flattered that you are in such haste to be rid of me that you will risk the horses in this fashion,' she said.

He was still smouldering over his confrontation with Andrew Bellamy. Never in all his life had he backed down from a fight. Bellamy would undoubtedly spread the word that he was a coward and had refused to meet him. That would hurt more than any physical pain. He was so tense, he could feel the muscles in his jaw twitching and his hand was gripping the leather strap on the door as if his life depended on it. Her voice only served to exacerbate his feelings of frustration.

'On the contrary,' he said, tight-lipped. 'You should be pleased that I am doing it for your sake.'

'It is not for my sake.' She rounded on him. 'You have some deep game of your own.'

'If I have it is one that you started, riding off after a man at dead of night like some common camp follower.' He did not know why he said it; it was cruel and untrue. What was the matter with him? Had he been so long out of feminine society he did not know how to treat a lady?

The pain in her expressive blue eyes and the way she shuddered told him clearly he had hurt her and he cursed himself for a fool. It was the unaccustomed responsibility for someone so vulnerable, his own ramshackle way of life which he had realised could not go on that had put the words into his mouth. And his pride. He had no cause to be proud. He reached out and laid a hand on hers. 'I am sorry, Molly. I did not mean that.'

She pulled herself away from him, curling up in the corner of the carriage like a wounded animal. 'Yes, you did. You have been saying so all along. And it is my fault, for I insisted on you taking me to London. Now I wish I never had. I am such a mopstraw and so ignorant, I am persuaded I should make a dreadful cake of myself in Society. It is no wonder Mama did not want me with her.'

'Humbug!'

She turned to look at him, puzzled by the expletive, but before either of them could speak again they heard galloping hooves and shouts and two riders suddenly appeared from nowhere and rode into the road in front of them. Frank was forced to pull the coach to a halt.

Moments later, a rider appeared at the door and, leaning down, opened it, pointing a pistol at them. 'Out! Get out!'

Molly gasped. The man was masked and wore a black riding cape. Silently Duncan got out and turned to hand Molly down. Neither spoke.

'Over there.' The man jerked his head to the side of the road. The other man had his pistol trained on Frank and Martha who sat on the box, perfectly still.

Molly looked at Duncan but all he did was nod. She stepped to one side and he followed her.

'Your money and your jewels,' the man demanded.

Molly found her voice. 'I have none.'

'Do you take me for a flat? Come on, hand them over or…'

'She is telling the truth,' Duncan said, realising that the men were probably ex-soldiers and not professional criminals. 'I have but lately taken her up. She is nothing, a nobody…' He ignored Molly's gasp. 'A ladybird not worth risking a hanging for.'

'No? Then perhaps you are, my lord. Turn out your pockets, if you please.'

Duncan complied, pulling out a purse containing a few coins and his watch.

'I hope you don't mean to persuade me that's all you have.'

'It is.'

'Lord Brancaster is known for being high in the stirrups, and he wouldn't stint his son and heir.'

Molly stole a sideways glance at Duncan but his expression was inscrutable.

'It is also known that his heir is a gambler,' he drawled. 'At this moment, he has pockets to let.'

The man received this news with incredulity. He bade his companion to keep them all covered and proceeded to pull the trunk and other baggage from the boot, which he emptied out all over the road. Molly watched in horror as all her lovely clothes were scattered in the dust. 'I told you so,' Duncan said when this search revealed nothing.

The man did not reply but turned to the interior of the coach and pulled out all the squabs, peered under the seats and behind the back-rest, even examined the roof. Nothing in the way of money or jewels was discovered. He forced Frank and Martha down from their perch at gunpoint and subjected them to a humiliating search.

'Now you,' he said, advancing on Molly.

'Please,' Molly pleaded. 'I give you my word I have no valuables. His lordship spoke the truth. He picked me up.' She smiled. 'And you are known for a chivalrous man…'

'Am I?'

'You are the Dark Knight, are you not? It is said he never robs ladies.'

The man looked at Molly and laughed. 'Then they say wrong, don't they?' He reached out to pull Molly forward.

'No, you don't.' Duncan stepped in front of her. 'You lay a finger on her and…'

'Thrash me? I should like to see you try.'

Duncan was still smarting from the humiliation of refusing

Andrew Bellamy; he could not be seen to back down again. He launched himself at the man, knocking the pistol from his hand and pulling him in front of him so that the accomplice dared not shoot. When the second robber turned to see what was happening, Frank seized his chance to dive for his legs and pull him to the ground. In a moment he, too, was disarmed.

Molly, quicker-thinking than even Duncan would have credited her with, picked up the pistol and handed it to him. 'Thank you, my dear,' he said calmly, pointing it at the robber. 'Now, put everything back in the carriage as you found it.'

Reluctantly they obeyed, bundling Molly's clothes back into her trunk and forcing the lid shut, then replacing Martha's few belongings in her portmanteau. They looked round when they had done this but Duncan was still watching them. 'And the rest. And the cushions.'

When they had finished Duncan strode over and pulled the masks from their faces. 'So that I remember what the Dark Knight looks like,' he said, smiling. 'Now it is your turn to empty your pockets for me.'

This revealed a purse of coins, a ring, a watch and a gold cross on a chain which Duncan took and put into his own pocket.

'What are you going to do?' the man asked, trembling.

'What do you think I should do?' Duncan was affable. 'It might be quite a feather in my cap to be the means of apprehending the Dark Knight, don't you think?'

'Yes, but…'

Duncan turned to Molly. 'What do you say, my dear? Shall we take these two incompetent snafflers to the law?'

Molly was so relieved to learn that Duncan was not the

Dark Knight after all, she was inclined to be lenient. 'Not if they promise to turn over a new leaf. I should hate to be the one to bring them to the gallows.'

'Oh, thank you, miss. God bless you.' The second man spoke for the first time.

Duncan smiled at Molly. 'I think you are too kind-hearted, but as we are in some haste to continue our journey and I have no wish to waste time answering questions I shall do nothing.' He used the gun in his hand to point to the bank at the side of the road. 'Now, stand over there.'

They shuffled back, looking chagrined. 'Further,' Duncan commanded.

They retreated another pace and fell backwards into the stream. There had been no rain for some time and there was more mud than water in it. While they scrambled to their feet, covered in stinking slime and weeds, Duncan ushered Molly back to the coach. Not until they were on their way again did he sit back and roar with laughter.

'It is not funny,' she said, realising she was trembling all over now that the danger had passed.

'Oh, it is; it certainly is. You will never know how comical it is. To be held up by the notorious Dark Knight in broad daylight and best him. Oh, that is the greatest entertainment I have had in years.'

'Entertainment!' She could hear Frank, on the box, chuckling too and Martha protesting. 'I begin to think you are both a little touched in the attic. We could all have been killed.'

He attempted to be serious and for a moment stopped laughing, but then the thought of those two men set him chuckling all over again.

'You *are* mad,' she said. 'You should be giving thanks for our deliverance.'

'Oh, I do, I do.' He chinked the man's purse in his pocket. 'In more ways than one.'

'You can't keep that; it should go back to the poor man from whom it was stolen.'

'And you know it was stolen, do you?'

'Of course it was. So was the ring and the crucifix. You should hand it to the watch at the next place we stop.'

'They would not pass it on, even if they knew who had lost it, and I had as lief it was in my pocket as theirs.'

'That man thought you were Mr Bellamy.'

'I rather fancy he did, but it is hardly surprising; we are travelling in the Brancaster family carriage.'

'And you are not the Dark Knight,' she murmured pensively.

'Did I ever say I was?'

'No, I allow you did not, but…'

'You thought I was and now you are disappointed.' He spoke softly, not laughing now. 'Captain Duncan Stacey is no more than he claims to be—a half-pay officer with as little romance in him as a tin kettle. I am afraid, my dear, I am no Don Quixote, not a bit of good at tilting at windmills.'

She smiled suddenly. 'You defended me very well when that man threatened to lay hands on me.'

'Oh, that was nothing.'

'He could have shot you.'

'No, my dear, I do not think so. But you are shaking.' He put his head out of the door and shouted up at Frank. 'Stop at the next respectable hostelry, Sergeant. We'll rest the horses and have something to eat and drink before going on.'

There were several people in the dining room of the inn they chose in Saffron Walden, but they were quickly served. Frank and Martha finished their meal first and went to the stables to see that the horses were being well looked after and made ready again for the road, leaving Duncan and Molly talking to a clerical gentleman and his wife.

The Reverend was as thin as his lady was fat; he wore generous side whiskers but was otherwise quite bald and he was holding forth to all who would listen about the evils of travelling in a country that was rapidly going to the devil.

'Beggars and thieves everywhere,' he said, waving his spoon about. 'A man of the cloth should be able to travel freely in his own coach without fearing for his life. Forced from our carriage at pistol-point, we were, and all our belongings taken.'

Molly looked at Duncan, but he was concentrating on the plum duff on his plate. 'Sir, I am sorry for your misfortune,' she said. 'Tell me, when did this happen?'

'Early this morning,' he said. 'On the way here from Cambridge. We had set out early because I wished to make one or two pastoral calls on the way. We had just left the town behind and were making good progress over the Gog Magog hills when the two men sprang out at us. They took everything we possessed—my purse and watch, my wife's betrothal ring with a fine ruby in its centre. Even my crucifix.'

'It is a very frightening experience, I know,' Molly said. 'We, too, were stopped on the road by two such evil-looking characters as you are likely to meet in a twelve-month.'

'Why, ma'am, it sounds very much like the same two,' he said. 'I am a man of peace and I expected my cloth to protect me. I begin to wonder what the world is coming to, when no one has any respect for a man of God.'

'No, it is to be deplored,' Duncan said. 'We were stopped, 'tis true, but the rogues took nothing. We were able to turn the tables on them.'

'Then you were indeed fortunate,' the Reverend said. 'I

should have put up some resistance, but they threatened to harm my wife if I attempted it.'

'You lost a crucifix and a watch, you say?' Duncan asked.

'Yes, the crucifix was of solid silver on a silver chain. The watch was presented to me by grateful parishioners when I left my last living and is inscribed.'

'I do believe we have them safe,' Molly said. 'The Captain relieved the robbers of them when he retrieved our own belongings.'

Duncan took the watch from his pocket and examined the inscription. 'Be so good as to tell me your name, sir.'

'Josiah Appleby.' He called the landlord over to him. 'Gilpott, tell this gentleman my name, if you please.'

Mr Gilpott looked startled, but furnished the information, adding that he had known the Reverend gentleman some years and he was a regular customer of the inn. Duncan smiled and handed over the watch together with the money and the other items he had taken from the highwaymen. 'One cannot be too careful,' he said.

'Oh, thank you, sir!' Mrs Appleby exclaimed as the landlord went to look after a new arrival. 'How very fortunate we met up with you.'

'Let me recompense you,' the Reverend said, opening the purse and extracting two guineas.

'No, not to be thought of,' Duncan said. 'Glad to be of service.' Though he was speaking to the Reverend he was not looking at him, but at a man in a frieze coat and a shallow hat who had just entered the room. He was accompanied by the innkeeper who brought him across to where the parson sat.

'This 'ere's a Bow Street Runner, Reverend,' the landlord said. 'He's investigating this 'ere Dark Knight on behalf of

Sir John Partridge what was 'eld up by 'im some few days ago. I told 'im you could, like as not, furnish 'im with details.'

'Indeed I can, and so can these people here, for we have both been victims of that gentleman and his accomplice.'

'Is that so?' The Runner looked at Duncan.

Duncan cursed inwardly but produced a lazy smile. 'Yes, but they took nothing from us and I can tell you no more about them than the Reverend. I fancy they rode off towards Newmarket.'

'One of them admitted to being the Dark Knight,' Molly put in.

'Are you sure they were both men?' the Runner asked. 'There is some doubt that one might be a female. There was a woman at the inn in Aylsham who turned up in the middle of the night, bold as you please.'

'Gammon!' Duncan said, ignoring Molly's splutter as she tried not to laugh. 'Two men, you may depend upon it.'

'And did one have a scar on his face?'

'I saw no scar,' Duncan said, praying that Frank would not enter the room just then to tell them the carriage was ready for departure.

'I wonder,' the Runner said thoughtfully. 'Can there be more than one Dark Knight?'

'I shouldn't be surprised,' Duncan said. 'The country is full of scamps.'

'May I ask your business, sir? Where you came from and where you are bound?' And, seeing Duncan's frown, he added, 'My duty, you understand, sir; no wish to pry. Discretion's my name. Little lady's name will not be mentioned.'

Molly held her breath, but Duncan simply changed his frown to a benign smile. 'It is no secret, sir. I am escorting Miss Martineau to her mama in London from Stacey Manor, at the request of Lady Connaught, her godmother. You may check with her ladyship if you wish.' He stood up and turned to Molly. 'My dear, we shall be late arriving at your mama's, if we do not leave at once.' Bowing to the parson's wife and bidding her husband good day, he hurried Molly from the room, giving her no time to protest that she had not finished her meal.

'That was very uncivil of you,' Molly protested as she was bundled into the carriage and Duncan climbed in behind her. 'You could have described those two ruffians much better than the Reverend, for you pulled the masks from their faces.'

'If we had stayed we would have been there until supper time answering questions,' he said as they moved forward with the riding horses tied on behind. 'The episode has already delayed us.'

'But you could have helped the Runner to catch the Dark Knight.'

'So I could,' he said, a quirky smile playing about his lips. The two robbers were an unexpected blessing; they would keep the Runner busy for a good day—long enough for him to deliver Molly to Holles Street and report to the War Department. 'But I did not choose to. He will manage well enough.'

'I wish I knew what deep game you are playing,' she said. 'You are not at all what I expected of a romantic hero.'

'And I never expected to be obliged to play the role,' he retorted.

She sighed. 'I know that for you are singularly ill fitted for it.'

'I am a soldier—or I was until Boney decided to throw in the sponge. Now I am a common man with pockets to let. Mayhap when you find yourself in among the *ton* you will meet someone who fits your bill.'

'Oh, do you think I will?'

He shrugged, unwilling to admit that he envied whoever it might be. 'I do not know, for it is years since I was in Society. But I will tell you this. It is no good puffing a man up in your imagination and then complaining when he don't live up to it. We are all human with human frailties, whatever those novels you read say to the contrary.'

'No, I can see if I did that it might cause disappointment,' she said, so seriously that he found himself smiling. 'You think I should be a little sceptical?'

'It might be wise. But tell me, Molly, exactly what are you anticipating?'

'I do not know. To be introduced into Society, to go to routs and soirées and to the theatre. Above all, I should like to go to a ball and have all the eligibles at my feet.' She sighed. 'But I know that is only a dream because I am not at all beautiful and I do not know how to converse with all the latest *on-dit*, and the ballgown you bought for me is so dirty and creased where those men trampled it in the dust that I have nothing to wear. But it would be so gratifying if just one gentleman paid me a little attention.'

'Only one?' he queried a little pensively. 'Such modest expectations! But I collect he would have to be rich and have a title, or the prospect of one?'

'No. It is not at all necessary, though perhaps Mama might think so.'

'Oh, undoubtedly your mama would think so,' he agreed.

'But that would be unrealistic, don't you think? I have no fortune which, I am persuaded, would make up for all the other deficiencies.'

'It might indeed,' he said. 'It seems you must settle for a man of no particular importance, without a fortune or a title—

in short any tulip who pays you his addresses.' He stopped when he saw the distress on her face. How could he be so insensitive? Was it because Bellamy had been so particular towards her and she had obviously been delighted by him? Or was it because they were so near to Foxtrees, his ancestral home? Not five miles from here, his brother enjoyed what should have been his and which would have made him someone of consequence, able to pay his addresses to any lady he fancied in the proper manner.

But it was grossly unfair of him to take his disappointment out on his young companion. He turned to her, speaking softly. 'Molly, I am sorry. I had no right to speak like that. I was simply trying to point out the pitfalls of being too trusting. I am not the only rakeshame you are likely to meet.'

'No, but I am not such a sapskull as to think you are. And I am not at my last prayers yet.' Which, without her realising it, put him firmly in his place.

'Captain,' Frank called down from the box. 'I fancy we are being followed. There have been horses behind us for several miles.'

Duncan put his head out of the door and looked back. 'Slow down and see if they pass.'

Frank did so and two horsemen rode up alongside them. One doffed his hat and grinned at Duncan as he came level with the door of the coach.

'Bellamy!' Duncan exclaimed.

'I shall be waiting for you,' he shouted as he galloped past. 'That is if you can find the courage.' His last words were carried on the wind.

'What did he mean?' Molly asked.

Duncan made a valiant effort not to betray his fury. 'I

expect he is just making sure we do not damage his carriage or spoil his horses.'

'I am sure he has no need to worry on that score, though you have been galloping the cattle very hard today.'

'For heaven's sake, can you not keep quiet about anything?' he demanded. 'You must have your say and state your opinion on every subject from highwaymen to horse-flesh and I am sick of it.'

'I am sorry,' she said. 'I will not say another word.' And this time she meant it. He had never spoken to her like that before, however annoyed he had been, and she was confused and hurt.

The nearer they came to their destination, the more gloomy he seemed to become. Perhaps he was anticipating a jobation from her mother or perhaps he had realised he ought to do something about his ramshackle life. He had been very quick and brave when the highwaymen had held them up and he was used to taking command—anyone could see that—so why could he not find useful employment? Surely it was not so difficult for officers as it was for the men?

They travelled in silence until they arrived in Bishops Stortford, where they pulled into the yard of an inn. Duncan bespoke rooms for them and they went up to change for supper.

When Molly returned downstairs, he was waiting to escort her into the dining room. He smiled at her, his ill humour apparently forgotten, and opened the door for her to precede him. They were followed by Frank and Martha.

'Why, here is Mr Bellamy and Mr Lampson!' Molly exclaimed, spotting the two men at one of the tables.

Andrew rose, smiling, and took her hand to raise it to his lips. 'Miss Martineau, what a great pleasure it is to meet you again so soon.' He held onto her hand and looked into her eyes, making her blush. 'You are still in the same bad company, I see.'

'Now that is very unkind of you, sir,' she said. 'What has the Captain done to deserve such animosity?'

'He knows. But we will not speak of it in company. Please join me.' He indicated seats at his table.

Duncan was silent and she looked round for him. He was making his way to another table. 'Thank you, Mr Bellamy, but not tonight,' she said. 'We are all very tired from travelling and shall undoubtedly retire early.'

He bowed. 'Another time, perhaps, when you are not so constrained.'

'I am not constrained,' she said. 'But yes, perhaps another time.'

She turned and walked slowly over to where Duncan, Frank and Martha had settled themselves and were ordering food.

'You could at least have been civil to him,' she said to Duncan, taking her place next to him. 'He has been very obliging, after all, and it is not fair to take your dismals out on him.'

'Miss Martineau, you do not know the truth of it,' Frank put in. 'The Captain...'

'Sergeant, be silent!' Duncan commanded.

Molly had never heard Duncan speak to Frank like that and she felt very embarrassed on his behalf, though he said nothing, but subsided into his seat and concentrated on the mutton chop and sausages on his plate.

It was a very silent meal, fraught with tension, and Molly was glad when it was over and she could retire to her room.

'Do you know what all that business with Mr Bellamy was about?' she asked Martha as they climbed the stairs.

'No, I don't. It has something to do with what happened in the past, I think. But it has certainly put Captain Stacey into a bad temper. I shall be glad when we are on our way again. I believe the Captain means to reach London by night-fall tomorrow.'

Duncan and Frank were finishing off the wine, before retiring themselves, when Bellamy strolled over to them. 'Well, sir,' he said, addressing Duncan. 'How does it feel to hide behind a woman's petticoats? I'll wager you won't feel so comfortable about it when you reach London. News of your cowardice will go before you. What excuse will you have then for refusing to meet me?'

'There will be no excuses,' Duncan growled. 'Now, if you will allow me.' He stood up and made to leave.

Bellamy seized the sleeve of his coat to detain him. 'You call yourself a Stacey. No Stacey I ever heard of backed away from a fight.' He laughed and pulled a glove from his coat pocket and flung it into Duncan's face. 'Refuse again, if you dare.'

Slowly Duncan stooped and picked up the glove, while the other diners looked on, their faces alive with interest. 'I shall look forward to receiving a visit from your seconds,' he said. 'Come on, Sergeant.'

'Now you've done it,' Frank said as they left the room and climbed the stairs. 'You should not have allowed him to taunt you into accepting his challenge.'

'I can't not accept it. I did it once before for Molly's sake, but now I must act for my own sake.'

'There were several witnesses in the dining room; someone is bound to send for the watch or a magistrate and there'll be hell to pay. And if you should kill him…'

'I have no intention of killing him. I merely wish to teach him that he cannot, with impunity, insult my good name or the honour of a lady who is under my protection.'

'What do you think Miss Martineau will say when she hears of it?'

'She need not know.' He realised, as he spoke, that keeping Molly out of it was going to be very difficult, if not impossible. He had no idea what her reaction might be. Was her love of adventure such that she would be excited, rather than frightened, by the prospect? After all, she spoke gaily of highwaymen and holding up coaches, but then that was fantasy. She had no experience of death or severe injury and he did not know what she would do when faced with reality. 'You do not have to stay.'

'Captain, if you think I will leave you now when you need me, then you must have a very poor opinion of me. Who else will you find to act for you?'

Duncan grinned. 'Thank you, my friend. Now, see if you can procure someone else to make a second. I do not think Mr Bellamy will delay in sending his men.'

He was right. He went to his room to prepare himself for what he knew was a highly risky and illegal undertaking, and in a few minutes Frank returned with a scrawny youth he had found in the tap room, followed by Andrew Bellamy, his valet and George Lampson.

'You have the choice of place and weapons,' Lampson said.

'Pistols,' Duncan said. 'At dawn. In the clearing in the wood on the London road. It is about three miles from here. Far enough away not to attract attention.'

Bellamy smiled, though now the challenge had been accepted he was looking decidedly shaky and rather pale. 'Until tomorrow, then.'

'Why did you choose pistols?' Frank asked, when the others had left. 'You are the best swordsman I ever met.'

'I don't have my sword with me and, besides, pistols will have it done more quickly. One shot each and it will all be over.'

'And you might be lying dead or mortally wounded.'

'I do not think so. It is not so easy to look a man straight in the eye and fire a pistol at him with any accuracy. Not in cold blood. Especially if your opponent has deliberately missed. Bellamy is a young pup; I'll wager he has never fired a shot in anger. He will be shaking so much he will miss.'

'That is a monstrous gamble.'

'I have taken bigger risks.'

'Are you coming back here afterwards?'

Duncan smiled. 'If I survive, you mean?'

'I didn't like to say it, but yes.'

'We have no choice. I cannot abandon Molly and I know you will not leave Martha.'

'No, but there will be a hue and cry and if Mr Bellamy is wounded this is the first place anyone will look.'

'You can come back for the ladies alone and bring them to me and we can go on as before.'

'And if…?'

'You still come back for them. Take Molly to Holles Street as planned. It is only one day's ride from here. You should have no trouble.'

'Very well, though I could wish this business had never been begun.'

'You expect me to take that young pup's insults?'

'No, of course not, but…'

'Let us get some rest, then. It will soon be dawn.'

Molly was woken from a deep sleep by voices in the room next door, the one occupied by the Captain. Curious, she rose and put her ear to the wall, but the voices were too low for her to hear more than a single word here and there. She heard the murmur of the Captain's voice and this time her own name came to her clearly through the woodwork, then Mr Upjohn's voice, raised in protest. Pistols; she heard that word very clearly. If someone was going to shoot off a pistol, she hoped no one would be hurt by it. More than anything she hoped it would not be the Captain. The thought of him lying bleeding, perhaps dying, was more than she could bear.

A door was opened and shut with a soft click. She scrambled out of bed and opened her own door. The Captain and Mr Upjohn, dressed for outdoors, were disappearing down the stairs; she could just see the tops of their heads in the light from the lamp left burning on the landing.

She scrambled into the breeches she habitually wore under her old habit, pulled on a shirt and stuffed her hair under her riding hat. Picking up her boots, she tiptoed from her room and down the stairs. Pausing on the step to pull on her boots, she heard, rather than saw, two horses leave the yard and gallop off down the road.

It took only a couple of minutes to saddle Jenny and then she was galloping after them, digging her heels in and urging Jenny to go faster.

It was a clear moonlit night and it was easy to see the ribbon of road winding ahead, but there was no sign of the horses in front of her. Already the horizon to the east was tinged with pink. Soon it would be day and then everyone would be astir, going about their business. Why had the Captain and Mr Upjohn left the inn in such a hurry, abandoning her and Martha? It did not seem the sort of thing they would do voluntarily. If she had not known that he was not the Dark Knight, she would have thought he was going to hold up a coach.

Galloping along the empty road, she could easily believe the whole adventure was fantasy, a dream from which she would soon wake to find herself in bed at Stacey Manor with the sun shining through the window and the birds twittering in the eaves. But that would mean the Captain was a figment of her imagination too and she did not want to believe that. She wanted him to be real. He was becoming a necessary part of her life. Without him she would be lost.

The road ahead disappeared into the gloom of a copse of trees and she was forced to slow down. It was as well she did, for she heard the unmistakable snuffle of a tethered horse among the trees to her left. She pulled up sharply and dismounted. Leading Jenny by her bridle, she walked slowly forward, eyes and ears alert.

There was a clearing in the trees and in the clearing were six men, standing in a circle. Molly gasped as she recognised the Captain and Mr Upjohn, Mr Bellamy and his cousin. The other two she did not know, though she thought one of them had been with Mr Bellamy the first time she had seen him.

She watched as the Captain and Mr Bellamy took off their coats. Mr Upjohn offered Mr Bellamy an open box from which he extracted a pistol. Duncan took another from the same box and the two men moved to the centre of the clearing and stood back to back. They were going to fight a duel!

She stood, hidden by trees, clinging to Jenny's bridle as the two men paced away from each other while Mr Upjohn counted: one, two, three… It seemed to take an age, but could only have been seconds before they reached twenty, turned to face each other and raised their weapons. She plunged her fist into her mouth and looked away as two shots echoed in the morning air, one some seconds after the other.

They were followed by a deathly silence and then she

heard Andrew Bellamy laugh. It was a shaky kind of laugh, a laugh of relief, a laugh that told her he had not been hurt.

She swivelled round to see Duncan on the ground where he had fallen. She forgot her fear, forgot she was supposed to be asleep in her bed, as she ran out from her hiding place and sped across the grass to where he lay, tears streaming down her face.

'My, the filly was here all along,' Bellamy drawled. 'Such devotion!'

She ignored him and flung herself on the ground beside Duncan. He was still as death and there was a great deal of blood seeping into the ground beside him. 'Captain! Oh, you must not be dead. Oh, please God, don't let him be dead.'

'Touching,' said Bellamy.

'Get out!' Frank snarled. 'Get out of here. Think yourself lucky he did not put a bullet through your heart.'

Molly, intent on feeling for a heartbeat through the blood-stained shirt, was hardly aware of the young man's going, but soon the echo of several sets of hoofbeats faded and she realised that only Frank remained. She looked up at him with a tear-streaked face.

'He could have fired,' he said, kneeling beside Duncan and carefully cutting away his shirt to reveal the wound. 'He could have picked his spot, easy as eating pie, but he didn't. He fired into the air and waited.'

'He did it on purpose? Why? Did he want to die? Oh, Mr Upjohn, what was he thinking of?'

'He's not dead,' he said, looking up from his examination into blue eyes that no longer sparkled with mischief but with tears. 'Winged. The bullet passed right through his shoulder, which is a blessing, but it is making him bleed like a stuck pig.'

'Then we must get a doctor to him.'

'And have him arrested? No, miss, I think not.'

'But he will die if he is not attended to. I have never seen so much blood.'

He forbore to point out that she was inexperienced in such matters whereas he had seen worse—a great deal worse. 'At least you are not swooning at the sight of it,' he said, prepared to concede that much, just as Duncan stirred and moaned.

'Captain, thank God. But lie still, do, for you are bleeding badly.'

He opened his eyes and grinned lopsidedly at her. She had wiped her tears away with blood-stained fingers and her cheeks were smeared with dirt and blood. And the expression of tender concern in her eyes made his heart leap. 'It is only a flesh wound,' he murmured. 'I shall be as right as ninepence in no time.'

'You should never have had the wound in the first place,' Frank put in, his concern for his friend making him speak more sharply than a servant ought. 'Why in creation's name did you not wing him? If you had only put a ball in his pistol arm, he could not have shot you. But to stand there and invite him to do his worst…'

'His worst was not so bad. And now he has to live with his conscience and I have no such problem. How could I take Molly to London if the law was on my heels?'

'I thought it already was,' Molly put in as Frank stood up and went over to Caesar's saddlebag where he knew Duncan always kept a clean pad and bandage—a practice he had started while in the Peninsula. It had saved more than one life and he had made it part of his baggage on this particular mission.

'No one is on my heels, little one, not on Duncan Stacey's heels. Unless it be you. How come you to be here? Did you follow us?' He was making a valiant effort to speak normally, but it was obvious he was in pain.

'Yes. And it is as well I did. You need a doctor…' She started to rise, but he reached up with his good hand and pulled her down again. She almost fell on top of him. His lips were on hers before she could even draw breath.

Unwilling to hurt him, she did not struggle, and then she realised she did not want to. His mouth was warm and sensuous on hers, making her insides stir with a strange uncontrollable heat, which spread from her fluttering heart to her belly and down, down to her groin. She had never been kissed like that before, had never been kissed by any man that she could remember; neither of her stepfathers would have dreamed of kissing her, except perhaps an affectionate peck on the top of her head when she pleased them.

This was different—so different, she was lost to time and place. There was no hard ground beneath them, no blood-stained shirt between them, no onlooker in the shape of Frank Upjohn, no horses snuffling impatiently nearby, nothing but their two selves, floating on a cloud.

He released her at last. 'My poor sweet, what have I done to you?'

'Me?' she queried, her voice thick with the sensuality of what had happened. 'You have done nothing to me. It is you who are wounded, but Mr Upjohn will not fetch a doctor.'

He smiled. There had been no histrionics, no protestations of outrage, no maidenly blushes. She ought to have been scandalised; she ought to have been angry. Instead she was looking at him with loving, innocent eyes. He was a cur and deserved to be whipped. But somehow he could not form the words to apologise; apologies would spoil the moment, make it sordid and wrong and it had been neither. It had felt so right.

'I should hope not,' he said cheerfully to cover the depth of his emotion. 'I have Frank. He's a great one with wounds, is Sergeant Frank Upjohn. It will not be the first time he has bound me up.'

Frank came back with the bandage and began staunching the fresh flow of blood and securing the pad over the hole. 'Raise him up,' he commanded Molly. 'I have to get this round him.'

She did as she was told, putting her arm about Duncan and helping him to sit up, while Frank bound him tightly. 'There! That should hold it.'

'Good. Now help me up, old friend.'

'You think you can ride?'

'Well enough to reach Foxtrees.'

'Good idea. They will look after you.'

'Oh, I do not intend to go up to the house and embarrass them all,' Duncan said, grunting with pain as Frank stooped and lifted his good arm to put it round his shoulders and haul him to his feet. 'There is a deserted gamekeeper's cottage in the grounds. It is almost derelict but it will serve until I have recovered a little…'

He was standing now, but leaning heavily on his friend. His face, beneath the early morning stubble, was grey, his eyes too bright. He forced himself to stumble towards the horses. 'Get me up on Caesar, Frank, then go to your wife. When she wakes and finds we have all disappeared, there is no telling what she will do. The last thing we want is a hue and cry made of it.'

'Later. First we must find that cottage you spoke of.'

'It is only a five-minute ride. I can manage.' Mounting his horse set his shoulder bleeding again and he was all but fainting. 'Come,' he said, gritting his teeth and turning his horse deeper into the wood, followed by a watchful Frank.

Molly ran back to Jenny, hauled herself without decorum or elegance into the saddle, glad that Jenny was a good-natured beast and stood still for her. Her heart was racing and her hands trembling. This had been a night to remember, when she had been kissed for the first time. Oh, it had been magical. Nothing had prepared her for the sensations it had caused in her body, sensations over which she had no control—the tingling, the trembling, the warmth washing over her, the virile smell of him, the taste of his mouth, her own involuntary response. At that moment, nothing on earth would have prevented her from following him.

Chapter Eight

He turned in his saddle and gave her a quirky smile, as if to reassure her, before facing forwards and plodding on. His back was ramrod-straight, but she could guess the effort it was costing him to remain in the saddle and half expected to see him thump to the ground with every step the horse took.

She followed, every sense heightened by what had happened. It was as if the sun had exploded into a million pieces which were showering down on her in brilliant splinters of exquisite pain. She was vibrantly alive. If he had not been wounded and if she had not been so worried about him, she could have sung with joy.

Was she in love? But it was nothing like the love she had read about in the romantic novels she devoured. Indeed, if a man had tried to kiss the heroine of those pages in that way, she would have flown into the boughs, shouted for help, considered herself ruined. Was that why Captain Stacey had smiled? He was undoubtedly experienced in these matters and she was not.

On the other hand he was injured and only half conscious,

that was it—he had not known what he was doing. When he recovered he would be ashamed, apologise, swear never to let it happen again. And she would be the poorer. How confused she was and yet how unbelievably happy.

A five-minute ride, he had said, but that was five minutes for a healthy man who could canter. They had been riding slowly along this woodland path for at least ten.

And then suddenly the trees thinned out and there was another clearing in front of them. The sun had come up while they had been in the wood and now it bathed a little flint and stone thatched cottage in its light and warmth. It was a haven, even though all the windows were broken and weeds choked the flowerbeds.

Duncan slipped from the saddle and was caught by Frank who had dismounted as soon as they stopped. 'He's out again,' he said, picking the heavy man up and staggering with him into the little house. Molly followed.

Most of the furniture had been taken out; there was nothing but a broken chair and a slatted bed. A cupboard door stood open to reveal empty shelves. Frank lowered his burden onto the bed.

'Now go,' Duncan commanded, coming to his senses. 'Molly will look after me.'

'That I doubt. She is a young lady, unused to such things, and it is hardly…'

'Fitting?' Duncan finished for him. 'This is not the time to worry about decorum. Molly will do very nicely. And think of your wife, waking up in a strange inn all alone. She will be frightened or angry or both—you know better than I which it will be—but either way it ought to be avoided. Take my purse from my saddle and pay our dues and bring her back here. We will decide our next move when you return.' The effort of speaking left him breathless.

Frank turned to look at Molly. 'You think you can manage him? The ride has started him bleeding again and he needs a fresh bandage and something to drink, though heaven knows where you will find either without going to the house. And don't let him roll about, especially if he gets feverish…'

'Frank, go!' Duncan commanded. 'That's an order.'

As soon as his friend had gone, the wounded man sank back onto the bed and closed his eyes. Molly watched him fighting insensibility and knew he would succumb before long. She knelt beside him and took his good hand. 'Captain, what do you want me to do?'

'I want you to cease calling me Captain. My name is Duncan. Haven't we been together long enough for you to know that?' It was said slowly and breathlessly.

'Yes, Ca… Duncan. But where am I to find bandages and food and drink?'

'You have a petticoat under that skirt, haven't you?'

'No. Breeches.'

He gave a short laugh which turned into a grunt of pain. 'I might have known.'

'I can tear the hem off my habit. It is too long anyway, but I fear it is not very clean.'

'There is a well outside. Find a bucket. There's a drinking cup in my saddlebag…'

She ran outside to do as he suggested and was soon back with a bucket of sparkling, cold water. 'Here it is…' She stopped. He was unconscious again.

She tried to tear the hem off her skirt, but it was well stitched and she could not make a start. Looking round, she saw a shard of broken window glass and used that like a knife. Once the tear was begun it was the work of a moment to rip the rest. She stood there with her skirt barely reaching her calves and smiled. Indecorous or not, she was better without it.

She took it off, tore it into strips and immersed them in water. While he was still unconscious she peeled off the old dressing and washed the wound, trying not to notice his bare chest, with its dusting of dark hairs. The wound began to bleed again as she worked but she made a pad of damp material and bound it tightly with dry strips.

He moaned a little and murmured incomprehensibly. 'Be still,' she said, trying not to sound frightened. It would not do for him to think she was afraid of a little blood. 'I have nearly finished.'

She left him to throw away the pink-tinged water, clean the bucket and draw more from the well. She fetched his saddlebag from Caesar and found the drinking cup which she filled with fresh clean water and took to the bed.

'Here, drink this.' Putting her hand under his head, she raised it to help him to drink.

'Thank you.' He sank back again, but he looked more alert. 'My ministering angel.'

'Oh, no, for I am entirely ignorant of what to do. I still think you should have a doctor.'

'Why?' He smiled, touching the bandage. 'He would do no more than you have done and dose me with some foul concoction which would do nothing but make me sleep. And he would demand excessive payment for keeping his mouth shut. Duelling is illegal.'

'Oh.' She paused. 'Then why did you do it?'

'Sometimes a man has no choice.'

'He impugned your honour?'

'Not mine. I could have waived that without too much regret, but when someone I hold dear is insulted...' He stopped, fidgeting to make himself more comfortable. 'This bed is devilish hard.'

She rolled up what remained of her habit and put it gently behind his shoulder. 'A lady?'

'Never you mind. It is not for you to know.'

'And I think it is very uncivil of you to have secrets from me. Especially after…'

He reached out and took her hand. 'After I kissed you? Does that make a difference? Has the world stopped turning because of it? Am I no longer your reluctant escort?'

'You cannot escort me anywhere now,' she retorted, stung into retaliating. 'But perhaps that is what you wanted, though it seems to me a risky way of ducking out of it. Asking to be shot!'

He chuckled suddenly. 'That's what Frank said.'

'You should have listened to him. And if you are in pain, then you are well served. I have no sympathy.'

He looked at her for several seconds, his eyes moving over her face as if reading the expressions that flitted across it: perplexity, because she had not meant to be so acerbic, worry, anger, concern. There was real anxiety in her blue eyes. A tear glistened on her lashes and she blinked hard to dispel it, making it roll slowly down her grubby cheeks.

He lifted his good hand and wiped it away with the back of his finger, making her shiver. 'I am sorry, my dear. I have not served you well, have I? I have dragged you about the countryside, compromised you, taught you to prevaricate and gamble, and now this.' He looked about the tumbledown hovel. 'Is this adventure enough for you?'

'More than enough,' she said crisply. 'Adventure is all very well, when it is no more than a lark and no one is hurt by it. But this is altogether more serious. I was afraid you would die…'

'It will take more than a pinprick to kill me, Molly.'

'It is more than that, and if it should fester or you develop a fever, what must I do?'

'Neither is likely.'

'You said something about a house…'

'Did I? I must have been dreaming.'

'No, you were wide awake. And Mr Upjohn thought we might obtain help there.'

'No. And I forbid you to go. I need you here.'

'But you need proper bandages and food and drink.'

'Not so much that I cannot wait until Frank returns. He will bring all we need.' He looked quizzically at her. Even with her dirty, blood-smeared face and her hair in a tangle, she was beautiful, and the breeches she wore outlined her firm young thighs and tiny waist. It was as well that every movement was painful or he would be tempted to take her in his arms again and declare his love for her. 'Are you afraid I will kiss you again?'

She felt the colour flare into her cheeks. 'No, I think you were not yourself and did not know what you were doing.'

'Oh, I did, believe me. The temptation was too much to resist, but I apologise unreservedly. It will not happen again.'

Which was not at all what she wanted to hear.

A silence fell between them and a few minutes later he fell asleep. She sat on the edge of the bed, watching the rise and fall of his chest, the twitching of his nose and lips, as if he was dreaming, and decided he was not about to die. The terrible tension she had been feeling ebbed away, leaving her exhausted. She could not keep her eyes open. For want of anywhere else to lay her head, she stretched out beside him and in seconds was slumbering.

That was how Frank and Martha found them, her arm

flung across him, her head nestling in the crook of his good arm.

'Disgraceful!' Martha said, but Frank only smiled knowingly and bent down to touch Molly's arm.

She woke instantly and sat up, looking round, wondering for a moment where she was. 'Oh, Mr Upjohn, you are back.' She scrambled from the bed, her face on fire with embarrassment.

'Yes. How is the patient?'

Molly turned to look at Duncan and a slow smile lit her face. 'I think he will do. I think he will do very well.'

Duncan woke at the sound of her voice. Forgetting his injury, he tried to sit, and winced when it hurt him. 'Damn this confounded shoulder; it is as stiff as a board.' He looked up at Frank. 'Any trouble?'

'If you mean did I see Brancaster's son and heir, no, I did not, though I do not doubt you have made an enemy there. You humiliated him in front of his cousin and his valet and he will not easily forget it.'

'I am quaking in my boots.'

'It is not a matter for jest. You might not be so lucky the next time.'

'At the moment we have more important matters to deal with.' They must reach London before that Runner caught up with them.

'I've brought food and drink and Martha has some salve in her bag which will help your wound.'

'Good. And the carriage?'

'Outside.'

'Then the sooner we are on our way again the better.'

'Not today, surely?' Molly protested. 'You are not well enough…'

'I say when I am well enough and my first concern is

to see you safely into the hands of your mama. We have dallied too long.'

Molly was disappointed. He really was wishful of being rid of her, after all, and she had hoped… She pulled herself up short; she did not know what she had hoped. 'You are singing a different tune from the one I heard the other day,' she said tartly. 'Nothing would serve then but we must go to Newmarket. You said you had not undertaken to go by the shortest route.'

'I have changed my mind. It is wonderful how a ball through the shoulder concentrates the mind. The sooner you are with your mama, the easier I shall be.'

'Amen to that,' Frank said, with feeling.

While they had been speaking, Martha had been taking the salve and some fresh bandages from her bag. She handed them to her husband and while he set about re-dressing Duncan's wound and putting the useless arm in a sling she fetched out a parcel of food: cold roast chicken, half a loaf and some little fruit tartlets.

Molly sat on the only chair and watched these proceedings. She was feeling rather glum but she could not explain why. Perhaps it was because Frank and Martha had taken over looking after her patient and there was nothing she could do for him, or perhaps it was because Duncan had made it very clear he did not want her and, if that were so, it had not been at all fair of him to kiss her.

What had the duel been all about? Someone else's honour, not the Captain's. A lady perhaps? The lady the Captain had spoken of, the one who had not returned his love? Had he, in the weakness caused by the wound, thought he was kissing her? Oh, how mortifying if that were so, for she had responded in a way which, thinking about it now, made her go hot and cold all over.

But he had seemed perfectly alert. Oh, she did not understand. She wished with all her heart he had not kissed her; they had been perfectly at ease with each other before that, and now there was a constraint between them and he did not seem to want to look at her.

After they had shared a frugal meal, the ladies went to the coach while Duncan changed his torn and blood-stained clothing for the biscuit-coloured pantaloons, blue superfine coat and canary-yellow waistcoat which he kept in his bag for those occasions when he needed to give the impression of being a man of means. Then Caesar and Jenny were roped on behind and Duncan joined her in the coach and they set off again.

Their progress was slow but that was to the good because Duncan, while pretending all was well, winced with every jolt.

'I wish I knew what you were duelling about,' Molly said.

'No need for you to know.'

'Was it about the carriage? Mr Bellamy didn't lend it to you, did he?'

'Yes, he did. Not willingly, I agree, but he did allow us to borrow it.'

'Then what was it about? You could have been killed.'

'That's what a duel is,' he said. 'One man trying to kill another.'

'Do you always reduce everything to the commonplace?' she demanded. 'You make light of even the most serious situation. I cannot believe it is not all a sham to cover your true feelings.'

'I have no feelings.'

'She must have hurt you very much to make you so bitter.'

'She?'

'The young lady you loved once. You said it had come to nothing.'

'Do you always store up things people tell you so that you may bring them out later to discomfit them?'

'I was not trying to discomfit you. I wish you to be perfectly comfortable. If you did not want me to speak of it, you should not have told me in the first place.'

'You are right. I must remember to hold my tongue in future.'

'But perhaps talking about it might help.'

'No.' He was very firm.

'What do you suppose has happened to Mr Bellamy?'

Her sudden change of topic startled him. 'Bellamy? I do not know. You saw what happened. He rode away.'

'Yes, and I am persuaded he was the one who stole the woman you loved. That's why you duelled with him, that's why you would not shoot him. It would have made her so unhappy and she would not have been persuaded to return to you. Why, I do believe it might have the opposite effect and drive her into Mr Bellamy's arms. On the other hand, if she thought you had desisted from firing at Mr Bellamy and put yourself at risk on account of her happiness, she would think more highly of you. She would know you were ready to die for her.' She stopped speaking suddenly. 'You are laughing again.'

'Oh, Molly, you are priceless. I do believe you could make a living as an author.'

'Do you?' she asked, diverted. 'Do you really?'

'Such an imagination! Such romantic notions!'

'Now you are bamming me.'

'No, not at all. I am full of admiration. Nothing seems to put you in a taking, not duels nor hold-ups, nor my grumpiness. You follow my lead, and pick up on everything I say, with the quickest wit imaginable. You have lied for me and you did not contradict when that scamp mistook me for Bellamy, you picked up the gun without the least distaste, you have dressed my wounds, and all that without quaking.'

'Oh, I was quaking, but I knew I must not let it show. The Colonel, one of my step-papas, always told me to stand firm and face my fears. He said it often when he was teaching me to ride.'

'And I collect you are a fearless rider.'

'I would not say that, but I enjoy riding and do not baulk at a fence unless it be very high.'

'Then how did you come to be thrown from a cantering mare?'

'When?'

'Why, the night we met. Jenny was hardly bucking, was she?'

'It was dark. The shadows of the trees…'

'And perhaps you were gulling me into believing you were hurt. I have seen no signs of it since.'

'I believe you are determined to quarrel with me,' she countered. 'It is not gentlemanly to question a lady's honesty.'

He laughed. '*Touché*, my dear. I apologise, for I would not for a second have been deprived of your delightful company since.'

She was confused. The compliments rolled easily from his tongue, almost as if he meant them, but he was also quick to upbraid her, to tell her she had no idea how to go on. He had kissed her as if he meant that too, but he had not denied the suggestion that Bellamy was the man who had stolen the woman he loved. And she did not know how she felt about that.

She did not think there was any hope of reaching London that day, but she did not mind. All at once it did not seem such a delightful prospect. She had forgotten how sharp her mother's tongue could be, how she disdained to notice her offspring unless it was to run errands or mend a tear in a petticoat or listen to the many difficulties she had had to contend with all her life. As if it were Molly's fault her father had died and her two stepfathers after him, and left them without a feather to fly with!

It would be much more fun to be a lady high toby and ride with the Dark Knight, taking from the rich to give to the poor and laughing at every attempt to bring them to book. Except, of course, that the Captain was not the Dark Knight; she had been glaringly abroad in thinking that. He was, as he had always maintained, nothing more than a scapegrace and a gamester. But there was more to it than that. Much, much more.

The memory of that kiss still warmed her. She was drawn to him, wanted to be close to him, to learn more about him, but sometimes he angered her so much she disliked him intensely. He was an enigma—a man with strange ideas about honesty, not averse to breaking the law and yet she knew instinctively that he was an honourable man.

She risked a peep at him from beneath the brim of her bonnet. He was sitting with his eyes shut, but the corners of his mouth were turned down as if he was in pain, which he probably was. He ought to be in bed, not racketing about the countryside.

He was not unaware of her scrutiny and wondered what she was thinking. Trying to decide when he spoke the truth and when he was hoaxing her, he supposed. But he didn't know that himself. He said things he did not mean, gave way to impulses that were far from gentlemanly and generally behaved in the rakeshame manner his grandmother had deplored.

But how could he change? He could not make himself into a man about town overnight. Or could he? Did he want to? What had he to offer someone like Molly? Adventure palled in the end and there was nothing else, no income worth the name, no title because he had relinquished it. Would he have done that if he had known Molly at the time? It was no good tormenting himself with that question; it was done and he had to live with the consequences.

How long would it be before retribution caught up with him? How many other Dark Knights were there riding about the countryside? They would all be tarred with the same brush. It was time he abandoned his scapegrace ways. His grandmother had offered him a way out, but was that fair on Molly, even if he did love her to distraction? It was because he loved her that he must part from her.

He must take her to her mother and quietly fade out of her life. He wished her happy. More than anything in the world, he wished her happy.

By the time they arrived in Great Chesterford his injury was hurting like the devil and he was more exhausted than he could ever remember being, except perhaps when he had been wounded and taken prisoner during the war. He was glad to abandon his earlier intention of reaching London that night and stop at the first coaching inn they came to, procure beds for them all and tumble into his.

'I advise you to do the same,' he said to Molly, bidding her goodnight on the landing outside her room. 'You look done in and you must not arrive in Holles Street looking not quite the thing.'

'Tomorrow?'

'Yes, my dear.' He was swaying on his feet. 'Tomorrow, your journey will be over.'

She did not know why the prospect of that depressed her. It was what she wanted, wasn't it?

She rose next morning and hurried downstairs. Frank was pacing up and down the parlour with a worried frown on his face. There was no sign of Duncan.

'Where is he? What has happened?' she asked breathlessly. 'Is he worse?'

'He started a fever in the night…'

'Then he must have a doctor, whatever he says to the contrary.'

'No, for I watched over him and the fever broke about an hour ago. He is sleeping now. I did not have the heart to wake him.'

'No, let him sleep as long as he can. There is no hurry.'

He did not agree. That Runner would tumble to the truth before long and they had to hand the evidence over to the War Department before Sir John caught up with them. Nor did he trust Bellamy to leave well alone. Duncan had tried to persuade him to go on ahead, but he would not leave him. He could only wait and hope. None of this could he explain to Molly; he had been sworn to secrecy.

She looked at him. 'You are exhausted, Mr Upjohn. You go and rest. I will watch over him.'

She went to Duncan's room and sat by his bed, watching him hour after hour, praying for his full recovery. He was breathing evenly and his colour was normal, so she was hopeful. But he must be an extraordinarily strong man to sustain a wound like that and still get up and travel for hours and then overcome a fever in so short a time. 'Let him get well,' she prayed. 'And I will never provoke him again.'

She dipped a cloth in a basin of water on the table by the bed and bathed his brow. He flung an arm out and muttered to himself but the words were unintelligible.

'Hush,' she said. 'Rest easy. You are safe and going to get well again.'

He opened his eyes slowly, smiling when he recognised her. 'All this for a kiss,' he murmured.

She felt her face go hot. 'It has nothing to do with that and it is unkind of you to remind me of it...'

'So it is. And I beg your pardon. Perhaps I was hoping...' He stopped suddenly.

'Hoping what?' she demanded.

'Nothing. What time is it?'

'Two o'clock.'

'Two!' He sat up with a jerk and winced when it hurt him. 'We must be on our way. Why did you let me sleep so long? Leave me, girl. Let me get dressed.'

'You ought to stay in bed at least another day.'

'Don't be foolish. I am perfectly well. Go on. Tell Frank to get the horses harnessed and saddled. I will join you in a few moments.' He had flung back the bedcovers and she fled in embarrassment.

Half an hour later, they were on their way again on the last lap of their journey. Frank had strapped Duncan's arm to his chest so that it would not be jolted, but apart from that he would not allow anyone to help him. He was pale and obviously in pain, but pretended it was nothing. Molly began to wonder what it was that was so urgent; she was sure it had nothing to do with taking her to her mama. He had been content with their leisured pace until the day before yesterday. But she had, at last, learned when to keep silent and leave him to his thoughts, and so she sat looking out of the window at the countryside as they passed, not speaking.

The excitement of the previous days and nights and her lack of sleep began to tell as the carriage rolled on, and, though she tried, she could not keep her eyes open. Her chin dropped and her head lolled. Duncan put his good arm round her shoulders and, with a little sigh, she nestled her head against his chest and slept.

For mile after mile he cradled her head, not even moving when his arm went numb. A little cramp was a small price to pay for her proximity, for the sweet smell of her hair in his nostrils, for her innocent trust. He would savour it while he could, for in a few hours he must relinquish her.

It was dark when the carriage pulled up outside the house in Holles Street and he woke her gently. 'We are here, Molly.'

She sat up with a start and tried to straighten her bonnet which was askew over one ear. 'Oh, dear, have I been asleep?'

'Yes. Come, we have arrived.'

'Already?' She peered out of the coach window at the house. There was a lighted flambeau at either side of the door and a light in an upper window, which was a relief for she had suddenly wondered if her mother might be from home.

He jumped down to open the carriage door and let down the steps, showing very little sign of his injury, except for the sling which held his arm to his chest. He held out his good hand to her, smiling reassuringly. 'Come, my dear, let us surprise your mama.'

Leaving Frank and Martha to wait with the carriage, he took her elbow to escort her to the door and knocked firmly. A moment later, the door was opened by a manservant who

stared at him in surprise as if he had been expecting someone else.

'Please tell Mrs Benbright her…' Duncan stopped. 'No,
tell her there is someone who urgently wishes to speak with
her.'

'Mrs Benbright is preparing to go out.'

'She will see me. I have come from Stacey Manor with a
package for her.'

Molly, who had come up behind him, chuckled at this, but
he reached back and took her hand, squeezing it so she lapsed
into silence.

'Your name, sir?'

'Stacey.'

The man knew the name of Stacey, for who in London did
not know of the Earl of Connaught and his pretty Countess,
though they had never graced the portals of Holles Street
before this, it being on the unfashionable side of Oxford
Street? Why they should choose to come visiting at this hour,
it was not his place to enquire, though his curiosity was
almost eating him alive.

He conducted Duncan and Molly to the withdrawing
room, where he left them to go in search of Mrs Benbright.
Duncan stationed himself in front of the firescreen, while
Molly wandered about the room looking at the furnishings
and ornaments.

There were two sofas upholstered in green brocade which
matched the curtains at the long windows. Several small
tables were set against the walls upon which were arranged
small china ornaments. There were several high-backed
chairs with spindly legs and, in an alcove, a shelf full of
books, which was a surprise to Molly, for she had never
known her mother to read anything but the *Lady's Magazine*

and the *Ladies' Monthly Museum* which were full of gossip, fashion and serialised novels. She was inspecting the titles when the door opened and her mother came into the room.

Molly's first impulse was to run to greet her, but the sight which met her eyes made her stop where she was. Harriet was dressed in costume. Her pink gown had the most enormous hooped skirt which was caught up at intervals with ribbon bows, revealing a pale blue satin underskirt, white stockings and red satin shoes. The bodice of rose-pink and amber stripes was so tight, Molly wondered how she could breathe. Indeed, she must have been having difficulty in the direction because she almost fell out of the low *décolletage* with every rise and fall of her bosom.

She was wearing a white wig of gigantic proportions interlaced with ribbons, beads and feathers over her dark hair and there was a great deal of jewellery round her neck and upon her arms and fingers. A lace handkerchief peeped from the end of her ruffled sleeves and a quizzing glass and a fan dangled from her wrist.

'Tony!' she exclaimed. 'Is it really you? I thought when Perrins said it was Stacey he meant the Earl.'

'I thought you might,' he said, moving forward lazily to take her hand and bow over it.

'They said you were dead. We all believed you were dead.'

'I know.'

'You have given me quite a turn. I declare I shall have to sit down.' She fell into a chair and began vigorously fanning herself. 'Where have you been all this time? What have you done to your arm?'

'A slight accident, no more.'

'Does Hugh know you're back? Oh, what a mull that will make. Beth won't like it by half. Oh…' She stopped.

Molly looked from one to the other. Clearly her mother knew the Captain very well, but why had she called him Tony? And what did her mama mean about him being dead? He looked very much alive and in command of himself.

'Hugh does know and so does Beth, so you may rest easy,' he said. 'I ain't here to ask you to break the news to them.'

'Oh, thank heavens, for I should not like having to do that, and indeed should feel obliged to refuse. But what is to be done? Are you going to turn them out? You know they have a son?'

'Yes, I know, and I have no intention of throwing them out, no intention of appearing at Foxtrees at all. I am a ghost.'

'You look very substantial to me. I would go so far as to say very agreeably in countenance.' She stopped. 'Why are you here? Perrins said something about a package from Stacey Manor. There is nothing wrong there, I hope? Lady Connaught is not ill? Or Molly? Oh, do not tell me the tiresome child has caught measles or some such.'

'No, her ladyship is in plump currant,' he said, nodding towards Molly, who stepped away from the bookcase which had been half concealing her. 'And so is Molly, as you can see.'

'Molly!' her mother gasped. 'What are you doing here?'

Molly came forward and kissed her mother's cheek, aware that it was heavily rouged and powdered. 'I have come to visit you, Mama. It was so dull at Stacey Manor and the Captain was so good as to escort me here and we have had such adventures…'

'Dull? Escort? Adventures?' she repeated faintly, wafting her fan ineffectually. 'What are you prosing on about?' She stopped to look suspiciously at her daughter. 'You have not run away from Stacey Manor, have you? Oh, what will her ladyship think of you, you ungrateful wretch? Tony Stacey,

I am surprised at you conniving in this. I knew you for a scapegrace, but this… Have you run quite mad?'

'It is not the Captain's fault,' Molly put in quickly. 'He was a most reluctant escort but I persuaded him that Aunt Margaret would not mind. And now I am here he will leave me with you.'

'And what am I supposed to do with you?'

Molly was very near to tears; this was not the welcome she had hoped for. But it was her own fault; she should not have arrived unannounced. 'I hoped you would let me stay with you,' she said. 'I should be no trouble. I should so like to see something of the town and go out and about with you.'

'Trouble! Trouble is nothing to it. You are enough to give me a seizure, arriving on the doorstep like a stray kitten. Look at you! Such a bedraggled chit I never did see. I cannot take you out looking like that and I certainly cannot afford to tog you out.'

'Captain Stacey has been so good as to provide me with a wardrobe.'

'Stacey?' She went into peals of laughter. 'What does he know of ladies' fashion? He is a single man and a soldier to boot.'

'I think they suit me very well.'

'So they might, for you will not be going out into Society…'

'But, Mama…'

'No more. I told you months ago that it would not be possible until next year. I explained it very carefully, so why did you have to throw away the only chance either of us will have on some cork-brained idea that I would welcome you?'

Molly choked back a sob. 'I should not be any trouble, Mama.'

Duncan could stand silent no longer, though he had promised himself he would not interfere but await developments. 'Miss Martineau, please do not distress yourself. Our arrival was untimely, that's all. Your mama has been taken by surprise.'

'That is the least of it,' Harriet put in tartly. 'I am going out. A long-standing engagement I cannot cancel. Nor will I for a wilful child who thinks she may order the world to suit herself.'

'Madam, I would as lief leave her with a dragon as you, but it is late and I suggest you give orders for a room to be made ready for your daughter and talk about it tomorrow,' he said. 'No doubt your escort will be here directly...'

The mention of her escort decided Harriet. She rang the bell for Perrins and instructed him to have Betty make up a bed for Molly in the green room. 'Tomorrow we will decide what is to be done with you,' she said. 'But not before the afternoon, for I do not expect to be home much before dawn and shall sleep late.'

Her orders had barely been given before they heard a knock on the street door and a few moments later the butler returned and announced the Marquis of Tadbury. If Harriet intended to tell Perrins to conduct him to another room to wait, she was thwarted because the gentleman himself followed the servant into the room and executed an exaggerated leg, sweeping his feather-decked hat off and bowing before her.

He was dressed as a cavalier, with a blue satin coat and a darker blue silk sash. There were frills at his throat and at his wrists and he wore a full-bottomed curly black wig. But what surprised Molly more than his costume was the fact that, in spite of being rather portly, he was so young. Why, he was younger than Captain Stacey!

'My love, you are in looks tonight,' he said, surveying Harriet's heaving bosom with more than a little interest. 'I shall be the envy of the whole *ton*.'

Molly's stifled laugh betrayed her presence and he looked round in alarm to find himself being subjected to the scrutiny of two merry blue eyes and two sardonic brown ones. 'You are not alone?'

Harriet sighed. 'May I present Miss Margaret Martineau? Molly, this is my friend, the Marquis of Tadbury.'

Molly curtsied demurely, conscious of her bedraggled appearance and wishing she could have been spared the encounter until she had been able to refresh her wardrobe. She supposed that was why her mother had not introduced her as her daughter.

He bowed. 'Miss Martineau, your obedient. I do not think I have come across the name before.'

'No, you would not,' Harriet said quickly before Molly could reply. 'She has lately come up from the country with my cousin, Captain Stacey.'

Duncan inclined his head in a curt nod. 'Your servant, sir.'

'Stacey,' the man repeated. 'Not one of the Connaught Staceys?'

'A distant connection,' Duncan said laconically.

The Marquis turned to Harriet. 'I did not know you were related to the Staceys, my love.'

'It is only very distant,' she said, her cheeks flaming beneath the *maquillage* she wore. 'It hardly signifies. I really think we should be leaving or Lady Bonchance will think we are not coming. It is excessively impolite to arrive after everyone has gone in.'

'You are right. Let us be off. My carriage is only a pace or two down the street—couldn't bring it to the door for the barouche standing outside. Is that yours, Stacey? Damn fine set of bloods in the shafts.'

Duncan smiled. 'Yes, aren't they?'

'Take them off your hands if you ever think of selling.'

'I have had numerous offers for them, but they are not for sale,' Duncan said. 'But you have reminded me that they have been standing too long. I will take my leave of you.'

Harriet turned to Molly. 'Bid the Captain goodnight, Molly, and then go to bed. You look done in.'

Molly would have liked Duncan to stay for a little while and talk to her. She was feeling confused and unhappy. Nothing was as she had expected but then when she asked herself what she had expected, she had no answer. The one she had given the Captain when he had asked the same question seemed trite and foolish.

She smiled a little wanly. 'Goodnight, Captain. I am much obliged for your escort.'

He took her hand and raised it to his lips, looking into her sad little face and wishing he could put the smile back on it. 'It was my privilege, Miss Martineau. Perhaps I may give myself the pleasure of calling on you tomorrow?'

'Not before three o'clock at the earliest,' Harriet put in. 'In fact, I would as lief you did not come at all tomorrow. I shall not rise before noon, I am engaged for tea, and in the evening I go to Almack's, and I cannot allow you to visit Molly unchaperoned.'

'I am sorry, Captain,' Molly whispered. 'Perhaps another time?'

'Yes, of course,' he said, though he could cheerfully have strangled Harriet. She had been less than pleased to see her daughter and he would not be at all surprised if she packed her back to Stacey Manor on the next available coach. How disappointed Molly would be! She had set her heart on seeing something of London Society and finding the husband of her dreams. He was not that man, he told himself. She was looking for someone younger and more in keeping with her romantic notions.

Having discharged his duty as the reluctant escort, he should put her from his mind. He smiled at her, a secret smile of sympathy. 'Goodnight, my dear.' And then he said, in a whisper only she could hear, 'Keep your ginger up. Tomorrow, I am sure all will be well.'

She watched him leave with her mother and the Marquis, heard the front door slam and both carriages driving away, and she was alone. She sank onto one of the sofas, realising that her mother had not offered the Captain any refreshment, nor her either, but Mama must have been so taken by surprise, the proper civilities had quite deserted her.

She looked up when the door opened and a young woman in cap and apron came into the room. 'I'm Betty, miss,' she said. 'I'm to take you to your room.'

'Thank you. But I am very thirsty and a little hungry. It was a long journey…'

'Bless you, miss, I thought you must have dined long ago, it being so late. There ain't much in the house, for Mrs Benbright don't eat in very often, but I dare say I can find some cold chicken and some bread and cheese, though I don't think you should eat cheese late at night, miss, on account it will give you nightmares.'

'The chicken will do very nicely, if you please. And perhaps a dish of hot chocolate?'

'I'll tell Cook and bring it up to your room. Now, if you'll follow me, I'll show you where that is.' She led the way up a second flight of stairs, chattering all the while. 'Goodness knows why her ladyship should put you in the green room, it being right at the back of the house, so far from her own, and such a sickly colour. But there, you won't be disturbed by the traffic in the street, nor Mrs Benbright coming home in the early hours, so like as not you'll sleep well there.'

'Her ladyship?' Molly queried.

'Mrs Benbright.' She giggled. 'That's what we call her behind her back, but like as not we'll be saying it to her face before long if the Marquis comes up to the mark…'

'I am not sure you should be calling her anything behind her back,' Molly said. 'It is disrespectful.'

'Oh, well, if you are going to be stiff about it, I'll say no more,' Betty said. 'But there's only the three of us and if you're to work here we must all get along and be friends.'

'I did not come here to work,' Molly said. 'Mrs Benbright is my mama.'

'Your mama?' Betty repeated incredulously. 'We never knew she had a daughter. She never said so.'

'There is no reason why she should,' Molly said. 'I do not imagine it is the done thing to discuss one's private business with servants.'

'Beg pardon, miss, I'm sure,' Betty said stiffly. 'Is there anything else you need?'

'No, thank you.'

Molly was so bewildered and exhausted and the candle the maid had left with her was so feeble, she saw very little of the room, except the bed. But her trunk had been brought up and stood against the wall, and she found her nightgown, undressed and slipped between the sheets. By the time Betty came up with the food and hot chocolate, she was already asleep.

Chapter Nine

Duncan, having watched the Marquis's ornate town coach drive away, turned to give Frank instructions to see that the carriage and horses were safely stabled and then find lodgings for himself and Martha. 'Meet me tomorrow morning at eleven at Stephen's Hotel in Bond Street,' he told him.

'Where are you going, Captain?'

'Home, Frank, home.' He untied Caesar and hauled himself one-handed into the saddle and picked up the reins. 'We will decide our next move tomorrow.'

'Are you fit to ride, sir?'

'Yes. Don't worry. It's not far. Goodnight to you both and my grateful thanks for all your help.'

He rode slowly towards Bond Street, glad to be alone. He was unaware of his surroundings, and the late-night traffic on the road; his mind was full of Molly. She had been delightful company, enjoying her adventure, teasing him with her seriousness one minute and her merriment the next, unconscious of the peril she was in. She had been cheerful and stoical, putting up with his temper and never complaining when he left her to play cards, nor when he insisted on travelling through the night. She had accepted whatever food he provided and was inordinately pleased with the few fripperies he had bought for her and seemed to thrive on risk. All for the sake of a Season.

But would her mother grant her wish? And if she did not, what madcap scrape would Molly get herself into? The capital was full of unsavoury characters and not all of them among the lower orders. She would never be able to distinguish honesty from treachery, gentleman from rogue, unless there was someone with her to point out the pitfalls. He found himself envying the young bloods who would be sure to flock about her once she had been seen about town. It wouldn't hurt him to stay for a few days to see how she fared.

His grandmother was right; it was time to put the past behind him and make a new life for himself. Now his mission had been accomplished, he could not go back to being a ne'er-do-well. He was not a criminal. But he ought to tell Hugh of his plans. They might meet socially and the last thing he wanted was to embarrass his brother and sister-in-law. He did not know how he felt about seeing Beth again, but he could not hide himself away for the rest of his life. He had done no wrong. He grinned ruefully; if you didn't count highway robbery, of course.

He turned Caesar towards Berkeley Square and five minutes later was sitting outside Connaught House, looking up at its façade. He was almost relieved to discover the knocker off the door. The family, so he was informed by an astonished Mr Birtwhistle who admitted him, were still in the country and not expected until later in the Season and there was only himself and the housekeeper in residence.

'No matter,' Duncan told him airily. 'Not stopping. Came for my mail. It has been kept for me?'

'Yes, sir…my lord.' The butler was clearly agitated.

'Captain,' Duncan corrected him. 'Captain Stacey will do very well.'

'My lor… Captain,' he amended. 'I didn't rightly know what to do about the mail; some of it came from the War Department. I left it in the library for the Earl to… Oh, dear… We thought you were dead.'

'Yes, I know. But as you see…' he spread his good arm '…apart from a slight injury, which is healing well, I am in the best of health.'

The man made an effort to recover. 'Would you like some refreshment, my lord?'

'Captain,' Duncan corrected him again. 'Yes, I should like something to eat and a glass or two of wine, while I go through my correspondence.'

He made a good meal and drank half a bottle of claret which he owned was very good; his father had always kept a good cellar and it seemed Hugh was following in his footsteps. He was feeling decidedly mellow by the time the butler came to clear the table and put a bottle of the best French brandy and a fresh glass in front of him.

'Tell me, Birtwhistle, how is everyone? In plump currant?'

'Yes, sir, very well. The young viscount is a delightful child.'

'Oh, yes,' Duncan mused. 'I had forgotten him for the moment. Viscount Stacey, the son and heir.'

'Sir, may I ask a question?'

'Fire away.'

'What do you intend to do? I mean, should I inform the…um…Earl that you are back and have been here?'

Duncan smiled. 'My brother knows I am back, Birtwhistle, and as for what I mean to do I am not exactly sure, but I'm not about to upset the apple cart if that's what's worrying you.'

'Thank you, sir. Will you be staying, sir?'

He could not resist the prospect of spending at least one night in a comfortable bed in his old home, and as his brother was not in residence he could see no harm in it.

Later, lying on a feather mattress in the big four-poster in the second best bedroom, he took stock of his situation and the euphoria left him.

This large, fashionable house should have been his London home and, if he liked to kick up a dust, it still could be. He could bring Molly here as his countess. It was ironic that if it had not been for that trick of fate which had deprived him of his inheritance he would never have been sent to Norfolk, never become the Dark Knight, never met Molly, never known the sweetness of a single kiss, the music of her inconsequential chatter, never succumbed to her scolding. That bullet had expunged all his old bitterness, leaving him cleansed of acrimony, a new man. Beth was not the woman for him, but Molly was.

She had come to London with the express purpose of finding the romantic husband of her dreams, though he was sure she had little idea of what that really meant. The thought of anyone else enlightening her filled him with helpless fury. He did not want her to marry anyone unless it was himself. But could he ask her to marry him when he was not the hero of her fantasies and had neither title nor wealth to offer her? He could not force his way back into Society now, could not take back what he had freely given. Would she settle for less? Had he the right to ask it of her?

The next morning, in his best uniform, he entered the imposing portals of the War Department and spoke to the man on guard. 'Captain Stacey to see Colonel Gadsby.'

The man disappeared along a corridor and returned to conduct him to the Colonel's room, where he flung open the door and announced him in a strident voice.

'Tony!' The Colonel, a huge man with long dark curls and a pointed beard, left the desk behind which he had been sitting and hurried forward, hand outstretched. 'I did not know you were back in town.'

Duncan grasped the hand. 'Arrived late last night, sir.'

'Sit down, Captain. How did it go? I see you sustained an injury.'

Duncan sat in a chair near the desk and the Colonel resumed his seat behind it. 'Oh, that came later, sir. It is nothing but a scratch.'

'But you did obtain the proof we need?'

'Yes, sir, though the man was no flat; he was suspicious of everyone. His house was like a fortress and his servants close-lipped. I could not have done it without Sergeant Upjohn. He obtained a position as a groom and managed to get into the house—something I could not have done because Sir John was bound to recognise me. Frank learned there were documents kept in a chest, but he could find no opportunity to search for them.'

Duncan had met Sir John Partridge when working as an agent in France. The man had come over from England in the middle of a war, as bold as you please, to negotiate the sale of guns and ammunition to the French army. At the time Duncan had been pretending to be a sympathetic American and was serving as an interpreter in the French intelligence service. He could do or say nothing without blowing his own cover, but as soon as he'd returned home he'd reported what he knew.

As a result, he had been asked to find documentary proof

a task he was more than happy to undertake, even without the added inducement of a reward. It was fortuitous he had run into Frank when he'd tracked the man to Norwich. Frank's help had been invaluable and if, at the same time, it had saved his sergeant from a life of crime, then it was a double blessing.

'Just when we began to think we were at a stand,' he went on, 'my sergeant learned he was making a journey to Cromer and taking his strong box with him.' He paused and then chuckled. 'We became high tobies.'

He reached in the pocket of his frockcoat and withdrew a bundle of documents which he handed to the Colonel. 'I think this is what you are looking for: letters, bills of lading, receipts. There is enough evidence there to convict him a hundred times over and the beauty of it is that he does not know he was robbed for those. He thinks it was the gold the scamps were after and has been making strenuous efforts to have the doers of the deed caught and brought to book before they realise the significance of what they have.'

The Colonel spent a few moments scanning the contents of the documents, before looking up and smiling at Duncan. 'You have done well, Captain. It will give me a great deal of personal satisfaction to see the traitor hang.'

'Indeed, sir. Publicly, I hope, so that everyone knows his treachery.'

'There will be a trial. We must allow him that. But what happened to the gold? I gave no orders for anything else to be confiscated.'

'No, sir, but if we had left him with his blunt he would have wigged what we were about. It was put to good use. We distributed it among needy ex-soldiers. It seemed a kind of rough justice.' He said nothing of Mr Grunston, the slave trader; that episode had been well outside his remit and just showed how far he had gone along the road of the ne'er-do-well.

'Did it indeed? I think perhaps I will conveniently forget you told me that. If there is a fastener out on you, I do not want to know about it.'

'Oh, I do not think anyone will make the connection,' he said, smiling. 'There are so many scamps about these days calling themselves the Dark Knight.'

'Quite so. What are you going to do now? Ain't it time you found yourself a filly and settled down?'

'I doubt anyone would have me,' he said with a wry smile. He was no nearer finding a way of making a living that did not involve gambling and though, for the most part, he was very successful at it, it was no way for a man wishing to marry to go on.

'I wish you luck, whatever you do,' the Colonel said. 'There is, as I told you at the outset, a considerable reward. will make sure a draught is taken to your bank by the end of the week.'

'Thank you, sir, but I wish half of it to be sent to Sergeant Upjohn. If possible I would wish him to be absolved of complicity in any illegal acts while acting under my instructions in this matter.'

'I think that can be arranged.'

Duncan thanked him, bowed and took his leave. He met Frank and Martha as arranged, paid them what little money he had and sent them home in Lord Brancaster's coach. 'Take it back to him,' he said. 'Thank him for its use and tell him will compensate him for any inconvenience. And you will hear from Colonel Gadsby yourself.' He smiled. 'It will be enough to start you off in a little business of your own.'

He brushed aside their gratitude and watched them go. I

was too early to call on Holles Street and as Caesar needed exercise he set off for Hyde Park. Avoiding the carriageway and the ride, he made for the wide area of grass beyond the lake and allowed the stallion to have its head. An hour later, he slowed to a walk and turned back to skirt the southern shore of the lake, making for the Curzon Gate.

The idea he had mentioned to his grandmother, that he might breed horses, had been growing slowly in his mind. After all, horses were always wanted for every kind of use—for riding, for carriage work, for the army; there was always a ready market for top quality animals. He knew a little about the subject and if he employed experienced help he felt sure he could make a success of it. Would Molly consent to be a farmer's wife?

It was daylight when Molly woke and the sun was shining through the curtains. She rose and drew them back to look out on a small back garden which had been untended for some time, judging by the length of the grass and the weeds in the borders among which a few flowers struggled to survive.

She had no idea of the time, but she was wide awake and anxious to explore her surroundings. There was water in the jug on the wash-stand and she washed quickly and dressed in the turquoise muslin gown Duncan had bought for her, brushed her hair and tied it back with a matching ribbon before leaving the room to find her way downstairs.

The house was very quiet and she supposed her mother would be as good as her word and would not rise before noon. Not wanting to disturb her, she crept along the upper corridor towards the stairs. Once in the hall, she opened all the doors one by one and peeped into the rooms. There were not many for it was not a big house.

There was the drawing room she had been in the night before, where a tray containing an empty bottle and two used glasses told her that her mother had invited her escort into the house on their return. On the other side of the hall was a bookroom which was so tidy and smelled so musty, Molly was sure it was never used. Towards the back of the house was a breakfast parlour and another small sitting room.

She was standing, undecided what to do, when she heard voices on the other side of the door which evidently led to the kitchen. She opened it shyly and saw three servants sitting round a table—Betty, Perrins and a red-faced woman in a large apron whom she took to be the cook. They sprang to their feet when they saw her.

'We didn't know you were awake, miss,' Betty said. 'Mrs Benbright don't rise afore noon.'

'No, I know. But it is such a lovely day, I wanted to be up and about.'

'You will be wanting your breakfast.'

'A little tea and toast, if you please, and I will take it in the breakfast parlour. I see the table is laid up.'

She had just begun her meal when her mother wandered into the room in a puce silk peignoir which did nothing to enhance a pasty complexion brought about by too many late nights. Her hair was loose about her shoulders and her eyes were heavy.

'Good morning, Mama,' Molly said brightly, and noticed her mother wince. 'I did not think you would be awake yet.'

'Well, I am not sure that I am,' her mother said, sitting down opposite her. 'I am not at all sure this is not some horrible nightmare.'

'What is?'

'You arriving like that without a by-your-leave. And with

Tony Stacey too. There will be the most prodigious scandal, especially when the *ton* learns that his lordship is not dead at all…'

Before Molly could comment on this, Betty came in with a tray containing a pot of chocolate, a plate of buttered toast, a dish of hard-boiled eggs and a jar of conserve. She set it all on the table. 'I didn't you know were up, ma'am,' she said, addressing Mrs Benbright. 'Do you want me to fetch you anything else?'

'No, this will suffice, thank you.'

Betty disappeared reluctantly. 'Now I suppose they will have a fine time of it, discussing our affairs in the kitchen,' Harriet complained. 'As if I do not have enough to contend with.'

'What do you mean, "his lordship"?' Molly demanded. 'Whom were you speaking of? Not Captain Stacey surely?'

'Captain Stacey, as you call him, is an earl, or he would be if his brother had not usurped the title, thinking him dead. He has always been called Tony to distinguish him from his father for whom he was named and who died two years since. He is Duncan Anthony Stacey, Earl of Connaught.'

'Duncan is an earl?' Molly queried in astonishment. 'But he never gave me even the smallest hint. Nor did Aunt Margaret. She introduced him to me as Captain Stacey and she called him Duncan, not Tony…'

'She always did.'

'Oh, dear, I wish I had known. I have not always been civil to him and I never addressed him as anything but Captain.'

'You referred to him as Duncan just now.'

'Did I?' Molly felt her face flush. 'Oh, that is because he told me to use his given name.'

'Did he, now? And what else happened on this highly

improper journey to London? I collect you mentioned adventures.'

'Well, there were,' Molly said. 'But nothing unseemly occurred.'

'The whole escapade was unseemly,' her mother said irritably, taking a slice of toast and looking at it as if it might poison her. 'I wonder at Stacey embarking upon it. Unless he don't care for his good name any more.'

'I don't suppose he does, if his brother has been too hasty in taking it over. Is it any wonder he prefers to be an adventurer and pretend to be the Dark Knight, which I know now he is not?'

'Is that what he said he was?' Harriet asked, barely following the gist of what her daughter was saying.

'The Dark Knight? No, he denied it, and later when we were held up by the high toby ourselves and one of them as good as admitted he was the Dark Knight I knew he could not be. I do not know if I was glad of it or not, for the Dark Knight has a romantic reputation, but I should not like the Captain to be hanged for a scamp…'

'Molly, what are you saying?' her mother asked weakly. 'I begin to think all those romantical books you read have turned your head. Such a Banbury Tale I never heard.'

'I am sorry, Mama; I did not mean to displease you, but there is so little to do at Stacey Manor, and when the Captain came to see Lady Connaught and rode out in the middle of the night…'

'Middle of the night? You left in the middle of the night?' Her mother's voice was almost a squawk.

'Yes, but I had no thought of coming to you then; it was only later, when my horse threw me and the Captain took me to an inn to recover, it came to me that it would be a prodigious adventure to come to London.'

'He took you to a common inn?'

'Yes, but he behaved very properly. After that we travelled in a coach with four beautiful bays and were never without a night's lodging though I own he sometimes had to play cards to pay for it. And he insisted on Sergeant Upjohn's wife travelling with us...'

'Sergeant Upjohn's wife! You think a common soldier's wife is an adequate chaperon, do you? My life! You might as well have had none at all.'

'Mrs Upjohn is clean and respectable and very polite and...'

'Oh, that is the outside of enough! Captain Stacey, as you call him, has cut himself off from his family and left himself without a feather to fly with, so how could he afford to hire a coach and four?'

'He did not hire it, he borrowed it. It belongs to Lord Brancaster.'

'Lord Brancaster? Where does he come into it?'

'He doesn't, but we met his son, Mr Andrew Bellamy, and he was kind enough to lend us the carriage.' She was very careful not to say anything about the duel.

'If I had known this last night, I would certainly have called him to account for it. He has quite ruined your reputation and mine along with it. What Tadbury will say when he hears of it, I dare not imagine.'

'What has it to do with the Marquis?'

'Are you a sapskull, girl, that you can say that? I had all but got him to the point of proposing, but he will think twice of it when he realises what a scapegrace I have for a daughter.'

Molly found it difficult not to smile at the idea of the Marquis of Tadbury becoming her third stepfather. Why, he was nearer her age than her mother's! 'Surely there are others just as eligible?' she said. 'He looks so...so young.'

'I am tired of being married to old men, Molly; they have a tendency to die on me. And the Marquis is very rich and very careful of me, which so many men of the *haut monde* are not. And I fancy myself as a marchioness. You would not ruin it for me, would you?'

'Of course not. But I do not see that we have to tell the world how I came to London. You need only say your daughter has come to keep you company…'

'My daughter!' Harriet wailed. 'No one knows I have a daughter—or if they do they think she is no more than a child.'

'You will have to tell the Marquis some time,' Molly said with perfect logic. 'You cannot deny my existence if you mean to accept his suit.'

'Yes, I know, but I was going to lead up to it when I was sure of him. Now he will hear of it from Stacey, you may be sure.'

'The Captain won't say anything. My goodness, he was a most reluctant escort.'

'Not so reluctant as to refuse,' Harriet said with heavy irony.

'No, but the circumstances made it difficult for him. There was all that business when the stage was held up and being questioned by the watch and there not being another stage until the next day. And I persuaded him that it would be better if he travelled with a wife…'

'Wife!' shrieked Harriet. 'You mean to say you have been passing yourself off as Stacey's *wife*?'

'Only for one night, and he did not come to bed…'

'Enough!' Harriet said weakly. 'I do not want to hear any more of this. You have given me a megrim and I shall have to go and lie down again.' She left the room, the back of her hand to her forehead.

Molly sighed and took Miss Austen's latest novel from the

shelf, thinking to take it out to the garden, then changed her mind. She went to the kitchen and asked Perrins to send the potboy round to the mews to have Jenny saddled and brought to the door.

Returning to her room, she scrambled into the new habit which Duncan had included in his purchases in Norwich, pulled on her boots and set her feather-trimmed riding hat on her fair curls. Ten minutes later, having asked Perrins for directions, she was riding her mare down Oxford Street towards Hyde Park, completely ignoring the fact that she ought to have had an escort.

It was a lovely summer day, the sort of serene day when everyone should be happy. Indeed the faces of those about her seemed cheerful enough as they went about their daily business. An errand boy was whistling, a young man and a girl were deep in a conversation which was making them smile, a bird sang from its perch on a railing, ignoring the cat that was sunning itself on a step.

The shops were open and people passed in and out of their portals, carrying packages; phaetons and tilburys and curricles went up and down the busy street; a stagecoach rattled along, the guard tooting his horn to let the next stop know they were coming. Even the barefoot beggars called cheerily. Molly's spirits lifted as she rode. How could she despair when the world was such a lovely place?

She turned in at the gates of the park which was crowded with people in carriages of every description, all dressed in the latest mode, going at a sedate pace, nodding to acquaintances, stopping every now and again to exchange pleasantries and the latest *on-dit*. Were they talking about her? Her mother seemed to think they would be and it had worried her more than a little. According to Mama, reputations could be lost with a single word, or even no word at all, if someone of importance were to cut one dead.

The carriageway was divided from the ride by a fence. She found her way round it and set off at a trot to try and dispel the image of her and her mother being the subject of everyone's gossip. It was foolish, she told herself after a few minutes; no one knew who she was; her mother had taken care of that.

Her thoughts occupied her so completely she was unaware of the rider coming towards her until he pulled up in front of her, forcing her to stop. 'Why, I do believe it is Miss Martineau,' he said, doffing his curly-brimmed beaver and bowing from the waist.

'Mr Bellamy.' She inclined her head in acknowledgement while controlling Jenny, who objected to being reined in so unexpectedly.

'All alone?' he asked, looking about for her escort.

'As you see.'

He was dressed in a single-breasted coat of bath cloth and buckskin riding breeches tucked into tasselled topboots. His starched muslin cravat fell over the top of a yellow and black striped waistcoat, reminding her of a bumble bee. He was, she supposed, what was called a pink of the *ton*.

'Then please allow me to accompany you.'

'I am sure you have other things to do.'

'Nothing of more importance, my dear. I am at your service.'

Molly wasn't at all sure she liked him addressing her as 'my dear' but she did not comment. The Captain did it all the time and she assumed that was how young men went on in the *haut monde*. 'Thank you, sir, but I was thinking of turning back.'

'Not yet, surely? Riding is a pleasure on a day such as this we should take advantage of it, for tomorrow it may well be raining. Do you not agree?'

'Yes,' she said doubtfully, wondering whether she ought not to give him a set-down. But how could she do that when he had been so good as to allow them the use of his family coach? 'I did not thank you properly for lending us your carriage,' she said as he turned and walked his horse beside hers.

'Think nothing of it.'

'Oh, but I do! And for the Captain to call you out was not at all the thing.'

'How is the gallant Captain? No permanent damage done, I trust?'

'He was recovering well when I last saw him. But it was unkind of you to shoot him when he had refrained from firing.'

'One of us had to do something; we could not stand facing each other for the rest of the day. And I only winged him.'

'Why did he call you out?'

'Do you not know?'

'No, he would not say.'

'Then neither will I.' He smiled. 'Where is he? I am surprised he is not with you today.'

'I don't know where he is. He was only my escort for the duration of the journey to London, you know. I do hope you will not put any other interpretation on it.'

'If you say that was all there was to it, then of course I will not.' He reached out for her reins and drew both horses to a stop. 'Shall we walk a little?'

He jumped down and held out his hands to help her dismount. She looked about her, wondering whether she ought to comply, but none of the riders who were hacking up and down was paying them the least attention, so she slid from the saddle and stood beside him.

'There, that is better,' he said. 'We cannot converse properly across the backs of our horses.'

They walked side by side, leading their mounts, but she felt uncomfortable about it and wished she had given him the right about when he had first approached her. What would her mother say if she knew where her daughter was at that moment? Would she put it down to another of her embarrassing scrapes or would she be pleased that someone was fixing an interest in her?

'Miss Martineau, may I call on you?'

She pondered this for a moment. Calling meant no more than paying respects, after all. 'If you wish. Mama will want to thank you for the use of the carriage, I am sure. But I do not know how long I shall remain in town.'

'Not remain! Oh, how could you be so unkind as to give the world a glimpse of your loveliness and then disappear again? I declare it is cruelty of the most severe.'

She laughed at this piece of nonsense and answered lightly. 'Oh, sir, you put me to the blush.'

'And a very pretty blush it is,' he said, caressing her cheek with his finger.

'I think we should mount again,' she said, turning away in confusion.

'So soon?' He took her shoulders in his hands and turned her to face him. 'We have hardly had a chance to converse at all.'

She refused to look up and he put a finger under her chin and raised it so that she was forced to look into his eyes. She shivered apprehensively and he, aware of it, smiled. 'Are you afraid of me?'

'No. Should I be?'

'Not at all.' He lowered his mouth to hers but he had hardly touched her lips before she realised what was about to happen and pulled herself away. 'Mr Bellamy, I must go. Mama will be concerned.'

'Very well.' He sighed melodramatically. 'Another time perhaps, when we can contrive to be alone and you have learned to relax in my company.' He stooped and cupped his hands for her foot and in a moment she was in the saddle again where she felt more at ease.

They had almost reached the gate when she saw Duncan approaching on Caesar and her heart suddenly seemed to beat twice as fast as usual and her hands to shake. He was riding leisurely, as if he had all the time in the world. He could not have seen what had taken place, could he? Oh, she prayed he had not!

He reined in when they met. He looked very impressive in the uniform of a hussar and she wondered if he had rejoined his regiment. Did that mean she would not see him again? The thought made her suddenly sad.

'Miss Martineau, I hope I find you well?' he said, searching her face, trying to read she knew not what, but she felt the colour flare in her cheeks and it put her on the defensive.

'Very well, thank you, Captain.'

He turned to Andrew, forcing himself to be polite for Molly's sake. 'Bellamy. I did not know you were in town.'

'How could I resist, when this lovely lady is here? We have been having quite a coze, you know. Delightful.'

'I am sure.' Not by a flicker of the eye did he betray his deep concern. 'Molly, allow me to escort you home.'

'I have Mr Bellamy to escort me,' she retorted. 'And I do not remember giving you permission to call me Molly.'

'It seems you have been given your congé, Stacey,' Bellamy said with a wide grin which made Duncan want to hit him again. 'I should accept it with a good grace, if I were you.'

'Miss Martineau?' Duncan appealed to her.

In spite of feeling uncomfortable with Mr Bellamy, Molly objected to being treated like a child by Duncan and so she smiled and picked up her reins again. 'Please do not trouble yourself, Captain. Mr Bellamy will see me safely home.'

He could not insist and was obliged to withdraw. She was still chasing her dream, still looking for her romantic hero. Did she think she would find him in Bellamy? He was sure marriage was not on the young man's mind, not to Molly, who had neither pedigree nor fortune, and he was afraid he was more likely to offer her carte blanche. Would Molly have sense enough to realise what was happening before it was too late? He doubted it.

There was nothing for it; he must join the *haut monde* and set out to try and win her hand in the way she dreamed of. But if he stayed in town, who was he to be? Not the Earl of Connaught; that was no longer possible. He supposed that Molly's assumption that he was a distant cousin of the Staceys was as good an identity as any and one which would be easier to maintain than a complete fiction, especially as he had always been known as Tony as a child to distinguish him from his father. Duncan Stacey was not a name anyone in today's *haut monde* would recognise, except Harriet who had known him since he was in leading strings, and she was too busy furthering her own ends to spread tattle about him.

Molly's escort chattered inconsequentially all the way back to Holles Street in spite of the fact that she was, for the most part, silent. She had been very rude to the Captain and she was burning with shame. Did he really think she preferred Mr Bellamy's company to his?

He helped her dismount at the gate and escorted her to the door. 'Thank you for your escort, Mr Bellamy,' she said, holding out her hand.

'Oh, you do not mean to send me away without introducing me to your mama, do you? I have been looking forward to meeting her.'

'I am not sure she is at home.'

'I understand,' he said, grinning. 'You do not wish her to know you were riding out alone. Your secret is safe with me.' He took her hand and bowed over it. 'But I shall expect to be rewarded.'

'Rewarded? But I have no money…'

He laughed. 'It was not money I was thinking of, my dear, but the opportunity to ride with you again. I shall call on you and suggest it. Adieu, my fair beauty.'

He turned and mounted his horse, just as the door was opened by Perrins. She hurried inside and up the stairs to change out of her habit.

'Molly, where have you been?'

She looked up, startled to see her mother at the head of the stairs. As she was obviously dressed for riding, there was nothing for it but to tell the truth. 'For a ride, Mama; it was such a lovely day I could not resist it.'

'Alone?'

'I set out alone, Mama, but I met Mr Bellamy and he gave me his escort.'

Harriet sighed with exasperation. 'Go and change into something more suitable for a young lady at home and then come into my boudoir. We must talk some more.'

Molly obeyed and a few minutes later was seated watching her mother, who stood beside her bed contemplating what to wear for a visit to the theatre that evening. The choice was between a green taffeta, trimmed with pink silk roses, and a ruby-red velvet banded in black and white braid.

'Now tell me exactly what happened this morning,' she said

'Nothing happened, Mama. We met while riding and Mr Bellamy offered to escort me, nothing more.'

'Who else saw you?'

'There were a great many people about, but they did no take any notice of me. Why should they? They do not know me.'

'Thank goodness for that. But you will not do it again, do you hear me? Until I decide what is to be done, you wil confine yourself to the house and garden…'

'But, Mama…'

'I blame Tony Stacey. When he does decide to put in an appearance—which give me leave to doubt, for he is assured edly more concerned with his own pleasures than the ruined hopes of a young lady—I shall ring a peal over him for leading you astray.'

'Mama, that is unfair! He has not ruined my hopes and he did not lead me astray. He was always very proper and kind and generous. I told you that. If it had not been for him would have had no clothes…'

'Rags!' her mother said, referring to Molly's purchases and not the velvet gown she had just picked up and was eyeing critically. 'I could wear my rubies with this. But I am not sure they suit my colouring. What do you think?'

Molly was fairly sure her mother did not own any rubies and the necklace which lay on her dressing table was almos certainly fake. 'I think they would look very fine.'

'But the green shows off my figure better, does it not?' She stood up and held the taffeta gown against her ample bosom, then clad in amber sarcenet. 'And the emeralds have more sparkle. The same colour as my eyes.'

'Whichever you like, Mama. They are both beautiful.'

'Of course they are! I am known for my elegance and would not be seen in such dowdy things as those Tony Stacey bought for you.'

'Oh, I know they are not of the first stare,' Molly admitted, 'for I have been looking at the pictures in your *Lady's Magazine* and *La Belle Assembly*, but they suit me very well.'

'Oh, they are quite good enough for someone living in the seclusion of the country, which is where you belong. I cannot think why he did not take you straight back to Stacey Manor when he first found you.'

'I think he had arranged to meet Sergeant Upjohn and there was no time. They had business together.'

'I am beginning to wonder if he is this Dark Knight you spoke of, after all. It is the sort of rig he would get up to. I collect he was always falling into scrapes when he was a boy. I would not be surprised if he weren't playing some deep game of his own.'

Molly was inclined to agree but did not say so. 'He cannot be that bad for Aunt Margaret is very fond of him.'

'That don't mean he ain't up to something. Are you sure you have told me the whole?'

'Oh, yes, Mama.'

Harriet looked closely at her daughter, wondering if she was as innocent as she sounded. 'You have not set your cap at him, have you? You will come home by weeping cross if you have. I believe he is still repining for Beth Gooderson and has forsworn marriage.'

'You mentioned the name of Beth before,' Molly said. 'And he did admit there was someone who disappointed him, which was excessively unkind of her.'

'She thought he was dead, killed at the Battle of Vittoria or some such, so how was it unkind of her?'

'She married someone else?'

'She married his brother.'

'Oh, poor Duncan! His brother took his title and his love! No wonder he is sometimes a little out of humour.'

'What I should like to know is what he is going to do about it. There will be a farrago over it, to be sure, and I wish we had not got mixed up in it.'

'I am not privy to his intentions,' Molly said, with a spirit intended to hide her misery. 'But I'll wager he will do nothing. I think he will go back to a life on the road. I doubt we shall see him again.'

The thought of never seeing him again made her feel very, very sad, as if something sweet and wonderful had slipped from her grasp before she had managed to catch it properly. And trying to convince herself there had never been anything between them and that he had kissed her when he was not feeling himself, and that her life from now on would be full of new experiences and new excitement, did not work at all.

Chapter Ten

Duncan took his mount back to Connaught House and then went shopping, taking in Weston's to have pantaloons and waistcoats made up and to Scott for a new frockcoat; they had made his uniform and he liked their military cut. He went to Hoby's for boots and Locks for hats and finally dropped in at Robinson and Cook in Mount Street on his way back to order a phaeton. None of it would be ready before the end of the week and by that time the money from the War Department would be safely in his bank to pay for it. Then he set out for Holles Street.

Molly was sitting with her mama in the small parlour when Betty announced his arrival.

'Oh, he has come,' she murmured, and found her heart lifting with pleasure.

'Show him into the withdrawing room,' Harriet instructed Betty, and then said to Molly, 'Stay here. I wish to speak to the Captain alone.'

'Oh, Mama, you are not going to roast him, are you?'

'Naturally I am. He need not think that I will allow him

to play fast and loose with my daughter and do nothing about it.' And with that she swept out of the room.

The last thing Molly wanted was to be excluded from the conversation and she followed to listen outside the door.

'Your obedient,' Duncan said, sweeping Harriet a bow. 'I trust I find you well?'

'I would be better if you had not saddled me with that madcap of a daughter. She tells me you passed her off as your wife, and in a common tavern too.'

'She told you that?'

'Of course she did; she has no idea how to dissemble, as you must know by now. She is no more than an innocent child and has no idea how to go on in Society, but you should have known better. You have ruined her reputation and mine along with it.'

'Oh, I would not say that,' he said wryly. It was not that he was not sorry for what had happened, because no one regretted it more than he did, but he would be a sousecrown if he admitted that to Harriet, who had done more to ruin her daughter's hopes than anything he had done. 'No one will think anything of it if you take her out and about, which is all she wants. She has talked of nothing else since I met her.'

Molly, creeping to the door and putting her eye to the keyhole, saw her mother sitting on the sofa fanning her flushed cheeks and the Captain standing with his back to the hearth, looking down on her. He was still dressed in his uniform, which set off his broad shoulders and long, shapely legs.

'That will only make matters worse. If any of this is whispered over the teacups, we shall both be undone.'

'No reason why it should,' he said reasonably. 'I'm not about to noise it abroad and I'll wager you will not. As for

Miss Martineau, all she wants is for someone to pay her a little attention.'

'Then I suggest you do it.'

'Perhaps I will,' he said, so softly that Molly, on the other side of the thick door, could not hear it.

'But not in town, not where we will be the laughing stock of the *haut monde*. Take her back to Stacey Manor.'

'Ma'am, you shock me. How could I do that? It would be highly improper and, besides, she would be so disappointed.'

'It is no more improper than the way you brought her here. I think your disappointment over Beth Gooderson must have addled your brains. You cannot suddenly come to life again and think everything will go on as before. You should not be in town at all. I wonder at your audacity.'

'Oh, I have audacity and to spare, ma'am,' he said, smiling lazily. 'But there is no need for you to disturb yourself over it. I am a distant cousin of the Earl up from the country.'

'And you would do well to return there post haste before Beth comes to town. And take my daughter with you.'

'I cannot do that, ma'am; I have other engagements. Things to do, you know. Besides, she would not go.'

'She will do as she is bid.'

Duncan was not so sure. Molly had a mind of her own and if she decided she would not go, only tying her up and carrying her to a coach would make her budge. That was no way to treat her. She needed to be handled with affection and humour and persuasion—all attributes he had never pretended to have, though he was learning fast. 'Then you may look to someone else to take her back, ma'am, for I will not do it.'

Molly was near to tears. She crept away and climbed the stairs to her room and sat down on the bed to stare at the hideous green wallpaper. No one wanted her, not her mother, nor Captain Stacey, and she had been a ninny to think that she could turn up on the doorstep and all would be well.

Now she would never have the opportunity to wear that lovely ballgown the Captain had bought for her, nor would she go on picnics and to the theatre or to Almack's, which she understood was the height of acceptability. Her mother would go out tonight and she would be left behind, just as she had been at Stacey Manor.

She heard the front door shut behind the Captain and it was as if the door had been shut on her happiness. He would go back to his life on the road with Sergeant Upjohn, to have more adventures, while she would be sent back to Norfolk and her humdrum existence there until her mama remarried. If she remarried; it seemed that her unwelcome arrival might well have put that in jeopardy.

She heard her mother come up the stairs and looked up as she opened the door. 'There you are, child! I have told Tony Stacey straight what I think of his behaviour and given him his right about.'

'What did he say?'

'Very little to the point. Not even an apology.'

'He has nothing to apologise for. Mama, I wish you had not scolded him; you will give him an aversion to me, for he will think I wanted you to do it, and I do not at all wish him to think that. He was very brave and clever and saved my life…'

Harriet peered at her daughter. 'I was right. You *have* developed a *tendre* for him.'

'No, Mama, there is nothing but cousinly affection between us.' She was deceiving herself, she knew. The way she felt about him, the tingling sensation in her limbs when he touched her, the enchantment of his lips on hers which made her melt inside, was not a cousinly feeling at all.

'You noddicock! He will not marry you, even if I were to insist upon it, which I will not, for I would not saddle you with a rakeshame such as he is. You would do better to cultivate Andrew Bellamy.'

'Mr Bellamy!' Molly protested. 'Oh, Mama, no.'

'Now I am going to rest,' Harriet went on as if she had not spoken. 'I must be in looks when I go out tonight. Cook has instructions for your supper. Tomorrow we will sit down and talk about what is to be done.' She smiled suddenly. 'Do not look so Friday-faced; we will come about.' With that she was gone, leaving Molly to her tumbling thoughts.

Her mother's strange smile had disturbed her. Had Mama suddenly changed her mind about giving her a come-out? Molly's spirits lifted, but were as suddenly dampened. Two or three weeks before she would have been overjoyed at the prospect but now she was not at all sure she wanted it, if it meant she had to drop the handkerchief to Andrew Bellamy.

The dream of going into Society seemed hollow now, meaningless, a sham. She had grown up, just as Duncan had said she would. Duncan, Earl of Connaught, soldier, highwayman, rakeshame. She would rather be dashing about the countryside with him, taking risks, enduring discomfort, than be the finest, the most desirable young lady in town. But it was not to be. Her mother had sent him away and she would not see him again.

Duncan was puzzled when Molly did not appear at any of the innocuous entertainments he would have expected her mother to sanction, though Harriet was very much in evidence, parading the Marquis of Tadbury like a trophy. She had probably passed herself off as a widow with a fortune. If that were so, they were both in for a shock; the Dowager Lady Tadbury was a pinchpenny and kept her son on very short commons. She would make stringent enquiries before she opened the purse strings sufficiently to allow him to marry.

'Where is Miss Martineau?' Duncan asked Harriet when he met her at a rout given by Lady Driffield. It was a dreadful squeeze and he had spent the better part of the evening wandering from room to room and even into the conservatory and the library looking for her and her daughter among the guests.

'At home, in Holles Street; where else would she be, considering you would not take her back to Norfolk? I see now why not. You prefer to racket about town. I shall be interested to see what happens when someone recognises you.'

'I do not see why they should. I was a mere stripling when I left home and war has a way of ageing a man.'

'I cannot think what game you may be playing, unless you are planning to reclaim your inheritance.'

'And if I were?' he queried.

'It would be seen as an act of vengeance. Your brother took your title and your betrothed and you cannot forgive him, but I doubt it would make you popular.'

'If there was anything to forgive, I forgave him a long time ago,' he said, deciding to say nothing of the fact that he had received a letter from Carlton House only that morning telling him that he had been awarded a baronetcy for services to his country; he could now call himself Sir Duncan Stacey.

'And Beth?'

'Beth is my brother's wife. I wish them happy.'

'Do you mean that?'

'Indeed, I do. And if I hear that you have had a hand in spreading tattle to the contrary I shall fetch Molly from the garret where you have imprisoned her and introduce her to the whole *ton*. You will have to acknowledge her.'

'I have not imprisoned her,' she said indignantly. 'Why, you know very well she has been out with Mr Bellamy.'

'Is he still dangling after her?'

'What a vulgar way of expressing it,' she said. 'But then I should not expect anything else from someone who has been out of Society so long—you have not the least idea how to behave like a gentleman.'

'Is he?' he persisted.

'He has called once or twice and taken her in the park in his phaeton. And do not look so shocked; she was chaperoned by Betty.'

'I am surprised at you allowing it, ma'am. His interest in Molly is not as a wife.'

'Oh, I think he can be brought up to the mark. Molly is not without breeding and she is a pretty little thing. I am persuaded she is already inclined favourably towards him. And anyone can see he is enamoured of her.'

Duncan was dismayed. 'You would not force her?'

'No, of course I would not force her. Do you take me for a monster?'

'Then you will give her a proper come-out?'

'There is not the least need for that; the whole thing can be managed very quietly.'

The interest in the evening's entertainment was gone and he took his leave, seething on Molly's behalf. How could Harriet use her daughter so? Not only was Molly not to have the Season she longed for, she was to be married off in a havey-cavey way which would break her heart. And his. He told himself he would not have minded seeing her at every Society function, beleaguered by eager beaux, if it meant she was happy. But to hide her away and only let her out with that rake, Andrew Bellamy, was an unkindness of the first water. He could not let it happen unless Molly herself told him she wanted it. If she did, he would withdraw, leave the country, die a second time.

Molly's disappointment was profound, but she did not blame anyone but herself. She should not have run away, nor inveigled the Captain into bringing her to London; her mother was right to be angry. Except for carefully orchestrated outings with Mr Bellamy, she was confined to the house and the overgrown garden and was expected to pass her time with no other company but the housekeeper and Betty, who accompanied her when she went for a walk in the park or to look at the shops or change her book at Hookham's library. How long would this punishment go on? Would she be sent back to Stacey Manor at the end of it? Would Lady Connaught even have her back?

It was at breakfast next morning that Harriet, enthusing to Molly about the rout which had, in the eyes of everyone there, been a great success, let slip that she had spoken to Duncan.

'The Captain is in town?' Molly's eyes lit up and then immediately clouded again. 'Why has he not called on us?'

'Why should he?'

'I hoped... Did he not even ask how I did?'

'No, but then I hardly said five words to him.' Harriet had no intention of telling her daughter the truth—that Captain Stacey had talked of nothing else; it would only unsettle her.

'How did he seem? Is he fully recovered?'

'I must admit he looked in fine fettle, flirting with every unmarried lady in the room, and even some that were not single.'

'Oh.'

Harriet looked closely at her daughter's dejected countenance. 'Molly, you must put him from your mind, you really must.'

Molly wished she could. Her obsession with the Captain quite spoiled her outings with Mr Bellamy when she found herself constantly comparing the two men. And though Mr Bellamy was the picture of elegance and his manners were excessively correct when they were in the presence of her mama she sensed a falseness about them.

He could turn a pretty compliment and brought her flowers and sweetmeats when he called, and she thanked him properly, but she did not think he was sincere. For one thing, she knew she was not the 'loveliest blossom in all of London', and it was a falsehood to say it. Mama said that was how things were done and she ought to learn to accept compliments in the spirit in which they were given. But what she could not fathom was exactly what was meant by that.

The Captain was different. He rarely praised, preferring to gammon her or even to scold, but when she thought about it carefully she decided she would rather that than Mr Bellamy's fulsomeness; it was more honest and easier to deal with.

'Will the Captain be at Lady Tadbury's masked ball, do you think?' she asked.

Harriet shrugged. 'I doubt it. He is, on his own admission, only a poor relation of Connaught's and only lately come to town, for all the silly articles swooning over him and calling him handsome and daring and mysterious. Her ladyship would have more sense than to include him.'

'Why?'

'Why? Because the ball is being given for her daughter

Letitia, the Marquis's sister, and she has only just come out
Only the top one hundred will be invited and as far as the
world is concerned Stacey is only a half-pay captain in the
Hussars.'

'You will be there.'

'Naturally I will; the Marquis and I have an understanding.' She smiled suddenly. 'I shouldn't wonder if the announcement were made at the ball.'

Molly sighed. 'I wish I could go.'

'You know you cannot. It is not the thing for a young lady
not yet out to attend a ball unless it be her own come-out ball.'

Molly concluded that her mother used the conventions
when it pleased her and disregarded them when it did not, but
she decided not to comment on that. 'I should so like to go
to a ball before I return to Norfolk.'

'No, Molly. But do not look so glum. I promise you that
if all goes as I hope it will I shall have a little supper party
and introduce you to a few select people.'

It was not a supper party Molly wanted. She wanted to
wear the lovely ballgown Duncan had bought her, to watch
all the guests in their silks and satins, dancing under the
chandeliers, to listen to the music and smell the flowers and
most of all, to dance herself.

It just wasn't fair that she should be left at home to dream
while her mother, who had been to hundreds of balls and
often pretended they were a boring duty, should go. It was to
be a masked ball so how would anyone know she had not yet
come out? No one of the *ton* knew her, except Mr Bellamy.
Would he be there? Would Duncan? But her mother had said
she was sure he would not be invited.

The more she thought of it, the more the imp of mischief
which habitually sat on her shoulder when she was thwarted

urged her to rebel. She would go. But how could she accomplish it? The problem occupied her mind to the exclusion of all else for the next three days.

On the evening of the ball, she sat on the bed in her mother's bedchamber and watched her dressing. She was going as Queen Elizabeth, in a brocade gown so impossibly tight over the bust, Molly wondered how she could breathe without popping out of it. She had fake diamonds in her great orange wig and a starched lace ruff about her throat which made turning her head difficult. Her skirt was four feet wide, looped and garlanded. The whole thing was finished off with a white satin mask, a chicken-skin fan and a quizzing glass dangling from a ribbon about her wrist.

'Lovely, Mama,' she said. 'Do you think anyone will recognise you?'

Her mother laughed. 'Not until we unmask at midnight. That is half the fun of it, keeping people guessing.'

'Does that always happen? I mean if someone knew you really well…'

'If they knew you well, naturally they would recognise you. Tadbury would almost certainly recognise me whatever I wore, but as I am going with him it is of no consequence. And I suppose if someone had a distinguishing mark, like a scar or a mole, or a figure you could not mistake, like the Prince Regent's…'

'But someone who was quite ordinary and had not been seen in Society before would remain anonymous?'

Harriet looked at her curiously. 'I suppose so. Why do you ask?'

'Oh, no reason. I was just dreaming…'

'That is half your trouble, Molly—you dream too much. Life is not like that. Now, I must go.'

She picked up her cloak and reticule as the front door knocker resounded through the house and Perrins came to tell her his lordship, the Marquis of Tadbury, was waiting for her downstairs. She pecked the air six inches from Molly's cheek, told her gaily not to expect her home before dawn and not to stay up reading too late, and disappeared.

As soon as she heard the front door shut, Molly raced to her own room where Betty was waiting for her. 'They've gone,' she said, stripping off her day gown and slipping into the ballgown which she had persuaded the maid to clean and press. It looked as good as new; the blue-green crepe had lost none of its translucence and floated about her slim figure like a gossamer cloud.

She had removed the flowers which had trimmed it and replaced them with woodland greenery. Betty put her hair up in the Greek style, finishing it off with a coronet of ivy. Her mask of green velvet was tied on with a narrow green ribbon. The last thing she wanted was for it to fall off.

'There!' Betty said, standing back to admire her handi-work. 'You will be a sure hit.'

Molly took a deep breath, slipped on her Greek sandals and picked up her fan and reticule, in which she had put the last of her Newmarket winnings; her mother had not thought it necessary to provide her with pin money. 'I am ready. What time did you tell the cab to come?'

'Nine. Are you sure you want to go alone?'

'Oh, yes, for if Mama ever found out you had helped me she would turn you off.'

Betty realised the truth of this and was grateful. She led the way down to the hall just as Perrins opened the door to the cabman. Molly sailed out into the balmy evening air and climbed into the hackney with all the aplomb she could muster. How to get in to the ball without an invitation she was not at all sure, but her adventures with the Captain had taught her self-reliance and ingenuity and she would manage that when the time came.

She arrived within three hundred yards of the Tadbury mansion in Bedford Row in no time but then they came to a stop. Looking out of the cab, she could see a long line of carriages all waiting to pull up at the door. As soon as one had deposited its occupants, the empty carriage rolled away and the next drew up. It was going to take an eternity to reach the entrance and she realised, too, that each arrival was being carefully scrutinised by a footman and invitations checked. She could not go in that way.

'I'll walk from here,' she called up to the driver.

He was glad enough of that; time was money and he did not like wasting it sitting in a line going nowhere. He jumped down and opened the door for her. She gave him the fare he asked for and the cab rattled away, leaving her standing in the road, wondering how to go on.

She walked purposefully up to the house and then, with a quick look round to make sure she was not observed, skipped round the corner of the building and made her way stealthily to the rear of the house, guided by the tuneful music of a country dance. It was a warm night and the windows onto the terrace were open, their curtains wafting slightly in the breeze. She crept up and gazed inside.

The ballroom was brilliantly lit and crowded. Every historical figure she could imagine was represented: kings, queens, pirates, highwaymen, harlequins and columbines, milkmaids, court jesters, Roundheads and Cavaliers, Greek gods and goddesses whose costumes were so revealing she was shocked.

There were a few matrons and old men sitting on the side-lines watching the younger ones dance. Little huddles of young ladies stood and giggled, peering over their fans at groups of young men who pretended indifference. The music was setting her feet tapping and she longed to be in among them. The windows were deep and it was only a matter of stepping over a foot of wall and she would be in, behind one of the curtains.

'What are you doing there, miss?'

She turned to see a liveried footman advancing towards her. Her first impulse was flight, her second to stand her ground; he could not know every guest when they were all masked. 'It was so hot indoors, I came out for fresh air,' she said. 'Now I cannot find my way in again.'

'You will ruin your clothes going in by the window, miss,' he said. 'And there is a door not ten feet away.'

She did not tell him she had seen it and seen the footman who guarded it as well. 'Oh, what a ninny I am!' She moved towards it, wondering what she would do if the second footman stopped her.

'There you are, my dear,' said a familiar voice. 'I have been looking for you everywhere.'

She spun round to see a highwayman, complete with black three-cornered hat, cloak and black mask standing beside a garden seat not six feet away.

'Oh, Captain.' Although she tried to keep her voice light and unconcerned, she could not disguise the fact that she was unashamedly pleased to see him. 'I lost myself in the garden.'

He had accepted Tadbury's invitation in the hope of meeting her, but when Harriet had turned up without her he had been sorely disappointed, assuming she had been sent back to Norfolk after all. He'd been as sorry for Molly as he was for himself, and very angry with Harriet. Wandering out into the garden to calm himself, he had seen Molly contemplating climbing in a window. She had not changed; she was still the madcap Molly he loved.

'And now you are found. Come along in, my dear; I do believe they are playing a waltz.' And with that he took her arm and sauntered past the footman who had accosted her and the one who stood at the door and she found herself in the ballroom.

'I cannot waltz,' she hissed at him, blinking in the bright light.

'Of course you can. Listen to the rhythm of the music, follow my lead and don't you dare tread on my toes.'

He put one hand about her waist, took her hand with the other and whirled her into the middle of the floor. She had no choice but to do as he said and suddenly found she was enjoying it.

Everyone else faded into the background and it felt as if they were alone, moving in perfect rhythm to the music, at one with each other. Her temerity in coming, her nervousness, her fear of being caught all disappeared in a haze of joy. He did not speak and, for once, she was silent.

But it came to an end all too soon and he led her to a quiet corner, pushing two chairs close together so that they might talk uninterrupted.

'Now,' he said, admiring her composure; any other young miss would have been shaking with nerves. 'Tell me what you thought you were about. Climbing in at the window of a ballroom crowded with people is not the way to remain anonymous, you know. Or did you wish to embarrass your mama in front of half the *haut monde*?'

'How could I? No one knows me.'

'Not anyone?' he asked in surprise. 'Then who brought you?'

'No one. I came in a cab but as there was such a line at the door I sent it away and walked.'

'Why?'

'I told you, there was a long line and I would have had to pay for every minute we stood idle…'

'No, you goose, I meant why did you come?'

'I am to go back to Stacey Manor but I did not want to go without wearing this beautiful gown you bought me. I thought as everyone was masked…'

So, she thought the gown was beautiful. On her it was, though he realised most young ladies of her age would decry it as too plain. It had a simple elegance that enhanced her delightful figure. 'They will unmask at midnight.'

'Oh, I shall be gone by then.'

'Have you asked the cabman to come back for you?'

She looked nonplussed. 'No, I did not think of it…'

He smiled. 'I think I had better take charge of you.'

'Oh, no, that will not do.'

'Why not? Oh, I know you think I am an old goat…'

'I do not think anything of the sort, my lord.' That was perfectly true. She no longer thought of him as old, nor of herself as young; somehow or other she had grown up to meet him.

'My lord?' he repeated. 'I am not your lord or anyone else's.'

'Yes, you are; Mama told me. She said you were really the Earl of Connaught come back from the dead. And you were a rakeshame and always would be and Beth Gooderson has had a lucky escape…' The words tumbled out breathlessly.

'Undoubtedly she has. And so have I.'

'You cannot mean that. Mama thinks you are still suffering over it and that is why you have been riding about the countryside calling yourself the Dark Knight.'

'You were the one who clung to that notion—something to do with Don Quixote, or some such romantical nonsense, I collect. I never said it. Highway robbery is not romantic; it is a crime for which the punishment is hanging.'

'Do you wish to be hanged? Is that why you take such risks, because you are tired of life?'

He smiled. 'Molly, I am not tired of life. I am very glad to be alive, especially at this moment.'

She did not recognise the compliment for what it was and ignored it. She looked him up and down, noting that his costume was made of the very best materials, that the frills that fell from the cuffs of his shirt were of handmade lace and that a diamond pin in his skilfully tied cravat twinkled in the light from the chandelier above their heads. 'No, for I perceive the cards have fallen successfully for you again.'

He laughed. 'How well you know me, Molly.' He was suddenly serious. 'Or perhaps you do not know me at all. Perhaps I am Don Quixote, after all, rescuing a damsel in distress.'

'I am not in distress.'

'You will be when your mama finds you here. Why do you do these foolish things, Molly?'

'For the same reason you do the hare-brained things you do—for adventure. Life would be very dull without it.'

'True,' he said. 'But I am a man and you are…' He paused and finished softly, 'You are a dream.'

'You know, I dreamed of being a female high toby,' she said, disregarding the second compliment she had received from him in the space of a minute. 'A daring rider, known the length and breadth of the country for taking from those who did not deserve their wealth and giving it to the poor. That would be an especially commendable adventure, don't you think?'

He laughed. 'An impossible dream, my dear, and sooner or later we have to face reality.'

'Yes, I know. I must go back to Stacey Manor and you… What will you do?'

'Oh, I shall contrive.'

'By gambling and taking risks. I wish you would not. I should hate to see you hang.'

'How did we come to be talking about me, when it is clearly you who have the problem?'

'Please do not concern yourself on my account. I have worn my ballgown and had my dance…'

'And is that enough?'

'You told me I had to face reality.'

'So I did, but I think we can prolong the dream for an hour or two. Come, let us take a last turn about the floor before we go.'

And for a second time that evening she was on the dance floor being whirled round in a rapture of joy which was not lost on the chaperons who habitually sat on the sidelines making comments on everyone. 'It's the second time he has danced with her,' they said. 'Who are they?'

'I believe he is the Earl of Connaught's relative,' said another. 'But who the young chit is, I have no idea. Some barque of frailty, I shouldn't wonder; she don't seem to have a chaperon.'

Molly did not want it to end, but when it did she was surrounded by young men, all clamouring to mark her card, including Andrew Bellamy, dressed as a Cavalier. Duncan stood back and smiled stiffly as she was claimed and whisked away. It was what she wanted and who was he to deny her a little happiness?

'Miss Martineau, how lovely you look tonight,' Andrew said as they stepped hand in hand into the dance.

'You know me?' she said in dismay.

'Of course. Did you think a scrap of velvet would be disguise enough? I would know your figure anywhere—such grace of movement, such perfection. It would put Venus to shame. And those eyes! Ah, the eyes! What can I say to do justice to their colour, their brightness? And rosy lips made for kissing…'

'Mr Bellamy, I beg you, desist,' she said, laughing. 'You will make me puffed up with your flummery.'

The dance took them away from each other as they paraded down the outside of the line of dancers. At the top of the room, they came together again. 'There is to be a firework display at Vauxhall Gardens on Saturday evening,' he said as they promenaded in a circle round each other. 'It promises to be very fine and there will be musicians and tableaux. Will you allow me to escort you?'

She sighed. 'I think I shall have gone back to Norfolk by then.'

'Oh, you must not; you must not deprive Society of one of the brightest stars in its firmament.'

'It is not my choice.'

They moved hand in hand down the long line of dancers. 'I shall go at once and speak to your mama.'

'No, please don't. She does not know I am here…'

'Then who brought you? Could it be the highwayman? I fancy when we unmask we shall see the face of that rake-shame, Captain Stacey.'

'He did not bring me. I came alone.'

'Really?' He looked closely at her and smiled knowingly. 'Then if you do not want your mama to know I think you should repay me for my silence by allowing me to escort you home.'

'There is no need; the Captain has already offered and I have accepted.'

'Give him his right about.'

'Oh, no, I could not do that. I promised...'

'And promises count with you, do they?'

'Oh, yes. I should never break my word.'

'Then I must accept that, but you will come to Vauxhall Gardens with me on Saturday?'

The intricacies of the dance separated them before she could frame a reply and when they returned to each other the music came to an end. He bowed and she curtsied and put her fingers lightly on his arm to be escorted from the floor. 'I will wait for you in my carriage on the corner of Holles Street,' he murmured as he returned her to her seat. 'Eight o'clock. Please do not disappoint me or you will break my heart.'

'Then I am afraid your heart will have to break,' she said crisply. 'I am not so lacking in sense as to agree to meet you in such a clandestine way.'

He did not answer because at that moment the Marquis of Tadbury bowed over her hand and requested the pleasure of dancing with her. She smiled at Andrew and allowed herself to be led away. The Marquis was hardly less fulsome in his compliments than Mr Bellamy, but he was certainly a much worse dancer for he trod on her toes several times, blaming her loveliness for his lack of attention. She was thankful that he had not realised who she was.

She could see her mother out of the corner of her eye dancing with an older man and coming perilously close. Surely she could not fail to recognise her? But her eyes were only for the Marquis. Could she be jealous? The idea would have amused Molly if she had not been so anxious to steer her partner away from her mother—a move which was not lost on Harriet and was entirely misinterpreted.

At the end of the dance, Harriet claimed the Marquis before he could conduct Molly to her seat. For a moment she stood alone in the middle of the floor, feeling lost, and then she saw Duncan leaning nonchalantly against a pillar, watching her from beneath his dark lashes, a smile playing about his lips.

She walked over to join him. 'Are you going to ask me to dance again?'

'Twice is considered enough for couples who are not engaged to be married, my dear. And you have had partners enough. You are the belle of the ball. I heard the tabbies whispering, "Who is she? Where has she come from?" They are all agog to see you unmasked.'

'Mr Bellamy knew me, but I made him promise not to tell Mama. He was vastly amused.'

'I'll wager he was,' he said laconically.

At that moment a drum rolled and a hush of expectancy descended on the company; it was time to unmask. Duncan grabbed her hand and marched her off the floor, out of the nearest door and into the garden. 'Home, before any damage is done,' he said, giving her no time to argue.

They walked quickly round the side of the house and along the alley to the mews where his horse and phaeton were being looked after until he was ready to leave. He helped her in, climbed in beside her and picked up the reins.

'I think the damage is already done,' she said, when they had safely negotiated the line of vehicles waiting to be called up, and turned into the street. 'I am sure Mama recognised me. She was certainly giving me some strange looks when I was dancing with the Marquis.'

'It would be an unnatural mother who did not know her

own offspring,' he said, though secretly he thought the reason
for the strange looks had another cause altogether. 'But you
will know soon enough. If I hear you have been locked in
your room, then I shall know the reason.'

'Mama would not be so cruel. After all, I have not spoiled
her evening. She danced a great deal and I could see her fluttering her fan and enjoying the latest *on-dit* with other guests.
Who was the older man she was dancing with just now? He
seemed very attentive to her.'

'That was Lord Brancaster.'

'You mean Mr Bellamy's father?' she asked in surprise.

'Yes.'

'Then I think you were very rash to come tonight when
you knew he could denounce you the moment you unmasked
if not before. I know Mr Bellamy knew you. You will be lucky
if he has not pointed you out to his father.'

'What has he to denounce me for? I returned his lordship's
coach and paid him for his inconvenience. And, like you, I
have left before the unmasking.'

'Why *did* you come? I was sure you would be on the open
road again with Sergeant Upjohn.'

'I think those days are numbered, Molly,' he said, his
spirits suddenly lifting to know she had been thinking of
him. 'A man must settle down some time.'

'Oh.' She was silent for a moment. Was that why he had
been attending Society functions and, according to Mama,
flirting with all the unmarried ladies in town? He was looking
for a wife. Another Beth Gooderson.

'Nothing to say, Molly?'

'I wish you happy.' It was said in a whisper, for she had
suddenly realised she could not bear to think of him married
to anyone else.

'My happiness lies in your hands, Molly.' He pulled up outside the house in Holles Street, but made no move to get out and help her down.

'Mine?' She was looking at him with those wide blue eyes, and a puzzled frown on her brow which made his heart lurch. Gambler he was, but suddenly he could not risk declaring himself. It was too soon, much too soon. And she still had not been invited to any Society gatherings and he was determined to see her wish granted.

'Yes,' he said, thinking quickly. 'You will make me happy if you will consent to accompany me to Vauxhall Gardens on Saturday. I shall ask your mama's permission, of course. She may like to come too. We will make a party of it.'

She had been holding her breath, but now she let it out in a great sigh of disappointment. He did not think of her as a wife at all; to him she was a hoyden, a fribble without a sensible thought in her head. And how could she blame him for that? It was exactly what she was; she had proved it over and over again with her madcap behaviour.

She pulled herself together and forced herself to sound light-hearted. 'Oh, so many suitors, all clamouring to take me to Vauxhall, but you know you are too late, Captain. Mr Bellamy has already asked me. I am to meet him at the end of Holles Street on Saturday evening.'

'Molly, you cannot mean to go in that havey-cavey fashion? It is unthinkable.'

His arrogant attitude annoyed her. Instead of telling him that she knew that perfectly well and had no intention of going, she demanded to know why she should not. 'He is very attentive. He says I am beautiful and though I know that is a hum it is nice to be told.'

'It is not a hum,' he said softly. 'You are very lovely.'

She turned in her seat to look at him in the light from the gas lamps that lit the London street, and was disconcerted to find him looking down at her with an expression in his dark eyes she could not fathom. Hurt? Disappointment? Tenderness? Amusement? But there was no laughter in his eyes. 'You do not mean that.'

'I am not in the habit of telling whiskers, Molly. Nor will I allow you to make a cake of yourself over that scapegrace...'

She laughed. 'Listen to the pot calling the kettle black.'

He smiled ruefully. '*Touché*, my dear.'

He was ready to wager Bellamy had no intention of requesting Harriet's permission, and asking Molly to meet him away from the house boded ill for her. But if he protested too much he would almost certainly throw her into the man's arms, and once she had been compromised she would be at his mercy. 'If he asks your mama first and you are well chaperoned, I suppose there is no harm in it,' he said, pulling up outside the house in Holles Street. 'But you are not to meet him clandestinely.'

Again she was disappointed. She realised she had only told him about Mr Bellamy to judge his reaction and all he had done was give her orders as cool as you please! 'Who are you to say what I must and must not do?' she demanded, scrambling down. 'You are not my keeper.' Without looking back she marched to the door.

He strode after her and took her shoulders in his hands, turning her towards him, resisting with a huge effort of self-control the temptation to shake sense into her. 'Molly, don't you realise the peril you are in?'

'From Mr Bellamy?' she asked. 'Or you? I collect you are not averse to taking a lady by surprise...'

It was too much. He pulled her roughly to him and lowered his mouth to hers. It was a kiss that started in exasperation, even anger, and ended in sweetness and tenderness. He understood the reason for it, but did she?

She made no move to draw away, did not squirm in his arms or lift her hand against him. She settled herself against his chest, her head tilted upwards, and loved it. Loved him. Knew she loved him.

He broke away at last and stood looking breathlessly at her, wondering what to say and saying nothing. What good would words do? He had lost his patience and made a mull of it.

She was too confused to understand. She ran from him and pushed open the door, glad she had asked Betty to make sure it was left unlocked so she did not have to summon Perrins.

He watched her go inside and the door close on her and murmured, 'Goodnight, my love,' before reluctantly returning to his carriage. Harriet had been right; he had been so long out of Society, he no longer knew how to behave towards a young lady of tender susceptibility.

Chapter Eleven

Feeling nothing but contempt for himself, he returned to Connaught House. Birtwhistle admitted him, still fully dressed. 'Oh, sir, I am glad you have come. Lady Connaught has arrived.'

He was startled. The last person he wanted to face was Beth. 'Is the Earl with her?'

'No, sir, I meant the Dowager Lady Connaught, not the Countess.'

'Grandmama! Why, she hasn't left Norfolk in the last ten years.'

'She is here now, sir. Before she retired she left instructions that you were to present yourself in the library at nine in the morning.'

'Thank you, Birtwhistle. Do you think you could rouse me at eight?'

'Yes, sir.'

He went up to the room he had been occupying for the last ten days and went to bed. He had a very good idea why his grandmother had come to town, but it was no good losing sleep over it.

At precisely nine o'clock the next morning, he strolled into the library to find Lady Connaught sitting behind the great oak desk from which her late husband had directed the affairs of his vast estates. Besides Connaught House, there was a parcel of streets in the metropolis, bringing in considerable rents, Foxtrees and several surrounding farms, a hunting box in Leicestershire and a grouse moor in Scotland, besides Stacey Manor and its surrounds in Norfolk, which had been left to his wife without encumbrance.

She looked up as Duncan entered, noting his brown single-breasted frockcoat buttoned to the waist, his nankeen trousers which were strapped under the foot, his biscuit-coloured waistcoat and perfectly tied muslin cravat. He had shaved himself and his hair had recently had the attention of a barber for it was arranged in the latest windswept fashion.

'Good morning, Grandmama,' he said, kissing the back of her bejewelled hand.

'Is it?' she queried. 'It is impossible to tell in this dreary city, what with the high buildings and the smoke and fog.'

Duncan had seen no fog, but he let that pass. 'What brings you here, if you find it so little to your taste?'

'You do. You seem to be in fine feather.'

'I am, thank you.'

'What have you done with that chit, Molly?'

'I have done nothing with her. I took her to her mother, as I said I would.'

'And what did Harriet say about that?'

'She was hardly in raptures. Molly is kept closely confined and Harriet will not even acknowledge her as her daughter. It is monstrous the way she treats her and I do not wonder that Molly rebels.'

'Harriet did not insist on you making an offer for her?'

'No. On the contrary, she told Molly she would not saddle her with a rakeshame such as I am. She has her mind set on pushing her onto Andrew Bellamy.'

'Bellamy. You mean Brancaster's only son?'

'Yes. We met him on the journey to London and since we arrived he has renewed the acquaintanceship, dancing attendance on her and paying her fulsome compliments, but I am prepared to wager that all he has in mind is carte blanche. Molly is a sweet and innocent child, a little spirited perhaps, but none the worse for that; she can have no conception of what the phrase means…'

'I thought so,' she said, nodding her head sagely. 'A few weeks in her company and you have learned her true worth. I knew you would. Why have you not offered for her?'

'Grandmama, have you forgotten I relinquished my inheritance, every last penny? I am a gambler and a scapegrace, as you yourself pointed out, and…'

'It is not the least use you blustering.'

'I have nothing to offer a young lady like Molly; I have nothing to offer any young lady.'

'I have been thinking of that. I came to bring you this. It might help.' She picked up a sheaf of papers which lay on the desk and handed them to him. 'As you and your brother have exchanged roles and he has the Stacey inheritance, leaving you with nothing, you shall have what I intended to bequeath to him as the second son. And you need not wait for my death; those are the deeds of Manor Farm. You always said you'd like to breed horses and it is ideal for that. But you offer for Molly, do you understand? I want to see you settled before I hand in my accounts. I shall call on Harriet this afternoon…'

'I hope you do not mean to press my suit for me,' he said, and there was a warning in his voice she perfectly understood.

He did not like being pushed even when it was in the direction he most wanted to go. If Molly ever got to hear of it, she would conclude he wanted to marry her for the sake of owning a farm and she would surely turn him down. She was too much of a romantic to consider wealth when choosing a husband, and she would expect the man she married to feel the same way.

'Do you take me for a noddicock, that I should do such a thing? I shall suggest taking Molly under my wing for the rest of the Season. She can live here with me and you can move into Fenton's Hotel; it would never do for you both to be under the same roof. Molly shall have her come-out; I know how much it means to her. What you do about it is entirely your affair. If you decide you would not suit, then find someone else.'

He smiled ruefully as she rose and swept from the room, her taffeta skirt rustling, leaving him to his thoughts. There was no one else; there never would be.

Molly spent what was left of the night in silent misery. She had been the worst kind of fool. Everyone at that ball had been talking about her; it was no wonder her mother pretended not to know her.

Duncan had rescued her, saved her from making a cake of herself, given her a little taste of what it was like to be the centre of attention, and for that she was grateful to him. More than that, she loved him. For one short minute, when he'd said his happiness was in her hands, she had thought he returned that love and was going to ask her to marry him, but he had not.

He had been no better than Andrew Bellamy, suggesting an outing which she did not think was at all proper. The fact that Duncan had said he would ask her mama and Mr Bellamy had suggested meeting him secretly she completely ignored.

Like Mr Bellamy, he had taken her for the kind of girl he could kiss with impunity. What was the phrase? A little bit of muslin? For all he pretended otherwise, he was a member of the aristocracy and he would not forget that when choosing a wife. She did not fit the bill.

She fell asleep as dawn lightened the sky and woke in the middle of the morning with a bad headache. She was not sure if it was caused by the unaccustomed champagne or the churning thoughts in her head, but whichever it was she could not lie abed.

As soon as she had drunk the hot chocolate Betty brought her, she rose and dressed in the plainest of her new gowns and went downstairs to eat a lonely breakfast. Then she went into the small parlour to finish reading her novel. But she could not concentrate and her mind kept straying to Duncan Stacey. Who would have thought that she would fall in love with a man who was not at all the lover of her dreams? Nor had she needed to come to London to meet him. But having met him, having melted under his kisses, having given him her heart, she had waited in vain to hear him speak of love.

All he wanted was an undemanding companion for whatever devious game he was playing, a ready accomplice. Once she would have been content with that, but not now. Now she wanted more. Don Quixote was not enough. She had grown up in the last few weeks and it was a painful business.

Going to that ball had been a mistake and now she would never have her longed-for Season. Not that it mattered any more. She would go back to Stacey Manor, which would please Mama, if no one else.

Harriet joined her at noon. Dressed in an undress gown of blue silk and with her hair loose about her shoulders, she sank onto a chaise longue in the small parlour with every appearance of exhaustion.

'Did you enjoy the ball, Mama?' Molly asked, affecting innocence. 'Were there many people there? Did you recognise anyone in their costume?'

'Oh, I knew most of them, they have been doing the rounds all Season, but there were one or two strangers who disappeared before the unmasking. Tony Stacey was there dressed as a high toby, though that was hardly a proper disguise; I knew him at once. I own I was surprised he should have chosen that costume considering what you told me about the Dark Knight. I am not at all convinced he wasn't bamming us all.'

'You said you doubted Lady Tadbury would invite him.'

'Oh, that was Tadbury's doing. He thinks we are related and as Tony is a Stacey…'

'Was the Captain alone?'

'No, he was not. He had a chit with him dressed as a wood nymph or somesuch and though I asked Lady Tadbury she could not put a name to her, for which I was vastly relieved.' She paused and looked closely at her daughter. 'Did you think I would not know you? I never felt so mortified in all my life.'

'Oh, you did recognise me.'

'Naturally, I did. It was a shock, I can tell you. It is a wonder I did not have a seizure. Whatever possessed you to do such a cork-brained thing?'

'I did so want to go and you would not take me.'

'No, and is it to be wondered at? You have no idea how to conduct yourself. Tony Stacey put you up to it, didn't he? It is the sort of rig he would indulge in. I think he finds pleasure in vexing me, though why he should I do not know. I have never done him any harm…'

'It had nothing to do with the Captain. I went alone.'

'Alone!' her mother shrieked. 'Oh, Molly, how could you? You do know you are the talk of the *ton*?'

Molly could not suppress a little smile. 'I do believe people were asking who I was. The Captain said I was the belle of the ball.'

'Thank goodness Stacey had sense enough to whisk you away before everyone unmasked. You must never do anything like that again. Never, do you hear? If the gabblegrinders find out it was you, we shall be undone. We might as well find a dark hole and live in it in penury.'

'Oh, Mama, why should they find out? No one knew me except Captain Stacey. And Mr Bellamy, but he promised not to say a word to anyone.'

'We must make sure he does not. If I could persuade him to offer for you…'

'No, Mama, no!' she cried. 'We should not suit; really we should not. I do hope you have said nothing to him.' Then, remembering her mother had been dancing with Lord Brancaster, she added, 'You did not speak of it to his father? Oh, do tell me you did not.'

'No, of course I did not. These things have to be done in the proper manner.'

'Then I beg you, do nothing. I will go back to Stacey Manor, I will never embarrass you again, but please do not make me accept an offer from someone I do not, cannot, love.'

'Love! What has love to do with it?' She stood up and shook herself determinedly. 'Now I am going to change. I expect Lord Brancaster to call.'

Molly was appalled. 'But you said you had not spoken to him.'

'Of you, no. You are not the only subject of conversation, you know. In fact, it is one I avoid if I can.'

'Then I think I shall go to the library, Mama. I have finished my book and need another.'

'You read far too much, and what you do read is a fribble. No wonder you have such romantic notions.'

'There is nothing else for me to do, Mama.' It was said with a heartfelt sigh.

When she returned, she was astonished to find Lady Connaught with her mother in the withdrawing room. Her ladyship was still dressed in her old-fashioned mourning clothes but they did not detract from her imposing presence. She sat bolt upright, sipping tea, determination on every feature of her face.

'Here she is,' Harriet said. Her face, Molly noticed, was as puce as the silk day gown she wore and she looked decidedly uncomfortable. 'Come and make your curtsey, Molly.'

Molly obeyed and went to kiss her godmother's cheek. 'Aunt Margaret, I am truly sorry that I worried you. I should not have run away as I did, but you knew I was safe with Captain Stacey, didn't you?'

'I did not doubt it.'

'Then why are you here? I thought you hated London.'

'So I do, but I could not stand idle, knowing he would be bound to make a mull of everything.'

'How? He has done nothing wrong…'

'Nothing right either.' She paused. 'Enough of that. Now you are here, tell me, have you been out and about with your mama, seen the sights, met some of the eligibles?'

'She has had one or two carriage rides in the park,' Harriet put in before Molly could reply.

'Incognito, I shouldn't wonder.'

'Not at all. But she is not yet out…'

'And when were you going to bring her out?'

'Soon. I have yet to settle my affairs.'

'And does this settling of affairs involve a certain marquis?'

'That is all over. I decided we should not suit. He is too young and I have discovered he is fickle.'

This was news to Molly, though she remained silent.

'So you have spent all your blunt to no good purpose.'

'There is some way to go to the end of the Season. And there is someone else…'

'Then you will be fully occupied, I do not doubt, and poor Molly will be left out in the cold, as usual.'

Molly was shocked to hear her godmother speak to her mother like that, and she could not let her mama take all the blame. 'Aunt, it is not Mama's fault,' she put in. 'I arrived inopportunely and spoiled it all for her. I will come back to Norfolk with you and not bother her again.'

'Fustian!' She paused to look at Molly. 'I ain't going back to Norfolk, not yet. And don't look so Friday-faced; you shall have your come-out.'

Molly looked from her godmother to her mother in surprise. Her ladyship was smiling but her mother continued to look uncomfortable. 'Lady Connaught has offered to sponsor you,' she said.

'Oh.' Her initial delight was tempered with doubt. The prospect of going out and about and meeting other young people was no longer the epitome of her ambition. In truth she would not have minded in the least if Lady Connaught had insisted on taking her back to Stacey Manor. The Season had lost its magic. It had faded the minute she realised how much she loved Duncan Stacey and how hopeless it was. 'But I do not wish to embarrass Mama and…'

'Any embarrassment she endures has been brought on by her own silliness,' her ladyship said. 'I should never have agreed to it in the first place. Now, Harriet, you will give up this house. I wonder at you taking it on when it is so far above your touch. You will be dished up before the Season is out…'

'I could not allow the world to think I was a pauper…'

Her ladyship ignored that. 'You will both come and stay at Connaught House with me. We will do the thing properly.'

'Did Tony put you up to this?' Harriet demanded.

Her ladyship gave a chuckle. 'Duncan is a mopstraw, doesn't know what's good for him, but that don't mean he'd come rattling to me to set things straight for him. He knows I can't abide maunderers.'

Molly could not see what begging had to do with it, but it seemed her mother had lost control of the situation and it was now very firmly in the hands of Lady Connaught. She sat by helplessly as the arrangements were made and the following Saturday accompanied her mother and a mountain of luggage, very little of which belonged to her, to Connaught House. She wondered if Duncan might be there, but he was not. He had moved into a hotel at his grandmother's insistence.

It was not because of lack of space, she soon discovered, for the house was huge and several families could have lived in it without encountering one another; it was done, so she was told, for convention's sake and because the Earl and Countess were expected soon.

In the next few days Lady Connaught took her shopping for clothes, all of which were modish and expensive, but she preferred the simple garments Duncan had bought her, just because he liked her in them. Rags, her mother had called them, but to Molly they were the stuff of dreams.

As soon as the *ton* learned that Lady Connaught was in town and sponsoring her god-daughter, the invitations began to flood in, but it was all too late. Molly found herself at tea parties, picnics and routs and being introduced to other young people, but instead of enjoying their gossip she found it shallow and meaningless. The young ladies simpered and the men were so excessively polite, she wanted to scream at them.

She saw Duncan occasionally at these gatherings, and sometimes he asked her to dance, or sat beside her at supper and made light conversation. But he was as bad as the rest; he talked inconsequentially about nothing, affecting a style and mannerisms which she was sure were completely alien to him.

'I wonder you are still in town,' she whispered to him when they chanced to be sitting beside each other at a musical evening. She had been enjoying the music, but was all too aware of the immaculately clad figure beside her.

Not so long ago he had had pockets to let, but now he was wearing a double-breasted evening coat of black brocade, a shirt and cravat of such whiteness they dazzled the eyes, and shining black shoes. Was he still gambling and winning? Or was the Dark Knight still about his business? But he was not the Dark Knight she reminded herself, so that did not signify.

'How could I leave while you are still gracing the capital with your presence?'

'That is flummery,' she said as the music came to an end and the audience began to applaud. 'It does not suit you.'

He laughed. 'I thought that was what you wanted. A little attention, you said. And Mr Bellamy seems to succeed with it.'

'I was a ninny to think that was important. I have grown up in the last month.'

'Oh, I do hope not.' He was looking at her quizzically with his head on one side, his eyes deep pools she could not fathom.

'What do you mean?'

'I liked you best as you were. Madcap Molly, game for anything.'

'The Dark Knight would think that, but you must have moved on yourself. Are you not thinking of settling down?'

'Indeed I am. I am going to breed horses.'

'Horses?' she queried, with an attempt at a laugh. 'Not children?'

'To have children one must have a wife. At least, if one is not to cause the most outrageous scandal.'

'And is that why you have been seen about town? You are looking for a wife?'

'I do not need to look. I have found the one I want.'

'Oh. Then I wish you joy.'

'Do you?' he asked softly.

She forced herself to sit still, though she longed to flee. 'Yes, naturally I do. And I hope we can still be friends…'

His laughter was so uninhibited, everyone turned to look at him, but he was unaware of it. 'Oh, Molly, Molly, you little goose…' He looked up as a shadow loomed over them. 'Oh, it's you, Bellamy. What do you want?'

Andrew ignored him and spoke to Molly. 'Miss Martineau, would you take a turn about the room with me?'

She rose and laid her fingers on his arm, anxious to escape from a situation and emotions she could not control. She hated Duncan Stacey for making her feel the way she did. It was unfair in him to take all her cherished dreams and wreck them with casual words, strew them at her feet and reveal their emptiness. Now she had nothing, not even a sense of adventure, for without him even adventure seemed meaningless.

She walked sedately round the room, following other couples doing the same thing, only half listening to Andrew's complaints that she had not kept their tryst and he did not intend to give up. Molly then became aware that Duncan had left his seat and was taking leave of their hostess. The next minute he was gone and the crowded room seemed suddenly empty.

It was next day she learned from Lady Connaught that he had left town. 'He has gone to Manor Farm,' she said. 'There are alterations he wishes to make and he has gone to put them in hand.'

'He told me he was going to breed horses,' Molly said, wondering how she was going to bear having him living with his new wife not two miles distant from Stacey Manor. She was convinced that was where she was bound. Her Season had been a total failure.

'What else did he say?'

'Nothing, except that he had met the lady he wanted for his wife.'

'Did he, now?' She peered at Molly short-sightedly. 'And how do you feel about that?'

'I said I wished him joy.' She spoke flatly. She could not put into words exactly how she felt. She wanted to berate him for his blindness, to shout at him in frustration, at the same time as she longed for him to put his arms about her and kiss her as he had done twice before. The memory of those two kisses would live with her for ever, though they could have meant very little to him.

'I did not ask what you said,' her godmother said. 'I asked how you felt.'

'I don't know. A little sad, I think. He is such a free spirit...'

'You mean a scapegrace.'

'No, I don't. He is chivalrous and caring and...' Her voice trailed off.

'I do believe you are wearing the willow for him.'

Molly sighed. 'Perhaps I am, but there is nothing I can do about it. I cannot make him love me and if there is someone else...'

'Fustian! He does not know his own mind. You must make a push.'

'Oh, no, I could not do that. It would not be fair.'

'All's fair in love and war,' her ladyship said bluntly. 'Men are all children at heart; they need to be told what is best for them.'

'My lady, I do hope you will not say anything like that to him. It will give him an aversion to me and I do so want to remain his friend.'

'Oh, give me patience!' her ladyship exclaimed. 'You should have your heads knocked together.'

Harriet came into the room then, bursting with energy. 'Lord Brancaster is arranging a party on Saturday to visit Vauxhall Gardens,' she said. 'We are all to go.' She stopped and looked at her daughter. 'Why the Friday face? It is ungrateful of you to look so solemn when everyone is doing their best to entertain you. Why, I do believe Mr Bellamy suggested the outing to his father in order to please you and you should be happy about it.'

Molly forced a smile. 'I am perfectly content, Mama.'

'Good.' Harriet took her at her word. 'Now we must decide what to wear. You must be in looks for Lord Brancaster will want to look you over.'

'Mama!' She was horrified.

But all her mother did was laugh gaily and take her off to the dressmaker to have a new gown made. It was an open gown of creamy muslin, decorated with pale lemon embroidery over a silk slip. There was a lemon caraco jacket and a chip bonnet trimmed with yellow flowers. 'The essence of spring,' her mother said, putting it on Lady Connaught's account, along with the ruby taffeta gown she had bought for herself. 'Unsullied youth—Lord Brancaster will like that.'

'What has it to do with him?'

'If you are to make a push to catch the son, you must impress the father, for he holds the purse strings. And besides, there are other reasons…'

'What other reasons?'

'His lordship is a widower and I've heard he is looking for a wife.'

'Oh. But I thought you were tired of old men.'

'He is not so very old and age has its compensations. It has a mellowing influence.'

Molly could not help smiling at this but decided not to comment. What concerned her more was her mother's conviction that Andrew Bellamy meant to offer for her. She did not want to marry him and must let him down as gently as possible; she hated hurting anyone's feelings.

The party, consisting of Lady Connaught, Harriet, Lord Brancaster and Andrew, Lord Tadbury and his sister, Letitia, Lord and Lady Bonchance and their daughter, Naomi, travelled in several coaches to have supper at Rules, before going on to Vauxhall Gardens to listen to the concert and stroll about the lantern-lit gardens before fireworks brought the evening to an end.

The musicians played with verve and several of the songs

were tuneful enough for the audience to join in, but Molly's thoughts were far away with Duncan in Norfolk and were only brought back to the present when the applause at the end of the concert impinged on her reverie.

'Miss Martineau,' Andrew said, jumping to his feet and holding out his hand to her. 'Tadbury and Miss Bonchance are going for a walk before the fireworks start; shall we join them?'

She looked at her mama, who was sitting beside her with Lord Brancaster on her other side. 'Go on, child,' she said, before turning her smile on his lordship again.

'What do you think of the Gardens?' Andrew asked as they walked slightly ahead of the Marquis of Tadbury who had soon got over his disappointment with Harriet and had fixed his attention on Naomi Bonchance. They were deep in conversation and not paying the least attention to Andrew and Molly.

'I find they are fascinating—so much going on at once and so crowded.'

'They are only crowded near the pavilion, and in the more common walkways. There is more to see than this.' He waved his arm around him to encompass the pavilion and mown grass, the little hedges and pergolas. 'Come, I will show you.'

The Marquis and Naomi had fallen so far behind, they did not notice Andrew take her arm and draw her into one of the less frequented walks where the light of the lanterns did not reach. 'This is better, don't you think? I dislike an audience when I have something serious to say.'

Her heart began to beat uncomfortably; she could see that the walkway was dotted with little arbours and in almost every one there was a couple in each other's arms and their antics dismayed her. 'Mr Bellamy, I beg you, let us return to the others. I am not at all sure we should be here.'

'Why not? You know I have lost my heart to you
don't you?'

'No, I do not.'

'How can you not? I have been most attentive; you canno
deny that.'

'Yes, but I thought… I did not think…'

'Come, let us sit on this seat, while I show you just hov
much you mean to me.' He took her hand and pulled her int
one of the arbours. 'I adore you. I need you in my life.
cannot conceive of anything more pleasurable than lovin
you. The idea consumes me with passion.'

'Mr Bellamy…'

'Call me Andrew, please,' he murmured, burying his hea
in her neck and kissing her. 'If we are to deal well togethe
you must learn to be easy with me.'

'Mr Bellamy.' She tried again. 'I am very sensible of th
honour you do me, but I cannot accept…'

He laughed suddenly but it was not a happy sound and sh
shivered with apprehension. 'What a pretty speech, learne
by rote, I shouldn't wonder. And that before you have eve
heard my offer.'

'Then I have saved you the trouble of making one.'

He smiled and stroked the back of his finger down he
cheek. She was so rigid with inner tension, she could d
nothing to prevent it. 'You are not such a ninny as to believ
I had marriage in mind, are you?'

'You haven't?' Her words were whispered.

'Of course not. You have nothing to commend you as
wife, no fortune and no breeding, but as a ladybird—that i
a different matter. You have exactly the right attributes—
beauty, the figure of a goddess, the necessity of making you
way in the world, and you do not care what people think c

ou or you would not go racketing about the countryside
ith a half-pay soldier and riding in the park astride a horse
here the whole *ton* can see you. Such aplomb! Only a high-
lass impure could carry it off.'

She was beginning to understand. That was why Duncan
id not want her! Not as a wife, not as anything. No wonder
er mother did not wish to own her! But that did not mean
ne would succumb to Andrew Bellamy's blandishments.
Sir, you have quite mistaken the matter.'

'No, I do not think so and I will prove it to you.' He took
er face in both his hands and kissed her with more force
an finesse.

She squirmed as his mouth opened and his tongue forced
s way between her lips. It was horrible. She grunted and
ushed at his shoulders, forcing him to lift his head. 'Mr
ellamy, please…'

'Oh, I do please. Very much. And so do you.'

'I certainly do not. Let me go at once.'

'Not until you've heard me out. You shall have everything
woman could desire, all the clothes and knick-knacks you
eed, a well-furnished apartment and a carriage. All you have
do is to be there for me when I need you and be agreeable
my friends.'

'If you think I would agree to such an arrangement you
e a bigger sousecrown than I took you for,' she retorted, as
ngry with herself as she was with him. How could she have
een such a fool? 'I am not at my last prayers yet, and even
I were I would not consent to that.'

'You are unlikely to get a better offer, certainly not from
uncan Stacey, and you would do well to consider it.'

She stared at him in the gloom. His eyes were pinpoints
f light in a dark face; the rest was shadow. She began to be

very afraid, but determined not to let him see it. 'I never wil
Please take me back to my mama.'

'Mrs Benbright! She is a demi-rep herself; she will than
me for taking you off her hands. I'll wager she told you
encourage me.'

She did not answer; her mother had said something lik
that, but she had surely not been thinking of anything les
than marriage?

All she wanted to do was escape, but he held both he
hands. She forced herself to relax because only that wa
would he loosen his grip. As soon as he did, she kicked h
shins very hard and stamped on his toes. While he yelped wit
pain, she made good her escape. Down the dark paths sl
fled, making for the lights she could see in the distance.

She stopped when she realised she could not go back
the party in the state she was in, nor tell anyone what ha
happened. It would cause no end of a scandal, and though sl
was innocent no one would believe she had not enticed M
Bellamy. Her mother might even be pleased and insist on hir
marrying her. The very idea was abhorrent.

She was standing, trying to compose herself, when a ta
figure loomed in front of her and grabbed her. She opene
her mouth to scream, but he forestalled her and put his han
over her mouth. 'Not so fast, my pretty,' he said.

She struggled in vain. And then she heard Andrew's voic
behind her. 'Oh, you foolish wench, did you think you coul
escape from me?'

'She's yours?' the man queried.

'Indeed, she is. A little firebrand too. I thank you fe
stopping her, for there is no telling what she would do if le
to herself.'

'She is certainly a handful,' the man went on, holdin

Molly at arm's length while trying to avoid her kicking feet. 'You should teach her manners.'

'So I shall. My carriage is on the road, will you help me get her to it?'

'No! No!' Molly yelled, and was immediately cuffed about the ear. She spat in his face which was a bad mistake. He hit her so hard she lost consciousness.

When she came to her senses, she was riding in a closed carriage. Andrew was sitting beside her and the man who had captured her was sitting opposite her; beside him was another man. They were talking quietly together and she decided not to let them know she had regained her senses.

'It was a stroke of luck bumping into the little lady,' the first man said.

'Why?' Andrew asked warily. 'What is your interest in her?'

'Oh, we ain't interested in her,' the second man said. 'But she can lead us to the man we want. Been tracking him for weeks…'

'Who might that be?'

'The Dark Knight.'

'The Dark Knight,' Andrew repeated, while Molly held her breath. 'You mean the high toby who has been terrorising the countryside?'

'Yes. This little one is his accomplice. You would never think it to look at her, would you? Demure as a whore at a christening, she is.'

'That's ridiculous. No one knows who he is.'

'She does. An' so do we. She's goin' to fetch him to us.'

'What do you want with him?'

'He's got property that belongs to our master. Took it off him, he did. We've been sent to fetch it back.'

'Why don't you go to a magistrate and have him arrested?'

'That won't serve, not at all.'

Molly was beginning to realise that Andrew had lo
control of the situation. She could tell by the tone of his voic
he was afraid, and yet he was ready to bluff his way out o
trouble. 'The lady is my mistress,' he said. 'I say where sh
goes and she goes with me to a little house I've got prepare
for her…'

'A love nest. So be it. You keep her there. We will do the rest

Molly stirred a little and the first man leaned across an
poked her ribs. She flinched. 'She's coming round,' he sai

'Where am I?' She struggled to sit up and stared at the tw
men. She could see little in the gloom of the carriage, excep
that they were both dark and wearing dark clothes. One ha
long hair and straggly moustache and the other was ver
thin. 'Who are you?'

'No need for you to know,' the long-haired one said, wit
a grin.

'What do you want? Where are you taking me?'

'Bless you, we ain't takin' you anywhere. Lover boy is th
one who's doin' the takin'. We're just going along for the rid
so to speak.'

'Oh.' She turned to appeal to Andrew. 'Mr Bellamy, pleas
take me home.'

'Home?' he repeated. 'Why, of course, my dear. I'll tak
you to the prettiest little home imaginable. Be patient.'

'I meant Connaught House.'

'I'm afraid that is out of the question.'

'But Mama and Lady Connaught will be searching for m
You cannot simply abduct me and think no one will look for me

'They will not find you until it is too late.'

'Too late?' she queried, wondering if he meant to murder he

'Too late to save your reputation,' he said, then smile

'Once you have spent a night in my company, you will be ruined in the eyes of the *haut monde*, a fallen woman—not that you aren't already, for you spent a week on the road with Captain Stacey...'

'Nothing happened,' she protested.

'Then he is a bigger clunch than I took him for.'

'He is more a gentleman than you will ever be.'

'Such touching loyalty will not serve you when it comes to asserting your innocence, you know. Society can be very cruel. By the time the gabblegrinders have done with you, you will be pleased enough to accept my offer.'

'Never! I would rather die.'

She heard the dark man laugh and turned angrily on him. 'And you will be in worse trouble when you are caught. I have powerful friends.'

'Captain Duncan Stacey!' The man laughed. 'Yes, I do believe he will ride post haste to the rescue.'

'Stacey!' Andrew repeated, and burst into laughter. 'Is that the Dark Knight? A common highwayman! Oh, what a rig!' He slapped his knees. 'Why, my friends, nothing would give me greater pleasure than to have him done for a scamp. Double vengeance, that would be.'

'Not before we've done with him,' the second man growled. 'Then you can do what you like.'

They left the lights of the town behind and Molly could see nothing but hedgerows and realised she was being taken into the country. But where?

Fifteen minutes later they turned into a rutted drive and drew to a stop. Andrew jumped down and let down the step for her. 'Come,' he said, holding out his hand. 'It will not be so bad, I promise you.'

Neither of the other two men moved and she assumed

they were going to take possession of the coach. Between the devil she knew and the unknown terror of the two ruffians, she preferred the devil, and, taking his hand, stepped down to stand beside him.

'Mind you keep her safe here,' the dark man said. 'We will be back.'

She watched the coach disappear into the darkness and then turned back. They were standing outside a small cottage.

'Where are we?'

'Home,' he said, taking her hand and leading her to the door. She tried to free herself but he whipped off his cravat and tied her wrist to his. 'I do like a little spirited resistance: it makes the conquest all the sweeter,' he said cheerfully as he unlocked the door and ushered her inside. 'You will be all smiles and womanly wiles tomorrow.'

She did not answer; her whole mind and body was centred on keeping her head and taking stock of her surroundings. The cottage was clean and neatly furnished and they were evidently expected, for the lamps were lit and a meal was set out on the table, with wine and glasses. But there was no sign of servants.

'This will do for a few days, until we are at ease with each other, then I will set you up in town.' He moved towards the table and because she was tied to him she had perforce to follow. 'Now we will eat and drink and after that…who knows?'

'It will be difficult,' she said, raising the hand that was bound to his.

He laughed. 'It will be a pleasure trying.'

'Please untie me.'

'So that you may run?'

'No, for I have no idea where to run to. I am persuaded we are miles from civilisation.'

'You are right.' He went to the door, turned the key in the lock and put it in his pocket, before releasing her. She stood rubbing her wrist, wondering how she could escape before he compelled her to agree to his outrageous proposal. Not only that, but she must warn Duncan of the danger he was in. But how?

'Sit down, my dear,' Andrew said. 'Now we are alone, we may enjoy each other's company and get to know each other.'

She decided it would be expedient to obey. He served her with food and though it was well-prepared and looked delicious her throat was so dry she could not swallow. He ate well and drank copiously.

'Come, try this wine,' he said, filling a glass for her. 'It really is very good.'

'I do not want it.'

'And I say you shall have it. It will make you more relaxed. You are as stiff as a starched cravat.' He stood up and came to stand beside her, holding the glass. 'Drink.'

'No.'

He held her nose so that she was obliged to open her mouth, and then poured the wine down her throat. She had to swallow or choke. 'That is better.' He made her take more until the glass was empty. It made her dizzy, through drinking it too quickly, but it did not make her feel any easier about what was about to happen.

'Now, come with me,' he said, picking her up and flinging her across his shoulder. She kicked in vain; he held her by her legs and marched from the room and up the stairs, where he took her into one of the rooms and flung her onto the bed.

She started to thrash about and scream. He stuffed a handkerchief into her mouth. When her flailing legs made contact with his shin, he swore. 'You are being a very silly chit,' he said. 'Tomorrow, when the world knows you for what you are, you will be happy to oblige.'

The door opened behind them with a crash. He looked up and swung round, allowing Molly a moment's respite. But if she hoped it would be someone come to deliver her she was disappointed. The figure in the doorway was not a rescuer but the second of the two men who had helped Andrew abduct her. And he was grinning.

'Jeremy wants you,' he said, jerking his head backwards. 'Go on and be quick about it.'

Andrew hesitated, but one look at the man's murderous face decided him. He took Molly's hands and tied them to the bedpost. 'I fear I must leave you for a little while, sweetheart, but rest assured I shall be back.'

And then he was gone, followed by the other man, to her immense relief.

She struggled for several minutes, then lay back exhausted. The wine she had been forced to drink was taking its toll and though she tried to stay alert she was becoming more and more drowsy. How could two glasses of wine send her to sleep? Unless they had been drugged... Her head lolled on the pillow and her eyes closed...

Chapter Twelve

⁓⁓⁓⁓

'Here's to you, sir.' The man raised his glass to Duncan. 'God bless you and grant you long life and prosperity.'

'Here! Here!' came a chorus of assent from the half dozen men in the taproom of the Lamb and Flag.

'If there's anything we can do for you, you have only to tip us the wink.' This from one of them who had identified himself as ex-Sergeant Ben Brightman.

'Thank you.' Duncan was in beneficent mood, having come from Manor Farm, where he had engaged a builder to make the alterations to the stables he needed and to refurbish the farmhouse. He had returned to London and gone straight to Tattersalls to look over some breeding mares. Coming upon the ex-soldiers on his way home, he had invited them to the inn to join him in a celebration and, realising he would need help on the farm and these were men accustomed to looking after horses, he had offered them work.

He left them singing 'Over the Hills and Far Away', with more enthusiasm than tunefulness. Now he could put the past behind him and make something of his life. Tomorrow he

would tell Molly that he had only a few acres and his strong
arm to offer her, and a heart full of love, and that if she consented to marry him he would cherish her for the rest of their
lives.

Leaving Caesar at the mews behind Connaught House, he
set off to walk to Fenton's. He would be glad when he need
no longer spend his nights at the hotel; the beds were hard and
he was sure there were bugs. Turning the corner, he paused
outside Connaught House. He did not see why he should not
sleep there; he had not been banned and everyone would be
in bed and would not know he was there until the morning. And
he would be near Molly. Near Molly, ready to speak to her.

He bounded up the steps to the front door, only to find it
standing wide open. His grandmother was in the grand hall
furiously directing the servants, sending them hither and
thither; Harriet was weeping into her handkerchief, crying
'My baby! My baby!' while Lord Brancaster stood over her
trying to calm her.

Andrew Bellamy, who had just that moment arrived, was
in the middle of explaining that he had seen Miss Martineau
snatched by a band of ruffians who had knocked him to the
ground when he tried to intervene and had then carried her off.

'Why? Why?' wailed Harriet.

Duncan pushed his way forward. 'What has happened?'

'Molly has been kidnapped,' Harriet cried, turning a tear-
streaked face up to him. 'We were at Vauxhall. Why should
anyone want to take Molly? She has no fortune, no prospects.
Oh, my baby.'

'Hush, ma'am,' Lord Brancaster said. 'Calm yourself. No
doubt we shall hear the kidnappers' demands in due time.'

'What is the good of them making demands?' Harriet went
on. 'I have no means to pay a ransom.'

'Stacey has,' Andrew put in, looking at Duncan. 'I heard them mention his name.'

'Mine?' Duncan queried. He had made a good many enemies in his life, but he was dismayed to think that Molly should be made to suffer because of anything he had done.

'Well, not exactly.' Andrew, in spite of the seriousness of the situation, seemed to be grinning. 'It was the Dark Knight they wanted.'

'Good God!' The exclamation was wrung from Duncan, but it was no good flying into a panic. He forced himself to stay calm. 'Have you any idea where they might have taken her?'

'None. They took my carriage which is why I have been so long arriving.'

'Oh, pray they do not harm her,' Harriet went on. 'Or worse… Oh, the shame of it.' She resorted once again to her flimsy lace handkerchief. 'No one will offer for her if she has been despoiled. It is all your fault, Stacey, for encouraging her madcap ways. She said you were not the Dark Knight, but I always thought there was something smoky about the way you brought her to London.'

'There is no sense in blaming anyone,' Lady Connaught put in, losing patience with her. 'Duncan, have you any idea who these men might be?'

'No, unless they be connected with Sir John Partridge…'

'I have heard of him,' Lord Brancaster said. 'He has only today been arrested and thrown into the Tower. I believe he is to stand trial for treason. We heard of it in Parliament today.'

'Then you must use your influence to speak to him and ask him where the men have taken Molly,' Duncan said. 'In the meantime, I will make my own enquiries. And Bellamy, if you want to be useful, organise a search round Vauxhall Gardens; they might not have taken her far.'

'Where are you going?' Andrew demanded. 'There's no sense in both of us searching the same place.'

'To the Lamb and Flag in Covent Garden. There are some fellows there who will help.'

He did not wait for a reply, but hurried from the house, fetched Caesar from the mews where he had left him only a few minutes before, and set off for the inn where he had left the ex-soldiers. He dared not think of what might be happening to Molly, but if it was the Dark Knight the men wanted, then the Dark Knight they should have. And if the worst was to come about and he could not free Molly any other way he would barter her life for his and it would be a small price to pay. But he needed allies.

He had given the men enough money to keep them drinking the rest of the night and he hoped they would still be there. Some of them were and, though they were well disguised, they had enough wits about them to listen to what he had to say.

'We'll look for her, Captain,' Ben Brightman said, speaking for them all. 'We know all the kens hereabouts.'

In no time they had organised themselves with military precision and set off to scour the capital. Duncan was about to leave to resume his own search when he was approached by a dark man with a straggling moustache and long greasy hair who had just entered. He was wearing a suit of black clothes, shining with dirt. 'Heard you were looking for a certain ladybird,' he said.

'Yes, yes,' he said, ignoring the implied insult to Molly; it would not help him to find her to quarrel with a potential bearer of news. 'What do you know?'

'Small, hair the colour of ripe corn, eyes like bluebells and a fierce temper, goes by the name of Molly.'

Duncan grabbed him by the coat collar and nearly lifted him off his feet. 'Where is she? If you have harmed a hair of her head, I'll…'

'Hold hard, old fellow,' the dark one said. 'It don't pay to shoot the messenger.'

Duncan released him. 'Who are you?'

'Box is the name. Jeremy Box.'

'Then, Mr Box, I suggest you tell me what you know. And then tell me where I can find Miss Martineau. Fast.'

The man looked at him, smiling. 'Now, as to that, it depends…'

'Very well. Name your price.'

'Money? No, money ain't the thing, but me and Danny wouldn't say no to a monkey apiece. But what's more important is them documents you took from a certain gentleman on the road to Cromer.'

He was about to say he no longer had the documents and Sir John had already been arrested on the strength of them when he realised that they were the only bargaining power he had. 'Oh, those. Bits of paper. No good as currency; can't exactly recall what I did with them.'

'Then you had better start remembering. No documents, no girl.'

'No girl, no documents,' he countered, hiding his impatience. 'Take me to her. It will have a wonderful effect on my memory to see her safe and sound.'

The man looked pensively at him and Duncan could almost see his mind working. 'You write home. Tell them to send someone with money and the papers.' He called the landlord and asked for pen, paper and ink, which was produced after a search which had Duncan hopping from foot to foot with impatience.

'Now write.'

Duncan sat, pen in hand, wondering how to word the note. There were no documents, except the mail he had left there when he'd first returned to London with Molly. None of it was of any importance. He dipped the quill in the ink and began to write, addressing the missive to his grandmother who seemed to be the calmest of the people at Connaught House. She also knew his connection with Sir John and might understand his predicament.

He wrote: 'My lady, I am unavoidably detained. Please give…' He stopped to look up at the man who stood reading over his shoulder. 'Who are they to be given to?'

'Mr Andrew Bellamy.'

'Bellamy!' he repeated in surprise. 'Why him?'

'The little lady trusts him and who are we to argue with her? Write.'

Duncan continued. 'Please give to Mr Bellamy the bundle of papers from the top drawer of the chest in my room and a thousand pounds which you will find in the same place.' He stopped writing again. A servant would not dare read the papers but Bellamy most assuredly would and he would know they were worthless as bargaining instruments. He dipped the quill again and added, 'Seal them carefully and tell him that he must deliver them with the seal unbroken…' Again he stopped. 'Where?'

'He will know.'

Duncan was puzzled. How had the man who stood over him now known where to find him, unless he had been told by someone who knew? Andrew Bellamy! Had he had a hand in Molly's disappearance? Frank had been right in saying he had made an enemy there. But to use Molly! There was no time to waste asking questions he knew would not be answered. He finished the letter and signed it.

The dark man snatched the paper as soon as he had dusted he ink and read through it. 'A sensible precaution, Captain; ve don't want to give anyone any ideas, now, do we?' He alled the innkeeper and gave him a handful of coppers. 'Send a servant to Connaught House with this. It is urgent.'

The innkeeper called to someone who was washing pots ehind the counter. 'Hey, you, Abraham or whatever you call ourself, come here.'

A big black man joined them and was given the letter. 'Can ou find Connaught House on the corner of Berkeley 'quare?' the innkeeper asked him, speaking very slowly as f the man did not understand English.

'Yes, sir.'

'Then off you go. And mind you come back. You ain't inished those pots.'

Duncan, glancing briefly at the man, was taken aback vhen he recognised the slave he and Frank had freed, not so nuch by his looks as the ill-fitting garments he wore, lthough now they were filthy and ragged. It was evident the nan remembered him, for his eyes widened, but he did not peak. Duncan wished he could have given him a verbal nessage, but the kidnapper, if that was what he was, was too vary to allow that.

As soon as the messenger had gone, Duncan turned to him. 'Now you fulfil your part of the bargain, Mr Box.'

Molly woke feeling stiff and cramped and her wrists hurt. 'he realised why when she tried to move her hands. How long ad she been asleep with her hands tied to the bed-rail? Where vas Mr Bellamy? Was he downstairs drinking, or had he left he house? Could she free herself? She struggled but only suc-eeded in tightening her bonds. She twisted her head to look

up at her hands. They were tied with Andrew's cravat and tha
was made of starched muslin. It would rip if she could onl
make the first tear.

Slowly she inched her way up the bed, thankful that he
hands were tied in front of her and not behind her back
Craning her neck, she was able to get her teeth into th
material. It was stronger than she expected and her jaw an
neck began to ache. She gave herself a few moments' respit
and began again, her senses alive to any sound from down
stairs which would tell her Mr Bellamy had returned fron
wherever he had gone.

A tiny split appeared in the muslin. She strained her wrist
apart with every sinew of her strength. And then it tore. Sh
was free! But that was only the beginning; she had to escap
from the house. She rubbed her wrists and padded across th
floor to the window and looked out.

It was still dark, but the sky to the east was tinged wit
pink, and away to her right there were lights. They were th
gas lamps that lit the West End of London and there wer
others that could only be the lanterns on moving carriages c
those carried by linkboys. She was not so far from civilisa
tion, after all. Below her a narrow lane, edged with bushes
led to the main road.

She re-crossed the room, picked up her shoes and carefull
opened the door, freezing against the wall when it creake
loudly. No one came. Slowly and silently, one step at a time, sh
made her way down to the ground floor in her stockinged fee

There was a sudden snort from the room where she ha
sat with Andrew and she nearly cried out, but managed t
stifle it. There was someone in there. Creeping slowl
forward, she peered round the door. A man was slumped i
an armchair fast asleep, but it was not Andrew. It was th

second of the two men who had helped Andrew abduct her. Beside him on the table was an empty wine bottle and a half-full glass.

She turned and made her way to the front door, hardly daring to breathe. Slowly she lifted the latch. The door opened and a blast of cool air hit her face. She ran down the path, her relief so great, there were tears running down her face and she could hardly see where she was going. It did not matter. Anywhere would do. The gravel was hurting her feet but she dared not stop to put on her shoes until she was safe.

She heard horses on the road and just managed to hide behind one of the bushes when two riders turned up the lane. She recognised the first one, even in the dark, and ran from her hiding place, crying with relief. 'Duncan! Oh, Duncan!'

He turned at the sound of his name and flung himself off Caesar. She ran forward and into his arms. 'Molly. Thank God!' He took her head in his hands and lifted her face to his. 'Are you hurt? Did they hurt you?'

'No, but I was so afraid…'

'Afraid? Madcap Molly afraid? Who would have believed it?'

His slightly bantering tone was enough to restore her spirit. 'But I wanted to warn you.' She turned towards the other man, who was standing beside his horse, smiling cynically. 'About this man and another one who is in the house. They are…'

'I know who they are, Molly.' He spoke calmly, but his mind was racing. How could he get her to safety?

'And Mr Bellamy…'

'I know about him too.' His tone gave nothing away. 'It is over now. Try to forget it. You are safe.' On the ride to the cottage, the man had enjoyed relaying what Bellamy had said to Molly in the coach. 'She will be of no use to you, Captain,' he had told him, grinning. 'Soiled goods, that's what she is by now.' He had been seething with fury ever since and not only with fury but disgust. Had she succumbed? Would she have had any choice? Did he still feel the same about marrying her? They were not questions to be answered now.

'Very touching,' the man said, producing a pistol from his belt. 'Now back into the house with you.'

She looked up at Duncan. He smiled reassuringly. 'Don't be afraid. We have to wait for a messenger.'

'The messenger is here,' said a voice from the darkness of the bushes.

Startled, their captor turned towards the sound and his mouth fell open. Two big men emerged, carrying muskets. 'Put the gun down,' one of them ordered him, lifting the musket to his shoulder.

Molly heard Duncan chuckle as more men appeared— some from the ditch beside the road, others from behind the house, pushing the second kidnapper, securely tied, in front of them. And standing beside Duncan's horse, as if he had appeared there by magic, was the big negro, grinning in the darkness and showing even white teeth. Jeremy Box dropped his weapon with a clatter.

'What do you want done with them, Captain?' Ben asked, forcing the man's hands behind his back and tying them securely with a length of rope he had brought with him.

'Take them to the Westminster magistrate and tell him they are accomplices of Sir John Partridge. He will know what to do. And my thanks to you all.'

'It was Abraham what put us onto you,' Ben said. 'He don't speak much English, but he made us understand.'

Duncan left Molly's side to shake the black man by the hand. 'You have my undying gratitude. Go with these men. They will take you to Norfolk. I can find work for you. Paid work,' he added. 'You are a free man; if it is not to your liking, you are under no obligation to stay.'

The man nodded, showing he understood English even if he did not speak it well. 'I serve you good,' he said.

'How did you all get here?' Molly asked, looking from one to the other.

'Oh, we had a guide who knew exactly where you were,' Ben said.

'Mr Bellamy,' she murmured.

'Yes.' Then he said to Duncan, 'What do you want done with him? He's sitting in his coach, awaiting your pleasure.'

'My pleasure would be to beat him to a pulp,' Duncan said.

'Oh, no, please don't,' Molly put in. 'I do not want anyone hurt. Send him away. I don't want to see him.'

'You heard Miss Martineau,' Duncan said. 'Turn him loose. Let him walk home.' He smiled suddenly. 'We will borrow his coach again.' Then he said to Molly, 'The sooner we get you home to your mama the better.'

Ten minutes later, Duncan and Molly were sitting side by side in the Brancaster coach, with the negro on the box. Ben and his companions were riding the horses and were slowly driving the two criminals in front of them with their hands tied behind them. The coach soon left them behind.

Molly was almost limp with relief that her ordeal was over, but she could not relax; she was taut with nervous tension. Any moment now Duncan would start to ask her about what had happened between her and Andrew Bellamy and how could she answer him? She did not know if anything had happened while she had been drugged. But perhaps he had guessed and that was why he was so silent. Was he condemning her, as Mr Bellamy had said everyone would?

'Captain,' she said, after they had been travelling in silence for several minutes. 'I am sorry to have been the cause of so much trouble, but it was not of my choosing. Please believe me.'

'Oh, I do,' he said, smiling at her. 'But it seems to me you are even more prone to fall into scrapes than I am—but I am persuaded that was one adventure you would rather not have had.'

'It was horrible. I never want to live through another night like it.'

'Are you going to tell me about it?'

'I…I can't.'

'I see.'

'No, you do not see,' she cried. 'You are blaming me, telling yourself that a well brought up young lady would never allow herself to fall into such a bumblebath…'

'How did you fall into it? Tell me from the beginning.'

'Mr Bellamy asked me to walk with him in Vauxhall Gardens while we were waiting for the fireworks to start. He said we would be accompanied by the Marquis of Tadbury and Miss Bonchance and I did not think it was wrong, especially as Mama agreed I could go.'

'Then what?'

'We became separated from the others. He…he tried to kiss me.'

'The scoundrel.'

'It is no more than you have done.'

'So I have.' He smiled, trying to lighten the feeling of gloom which pervaded the coach. 'And how did we compare?'

'I do not know how you can make a jest of it.' She turned on him. 'It is not the least amusing.'

'No, of course not. I apologise. What happened then?'

'I was angry and I left him. That big dark man suddenly appeared out of the bushes and grabbed me. Mr Bellamy came up and they put me in the coach and there was another man there. The other two men left when we arrived at the house. Mr Bellamy took me inside. He wanted me to have supper with him and afterwards…'

'Never mind,' he said. 'You do not have to tell me if it is painful for you. I understand.'

He *was* disgusted with her. She had never been more miserable, but she refused to be cowed. 'No, you do not. I did not want it. I never asked for it. I fought and was tied up for my pains.'

'Oh, my poor, poor Molly.'

'But he left me, said he wanted me to be willing and I would be, too, the next day…'

He looked at her and put his arm about her shoulders, squeezing her to his side. 'My poor, brave darling. How did you escape?'

'I bit through my bonds.'

He laughed. 'Bit them? Oh, you are priceless.'

'It is not in the least funny.'

'No, it would have been terrifying and my admiration is unbounded.'

Admiration, she noted, not love. 'Now you have heard my story, don't you think it is time you told me how you knew where to find me? How did you meet that dreadful man and who were all those other men and the big black man?'

He told her the whole truth, speaking gently to her to reassure her. His disgust was directed at Andrew Bellamy and not her. None of it was her fault. The blame lay with those around her, including and more especially himself. He should have spoken to her of his intentions before going back to Norfolk, should have asked her to marry him the moment he could see the way forward. His delay had cost her pain and misery.

'We are two scapegraces together,' he ended, smiling. 'I think there is only one way to cure us.'

'How?'

'To marry.'

'Yes, I collect you said you had found a wife,' she said solemnly. 'I wish you joy of her.'

'I meant each other,' he said.

She twisted in her seat to face him, wondering whether he was bamming her, but his expression was perfectly serious. 'Marry you?'

'Do you still think I am too old?' he queried.

'No, I have decided age is not so important, after all, but Mr Bellamy said that after last night no one would marry me and I would have to be his ladybird. I do not know exactly what that means but I do not think it can be respectable. I think I would rather be an ape leader and live in seclusion for the rest of my days. I know you are always pulling me out of scrapes, and I am grateful, but this is one too many.'

'Scrapes. Do you think that is the only reason I spoke?'

'Only a moment ago, you said…'

'Then I am a clumsy oaf. I love you. I will always love you.'

She could hardly believe her ears, did not dare believe them. 'After all that has happened, I would expect you to have a disgust of me.'

'Oh, Molly, how can you say that?' It did not matter what had happened, if she loved him; he had been a cur even to think about it. 'All I need to know, all I want to know, is do you love me?'

'Of course I do. With all my heart. How can you doubt it?'

'And will you flinch and turn away if I kiss you?'

She laughed suddenly. 'Try it and see.'

So he did and it was as wonderful as it had been the first time and the second, and when he kissed her again it was still glorious. They would have gone on doing it, if the coach had not drawn up outside Connaught House.

They walked into the house together and were bombarded with questions by Harriet, weeping and full of contrition, and Lady Connaught who had a sparkle in her eye which could have been a tear. Lord Brancaster was there too, looking white and drawn. Molly felt sorry for him and made up her mind she would not distress him by telling them what really happened.

It was almost as if Duncan could read her mind, for he pretended Andrew had only been allowed to go free if he agreed to lure Duncan into a trap. 'He is on his way home and will be at Brancaster House very shortly,' Duncan ended. 'I am indebted to him for reuniting me with Molly.' He took her hand and smiled conspiratorially at her. 'You may offer felicitations.'

'Then I do, most heartily.'

And so did everyone else. After that, Lord Brancaster left and an exhausted Molly was packed off to bed with a tisane, leaving Duncan to fill in the details of what had happened for the benefit of his grandmother and Harriet, and then go back to his lodgings for a few hours' sleep before returning.

Her mother came to her as she was climbing into bed. 'Tony has just told me the whole and I am mortified,' she said. 'It was all my fault. I thought Bellamy could be trusted to look after you. I thought he would marry you. Can you ever forgive me?'

'It was not your fault, Mama. I should not have come to London and put you to the blush. I must have spoiled every thing for you.'

'Oh, it has come out well in the end. Brancaster proposed during the fireworks. I was so pleased and longing to tell you but you had disappeared. Thank heaven you were not harmed. And Tony Stacey has offered for you. Who would have thought it? 'Tis a pity about the earldom, but Aunt Margaret tells me he has been awarded a baronetcy, so you will not be without a title.'

'Mama, how can I marry Duncan? I know I did not spend the whole night alone with Mr Bellamy but surely it was enough to ruin me? He said it would be.'

'No, of course you are not ruined.'

'Duncan said it made no difference,' she said. 'But he does not mean that. I am disgusted with myself and I cannot go through with a marriage which will cause him distress. He will never be able to forget it and neither will I.'

'Fustian! He rescued you, did he not? And he said Andrew had been kidnapped too. Nothing will be said, you may be sure, certainly not by Andrew. He has too much to lose. Now go to sleep and forget all about it. Tomorrow we will discuss weddings. Though I think mine must come first, don't you think?'

'Of course, Mama.' Molly smiled as the tisane began to work and she drifted off to sleep; her mother would never change.

It was the middle of the afternoon when she woke and the whole ordeal came flooding back to her. But that was followed by a wonderful sense of well-being. She was loved. She had found the man of her dreams, her Don Quixote, and he loved her. It had not been the least necessary to have a

eason; he had been there all the time. Sir Duncan Stacey,
ero and highwayman, farmer and horse breeder, was to be
er husband. She would be Lady Stacey. Her dreams had
ome true.

She could not lie abed when there was a glorious day to
e lived, and not only one but many, a whole lifetime of
hem. She rose and dressed and went downstairs.

Duncan had returned and was sitting in the drawing room
ith her mother and Lady Connaught. There were also two
thers in the room she had never met before—a young man
ho was stationed in front of the hearth and a young lady who
tood with her back to the room, gazing out on the garden.

Duncan jumped up when she entered the room and strode
ver to take her hand and kiss the back of it, his eyes dancing
ith something akin to mischief. Or was it simply happiness?
Molly, how are you?'

'Quite recovered, thank you.' She knew she was blushing
ut could not stop herself.

'Good. Come and be presented.' He led her to the young
an who stood by the hearth. He was very like Duncan in
ooks though not quite as tall and very much thinner. 'Hugh,
is is Molly. Molly, my brother, the Earl of Connaught.'

Hugh smiled and took her hand, raising it to his lips. 'I am
harmed to meet you, Miss Martineau.'

'If it please you, my lord, I am Molly.'

'Molly it shall be,' he said. 'And no more "my lord". It is
naccurate to say the least.'

'Hugh, I said we would speak of that no more,' Duncan
ut in, before turning to present Molly to his sister-in-law,
ho had turned from the window.

She was, Molly noted, tall and graceful and her elegant
lothes set off a figure she envied. So this was the lady who

had disappointed Duncan. She searched their faces for sig⹀
that the attachment still lived, but either they were skilled ⹀
hiding their true feelings or he had been telling the trut⹀
when he'd said it was all in the past.

Molly moved forward and curtsied. 'I am very pleased ⹀
meet you, my lady,' she said.

'And we you,' Beth said. 'Such tales we have heard…'

'Oh, I beg you, take no note of them. They are bound t⹀
have been exaggerated.'

'What? No abduction, no gallant rescue?' Hugh put in.

'Yes, but it is over now.'

'I must say you look remarkably calm about it all.'

Duncan laughed. 'It takes more than a kidnapping t⹀
unsettle Molly. She is the match of any ne'er-do-well, as ⹀
know to my cost. You may felicitate me.'

'Then I do. Heartily.'

'I wish you happy,' Beth said, moving forward to kis⹀
Molly's cheek. 'It is time Tony settled down.'

'Oh, we plan to do that,' Duncan said. 'On Manor Farm⹀
breeding horses.'

'No, that is not fair,' Hugh said. 'You must take up you⹀
rightful place as the Earl. I am an impostor and have n⹀
right to the title or the estate. I came to London to make ⹀
public announcement of the truth. Beth agrees with m⹀
don't you, dear?'

'Of course.' She turned to Duncan. 'Since you came bac⹀
from the war, Tony, we have been feeling so guilty. Hugh ha⹀
been quite ill with it. I would rather have a healthy, happ⹀
husband than any title…'

'Then he should be happy. He is not depriving me ⹀
anything I want.' He reached out and took Molly's hand. ⹀
have my heart's desire.' He paused and turned to look ⹀

Molly, searching her face. 'What say you, my love? Do you wish to be a countess?'

'Seems to me she doesn't have any choice in the matter,' Lady Connaught put in. 'You cannot throw away the laws of progeniture to please yourselves. Duncan, you are the Earl of Connaught, whether you will it or not. And you will have children…'

Duncan smiled at Molly. 'I certainly hope so.'

'Whatever you do, you cannot deprive your son of his inheritance.'

'No, you are right, but I do not want to live at Foxtrees. Hugh, you will stay there and manage the estates on my behalf, until such time as my heir is ready to inherit. Molly and I will live at Manor Farm and I will be Sir Duncan Stacey. After all, it is a title I have earned for myself.' He smiled again at Molly. 'Does that suit, my love?'

'Yes, yes. As long as I am with you, that is all I care about.'

'Then that is the end of the matter,' Duncan said. 'Now, Molly and I are going to stroll round the garden. We have a lot to say to each other.'

But it was not words that passed between them once they were out of sight of the house and sitting in a little green bower at the end of the garden. It was smiles and kisses, and a great many of them.

* * * * *

Regency

HIGH-SOCIETY AFFAIRS

*Rakes and rogues in the ballrooms – and the
bedrooms – of Regency England!*

Volume 1 – 6th March 2009
A Hasty Betrothal by Dorothy Elbury
A Scandalous Marriage by Mary Brendan

Volume 2 – 3rd April 2009
The Count's Charade by Elizabeth Bailey
The Rake and the Rebel by Mary Brendan

Volume 3 – 1st May 2009
Sparhawk's Lady by Miranda Jarrett
The Earl's Intended Wife by Louise Allen

Volume 4 – 5th June 2009
Lord Calthorpe's Promise by Sylvia Andrew
The Society Catch by Louise Allen

Volume 5 – 3rd July 2009
Beloved Virago by Anne Ashley
Lord Trenchard's Choice by Sylvia Andrew

Volume 6 – 7th August 2009
The Unruly Chaperon by Elizabeth Rolls
Colonel Ancroft's Love by Sylvia Andrew

Volume 7 – 4th September 2009
The Sparhawk Bride by Miranda Jarrett
The Rogue's Seduction by Georgina Devon

NOW 14 VOLUMES IN ALL TO COLLECT!

M&B

Regency

HIGH-SOCIETY AFFAIRS

Rakes and rogues in the ballrooms – and the bedrooms – of Regency England!

Volume 8 – 2nd October 2009
Sparhawk's Angel by Miranda Jarrett
The Proper Wife by Julia Justiss

Volume 9 – 6th November 2009
The Disgraced Marchioness by Anne O'Brien
The Reluctant Escort by Mary Nichols

Volume 10 – 4th December 2009
The Outrageous Debutante by Anne O'Brien
A Damnable Rogue by Anne Herries

Volume 11 – 8th January 2010
The Enigmatic Rake by Anne O'Brien
The Lord and the Mystery Lady by Georgina Devon

Volume 12 – 5th February 2010
The Wagering Widow by Diane Gaston
An Unconventional Widow by Georgina Devon

Volume 13 – 5th March 2010
A Reputable Rake by Diane Gaston
The Heart's Wager by Gayle Wilson

Volume 14 – 2nd April 2010
The Venetian's Mistress by Ann Elizabeth Cree
The Gambler's Heart by Gayle Wilson

NOW 14 VOLUMES IN ALL TO COLLECT!

Immerse yourself in the glitter of
Regency times and follow the lives
and romantic escapades of
Stephanie Laurens' Lester family

Sparkling ballrooms and wealthy glamour in Regency London

millsandboon.co.uk Community

Join Us!

he Community is the perfect place to meet and chat to
ndred spirits who love books and reading as much as
u do, but it's also the place to:

Get the inside scoop from authors about their latest books

Learn how to write a romance book with advice from our editors

Help us to continue publishing the best in women's fiction

Share your thoughts on the books we publish

Befriend other users

orums: Interact with each other as well as authors, edi-
rs and a whole host of other users worldwide.

logs: Every registered community member has their
wn blog to tell the world what they're up to and what's
n their mind.

ook Challenge: We're aiming to read 5,000 books and
ave joined forces with The Reading Agency in our
augural Book Challenge.

rofile Page: Showcase yourself and keep a record of
ur recent community activity.

ocial Networking: We've added buttons at the end of
very post to share via digg, Facebook, Google, Yahoo,
echnorati and de.licio.us.

www.millsandboon.co.uk